THE MIRROR THIEF

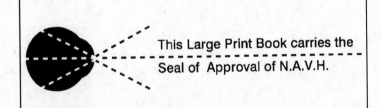

This Large Print Book carries the
Seal of Approval of N.A.V.H.

THE MIRROR THIEF

MARTIN SEAY

THORNDIKE PRESS
A part of Gale, Cengage Learning

GALE
CENGAGE Learning·

Farmington Hills, Mich • San Francisco • New York • Waterville, Maine
Meriden, Conn • Mason, Ohio • Chicago

GALE
CENGAGE Learning®

LIBRARY OF CONGRESS CATALOGING-IN-PUBLICATION DATA

Names: Seay, Martin, author.
Title: The mirror thief / by Martin Seay.
Description: Large print edition. | Waterville, Maine : Thorndike Press, 2016. |
    Series: Thorndike press large print guy reads
Identifiers: LCCN 2016022457 | ISBN 9781410493514 (hardcover) | ISBN 1410493512
    (hardcover)
Subjects: LCSH: Large type books. | GSAFD: Mystery fiction.
Classification: LCC PS3619.E2593 M57 2016b | DDC 813/.6—dc23
LC record available at https://lccn.loc.gov/2016022457

Published in 2016 by arrangement with Melville House Publishing

Printed in Mexico
1 2 3 4 5 6 7 20 19 18 17 16

For
Kathleen Rooney
and
in memory of
Joe F. Boydstun

"Did you ever happen to see a city resembling this one?" Kublai asked Marco Polo, extending his beringed hand from beneath the silken canopy of the imperial barge, to point to the bridges arching over the canals, the princely palaces whose marble doorsteps were immersed in the water, the bustle of light craft zigzagging, driven by long oars, the boats unloading baskets of vegetables at the market squares, the balconies, platforms, domes, campaniles, island gardens glowing green in the lagoon's grayness.

•

"No, sire," Marco answered, "I should never have imagined a city like this could exist."

— ITALO CALVINO, *Invisible Cities*

1

Listen. This is what you see:

A tall casement window. Floorlength drapes of green brocade, parted along the curtainrod. Gray halflight seeping through. Tasseled valance, sheer lace beneath. The wind shakes the glass, and the curtains sway into the room.

Chairs. Desk. Chest of drawers. Wardrobe — they never have closets, these old places. Whitewashed walls. Polished parquet floor, too slick for socks. Nightstands, frilly lamps. White telephone. Tacky glass chandelier: aqua petals, frosted forty-watt bulbs. Hotel shit. The type of shit they always put in hotels. Doesn't matter where.

The bed, of course. Queensize. Canopied. Fancy pillows stacked in the corner, like somebody's weddingcake. Linen sheets. Every blanket the innkeeper can spare. *Coperte, per favore! Più coperte!* Still, it never gets warm.

Coperta. Add it up. Two hundred ninety-nine: to overthrow. Or twenty: to breathe, to hide, to sweep away dirt. An illness. A sickness at heart. In Hebrew, מעטה: that's a hundred and twenty-four, which can mean a torch, or a lamp. A forsaking. A passing-by. A delay, maybe. How long?

Clothes laid out on the dresser: gray slacks, black socks, blue oxford shirt. Hat. Wallet. Bunch of weird coins. On the floor, your new white sneakers and your suitcase. Propped in the corner, your ironheaded cane.

Another minute and you'll sit up. Stand. Go to the window. Steady yourself for the long look across the rooftops: the sliver of the Calle dei Botteri on one side, the Calle dei Morti on the other, emptying the quiet campo. You'll stand there and you'll watch. Like you always do.

In this city, nobody's supposed to know you. Though you've walked its streets in your head a million times, you're a stranger here, a tourist. That's a big part of why you came. But somebody down there knows you, and he's headed your way: a bug crawling up your pantleg, making it tough to concentrate. Before he shows up at your door you want to spot him, to sieve his shape from the sparse Lenten crowds. Buzzcut head. Cadenced step. Muscled frame. Easy enough to notice. Just go to the window and wait.

But not right now. Maybe in a while. Not

feeling too good now. No pain, just a funny heavy feeling. The layered blankets rise and fall.

On the wall above the headboard — upside-down at this angle, can't quite see — there's a framed print. Muddy watercolor. Rickety boats. Smeared sky. San Giorgio Maggiore in the background. A view from the Riva degli Schiavoni, probably. J.M.W. TURNER: black letters in the white margin. Some guy who didn't know when to quit. Looks like he tried to erase it with a wet toothbrush.

Turner. That's five hundred and five. Drinking vessels. To declare perverse.

Another gust: the sashes rattle. Three days of cold, late in the season. At low tide the canals are bled out, the gondola-keels stuck in the mud. The whole city kashered. Yesterday at noon you could just about walk to Murano from the Fondamenta Nuove. Imagine it: wading through the muck under the white stones of San Michele. God, what a smell. Slick worms and snailshells. Black ooze between your toes.

Through the angled glass, the fat brick belltower of San Cassiano, dark against damp gray clouds. Crumbling apartments under it: painted stucco flaking from red bricks. Pigeons coo under the eaves; pale shit glues downy puffs to the sill. Seagulls glide by like kites, their little heads moving. So white they seem cut from a different sky.

11

What did this place use to be? Everyplace here used to be something.

On the wall opposite the window is the mirror. Big, in a heavy wood frame. Nothing special about it. More than adequate to your needs. In some crazy way, it's what started everything.

What does a mirror look like? What color is it? Who ever *really* looks at one — and how would you, anyway? You know when it's there, sure. But do you ever really see it? Sort of like God. Or maybe not. But that's the mirror, all right. Invisible commonplace. Machine for unseeing.

That's pretty much what you've wanted all along: to see the mirror. Only that. Not too goddamn much to ask. Is it?

Bells again. One church always starts up as another's nearly finished, so it's tough to keep the count. Plenty late, anyway. The girls at the Biblioteca are probably worried. Wondering where you are. Wondering whether today is the day. Well, ladies, maybe it is.

After the window, the commode. Then dressed. Bite to eat. The phone, maybe. Couple of calls. Night now in Vegas. No sun yet on the East Coast. Wait a little longer. No big rush. You've got time to settle things. A few good cards left to play. No matter what your friend outside thinks: the lovely soldier-boy sniffing your trail from the narrow streets, who's worked so hard and come so

12

far just to kill you.

Plenty of time to deal with him, and with the rest. To go to the window. To look. Meantime, *think,* why don't you? Put it together, as well as it'll stick. Shut your eyes. *Listen.* The old voices. There's a trick to it, just like everything. Never too late to learn. Remember everything you can. Imagine the rest.

You wish like hell you'd brought the goddamn book.

■ ■ ■ ■

Solvtio

MARCH 13, 2003

■ ■ ■ ■

All cities are geological; you cannot take three steps without encountering ghosts bearing all the prestige of their legends. We move within a *closed* landscape whose landmarks draw us constantly toward the past. Certain *shifting* angles, certain *receding* perspectives, allow us to glimpse original conceptions of space, but this vision remains fragmentary. It must be sought in the magical locales of fairy tales and surrealist writings: castles, endless walls, little forgotten

bars, mammoth caverns, casino mirrors.
— IVAN CHTCHEGLOV,
"Formulary for a New Urbanism"

2

A little farther up the Strip the pirates are at it again: their last cannons boom as the taxi drops him at the curb, and he crosses the Rialto Bridge to the sound of distant applause. A whiff of sulfur in the scattered air turns the early-evening breeze slightly infernal. He wrinkles his nose, fights the urge to spit.

Picture him there, on the moving sidewalk: short and broad-shouldered, high-yellow skin and black freckles, around forty years old. He wears wraparound sunglasses, new bluejeans, a leather blazer and a slate-gray T-shirt. A Redskins cap perches on his freshly shaven head, brim low on his brow. His feet move across the walkway's textured surface, weaving around tourists who stop for photos, cluster at the rails. Below, somewhere out of sight, a gondolier sings in a high clear voice — *o mia patria sì bella e perduta* — as he turns his boat around. A gust comes from the west, and the song fades like a weak broadcast.

The man — his name is Curtis — enters

the hotel beneath the lancet arches of a portico, then walks through the slot machines to the elevators. A blast of perfumed air from the HVAC raises gooseflesh on his sweaty neck. He eyes the blackjack tables as he passes, studying every gambler seated there. He's tense, fretful, afraid he's missing something.

He punches the button for Floor 29 and begins to rise. Alone for a moment. His reflection wavery in the copper-tinted doors. He swaps his shades for a pair of black-rimmed safety glasses, fishes his keycard from an inside pocket.

His suite sports two televisions and three telephones, a canopied kingsize rack, vast curtained windows looking south down the Strip. A murky and puzzling painting — the brass plaque on the frame reads J.M.W. TUR-NER — hangs over the fold-out couch in the sunken living area. At six hundred fifty square feet, this is the smallest room the hotel offers. Curtis doesn't like to think about what it's costing Damon to put him up here, but Damon won't object; they both know he's in the right place.

He checks the phone and the fax machine, but nothing's come in. He pulls the new box of hollowpoint hotloads from his jacket pocket and puts it in the little safe in the armoire, then sets his snubnosed revolver on top of it. It's getting dark: the city's vanishing from the windows, replaced by the reversed image of the room itself. Curtis switches off the overhead lights, looks out at the view: Harrah's and the Mirage down the Strip, the belltower and turquoise canal below. A flash of memory, from three years ago: Stanley leaning on the balustrade above the moored gondolas. Tweed driver cap cocked on his bony head. Stirring the air with small gnarled hands. The new moon low in the west, a washed-out circle in the black. Stanley reciting a poem: *Burn, thief of images, on the amnesic sea!* Something like that. Before Curtis can get a fix on it, it's gone.

Lights are coming on all over the city, trembling in the rising heat. The blue-white beam of the Luxor is just visible in the distance, a streak in the indigo sky. Curtis thinks about home, wonders whether he should call, but Philly is three hours ahead: Danielle will already be asleep. Instead he undresses to his boxers, folds his clothes, tries to find something sexy on the widescreen TV, but all he seems to get are computer graphics of cruise missiles and 3-D rotating maps of the Gulf. After a while he puts down the remote and does pushups and situps on the carpeted deck as the talking heads drone on above him, speculating eagerly about the war to come, their jerky pictures freezing up from time to time, glitching out into flat digital mosaics.

When he's done, Curtis mutes the television and opens the safe again. His wedding ring is there, next to the box of ammunition, and he slips it on, takes it off, puts it in his mouth and sucks on it, clicking it against the backs of his teeth. He unholsters the little revolver, unloads and checks the cylinder, and dry-fires it at the flickering TV, one hundred times with his right hand, eighty with his left, until his forearms burn and his index fingers are raw and chapped. It's a new gun; he doesn't know it as well as he should.

His stomach turns over with a gurgle, still upset by the long flight and the many sleepless hours before it. He locks up the ring and the pistol and walks into the fancy marble head, where he sits on the commode and fishes through his shaving kit for his nailclippers. His hands smell like gun-oil and are cracked from the dry air, and for the first time today Curtis remembers, really remembers, what it was like being in the Desert.

3

Later that night, on his way back from dinner, Curtis spots Stanley's girl at a blackjack table downstairs.

He stops for a second, blinking in surprise, then begins a slow clockwise orbit of the gaming floor, keeping her on his good side, in his periph. Picking up a ginger-ale along the way to busy his hands. She's looking around, but not at him.

Two hundred eighty degrees later he parks himself at a video poker machine, breaks a roll of quarters, wets his lips from his clear plastic cup. He's been worried about recognizing her — he has no photo to go by, and only saw her once before, nearly two years ago, at his dad's wedding — but now he's surprised to find he knows her right away. She still looks like a college student, although she must be near thirty by now. She reminds Curtis of some of the white kids who used to Metro in from College Park to hear his dad's combo play in Adams-Morgan, or on U Street. Cool, smart, a little cagey. Toughened up by a few hard knocks — brought on by bad decisions, not by circumstances or bad luck. Thin. Wavy brown hair. Big eyes, widely spaced. She should be pretty but she's not. A mistaken idea of pretty. Pretty sketched by somebody who's never seen it, working off a verbal description.

Curtis watches her for the better part of an hour: her shifting eyes, the trickle of people behind her. Waiting for her to move, or for Stanley to materialize from the crowd. Stanley never does, and she doesn't budge. She's definitely counting cards, but she doesn't seem to be after a big score; her bets don't change much as the count goes up and down.

21

She seems distracted, like she's just killing time.

The machine deals Curtis three queens, and he dumps one, afraid of hitting a big payout and drawing attention to himself. The girl is playing just like he's playing. Does she know she's being followed?

Then, off to the right, an old man in a sportcoat, slender and compact, hurrying along the patterned maroon bulkhead. It's not Stanley — too gawky, too nervous — but the girl stops in mid-play, her eyes widening. She tracks the old man for a second, her brow furrowed, and then slumps in her seat. The dealer says something to get her back in the game, and she shoots him a glare. It's all over in an instant.

But now Curtis knows: he'll be able to find her here whenever he needs to. She's looking for Stanley too.

He drops the last of his quarters and heads back to his room. A fax is waiting for him: a cartoon drawn on *SPECTACULAR!* hotel letterhead, showing a muscular dark-skinned man sodomizing an older guy with exaggerated Semitic features. The cartoon Curtis's expression is grim, determined; his face and arms are densely shaded with slashing diagonals. Comma-shaped teardrops shoot from the panicked Stanley's wrinkled eyes. Across the top of the page, Damon has written in block capitals, *GO GITTIM!!!* Across the bot-

22

tom, *THAS MAH BOY!!!!!*

Curtis crumples the fax and drops it in the trash. Then he fishes it out, rips it into small pieces, and flushes the pieces down the toilet.

4

It rains overnight. Curtis wakes to see lightning flash against the bathroom door, rolls over to get a better look, and dozes off again right away. He remembers hearing drops against the glass, but in the morning there's nothing, no sign of moisture at all.

He's already dialed before he thinks to look at his watch — it's Friday, nearly noon now in D.C. — but Mawiyah picks up anyway. Curtis! she says, a broad smile in her voice. *As-Salaam-Alaikum,* Little Brother! I didn't recognize your number on the Caller-ID. You get a new phone?

I did, Curtis says. I sure did. Say, I just remembered what day it is. I'm surprised to find you home. I figured you'd be on your way to the temple by now.

Well, we're running a little late this morning. And thank God for that, or we would have missed your call! How are you?

I'm doing all right. I don't want to hold you up too much, though. I was hoping to catch my dad. He's around?

Curtis hears a soft tap as Mawiyah sets the receiver down. Her whippoorwill voice grows distant, abstract, as she moves through the house. As he waits, Curtis is struck by a couple of memories in quick succession. First, her photo, hung outside the library at Dunbar: six years ahead of him, still a legendary presence there. Four days a week he passed it on his way to the practice field and another asskicking courtesy of the defensive line. Second, years later: her singing "Let's Get Lost" in a tiny 18th Street club, eyes closed against the blue light. His father behind her, in shadow, leaning on his bass. Out of prison, not yet cleaned up for good. She was Nora Brawley then; his dad was still Donald Stone. Curtis had come straight from National, on leave from Subic, jetlagged and exhausted, still wearing service-alpha greens. He remembers a beerbottle's sweat beneath his fingers, and the way everything seemed to be tipping over. Stanley was there somewhere, too. Invisible. His voice a loose thread in the dark.

Curtis hears his father's heavy footsteps, telegraphed through the floor, the table, the phone. Little Man!

Hey, Pop.

Real smart, calling when you know I can't talk for too long. Let me call you back on my cell.

No, that's okay, Pop. I just want to ask a quick favor. I'm trying to get in touch with Stanley.

Curtis feels a bubble of silence open between them. Stanley? his father says. Stanley Glass?

Yeah, Dad. Stanley Glass. I need to get a hold of him. Do you maybe have a telephone number, or —

What in the hell you need to talk to Stanley Glass for, Little Man?

It's — I'm just trying to help somebody out, Pop. Friend of mine's looking for him. This is the guy I told you about, the one who's gonna hook me up with that job at the Point.

At the what? I thought you said you're gonna be working for —

The Spectacular. I am. It's the same thing, Dad. Everybody who works there calls it the Point, because —

Well, then what does your *friend* want with Stanley Glass? And has he ever heard of dialing 4-1-1? Stanley's right there in the Philly White Pages. You just gotta —

I don't think Stanley's in Philly anymore, Dad. Or in AC. I think he's out here.

Wait wait wait. Out where?

Vegas, Curtis says. I'm calling you from Las Vegas.

His father draws a heavy breath, lets it out. Curtis has made a mistake by bringing him into this. Look, Dad, he says. I know you don't have time to talk —

I haven't kept up with Stanley too much, Curtis, his father says. Stanley is a great man

25

and a great friend, one of my oldest friends in the world, but I haven't talked to him too much since Mawiyah and I got married. I don't judge him, and I don't bear him any ill will, but the fact is, Curtis —

I know, Dad.

The fact is — if I may finish — the fact is that Stanley is a professional gambler. And Mawiyah and I are good Muslims now. Or I'm trying to be one, anyway. And the teachings of the Prophet, peace be upon him, very specifically prohibit —

I know all about this, Dad.

I know you know. But you need to understand. Stanley is a gambler all the time. He is a pure gambling machine. To be with Stanley is to gamble with Stanley. And so: I cannot be around Stanley. I love him, he's my brother, but —

Look, Dad, I'm making you late. This is not that important. I understand what you're saying, and —

I just need you to hear me out on this, Curtis.

I'm hearing you out, Dad. All right? I'm sorry I bothered you. I gotta go. Tell Mawiyah goodbye for me.

Curtis hangs up. He stares at the new cellphone for a moment, pondering his own apparently limitless capacity for misunderstanding and foolishness. He still hasn't called his wife.

He makes the big hotel rack to calm himself down, pulling the sheets flat and tight. This provides a kind of cheap satisfaction and solace. Outside, the rinsed-and-dried city buzzes in the morning light, inventing itself for the coming day.

5

The Strip trolley picks Curtis up at Harrah's, four hundred yards south of his own hotel. He pays his two bucks, takes a seat near the front, and scans the sidewalks as they roll along: Slots A Fun, the Crazy Girls billboard, the fat blue tentacles of the Wet 'n Wild waterslides. Stooped yellow cranes tend the grave of the Desert Inn, swinging steel girders over pale mounds of earth. Guys with firehoses spray everything in sight, trying to cut down on the dust, but it isn't working: the ground just drinks it up, and the still air is hung all around with wisps of silica.

The trolley is nearly empty at this hour, silent but for the diesel's lulling chug, and Curtis finds himself twisted in his seat, craning his neck to catch a glimpse of Mount Charleston through the rain-washed morning air. Lots of snow still left at the peak. Even at this distance it's fiercely white in the blinding sun, a gap at the horizon, a space intentionally left blank.

The mountain vanishes behind the three-legged tower of the Stratosphere, and Curtis turns forward again. The big casinos are all behind them now, the streets lined with motels, wedding chapels, lingerie shops. The Boulevard between here and downtown always reminds Curtis of Subic, the bridge into Olongapo, minus the shit-smelling river, the moneychanger booths, the boys begging for centavos. A few hard-eyed and ragged leafleteers have already reported for duty, sipping coffee from paper cups, satchels bulging at their feet. Last night's handbills and magazines blow across the sidewalks: ads for sex clubs, escort services, brothels in Pahrump. The palmtrees are thinning out, replaced by billboards: the city advertising itself to itself. Curtis is surprised by a quick tremor of glee; he catches his breath, fights back a smile. *What happens here stays here.* He's alone, at risk, alive in his own skin for the first time in years.

The trolley unloads him near Fremont Street, the main downtown drag, lately closed to vehicular traffic and spanned by a steel canopy studded with concert speakers and tiny colored lights. The lights are off now, the speakers silent. A few earlybird dayshifters drift in from the sidestreets: waiters and dancers and dealers in streetclothes, uniforms stuffed into backpacks or duffelbags. Curtis is still operating on Philly time; he feels foolish for starting so early. Wherever Stanley is

28

now, he's asleep.

Curtis walks up Fourth to the restaurant at the Gold Spike, amused and a little disappointed to find that the price of a two-egg breakfast has more than doubled since his last visit: they now ask a buck ninety-nine. He places his order at the counter, sits in a booth by the window, watches as delivery trucks and taxis and armored cars move across the dust-flecked glass.

Nearly three years gone by. In the summer of 2000, coming off his first Balkan tour, Curtis got TDY'd to Twentynine Palms to help with combined-arms exercises: six months of grit in his molars, charred rock and crucible sun. The way the Corps saw it, Curtis was a combat veteran who'd been in the Gulf in '91, who'd done counterinsurgency in Kosovo and Somalia, and they wanted him to share his experience with their green recruits. Curtis had been a terrible teacher, reluctant to revisit operations he felt he'd done a halfassed job on in the first place, unable to come up with anything that felt like wisdom in his mouth. He tried to pass along what he'd learned — battlefield circulation control, rear-area security, processing EPWs — but it all came out as textbook stuff, the same standard-issue post-Vietnam bromides he'd scoffed at himself at his first CAX back in '84, and he could tell the boots weren't hearing it. And anyway, nobody really

29

wanted to think about how to handle fifty Iraqi soldiers surrendering to a four-man scout team, or to a water truck. People are always ready to prepare for the worst, not so much the ridiculous. How many of those fresh-minted marines are in the Sandbox now? Curtis wonders. In Kuwait and Saudi. Waiting for the whistle to blow, for the second half to start.

Twentynine Palms reunited Curtis with guys he went through MP school with at Leonard Wood, guys his own age, and they got to be pretty tight, keeping each other entertained, driving to San Diego or TJ or Vegas on weekends. Damon always organized the Vegas trips: caravans of marines speeding across the desert, taking over whole floors at Circus Circus or the Plaza, *semper fi*'ing back and forth over craps tables and handing fist-fuls of taxpayer dollars over to the girls at the Palomino and Glitter Gulch. Damon's excursions always drew new faces, younger guys, marines Curtis had never met, and they all wanted to talk about Damon. Shit, they'd say, that guy's the craziest MP in the Corps. But Damon wasn't crazy. He always kept it together: pacing himself, quarterbacking, pulling the strings. Always in good working order when everybody else was throwing away their money, puking on their shoes.

On the last trip, they were moving in a pack through one of the big casinos — Caesars, or maybe the Trop, scaring civilians, razzing fly-boys from Nellis — when Curtis felt a tap on his shoulder and turned to find Stanley there. Stanley looked thin, even gaunt, but still dialed in tight; he was lithe and strong in Curtis's awkward embrace. When Curtis asked what brought him to town, Stanley just gave him a funny grin that could've meant *do you have to ask?* could've meant *you'd never guess.* They talked for a minute about Curtis's dad, about the Corps, about people they both knew back East, and then the conversation turned a corner and Curtis, maybe three-quarters drunk, found himself unable to keep up. Stanley was telling a story about a hand of blackjack he'd played at the Barbary Coast — about something that happened during it, or something it made him think of — and then about an English magician named Flood, and a famous trick he did in which unrelated objects moved in ghostly parallel, as if linked by invisible threads. Curtis kept expecting Stanley to explain how the trick was done, or to connect it back to the black-jack game, but he never did, and suddenly he was silent, watching Curtis, waiting for a response.

Now, sitting in the booth at the Gold Spike, sponging spilt yolk with folded-over toast, Curtis is shaken by the memory: it cools his blood, stifles his appetite. It's hard to say why.

Partly it bothers him that he could fail so completely to understand a man he's known his whole life. But that's not it, or not entirely. Something else is poisoning the recollection: a nightmare feeling, irrational and uncanny. A sense of menace hidden in plain sight. The presence of an impostor. As if it wasn't really Stanley that Curtis met in the casino that night. Or, worse, that it was Curtis who was off, who wasn't really himself.

At the time, of course, he didn't feel any of this: it was just an awkward moment. He and Stanley stood there; Curtis looked down, shuffled his feet. Then Damon walked up, and Curtis introduced them.

And that was it: the first time the two of them met. It seemed like such a small thing then. Like nothing. Now Curtis can barely track what has followed from it.

The rest of that night is a drunken blur in his memory, but he retains one last lucid image: Damon sitting at a $25 table, bright-eyed and focused, smirking at his cards as Stanley hovered behind him, a hand on his shoulder, whispering into the shaven base of his skull.

So in a way, Curtis figures, all of this is his own fault.

6

The dayshift comes on at noon, and Curtis begins walking down Fremont, from the ElCo to the Plaza, stopping at every casino along the way. He talks to croupiers and dealers, waitresses and bartenders, floor people, security guards, and every pit boss or casino host whose ear he can bend. In each case he tailors his story to his audience, mostly blowing variations on *I'm looking for a friend, he's staying somewhere in town, I'm hoping to throw some action his way.* Everybody gets Curtis's cell number, and he drops a few double sawbucks where he thinks they might do some good. A couple of people say they've seen Stanley in the last week or so. Everyone over the age of forty seems to recognize his name.

Curtis was nervous at first about operating in the open, laying such thick spoor, but he's over that now. If he's not visible, then this isn't going to work, not in what little time he's got. He's never been wired for cloak-and-dagger shit anyhow, which by now Damon should know. Sneaking around, in Curtis's view, generally amounts to time-wasting; better to just say what you want, then own whatever comes with wanting it. If Damon has a problem with that approach, he could have called somebody else. Out here Curtis has done nothing wrong, has nothing to hide

Not yet, anyway.

each place he stops, he makes the same ckwise circuit of the tables, scanning the crowd for Stanley's bald head, his narrow shoulders, his beaked nose. He comes up empty every time, but always feels like there's something he's not seeing. He's rusty, and still doesn't trust his eye.

He leaves Main Street Station with two rolls of quarters in his pocket and catches the trolley to the Stratosphere. Starting his long trek south. He's making better time, zeroing in on the right people: pit bosses with ten-dollar haircuts, middle-aged bartenders, valets who look him in the eye. Damon's cash is going fast, but Curtis feels like he's buying something with it now.

Nobody's asked him any tough questions, but he runs through his story anyway, rehearsing made-up dialogue as he's passing between casinos, crossing the boulevard. Thinking back to ten days ago, South Philly, Damon in a booth at the Penrose Diner. Swirling the dregs of his third coffee, brown parabola lapping the bone-white rim. *I'm not asking you to lie. Just keep it simple. If anybody presses you, you just tell 'em you're collecting on a marker. That's the truth, right?* Yellow hair trimmed to a uniform half-inch, longer than Curtis had ever seen it. Beige houndstooth suit wrinkled like it'd been slept in, though Damon clearly

34

hadn't slept in days. *The trick is to have layers. See? You give up a little, they think they got the whole picture.* Dark eyes watery but alert, like greased ballbearings. One obsidian cufflink in his black poplin sleeve, a few raveled threads where its mate was torn out. *It's fine to drop my name if you think that'll help. Nobody's gonna know what happened in Atlantic City. Or, if they do know, they won't make any connections.* A new mobile phone atop an unmarked #10 envelope. An e-ticket printout inside — UA 2123 dep PHL 07:00 arr LAS 09:36 03/13/2003 — wrapped around three packs of hundred-dollar traveler's checks. *What you tell your wife is your business. Look, this is not dangerous. Nobody's breaking any laws. You find him, and you call me. You do it no later than twelve a.m. next Tuesday night. It's that simple.*

Curtis watched Damon's Audi pull out of the lot and disappear up the onramp toward the Whitman Bridge. He finished his slice of apple pie along with the chocolate napoleon that Damon had barely touched, ordered himself another coffee, and sat not reading his newspaper until nearly rush hour, when he walked back to the subway. The next morning he awoke at four with Danielle's alarm, listened as she dressed and left for work, and lay sleepless and staring at the sky through the miniblinds as it went from black

35

to red to yellow to white. Then he rose and cleaned up and caught the bus down to Collingdale, where he bought the gun.

South of Fashion Show Mall the casinos are bigger, busier now that it's later in the day, and everything takes longer. By eight o'clock he's past the airport, leapfrogging places that seem unlikely, feeding quarters to the southbound trolley as it carries him from block to block to block. He stops at the buffet at the Tropicana to load up on prime rib and peeled shrimp by the glow of heatlamps and coral-reef aquariums, then sits for an hour above the deserted pool and watches the reflections of palmtrees nod in the wind-purled water. Once his food has settled, he humps it east to the Hôtel San Rémo, west to the Orleans, south to the Luxor and Mandalay Bay.

On the long ride back to his own hotel he nods off for a second, then jolts awake, his heart skittering. Outside the streaked bus windows the city seems different, alive in a way that it wasn't before. There's steady foot traffic along the boulevard, laughing and shouting and acting out, and the street is full of high-end rental cars, windows down, stereos rattling. Stretch limousines idle at curbside, sly and circumspect, while the sidewalk procession slides backlit across their mute black windshields. Time seems to pass in a hurry. Curtis thinks of bad places he's been, of nights he's spent along razor-taped perimeters, eyeing burning wells and distant winks of small-arms fire. Very different from this. But the same nervous thrill, the same sense of something gathered just beyond the lights, waiting for a signal to move. For the first time in a long while Curtis feels as if he's in the world again — the real world, inhuman and unconstructed — where he can be anybody, or nobody, and where anything is possible.

He's reached the door to his room, is swiping his keycard, when his cellphone throbs to life. The unfamiliar ringtone startles him; he jumps, the door swings open, and the keycard drops and slides along the tile just inside the jamb. Curtis digs for the phone as he stoops to retrieve it.

A loud voice on the line, not one he can place. Curtis! it says. How you been, man?

I'm good. What's up?

You know who this is? You recognize my voice? It's Albedo, man! Remember me? I hear you're in town!

Curtis doesn't know anybody named Albedo — or Al Beddow, for that matter. A white guy, probably his own age. Blue Ridge accent: North Carolina, Virginia. Crowd noise in the background. Yeah, Curtis says. I'm here for a few days.

That's great, man. We gotta hook up, we gotta hang out. What are you doing right now?

I'm — I just got back to my hotel.

Your hotel? Fuck, man, it's like eleven. You can't go back to your hotel. Look, I'm at the Hard Rock right now with some people. You need to get your ass over here. You know where it is?

Curtis knows where it is. He's half inside his doorway, dead phone cradled in his hand. Trying again to place that voice. Maybe somebody he talked to earlier. Maybe somebody who's watching what he says because of who he's with. Curtis closes his eyes, tries to form a picture of Albedo — shrouded in dim light, loud music, the clamor of raised voices, Stanley's maybe among them — but at the center of Curtis's picture is an absence, a void in the smoky air, and he quickly gives up.

Leaning farther into the dark entryway, checking the fax and the message-light, he hears a door slam somewhere down the corridor and is suddenly uneasy, an interloper in shared space, aware of the closeness of unseen others. Somebody's been here while he was out: housekeeping, of course. For a second he can sense the strata of odors in the room — a hidden history of cleansers, perfumes, sweat — before his nose habituates and they're blended, gone. Due south, a block off the Strip, some kind of event is going on, the grand opening of something. Four times a minute the beam of a swiveling searchlight falls through the open curtains; the suite's furnishings appear, disappear, appear. With each sweep, the air over the city turns a solid blue, flat and opaque, and the room seems telescoped, shallow, a diorama of itself.

After a couple of passes, Curtis pulls his revolver and checks it in the wan light that leaks from the hallway. Then he hurries back to the elevators, and the door shuts itself behind him.

7

The Hard Rock is on Paradise Road, between the Strip and the UNLV campus — not far, but Curtis doesn't want to risk missing Albedo, so he hops a cab and is there in minutes.

He's been here before, but only briefly and drunkenly, and he doesn't remember it well. It's small, chalk-white and curvy, lit from below by purple-gelled spots; the glowing diodes of a streetside readerboard flash OZZY OSBOURNE! as the cab turns onto the palm-lined drive. A parade of revelers — off-duty dancers and bartenders, highrollers from the coast — pours inside by the light of an enormous neon-strung guitar.

As soon as he's stepped through the Gibson-handled doors Curtis knows Stanley won't be here. It's all young MBA types inside, college kids on extended spring break: aside from Ozzy, Curtis is probably the oldest guy in the place. On his way through the crowded lobby he passes a cardigan-clad Britney Spears mannequin, somebody's glassed-in drumkit, a chandelier made of gleaming saxophones. Aerosmith blasts from speakers overhead. In the circular casino Curtis stops to read the mulberry baize of a blackjack table: there, above a line of lyrics he can't place — something about getting lucky — is a notice that dealers must hit soft seventeens. Stanley wouldn't be caught dead within a hundred yards of this joint.

Close to the disc-shaped bar it's even louder. The crowd, the machines, the PA blend and collide into an indistinct roar, a new silence. Curtis only gradually becomes aware of someone screaming his name from a few yards away: a longhaired white guy. Ripped jeans, Guns N' Roses T-shirt, motorcycle jacket. He's grinning, half-silhouetted against the wavery light of a flatscreen TV, one splayfingered arm swaying over his head like a strand of kelp. Curtis is certain he's never seen this guy before in his life.

Up close, Albedo looks like a bad blend of Chet Baker and Jimmy Buffett. His fingers are sepia-stained; his grip is firm but clammy, tentacled, and Curtis is quick to release it. He's tall, six-three at least, but soft in the middle. His thin brown hair is pulled back in a curly ponytail, gray at the temples. His eyeballs are rose-rimmed, watery, and he smells of whiskey and pot.

Albedo's sitting with two young women — one pale, blond, the other dark, probably Hispanic, both wearing sequined halters. Curtis can't read anything in their faces aside from exhaustion and low expectations. The women move apart and leave two empty bar-chairs between them; Albedo claps a hand on Curtis's back and steers him into the one on the right. As he sags into his own seat, his fingers drag drunkenly down Curtis's blazer and brush the shape of the revolver at his waist, and Curtis knows immediately that this is wrong, that he ought to get out of here.

Albedo's ordering him a Corona; he introduces him to the women as if they're old friends. We were in the Desert together, he says. The first Iraq war. The women's names are unusual, foreign; Curtis is thinking fast, trying to keep his shit together, not really paying attention, and he forgets them immediately.

You been keeping up with the news from over there? Albedo asks. You believe all the bullshit that's going down?

What? Did it start?

Any minute, man. Albedo nods sagely, as if privy to secret knowledge. And I tell you what, he says, raising his glass. Better them than us. Right, my brother?

Curtis nods, sips silently.

I was just now trying to articulate to my two young companions, Albedo says, neither of whom has the good fortune to be a citizen of this great nation of ours, the magnitude of the fucked-up-ness going down in the Middle East tonight. Because, see, the first war — *our* war? — *that* was total bullshit. No doubt about that. But *this* just takes the proverbial cake. Am I right, Curtis?

Curtis picks up his beer, then rotates the cardboard coaster under it, aligning the text with the edge of the counter. He sets the beer down again. He doesn't want to talk about this, or think about it. It's a messed-up situation, he says.

Truer words were never spoke, my man. You are putting that shit mildly.

A pack of cigarettes and a silver Binion's lighter appear on the bar, and Albedo lights up with a flourish. He's leaning way back in his chair, balancing it on two legs; Curtis has to crane his neck to keep him in sight. The blond girl to Albedo's left is looking back and forth between them, her brow wrinkled, like she's trying hard to understand. Something about her reminds Curtis of the Balkans, almost but not quite, and he figures her for Ukrainian, or maybe Slovak. He's calming down now, assessing. His beer is still three-quarters full.

So how's civilian life treating you, Albedo?

Real good, man. Real good. I am every day relishing my freedom. And I'm telling you, this is the *place*. Shit is *happening* out here. Lots of opportunities for guys like us. I oughta make a few calls while you're in town. Introduce you to some people. Would you be into that?

Sure, maybe. How long you been out here?

Albedo flashes a sharky grin. Long enough to get the lay of the land, my friend. To learn the ins and the outs. This town is all about the *juice,* man.

So's everywhere else.

Well, okay, sure, man. Touché. But *here* especially. And it's different here. It's wide-open, entry-level. There ain't the antidemocratic bullshit you get most other places. No country-club secret-handshake jive. No artificial barriers to trade. Everything just is what it is.

What are you doing now?

What? For dollars, you mean? Albedo smirks, shaking his head, like this is a dumb question. I'm doing *lots* of shit, man. I'm just taking it as it comes. And lately it's been coming faster than I can reach out and grab it. I got action to give away.

Anything steady?

Some of it is. A couple nights a week I been chauffeuring these lovely ladies around town. To their various assignations. Them and a number of their professional cohorts. And that earns me enough to live on: two nights a week, eight or ten hours a night, chauffeur and security. Shit, the fucking *valets* out here pull down six figures per annum. It's a boomtown, baby. For the right kind of guy. Boom boom boom.

Curtis gives Albedo a thin smile. This is a bunch of static, and it's good to see him dishing it out, overplaying his hand. The guy's dumping a lot of chum, but he can't seem to figure out how to get any hooks baited, and Curtis starts to think that maybe he's not in trouble here after all. Unless Albedo's just stalling, lining him up for the blindside. Curtis turns away, scans the screaming crowd. Somewhere behind him a slot machine is playing a tinny rendition of "Tequila"; the familiar melody emerges from the surrounding noise like light coming through a pinhole. His beer is half-empty now.

The Hispanic girl is smiling, watching him, and he gives her a polite nod. He wonders what she and the other girl are doing here with Albedo when they could be out earning, and then he thinks maybe they're earning right now. She's leaning close to him. I like your glasses, she says. With each syllable Curtis feels a tiny puff of air on his neck.

Her accent isn't bad; she's been in the States awhile. I wear contacts, she says. Her irises are the color of Windex, so Curtis isn't surprised to hear this. She reaches for his

44

face. Can I try?

Curtis lets her. They are not so strong, she says, handing them back.

They're nonprescription.

So are my contacts, she confides. Also nonprescription. She sleepily bats her mascaraed lashes.

¿De dónde eres? Curtis asks.

I am from Cuba.

He wouldn't have guessed, but it's there in her voice, in her stretched vowels and dropped *s*'s and *nonprescrikshun.* He wonders how she ended up here instead of Miami or Tampa or NYC but has neither the vocabulary nor the inclination to pursue the topic.

¿De qué región?

Santiago de las Vegas. You know where is Santiago de las Vegas?

Está cerca de la Habana, ¿verdad?

Yes. You have been to Cuba?

Sí, Curtis says, *he estado en Cuba,* but he doesn't say where, or why. If he hadn't taken his retirement he might be there right now, and he thinks about that for a second. Recalling a bright morning last April in the hills above Granadillo Bay. Looking down at the camp. All the orange jumpsuits like cactus-flowers caught in the wire.

You speak good Spanish, the girl says. She's not very convincing; her smile has started to wilt. She has fingers on his thigh now, a foot brushing his ankle. Moving automatically,

45

like this is something she learned from an instructional video, which for all Curtis knows maybe she did.

He pats her roaming hand and turns back to Albedo, who's trying to explain to the blond girl who Condoleezza Rice is. Taps him on the shoulder.

What's up, my man? Albedo says. You need another beer?

How'd you find out I'm in town?

Albedo looks surprised, nonplussed; he sputters theatrically for a second. It ain't exactly a secret, he says.

No. It's not. But how did you find out?

They stare at each other. Albedo's face is empty, frozen between expressions. A big vein flutters on his throat; Curtis half-consciously counts the throb: one-two, three-four, five-six.

Damon, Albedo says. He told me. Called me up last night. Gave me your cell.

Curtis narrows his eyes. And how do you know Damon, again?

What do you mean? I know him from the Desert, man. Same place you know him from. What are you talking about?

I know Damon from Leonard Wood, Curtis says. I was in Saudi during the war. He was on float, on the *Okinawa*. I wasn't with Damon in the Gulf.

Albedo grinds out his cigarette, drinks from his empty glass, leans back farther into Cur-

46

tis's blind spot. Well, whatever, man, he says.
That's where *I* know him from.

Curtis waits for him to tip forward again.
He's dropping his baffled act; there's a challenge in his eyes. He's not as drunk as Curtis
thought. Okay, Curtis says. Where do I know
you from?

Albedo looks at Curtis, shrugs, and turns
away. His index finger shoots up like a snail's
eye. Corona, he says across the bar.

Do I know you?

Albedo turns back, an oilslick grin spreading across his face. Well, he says, you goddamn sure know me now. Don't you? Bar-
keep, get this gentleman another —

No thanks. I'm done.

Hey now. Chill out, Curtis. Any friend of
Damon's is a friend of yours. Right?

Curtis kills the last of his beer, pushes the
bottle away, rubs the condensation into his
chapped fingers. Did Damon tell you why
I'm in town?

Just that you're doing some work for him at
the Point. Looking for a guy who skipped on
a marker. That's about it.

Did he tell you who I'm looking for?

Albedo's little black eyes flit in their sockets.
I don't think so, he says after a while. I don't
believe that he did. Anybody I'd know?

No. Nobody you'd know.

I know a lot of people, Curtis.

I'm sure you do.

47

Albedo takes his beer from the bartender, then fishes out his lighter and another ciga-rette. He cups his hand around the flame, and he and Curtis study each other through the curling smoke. Curtis feels his eyesocket twitch, tear up. He swivels, scoots his chair back, and moves the Cuban girl's hand into her own lap. She jerks like she's been asleep. Goodnight, he tells her. Good to meet you.

Albedo's getting up too, juggling his ciga-rette, coughing a little on an errant breath. Whoa now, Curtis! he says. Where's the fire, son?

I'm gonna hit the road.

What are you talking about? The night is still young!

I've had a long day.

I got stuff I want to show you. Very interest-ing things.

Maybe next time.

Albedo laughs and nods — all right, all right, he's saying — but he's also trying to block Curtis's exit, and Curtis shifts his weight, starts thinking about where to hit him.

At least let me give you my cell number, man.

I got it. It's in my phone.

Some of the people at the bar are looking at them now. Albedo glances around, then grins, relaxes, becoming harmless and dif-fuse. Okay, he says. Okay, kemosabe. You're hurting my feelings, man. But look here. I'm gonna tell you just what I told Damon. I know this town. This town knows me. I can open up a lot of doors for you. This is not bullshit. You can ask Damon if you don't believe me.

I'll do that.

Albedo steps aside. His big right hand flutters to his mouth, leaves his cigarette there, drops and hovers in the space before him. Curtis stares it for a second, figuring distance; Albedo's face floats above it, blank and watchful. And now, at last, the man does seem familiar. Curtis has never met him before, but he's met guys like him — in the Desert, in Mogadishu, at Gitmo — and he's been sorry for it every time.

He wants to take Albedo's hand while looking him in the eye, but he's tired and rattled and can't do it: he looks at the hand. Goodnight, he says, shaking it. Thanks for the beer.

He turns on his heel and goes. There's a band of towering NBA types headed his way; he steps among them and lets himself drift toward the saxophone chandelier, the lobby, the marquee. Hearing Albedo's lubricated voice somewhere behind him — *You're never gonna find your guy if you can't stay up past two a.m., marine!* — before it's drowned out by the conversation shouted a foot above his head. A few yards on, he shoulders past a couple of college kids in tennis shirts and

49

vanishes, anonymous again, encoded into the crowd. Everyone looking everywhere. He feels eyes sliding off him, water beaded on wax.

The pack of people just ahead slows to look at a gleaming black-and-chrome Harley on a raised platform, and Curtis turns back for an instant. Albedo's still standing there, flanked by the two women, scanning the round room with squinted eyes. One big hand is pressed to his left ear, his cellphone is in the other, and he sways like an anemone on his planted feet as passersby jostle him. When Curtis looks forward again his path has cleared, and he steps swiftly and lightly to the hotel exit. Walking into the neon glow, the clean night air.

8

When the cab hits the Strip about a mile down Harmon, Curtis drops a twenty through the gap in the plastic divider and is on his feet before the wheels have stopped. He doubletimes to the squat twin domes of the Aladdin, through a horseshoe arch and into the Desert Passage mall, zigzagging between shoppers, catching details from the blur of ornaments and signs: tunnel vaults, porticos, jeweled mosaics, screens and lattices, eight-pointed stars. Hookah Gallery, Pashmina by Tina, Napoleon Fine Fashions,

Lucky Eye Design. Fake rain falls from a fake sky. Patterns proliferate, as if in terror of blankness: geometric, vegetal, endlessly elaborated. Every surface seems vented, weightless, shot through with numberless holes.

Curtis makes a right at a twenty-foot hurricane glass — he mistakes it at first for a neon minaret — and finds himself in a parking lot on Audrie Street, a block off the Strip, alone and exposed under the humming monorail tracks. He crosses to the back entrance of Paris and takes the skywalk to Bally's, cuts through their casino to Flamingo Road, hops another cab. He doesn't think anyone's following him but he wants to be sure; he's spending a lot of Damon's money now but fuck it, fuck Damon for putting some sketchy shitbag onto him without giving him a heads-up. He's digging out the new phone, dialing the only name on the CONTACTS list.

He's not sure if the number Damon gave him is home or work or cell or what, and there's no greeting when it picks up, just a beep. Damon, he says. It's Curtis. I just met up with some guy called Albedo who says he knows you, and who says you told him to call me. I've never seen him or heard of him before, and I hope you'll call me back and tell me what this is about, because the dude seems wrong to me. All right? It's five a.m.

your time. Sorry if I'm waking you up. Later.

To be careful, and to give himself time to think, Curtis has the cabbie drive him as far south as the airport before turning north again. The cab nudges doggedly through the slow after-midnight traffic; Curtis adjusts his cap, settles in his seat, leans his head against the side panel. Staring at his phone's display till the blue light goes out. A nasty down-elevator feeling in his gut.

This doesn't mean anything. Not necessarily. It doesn't mean anything's wrong. If Damon's been making moves without keeping Curtis in the loop, well, that would be SOP for Damon, who is loath to so much as circulate a shopping list prior to a grocery run: everything always has to be need-to-know. It drives Curtis nuts, but it's also partly why Curtis loves him, partly what makes him such a blast to roll with — and partly why Curtis agreed to come out here at all. With Damon, any routine errand could turn into an adventure you'd tell your grandkids about; being kept in the dark was the price of the ticket. Signing on meant drinking a little Kool-Aid, suspending a little disbelief. By now Curtis should know to expect it.

Not everybody finds it charming, though. *Slim Shady:* that's Danielle's nickname for Damon, and not because he looks all that much like Marshall Mathers. He's *that cracker scoundrel friend of yours* when she's pissed

52

off, which lately has been pretty often.

Curtis squashes the phone's keypad with his thumb. The display lights up again: 2:06 a.m. Three timezones east, Danielle's probably leaving for work. This is a good time to catch her, but Curtis can't bring himself to dial, can't begin to imagine what he'd say. He's not even mad anymore, not really. He puts away the phone, presses the heels of his hands to his eyesockets. The taxi rolls to a stop at a traffic signal, rolls forward again when the light changes; inertia tips Curtis forward and back in his seat. He turns to the window, opens his eyes.

The first big blowout since they got married. He's walked out on her before — a few times, not long after they first moved in — but those times he always came right back: home before she'd changed into her PJs. He had no place to run then, nowhere he could imagine himself going. This time he did. And he went.

To keep himself from remembering the argument, he tries to think of the airport: sleepless hours slouched in the cushioned seats at the concourse gate, alone amid a scattering of laid-over travelers. Concentrating hard on the urgent monotonous drip of news from ceiling-bolted televisions. Barely noticing the sunrise in the windows behind him, doubled by the surface of the Delaware. Watching the war take shape.

That's something else she said: one of her pent-up gripes. *Why can't you just admit that it's getting to you?* Okay, sure. She's not wrong. The jumpiness and the short temper, the bad dreams and sleepless nights that he shook off after the Desert, after Mogadishu, after Kosovo — shook them off each time, shook them right off, no trouble — sure, they've come back a little bit. *I see this at the VA all the time, Sammy D. It's a normal thing. There's a war coming on, and you're not in it, and that's gonna bother you.* But it's not the war that bothers Curtis: it's everything else. Everything *but* the war bothers him. The war he knows what to do with. The war makes sense.

This favor Damon's asking — this is not how people get jobs, Curtis. Are you even listening to yourself? Flying to Las Vegas, sneaking around casinos: this is not any kind of career track you want to get on. If you don't want to think about your future, you can think about mine. All right? Because I goddamn sure am not gonna sit around for the next thirty–forty years to watch you cash disability checks. You hear me? This is not the way a grown-up man acts. Not in the real world.

The real world: that's the jab she's leading with nowadays, the power halfback in her offensive pattern. She always says it like there can be no argument about what it means.

But to Curtis, the stuff she talks about —
cover letters and résumés, community college
classes, refinancing the mortgage — it all
seems about a million miles removed from
what he thinks of as reality. Six thousand
miles, anyway. The fact that these are ordinary
concerns for every functional adult in
America just makes him feel worse. Still, he
can't shake the sense that there's something
inane, something thoughtless, in worrying
over stuff like this while another war is coming on. It feels babyish, inconsequential, like
playacting that Curtis never took part in and
has now long since outgrown.

War is a game too, of course; he knows that.
But at least in war the stakes are serious, the
horizon of what's possible vastly expanded,
the immediate objectives as unarguable as a
white stripe across bermuda-grass. You ready
yourself; you go to the war or the war comes
to you; you live or you die. Curtis wonders
whether he'll ever feel so alive in this world
again.

His eyes have closed; he forces them open.
At the stoplight at Flamingo, a group of kids
is crossing, led by a barechested boy with
blue hair and vinyl pants and a cyalume glow-
stick that swings by a cord around his skinny
neck. The boy dances and spins, the glow-
stick appears and disappears like a beacon,
and Curtis remembers a column of flexi-
cuffed Iraqi EPWs that he moved through a

cleared minefield south of Al Burgan back in '91: the way he felt out the safe route in the sand, searching for the bowls of cool green light in the smokeblack petroleum darkness of late afternoon. This strikes a spark off another memory: two nights ago, flying into McCarran, the way the lights came up out of the desert, out of nothing, as if the city were made of nothing but light, and all of it radiating from the Strip.

Then the cabbie is waking him, the taxi door is opening, and Curtis has stepped out into the porte-cochère of his own hotel, pinching his wallet with sleep-numb fingers as he watches the cab's taillights dim and fade under the smug white span of the Rialto Bridge. For a while he just stands there. People step around him. He shakes his head and moves out of the way, adrift on the pavement, rotating to look at the buildings. Rows of trefoils and quatrefoils and crenellations. A gold zodiac ringing a clock's blue face. Above the clock, the casino readerboard, flashing its loop of news down the Strip. The tinted hotel windows catching whatever news flashes back.

When Damon asked him to find Stanley, Curtis thought of this hotel right away, before the sentence had even cleared Damon's teeth. For some reason it's hard now to remember why he thought that. It's like being here in the flesh is tangling him up — like the place itself is blocking the *idea* of the place.

Near the end of that last Vegas trip, Curtis and Stanley walked together to exactly this spot. They stood on the bridge, and they watched the gondolas pass in silhouette over the green coronas cast by underwater lights. The new moon lurked in the east, erased by the earth's shadow, still somehow visible. Stanley kept talking, talking. Curtis was very drunk. He remembers leaning stiff-armed against one of the twin white columns by the boulevard sidewalk, sucking in deep breaths to hold his liquor down.

The Doge, he brought these two columns back from Greece. The real ones, I'm talking about. Not this fake shit here. Twelfth Century, it would have been. The Doge — this guy was like their king, see? — he brought 'em back from a campaign against the Byzantines. Disastrous campaign. He brought back the plague, too. People weren't too happy about that, so they rose up, and they killed him. For years these two columns, they were just lying there next to the water. Every so often, somebody'd say: Hey, you think we ought to raise these things up? But they were so big, see, that nobody could figure how the hell to do it. But then this kid comes along, this engineer, and he says, sure, I'll put these upright for you. But if I can do it, I want the go-ahead to run dice games between 'em. People said okay, and the two columns went up, right there on the Piazetta. And that is where it all began, kid. Fast-forward four hundred some-odd years, 1638. That's when the first casino opens on the Grand Canal. I'm talking about the first modern casino, the first casino as you and I know it. The casino as a business. The casino as an institution. The institution that has fed and housed my ass for the last forty years, my whole grown-up life. These other joints, these other bullshit cities they keep building on the Strip — I'm talking Paris, I'm talking New York — I look at that, and I think: what the fuck? But this place here, this place makes some god-damn sense. It's the holy city, kid. The gambler's Jerusalem.

Is that really what Stanley said? Or did Curtis conjure this memory from other half-recalled conversations he half-listened to through the years, adding detail from his own Italy trip back in — what was it, '98? And why should it matter anyway what Stanley said? Does it relate in some way to the fix he's in now? Where does that trail lead?

Goddamnit, kid — I forgot the most important thing! The whole reason I started telling this screwy story. Listen: the Doge brought three *columns back from Greece. Not two: three. The longshoremen fucked up, and one of 'em wound up in the drink. It's still down there, stuck in the muck at the bottom of the lagoon. And that's the lesson you gotta learn, kid: there's always gonna be three. Anytime you think you see two of something — doesn't matter what — you start looking around for the third. Likely as not, you're gonna find it. This profound secret I now entrust to you.*

Curtis yawns, stretches, turns back toward the entrance. He trudges past the gold armillary-sphere fountain in the domed lobby, heading for the elevators. Then he slows to a stop.

On the wall behind the registration desk hangs an old-style perspective map: a turkey-leg island viewed from midair, imagined onto paper by some ancient earthbound cartographer, now repurposed by hotshot design consultants into this great gilded frame. Swarmed by tall ships, crowded with palaces and domed churches, bristling with bell-towers and spires. The blue reverse-S of a canal slashes through its thick western end From the corners, cherub-headed clouds blow favorable winds. A couple of bearded gods look down. MERCVRIVS PRECETERIS HVIC FAVSTE EMPORIIS ILLVSTRO. Curtis stares at the map for a long time before he realizes that he's looking for Stanley there, expecting to spot him loitering in a tiny piazza, smirking. The clerks at the desk are eyeing Curtis nervously. He shakes his head, turns to go.

And not toward the elevators this time, but

into the grand galleria. Strolling between marble columns, below meticulous fake frescoes: plump foreshortened angels vaulting through white cumulus. Feeling like maybe he's onto something, though he's not yet sure what. His rubber soles are silent on the cube-patterned stone deck as he passes the entrance to the museum — *ART THROUGH THE AGES extended through May 4th!* — into the casino beyond.

He finds her without much effort, alone at a $25 blackjack table near the baccarat pit. She's wearing jeans and a loose pink tanktop; her hair is up in a clip. She and the dealer — a stocky South Asian kid — have fallen into a comfortable rhythm, barely looking up or speaking, moving cards and chips. She's playing two spots, with a nice pile of green and black in front of her. It looks like she's given up on Stanley for tonight.

Curtis picks up a plastic cup of orange juice and watches from the slots, writing on the back of one of Damon's *SPECTACULAR!* business cards with a hotel inkstick. Then he moves in closer until he's a short distance behind her. She's in good shape: back and shoulders well-muscled, posture ramrod-straight. Pro gamblers have to be athletes, Stanley always said; poised enough to sit for hours, waiting for the right cards. Curtis tries to remember how long the two of them have been a team.

The dealer — his nametag reads MASUUD — looks up at him. A minute later he looks up again, and Curtis steps forward, reaches into the pocket of his jeans. He colors in two hundred of Damon's dollars and takes a seat a couple of spots to her right, far enough along the table's curve to keep her in view. He keeps his eyes trained on the cards at first, but within a dozen hands he's down to two green chips, and she still hasn't recognized him, hasn't even looked at his face.

On the next round she stands on a twelve and a sixteen with the dealer showing an eight; Masuud turns over a six, busts with a jack. If this was his joint, Curtis thinks, he'd bounce her right now. He glances over as he collects his single chip: she had four hundred dollars on the line.

Thanks, he tells her. That was a gutsy play.

She shrugs. Glad it worked out, she says.

How you doing tonight?

She doesn't answer right away, doesn't look up at all. I'm doing okay, she says. And yourself?

Not too good tonight, Curtis says. Can't seem to get anything started.

Well, she says, meeting his gaze at last. I hope your luck changes. Her face is blank. She turns back to her cards.

Three rounds later he's wiped out. He tokes Masuud with the last bill in his wallet and retreats, hiding in the slots again. He thinks

61

about going to the cage — cashing one of Damon's traveler's checks, coming back — but he doesn't want to lose sight of her, and at this point he's pretty sure he can wait her out. It's nearly four a.m. The casino is still hopping; he keeps forgetting it's the weekend.

He stops at the Oculus Lounge to get ice-water for his empty cup. As he steps back onto the carpet, he sees Masuud clap out, receive his toke, and go. A middle-aged Filipino woman takes his place: the graveyard shift coming on. Stanley's girl plays a few more rounds — out of courtesy, and to make sure the new dealer isn't running cold — then gets up, stretches impressively, and heads toward the cage with her chips.

He waits for her to cash in, tracks her through the tables, and falls into step beside her as she approaches the slots. Coming up on her left. Hello again, he says.

She glances over, flashes a thin smile. Doesn't slow down.

Looks like you did pretty well tonight, Curtis says.

Yeah.

You win everything on blackjack?

Yeah, she says. Hey, listen — I'm not looking for any company tonight. Okay? No offense.

None taken. You're Veronica, right?

She jerks to a halt. He steps into her path, turns to face her. Her hands come up, then move to her hips. Excuse me? she says.

Can I talk to you for a second?

What is this? she hisses, her lip curling into a sneer. You're security? Jesus. Okay, I want to see some ID, and I want to talk to the shift boss, because this is bullshit.

Curtis backs up a step, palms out. I'm not security, he says.

Then what is this?

You don't remember me, do you?

She looks at him. Squinting, like it's dark, like they're underwater. Then her eyes widen, go to his jacket, his belt. Her pupils dilate. Blood flees from her face.

Hey, listen, he says. I'm not —

You're from back East. Atlantic City. Right?

He shakes his head. Not AC, he says. Philly.

She's shrinking away: shifting her weight, not backing down. Quick, shallow breaths. So? she says. What do you want?

I'm looking for Stanley.

She snorts. Her eyes drop to the deck for a second, scanning the patterned carpet. Yeah? she says. Well, join the fucking club, pal.

You don't know where he is?

I have no *idea* where he is. Okay? I haven't seen him or heard from him in days. And I don't know how to reach him. Understand? And if I did — if I *did* know — then you better fucking believe I wouldn't tell you. You got it? Am I being clear?

Hey, whoa, ease up a second. I'm not —

63

Who sent you here?

Curtis blinks, confused. This sounds wrong, but it isn't. Until now, he hasn't thought of himself as sent.

Who sent you? she asks again. Who are you working for?

I — I'm not working for anybody. I came out here on my own. I've known Stanley for years.

Bullshit.

Okay. Look. I know Damon Blackburn at the Spectacular. He's an old friend. And he asked me to help find Stanley.

She's calming down now, more sarcastic than scared. Angrier. Really, she says. Damon Blackburn. Imagine that. Small fucking world.

But I *do* know Stanley, Curtis says. That is not bullshit. I've known him my whole life. He and my dad used to run together.

She's squinting again: Curtis can see her trying to remember.

Badrudin Hassan, Curtis says. Used to be called Donald Stone. You and I met one other time, at his wedding, couple years ago.

She nods. Okay, she says. Sure. Hey, I don't suppose Damon Blackburn told you *why* he's looking for Stanley? Did he happen to mention that?

Curtis widens his stance, settles on his feet. Yeah, he says. A couple months ago, Stanley came into the Point and took out a marker

64

for ten grand. Damon signed off on it. Stanley hasn't made any payments, and in four days it's going to be delinquent. Damon doesn't want any problems, for Stanley or for himself. He wants to get in touch so they can work something out.

Her mouth falls open, in disbelief or disgust. She's too far into this to buy the story Damon gave him. Way farther into it than he is himself. She knows everything he knows. He's got no leverage, nothing he can use. A delinquent marker, she says. That's what Damon told you?

That's what he told me.

It's that simple.

Curtis stares at her for a second, then sighs. Well, he says, it's a little bit more complicated than that.

Neither of them moves. Streams of people pour past them, coins rattling in their plastic pails. Soft chirps and beeps from slot machines fill the treated air like birdsongs. Tiny unblinking lenses look down from high above.

Are we finished here? she says. Damon wants Stanley to call him? That's it?

Yeah. If you give him the message when you hear from him, I'll be grateful.

I don't think Stanley's in a real big hurry to talk to Damon Blackburn right now, she says. I think he's mostly inclined not to do that. Just to let you know.

Maybe he'll talk to me, Curtis says. He

knows me. He's a reasonable guy.

She laughs. Reasonable! she says. That's good. Reasonable.

Curtis reaches into his inside pocket, slowly, for Damon's card. Holds it out to her. My cell's on the back, he says. So's my room number. I'm staying upstairs. Tell Stanley to call me. Maybe I can talk sense to him.

Good luck, she says. Good fucking luck on that one, pal.

She crosses her arms, looks out across the casino floor. There's an old couple at a craps table nearby, the old man laughing hard, the old lady waving her arms and going *woo woo woo,* both of them drunk, both better than seventy years old.

Veronica smiles. Stanley's totally crazy now, she says. You know that, right?

I been told that, yeah.

She keeps staring at the old couple. Now she looks tired, really fundamentally exhausted. Curtis remembers that he is, too. He keeps the card in the air, unmoving.

So, she finally asks, did Damon send anybody else out here?

Curtis thinks about that. No, he tells her. Just me.

Veronica uncrosses her arms. Then she reaches out and plucks the card from his fingers. Looks at his face, his chest, his face.

Your name's Curtis, she says. Right?

9

His first couple of swipes miss the card-reader, and he stops for a second, fuming, before closing his eyes and using both hands, brushing the card's edge along his left index finger, guiding it into the slot. The door unlocks with a soft interior click.

No faxes, no messages. Curtis puts away his gun, strips down to his skivvies, collapses onto the big rack. Too tired to sleep. Too keyed-up. Thinking too much. His brain revs and revs, but won't drop into gear. The clock on the nightstand glows like a hot coal. Ninety-one hours to go. And counting.

He gets up, goes to the head, washes his face and hands. The water tastes of stone, is hard to lather. Not like home, where the soap never seems to come off. He dribbles it over his stubbly scalp, across his eyelids. Rubbing it in.

The girl — Veronica — doesn't seem like somebody apt to spook easily. But tonight, when Curtis first called her by her name, her fear seemed out of proportion to anything Damon told him about the current circumstances. He wonders what she knows that he doesn't. It worries him, but it excites him, too. He did right by coming out here.

The searchlight that swept his window earlier is gone now, switched off, and the suite is lit by a low steady glimmer from outside.

Curtis puts on one of the hotel's white robes and sits at the table in the sunken living area, looking out at the city. Columns of headlights glide down the Strip and the interstate farther west: swingshift traffic headed home. Beyond that, the redundant moon, dilating as it drops. Mount Charleston somewhere under it, erased by ambient glow. Curtis pictures soft light falling on the snowcap, cold wind blowing around the peak. The view of the city as it shines up from the desert. Phosphorescence in a ship's wake. Firelight glimpsed through a copper screen, or a worn black curtain.

Bright streaks move beyond the window-glass: early flights taking off and landing at McCarran. Curtis yawns and watches their navigation lights — dim reds and greens — cross the Luxor's beam. He closes his dry eyelids and imagines, for no good reason, the city as a living creature: the airport its mouth, sucking stars from the sky, spitting them back like husks. The roads and highways its veins and intestines. The Strip its aorta, or colon.

He wakes not much later to the sound of the fax machine and to the night outside gone blue. His uncomfortable forehead has come to rest on the cool wood of the tabletop. He stumbles as he stands, draws the curtain with a jerk, shrugs off the white robe, and falls into bed without bothering to check the fax. Recalling nothing of it when he next stirs, which is shortly before noon.

No memory of dreams, or of dreaming. He rises with a gasp, as if he's just nodded off. Looks at the clock, curses, slides from bed. Picks up his jeans, pulls them on. Stands in the middle of the room. Breathing hard, certain that he's late, that he's slept through something. Gradually remembering other-wise. Remembering yesterday like he watched it happen to somebody else. He sits on the edge of the rack and pulls his trousers off again, slowly.

He draws back the curtains. Flat hazy light. Thick Saturday crowds below, thronging sidewalks and bridges, shooting photos of the belltower, the boats, the twin columns. Cur-tis switches on the TV: Bush and Blair meet-ing in the Azores, a kidnapped girl rescued, some new disease in China. No bombs drop-ping yet.

He's in the shower when he hears the cellphone ring; he can't get to it in time. Wrapped in his towel, dripping on the carpet, he's surprised to see he's missed three calls: Danielle, Albedo, his father.

Danielle's voicemail is fake-cheerful, a little sheepish, scared underneath. Much as I hate to spoil a good fight, it says, I'd like it if you'd call me when you get the chance. Just so I know you're still breathing, and not locked up. Trying to plan my week, is all. I love you, Sammy D. Don't do anything stupid.

Curtis erases the message, and Albedo's voice comes through the phone. Hope you got plenty of beautysleep last night, it says. My girl Espeja was real disappointed y'all didn't get to get better acquainted. But I'm glad you and I could catch up on old times. Reminisce a bit. Hey, you find your skip yet? I think maybe I got some leads. Gimme a call.

Then his father. I hope you're staying out of trouble, Little Man. I been thinking about what you said yesterday, and I remembered something, somebody you ought to get in touch with. Back in the old days when Stanley and I would go to Vegas, we'd meet up with this Japanese fellow Stanley knew from California, name of Walter Kagami. He was a cardsharp back in the day — professional gambler, just like Stanley — but I think he gave it up. Last I heard he's still living out there, managing some locals joint. Place is called Quicksilver, I think. I don't believe you ever met Walter. You'd've been real young. Haven't talked to the man in years myself. But I think maybe Stanley still keeps in touch. Just a thought. Hope it helps. Anyhow. Love you, kid. Mawiyah sends her love too. You watch your back out there.

Curtis drops his towel and picks up a pen and notepad. He writes down Kagami's name, and the name of the casino, and is going through drawers for a phonebook when he spots last night's fax in the machine, the *SPECTACULAR!* logo visible upsidedown at its bottom.

Flattened on the desk, Damon's blocky handwriting:

Albo al be
Beddow a bedo cool.
Let him help.
Proggress???????

Below the message, another cartoon Curtis, staring in bug-eyed horror at an oversize stopwatch in his left hand while frantically jerking himself off with his right. The pupil of the left eye grotesquely askew. The enormous ejaculating penis heavily shaded, minutely detailed.

Curtis flushes the bits down the toilet on his way out the door.

10

The taxi that picks him up has jazz on the radio — "Invisible," from the first Ornette album — and this puts Curtis somewhat at ease. He stretches his legs as they turn right on the Strip; the cab's interior smells like cigarettes and mint.

The driver is Middle Eastern, in his late fifties, with a full head of gypsum-white hair. Careful and patient behind the wheel. He has an air of certainty that Curtis envies. The ID card in the backseat gives his name as Saad; Curtis can't make out the last name without staring, and he doesn't want to stare.

So how are you doing? the cabbie wants to know.

Not too good, Curtis says. Can't seem to get anything started.

The cabbie aims an accusatory finger at the Mirage on their left. You are smart to leave the Strip, he says. Very smart.

Oh yeah?

It is true. It is always good to move around. People always say, oh, my luck is good, oh, my luck is bad. But places have luck too. The casino has luck. Everyone forgets this. If the casino is being lucky — if the dealers are hot, as you say — then you must go someplace else. Not to do so is foolish.

I guess that's right.

The stoplight on Industrial Road catches them. Chartered buses pass by. The radio rolls Ornette Coleman into Art Pepper. Curtis looks down again at the ID card. Your name's Saad? Curtis says.

Yes. Saad. That is correct.

You a Muslim, Saad?

The driver shoots him a hard look in the rearview: flinty eyes, deeply lined from squinting. Why do you ask me this, my friend? he says. You are from the Homeland Security Department, maybe. You think I blow up your casino with my taxicab.

No, no. I just — my dad is a Muslim. And he won't set foot in this town.

Ah. I see. Islam says no gambling.

Saad flips on his turn signal, merges onto the northbound lanes of the interstate. I am Muslim, he says. But I sometimes like to play roulette. And sometimes also the video poker. And I like to drink a glass of wine. I do not pray very often as I should. So maybe I am not a very good Muslim. Your father is Muslim, you say?

That's right.

Like Malcolm X?

Yeah, sure, I guess.

Or Muhammad Ali? Kareem Abdul-Jabbar?

More like Ahmad Jamal.

Ahmad Jamal! Yes! Very good. Or Tupac Shakur?

No, Curtis laughs. Not like Tupac Shakur. I don't think Tupac was a Muslim. His mom was, maybe.

You like jazz? Saad reaches for the radio, turns it up a little. Cool jazz? Bebop?

Sure. My dad plays jazz. He plays the bass.

Saad drums along with Philly Joe Jones on the battered steering wheel for a few bars before he speaks again. I was working on the Strip the night they shot Tupac Shakur, he says. I was less than one mile away.

Is that so.

I did not hear the shots. But I saw the

73

police arrive. The ambulance. The black car, full of holes. It was a terrible sight.

Curtis doesn't respond. He's looking out the window, not really seeing anything, remembering. Ladder drills on the practice field at Dunbar. The smell of new grass crushed underfoot. Sirens everywhere. Policecars speeding down Florida toward Adams-Morgan. Helicopters in the air, circling. The assistant principal jogging out, waving to Coach Banner. More than twenty years ago now. Twenty-two, this month.

Many people come to this city to die, Saad is saying.

Yeah, well. I don't think that's exactly what Tupac had in mind. I think he just wanted to catch the Tyson fight.

Maybe this is so. Who can say?

Saad's turn signal clicks again; he's exiting at Lake Mead Boulevard, turning right, toward Nellis and Sunrise Manor. The white spires of the Mormon temple gleam in the distance. Frenchman Mountain looms beyond.

Maybe your father is smart, Saad says, or is wise, maybe, to think of these things. Everything in this city is made by gambling. Yes? It builds the buildings. It builds the roads. It pays the people. It pays me. All of these things. And always with gambling there is death. You see?

Okay.

This is why we gamble. To face what is uncertain. To confront the unknown, the great unknown. You make your wager. The wheel spins. What will happen? To gamble is to prepare for death. To rehearse. This is the appeal.

You do this rap for all your fares, Saad?

Saad cackles, a rough smoker's laugh, slapping his palm on the wheel. Only for you, my friend! Only for you. Because you are a serious man. Concerned with serious things. I know this about you. It is in your eyes.

Curtis smiles, doesn't respond.

Or the man who died here last year! Saad continues, picking up a dropped thread. The Englishman. The rock star.

I don't know who that is.

The Ox. The one who stands very still.

A thin electronic rendition of "La Marseillaise" is playing below the radio: the ringtone of Saad's cell. Forgive me, he says, and answers it. Speaking first in English, then switching to Arabic. Curtis tries to follow but soon gives up; some phrases sound familiar, but he can't recall their meanings. The cab rolls through the light at Pecos Road, passing over the depleted river in its concrete channel. Fewer houses on the sidestreets now. A low roar of jet engines overhead. Curtis settles back in his seat, tries to relax, to think. To get his mind back on Stanley.

But Stanley is slippery, and seems to go

75

everywhere, spinning Curtis back onto himself. His father. Kagami. Los Angeles, in the late Fifties. Art Pepper, dragging himself into the Contemporary studios, white junkie with a dried-up horn, Band-Aid on the broken cork. *Pepper was an MP too, Little Man. A prison guard, in London during the war.* Columns of orange flame off to the north. The sky burnt black at two in the afternoon. Oily poisoned rain. *Ijlis.* Sit down. *Inhad.* Stand up. *Sa tuffattash ilaan.* Now you will be searched.

Saad is still on the phone, becoming more animated, shuffling in bits of English and French: orange alert, Air Canada, *maison de passe,* Flamingo Road, *dépanneur,* oh my god, the Aladdin, *une ville lumière,* he's a shithead, forget about him. An F-15 passes directly overhead; Curtis can't see it, but he knows the sound of the engines. They're due south of the airbase now, nearing the northeastern edge of the valley. Ranks of white stucco houses topped with orange mission-tiles perch on the foothills ahead, crowding the borders of the government land.

Curtis is wondering if Saad is distracted, if maybe they've missed their turn, when they veer onto a sidestreet just past a Terrible Herbst gas station on the corner of North Hollywood Boulevard. The neighborhood is getting anonymous, purely residential; the houses are bigger, newer, farther apart, and suddenly there are none to be seen at all, only steep gated driveways sprouting off the road. The taxi's transmission downshifts as they climb past cleared gravel pits and an old cement plant, winding slowly through slumps and dry washes and mounds of talus stanched by gabions. Then they crest a rise on a sickening turn and the entire valley is arrayed before them: a sea of roofs and palmtrees, the Strip towers flanked by the Luxor and the Stratosphere, the snows of Mount Charleston in the distance, white blotches hung in midair, the mountain itself vanished in the afternoon haze.

A flashing traffic signal comes into view — a two-lane road with a wide shoulder, cars towing fiberglass boats — but Saad hangs a sharp left before they get there, into a fresh and narrow roadcut marked by a blond limestone sign: QUICKSILVER CASINO & RESORT. The parking area is modest, crescent-shaped, following the curve of the hillside; it's at maybe a quarter capacity, with Cadillacs and Town Cars and the odd Lexus or Mercedes clustered near the top. Wheelchair ramps stretch downhill like exposed roots, and the handicapped spaces are all full.

They bypass the parking lot and roll up to the entrance: a massive oak portico held aloft by thick columns of smooth riverstone orbs. A little pack of bluehaired white ladies is waiting in the shade, bingo bags and plastic coinpails dangling from their folded hands. A green-and-white placard by the entrance says FIND YOUR POT O' GOLD AT QUICKSILVER! ST. PATRICK'S DAY IS MARCH 17TH.

Saad is ending his call. We have arrived, my friend, he says. This place will be lucky for you, I think.

It's farther out than I thought, Curtis says, digging some of Damon's cash from his wallet.

There is nothing farther. Government land, and then the lake. That is all.

I didn't think you could build up here.

Saad shrugs. What can you pay? he says. Who is your friend? You can do what you want.

Curtis hands the folded bills over the seat and Saad takes them with practiced ease, watching Curtis in the rearview mirror. Smiling conspiratorially with his eyes. As if they share some secret knowledge about the world.

Curtis opens his door, steps out, leans back in. Hey, Saad, he says. You got a business card?

11

He glances at the card as the cab is pulling away: SAAD ABOUGREISHA, it says, and a phone number.

The sidewalk beneath Curtis's feet, which

had looked like mortared flagstones from inside the car, is really some kind of springy padding composited from shredded rubber; it gives a little under his weight. He rocks back and forth on his heels, testing the surface, thinking of the deck of the physical therapy room at the Naval Hospital in Bethesda, where he first met Danielle.

A boxy shuttlebus sporting the Quicksilver logo — a jazzed-up Indian pictograph of a raven in flight: gaping beak, gleaming reflective eye — pulls into the space Saad vacated. A group of old people exits the bus with the help of a pair of minders, young kids with big smiles and loud voices. The ones standing under the portico wait patiently to board. Curtis watches all this for a while, not sure what he's looking for. Then he turns and walks to the entrance.

The Quicksilver is high-class for a neighborhood joint: small, rustic, more country club than bingo parlor or shopping mall. The building looks like an Anasazi cliffpalace reworked by Frank Lloyd Wright: lots of exposed beams and slender limestone blocks. The whole thing's built around an old quarry or open-pit mine, now converted into a sunken courtyard with a pond and a waterfall and a recirculating fountain in the middle. Through the bow window behind the gaming pit Curtis can see madrones and junipers, pergolas twined with wisteria and passion-flower, the towering blooms of a couple of century-plants. A halfdozen plump guinea-fowl peck at the rubber sidewalks, and aside from them the courtyard is deserted.

Kagami is running late, stuck in a meeting, so Curtis gets a cup of grapefruit juice and plays a little blackjack to pass the time. The dealers are fresh-faced, easygoing, slow with the cards. Most of the action is at the machines and in the large bingo room; there are only four tables. Curtis's sole companion is an elderly gentleman wearing a silk neckerchief and an oxygen mask. There's a separate area for high rollers behind the bar, dim and sunken, and it's busier than Curtis would have expected for a joint this far out of town. The players down there look like whales: East Asian heavyweights, the kind of guys who keep casinos in business. From time to time their cheers and shouts rise over the new-age flute music on the PA. Somebody like Stanley Glass could walk in and tear this place apart inside of an hour, Curtis thinks. Which is probably why the owners hired somebody like Walter Kagami as the manager.

Saad's prediction is coming true: Curtis is up by nearly four hundred dollars when he feels a gentle hand on his shoulder. Mister Stone? Mister Kagami's very sorry for the delay. If you'd like to wait in his office, he'll meet you there in a few minutes.

Kagami's office is small, cluttered, tucked

away off the gaming floor. Nice oak desk. Navaho rug over scuffed parquetry. Picture window with a southern view: the Boulder Highway, toward Henderson and the dam. A sink and a tiny closet. A little slept-on couch. On a patch of bare wall between two over-flowing bookcases hangs a column of old photographs, and Curtis spots his father's laughing face in one. It looks like it was taken at the Trop; the clothes and the eyewear seem to put it in the late '70s, though with gamblers it can be hard to tell. Curtis's dad is posed with an aloof-looking Stanley, an Asian guy who must be Kagami, some men Curtis doesn't recognize, and, in the middle, Sammy Davis, Jr. Curtis blinks, leans closer, touches the frame. Smiling wryly. Thinking of Danielle: her favorite pet name for him. But his smile collapses, and he starts to feel uneasy. Self-conscious. Fraudulent. Like he's performing as expected for the benefit of some unseen audience. Or for himself.

He shifts his attention to the shelves. Math and physics paperbacks with drab two-tone covers. Thick illustrated works on American Indian art and archaeology. Books on the history, the economy, the architecture of Las Vegas. A Peterson's guide to western birds. A Jane's guide to aircraft identification. Everything ever written on card counting, including fifteen different printings of Edward Thorp's *Beat the Dealer,* most from prior to the 1966 revision.

A voice from behind him: That's the book that started it all, you know.

Curtis has been standing with the door in his blindspot and didn't see Kagami come in. He curses inwardly, tries not to register surprise. I read it a long time ago, he says, turning around. An old copy of my dad's. I don't remember it too well. I never had too much of a head for that stuff.

You know where that guy is these days? Ed Thorp, I mean?

Curtis shakes his head.

Take a wild guess. Shot in the dark. C'mon.

The yellow-edged paperback that Curtis was looking at protrudes slightly from the shelf; he extends a blunt finger, pushes its cracked spine flush with those of its siblings. Wall Street? he says.

See? Kagami says, grinning, moving into the room. You always were a smart kid.

Kagami is about Curtis's height, stocky, in good shape for his age — probably older than his dad by a couple of years, though he looks younger. Gray herringbone trousers, brown tweed jacket, fawn shirt, classy tie with a gold pin. A pokerplayer's tinted eyeglasses. Big rings on both hands. He gives Curtis's upper arm a friendly squeeze as they shake. Last time I saw you, Kagami says, you were probably about six years old. You're looking good, real good. You're a married man now, I hear.

Yes sir. It'll be a year next month.

You still in the Marine Corps?

Just took my retirement.

Well, congratulations! That's good. Looks like you got out just in time, too.

Kagami steps back, studies him. I heard you took a pretty good hit a couple of years ago, he says. Bosnia, was it?

Kosovo.

Well, it looks like you bounced right back.

Yeah, Curtis says. It took me a little while. I appreciate you seeing me on such short notice, Mister Kagami.

Walter! Christ, call me Walter. I'm glad you stopped in. Don't know how much help I'm gonna be, though. You're looking for Stanley Glass?

Yes sir. I'm trying to put him in touch with a friend of mine, and I heard he might be out here. Do you know how I can reach him?

Kagami moves behind his desk, looking out the window. Sunlight pours in sideways, and as he draws closer, his reflection meets him in the glass. I don't know how to get in touch with Stanley, he says. But he has definitely been around. I had dinner with him just last week.

Did he say how long he's going to be in town?

He didn't. He said he was waiting for a connection to come through. Something he had going back East. He and Veronica had just

83

flown in that afternoon: Wednesday, it would have been. Nine days ago. I remember because our waitress had the black smudge on her forehead. Stanley made a joke about it. Anyway, I comped them a suite, told them they could stay the week, but they were gone by morning. Didn't say where to.

Kagami leans a little to the side, as if he's trying to get a better view of something down below. Veronica was in college out here, he says. She used to be a dealer at the Rio, and I think maybe at Caesars before that. Stanley could be staying with her people.

I talked to Veronica last night. She says she doesn't know where Stanley is. She's looking for him, too.

You believe that?

Curtis tries to find Kagami's eyes in the window reflection but can't. I don't know, he says. I don't know why she'd lie.

She seemed pretty goosey when I saw her. Nervous.

Yeah. When I saw her, too. How did Stanley seem?

Kagami is quiet for a second. Then he laughs, turns back around. How does Stanley ever seem? he says. Listen, Curtis, I tell you what. If I can't tell you where Stanley is, I can at least feed you a decent meal. We got the best restaurant in the state of Nevada right upstairs. My treat. Those Strip buffets'll kill you.

The corridor outside Kagami's office leads to an art-nouveau glass elevator that runs up the rocky hillside. The car is walled with lead-crystal, topped by stained-glass tracery in blazing sunset colors; it bears them smoothly toward a benchcut terrace about twenty feet overhead.

Real nice place you got here, Walter. How long you been doing this?

We've been open for two years now. I've been on board since we broke ground.

How's business?

It's terrible. Maybe you didn't notice, but most of our regulars are older than me. And I'm no spring chicken. On the upside, our owner's a fruitcake. Silicon Valley zillionaire. He plans to operate this place at a loss for ten years, for fifteen: however long it takes the city to grow up to us. He's a young guy, and he thinks he's got the bankroll to make it work.

You think he's right?

Kagami laughs. That depends, he says. It's like anything else: there's a window. If you're there when the window opens, and you can get out before it closes, then you do real well. The city is growing in a hurry, that's for damn sure. But here's the other thing: we got no water out here. People tend to forget that. I'm talking about the entire valley. Lake Mead's at a thirty-year low. That's climate change: the water's not coming back. Eventually we're gonna dry out. And that's assuming we're even around long enough to have that problem. We could get avalanched onto North Hollywood by an earthquake long before then.

You get earthquakes up here?

Haven't had one yet. But one is all it would take. We're about two hundred yards from the Sunrise Fault. That's an active fault. You saw the river rocks on the pillars at the entrance, where the nursing-home shuttles drop off? The big round ones? We've already had to mortar five of those bastards back into place. If the ground ever really starts to move, and Doctor Richter weighs us in anywhere north of five and some change, it's gonna be Bowling for Biddies out there.

Damn.

Yeah, Kagami says, I figure one way or another, I'll be long dead before this place ever turns a profit.

He wipes a hand on his jacket, reaches out to touch the spotless glass. The Mormon temple is below them, edging into view as they rise. All around it Curtis can see roofs of new houses going up: blond wood of exposed sheathing, patterned rows of underlayment.

This is the first straight job I've had since I was nineteen years old, Kagami says. I used to be a gambler, just like Stanley. But the grind finally wore me down. Trying to make a living off a two-percent edge — it's too much for a senior citizen like me. Unless you're working with a good team. And teams always come apart.

Curtis shifts his weight a little. I don't know how Stanley does it, he says.

Well, Stanley's got Veronica. And besides, Stanley doesn't know anything else. Kagami smiles to himself. Stanley also has a supernatural gift, he says. You did not hear that from me.

The doors slide open on a little glassed-in chamber, which opens in turn onto a rubber-flagstone path bordered by rosemary and budding desertwillow. A tiny restaurant at the terrace's edge: RAVENCREST branded on a wooden sign. White tablecloths flutter in the light breeze.

Kagami walks slowly, hands in his pockets. So, he says, how's old Donald doing these days? I haven't talked to him in years.

He's doing real good. He's not Donald anymore, though.

That's right, I forgot. What is it now?

Badrudin Hassan. He remarried a couple years back, too. He's playing gigs again. Being Muslim and being married both seem to suit him real well.

His wife's a young little thing, isn't she?

I don't know about little, but she's younger, yeah.

Kagami chuckles, kicks a stone chip from

the rubber path. What about you, kid? he says. What's a young fellow like you do after retirement? Work on your golf game?

Curtis smiles. A friend of mine is setting me up with a job, he says. Security supervisor. He's a shift boss at a joint in Atlantic City, a new place. I know him from the Corps.

He anybody I'd know?

Damon Blackburn. He works at the Spectacular.

That's in the Marina District, right? Kagami pulls the restaurant door open, holds it for Curtis. I don't suppose, he says, that he'd be the friend of yours who's looking for Stanley?

Yeah, Curtis says. He is.

The maître d' greets Kagami deferentially and seats them at the terrace's edge. Curtis chooses the strip steak from the succinct leatherbound menu and looks down into the valley, shading his face with a cupped hand. Somewhere on the ridge above them a pair of ravens calls back and forth; Curtis can't see them at first. Then one flutters down and lands atop the restaurant. The Mormon temple is in full view, below and a little to the north, like a dead bug at this angle, with its six spires and its battened brown roof. The spires' golden tips blaze orange in the late-afternoon light.

Kagami's talking to the waiter, ordering appetizers and wine. The waiter nods, walks away, and Kagami looks across the table, leans forward in his chair. So, Curtis, he says. I gotta ask. Are you sorry to be missing out on all the action? In Iraq, I mean?

Did the war start?

Not that I've heard. Sounds like pretty soon, though. I guess you probably know a lot of people who are over there.

Curtis takes a sip of water, then another one. It's ice-cold, but the glass is barely sweating. The second raven joins its mate on the gambrel roof.

It's complicated, Curtis says. In a lot of ways, sure, I wish I was over there. I trained for it. I trained other guys to do it. I'd like to be there taking care of my people. But in most ways — most ways that matter — I'm glad to be sitting this one out. I'm not a kid anymore. I got a wife to think about. And when I got hurt in Kosovo, that rearranged my thinking on a few things, I guess.

If you hadn't retired, you think you'd be over there now?

Hard to say. Probably I would.

You were a military policeman, weren't you?

I was an MP, yeah.

Stationed in the Philippines?

That was a long time ago. When my dad got out of prison in '89, I put in for a transfer to the Second Marines. I wanted to be closer to him.

You've been at Camp Lejeune, then?

That's right.

You ever spend any time at Guantánamo Bay, Curtis?

Curtis feels his stomach tighten — up high, under his ribs — and he takes a quick involuntary breath. Kagami sees it, was waiting for it. Yeah, Curtis says. A little bit.

The waiter reappears, sets down a plate of frybread, some jalapeños stuffed with goatcheese, a tiny baked pumpkin. Opens and pours the wine. Across the table, the sun is doubled in the lenses of Kagami's spectacles; Curtis can't see his eyes at all.

Kagami waits for the waiter to go before he speaks again. How long ago were you there? he asks.

I got TDY'd to Gitmo about a year ago. I was there for six months.

Because of the prisoners?

The detainees, yeah. They were moving them to the new facility.

Camp Delta.

That's right.

Kagami cuts himself a slice of pumpkin, takes a piece of frybread. So what's it like? he asks. The facility? He says *facility* like he's handling something dead.

Curtis lifts his glass, takes a sip of wine, then another sip of water. Steel mesh enclosures, he says. Eight by eight by six-and-a-half. They have flush toilets, bedframes, sinks.

An exercise area.

Pretty luxurious.

At Camp X-Ray they were using Port-A-Cans and sleeping on the deck, so it's a step up. These are bad dudes, Walter. Really evil guys.

I hear they got kids locked up there. Twelve, thirteen years old.

Juveniles are in a separate facility, Curtis says.

One of the ravens arcs past them, lands with a thump in the middle of a table a few yards away. The waiter calmly shoos it off with a dishrag, and it hops onto the rock wall at the terrace's edge. Up close, it's much bigger than Curtis had realized. He and Kagami watch it awhile.

Look, Curtis says. I don't think anybody's happy with the way things are. I don't like it myself. It's one reason I decided to retire.

Curtis has never told anyone this before; he's surprised now to hear himself say it. He pops a stuffed pepper in his mouth, feels the sting on his palate and in his sinuses.

I'm not trying to cross-examine you, kid, Kagami says.

I don't know all that much about it, Curtis says. To tell you the truth. Gitmo's a Navy base, but the Army's responsible for security inside the camp. I was just there to handle the logistics of the transfer. I never had a lot of contact with the detainees.

Well. It's somebody else's problem now, right? You're joining us in the gaming industry.

Yeah. Honest work at last.

Kagami laughs. I see a lot of you ex-military guys in security, he says. Lots of former MPs. Your buddy at the Spectacular — Damon, right? Was he an MP, too?

An MP, then later an MSG. An embassy marine, in Bolivia and Pakistan.

Sounds like serious business.

Damon's a sharp guy. I'm looking forward to working with him.

That's good to hear. You know, Kagami says, I don't think you told me *why* your friend is trying to get in touch with Stanley Glass.

Kagami is smiling, slowly tearing his frybread; it falls to his plate in nickel-size chunks. His eyes are still hidden by the reflected sunset, but Curtis can tell from the tone of his voice that he already knows the answer to his question, has heard the news from somebody in Atlantic City and figured it out. He's probably known since they walked into the restaurant. All that stuff about Gitmo was designed to rattle Curtis, to make him sweat a little. A soft spot Kagami knows about somehow. How?

The waiter comes with their entrées, unfolds a stand, sets his tray down. Kagami has ordered braised duck with blackberry sauce;

Curtis's steak is served with a tiny bowl of steaming posole. Everything is very good.

They eat in silence for a moment. Curtis chews slowly, sets his fork on the edge of his plate, looks down into the valley. He opts to stick to the script, see how far it gets him. Damon's trying to clear up a misunderstanding, he says. Two months ago he wrote Stanley a marker for ten grand, and Stanley hasn't made any payments on it. On Tuesday night — midnight Eastern — it's going to be delinquent. That'd be bad for Damon and for Stanley both. Damon just wants to work something out.

And that's why he asked you to come out here.

Yes sir.

Kagami takes off his glasses, polishes them on the edge of the tablecloth. Curtis, he says, you and I both know that doesn't make a goddamn bit of sense. Ten grand is not a lot of money, not for a joint like the Spectacular. And there's a hell of a difference between delinquent and irrecuperable. Your friend won't take any heat for writing that marker. Sure, it's cute that he's worried about Stanley — but at this point Stanley is a celebrity, a goddamn institution. Casino hosts and credit agents from one end of this country to the other will comp him six ways to Sunday just for darkening their door, no matter whose black book he shows up in. Casinos love professional gamblers, Curtis. They're great for business. They're like saints. Proof that salvation is really possible.

Curtis looks up, doesn't say anything. He knows there's more coming, and he's just going to wait for it. A raven strides into view from under the tables, disappears again. The wind shifts. From somewhere in the mountains he can hear the engines of a lowflying A-10; he thinks about the Gulf again, but only for a moment.

Kagami eases his glasses back onto his face. I heard an interesting story recently, he says. About two weeks ago, a team of cardcounters hit a string of casinos in Atlantic City. Like you'd expect, the bosses are being pretty tightlipped about how much these guys won, but the rumor mill's been throwing around some pretty goddamn unbelievable numbers. In any case, the managers could look at their counts at the end of the night and see right away that something bad had happened. Do you know how often cardcounters make hauls like that without getting burned, Curtis?

No idea.

Never. In all my years, I've heard of it happening maybe three or four times. Always to a *single* casino. These guys clobbered four or five places inside of twelve hours. That is unprecedented.

Kagami lifts his wineglass, drains it, refills it from the bottle. I'm bringing this up in the present context, he says, because — funny thing — the joint that got nailed worst of all was the Spectacular. What strikes me as *really* strange is that the Point was also the *last* joint to get hit. Hours after the other ones. Is this ringing any bells with you?

You just keep going, Curtis says. You're doing real good.

I have it on pretty solid authority that security at the Point was tipped off in advance that these guys were coming, and they thought they were ready. All hands were on deck. In AC, of course, you guys aren't legally permitted to bar counters the way we do out here, but there are other defenses, as I'm sure you know. From what I hear, the Spectacular threw out the whole bag of tricks: lowering table limits, reshuffling decks, the works. Pissed a lot of people off. And they *still* got massacred. From where I sit — and I'm speaking now from the perspective of a casino manager — that does not look too good.

Yeah, Curtis says. You could say that.

Kagami grins, shakes his head. I'll tell you a secret, he says. I'm jealous as hell of these guys. I used to put teams like that together, you know. Some of them were pretty good. But these guys! This was the kind of score people make Hollywood movies about. Weekend before Mardi Gras. Right? Very heavy traffic at the tables. Way I hear it, they were dropping out of nowhere. Tracking shuffles, cutting cards to each other, moving counters and spotters around as much as bettors. Totally invisible. At our best, we were never anywhere close to that good.

Kagami snaps his fingers, as if suddenly remembering something. But, hey! he says. You know who *could* put a team like that together?

Don't make me say it, Walter.

Stanley goddamn Glass, is who. And now you're telling me that your buddy, Damon Blackburn of the United States Marine Corps, loaned Stanley — a notorious professional gambler and known associate of hotshot cardcounting teams like the very one we're talking about — ten grand of his casino's money just six weeks before they got their asses kicked up and down the Boardwalk. And I'm wondering if maybe right about now Damon isn't a little worried about his job.

That may be a consideration, Curtis says.

The grapevine's been telling me that heads are already rolling at the Point. They got the Jersey State Police looking for one of the dealers who was on duty that night. Management fired a pit boss on the spot, then they fired the chief of security the next day. I don't suppose that's the vacancy *you're* planning to fill, is it, Curtis?

Curtis forces a sour smile.

96

Now naturally you're not going to get that gig unless Damon's around to give it to you. So far, he's staying afloat. But if Stanley's name shows up on the Spectacular's delinquent list Wednesday morning, alarm bells are going to go off, and Damon can start cleaning out his office. Since you know Stanley — because he and your dad are old pals, right? — Damon wants you to track him down and remind him to settle his account before it's too late. You get nice new job out of the deal. Am I on the fairway here, Curtis?

Yes sir, Curtis says. That's about how Damon's got it figured.

Curtis swirls the dark puddle in his wineglass. Not nervous anymore, just ill at ease, ready for Kagami to finish. He thinks back as he waits: the look on Danielle's face when he told her he was going to work for Damon. His father, years ago, behind the plexiglass in the D.C. Jail, after Curtis said he was quitting college to enlist.

Kagami laughs, wipes his mouth on his napkin. This is really nice, he says. Let me just throw something on the table. Okay? What if this *isn't* a big misunderstanding? What if Stanley hasn't been returning Damon's calls because he just finished screwing him? What if Stanley really *did* hit the Point, and all those other places? What if he put that team together, and he used the Spectacular's own money to help bankroll it? He's

97

done stuff like that before, kid. Many times.

Sure, Curtis says. Thirty years ago. But Stanley doesn't work with big teams anymore. You said so yourself: he doesn't have to, he's got Veronica. Besides, Stanley and Damon are friends. You know how loyal Stanley is, Walter. You really think he'd take advantage of Damon like that? That's just not Stanley, man.

Okay. I also know Stanley doesn't take any shit off anybody. Has Damon done anything to piss him off?

Not that I know about.

Well, you *wouldn't* know, would you? Damon's the only one you've been talking to. Right? When's the last time you saw Stanley, kid?

Curtis looks down at his plate. Picturing Stanley on a bench by the Tidal Basin, fanning a deck of cards for Mawiyah's little cousins. Mawiyah and Curtis's dad shouting from their pedalboat in mostly mock disapproval. Foamy clumps of cherryblossoms adrift on the water. Danielle beside him, laughing, invisible, on his left. Her fingers laced in his own. It's been a couple years, Curtis says.

Kagami looks off into the sun for a while. He's changed a lot, you know.

How do you mean?

For one thing, he's sick. I don't know what's wrong, but he was walking with a cane when I saw him on Wednesday. He didn't look too great.

Stanley's never been sick a day in his life.

For another, Kagami continues, he's crazy. For the past couple of years, Stanley has been losing a tremendous amount of money. Just throwing it away at the tables. He comes up with these new systems that don't make any sense at all, that have nothing whatsoever to do with probability. He's gotten really strange, Curtis. He dropped six grand in here the other night without batting an eye. I shouldn't have done it, but I pulled him aside, asked him what the hell he thought he was doing. I told him to knock it off with the metaphysical mumbo-jumbo. I told him to stop believing his own bullshit.

You told him that?

That's what I told him.

What did he say?

He told me a Zen story.

Say again?

He told me this story about a famous archer who lives in Japan. The guy is known universally as one of the great masters of his art. People come from all over the world to study with him. And although he's very old, and he's been shooting for many years, the guy has *yet* to hit the bullseye.

That's the story?

Yeah. Stanley likes telling me Zen stories. It's a little joke we have.

Is it true?

Kagami gives Curtis an exasperated look, opens his mouth to say something, closes it again. Stares down into the valley.

Walter, Curtis says, Stanley is always going on about that mystical stuff. It's all just part of his act. He doesn't really believe any of it.

Kagami shrugs. Maybe when he first started it was an act, he says. Maybe there was always a grain of truth in it. Sincerity. Fantasy. Wishful thinking. Maybe he's been doing his act for so long now that it's *become* who he really is. Or, hell, kid, maybe all *any* of us do is just an act. Who knows?

Kagami swirls a bit of duck in its blueblack sauce, lifts it to his mouth. You ever counted cards, Curtis? he asks. Seriously?

No sir. I understand how it works, but I've never tried to do it myself.

Kagami chews very slowly, washes down the mouthful with water and wine. If you're running hot, he says — and when I say *hot* I'm not talking about luck; I mean you got a solid true count, you're shuffletracking, you got a weak dealer and nice deep penetration in the shoe — there comes a moment when you are in complete control of the game. You know what your cards, the dealer's cards, even the guy down at first base playing basic strategy's cards are going to be, as well as how they'll be played, until the cutcard comes up. It is very difficult to describe this feeling.

It's almost like —

— and here Kagami looks up and reaches abruptly into the air above their heads, as if to pluck a word floating there, his face at once alive and very old, the sunset igniting his gold rings and wire-rimmed glasses and thin black hair, a few stars peeking out of the deep blue behind him —

— *omnipotence,* he says. Take it from me, kid, this feeling can do funny things to your head. It becomes very easy to fool yourself into thinking that the whole world might be a big blackjack game. If you could just recognize it, see the correspondences, learn to read the cards. Even the best players — and I hope you'll forgive me for saying that I am one of them — hit this moment only very rarely. Stanley *lives* there. In that moment. All the time. And I believe that this has gradually driven him out of his mind.

Curtis isn't sure what to say to this. He nods, looks away.

I'm not making a lot of sense, Kagami says. That's okay. It doesn't matter. All I'm saying, Curtis, is that you should never underestimate people's capacity to believe weird things. I mean, let's just take a look around.

Kagami jerks a thumb toward the Mormon temple. The folks in that building, he says, believe America was first settled by a lost tribe of Israel. Your dad thinks white people were created by an evil scientist. You never

101

know what somebody's going to grab onto when he starts to sink, kid. Don't be too sure you know where Stanley's coming from these days.

Curtis thinks about that for a moment. I figure it like this, he says. Maybe Stanley's lost his mind. Maybe he hasn't. Maybe he was part of the team that hit the Point, and maybe he wasn't. None of that really matters to me. What matters is, he's either running from me, or he's not. If he's running, then there's no way in hell I'm ever gonna catch him. If he's not, then I believe he'll talk to me.

A sudden gust comes down the mountain, flapping the tablecloths and toppling an empty tray; somewhere nearby one of the ravens squawks in surprise. For the first time since he arrived, Curtis is glad he's wearing a jacket.

Kagami is smiling: a warm smile, with no malice in it, but it could be hiding anything. Well, he says, good luck to you, kid. If I hear anything from Stanley, I'll tell him to call you up.

I'd appreciate that.

One of the ravens hops onto the rock wall just behind Kagami's back and preens for a moment, looking satisfied with itself. It caws, and its voice echoes in the darkening valley. Then it launches itself into the air, circling, flying back up to the ridge.

Curtis nods toward it. These guys are a nice touch, he says. How do you get them to stick around?

Stick around? Kagami laughs. Christ, we can't get rid of 'em. They were here before we laid the foundations. That's where our logo came from. The owner calls 'em Bill and Melinda. I can't tell which is which.

Kagami doesn't look up; his knife and fork snicker quietly on his plate. There was a third one, he says between bites. But he was too aggressive. He liked shiny things, and he'd get right up on your table. Some of these old ladies, you know, they wear some pretty gaudy jewelry. He was a real character. The boss named him Larry Ellison.

What happened to him?

I came up here one morning about dawn with the rearview mirror out of my car and a Remington twelvegauge I borrowed off a buddy of mine. Flash-flash, flash-flash, blam. The head chef made old Larry into a plate of *mole* enchiladas for me.

Kagami wipes his mouth on his napkin, smiles sadly, shakes his head. Hell of a lot of meat on that bird, he says. Tasted like shit. But what I kill, I always eat.

12

One of the Quicksilver's shuttlebuses makes an hourly run back to the Strip, and Curtis

103

buys himself a club soda and finds a quiet spot near the bingo room to wait for it.

The rich, spicy food has settled unevenly in his stomach, and he thinks about looking for the head before the bus arrives. He tries to sort through everything Kagami just told him — to line it up against the stories he got from Veronica and from Damon, to spot contradictions and coincidences — but it's hard to concentrate among the frantic warblings of the casino floor, and eventually he finds himself peeking through the bingo room's doorway, drawn by the intense calm he senses there.

Maybe twenty old ladies inside. Most playing five or six cards at once, some with fifteen or more, holding them in place with PVP gluesticks or blobs of adhesive putty. The caller is a young white girl with braces and a clear empty voice; her announcements pass through the room like swells. The air seems denser here, the transmissions clearer. The women stoop like oracles, their blue and pink perms intently bobbing. Knotted nimble fingers placing daubs in atavistic patterns. The numbers eclipsed even as they're revealed. Curtis watches, transfixed, until he has to rush to catch the shuttle.

On the long downhill ride back to the Strip he thinks of Stanley. He thinks of what Kagami said about blackjack — about the illusion of total control — and then he thinks of the bingo ladies in their quiet room, their fierce mastery of cards and daubers. It all begins to make a kind of desperate sense to Curtis, and as the shuttle slows to a stop in front of his hotel, he remembers a late-season football game from his junior year — how he saw the blitz coming well before the snap, saw it in the faces of the Banneker kids, the way they carried themselves. Recalling with his whole body the calm that came upon him then, the clarity. Empty and weightless. Everything moving on rails only he could see. He pivoted away from the defensive end that mirrored him across the line of scrimmage, just letting the guy drop. Shaking himself loose. Backpedaling into the path of the blindside. Arms windmilling. Unpretty. In the way. The cornerback running flat out — helmet down, rocketlike — right over him. Knee dropping on his wrist. The dull crack somehow right, somehow perfect. The sweetness of it. Hammerblow on a box of chalk. The pain transfigured him, lit him from inside. He knew without looking that the pass got off, connected. His cast stayed on until the end of February.

A month after it came off, Reagan got shot coming out of the Washington Hilton, and Curtis knew then exactly what he wanted to do with his life.

The elevator has never seemed so slow, rising balloonlike and unhurried through twenty-eight floors before discharging him. By the time he reaches his door he's already unbuckled his belt, and he slides his keycard and drops his trousers and tears the paper ring from the sanitized toilet in one smooth motion. He sits for a while in the scented dark — goosepimpled, tasting vitriol, wiping his clammy scalp — before shrugging off his blazer and setting his holstered revolver in the marble sink. The curtains are drawn from the windows at the end of the suite, and a dim wedge of light leaks through the door, multihued and pulsing. Watching it, Curtis thinks of Christmas lights, Christmas trees, and he thinks for probably the twelfth time today that he really ought to call his wife. He thinks about what he'd say, what she'd say, how he'd explain. Imagining her on the phone in the kitchenette. Warming milk, maybe, for hot chocolate. Her short white robe falling open. Fuzzy red socks. Tomorrow's uniform pressed and laid out on the dresser. Leaning against the fridge with one stiff arm, like she's holding it shut. Cowrie shells clicking against the handset. Her brow furrowed. The little wrinkle there. That and a couple of rings are all he's given her.

I'm real sorry, Dani. Hell yes, I miss you. I just can't talk right now. That's about it: the extent of what he's got. Can't say what the plan is because there is no plan — hasn't really been one since he got hurt, since he shipped home from Kosovo, since before he met her. Two years adrift, reacting. He'd have to be able to explain it to himself first. He flushes, undresses, showers, lies down on the rack and thinks about it.

He's thinking about it when his cell chirps to life, his home number in Philly on its display. He thinks about it as it rings, and as it stops ringing, and a minute later when the phone beeps and the *message* symbol appears, he's still thinking about it.

He turns on the TV and mutes it and tries to concentrate on the text that crawls across the bottom, flipping between CNN and CNBC and Fox, dozing off from time to time, until a few hours have passed and he's hungry again. Then he rises and dresses, locks up his pistol, heads down below to get a sandwich.

The elevator puts him out on the second floor, the shopping level, and he strides over black cobblestones toward the cool light of a painted sunless sky. At the wide terminus of the hotel's indoor canal a gondolier is bringing his craft around, shouting songs over his passengers' heads as they film him in wobbly digital video. The blue of the water is uncompromised, void, a screen for projections.

An arcade opens to Curtis's right, and he follows it toward the food court. Somehow he makes a wrong turn; even after he realizes it he keeps moving forward, letting himself be swept along by tourists and conventioneers into the great indoor piazza of Saint Mark's Square. Browsers fondle trinkets in umbrella-shaded carts; a string quartet duels with an unseen opera singer on a balcony; sidewalk patrons dine on gnocchi and tuna niçoise. Up ahead, in the middle of the square, a knot of people surrounds a living statue.

Curtis draws closer. The statue is dressed entirely in white — white gown, white sash, round white cap, a fat little loop of fabric — and white makeup pancakes its arms and face. Curtis can't guess its sex with any certainty. For a few minutes he watches it between the heads of the people in front of him; he never sees it blink. Its eyes are empty, focused on some invisible thing. After a while he realizes that many of the spectators, himself included, are nearly as motionless as the statue. A creeping paralysis. Curtis shakes himself, turns back the way he came.

He wonders whether he should try to find something for Danielle — a guilt gift — but everything he sees is handmade and imported, too expensive, nothing Dani would want anyway. Jeweled masks, leatherbound books, glass pelicans. A silver mirror framed in crystal. A wooden marionette with a foot-long nose.

As he's going through the menu at Towers Deli he starts to get nervous, worried that he's in the wrong spot. Stanley might be in the building now, but he'd never be up here. There's another food court down below, just off the gaming floor. Curtis doubles back, retraces his steps.

As the escalator carries him down, the classical music on the shopping level's PA fades into a Phil Collins ballad, and the white noise of the gaming area engulfs him like a steambath. Everything seems vague and equidistant. With the war brewing, and all the active-duty guys either in Kuwait or locked down on base, Curtis figured tonight would be a slow night, but it doesn't look slow. He doesn't see any crewcuts or high-and-tights in the crowd, but there are lines at all the ATMs, the high-roller area looks active, and traffic to and from the cage is steady. This isn't a jarhead joint anyway, Curtis thinks, so it probably doesn't matter. By the entrance to the washrooms, a group of men waits for wives and girlfriends, rattling coinpails or studying basic-strategy cards to pass the time. Most of them are Curtis's age or younger.

He makes his clockwise loop on autopilot, picking out details he's missed along the familiar route: massive chandeliers, colors in the carpet, the placement of surveillance cameras overhead. He checks the tables, the machines, the sports-book room, the high-limit slots, the video poker games in the Oculus Lounge. Stanley's not here, and neither is Veronica, at least at the moment.

He buys a Philly cheesesteak at the San Gennaro Grill and finds himself a table near the food court's entrance. He finishes half, washes it down with a gulp of iced tea, checks the message on his cell while starting in on the rest. Danielle's voice, punctuated by the soft clicking of his teeth. Sammy D, it says, this is your wife calling again. You remember you got a wife, right? That thing we did at the church, with the music and the flowers? You had to wear a tux? You remember that? See, since I hadn't heard from you, I'm wondering if maybe you got hit on the head or something. It is Saturday, nine o'clock in the p.m. Philadelphia time, and I would sure as shit like to hear from you, Junior. I know we're supposed to be in a fight, and if you don't want to talk right now, I guess I understand. But call and let me know that you're okay, at least. If you can't —

She cuts herself off with a sigh, then starts over. Look, she says. Curtis, I know I shouldn't have said all that stuff I said. But I think you understand why I said it. I just think you're selling yourself sh—

Curtis deletes the message, hangs up. The clock on the phone's display says 10:42. Nearly two a.m. Philly time. It still feels early. He stares at the phone until it says 10:43, then 10:44. Then he picks it up again to send a text. Im ok, he types. He examines the letters, the blinking cursor. The message seems inadequate. Ill call soon, he adds. Luv u.

He eats the last of his sandwich and drains his tea and walks back onto the casino floor. He makes another survey of the blackjack tables, taking more time, looking closer. Fifty-odd eight-deck games going, plus a handful of six-decks and two-decks. Curtis pays particular attention to those tables — that's where cardcounters will congregate — but none of the faces looks familiar. The swing-shift's been on duty for three hours now. He wonders where Veronica is.

Back in the Oculus Lounge he finds himself a Deuces Wild machine with a good sidelong view and stops a passing cocktail waitress to order a cranberry juice. He thinks she's the same one who served him last night, but he can't be sure. Like all the girls here she's tall, pretty, sharp-eyed. Dressed in an absurd burgundy-and-gold corselet with chiffon ruffles at the hips. The bridesmaid of a trapeze artist. She probably clears eighty grand a year in tips alone. A vast smile is drawn across her face like a curtain.

Curtis watches the casino floor for twenty minutes, scanning, then drifting, then scanning again. Thinking about Danielle. The strange and vital smell of her, tangled up with sweat and Bactine and isopropyl alcohol. Recalling his forearm tight across her lower back. The weight of her hips. A sound she made.

His phone wriggles to life, and he jumps, looks at the display. A number he doesn't know, a 609 area code. Damon, maybe. He switches the phone to his right hand, plugs his left ear with a finger.

Hello?

Silence on the other end. He can hear crowds, raised voices, music, electronic murmurings. Another casino. Atlantic City? He holds his breath, listens.

Then a voice. I don't think she's coming tonight, pal, it says. I think you scared her off.

Albedo, Curtis thinks at first. But it's not Albedo. The pitch is too high, and the accent's wrong: Ohio or Western PA, not Appalachia. Who is this? he says.

This is the guy you're looking for. Who do you think it is?

Stanley?

Curtis can't help saying it, although he knows it isn't Stanley. A younger guy, white, probably on the small side. He whistles a little on his *s*'s. Curtis tries to listen around his voice for other sounds, clues to where he's calling from.

Look, the voice says. Spare me the Stanley shit, okay? I'm the guy you're *really* looking for.

How'd you get this number?

Are you kidding? C'mon, Curtis. You gave your number to every bartender and blackjack dealer on the Strip.

So the guy's here in town. Curtis starts running through casinos in his head, thinking of their signature background noise. Nothing falls into place. He needs to buy more time. What do you want, man? he says.

The guy's voice is tense, coiled and snake-like; he's fighting hard to sound calm. What I really want, he says, is to talk to Veronica. But it looks like that's not happening tonight. Thanks to you.

A few feet in front of Curtis, a skinny middle-aged Hispanic woman has just hit the jackpot on a Double Double Diamond machine; she's hopping up and down, bug-eyed, screaming *I won I won I won I won,* and Curtis wrinkles his brow and jams his finger farther into his ear before he realizes that he's hearing her over the phone, too. He jerks in his chair, blinking hard, staring into the huge room.

There's a slight intake of breath on the other end of the line, barely audible. When the guy speaks again, his voice is steady. Well, he says, at least it's *somebody's* lucky night.

The whistle on *somebody* is canary-clear. Curtis stands up slowly, trying to be patient and careful. Leaving five unplayed dollars in his machine. Nobody's watching him that he can see. He needs to get the guy talking again, to look for moving lips. Quit messing

113

with me, man, Curtis says. Tell me where you are.

The guy forces a dry laugh. Where's your jacket, Curtis? he says. No gun tonight, huh? Probably a good idea. Veronica didn't like it too well when she saw that jacket last night, did she?

Curtis's back has been turned to the high-limit slot area, and although there's no one standing there now, the guy could be hiding inside. Curtis moves, checking all the faces, keeping the round bar on his left. Sure, man, he says. I left the jacket topside tonight. So come on out. Let's talk.

Curtis steps into the high-limit area, clears it in a couple of seconds — there aren't many people — and moves back to the casino floor, watching for eye contact or unusual movement, heading toward the food court. His vision scrapes away layers of detail as they emerge from the roiling background.

That is not how it works, Curtis, the guy says. You don't get to see me. Not yet. Besides, we're talking now, aren't we? Is this not good enough for you?

Through the whistle at the end of *this,* Curtis hears it: a canned recording of a crowd shouting in unison *WHEEL! OF! FORTUNE!* The sound fades toward the end. The guy's in the slots, and he's in motion.

Curtis hangs a sharp left into the path of a cocktail waitress who's approaching in his blindspot; she slams on the brakes, his extended elbow misses her nose by inches, and three of her drinks — two strawberry daiquiris and a screwdriver — slide from her tray and land on his shoes. She swallows a curse, screws her smile back into place, and starts spitting apologies through clenched teeth. Another waitress and a couple of janitors are already moving in. My fault, my fault, Curtis says, and sidesteps them.

His phone snickers at him. Better watch your step there, it says.

Curtis hoped his sudden turn would spook the guy, make him change position, but nobody's moving in the slots that he can see. A casino suit is hustling over, concerned and irritated, and Curtis cuts him off before he starts talking. I'm fine, Curtis says. It was my fault. I'm sorry, but I have to take this call.

Listen, the voice on the phone is saying, I've obviously caught you at a bad time. I'm going to let you go. But first I'm going to ask a favor. Would you give Damon a message for me? Curtis? Hello?

Curtis puts a hand up in the suit's face, turns back to the slots. Yeah, he says. Yeah, I'm here.

Would you tell Damon — are you getting this? — would you please tell Damon that I know what happened in Atlantic City? I know what happened, I know why it happened, and I have kept my mouth shut about it. Please tell your boss that I am a professional, that I am willing to deal, but only on my own terms, and only with a reasonable guarantee of my safety. Can you remember all that?

What movie'd you get that from, man? Curtis says. I think I saw that movie.

He's among the machines now, eyeing the crowd. Three Japanese ladies playing Beverly Hillbillies. A fat guy yelling at his wife, mouth half-full of burrito. A pregnant girl in an Eisenhower Lions T-shirt, sitting alone at a 24 Karat machine. Nobody's lips sync with the voice he's hearing. Every sound is swaddled in inane electronic chatter.

On the phone, the guy's coming unglued. I will contact you soon, he says. I will let you know what my terms are. Until I do that, you lay the fuck off of me. Just stay the fuck away. You may have Stanley and Veronica and Walter Kagami duped, but I know what your game really is, and I am not gonna go quietly. You tell Damon —

At the edge of the machines, about a hundred feet away, there's a blond kid, a pudgy fratboy type, leaning against an ATM. He's wearing a ballcap and a Mirage T-shirt; he's turned away from Curtis, reading a travel guide. And inside the travel guide is a mirror: about four inches by six, catching a little light from the chandelier over Curtis's head. Curtis freezes, lowers his phone from his ear,

116

takes a couple of quick steps, and the guy's gone.

The gaming floor is crowded, Curtis is out of shape, and getting there seems to take forever. He's got the guy in a corner, but it's a big corner: Curtis hasn't seen him pop up at the escalators, or at the Noodle Asia, so he figures he must've ducked into the sports book area. After quick glances left and right, that's where he follows him.

It's darker inside than on the casino floor: most of the light comes from dozens of flickering TVs, and Curtis's vision takes a moment to adjust. A few Australians are glued to a soccer match; most other screens are recapping NCAA basketball. In a far corner, Curtis can make out a single luminous map of Iraq.

He looks around for a baseball cap, then for blond hair, then for a Mirage T-shirt, but strikes out across the board. Moving into the room, he spots the brim of the guy's cap sticking out of a wastebasket. He picks it up, and finds the guy's blond hair sewn neatly inside. As Curtis lifts it to his face, there's movement somewhere to his left: someone making for the exit.

The guy is light on his feet. Curtis just catches a glimpse of him as he's rounding the corner up ahead, blackhaired now, an MGM Grand hoodie pulled over his T-shirt. By the time Curtis thinks to look at his shoes, he's

117

already vanished. Curtis makes the corner not far behind him, feeling winded, and ducks through the first opening to his left.

It's a little lounge, a salsa band playing to a crowded house. Colored lights sweep the floor; middle-aged white people shuffle and grin. Curtis knows right away that it's over. No telling how many changes of clothes the kid's got. If only he'd looked at the shoes. He stands there for a moment, fuming, catching his breath. His left foot is cold and sticky where the spilled drinks soaked through. After a while, he steps back onto the gaming floor and dials the number the guy called him from.

No answer, no voicemail set up. After five tries Curtis quits, then takes a moment to save the number in the phone. His fingertip mashes the small buttons. Whistler appears on the LCD screen.

He calls Damon on his way back to the elevators. As before, there's no greeting, just a beep. Damon, Curtis says. It's me. You got some explaining to do. I just had a very fucked-up phone conversation with some little freak who's here in Vegas dialing me from a 609 cell, who wants me to give you some message about how he knows what went down in AC and how he wants you to guarantee his safety, but I'm having a hard time doing that, see, because I don't know who the fuck he is or what the fuck he's talking about. All right? Now I am tired of being jerked around by you, motherfucker. You need to call me — on the *phone,* not any more of this fax machine bullshit — and give me the poop. Until you do that, I am suspending operations, effective immediately. I am sitting by the swimming pool, and I am spending your goddamn dollars. Hear me? You need to be straight with me, man. Because this is fucked up. Later.

The keycard slides; Curtis steps into his room. There's a rasp along the tile, something stuck to the damp sole of his shoe: a folded-over sheet of hotel stationery. He catches whiffs of rum and orange juice as he stoops to peel it off.

> We need to talk
> I'm upstairs in 3113
> Come by tonight after 11:30
> **VERONICA**

It's past 11:30 now. Curtis half-turns toward the door, then stops, thinking. Feeling suddenly very happy. Feeling like himself. Things are happening.

He turns, crosses the unlit suite, opens the safe. Checks the revolver's cylinder — five brass caseheads, a neat gleaming ring — and clips it to his belt. His leather blazer is draped over a chair by the window; Curtis slips it on, smoothes the hem to hide the pistol,

119

turns to check his silhouette in the mirror on the wall.

A second pair of eyes stares back at him. Black eyes in a waxen face.

Reflex puts the pistol back in his hand, but aims it automatically at the image in the glass; Curtis curses, wheels to look over his shoulder. As he moves, the phantom in the mirror wavers and warps — like a TV screen raked by a magnet — and dissolves from sight. Curtis feels the sickening, not-unfamiliar sensation of his brain losing its grip on his body: he sees himself wild-eyed, half-crouched, jabbing the pistol at dark corners, although he knows full well that he's alone. His eye has tricked him, or his mind has.

He straightens up, holsters the gun. His wrists and jaw quiver a little from adrenaline, and he clears his throat, shakes his head roughly, scowls at his solitary reflection. This has happened before, though not for a long time. When he first returned from the Desert, he saw ghosts often: dead faces, dead bodies or parts of bodies, what remained of the enemy after the daisycutters and FAE clusters fell on them. In Kuwait the dead were an annoyance, something not to step in, but when he shipped home they came to haunt him — charred skulls peeping from car windows, shriveled arms curled in flowerbeds — and bothered him badly for many days, until one day they didn't anymore. Now it seems they're back, which doesn't surprise him. These days it seems like everything is coming back.

What's strange, though, is that the face in the mirror didn't look like any memory from the Desert. It was a dead face, that's for sure, and also a familiar one, but not a face from any battlefield he's known. It looked like Stanley.

Curtis doesn't know what to do with that; doesn't want to think about it. He clears his throat again, rubs his face. Disgusted with himself. Topside, Veronica is waiting.

He pauses in the doorframe on his way out, just long enough to reach and turn on the lights. Checking to see if the room really is empty, which of course it is. Pointless. Curtis's gaze tracks the tile floor, the mahogany armoire, the wrought-iron divider, the tables and the couches, until it arrives at the windows, which show him the parts of the room he can't see from where he stands: the big rack, the door to the head, his own small shadow in the corridor. The fancy room reminds him of the waitress who took his order in the Oculus Lounge, and also of some of the nurses at Bethesda: good at what they do, so good that their skill becomes a screen that conceals the fact that they don't care. It's a plush room, but it's not comfy. Nobody's home.

For an instant — only an instant — Curtis

is scared that he might die out here.

The room seems ready for him to leave, so he does. He switches off the light, and the dark comes in behind him.

13

From the way the numbers run on his floor, Curtis can hazard a guess as to where Veronica's suite is, and he climbs the stairs at the opposite end of the building.

Four flights. Taking his time. The door opens on a hallway identical to the one he just came from. He moves silently down the corridor, past the elevators, counting the numbers down, listening hard as he goes. There's no sound beyond the drone of air ducts. Curtis is thinking that everyone must be at the tables down below when a door opens ahead, and two women in floorlength fur coats step out. They exchange parting words with a male voice inside, and the door closes behind them. Both women wear shiny red latex gloves; one carries a black attaché case. They smile brightly at they pass. Hi! they say.

When Curtis reaches 3113, he stands outside for a long time. A soft ding comes from down the corridor: the elevator opening for the women. Curtis steps back, listens at the door on the left, at the door on the right, at the door across the hallway. Overhead, the

HVAC system switches off. After a while it switches back on.

Curtis knocks. The tiny point of light in the convex peephole goes dark. Then the door clicks, swings open.

Veronica is wearing an ornate gold cat-face mask. Curtis can't help himself: he gasps when he sees it. She laughs at him, a nervous laugh, and backs into the room. The mask clashes badly with her bare feet and frayed bluejeans and baggy Cypress Bayou sweatshirt. Hey, Curtis, she says. Little jumpy tonight, huh?

You gave me a start there.

Sorry about that. Come on in. Oh — make sure that door pulls shut, okay?

Curtis turns to tug the handle and instantly gets a bad feeling, but it's already too late; there's a rustle of fabric, the rapid creak-and-click of a spring and a slide, and her pistol is just behind his ear. Smooth and quick.

Arms up, she says. Spread your legs wide. Toes out. Do it! Now fall forward. Put your hands on the doorframe. Higher! Do not fucking move.

Curtis feels a tremble in his bladder and a few hot drops on his thigh, and he fights hard to keep the rest inside. This is something that has always happened, every time he's been shot at, or thought he was about to be. It used to shame him badly afterward: the memory of coming out of situations with wet legs and darkened trousers. Now he's surprised to find that the feeling is almost a comfort. It calms him down, reminds him that he knows what to do.

Curtis? Veronica says. You still with me? You doing okay?

Curtis takes a deep breath, lets it out. I been better, he says.

I'm not gonna shoot you. Okay? I have to pat you down. Do not move at all.

He's scared she'll search him with the gun in her hand, but she knows what she's doing: it goes away, and there's a swish as she secures it at her waist. She reaches under his arms, unclips his revolver from his belt, sets it on the deck behind her and pushes it away with her foot, off the tile, onto the carpet. Then she works front to back, top to bottom, crushing and twisting each pocket before she reaches into it. She finds the speedloader in his jacket and the wallet in his jeans, and she drops them on the deck by the revolver. Then she pats down his groin, his legs, his ankles. She does all of this while wearing a gold cat-face mask.

She's backing off now, collecting his things, retreating farther into the suite. Leaving him there. He wants very badly to open the door, to walk down the hallway, to run. Hey, he calls to her. We finished?

Her voice, muffled a little by the walls: Yeah, she says. Sorry. Come on in. Make yourself at home.

He pushes himself upright, straightens his clothes, turns around. The reflector bulb directly overhead is lit; a table lamp glows at the far end of the room. Aside from that the suite is dark.

He steps forward. Veronica's suite is a looking-glass version of his own: higher up, maybe a little bigger — she's got two queens instead of one kingsize rack — but he's got the nicer view. One of her closet doors is ajar; nothing's inside. He looks around for luggage, but there isn't any.

She's on the couch in the sunken living area, with his gun unloaded on the coffee table before her, speedloader and five loose bullets beside it. Her own pistol — a black SIG, small enough to fit in a purse — is on the cushion next to her, in her shadow, about an inch from her hand.

He pauses on the steps. Her mask glitters in the dim light: gold paint and rhinestones, tufts of peacock-feather at the ears. She's flipping through his wallet: his VIC, his TRI-CARE card, his Pennsylvania ID and concealed-carry permit. I thought you were married, she says.

That's right. I am.

She closes the wallet, holds it out to him. Her eyes, dull amid the filigree, flit between his face and his left hand. No wedding ring, huh? she says. I guess what happens here stays here. Right, cowpoke?

Curtis doesn't move, doesn't respond.

Come on, Curtis, Veronica says. Don't act like you're upset. What did you expect me to do?

He steps down, retrieves the wallet. Next time you do a body-search, he says, you ought to ask your detainee if they're carrying any needles or sharp objects.

Hey, that's great advice. Thanks. You know, I was planning on talking to you about Stanley and Damon, but if you want to turn this into some kind of squarebadge best-practices seminar instead, then that's just awesome. I'll take some notes.

Curtis lowers himself into an armchair and looks at her. He sweeps a finger before his eyes like a tiny windshieldwiper. Could you take that off, please? he says.

She reaches back and unties the black ribbon knotted under her ponytail. The mask sinks to her lap. She's wrecked. Curtis thinks of a truckload of Romany refugees he stopped one time near the Serbian border: sleepless for weeks, shot at by everyone, they'd been stealing gas when they could, hiding in barns, traveling by night, with no notion at all where they were going. Veronica's not that bad yet, but she's on her way.

Stanley bought this for me in New Orleans last week, she says. It's a *gatto*. A carnival mask. We were there for Mardi Gras.

126

I heard you were in Atlantic City for Mardi Gras.

She gives him a cool glare. We were in AC on *Vendredi* and *Samedi,* she says. We were in New Orleans for Lundi Gras and Mardi Gras. Stanley was pissed we didn't get to see the Krewe of Thoth march. But what can you do? Gotta earn a living.

Veronica winds the ribbon around the mask, blindfolding it. She shifts it to her left hand, keeping her right hand near the gun, and sets in on the table. Curtis's vision has grown accustomed to the dim light, and he notices two more objects there: a glass tumbler, mostly empty, and a slender brown chapbook. The book seems familiar. He tries to remember where he's seen it before.

Here's a suggestion, Veronica says. Why don't we quit fucking around? Tell me what Damon wants.

Curtis looks up from the table. Far as I know, he says, it's like I told you before. Damon just wants Stanley to get in touch —

No. Please do not start with that skipped-on-a-marker bullshit again, Curtis. It's insulting. Let's do some business. What's Damon's offer?

Curtis shakes his head. I don't mean to insult you, he says. But I can't make any deals for Damon. He didn't send me out here to negotiate. Just to deliver the message.

I don't believe this, she says. She leans

forward, furrows her brow. Stares hard at his face, like she's about to pick an eyelash off his cheek. You're fucking serious, she says. Stanley skipped on a marker. That's why you're out here. That is seriously all Damon told you.

No. He also told me about the cardcounters that hit the Point.

Did he tell you that Stanley put the counters together?

No, Curtis says. He didn't tell me that. *Did* Stanley put the counters together?

Veronica ignores the question, sinks back into the couch. Are you absolutely sure, she says, that you're the only one Damon sent out here?

I can't be sure of that, no. I'm the only one I know about.

Curtis looks down at the table, at the dull rectangle of the book on the glossy wood. Somebody else is looking for you, he says. But Damon didn't send him.

Veronica has grown very still. Really, she says. Do tell.

I ran into him about an hour ago. Little guy. Gap between his front teeth.

White guy?

I'm not sure. I didn't get a good look.

You don't know if he's white, but he's got a gap between his front teeth?

He called me on my cell. He whistles when he talks.

Wow, she says, raising an eyebrow. That's good. I am very impressed.

I was downstairs in the casino when he called me. He was, too. He could see me, but I couldn't see him. Not at first. When I spotted him, he cleared out in a hurry.

How fucking adorable. How delightfully Foucauldian.

You feel like telling me who he is?

Foucault? He was a French philosopher. Looked like Telly Savalas.

She lifts the tumbler from the table and drains it. Using her right hand this time. Curtis relaxes a little. He can tell she's thinking hard, and he lets her think. His eyes keep drifting back to the book. It's bothering him like a song he can almost remember the words to.

He's nobody, Veronica says after a while. Nobody I'm worried about.

You sure about that? He knew to look for you in the casino.

Well, he didn't find me, did he? she says. Neither did you.

She's smiling sweetly to herself, staring into space. Rocking back and forth like she's trying to stay awake.

Point taken, Curtis says. But I was just thinking. Most folks I know tend not to answer the door with a gun in their hand unless they're worried about something.

Well, that's a charming bit of folk wisdom,

Curtis. You should cross-stitch it onto a pillow.

I'm also starting to feel like there's something going on that I don't know about. Something heavier than cardcounting and delinquent markers. If you know what I mean.

Oh, I know exactly what you mean, she says. But you, on the other hand, have no idea what the fuck you're talking about. And I'd be more inclined to buy your Miss Marple routine had I not just pulled a .357 snub off your belt. If you're confused, you can take it up with your buddy Damon. I am not going to explain this shit to you.

She's looking around the room now, everywhere but at Curtis, and he thinks he sees an opening. She's been on her own for a while now, and she doesn't like it. She's ready to talk to somebody.

So, he says, you're telling me Stanley didn't borrow any money from the Point?

I'm not telling you anything. Look, Curtis, use your head. Why would Stanley ask Damon for a marker?

Curtis shrugs. Why would anybody ask anybody for a marker? he says. I had lunch with Walter Kagami today. Walter told me that Stanley's been on a real bad streak lately. Losing a lot at the tables.

Veronica laughs. Walter! she says. Christ. Listen, Curtis, Walter Kagami is a very sweet man. But he has a tendency to talk out of his ass.

Stanley's not hurting for money?

She's giving him a strange look. As if she can't decide whether he's being extremely subtle or extremely stupid. Curtis, she says, how well do you actually know Stanley Glass?

Curtis thinks about that. He doesn't really know how to answer. Stanley's like my uncle, he says. He's my dad's oldest friend. My mom died when I was real young. And my dad had some troubles. So Stanley helped me out. He found my mom's folks living in Shaw, and they took me in and raised me. He helped out with money, and with other things. I owe him a lot.

So you know him as family. Not so much as a friend.

I consider him a friend.

But you don't know him in any professional capacity.

No, Curtis says. I guess I don't.

She sits quietly for a moment. Tallying something in her head. You're the one who introduced him to Damon Blackburn, aren't you? she says.

Curtis nods. Veronica looks at him. Her face so blank it's like another mask. Then she picks up her gun.

Curtis shifts his weight to his toes, ready to tip the chair and roll, but the barrel is pointed at the ceiling. Veronica ejects the clip and sets it by the lamp on the endtable. Then she clears the chamber and puts the pistol and the loose round next to the clip. You probably think of Stanley as a professional gambler, she's saying. That's not correct. Gambling is not Stanley's profession. It's his mode of existence in the world. Do you understand?

I don't think I do, no.

She settles back on the couch, lifts her feet from the floor, crosses her legs. Her toenails are movie-star pink, and look freshly painted. You know he doesn't count, right? she says.

Say again?

Stanley doesn't count cards. Did you know that? You know how cardcounting works, right?

I know the basics, sure.

A while back, Veronica says, Stanley and I were working Foxwoods. I signaled him into a table that was heating up. When I came back twenty minutes later, he was into the next shoe, with this enormous pile of chips in front of him. Completely in control. Making perfect bets every time. The pit boss was starting to sniff the air, so Stanley colored up and we split. I asked him what the count was when he left, and he had no idea. He laughed at me. You have to realize how natural this is to him, Curtis. The man's formal education stopped in the fifth grade. He has no theoretical understanding of probability whatsoever. He doesn't even believe in it.

He doesn't believe in what?

Probability, she says.

She leans forward, lifts the tumbler from the coffee table. Stops, realizing it's empty. Stares at it, as if she can't figure out how it got that way. Want a drink? she says.

No thanks.

You mind fixing me one? I'd do it myself, but I'm still afraid you'll shoot me.

Curtis takes the glass from her hand. There's a bottle of bourbon by the minibar, the red wax peeled from its neck, and he pours her a couple of fingers. Then he unwraps a second tumbler and pours himself some, too. In Stanley's mind, Veronica's saying, about the least interesting thing you can do at a blackjack table is win money. Gambling without any goal beyond making smart bets is like —

She takes the tumbler from Curtis.

— it's like using the Yellow Pages exclusively for pressing flowers. Or it's like using an English-to-Latin dictionary to translate Latin into English.

Wait. Say that again.

Never mind. Bad example. It's more like William Blake's optics. *May God us keep from single vision and Newton's sleep!* Right?

I wouldn't know anything about that, Curtis says.

Okay. What do you know about the sephirot? Or gematria?

133

Curtis gives her a blank look.

What about kabbalah?

Just what Madonna tells me, I guess. Never paid it much mind.

Veronica pulls an ugly face, sips her bourbon.

It's a Jewish thing, right? Curtis says. Some kind of mysticism?

Originally Jewish. Primarily Jewish. Although goyim have been piggybacking on it since at least the Fifteenth Century. Primarily mystical, too, although it's also a system of practical magic. That's what most interested Stanley.

When you say practical magic, Curtis says, I get the feeling you're not talking about Siegfried and Roy.

No, I'm talking about the practice of using talismans, formulas, and incantations to invoke angelic and demonic entities and to cause them to do your bidding.

Curtis blinks. You have got to be bullshitting me, he says.

I'm not bullshitting. Is Stanley bullshitting? *That* is the sixty-fucking-four-thousand-dollar question.

Curtis isn't sure what to say to that. He sets his tumbler on the table. Then he reaches for the book: a paperback octavo, sewn at the spine. Its weathered wraps feel like soft leather, or an old dollar bill, and Curtis knows it belongs to Stanley the moment he touches it. It's dense in his hand, heavier than he'd have guessed. He loosens his grip, feels the downward tug against his fingers.

Walter's worried, Curtis says. He seems to think Stanley's gone off his rocker. You're saying he's just getting religion in his old age?

Lots of people get religion in their old age, Curtis. They go to church. They don't hit the tables at Caesars Palace. This is more complicated.

Veronica's eyes are locked on the book. Curtis can't tell how she feels about him holding it, but he's definitely got her attention. Maybe Walter's right, she says. Maybe Stanley ought to be locked up. Off playing cribbage in a home someplace. Maybe that'd be the best thing for him.

How long has he been interested in this stuff? Magic. Kabbalah.

Veronica smiles wanly. It's not totally accurate to say he's interested in it, she says. *I'm* interested in it. So I fall back on it to explain Stanley to myself. That's how I got mixed up with him in the first place. He was one of my regulars when I was a dealer at the Rio. We got to talking. He wanted to know about the post-Pico Hermetic-Cabalist tradition in early-modern thought. I wanted to know how to exploit the gaming industry to pay off my student loans. So we were pretty much thick as thieves right off the fucking bat. Stanley's never been hung up on specifics, though. The notion of creating a system or being enslaved by another man's — that's not what Stanley's about. He doesn't give a shit about gematria. He's only interested in what it can do.

What can it do?

According to the tradition, it can divulge correspondences hidden throughout all of creation, and ultimately reveal the secret names of God. Since the universe was created through the godhead's utterance of its name, knowing these names theoretically gives you direct access to the divine essence, and the power to transcend space and time. Which comes in pretty handy when you've got clients in from out of town and you need a couple dozen tickets to Cirque du Soleil.

You believe in that stuff?

Fuck no, Veronica says. But I am interested in what happens when people *do* believe it. When I was in grad school, I thought all those people dropped off the face of the planet not long after 1614, when Isaac Casaubon determined the correct date of the *Corpus Hermeticum.* Now I find myself raiding America's casinos with one of them.

She sips her drink and watches Curtis's hands. He tracks her gaze back to the book. Its coffee-brown cover looks blank in the dim light, but Curtis feels imprints in the thick paper, and leans toward the lamp to read what's stamped there.

THE MIRROR THIEF, it says. The writing must have been filled with something silvery at one time; tilting the book forward, Curtis can make out a few starlike flecks clinging to the edges of the letters. He remembers, or imagines, Stanley's fingers dusted with that fugitive silver, twinkling in the halflight of a smoky club, some dive in Chelsea or Bensonhurst or Jackson Heights. Stanley laughing, cutting the cards.

You know what you've got there? Veronica says.

I've seen it before.

That's Stanley's favorite book. He's had it since he was a kid. These past few months he's been reading it just about all the time.

Funny that he didn't take it with him.

Yeah. It is.

Curtis opens the book. On the first page, there's a handwritten message in faded blue ink. Crazy antiquated script.

Stanley —

Remember this always:

"Nature contains nature, nature overcomes nature, and nature meeting with her nature exceedingly rejoices, and is changed into other natures. And in another place, every like rejoices in his like, for likeness is said to be the cause of friendship, whereof many philosophers have left a notable secret."

Best wishes to a fellow lunatic! May fortune speed you toward your own opus magnum.

Regards,
Adrian Welles
6 March 1958

Stanley knew this guy?

I don't know how well he knew him. He tracked Welles down when he was living in California. Stanley never told you this story?

Curtis flips to the next page. *Turn away, you spadefingered architects of denunciation!* it begins.

Turn, you stern merchants of forgetfulness,
you mincing forgetters of consequence,
    turn!
Tend to your sad taxonomy, your numb
    ontology,
your proud happenstance of secular
    wheels!
Nothing thirsts after your pungent spray.
    Nothing
yearns to dry its hands in your grim
    catalogues.
Cast your auditing stares elsewhere! Bold
    Crivano,
the Mirror Thief, skips quicksilver on your
    ancient stones,
trundles his dark burden through viscera of
    cloud,

swaddled in the damp folds of
    linden-scented night.

Harry him not with your snares of causality!
Spare him the gnashing of your mad abaci!
Grant him safe transit, you squat sundial
    kings
(all of you polishing gold to shame silver)
for the treasure he bears in his butterfly
    sack
is none other than that foremost reflector
    itself,
the genderless Moon!
                Let him pass, and mark not
his passage,
        save by sleep-talking
            a quiet threnody
                in your dreamvoided dark.

What in the hell is this, Curtis says.

Adrian Welles, Veronica says — sounding bored, automatic, like she's spoken or heard this many times before — was a poet active in the 1950s and early '60s, loosely associated with the Los Angeles Beats.

Curtis flips ahead, across pages of verse, some in neat columns, some sprawling on the yellowed paper. Toward the end, his eye alights on a line — *his flute conjures a harvest of sleep from the little fields of the dead* — that he can hear clearly in Stanley's voice. He's sure he's heard Stanley quote it, though he can't recall when, or why, and after a moment the memory is lost. Curtis riffles backward, as if to shake Stanley's voice from the book again, until he's at the beginning; then he shuts the covers, presses them between his palms. The old wraps smooth, like taut skin. He almost expects to feel a pulse.

Veronica is looking out the window. Her eyes are bright, full, like she's on the verge of tears or panic, but her breath is steady. She's pulled her legs into full lotus, and she's absently waggling the big toe of her left foot between her thumb and her index finger. Its shadow appears and disappears on the cushion beside her. Its red nail glistens like a coral bead.

If you want to figure Stanley out, she says, which I do not recommend trying, then that book is probably as good a place to start as any.

This guy — Welles — he was some kind of beatnik?

More like a proto-beatnik. He was an older poet, sort of an also-ran, and he gave the bandwagon a push in the early days. He was on the scene, but not really *of* the scene.

Curtis shakes his head, sips his drink. The bourbon is sneaking up on him. It feels like he, the book, and Veronica's eyes are the only motionless things in the room. Everything else is drifting, leaves on a pond.

And Stanley got this from Welles?

140

Veronica closes her eyes. He thinks for a moment that she's gone to sleep. When she opens them again, they're trained on Curtis's face.

I can't believe Stanley never told you this story, she says.

■ ■ ■ ■

SEPARATIO

FEBRUARY 1958

■ ■ ■ ■

Nothing out of place and yet everything was, because there existed between the mirror and myself the same distance, the same break in continuity which I have always felt to exist between acts which I committed yesterday and my present consciousness of them.

— ALEXANDER TROCCHI, *Young Adam*

14

Low clouds gather over the Pacific, cushioning the winter sun as it drops, and the beachcombers are coming in. For a moment the colonnades are unshadowed, and a rosy glow lights the winged lions on the frieze of the St. Mark's Hotel.

Across Market Street there's a boarded-up gaming parlor — FORTUNE BRIDGO in faded letters on its southern wall — and this is where the boy has set up his game. The king of hearts, the seven of hearts, the seven of diamonds, each creased lengthwise up its middle. Three tiny roofs, gliding across a flattened Wheaties box.

Picture him there, kneeling under the roman arches: small and muscular, maybe sixteen years old, cropped curly head already balding. He's dressed in bluejeans and a freshly stolen pair of crepe-soled Pedwins; his pink seercheck sleeves are rolled past his elbows. A battered workjacket rests within easy reach, but though the evening air is cool

145

and gooseflesh rises on his arms, the boy doesn't put it on. The pavement is gritty with sand, littered with shards of windowglass and chunks of stucco from the crumbling façade. The boy rests his knees on a folded-over tabloid, a *Mirror-News* from last week. FAISAL, HUSSEIN PROCLAIM ARAB FEDERATION, it reads. DODGERS CLOSE TO COLISEUM DEAL. It's seawater-warped, already yellow from the sun.

The boy has lately taken to calling himself Stanley. When he hopped the southbound B&O in Staten Island last April he began using the alias Adrian Crivano, and that name carried him as far as Little Rock before he was rousted by cops twice in five hours and had to come up with something else; he pulled STANLEY off the side of a Rollorama coach parked at a mechanic's shop. He was Adrian Stanley in Oklahoma and Missouri, Stanley Welles in Colorado and New Mexico, and when he finally crossed the California state line in mid-December he briefly considered taking the name Adrian Welles — like certain spiders that lure their quarry by resembling it — before deciding that that could only cause problems for him.

Most of his names have come from a book in his jacket's inner pocket, a book of poems that he has read many times and now knows by heart. It's a strange book; there's very little in it that he can claim to fully understand.

146

But it has taught him one rule about which he has no doubt: calling a thing by its name gives you power over it. Therefore you must be careful. The boy's own given name he does not use and never has.

The boardwalk fills as the beach empties. The shadows of passersby lengthen and strobe, and the shuttling cards seem at times to hang in midair.

You are thinking these things; the boy is not. His mind contains nothing but the sensation of regular motion, the steady click of the falling cards. Memory is a skill, as well as a habit. The boy is still young. What do you remember?

15

The sun is gone. The cloudbank, now solid, erases the mountains, blotting out the lights of Malibu across the bay. The amusement pier on the Ocean Park town line is quiet, closed for renovations, but Lawrence Welk is packing them in at the Aragon Ballroom: stocky Rotarians and their wives from Reseda and Van Nuys, pulling up in Imperials and Roadmasters, hurrying through the shabby streets in the hope of getting themselves on television. A mile to the south, the boardwalk swarms with a different crowd — roughnecks from the oilfield, airframe welders from the Douglas plant, dredger deckhands from the new marina, furloughed airmen from Edwards AFB — looking for different entertainment.

Stanley keeps a wad of bills in his breast pocket — singles, plus two fins — and he takes small bets from people who stop, moving their money around, working the throw to keep his bankroll steady. It doesn't take him long to spot a mark: a broad-shouldered hotrodder with a duck's-ass haircut, a little too old for the style. The guy's getting towed around by a fast-looking teenage girl in a neckerchief and pirate pants; he seems sober enough to be alert, drunk enough to be cocky, in the mood to spend some cash. Stanley leans back, cracks the knuckles of his right hand.

Under a lamppost about fifty feet away, a young man has been smoking a cigarette; now he walks toward the arcades. He takes measured, unsteady steps — although he has not been drinking — and he buttonholes the hotrodder and his young date at the boardwalk's edge. He speaks to them for a moment, gestures at Stanley, then closes the rest of the distance, flicking his smoldering stub into the shadows as he staggers to a stop.

You want another shot, chum? Stanley says, not looking up from the three cards.

I feel lucky now, the young man says. I will win it back.

He pulls a new IN GOD WE TRUST dollar

bill from his pocket, drops it, and it flutters onto Stanley's cereal box.

The young man — his name is Claudio — is slim and angular, with large dark eyes and a neat black pompadour; he wears a thin tie, a crisp Van Heusen, and a brown-flecked gray sportcoat that hides the deep creases in the shirt. The fingers of his right hand tap nervously against his thumb, one at a time, ascending and descending.

Stanley flattens Claudio's dollar on the pavement, spreads out one of his own, and puts the cards in motion. His hands rise and fall languidly. The cards stop. Claudio picks one of the red sevens, and a dollar bill goes back into Stanley's pocket.

I will play again, Claudio says.

The girl walks over as Claudio is losing his second dollar; her date lags a bit behind. They watch as Claudio wins one, loses two more. The hotrodder is getting interested now.

The left, Claudio says.

No, the middle, the hotrodder says. The one in the middle, jack.

Stanley turns over a seven on the left and takes away Claudio's dollar.

Enough of this, Claudio says. Enough. He puts a five-dollar bill down on the Wheaties box, and the hotrodder's eyebrows rise a bit. Stanley matches Claudio with a second fin, then holds up the cards — the king in his left hand, both sevens overlapped in his right — and starts his shuffle.

The hotrodder points, whispers something to his girl.

Claudio stares hard at the three peaked rectangles, blinking, shaking his head.

The one on the right, the hotrodder says.

Stanley shoots the guy an angry look.

Claudio bites his lip, looks around. The right, he says softly.

Stanley turns over the king, hands Claudio the two bills, looks up at the hotrodder. Listen, buddy, he says. You better show me some cash, or keep your damn trap shut.

The hotrodder digs out his wallet.

The guy's following the king easily, and Stanley lets him win a couple of singles. Can I bet on him? Claudio asks. Can I bet on this man?

Stanley leans back, looks away, pretends to think about this. A short distance down the boardwalk, next to an icecream cart, a couple of greaser kids are watching him work. Slouching and smoking. Hard-faced and hungry-eyed.

Okay, Stanley says. But you gotta keep quiet. It's his play.

Claudio puts down another five. The hotrodder hesitates for a moment, then puts down a fin of his own.

Stanley holds up the cards: the king and the seven of hearts in his right hand, the king

150

in front. On the throw he switches their positions. So fast that not even somebody watching for it could see. The cards float like gulls in the shuffle. Stanley arranges them on the cardboard and looks up.

It's the one on the right, the hotrodder says.

Stanley turns the card over. It's the seven.

Shit! the hotrodder says.

What? Claudio says. How did this happen?

The hotrodder looks at Claudio, at Stanley, at Claudio.

My money! Claudio says.

Stanley takes another five from each of them on the next throw. Claudio curses the game, curses the hotrodder, and stalks off, reeling. The hotrodder stares after him, confused, his mouth working silently. Stanley takes a moment to look around. Down the boardwalk, the two greasers have disappeared. He gathers his cards and rocks back into a crouch, as if he's about to leave.

Hey! the hotrodder says. Wait a sec, buddy!

I gotta move, Stanley says. A plainclothes cop's been working this stretch.

One more round. Double or nothing.

Stanley settles onto his knees again, throws the cards, takes away the guy's sawbuck.

The hotrodder is giving him a hard look. The smart thing would be for Stanley to clear out now, but he's not ready to go. He's tasting blood: this clown is a choice mark.

Tough break, my friend, Stanley says. One

151

last round? Double or nothing?

The hotrodder is taking rapid breaths, tapping a foot, grinding a fist into his palm. He looks pretty comical, but Stanley keeps his face empty. There's a sloppy tattoo on the back of the hotrodder's hand: what looks like a crow. Stanley smells liquor each time the guy exhales.

C'mon, Mike, the girl's saying. Let's just go.

You're down twenty bucks, chum, Stanley says. You sure you want to walk away now? Look — I'll give you a real easy one.

Stanley holds up his cards — the king behind the seven of diamonds — and throws them, working the switch. The shuffle so slow a child could follow it. Are you watching me here, Mike? he says. Last chance. This is a good investment, chum.

The hotrodder looks up from the cards, narrows his eyes, and looks down again. He draws two tens from his billfold. The middle, he says. It's the one in the middle.

You sure about that?

Yeah.

Stanley takes the two bills from the guy, snaps them into a rigid rectangle, and turns over the middle card with their upper edge. The seven of diamonds.

What the *fuck*, the hotrodder says. His nostrils dilate; his hands wad into fists.

Well, shit, Stanley says, glancing away. Here

comes the goddamn cop.

The cards and the bills vanish into his shirt pocket; he slings the jacket over his shoulder. The girl is scared now, wild-eyed, looking around, but the hotrodder is sputtering in Stanley's face. Scram, Stanley tells him. Go the other way.

Stanley turns on his heel and walks. Claudio is right there behind him, coming in fast from the opposite direction, and he lurches past Stanley into the hotrodder's path, tripping him up. Did you win? Claudio asks him. Did you win back my money?

Stanley hears scuffles and shouts as the hotrodder shoves Claudio against another boardwalk stroller, but he doesn't turn around. Two quick consecutive right turns bring him to the Speedway, where he dashes in front of a slow-moving De Soto to the opposite side of the narrow street.

He's behind the Bridgo parlor now, out of sight of the boardwalk. A few blocks ahead a whitewashed enclosed footbridge spans the road, linking the second stories of two battered hotels; it frames the flashing neon of Windward Avenue like a view through a peephole. Pedestrians run against each other in the boxed space — figures in silhouette, crossing and overlapping — but nobody turns Stanley's way. He slows his step, waits for the De Soto and the line of cars behind it to pass, and turns left down the first sidestreet.

Horizon Court is truncated by T-junctions — the Speedway here, Pacific Avenue opposite — and like all the local streets it's lit down the center by incandescent bulbs that droop from fat electric cables. Halfway along the block there's a dark zone where a few days ago Stanley knocked out a streetlamp with a slingshot and an egg-shaped pebble of rose quartz; now he hurries to that spot — *skips quicksilver on your ancient stones,* he thinks — and slips through the shadowed doorway of a boarded-up storefront as soon as the coast is clear.

Once off the street, he wedges a two-by-six pinewood plank between the shop's wrought-iron doorknob and its rough concrete floor. Then he strikes his father's MIOJ pocket lighter, holding the flame to a candle stub mounted in a rinsed-out vienna sausage tin, and weak yellow light creeps into the corners of the room.

Stanley still can't figure out what this place used to be. The dusty glass-topped counter and the wallmounts for absent display cabinets remind him of his great-uncles' jewelry store in Williamsburg — he saw it once as a young kid, and again last year when he helped burglarize it — but he doesn't think that's what this was. In the backroom are two workbenches, finger-wide holes bored into their tops for bolting down heavy equipment, and strange objects keep turning up in dim corners: tiny screws, semicircles of wire, drifts of glittering white powder that Claudio says is ground glass, although Stanley can't think of why he'd know that.

The mile of oceanfront between Rose Avenue and Washington Boulevard is full of abandoned buildings — outlawed bingo parlors, fly-by-night factories, the hulls of other defunct enterprises — but Stanley picked this particular storefront as a hideout because it's small, inconspicuous, centrally located, and because its back window opens onto a parking lot. After two days of casing the place, two sleepless nights ducking beat cops and shivering on the beach, Stanley broke the streetlamp and jimmied the entrance, and he and Claudio set to work fortifying their new lair: cracking window-glass against their pillowed jackets, pushing a workbench against the back wall to ready an escape route, and knocking a hole through a gypsum panel to stash their scant possessions.

Now Stanley picks up the candle and kneels at the gap in the wall. His father's Army field-pack is there, tucked out of sight, and he unsnaps the canteen and gulps some water before tugging it out and opening it. He keeps everything he owns squared away and ready to go at all times — blanket, tinned food, change of clothes — in case he needs to dust out in a hurry; now he unloads enough to make space to hide the cash. He counts it, although he knows exactly what's there: fifty-nine dollars. He and Claudio just tripled their stake on a two-hour grift, and nobody collared them. Not yet.

But Claudio ought to be here by now. Stanley has no watch, hasn't been minding the time, but it shouldn't have taken more than a few minutes for Claudio to shake the hotrodder and return to base. It's possible that Stanley just didn't hear his triple-knock signal to unblock the door. Possible, but unlikely.

He flattens the cash and the three playing cards between a couple of sardine cans — keeping a fiver and some singles in his pocket, just in case — and repacks the bag, pulling *The Mirror Thief* from his jacket and placing it at the top before buckling it again. For an instant he pauses, feeling the book's shape through the worn canvas, reassured by its promise that all this will soon be very different. Then he shoves the pack behind the gypsumboard, and with a quick puff he kills the candleflame.

16

Stanley doesn't want to walk with his back to traffic — the hotrodder could be behind the wheel by now — so he jogs three blocks to Windward, crosses the street, and makes a right turn toward the ocean. His eyes echo the rhythm of his steps, bouncing between faces in oncoming windshields, amblers rotating to and from the boardwalk. By now the lights along the avenue have picked up misty halos, and the squarejohn crowd has all but gone home. Familiar 42nd Street types emerge from the darkness: rowdy sailors and soldiers, pavement princesses cruising for trade, sharp-dressed Negro hustlers, hollow-cheeked junkies looking to cop. Stanley studies their features as they're lit by the rescue mission's buzzing JESUS SAVES sign, each pair of eyes hooded in the red glow, each nose throwing a shadow like the gnomon of a sundial.

He crosses the boardwalk to the beach side, out of the foot traffic, and takes a long look in both directions. The hotrodder and his girl are nowhere in sight, but Stanley spots Claudio without much trouble: he's slumped on a wooden bench two hundred yards away, a block north of the Fortune Bridgo arcade. Three greaseheaded hooligans in pegged jeans and motorcycle jackets are gathered around him. At first Stanley thinks they're strongarming him, but then he sees how they're standing: at ease, bored, like they're waiting for someone. Claudio's cradling his head in his hands, still doing his lush bit. Stanley grins. The kid's no Brando, sure, but damn if he can't act a little after all.

Two of the thugs are the ones he saw earlier

while working the grift on the hotrodder. The third punk wouldn't have been larking around on his own. That means there's a fourth someplace — probably off meeting the rest of the gang. He'll bring them back here, and they'll muscle Claudio into leading them to Stanley, so they can brace him for the evening's take. It's a straightforward operation. Stanley's been on their end of it himself.

He zips his dark jacket to cover his light shirt and begins to walk toward them. Experience has taught him that people never pay attention to anything — they're practically blind even when they do — so he's not too worried about getting spotted. Once he's closed half the distance he angles left onto the beach; he bears right again when he's out of range of the streetlamps, moving parallel to the boardwalk. Mist has settled on the sand: it's coarse and mealy at the surface, powdery where his new shoes punch into it. Stanley stops for a moment and shoves his hand down, grabs a fistful of fine dry grains, then another, and stuffs them into the right front pocket of his jeans. He puts a folded dollar bill in the left.

With the fog thickening and the boardwalk people backlit by neon it's harder now to see, but he's still able to pipe the greaser cavalry nearly three hundred yards off: what looks like six or seven of them, pressing through the crowd at the corner of Brooks Avenue, visible mostly from the attitudes of people they displace. They're slowing down as the crowds get denser. Stanley figures they'll be here in four minutes, tops.

Hey fellas, he says, sauntering up to Claudio's bench. Let me take my buddy off your hands.

The three hammerheads look up at him, baffled. The two on the right turn to the third: the boss, a little older, stockier, swarthier, sporting a thin pink scar that splits an eyebrow and reappears at his hairline. The guy's got deep cuts on his hands, too, which Stanley takes to mean either that he's been in lots of knifefights or that he's not very good at it. His chums both look fresh-weaned: one's got a gluesniffer's red eyes and runny nose; the other is white-blond and pimply.

Stanley shoulders past the two punks and tugs on Claudio's arm. Man oh man, you're really bombed, he says. Can one of you guys help me stand him up?

Not so quick, asshole, the boss says.

Stanley ignores him, lifts Claudio to his feet.

I wan' go home, Claudio says. Sick.

Listen, the boss says, clapping a hand on Stanley's shoulder. We saw the little con you were running tonight. Tell your friend to drop his drunk act. We need to have a discussion.

Stanley doesn't shrug the hand off, doesn't stop moving either. From the way these goons carry themselves, Stanley figures they've all seen *The Blackboard Jungle* maybe a dozen times apiece, but he keeps the smirk off his face for now. Yeah? Stanley says. So discuss.

You know who we are, buddy?

Stanley swivels to face him. Should I? he says.

You damn well should. We're Shoreline Dogs.

Stanley gives the guy a slow up-and-down. Shoreline Dogs, he says.

That's right. This is our turf. Nobody operates here without our say-so. What was your take tonight?

Stanley looks away, shrugs. Twenty, he says.

Bullshit.

So what's your cut?

Our cut is all of it, jerkoff. You didn't ask permission. If you're gonna work the boardwalk it's half your take from now on. Turn out your goddamn pockets.

Bafoom, Claudio says, sagging against Stanley. Need bafroom.

Stanley stares evenly at the boss. Then he shifts his focus over the guy's shoulder to the rest of the gang, two blocks away, closing in. What if I tell you to go climb up your thumb? he says.

Well, then I guess we're gonna have to pound you. Right now, and again every time we see you. You and your faggot friend.

Yeah, the whitehaired kid says, pushing in close, breathing on Stanley's neck. We don't

160

tolerate fags around here.

He's got a little extra sparkle in his voice, like this is a favorite subject with him, but that's fine: Stanley knows how to play this now. Okay, chum, he says. But I'm keeping a couple of bucks. My buddy and me ain't had a meal today.

Stanley reaches into his jeans, palms the dollar, turns the pocket out. Then he tips Claudio toward the gluesniffer, and Claudio drapes over him, moaning. Stanley loads up his fist with sand from the other pocket, fakes a switch, and holds the dollar bill out to the boss with his left. A few grains leak between his fingers, but nobody sees.

The rest's in my sock, Stanley says. He lifts his foot to the bench.

The boss reaches for the bill, then stops, wary. Hold it, jack, he's saying.

The whitehaired kid has just spotted his pals up the block; he's raising an arm, opening his mouth. Stanley slings the sand in the boss's eyes, throws himself backward off the bench, and elbows Whitey in the face. His funny-bone connects just under the kid's nose, which starts spurting; Stanley's arm goes tingly. The boss is digging into his motorcycle jacket for a knife, swinging blind: his hand ruffles Stanley's hair. Stanley pops a crouch — just like his dad taught him — and kicks the guy in the balls. He can hear shouts now from up the block, sandy boots scraping

161

wooden planks.

Claudio has come to life, punching the gluesniffer in the breadbasket; now he's got the doubled-over kid stiffarmed, holding him off by the head. The two of them are drifting across the boardwalk, orbiting each other like a binary star. Stanley drops his shoulder and knocks the gluesniffer on his ass. Go, he yells at Claudio. Go go go go go.

Claudio's wearing a perplexed look as Stanley runs past him — he hasn't seen the real trouble coming — but his longer legs and easy stride catch him up in a hurry. Stanley sticks to the boardwalk, dodging people, zigzagging whenever he comes to a cross-street to try to fake a turn. The hooligans are way back, but closing in. Claudio could blow them off with no problem — his great-grandmother was a pureblood Indian from some tribe famous for its runners, or so he says, though he barely looks Mexican, never mind Indian — but Stanley's not so quick. The rubber soles on his new Pedwins speed him up, but he can already feel blisters rising on his heels. The faces of pedestrians flash by like funhouse images: shocked, angry, laughing. For once in his life Stanley half hopes they'll run across a cop.

But there are no cops, and now the greasers are barking. At first it's only a couple of them, but soon they're all doing it: a rhythmic chorus of low woofs and frantic yaps, in and

162

out of sync, echoing down the colonnade. It's a typical smalltime JD stunt, corny and dumb, but a worm of genuine fear still crawls down Stanley's spine to his tailbone, and puts extra spring into his step.

At the stopsign at Pacific Stanley bears left into the intersection and starts running down the middle of the street. Cars roll past him on both sides, in opposite directions. Motorists scream at him. Somebody honks. Claudio's gotten gummed up on the sidewalk, surprised by Stanley's sudden move to the center. Stanley glances back to make sure he's catching up, and when he turns forward again, there's the hotrodder's girl, just ahead to his left, her teeth bared, her finger pointing, standing in the passenger seat of a hopped-up Model A like a charioteer. He hears the driver-side door open as he barrels by, then the hotrodder's voice. Hey! the hotrodder says. Hey you!

Stanley hits the brakes, spins, jogs back a few steps, waiting for Claudio, who's still sprinting along the sidewalk. The hotrodder is in the middle of the street, waving an empty bottle by its neck, illuminated from below by the headlights of the Nash stopped behind his roadster. Farther back, Stanley sees the dark shapes of Shoreline Dogs under the hanging streetlamps, outlined against shop windows. One of them gets stuck behind the hotrodder's open door, scrambles around

163

it cursing, and the hotrodder swats him in the shoulder with the empty bottle. The driver of the Nash is trying to back up.

Stanley and Claudio run through a grassy traffic circle, across a parking lot, aiming themselves toward whatever pockets of darkness they can find. They make a right, then a left. The wide street ahead is all residential: small weathered bungalows, sagging porches with steel-pipe railings. The waterlogged air traps the city lights, and the sky glows seaweed-green; Stanley can see shaggy crowns of palmtrees figured against it, and the derricks of the oilfield maybe a quarter-mile farther on. There's no sound coming from behind now except the drone of distant traffic. Stanley slows down, lightheaded, to get his bearings.

Who was making that noise? Claudio says. He's not even winded.

The guys chasing us. Who do you think?

Claudio looks at him. But they were lying on the ground, he says.

Not *those* guys, shit-for-brains. The ten hoods coming right behind 'em. You didn't see 'em?

Claudio wrinkles his brow, takes a skeptical look over his shoulder. What hoods? he says.

The avenue is joined by a smaller street just ahead, and Stanley checks the streetsign in the corner lot: Cordova Court, running into Rialto Avenue. They're only a block off

Windward, but the neighborhood feels different, quieter. Maybe half of the nearby houses are lit up inside, some by the haunted flicker of television screens. Cool jazz plays on a hi-fi somewhere to the right. Through an open window, Stanley hears a woman laugh softly.

That was a real nice move, by the way, Stanley says. Grabbing that thug by the head. That was pretty slick.

You liked my move?

No, Stanley says. That was what you call sarcasm. Buddy, we are gonna have to do something to toughen you up.

Claudio's opening his mouth to object when a scuffle of shoes comes from behind them, and then a voice, wordless and half-human, baying like a bluetick coonhound, like hounds in movies bay. Stanley and Claudio turn and run across the untended lawns, Stanley's vision tunneling and going white, his footfalls hollow in his ears, like he's hearing them through an empty coffeecan. Cordova angles to the right, but Stanley continues straight ahead toward a dark and sagging cottage, grabbing Claudio's sleeve to make him follow, casting a glance backward to see whether the Dogs have made the corner yet. They haven't.

To the left of the bungalow there's a low wooden fence, the rotting slats strung together with wire, and Stanley jumps it, catches his foot, and lands facefirst in a weedy garden; his knees sink into loose earth, and a cedar trellis crunches under his shoulder. Behind him, Claudio hops the fence like an antelope, lands gracefully, and Stanley grabs his feet and brings him down, too.

Another howl comes from the street: the Dogs drawing close; he can't tell how many. He scrambles on top of Claudio, puts fingers across his lips. Soon he can hear the Dogs in nearby yards, whispering back and forth. Claudio's chest rises and falls evenly. Stanley's own ragged breath and pistoning heart beat against it in raucous counterpoint.

The porchlight of the house next door comes on, deepening the shadows in the garden, lighting up two Dogs as they slink past a patchy boxwood hedge. A door creaks, and then a man's voice: Who's out there?

The bushes crash as the Dogs retreat. Stanley knows they'll be in the clear now if they can just lie low for a few minutes. He lets out a long breath to calm himself. When he fills his lungs again, the air is a cloud of odors he knows at once but cannot yet sort out or identify: rosemary, horseradish, garlic, mint, lemon verbena, tomato vine, the plants crushed under their fallen bodies. In the absence of words, Stanley's mind retrieves a succession of kitchens — his grandmother frying latkes, his mother cubing lamb, the simmering cauldron of red sauce made by a neighbor woman whose name is lost to him

— and beneath all these, his grandfather's hands, tearing bitter herbs for Passover. It's as if this plot of disturbed earth a continent's breadth from his birthplace has recognized him, acknowledged him. Welcome, it says. We have been waiting so long.

Stanley is filled with such joy and such certainty that he has to bite hard on Claudio's lapel to keep himself from laughing, from screaming. Claudio's black eyes widen in shock, but he makes no sound. He places a smooth palm on Stanley's cheek, runs it through his tangled hair, and brings his head to rest in the pocket above his collarbone. Claudio's neck is warm beneath his forehead, sticky with mist. Stanley draws closer to him, and they lie that way for what seems like many hours, long past the time they know it's safe to rise.

17

The next week brings rain that drowns what's left of February and flushes out the waterfront streets. Stanley and Claudio spend the days huddled under blankets in their storefront lair, reading to stave off boredom, books and magazines propped against the hillock of their tangled legs. Claudio works through a stack of glossies that Stanley stole for him from a newsstand on Market Street — *Photoplay, Modern Screen, Movie Mirror* — scanning them as if in search of clues. He speaks up now and then to report a discovery. The talent agent of Tab Hunter is the same as that of Rock Hudson, he says. Also that of Rory Calhoun. I believe the names of these men are not their true names.

Stanley reads *The Mirror Thief.* It's a book of poems, but it tells a story: an alchemist and spy called Crivano steals an enchanted mirror, and is pursued by his enemies through the streets of a haunted city. Stanley long ago stopped paying the story any mind. He's come to regard it as a fillip at best, at worst as a device meant to conceal the book's true purpose, the powerful secret it contains. Nothing, he's quite certain, could be so obscure by accident.

As he reads, his eyes graze each poem's lines like a needle over an LP's grooves, atomizing them into letters, reassembling them into uniform arcades. What he's looking for is a key: a gap in the book's mask, a loose thread to unravel its veil. He tries tricks to find new openings — reading sideways, reading upsidedown, reading whitespace instead of text — but the words always close ranks like tiles in a mosaic, like crooks in a lineup, and mock him with their blithe expressions. The usual suspects.

On the book's second printed page — *a poetic narrative by Adrian Welles, Seshat Books, Los Angeles, copyright 1954* — is a brief inscription: a message from whoever gave it away to the person they gave it to, somebody called Alan. Stanley's never been able to make out what the fiercely slanted handwriting says; one word looks like *salad,* another *naked.* He's long since given up on deciphering it. Above the message, Adrian Welles's printed name has been struck through with a curving slash of black ink. Stanley used to flip to this page and wonder why somebody would cross the name out like that, but lately he doesn't think about it at all.

Sometimes he'll close his eyes and close the book, balancing its spine on the mounts of his palm. He'll picture a dark figure — Welles, Crivano, himself — slinking through the streets outside, cloaked in a slicker and a dripping hat, in pursuit of some unfathomable objective: a void errant in the blurred landscape. Stanley will hold this image as long as he can, until other concerns encroach — what if Welles has left this place? what if he's dead? — and then he'll let the book fall open and he'll read the first line his eyes fall on, hoping it will contain a clue as to where he should go, what he should do next. Stanley knows there's no real logic to this practice — or, rather, that the logic is the book's logic, not the world's — but this is as it should be. The point where the book and the world intersect is exactly what he's looking for.

Sometimes a line offers clear direction: I seek you in constant carnival, masked Crivano, along the waterline. More often not: *Omphale's husband has rendered his judgment! You sully your hands with occult burrowing, but the goldmaker's shame still whispers from the reeds!* Sometimes a passage seizes his attention for no reason he can name —

Aqua alta: Crivano's feet
fuse with those of his watery double.
Look not upon your confederates,
the knaves hung from the columns!
Two-headed, in two worlds,
your facedown likeness
finds his silent image in the sea.

— and lures him in, propelling him to the final page, the final lines. *17 February 1953*, followed by two names: this town, this state. The map that guided him here.

Whenever Stanley and Claudio become bored with reading, bored with each other and themselves, they go to the movies. The first-run theaters in Santa Monica are the best place to see the lush and earnest melodramas that Claudio favors, but Stanley prefers the Fox on Lincoln: it's nearby, half the price, and its B-grade westerns and horror movies are more suited to his taste.

But the Fox isn't safe in the rain. Stanley and Claudio visit it a few days after their run-in with the Dogs, crossing Abbot Kinney and Electric, following Fourth to Vernon, seeking shelter under the crowns of eucalypts and rubber trees, still soaked to the skin by the time they spot the theater's neon sign. Stanley shivers in his seat as the first reel begins, distracted as always by the projector's machinegun stutter, the quick drip of images splashed on the screen.

It's a monster movie: a volcano releases giant scorpions from their underground lair, and they attack Mexico City. Stanley picked this one because it has lots of Mexican actors in it that Claudio probably knows; also, he wants to see how the scorpions work. He doesn't generally have much patience for sitting in theaters, but giant movie monsters like the Ymir in *20 Million Miles to Earth* and the dinosaur in *The Beast of Hollow Mountain* fascinate him. The first time he saw one — it was *Mighty Joe Young* at the Lido on Fordham Road; Stanley was eight years old; his father had left him there while meeting a girlfriend around the block — he'd understood immediately how it was done, could sense the invisible hands reaching between the frames to imbue the figures with life, and he knew he'd discovered something important, a small secret that opened onto bigger secrets. The trick wasn't in the fake monsters, or even in the riffling spool of film, but right there in his own head the whole time. The

171

eye that tricked itself.

This movie begins with a corny fake-newsreel opening — stock footage of volcanoes — and then the two heroes take the stage: a wisecracking American geologist and his handsome Mexican sidekick. Stanley finds himself drawn in by their cool daring and easy banter, and for a while he's caught up in the story, because after all aren't he and Claudio just like these guys? Two explorers in a dangerous land, with only each other to fall back on? Stanley half-wishes the movie could go like this forever: the men taking turns at the Jeep's wheel, passing gnarled jungles and smoldering ridges under the weird light of an ash-laden sky; the killer scorpions always sensed but never named, never visible, and the whole landscape vivid and mysterious in their uncast shadows.

Soon, of course, the leading lady shows up — followed by the inevitable little kid with a dog, acting cute and making trouble — and Stanley's interest gutters. Things don't get any better when the scorpions finally make the scene. They look pretty good at first, creepy and realistic, but the filmmakers don't have much footage, so they keep repeating shots: one goofy closeup of a popeyed scorpion head drooling poison ooze gets reused so many times that Stanley loses count. The producers must have run out of money or something, because by the last reel they're

172

not even using models half the time, just a black scorpion silhouette laid over shots of Mexicans panicking in the streets.

Stanley's barely even watching the movie — he's trying to remember if the guy playing the American geologist is the same guy who played the geologist in *The Day the World Ended,* and wondering whether this is a co-incidence, or if maybe the actor has some geological expertise in real life — when a lit cigarette stings him in the back of the neck. He slaps his skin and turns around, but no one's behind him. As he scans the half-empty theater, shielding his swelling pupils from the bright screen, a second butt strikes his seat-back and sends a spritz of orange sparks past his arm, and now he can see them: six Dogs, seated across the aisle a few rows back. Whitey's hair glows in the projector's pulse, but Stanley can't make out any faces. Some have their dirty All-Stars propped on the seats in front of them, and they're all smoking or lighting up, readying their next broadside.

Stanley swats Claudio's knee and jerks a thumb, and the two of them walk to the front, cross below the screen, and exit the theater in the opposite corner. They wait in the lobby long enough to see whether the Dogs will follow them out of the movie; they do, but evidently aren't carrying enough of a grudge to give chase in the rain. Stanley blinks drops from his eyes, looks over his shoulder as he waits for a break in traffic: the Dogs huddled under the marquee, vague and shapeless through the downpour, clouding the air before them with their spoiled breath.

From this day forward, Claudio says, I believe that we should see films only in Santa Monica.

He's naked now, candlelit from below, standing tiptoe in the backroom of the shop on Horizon. Stanley has strung a length of twine between two wallmounts with a midshipman's hitch; Claudio is draping his soaked clothes over it. Stanley leans in a corner, peevish and aroused, wrapped in his father's Army blanket: his cock chafes against the rough fabric. Don't let those jokers rattle your cage, he says. Today was just bad luck. Back in the neighborhood, that's what we always did in bad weather — we saw bad movies. I should've figured those punks would be hanging around the Fox.

They will give us more trouble.

I don't think so. We made 'em mad the other day, but we made 'em look pretty silly, too. If we steer clear, they'll let us alone.

How will we do your con? How will we get money?

Money? Stanley laughs and shakes his head, like he's talking to a child. Money's the biggest con of all, chum. It's only good for making more money. Anything you can pay for, you can steal.

174

Claudio gives him a skeptical look, wipes his damp palms across his hollow stomach.

What's the matter? Stanley says. If you don't believe me, just name something. Anything you want, I'll be back here with it in less than an hour. I'll get you two of 'em. Go on and try me.

You will be caught.

I ain't gonna get caught. C'mon, what do you want? A watch? A fancy watch? I'll get us a couple of fancy watches. A matching pair.

You should not even go outdoors in the daylight. You need your hair to be cut. You look like a criminal.

Like hell I do, Stanley says. I look like an honest American boy. He pats his matted curls with an involuntary hand.

You look like a monkey. A dirty American monkey.

Claudio grins slyly, steps forward. He tugs a handful of Stanley's hair; the blanket slips. Stanley flails at Claudio's arm, shoves him away, pulls him back in, wriggling.

It's another two days before the rain blows through, by which time Stanley has grown stir-crazy, desperate to wander. He walks Claudio to the traffic circle through the cool morning air, sharing a stolen breakfast of Twinkies and oranges. The bus to Santa Monica pulls up as they arrive; Claudio shoves what's left of his fruit into Stanley's sticky fingers and runs ahead. He turns and smiles once he's crossed Main, and Stanley smiles back. The fleeting dialogue of their faces across the busy street conveys many things, trust not foremost among them. Claudio vanishes behind the coach, reappears in shadow through its windows, settles into a seat. Stanley watches the kid's sharp-nosed profile — eclipsed by the irregular beat of passengers in the aisle, cars on the street — until the bus rolls away.

He walks back to the oceanfront and crosses the boardwalk to the beach, swallowing the last of the luminous orange wedges, sucking his fingertips clean. He breaks the rind into bits and pitches it to a group of seagulls running in the swash; the gulls take the pieces, fly with them, and drop them into the waves, where other gulls swoop at them in turn. Aerated, the ocean is sky-blue, opaque, dotted with pulses of silver. A row of white surf breaks two hundred feet out, cracking like a heavy whip, hollowing a brief cavern in the foam. Its dyspeptic growl echoes down the waterfront.

Stanley wipes his mouth and smells the citrus oil on his hands, thinking of the winter harvest in Riverside. That first week of work he probably ate his weight in fruit: sweet clementines, brilliant valencias, navel oranges bigger than bocce balls. Last month, after he and Claudio snuck away from the groves and hitched a ride into Los Angeles from a Fuller

Brush man, they both swore they'd never touch citrus again. Now they find themselves craving it.

Stanley met Claudio on a mixed picking crew. He didn't like him much at first. The kid seemed too smooth for harvest work, too cagey, no more born to it than Stanley was himself. Stanley made him out to be on the run from trouble, or maybe just slumming: a prodigal outcast from some mansion on some hill. He also figured Claudio for a sandbagger, feigning ineptitude to duck the worst work, certain his job was secure since the crew boss spoke no Spanish and needed him to translate. They ignored each other at first. But the whites on the crew were all older than Stanley, closemouthed, and the Mexicans seemed to steer clear of Claudio. Eventually the two began to talk.

Stanley never asked questions, so Claudio's story came out slowly, in no special order. The youngest of thirteen by two mothers, he'd grown up comfortable and invisible in a big house outside Hermosillo. His father was a famous general — he'd fought Pancho Villa at Calaya, the Cristeros in Jalisco — and his brothers left home to become lawyers, bankers, statesmen. Claudio spent his days in the cinema in town, learning English from Cary Grant and Katharine Hepburn, raising his small hands to hide the subtitles. He grew older, made quiet plans to travel north. Claudio told Stanley these stories as they worked, whispered them at night in the bunkhouse, and later, when they slipped into the dark groves to plot escape under moon-silvered citrus leaves, Stanley lay still and watched Claudio's lips move until he no longer understood anything at all.

He likes Claudio a lot. He's not sick of having him around. At idle times on his long cross-country drift he's often wished he had somebody to share his adventures — somebody who'd listen to him, who'd believe the stories he tells himself about himself — and then this oddball Mexican kid came along and seemed to fit the bill. And it's been great, having a partner. It's made things possible that otherwise wouldn't be.

But there are also things that Stanley wants to do alone.

When the rind is gone and the gulls are scattered, Stanley takes a deep breath and turns back toward the boardwalk. The late-morning sun is high over the city: buildings and streetlamps and palmtrees angle their shadows at him, marking channels in the sand, and the storefronts are blacked-out beneath their porticos. Stanley checks the signs over the arcades as he draws closer: Chop Suey, St. Mark's Hotel, Center Drug Co. On the corner of Market Street, blue and red stripes coil around a white column; he smoothes his frizzed hair as he passes it by.

Beachfront characters are out enjoying the weather — an old lady in an opera coat, stooped under her parasol; a bearded man in paint-spattered chinos, chasing two laughing women across the sand; a stout burgher walking an ugly dog, singing to it in a strange language — but Stanley pays them all little mind. He broadcasts his attention among the buildings, mindful of shapes and textures, of the attitude of sunlight on walls and streets. Patterns catch his eye, then slip into the background: rows of lancet windows, bricks emerging from stucco, mascarons grinning atop cast-iron columns. There's an absence here that he's training himself to see, something he can only glimpse sidelong, as if by accident. It's bound up with the past, with the lapsed grandeur of this place, but even that is insubstantial, a shadow cast by the thing itself, flickering behind the scrim of years like the ghost of a ghost.

This is Welles's city, so named in the book — which makes it Crivano's city, too, as much as any earthly city can be. Stanley will learn to move through it as Crivano would: silent, catlike, on the balls of his feet. Unhidden yet unseen. Whenever his path clears, he shuts his eyes to walk a few blind steps, imagining the feel of cobblestones under soft boots, of a slender blade at his hip, of a black cape fanning his ankles, billowing in the night air. The night itself another cloak. He's not

179

sure how he came to have so clear a picture of Crivano; in the book, Welles never really says what he looks like. It occurs to Stanley that he could have gotten this idea from someplace else: from Stewart Granger in *Scaramouche,* maybe, or even from a corny Zorro movie that he saw when he was a kid. He opens his eyes, blinks and winces in the sun, corrects his course.

Ahead is a cluster of old Bridgo parlors, some boarded up, some converted to penny arcades. Young men's voices inside. The frantic chime of pinball machines. He'd like to go in, play a few balls — he's good at it — but Dogs will be nearby, and he's not quite ready for another scrap. He hasn't yet settled on a strategy with those guys. He'll go to war if he has to; he'd probably only need to take two or three of them out before the others would fold. But he'd have to hurt those two or three pretty bad — hospital bad, maybe graveyard bad — for the rest to take him seriously, and he's not sure he wants the trouble that would come with that. For now he'll just steer clear and lie low.

He crosses the Speedway and heads inland, past dilapidated shops and orange brick apartments. The avenues are rain-washed, weirdly bright, laid out for inspection. The usual boardwalk sidestreet smells — fried food, spilled liquor, puke and piss — are erased, but this just uncovers the subtler ripe-fruit and rotten-egg odors of the oilfield. Past Abbot Kinney the buildings fall away, opening space for weedy lawns fenced by splintered pickets, gardens bordered by railroad ties. Flowers and green leaves are everywhere, even this early in the year: myrtle and boxwood, bottlebrush and oleander, jasmine and clematis on trellised porches, cosmos and hollyhocks at fencerows. The plants are long-stemmed, unsteady in the sandy soil, slouching against clapboard with scapegrace charm, ready to take ruthless advantage of any kindness shown to them.

Across the street, a geriatric with a shaggy white mane pushes an old-fashioned gang mower over a tiny lawn; damp grass clumps at his sandaled feet. He stares at Stanley, his eyes reduced to flecks by his spectacles' thick lenses. Stanley looks away.

He has no means of recognizing Welles. He could pass him on the street — maybe he already has — and he'd have no idea. This is obvious, but it's hard for Stanley to keep in mind. In his daydreams he always knows Welles by sight: their paths cross, their eyes lock, Stanley catches the impish and ironical expression on the older man's face and knows him immediately. He always imagines that Welles recognizes him, too. As a confederate. As the boy he has been looking for.

Stanley knows that this is childish. He needs to start asking around, and he's not sure of the best way to go about it. He's got good front going now — not an easy thing to maintain — and the idea of becoming more visible bothers him. Aside from running grifts and hustling occasional work, he hasn't had any real traffic with the squarejohn world in years. These people — walking their dogs, mowing their lawns, going about their ordinary business — seem almost like a different species.

As Stanley thinks this, he can hear his father's voice saying it, and he smiles. Remembering his dad seated in the kitchen of the apartment on Division, in full dress uniform, sipping buttermilk. Everybody else — his grandfather, his uncle, his mother, Stanley himself — was standing, and nobody else spoke. Stanley kept staring at the decorations on his dad's chest: the Pacific Campaign Medal, the Bronze Star. They flapped against his olive tunic every time he laughed. Later he let Stanley drag his new fieldpack partway to the Bedford Ave station, then tipped him a palmful of mercury dimes. *Get out of there quick as you can,* he said. *Those fuckers will bleed you dry.*

By the time the Red Chinese finally killed his father, as he'd promised they would, Stanley was living in the apartment like a cockroach, sneaking in whenever he needed food or shelter, creeping out again to forage.

He thought this at the time: a cockroach. The idea made him proud. A year after that, when his grandfather died and his mother stopped speaking forever, Stanley quit coming home at all.

The house ahead on his right is entirely overgrown by bougainvillea: only a slumped porch and a pair of dormers still hold off the emerald leaves and vermillion bracts. Stanley's thrilled to see a building obliterated like this in the midst of a city. Something moves in the vine-snared yard — a cat — and now he can see several, maybe a dozen. One emaciated gray persian watches from the porch, so thin it seems to lack a body, to be nothing but yellow eyes and a snarl of fur.

Stanley walks on. The ocean recedes behind him. He thinks about the cats, and about the anonymous neighborhood houses. About Welles. About Crivano. About black scorpions, and hidden watchers in dense jungles.

He comes to a dead stop on the sidewalk. Barber shop, he thinks.

18

When the bus from Santa Monica pulls up two hours later, Stanley is waiting at the curb, the combat unit from his father's fieldpack dangling from his fingers. He catches Claudio as he's stepping from the door, shoves him back inside, and climbs in after him, paying the fare, shrugging into a seat. Stolen sardine cans in the pack scrape together as he settles it in his lap. We're going to Hollywood, Stanley says.

Claudio stands in the aisle, slackjawed, then puts out a hand to touch Stanley's fresh buzzcut. Your hair, he says.

Stanley catches him by the wrist, jerks him into the seat. Knock it off, he says. Did you hear what I just told you? Hollywood, chum.

You look like a soldier, Claudio says.

As the bus rolls south to the end of its route and swings north again, Stanley fills Claudio in on what the barber told him. Adrian Welles, it turns out, is now mixed up with the movies: writing, sometimes even directing them. A big production of his just finished filming nearby — right along the boardwalk, in fact — and now he's in Hollywood editing it. It had a bunch of big stars in it, Stanley says. Even I knew some of the names. This could be your big break, kid.

Claudio's trying to seem cool and appraising, but Stanley can see the gooseflesh on his forearms. With what studio is he contracted? he asks.

Universal Pictures, I think, is what the guy told me.

I do not believe that the headquarters of Universal-International are in Hollywood, Claudio says. I believe they are outside the city. Do we know how to find this place?

Sure we do, Stanley says. How tough can it be?

They transfer at Santa Monica Boulevard and ride inland, past the boxy white spire of the Mormon Temple, past the Fox Studios and the Country Club, across the Beverly Hills town line. Stanley still can't figure how anybody can call this place a city. To him, it's like a real city got cut to pieces and dropped from a plane: tall buildings litter the valley in no real order, and streets and shops and houses stretch between them like a fungus. Every time Stanley thinks they're downtown, they're not.

At Wilshire they swap seats. Claudio takes the window to watch for famous faces in passing Rolls-Royces and Corvettes; Stanley slouches and half-listens to Claudio's commentary while he thinks about what to do next. He should be glad to have a solid lead on Welles, but this feels wrong, and he's not sure why. It's not that he doubts what the barber told him — the guy had no percentage in putting him off the trail — it's just that none of it fits with the image of Welles in his head. That scares him a little. The *movies,* for crying out loud! Stanley feels betrayed, but can't justify it. The idea that Welles didn't so much misrepresent himself in his book as somehow avoid representing himself at all leaves him queasy.

After half an hour of pointless wandering,

Claudio gets directions from a Mexican valet at the Sunset Tower — talking to the guy a lot longer than seems necessary — and leads Stanley to a spot where they can catch the Number 22 up Highland into the hills. They stroll the boulevard while they wait. Stanley points out details on the old theaters' weird façades: thick columns and pharaoh heads on the Egyptian, Moorish battlements on the El Capitan. Claudio listens, nods, but keeps glancing nervously at the white letters on the hillside to the north, as if he expects them to evaporate in the gathering haze.

When they reach Grauman's Chinese, Claudio gives a start, mutters something in Spanish, and dashes into its patchwork fore-court. Stanley follows at a skeptical distance as Claudio scans the pavement in a half-stoop, like he's looking for dropped coins. Stanley sees handprints and footprints in the cement, left when it was poured, with names and messages scrawled around them. For a moment he thinks of a sidewalk back home in City Park: G G + V C gouged into its set-ting surface, alongside the winged imprints of mapleseeds. Then he starts to read the writing at his feet, and he slows to a stop.

Carmen Miranda. Janet Gaynor. Eddie Cantor. *Here's looking at you, Sid.* Mary Pick-ford. Ginger Rogers. Fred Astaire. The paral-lel furrows of Sonja Henie's skates. *To Sid, Tillykke, Always.* Harold Lloyd's doodled spectacles. Loretta Young. Tyrone Power. *To Sid — Following in my father's footsteps.* As Stanley steps over each section of pavement, he imagines the moment it was made: movie-stars laughing in a fusillade of flashbulbs, waving their dirty hands. Kids playing in the mud. So this, he thinks, is what it means to be famous.

He turns to make a snide comment, but the look on Claudio's face brings him up short. The kid's expression is so transparent, so supersaturated with longing and awe, that Stanley immediately cracks up laughing. He has to sit down for a minute — next to the hoofprints of Champion, Gene Autry's trusty horse — to catch his breath.

The 22 makes a brief stop at the white shell of the Hollywood Bowl before climbing the dry hillside and dropping them near the entrance of Universal City Studios. Stanley expects a steady stream of cars from the other direction — showbiz footsoldiers knocking off work — but nothing's coming in or out of the gates. One look at the guard's booth convinces him that this is a waste of time, but he and Claudio stroll up anyway.

Excuse me, Stanley says. I'm here to see Adrian Welles.

The guard is a flat-nosed man with deeply lined skin. He marks his place in his Herman Wouk novel with a pencil from behind his ear and looks at Stanley and Claudio. His eyes are blue, sharp, devoid of judgment. Adrian Welles, he says.

That's right.

I don't think I know him, the guard says. Where does he keep his office?

He's editing a movie here. He's a writer. And a director.

The guard shakes his head slowly. He's not one of ours, he says. Maybe he hired out one of the cutting rooms?

Maybe so.

Well, the guard says, if you find out what building he's in, and then you have him phone me and put your name on the cleared list, I can let you through.

Stanley has been trying to figure out what he'll say if the guard asks if he's got an appointment, but now it's clear he isn't even going to ask that. *You can always tell a man who's been to war,* Stanley's dad used to say, although he never said exactly how to do it. Stanley's pretty sure this guy has been to war.

I don't want to make no hassle for nobody, Stanley says. If you just let me and my pal poke around a little, I'm sure we can hunt him down.

The guard gives him a tiny smile. Well, he says, I'm not so sure. I got better than two hundred acres of property over my shoulder. I don't want to have to come looking for you when you get lost.

Stanley nods, looks down at the concrete.

Tiny hairs left by the barber's electric razor are pricking him around his collar. He looks up again. Listen, he says. I came a long way to see this man. And I'm not going to bullshit you. I know your whole job is to keep people like me out. But I'm giving you my word. If you let us through, we are not gonna be a problem for you. Okay?

The guard's expression doesn't change. You know, he says, your friend's probably going to be punching the clock soon anyway. Maybe you fellas should just meet him someplace for a drink. The guard's eyes move from Stanley to Claudio, then back. Or a milk-shake, he says.

Thank you for your time, Stanley says.

He and Claudio turn and walk. A few hundred yards south along the Hollywood Freeway a road climbs the western edge of Cahuenga Peak; they hike its incline through a eucalyptus glade into a quiet neighborhood of narrow streets and widely spaced houses. One house that backs up on a scrubby rise has three days' newspapers scattered in its weedy lawn; Stanley crosses the flagstone path and opens its wooden gate.

The backyard is strewn with gnawed tennis balls and dry lumps of dogshit, but there's no dog. A gap interrupts the picket fence — two boards wide, worn on both sides, tufted with black hair in its rough spots — and Stanley slips through while Claudio vaults over. A short scramble among yucca and needlegrass brings them to a wedge-shaped cliff over a small arroyo, a vantage from which they can watch the sun nestling into the mountains, the Los Angeles River in its concrete channel, and the great oval of the Universal property just below. A chattering swarm of bushtits bursts from a sumac, disappears down the slope. Swallows streak the air, returning to roost along the freeway. Far below, a pale stretch of cyclone fence peeks between sagebrush and liveoak; Stanley sees a spot a quarter-mile northeast where it's sagging inward. Scanning the streets between the studio's lots and buildings, he sees nothing moving at all.

They sit for a while, eating bruised apples as the shadows of the mountains creep over them. Then they throw the cores into the arroyo and start their descent.

For another half-hour they hide in the bushes, watching the studio property through the fence until the sky goes deep blue and the streetlamps inside glow. Aside from a single sweep of headlights against a faraway building there are no signs of life. Stanley and Claudio take off their jackets. Stanley puts one inside the other, pulling the sleeves of Claudio's through the sleeves of his own. Beach sand left over from their first night in town trickles from the pockets, and he thinks for a moment about places he's been, distances he's crossed. Then he hands the jackets to Claudio and runs hard at the fence, hitting it square on its leaning post.

Claudio catches his foot, boosts him upwards. The concrete plug at the linepost's base shifts in the dirt, and Stanley tips forward. When he's reached the four strands of barbed wire over the toprail, Claudio hands up the jackets; Stanley drapes them over the three lower strands, pulls himself over the topmost, and drops, rolling on the dusty incline. By the time he's upright and brushing himself off, Claudio is over too, jumping to pluck the jackets from the wire.

They pass a courthouse's imposing façade — no building behind it — and detour around a paved lakebed, its sides slick with black algae. A breeze blows through Cahuenga Pass, swaying the crowns of trees; the screen of their leaves sieves the light of scattered streetlamps. More façades emerge as Stanley and Claudio head west: thatched jungle huts, a decrepit mining town, a rustic Mexican village. Here and there they find scatterings of cigarette butts, slashes of black graffiti: they're not the first ones to hop the fence. Headlights wash over them from somewhere in the distance — the double-tap of a slow pulse — and they freeze for a moment before moving on.

A rushing hum is everywhere around them; it seems to come from falling water, or the

191

rumble of hidden machines, or just the wind, though they're never able to decide which. They pick up their pace, crashing through a ribbon of trees to discover more fake buildings, more elaborate now: the hulk of a steam locomotive, the parapets of a medieval fortress, a quaint city street. Hey, Stanley whispers as he hurries over the cobblestones. Is this supposed to be Paris?

Yes, Claudio says, glancing around nervously. Europe. I believe Paris.

You ever been to Paris?

I have never.

Well, then how do you know it's supposed to be Paris? There ain't no Eiffel Tower. There ain't no whaddya-call-it.

Claudio doesn't look at him. You said Paris, he says. I said Paris only after you.

Do we think it's Paris just because it looks like Paris does in the movies? Maybe the Paris in the movies has got nothing to do with the real Paris. Maybe the real Paris looks like China. How'd we ever know?

There's a circular fountain ahead, decorated with four winged lions, its dry basin filled with stray tumbleweeds from the fake mining town nearby. The wind wavers, shifts, and a charred smell comes from somewhere in front of them, stinging Stanley's nose. It all seems deserted, he says.

No one lives here. Everything is not real.

Yeah, no shit. I know. That ain't what I

mean. I mean it's like nobody's been using this stuff. Like everything's shut down.

Claudio looks around, preoccupied. The films of today often shoot on location, he says. To seem more true. Do you smell a burning?

Around the next bend they find themselves in front of a mountain of scorched plasterboard and twisted girders: a fake city block, recently up in flames. The street and its gutters are silted with black mounds of ash and soot; it hisses around their ankles when the wind blows. The air is painful to breathe. Stanley looks at the adjacent structures to figure out what this used to be — what it was supposed to be — and sees department stores, theaters, the granite bases of skyscrapers. New York.

Stanley and Claudio push ahead to get past the burn. They come to a block of brownstones with black banisters and barred windows and crooknecked streetlamps lining their sidewalks: a looking-glass Brooklyn. It's nothing like the city he grew up in, not really, but Stanley knows that if he saw this place on a movie screen he'd buy it as New York, no questions asked. He thinks of movies he's seen that were supposed to happen on streets he knows well. Some of them were probably shot right here. Looking back, they always looked fake, every time, but he never questioned it. It makes him feel like a sap.

193

Stanley! Claudio hisses, motioning him toward the stoop he's crouched behind, but it's too late: headlights catch him. They pass over, leaving him in darkness again, but then jerk to a halt with a squeak of brakes.

He and Claudio dash around the corner, across a street, and hide in the bushes beside a fake New England church. Behind them a car door slams, then another. Did they see you? Claudio asks.

Oh, they saw me, all right.

What will we do?

Stanley doesn't answer. The cyclone fence isn't far, but he doubts they could clear it in time; anyway, they'd have to drop straight into the sloped channel of the LA River to get away, and he doesn't want to try that in the dark. But moving farther into the backlot is no good, either: they're apt to get tripped up or boxed in if they can't see where they're going. And now the way they came from is blocked.

Two white beams are moving down the street of brownstones: heavy flashlights, the kind with big square batteries slung beneath. The two studio guards are moving like cops move — keeping plenty of space between them, holding their lights away from their bodies — and Stanley can tell they'll be tough to shake. He didn't see whether the guard at the gate was wearing a pistol, but he'd bet that these two are. They're coming through

194

the darkness like men with guns.

We have to run away, Claudio whispers. They will find us.

Just sit tight. We ain't done here yet.

It is no good to sit tight. We can't see where to hide. They know this place.

They damn well *will* see us if we run. That's what they want, is to flush us out and shoot us. I didn't come all the way out here to get rousted by these clowns.

Stanley, Claudio says. Your man is not here. No one is here but them. It is stupid for us to stay.

The guards are close enough now to make out their faces: handsome, cold-eyed, unworried. Each has what looks like a thirtyeight special revolver in his right hand. Off-duty cops, Stanley figures, moonlighting for extra cash. They won't be slow to pull the trigger. He could use Claudio as a decoy, split them up, ambush one, take his gun away. If he can circle back to the mound of debris, there's bound to be something there he could crack a skull with. A piece of rebar, maybe.

I will go to them, Claudio says.

Huh?

I will go to them. When they take me away, you will go back through the fence. I will meet you on the road. Where the bus dropped us.

Stanley unglues his eyes from the moving lights and looks at Claudio. Have you flipped your wig? he hisses. Whaddya mean, you'll go to them? And do what?

Claudio's still watching the guards; Stanley can see his dark irises click from one to the other. His right hand is firm and warm on Stanley's shoulder. His expression is calm, alert. I will talk to them, he says.

Stanley takes a deep breath. Kid, he says, if they call in the cops, you're done for. They'll ship you back to Mexico. If you're lucky. Is that what you want?

They will not call any cops.

Yeah? How do you figure that, smart guy?

I will be very sorry to them. It will be no problem. He turns to Stanley and grins. I have a nice front, he says.

Stanley opens his mouth to speak, but Claudio is already standing up, stepping from the bushes. If you do not see me in one hour, he says, go back to the ocean. I will meet you at our headquarters.

He's walking down the middle of the street now, his arms above his head, his toes turned out in a slow saunter. Stanley watches him go. The flashlight beams rake the pavement and converge on him, and in their light his black perfect shape is trimmed by a white corona. Hello, my friends, he calls out. I think that I have become lost.

Stanley's pulse scolds him in his throat and in his temples. He keeps very still. The guards draw close to Claudio; they vanish at the edges of the light he's stopping. Stanley can't hear what anybody says. One of the beams sweeps his way, tracing Claudio's path back toward the bushes, and Stanley lies flat and buries his face in the redwood mulch.

The light flashes over him: once, twice, three times. When he hasn't seen it in a solid thirty seconds he looks up again. The guards have put their pistols away; one holds his flashlight at Claudio's back, while the other stands in front, a hand alongside his neck. He seems to be pinching Claudio's ear like a schoolmaster, though the gesture could also be a caress. His light is aimed at Claudio's throat, making his face unreadable, his eyes and mouth into black voids. After a moment, the three of them turn, walk, and vanish around the corner.

Stanley waits for the guards' engine to start, for the crunch of their wheels, for the spill-over from their headlights to fade from the canyons of façades. This seems to take a long time. When everything is dark and silent again, he jogs toward the burn, retracing his steps as best he can.

He's back to the spot where they jumped the fence in what seems like no time at all, but after a couple of tries he realizes he'll never clear it on his own: it's bowed badly inward, and he's neither strong nor heavy enough to bend it back without Claudio's help. There are too many lights to the south, too many houses, so he heads toward the river instead, looking for a spot where he can slither under. This is hopeless — there's a tension wire strung along the base, an inch above the ground — but eventually he comes to a tight corner with an endpost he can climb. He throws his jacket over, throws the combat pack after it, and winces as it clatters on the dry ground. Then he grabs the rough loops of wire, digs in with the toes of his shoes. Scared and impatient, he catches his leg on a barb as he's coming over the top; his jeans tear, a gash opens in his calf, and for a bad moment he's tangled, tipping forward, about to be flayed by his own weight, slammed facefirst in the dirt. Then he rights himself, measures out his breaths — staring at the black ridge of Mount Lee, a spillway impounding the lights of the city — frees his leg, and drops.

He backtracks until he finds streetlamps, pavement, houses with lit windows: old couples playing gin rummy, families gathered around TV sets. The neighborhood streets lead him to the freeway. He's jogging now, blood drying on his ankle, uncertain of the time; Claudio said to meet in an hour, but of course they have no watches. Stanley feels like it's been at least that long since they split up.

When he comes to the bus-stop, Claudio's not there. Stanley throws the combat pack on a bench and sits and waits. Then he stands up. Beyond the padlocked studio gates he sees no movement, not even the occasional glint of headlights. To the east, the dark form of Cahuenga Peak slowly takes shape against the purple night sky, and after a few minutes a reddish moon bubbles up behind it, not quite full. Stanley watches as it rolls across the sky, going yellow, then white.

He sits again, opens the pack, takes out *The Mirror Thief.* A streetlamp overhead gives plenty of light, but Stanley doesn't read, can't concentrate. For a second he has the urge to throw the book, as hard as he can, at the studio gates. He imagines it flying from his hand and flaring into a wall of fire that sweeps the whole valley clean — or taking wing, swooping through the dark like a great brown owl, finding Claudio and carrying him to safety. Stanley believes the book to be capable of such feats. He believes it has promised him as much.

But Stanley doesn't throw the book. *The Mirror Thief* stays shut in his lap, inert like a jammed pistol, as Stanley revisits its contents from memory.

Westward rise the twin oneiric gates, horn
and ivory, each one skull-sprung from
    sleep.
Half-awake, Crivano laughs at the asperity
of fire. So spake the alchemist, "Calcination

is the very treasure of a thing; be not you
weary of calcination!" In this manner only
can the foul substance by red levels be
   reduced:
bot   *bar*   *bot*
unglimpsed behind the white-hot furnace
   door,
made new behind the unfurled cloak of
   night.

How would Crivano handle a fix like this?
It's a dumb question, for a bunch of reasons.
Crivano would have come alone, for one —
or at least he wouldn't have come with
anybody he'd think twice about leaving
behind. Stanley may not know all the stuff
that Adrian Welles knows — history, alchemy,
ancient languages, magic — but he ought to
understand this much. He ought to know
how to act like a thief.

The bus has stopped running for the night.
Stanley wonders how he'll get back to the
waterfront. He puts away the book and stands
up again to pace around the bench, stopping
sometimes to scrape crusted blood from his
leg. A police cruiser swings by, slows down.
The cops stare at him; he stares back. They
stop for a moment, then pull away. He curses
them aloud as they go. Then he curses Claudio, then himself, muttering obscenities as he
makes his tight oval circuit. After a while he
folds his arms across his chest and moans,

doubled over by a feeling that's entirely strange to him, less a fear than an urge, like the need to sneeze or shit.

Headlights shine from the studio lots. Stanley sinks onto the bench and watches them come. A white sedan, unmarked, draws parallel to the gates. Its rear door opens. Claudio gets out. He leans to talk with the driver for a moment, then raises a palm in goodbye and steps over the low gate. The white car turns back into the studio property, accelerating as it drives away. Claudio walks toward Stanley, his hands in his jacket pockets. Stanley waves to him. Claudio doesn't wave back.

When Claudio reaches the edge of the circle of light shed by the bus-stop's streetlamp, Stanley rushes forward and grabs him by the shoulders and shakes him. Goddamnit, kid! he says.

Claudio breaks his hold, shoves him away. Stanley backpedals until he's sitting on the bench again. Claudio's chin juts; his mouth bunches with rage. Do not touch me, damn you, he says.

Hey! I'm just glad to see you in one piece, is all. What's the matter?

Claudio turns his back, shakes his head. Then he faces Stanley again. The film your man was making by the ocean, he says. What is the name of it?

I don't remember, Stanley says. I don't

201

think the barber told me.

It had big stars. You said this, yes? Even you knew their names. Now, tell me, Stanley, what stars did it have?

Ah, shit, kid, I don't know. That Hollywood stuff doesn't mean —

Was Mister Charlton Heston perhaps one of these big stars?

Stanley thinks about that for a second. Yes! he says. It was Charlton Heston! The barber said he even met him. He came right into his shop. Charlton Heston, and some famous actress, too.

Marlene Dietrich? Claudio says. Janet Leigh?

The second one. Janet. I think.

Claudio steps in very close. His breath is shallow and rapid. He glowers down at Stanley with bottomless eyes. Are you *quite* certain, he hisses, that the barber said *Adrian Welles*?

19

On foot they work their way back toward the city, navigating by moonlight, the earth's downgrade, periodic glimpses through the trees of the HOLLYWOOD sign. By the time they reach Santa Monica Boulevard they're stupid with exhaustion, and they hop the stone wall of a cemetery and break open a mausoleum door and spend what remains of the night half-asleep on its hard marble slab, without so much as a word passed between them.

In the morning the fog is thick but burns off quickly, sliding off the city like a drape. While he waits for Claudio to wake, Stanley shakes out his stiff legs and walks among the graves: low rectangles flush with the trimmed grass, angels and obelisks and boxy sepulchers among them, poking between dark trunks of cedars and palms. He has never imagined a place like this. Crossing his arms, rubbing his shivering elbows, he thinks of dead people he's known and wonders what happened to them, where they went.

In the combat pack he locates the canteen and a mostly clean rag, and he washes and bandages his wound. The rip in his jeans is already fraying, brown with crusted blood; he'll need to steal a new pair soon. Once he's tied the rag he digs out some crackers and a tin of sardines and *The Mirror Thief,* and he sits and eats and reads and listens to the drone of cars on the boulevard, the bawling of gulls lost in the clouds: the sounds of the city waking up.

> Crivano hides among
> the bones and serpents.
> On the wings of Argeiphontes
> he passes the White Rock,
> the shadow-land of dreams.

203

There, Okeanos, where Arian drowned!
No such martyrdom for Crivano.
                    Brave traitor!
His flute conjures a harvest of sleep
from the little fields of the dead.

When he finally emerges from the tomb, Claudio seems glum, preoccupied, uncharacteristically reserved, but Stanley shakes him from his funk by enlisting him in the problem of returning to base. A few blocks into the neighborhood they spot two bags of empty soda bottles on the doorstep of a duplex, and they lift them gingerly, wincing at the clatter of glass as they hotfoot to the boulevard. It's nearly a mile before they find an open drugstore, but the deposits are enough to cover their fares back to the beach and a proper breakfast besides.

They find a bustling roadhouse, Barney's Beanery, at the spot where Santa Monica ends its east-west run and tacks toward the coast, and they stop in to get coffee and split a plate of bacon and hotcakes. It's mostly suits and hats inside: movie execs on the way to Paramount or Goldwyn, Jewish doctors bound for Mount Sinai. A pack of bleary-eyed hipsters still up from last night sprawls in a corner booth, smoking slowly and intently. At the bar, the proprietor chats with a pair of slender men in matching ricky jackets, obvious queens, standing inches from a black-on-pink sign that reads FAGOTS – STAY OUT. Stanley and Claudio trade puzzled looks. Is it a joke? Does he know?

As the westbound 75 is rolling to the curb, Claudio glances back at the restaurant and pulls a doubletake. Ramon Novarro, he whispers.

Who?

Ramon Novarro! There, entering the beanery!

Claudio does an about-face; Stanley plants a hand on his breastbone and shoves him into the coach before he can bolt. C'mon, kid, he says. Let's move it along.

Claudio's craning his neck, pressing his nose to the grimy glass as they settle into their seats. I can't believe this, he says. Ramon Novarro eats his breakfast at this same restaurant. We should have spoken to him.

What the hell are you on about?

Ramon Novarro! Star of *Ben-Hur*! Star of *The Arab,* and *The Prisoner of Zenda*! These are films of great importance.

As the bus rolls past the fountains and the arbors of Beverly Gardens, Claudio summarizes the career of Ramon Novarro and recounts the plots of his many movies, proceeding with such abandon that they all blend into a single swashbuckling epic of hysterical complexity. Stanley only half-listens. He's hunched in his seat with his eyes closed, letting the engine's rumble massage him toward sleep. He pictures Claudio as a lonely boy in Hermosillo, his small fingers flipping through faded American screen magazines, his black eyes going wide as the lights of the cinema darken.

It's nearly noon before they see the ocean. On the way through Santa Monica they hit a couple of grocers' shops: Claudio pesters the proprietors while Stanley picks through the shelves — *spic doesn't understand a word of English* — and soon they've replenished their supply of fruit and crackers and potted meat. Stanley even comes away with a quart of milk and a couple of Heath bars, but Claudio is unimpressed. He's growing weary, short-tempered. The fog is gone. The day is warming up.

Claudio washes down the chocolate with a swig from the bottle and passes it back to Stanley. Now what will we do? he asks.

I don't know. Lie on the beach, maybe. Get some shuteye. What do you mean?

I mean, now what will we do for money?

Claudio sounds detached, automatic, like he's starting up an old fight again out of habit, or just to keep from thinking about something else. Stanley shoots him a look. Money? he says, and gives the combat pack a shake to rattle the tins inside. We got three days' worth of food here. I can hardly carry this thing. What do we need money for?

Claudio's face pinches in consternation, but his eyes are steady. We need money for a place to stay, he says. A proper place. So that we can become established.

Established? Stanley says. What's this *established*? Do you even know what that word means?

I know what it means. I know we cannot keep on like this.

Stanley glares at him, hitches up the pack on his shoulder. Yeah? he says. Speak for yourself, chum. I been keeping on like this since I was twelve years old. If you don't like it, that's too bad. You fucking pansy.

Claudio blanches, but doesn't take the bait, and Stanley feels a little sick for having said it. I helped you, Claudio says. I helped you look for your man. Now you help me.

Sure, you helped. You had *no desire at all* to see Hollywood. Right? What a terrific sacrifice you made. How can I ever repay you?

Silent gulls bank overhead in the clear air; their perfect shadows drift across the pavement with motionless wings, like outlines hung from a child's mobile. Stanley steps off the boardwalk, onto the sand. Claudio follows him. The wind is cool by the water, the beach all but deserted. Two old ladies pass with bundles of polished driftwood. Farther up the beach, a thin and shirtless man in a black beret stands before an easel, daubing at a canvas. A crowd of sandpipers runs ahead of Stanley and Claudio, then stops until they close the distance, then runs ahead again.

The beach widens as they walk south, and when they're far enough from the boardwalk — too far to be worth a vag bust for a cop — Stanley sits down. The tide is in: there's a towering surf, and waves are erasing the domed temples and square towers of an elaborate city built in the sand. A piece of blackened wood is trapped in what's left of its central plaza, and Claudio stoops to pick it up. It looks like a burnt plank from an old ship, heavily encrusted with dogwinkles and goose barnacles, afloat maybe for years. Claudio lets it drop into the next big wave and it glides away. In the distance, beyond the line of breakers, the sea is featureless, a shimmering silver band.

After a while Claudio sits down next to Stanley. Stanley brushes the sand from his palm and slips it under Claudio's shirt, against his narrow back. Claudio flinches, then relaxes. You will help me get money, he says.

Stanley studies the horizon, the pattern of flashes there. His eyes are tired. You want to go back to the three-card routine? he says. That made some good money.

Those hoods will bother us again.

We could take the game into town. Back into Hollywood.

No. Hoods are everywhere.

Claudio slides up the cuff of Stanley's jeans to expose the bandaged cut. He looks at it without comment, then covers it again. Moves his hand to Stanley's knee. Runs it slowly up his thigh.

Stanley's leaning toward him when he spots something in the waves off to the right. Did you see that? he says.

What?

Look, Stanley says, pointing.

Three black spheres are floating in the smooth sea halfway to the breakers, appearing and disappearing between the swells. They look like the heads of frogmen, surfacing for a moment to spy on the land.

I don't see.

Look! There's three of 'em.

Stanley scrambles to his knees, kneels behind Claudio, rests an outstretched arm on his shoulder, sighting down the length of it. Look, he says. Right there.

They sit like that for a moment. Stanley's arm rises and falls with Claudio's breath. One of the spheres vanishes, followed by the second, and the third.

There they go. See?

Claudio is quiet for a moment. There is nothing there, he says.

Stanley slumps backwards, flat on the sand. Closes his eyes. Goddamn, he says. I need some sleep.

The sun is warm on his face, his eyelids.

He feels Claudio's hand on his bare stomach. How did you get money in New York? Claudio asks.

He can feel the crash of the surf through the sand beneath him, rocking him like the engine of the bus. Lots of ways, he says.

What ways?

Ways you need a gang to make work. Ways that ain't gonna help us here.

No ways that can work with two people? You are certain of this?

Stanley takes a deep breath, lets it out. The seashell hiss of sleep fills his ears. Maybe we can roll lushes, he mutters.

What does this mean?

Lushes. Drunks. You find 'em, and you take their wallets. Simple.

Do you hurt them?

Not unless they make a fuss. Even then they usually fall down on their own. Most times they don't even know what's going on.

I don't think this is a good idea.

Fine. Let me know when you got a better one.

I have ideas, Claudio says.

Stanley thinks he's only been asleep for a second, but when he jerks awake with the sensation of falling his throat is sore, his lips speckled with sand, and everything is glowing orange. The sun is enormous in front of him, its cool disk split across the bottom by the horizon, and Claudio is gone.

He staggers to his feet, heart thrashing. The tide is going out. Big waves are still breaking a few yards away, and Stanley sees a dark shape — a log, or the trunk of a washed-out palmtree — just beyond the spot where they crest. As he watches, a pair of bright black eyes appears; then the shape jerks, arcs into a bow, and rockets into the depths. A little farther out are two more, rolling and swimming in the black water. Seals. Sea lions. Stanley's frogmen come to shore. He laughs at himself, shaken.

The streetlamps are coming on along the boardwalk, and knots of people are milling around in front of the arcades, laughing, shouting, huddling close. A sinister few stand in the shadows, nursing bottles, surveying the crowd. Stanley spots a couple of Shoreline Dogs loitering by the Bridgo parlor: young kids, new recruits, not faces he knows. He stops to rest the combat pack on a bench and shuffle through its contents. Coiled at the bottom among the tinned meats is his black-jack, two tapered strips of leather stitched into a long pouch and filled with a halfpound of double-ought buck, something he fashioned in his spare hours a few months ago while working on a ranch in Colorado, or maybe New Mexico. He tucks it into his blue-jeans at the small of his back and buckles the pack again.

As he strolls the boardwalk, Stanley scans

the crowd, concentrating on groups; he has a feeling Claudio won't be alone. The kid's nowhere to be seen under the arcades or on the benches, so Stanley turns around at the Ocean Park pier and heads south again, checking the sidestreets as he goes. The roar and sputter of motorcycles echoes from a few blocks away: a gang of bikers passing through. This will bring the Dogs closer to the water tonight, looking for fights they can win. He quickens his step.

A pack of shaggy hipsters is coming up the boardwalk: two bearded men in sandals, a dirty-blond girl in a black leotard, a white guy with a saxophone case, a Negro with a trumpet. Just before Stanley meets them, they make a right on Dudley. The blonde turns and gives him a weird knowing look as he crosses the street. He walks on, the hipsters' rough voices ricocheting in the shadows behind him. This bunch reminds him of the menthol-and-turtleneck crowd he used to see in the Village, but wilder, more sunburnt and desperate. The sight and sound and smell of them trouble him for blocks, though he's not sure why.

He's so distracted that he nearly misses Claudio, seated on a bench off Wave Crest Ave, next to a lean and handsome man. The man is dressed in a wrinkled Bali Cay shirt and what was once a nice pair of trousers; he's speaking Spanish with a flat American accent. The man laughs as he talks, gesturing with his left hand, which alights now and then on Claudio's lithe shoulder. Stanley steps to the corner and stands there until he's certain that Claudio sees him. Then he crosses to the opposite side of the street. Claudio doesn't meet his gaze. He's leaning in close, flashing his eyes, beaming into the handsome man's face.

A shiny black and silver Montclair squeals through a stopsign on the Speedway, Chuck Rio's saxophone blaring through its open windows, and now the handsome man is dancing in his seat, singing along, screaming *Tequila!* into the seething night. Claudio laughs and pats his leg. The man reaches for a bag-sheathed bottle at his feet, and his long fingers miss the neck by a full inch. Stanley crosses his arms, leans against a column, breathing steadily. His pulse throbs in his injured calf, pressing against the knots of the bandage. The blackjack is heavy at the base of his spine.

Claudio is looking up, beckoning with a curled finger. Stanley crosses the street again and saunters over. He pastes on a smile, narrows his eyes.

Charlie, Claudio says to the handsome man, please meet my good friend Stanley. Stanley, this is Charlie.

Encantado de conocerle, Señor, the man says, and extends an unsteady hand. His grip is damp, pickled. Claudio laughs.

Pleasure, Stanley says.

Charlie works in advertising, Claudio says. He is an ad man.

Have you noticed how many of your neighbors are using Herman Miller furniture these days? Charlie says, feigning a radio voice. *It's an open secret in Detroit — the Edsel is going to be copied!*

Stanley squats on his haunches and looks Charlie in the face. The man's eyes are bobbing, floating like June fireflies. Hey, Stanley says, what are you drinking there, Charlie?

Buh-BAH buh-buh BAA-buh BUH-buh! Charlie sings, misting Stanley a little on his *b*'s. *Lemon and salt in a martini? Caramba!*

But Stanley can smell the gin on his breath: it's a bottle of Seagram's in the bag. He gives Claudio a hard look. Claudio returns it, his eyes full and glassy. Stanley can't guess what's behind them. Let's go down to the water, Charlie, he says. What do you think?

Charlie is inviting me to go back to his pad, Claudio says.

His what?

Hey, you should come, too, man, Charlie says. Two's company, three's more company. More the merrier. Dig?

No, Stanley says. Let's go down to the water. The water's nice, Charlie. It's cold. It'll wake you up.

That's good, that's good, Charlie says. That's a good idea. I *love* the water, man. I love to just get out in it and —

He turns back to Claudio. Is that cool, man? he says. Is that okay? José? Sorry! I'm sorry. Uh — your name again? Cassius? My lean and hungry friend. No. Claudius? C-C-Claudius? No, man, wait — I got it, I got it. Bait the hook well, this fish will bite. Let's go the water. Where deeper than did ever plummet sound I'll drown my book.

Stanley takes hold of Charlie's right arm and tugs. It's like pulling taffy: he feels like he's making progress, but Charlie's still on the bench, fishing for his bottle. Claudio closes his hands around Charlie's left arm, and in a moment he's on his feet.

They steer him across the boardwalk, aiming him toward the sound of the surf. Their arms interlock at his waist. They don't look at each other. Now that Stanley's this close, he can tell Charlie's a serious drunk, well along the skids: he's a wisp, scarecrow-thin under his clothes, and his shaggy blond hair is brittle and dry. Stanley knows he won't have anything but pocket change on him, if that. He wonders why he started this.

A few yards into the sand, near the edge of the light from the boardwalk, Charlie's feet start to drag. You okay there, buddy? Stanley asks.

Don't go to the water, Charlie whines. Not ready.

What's that?

I *said* —

Charlie's feet are dug in hard now, his back straight: he's standing at parade rest. The slur has vanished from his speech, and his accent is pure Boston brahmin.

— that I am *not ready to go to the water yet.* If you don't mind.

Stanley's hand reaches under his shirttail, closes on the blackjack's braided handle. As he unwraps his arm from Charlie's waist, the man drops facefirst, pulling Claudio with him. Both of them are down before the bludgeon clears Stanley's belt. Odors of alcohol and juniper rise to his nose, and he hears the soft gurgle of the dropped bottle emptying. Charlie's laughter is muffled by the sand.

Stanley looks around, then stuffs the blackjack in his pocket. Let's be quiet now, Charlie. Okay? he says.

Claudio is rolling Charlie over. *Quiet!* Charlie says, spitting sand, palming Claudio's lean cheek. *Shhh!* Silence is the perfectest herald of joy. Ain't that right, Tadzio? Speak *low,* man. Speak low, if you speak love.

Stanley kneels by Charlie's side and pats his trouser pockets, looking for a wallet, looking for anything. The sky is dark except for a blue line at the horizon. The half-built amusement park on the pier to the north makes strange silhouettes against it. Stanley tries to keep Charlie distracted while he works. So, he asks, how do you like being an ad man?

No no no no *no,* Charlie says. *Atman.* I'm an atman, man. I'm an *anima,* a soul, a psyche. Like you are. Like him is. Like *all* of us. Dig?

You don't write ads?

Not anymore, man. I absolutely do not do that anymore.

So what do you do, then, Charlie? Aside from drinking?

I am a poet, Charlie says.

Stanley withdraws his hand from Charlie's pocket, then absently smoothes the wrinkled fabric. Somewhere to the south, a foghorn sounds its two long notes. A full yellow moon has bloomed over the city; Stanley can see its reflection in front of him, scattered among the waves. Of course, he thinks. Of course it would happen like this.

Charlie, Stanley says, I don't suppose you know of a guy called Adrian Welles?

20

A cavalcade of bikers is making the curve at Brooks as Stanley and Claudio march north along the boardwalk. Girls in circle skirts and pedal-pushers jam fingers in their ears and stare openmouthed while the oscillating line of headlamps sweeps the buildings, the reports of V-twin engines reshape the waterfront air. A pair of panhead Harleys is parked outside a liquor store on Breeze Avenue, their chrome-plated pipes and chassis so polished that they're visible only by the deformed images they return of the night around them. Stanley picks up the pace without sparing the bikes a second look.

You see? Claudio is saying. I am a great detective.

You're a lucky detective, is what you are.

Claudio shrugs. I don't think I understand what is the difference, he says.

You're not even lucky, Stanley says. You got the dope on what *I'm* looking for, not on what *you're* looking for. That guy didn't have one red cent on him.

Then it is you who are the lucky one, yes? To have such a great detective for your partner.

Don't talk to me about luck, Stanley says.

A few blocks up he spots two familiar faces coming out of a ramshackle amusement parlor: the boss Dog from the run-in a couple of weeks ago, along with Whitey, out for a night on the town. Both greasers have dates — a topheavy pinch-faced skirt for the boss, a Mexican halfbreed for Whitey who looks fresh off the playground — and they aren't paying much attention to anything else. Stanley and Claudio hesitate, then walk on.

The boss pipes them as they draw closer. Stanley meets his gaze, keeping his eyes steady, his face blank. The boss's eyes go narrow. Then he gives Stanley a tight smile and a nod — nasty, but respectful — and turns back to his girl. Stanley and Claudio hustle on by.

The moon is higher and brighter now, silvered blue, and over the roof of the Avalon Ballroom Stanley can make out structures on the amusement pier: a rollercoaster, a tilt-awhirl, a magic carpet ride with painted-on minarets and onion domes. They're getting close. Charlie's directions were a drunken mess, but Stanley knows exactly where they're going. He remembers Dudley Avenue from earlier, and he spots the coffeehouse as soon as they make the corner: ahead on the left, bright and bustling. They cross the street. Stanley tugs open the door.

It's a long room, lit from above, with an aisle up the middle and small octagonal tables along the sides. The whitewashed walls are painted with words and phrases in jagged black letters, and elsewhere hung with stretched canvases: splashed-over, squiggled-on. A narrow counter topped by a copper espresso machine juts partway across the far end; an old stove, a buzzing refrigerator, and a bespectacled man in a coffee-stained T-shirt slouch behind it. The hipsters from the boardwalk are scattered through the room:

musicians in the back, blond girl against the left wall, giving him a heavy-lidded stare. Nobody else seems to notice him. Coils of cigarette smoke rise from every place at every table. The milky air seems gradually to solidify into the white globe lamps that hang from the ceiling.

A drumkit is set up in front of the counter. A young man in bluejeans and a sweater stands in front of it, facing the tables, reading aloud from a folded-over notebook. He clutches a pencil in his right hand, as if he's just written the words he speaks. *I see the holy city through your eyes, Herman Melville,* guy says. *This new moonlight is your moonlight, Herman Melville, and my feet always find your cadences.*

Poetry, Stanley thinks. Then he wonders why he thinks this. It's nothing like the language in *The Mirror Thief,* and apart from a few lines he used to hear the 42nd Street grifters quote to rope in Columbia kids, *The Mirror Thief* is the only poetry he knows. So how come he's so quick to peg this stuff as verse, and not just as some hipster talking?

The guy in the sweater goes on for a while — ranting and jiving about Buddha and Zoroaster, Sputnik and General Motors — and Stanley tunes out, scans the room. The tables are three-quarters full; people are still filing in, shouldering by to find seats. Stanley squints through the smoke like he's blind-folded with waxpaper. At a table by the drumkit he spots an older man in hornrims and a Donegal cap; he's maybe sixty, twice the age of anyone else in the room. He's listening to the poet, nodding along. A fierce-looking character with a black beard and thinning hair sits to his right. The chair across from him is empty.

Stanley nudges Claudio. Wait here, he says. I'll be back.

The path to the empty seat is blocked by the guy reading, so Stanley steps around him, crossing in front of the drums. The poet looks up from his notebook, shoots Stanley a baffled glance, stumbles to find his place again. Stanley glides into the empty chair. The bearded man glares at him, bunches his heavy eyebrows, and looks away.

Stanley leans across the table toward the older guy. Excuse me, mister, he whispers.

Shhhhh, the older guy says, putting a finger to his lips. Tut tut.

The poet has hit his stride again; he's shouting something about towers and pyra-mids, about a new Renaissance, about Atlan-tis rising from the Pacific. People in the crowd cheer and shout *go go go,* but it sounds phony to Stanley, rehearsed. He taps his heel on the smooth concrete floor as the guy builds to his big finish and the hipsters all snap their fingers in applause. Then he leans across the table again. Excuse me, he says.

The old guy gets in a few more slow snaps before turning to Stanley and arching an imperious eyebrow. Young man, he says. How may I help you?

Are you Adrian Welles?

The eyebrow sinks, and the guy's face knots in irritation. The bearded man stifles a laugh, looks at the ceiling. My dear young friend, the old guy says. I am Lawrence Lipton.

He says it like Stanley's supposed to recognize the name right away. Over Stanley's shoulder, somebody's lurking: the poet, wanting his chair back. Stanley gives the old guy a thin smile. Okay, jack, he says. Do you *know* Adrian Welles?

Lipton stares at him for a second, doing an affected slow-burn, then raps twice on the white formica and pushes himself away from the table. I know *everyone,* he growls. He looks past Stanley and calls to the poet. Here, John, he says. Take my seat. I need to have a word with the musicians.

Stanley's rising to intercept him when the bearded man gently but firmly takes his arm. Wait up a minute, he says. Adrian Welles comes in here sometimes. He comes to hear the jazz canto.

Is he here tonight?

Not yet.

What's the jazz canto?

Lipton, circling the table, comes to a stop in front of the drumkit. He turns and spins in a slow circle, spreading his arms like a stage magician or a gameshow host. His open hands seem to indicate the room, the scene, the entire waterfront. *This!* he says. *This* is the jazz canto!

The bearded man holds out a thick, square hand to Stanley. I'm Stuart, he says.

Stanley, Stanley says.

So what do you want with Adrian Welles, man? Are you, like, his long-lost son or something? Here to claim your legacy?

I read his book, Stanley says. I want to meet him.

He published a book?

Across the table, the poet is lowering himself into Lipton's seat. Who published a book? he says.

Adrian Welles.

Never heard of him.

He lives in the neighborhood, Stuart says. Larry knows him. He read some work for us right after the café opened. You've seen him around. Seems square at first, but if you butter him up a little, he'll really beat his chops. Oh, Stanley, this is John.

The poet warily offers him a hand. Stanley looks over just long enough to take it.

You dig Welles, huh? Stuart is saying. Who else do you like?

I don't understand your question, Stanley says.

Poets, man. Who else do you read?

Stanley looks down at the tabletop. It's dappled all over with candle-wax, chipped around its edges, blistered by cigarettes in a few spots. He looks up again and shrugs.

Stuart strokes his beard, watching the smoke swirl past the light globes overhead. I like Welles all right, he says. I think he's sharp. But I gotta say, man, his verse is strictly off the cob. I mean, I dig T. S. Eliot just fine. *The Waste Land* is crazy. But it's just reactionary, man, to keep chasing the old possum's tail. All these old farts — Patchen, Rexroth, Adrian Welles, Curtis Zahn, shit, even Larry sometimes — they all got their boots on, sure. Their heads are in the right place. But they're screwed up under the ribs, man, and they don't even know it.

Near the center of the table, partly obscured by the base of a thick red candle, a lozenge of formica has been cut away to expose the wood-pulp beneath. Someone has glued a three-cent RELIGIOUS FREEDOM IN AMERICA stamp in the cleared area and inked a ring of symbols around it: stars, moons, crosses, ankhs, sigils. They all seem familiar, but most of them Stanley can't quite place.

Their kind of poetry, Stuart says, it's like cool jazz, dig? Same situation. Cats get so good at articulating the problem that they forget to look for the solution. And the whole scene just turns into a death trip. Poets today, we gotta pick up where Eliot left off, with what the thunder said. *Shantih shantih shantih,* man.

John jerks a thumb toward the entrance. Speaking of death trips, he says, look who just walked in.

Stuart pans toward the door. Stanley tracks his gaze. A small black-haired woman stands there, wearing a lost and sleepy expression. A man with a beaked nose and a simian brow looms behind her, his hand on her neck. The man's skin is a uniform gray, the color of boiled meat; tiny eyes flash in his otherwise lifeless face. The girl is slim, wide-hipped, broad-shouldered — pretty, though she won't be for long. Even through the haze Stanley can make them both as junkies. Together they look like a ventriloquist act.

That's not him, Stanley says. Is it?

Welles? Stuart laughs. No, man. That's, like, the *opposite* of Welles.

What's he doing here? John says. I thought he'd already hit the road. Weren't him and Lyn going back to New York?

They were, but I talked him into hanging around till after the fish run, Stuart says. Alex wouldn't pass up a free feast.

The fish? That's another two weeks yet.

No, man, they run tomorrow. Full moon tonight, dig?

225

Aw, you're full of shit, Stuart. Nothing's running tomorrow night. It's too early. The water's still cold.

Stuart grins. You got it all wrong, jack. Me and Bob and Charlie went down to the ocean last night and communed with Neptune and his nymphs. We got the report direct from the king. It's the bible, man: the fish *will* run tomorrow night.

Behind Stanley the Negro plays scales on his muted trumpet; the saxophonist sucks the reed of his alto. The blonde and a few of the other hipsters crowd around the counter and sit on the floor, their backs pressed to the walls. Lipton beckons to Stuart, a wrinkled sheaf of foolscap fluttering in his other hand. Uh oh, Stuart says. Showtime.

Stuart rises, pulls a notebook from his back pocket, and takes his place in front of the drumkit. Afoot, he's shorter than Stanley would have guessed: not much taller than Stanley himself. Lipton claps Stuart on the back, moves to take his empty seat.

Stanley gets up, pushes past the old man, taps Stuart on the shoulder. Stuart, he says. I need your help. How do I find Welles?

Stuart flips through his notebook, doesn't look up. If he stops in tonight, he says, I'll introduce you.

Can you tell me where he lives? Or where he works? Do you have a phone number for him?

I don't know about any of that, man, Stuart says. He sighs, closes the notebook, and looks Stanley in the eye. Listen, he says. I gotta do this thing now. I'll help you find Welles later. Just cool it, okay?

Stanley looks at the floor. A few feet to his left, the blond girl is staring up at him. Her eyes — dun-colored, kaolin-pale, a doll's eyes — are open wide. The sight of them makes Stanley uneasy, and he blinks. Then he shoves his hands in his pockets, turns, and crosses the room to stand by the entrance.

Claudio is at a table on the other side of the aisle, among a younger group: three girls, seated, and two guys, leaning on the backs of the girls' chairs. Claudio's doing his bashful act, sheepish and shrugging, in the middle of some story, recounting his wetback adventures in the Arizona desert, probably. The two guys have their ears cocked to hear him better, and the three skirts look like they're all set to take him home, bake him cakes, dress him up in fancy outfits.

Someone sidles up on Stanley's right: the beak-nosed man. As he draws close a wariness comes over Stanley, sharp and not unpleasing, a feeling he hasn't known since he left the city: this guy clicks as a true grifter. The familiarity feels good, even if it's apt to mean trouble. Stanley plays it cool, doesn't meet the man's gaze.

You're a fresh face, the man says. I'm Alex.

227

Stanley.

Alex nods his big head in Claudio's direction. That handsome bugger's got the run of the place, he says. Wastes not a minute, does he?

Stanley smiles, says nothing.

Your partner, Alex says. Is he a good man to work with?

Stanley takes a second to remember that Alex just walked in, has never seen the two of them together. Not that Stanley knows of, anyway. Stanley turns to face him.

Alex is giving him his old-man-of-the-mountain profile, staring into space. You and your friend are down and out, he says. Is that not so? You're on the street.

His accent is foreign: English but not English, Irish or Scottish, Stanley can never tell the difference. There's no shame in it, Alex continues. Though it can be very hard. I've been down and out myself. More than once. Each time because I've *chosen* it. You understand, I'm sure. Tell me, your friend — is he working as trade?

Stanley feels a jolt of anger, but keeps it out of his face, his voice. No, he says. He ain't. How come? You in the market?

He could do very well, Alex says. Not here, of course. But I know many places.

He ain't interested.

Alex glances over at Stanley for a second. His eyes narrow to slots. You're from New

228

York, he says. I hear it in your voice. What borough?

Brooklyn.

Flatbush? Borough Park?

Williamsburg.

You're a Jew?

Yeah, Stanley says. Sure.

Done a bit of wandering, have you?

No more than you, I guess.

True enough. What brings you to California?

Business.

And what business is that?

Stanley gives him a deadpan look. Batboy for the Dodgers, he says.

Alex seems confused; then he begins to laugh loudly, and now the whole place is looking at them. Stanley hadn't planned on getting this kind of attention. He keeps his eyes lowered, his face blank, until the stares scatter and fade.

Alex's laugh gutters. He's quiet for a second. Over there's my wife, he says. Lyn's her name. Common law; no ceremony. But we are married, nevertheless.

He doesn't point, doesn't even look at her. She's leaning against a wall at the far end of the room next to three seated women; the women talk among themselves, ignoring her, as if she's invisible.

We're leaving town in a few days, Alex says.

Going to Las Vegas. Have you ever been there?

I don't think so.

Lyn will find work there as a dancer. A stripteaser, I should say. For extra cash she'll turn tricks. There is no shame in it. All of us, we can only do as we're doing. Always.

What'll you do?

I am a writer, Alex says. I intend to write.

Across the room Lipton is waving his papers around, belting out some kind of introduction. Stuart stands next to him, his arms at his sides, his eyes closed, his nose aimed at the ceiling. A hairy white kid is seated at the kit, working brushes across the ride cymbal and the snare. The blond girl rises to her feet, sliding up the wall. A slanted line of black text above her head reads ART IS LOVE IS GOD.

Alex speaks softly; Stanley strains to hear him even as he feigns disinterest. Provisions for our journey, Alex says, have been difficult to find. You seem a wise and capable fellow. I think we can help each other. I have connections that could be useful.

I don't have a connection here, Stanley says. You're wasting your time on me.

You are welcome in this place, Alex says. Everyone who is not small-minded and conventional is welcome here. But this is not your world. It never can be. Likewise, your world is not mine. You are called a juvenile delinquent. It's a stupid label, it insults and inters a treasure-house of undocumented human experience, and it cannot easily be put aside. I don't offer you my understanding. I know you don't want it. But I do offer you my respect. We can help each other. Of that I am certain.

Alex's words are all but drowned out by a short fanfare from the two horns; he claps a heavy hand on Stanley's back, tips the brim of an invisible cap, and slouches off toward the music. The drummer scrapes a lurching stutter from his kit, and Stuart — his eyes still closed, his notebook sweeping the air before him — begins to shout across the room. *Silver!* he says. *Darkness! Echo! Ocean! Gather up the things that are yours, O Lady! I offer my voice for the gathering.* The room seems to contract, the air to grow more dense, and the shaved hairs on the back of Stanley's neck rise up like ghosts.

Stuart's language is plain, almost conversational, but his voice is melodic, incantatory, completely transformed, and Stanley catches almost nothing of what he says. His rhythms sometimes follow the drums, sometimes strain against them. The horn players are off-balance, at a loss, bleating awkward figures between his pauses for breath. A passing phrase snags Stanley's attention — *I reach for the hot coal, and suck my burned fingers* —

and dredges up the memory of a story his grandfather often told about the young Moses in Egypt. Stanley imagines Stuart bathed in light, hauling stone tablets down from a sacred mountain, and he smirks at the thought.

The smoke chafes Stanley's throat, making him lightheaded. His damaged leg is unsteady, trembling, and he steps back to lean against the wall by the café's entrance. Another man — potbellied, ginger-bearded, middle-aged, wearing black-framed spectacles and a tweed driver's cap — is standing on the doorway's opposite side. The two eye each other for a moment. Then they turn and stare across the room again, motionless as telamons, the bass drum pulsing lightly on their guts and faces.

Last night on Abbot Kinney Boulevard I met the archangel Sariel, Stuart is saying. *Dead-ringer for Robert Ryan. Worn-out, in need of a shave.* Up front, Lipton nods along to the music, punches his fist into the flesh of his palm. Alex has found Lyn along the left wall; his body eclipses her from view. Just ahead, Claudio sprawls between two hipster girls; he turns to give Stanley an easy grin. The kid has no recollection at all of why they came here tonight, Stanley realizes. Maybe he never really understood.

The blond girl is moving across the room

now, headed Stanley's way, drifting between the tables like a paper cup down a rocky brook. She keeps her flat stare trained on him till she's within a few feet. Then she veers to take the arm of the ginger-bearded man. She leans in as Stanley watches, resting a hand on his stomach, standing on tiptoe to whisper in his ear. Her posture — waist bent, black-sheathed knees locked, ass angled out — reminds him of a cheesecake pinup, and he wonders if the performance is meant for him. Aside from a few rapid blinks, the bearded man's face remains static, vacant.

When she's done speaking she gives the man a peck on his ruddy cheek and returns to her spot at the far end of the crowded room. It takes her a while to get there. She doesn't look back, at Stanley or at the bearded man. When she comes to a stop the man tips himself forward, turns, pulls open the café door.

Stanley watches him between the backward letters painted on the glass. The man stands at the curb, filling and lighting a pipe. Then he crosses the street. On the opposite side a small bowlegged dog is tied by its leash to an ashcan; the bearded man unhitches it, and they walk toward the beach. Wispy tendrils of fog reach in from the ocean, and the man and his dog vanish before they reach the boardwalk.

Inside the café the Negro trumpeter has

stopped seeking openings between Stuart's lines; he now plays an eerie looping riff under the poet's chants, and the altoist follows suit with a moaning ostinato of his own. The bass drum hits grow more frequent and forceful until they merge into a great subterranean tremor, and now Stuart seems not to be speaking words at all, just a torrent of gibberish that sounds as if it should make sense but resolutely does not. Stanley's eyes sweep the crowd — John standing on his chair, Alex sliding a hand under Lyn's skirt, the blond girl sinking down the wall and disappearing — then close their lids. The music that comes across the room seems to pin him to the brick. He can no longer distinguish the sax from the trumpet, the trumpet from the drums, the drums from Stuart's voice. And now all the sounds are gone, vanished into themselves, into a sheet of uniform noise that encompasses everything.

A moment later Stanley's on the curb outside the café, gulping cool air, uncertain of how he got here. Music comes from behind him in a muffled blur, clarifying briefly whenever the door opens. His fingers are curled around his bandaged leg; the gash on his calf has opened again. A brown shadow streaks the middle of the white bandage, wider and darker at the bottom.

Dudley looks deserted all the way to the boardwalk. In the glow of beachfront streetlamps Stanley can see pedestrians in the gap between storefronts, none of them walking a dog. Fog spreads over the ocean, and the full moon slides behind it, smeared and haloed, as if wrapped in a nylon stocking. As Stanley watches, the promenade clears. No one is visible in any direction. The atmosphere is heavy, stagnant, like air trapped in an unlit room. Everything seems unreal: a movie set, built just for Stanley and the ginger-bearded man.

His head swims as he rises from the pavement. He shuts his eyes and waits for the colors that swirl behind his lids to dim and slow. Then he opens them, and begins to limp as quickly as he can toward the beach.

21

The tips of breakers wink in the dark, copper-tinted by the light from shore, and the waves sound like the breath of hidden sleepers. Stanley's skin is filmed with sweat by the time he's reached the boardwalk, but his legs are firm beneath him and he's making good time. The streetlamps shine through the fog — a string of dull rhinestones linking Santa Monica to the oilfield — and beneath them the ginger-bearded man and his dog are nowhere to be seen.

Patchy crowds are gathered at Windward to the south and the Avalon Ballroom to the north, but this stretch of boardwalk is nearly empty. Two dismounted bikers in leather jackets and tight bluejeans come up on Stanley's right, lapping at icecream cones, and one of them gives Stanley a long look as they pass. Fuck you, Stanley says.

The biker shrugs, walks on, and now Stanley is alone. He wonders what time it is. Late, he guesses: after midnight. He wonders whether he shouldn't go back to the café. Shoreline Dogs are bound to be in the neighborhood, cruising for trouble, and it'd be ugly to run across them in his current shape. Besides, the ginger-bearded man is probably asleep at home by now.

Stanley takes a long look south, sifting figures on the boardwalk one by one to the limits of his vision. Dim green lights on the crowns of distant oil-derricks poke over the roofs of shops. Stanley hears the drone of twin engines, then sees landing lights angle toward the airport: backward comets streaking the fog. He watches the plane till it's gone. Then he steps onto the beach, hooding his eyes to expand their pupils. The moon is a blue smudge high over the water, lighting up the whole western sky.

When the sand feels firm and damp beneath his feet he sinks to his knees and sights up and down the shore, scanning the pattern of light at the sea's edge: the white sand, the black water, the reflections splintered in the waves. This is a trick he has taught himself. As he kneels, he thinks of his long trip across the country, of a simple game he'd play to pass the time in boxcars. He'd look through the narrow gap of the sliding door and try to keep a count of what he saw: bridges, roads, barns, roosting hawks. At first, he played in competition with other bored hobos — it was something everybody did — but the game soon became frustrating, awkward. No one was ever any match for him. In fact, the other tramps were often unwilling to concede that things he spotted with little effort were possible to see at all. Stanley kept playing, but kept the game to himself, and over time he grew more ambitious, trying to count telephone poles, doves startled into flight, bathtub gondolas on passing trains — even, during one particularly slow stretch, all the crossties from Winslow to Flagstaff. The trick was to synchronize his vision to the rhythm of light as it flashed between objects. That pulse became a kind of code for Stanley. With it he could read just about anything.

Early last September, over a Sunday poker game in the bunkhouse of a cattle ranch in New Mexico, or maybe Colorado, it occurred to him that there might be a way to apply this same idea to the shuffle of a deck of cards. So far he's been lax about pursuing this theory, preoccupied by other concerns.

The image of the full moon bobs on the

water, multiplied into a lattice of ovals and oxbows, and Stanley's eyes gradually translate it into a neutral screen. Two hundred yards south, maybe halfway to Brooks, a shapeless patch of black emerges: the ginger-bearded man and his dog. They're meandering, changing direction. Stanley moves to put himself between them and the boardwalk, keeping them skylit as he goes. He can't make out the man's features but his outline is clear. The blackjack in Stanley's pocket is chafing his thigh; he pulls it out, returns it to the small of his back.

A thread of pipesmoke carries on the shifting wind. The man is singing to himself, or maybe to the dog, in a language Stanley can't place. It's not Claudio's Spanish, nor the Italian of the neighbor lady back home, but it's like them. The man is walking toward Stanley now, closing the distance. Stanley keeps silent, holds his ground. He can see the orange glow of the man's pipe as he sucks on it, the trail of smoke, the quavering air above its bowl. The night seems brittle, as if held together by an invisible armature of glass. A single word could shatter everything.

When he's about fifteen feet away, the man spots Stanley. He gasps, comes to a halt. The dog strains at its leash, snuffling, then springs as if snakebit and starts to bark.

Hello, Stanley says. Excuse me.

The man switches the leash to his left hand;

his right hand goes behind his back. He wears a tweed jacket over a sweater, the textures of the fabrics barely discernable in the dark. Stanley swallows hard.

I didn't see you there, the man says. You gave me a start.

It's okay, mister. I don't mean you no trouble.

The man's voice is tight, but steady. He seems scared. His right hand remains hidden. You shouldn't be alone on this beach at night, he says. It's not safe.

Stanley holds his arms out, spreads his fingers, but the man isn't relaxing. His outline is shrinking back, balling up, and Stanley is pretty sure he's about to get shot. For so long he has thought of what to say at this moment, but now nothing comes. All words seem to flee from him. He feels his mouth opening, closing. Adrian Welles? he says.

The man is stock-still, silent, an inert blot on the ocean's silver curtain. The two of them stand there, not breathing, for what seems like a long time. Stanley is aware of the dog as it growls and paws the sand.

Who are you? the man says.

When Stanley speaks again, the voice that rises to his throat is utterly unfamiliar. In past moments of mortal terror his voice has sometimes reverted to that of his younger self; at other moments, when he's been sad or tired, he's heard his voice grow suddenly older, as if presaging a person he might one day become. But the voice that speaks now is neither of these. It belongs to someone unknown, from another life. Listen to it closely. You will never hear this voice again.

Are you Adrian Welles? Stanley says.

But he already knows the answer, and he is no longer afraid.

22

Welles is backing up, winding and bunching the dog's leash. Trembling a bit. An old man in the dark. Don't come any closer, he says. I have a pistol, and I will use it.

I been looking for you, Mister Welles, Stanley says. I don't mean you any harm. You or your dog. I just want to talk about your book.

Welles takes a shallow breath, lets it out. My book, he says.

Yes sir. Your book. *The Mirror Thief.*

Stanley has never spoken the title aloud before. It feels clumsy in his mouth, and he regrets saying it. Loosed on the air, the words seem lifeless, insufficient for what they name.

Who are you? Welles says. Who sent you here?

This strikes Stanley as an odd question. Nobody sent me, he says. I just came.

Welles adjusts his footing on the sand. Then he says something in a foreign language. It

240

sounds like Hebrew. Pardon me? Stanley says.

Welles repeats the phrase. It's not Hebrew.

I'm sorry, Mister Welles, but I don't have any goddamn idea what you just said.

What is your name, son?

I'm Stanley.

Your full name. What is it?

Stanley can't see the man's face well enough to read his expression. His short fingers are still absently gathering his dog's leash. His spectacles pick up the coppery glare from the boardwalk, and both lenses are split down the middle by a dark shape, like the pupil of a cat's eye, which Stanley realizes is his own shadow.

Glass, Stanley says. It's Stanley Glass. Sir.

Welles's right hand comes back into view. He wipes it against his jacket, rests it on his hip, lets it drop to his side. I saw you tonight, he says. In the café. Why didn't you say something to me then?

I wasn't sure it was you at first. I thought maybe, but I didn't know. You, uh, probably oughta slack up on that leash a little bit, Mister Welles.

The leather braid has spooled thickly around Welles's first two fingers, and the dog is twisting and backpedaling, thrashing the air with its forelegs, winched partway off the sand. Its growls have faded to a jowly sputter. Oh, Welles says. Yes.

Stanley looks out to sea, then down at the

beach. He shuffles his feet, nervous again. He has so many questions, a labyrinth in his mind, one that seems at no point to intersect with the realm of normal human speech. This is much harder than he expected. I read your book, he says.

Yes.

And I have some questions about it.

Yes. All right.

I'm not real sure how to ask them, though.

At Welles's back, the waves mutter softly. Down the shore, the foghorn sounds. It must have been sounding all night, but Stanley hasn't noticed it.

Would you mind, Welles says, if we went back to the boardwalk? There are a lot of dope addicts and juvenile delinquents on this beach at night, and it's better not to stay too long in the dark.

Uh, sure. That's fine.

Welles sets out on a diagonal path away from the water; the dog scurries after him. Stanley follows, then pulls forward to walk by his side. I'm sorry if we've gotten off on the wrong foot, Welles says. Recent events have made me preoccupied, perhaps overmuch, with my own safety. Although not without some justification. At any rate, I hope you'll forgive me. My evening stroll is generally south to Windward Avenue, at which point I turn back. But tonight, provided Pompey will oblige us, I think we should walk through town. I can give you a little tour. What say you, old chum?

Stanley's opened his mouth to answer before he realizes that Welles is speaking to the dog. It marches on, not acknowledging the question, announcing every step with a tiny snort.

As they approach the streetlamps Welles's broad face takes shape: tanned, small-nosed, creased around the mouth and across the forehead. Large blue eyes. Hair and beard flecked with white. Nothing about him is remarkable. Stanley figures him for about fifty.

They hit the boardwalk at the point where the storefront colonnade begins its long southward run. Welles stops, empties his pipe over an ashcan, and pulls a tobacco tin from an inside pocket. The dog pisses against the side of the can, stretching its hind leg skyward like a midway contortionist. Its fur is lustrous red and white; its small face is bug-eyed, short-snouted, terrifically ugly. It peeks from under velvety ears like Winston Churchill in a Maureen O'Hara wig.

You say you've been looking for me, Welles says. I don't think I've seen you in the café before. Do you live nearby?

We're staying in a squat off Horizon Court. Me and my pal. We been here going on three weeks now. We were working the groves in Riverside before that.

But you don't come from Riverside originally.

No sir. My partner's a wetback Mexican,
and I'm from Brooklyn.

Brooklyn! You're a long way from home.
How old are you, if I may ask?

I'm sixteen.

Do your parents know where you are?

My dad died in Korea, Mister Welles, and
my mother's pretty well lost her mind. There's
nobody back home who's missing me.

I am very sorry to hear that. What branch
of the service was your father in?

The Army. Seventh Infantry. He fought the
Japs in Okinawa and the Philippines, and he
reenlisted. He got killed at Heartbreak Ridge.

He must have been very brave. He must
have loved his country.

He was brave. He was good at being a
soldier, and he liked it. He never said too
much about his country.

Welles smiles, puts the pipe in his mouth.
He strikes a match, lets it burn for a second,
and moves it in tight circles over the briarwood bowl. When the tobacco is smoldering,
he tamps it out, packs it again. I was in the
Army myself, he says. I was at Anzio, in the
summer of 1944. But I was in payroll — I
am by trade an accountant — so I was able
to avoid the worst of the fighting. I was very
glad when the war ended. It upset me pro-
foundly.

He looks up from the pipe and narrows his eyes. I met you once before, he says. You were running a card game on the boardwalk.

Yeah. That was me.

I won a dollar from you.

Stanley looks down, bashful. You were smart to quit when you did, he says. I don't let nobody win more than a dollar.

You're a gambler! Welles says. You live by skill and fortune. Goddamn it, I'm intensely envious of you. That's been one of my romantic fantasies, ever since I was a lad. To be a riverboat gambler. With a white linen suit, and a derringer in my pocket.

You got me pegged wrong, Mister Welles. That boardwalk game is a straight con. I play cards a little bit, sure, but I'm no gambler.

Oh, of course you are, Welles says. Of course you are. At any given moment, you may be certain of the cards, but the other man — your opponent, your mark — you can never be certain of what he perceives, what he thinks, what he will do. You still place yourself, more or less reverently, at Fortune's behest. And that's all gambling amounts to. Isn't it?

Stanley furrows his brow. I guess so, he says.

Welles lights his pipe again, puffs to get it going, slowly shakes out the match. He drops the blackened curl of the matchstick in the ashcan, stares at the space where it fell, smoking intently. Then he takes the pipe from his teeth and points its stem toward the arches and columns of the penny arcade on the corner.

This may be of interest to you, he says. These buildings along the boardwalk all date from 1905. Abbot Kinney's original construction. They've changed quite a bit over the years — fallen into disrepair, as one says — but you can still get a sense of how it was. Notice the quaint approximation of Byzantine-Gothic architecture in the loggia. Done, if I'm not mistaken, in the style of Bartolomeo Bon. Shall we walk to Windward?

The dog lurches ahead as if it knows the route. Fog rings the streetlamps with aureoles; a few figures huddle beneath them. Two blocks up, a group of five bored Shoreline Dogs is playing mumbledypeg in the sand. Some look familiar: from the Fox theater, or maybe from the chase through the neighborhood, Stanley can't be sure. They sneer and glare at Stanley as he and Welles pass, but Welles seems not to notice.

The Fortune Bridgo parlor is coming up on the left, and Welles gestures toward its boarded-up windows. You picked a good spot to run your game, he says. An historic spot, even. That was Bill Harrah's old place. At one time — this would have been the 1930s — Bridgo was a big draw around here. Bridgo, Budgo, Tango. All those bingo games. Are you familiar with bingo?

Not really. I heard of it. I never played.

I thought not. You don't seem the type, frankly. It's an odd game. Unusually authoritarian, as games of chance go. You pay your money, you take your cards, you sit and listen and await revelation. You accept what is given to you. Since the game's origins are intertwined so closely with those of the Italian state, I suppose this shouldn't be surprising. In any event, despite this strict assertion of authority — or maybe because of it, who can say? — the municipal apparatus here in Los Angeles has been rather hostile to it, which is why Bill Harrah eventually moved his operation to Nevada, where he met with quite a lot of success. This is a pattern that recurs. Tony Cornero, the mobster who operated gambling boats just off the coast here, also in the 1930s, went on to found one of the largest casinos on the Las Vegas Strip. Have you ever visited Nevada, Stanley?

I'm not sure. I maybe passed through it.

I used to go there quite often. On business, after the war. Its present territory used to be covered by great lakes. Did you know that? Inland seas, really. This would have been during the Pleistocene Epoch, which is fairly recent in geological terms. Nevada is quite dry now. A desert, in fact. Where did those lakes go? Might they return one day? Let's turn left here.

They cut through the portico of the St.

Mark's Hotel and head inland, passing department stores, the Forty-Niner restaurant, a hotdog vendor, a Tee Pop stand. Everything is closed down, dark, and has been so for several hours. The illuminated clock on the hardware shop gives the time as nearly one a.m. Down the block, in the shadows cast by the JESUS SAVES sign, a figure is moving: a very large dog, or a person crawling on all fours. Before Stanley can decide which, it's gone.

So, Welles is saying, what brought you to Los Angeles?

Stanley guesses it would be unwise to tell the truth, at least until he's figured out how to ask Welles what he wants to ask. Just drifting, he says. Seeing the country. I happened to be in L.A., so I figured I oughta track you down.

Well, I'm very flattered that you did. Where did you come across my book?

I picked it up from a guy I knew on the Lower East Side.

Manhattan? Welles says. That's remarkable. We only printed three hundred copies, you know. A hundred of those are still sitting in my attic. How on earth did it find its way to New York, I wonder?

I got it from a pile of books that belonged to a fellow who'd just started a hitch at Rikers Island. There was a bunch of poetry books in the batch. But this fellow was getting sent up for trafficking stolen goods, so it's hard to say where he might've got it.

Perhaps the title appealed to him.

Maybe so.

A halfdozen Harleys are doing laps around the traffic circle, and Stanley and Welles fall silent in the thunder of their engines. Welles follows the curb clockwise to the circle's opposite side. The dog stretches the leash to its full length, straining away from the street, lowering its head and cocking back its ears against the roar.

When the bikers are two blocks behind them, Welles speaks again. It's a bit silly of me to ask, he says, but I'm curious. You said that there were several collections of poetry in the group of books that your friend had. Did you take any of the others?

No sir. Just yours.

I'm wondering why that is. Why you took mine. Not the others.

Stanley takes a few paces before he responds. I wonder about that myself, he says. I remember I liked the way it looked, for one thing. The rest all looked sort of cheap. Either that, or like you were supposed to be in awe of how great they were. But something about 'em was fake. Your book looked like somebody *made* it. I liked that.

My publisher would be gratified to hear it, Welles says. Were he not in Mexico avoiding his creditors I would certainly pass your comment along. Let's cross here.

When they reach the other sidewalk, Stanley speaks again. Something else, he says. When I opened up your book, I couldn't follow hardly any of it. I couldn't figure out what it was supposed to *be*, even. I could tell somebody worked on it really hard, and spent a lot of time on it. And that really got on my nerves. Because, okay — here's this complicated thing that somebody made. And I come across it just by accident, in a pile of crap on some hoodlum's floor. And I can't understand any of it! It made me mad, to tell you the truth. I'm not saying I rescued it or anything. It didn't seem like it gave a damn what happened to it, whether anybody read it or not. But every time I open it up, it makes me think of all the crazy stuff in this world that I don't know nothing about. That I never even heard of. And I guess that's a feeling that bothers me, Mister Welles.

Welles laughs softly: a smug, paternal chuckle that Stanley doesn't like. You mind telling me what's funny? Stanley says.

Welles shakes his head. Let's bear to the right here, he says.

The sidewalk carries them off Windward onto Altair Place. Streetlamps are fewer, occluded by palmtrees and eucalypts. The shadows make Welles's face harder to read. I'm not laughing at you, he says. I was surprised by your description of my book, that's all. The reason you cite for your choosing to read it was very similar to my reason for wanting to write it in the first place. A fascination with what is unknown. More specifically with what is invisible. It took me several years and quite a number of drafts to recognize that impulse. Now it's pleasing to hear you say it. Let me ask you another silly question. Do you *like* my book, Stanley?

Stanley can't figure out why Welles would ask this. Then he can't figure out how to answer. He's aware of the silence measured by their footfalls, the grunts of the little dog. To tell you the truth, he says, I never thought of it that way. I don't know what to say to that. I read it all the way through probably two hundred times. I think I could say the whole thing out loud to you right now, from memory. But do I like it?

They've come to a spot where the streetlamps' glow falls unimpeded between trees. Stanley takes a moment to scan the weedy yards of the nearby cottages. They're near the neighborhood where he and Claudio hid from the Dogs: it feels familiar.

I like it sometimes, Stanley says. I hate it sometimes. I don't ever get bored with it. I guess I should probably tell you that I came all the way out here to see you, Mister Welles. I told you a minute ago I was just drifting, but that ain't the truth. About the last thing I was doing was drifting. I had to leave New

York City, for some reasons that I'm not gonna get into right now, and I decided right then to track you down. It took me a lot longer than I figured. I hope it don't upset you that I'm telling you this, or make you want to stop talking to me.

Of course not, of course not, Welles says, but Stanley can feel discomfort radiate from him in the dark. He wonders whether he's made a mistake by not playing it cool. Then he thinks: fuck it. His leg hurts. He's tired of pussyfooting with this guy.

Welles is quiet for a while. His pipe has gone out. Altair Place merges into Cabrillo. About half the streetlamps on the blocks ahead are burnt-out or broken. At the edge of the dim circle cast by one of the survivors two large rats are fighting; the dog tenses and raises its ears at their inaudible shrieks and squeals.

I'm glad you came to see me, Welles says. I am worried that I'm going to disappoint you. It is difficult, but probably necessary, to remember that books always know more than their authors do. They are always wiser. This is strange to say, but it's true. Once they are in the world, they develop their own peculiar ideas. To be quite honest, I haven't revisited the poems in *The Mirror Thief* in more than a year. The last time I did, I couldn't remember quite what I'd meant by much of it. A few lines have been mysterious to me since I wrote them. Let's turn right on Navarre.

The sidewalks are badly cracked, reduced in spots to rubble, overgrown with grasses and creeping plants. On the left, the lots slope away from the narrow street; one house has a pond in the middle of its swampy lawn, overgrown by bulrushes. As Stanley's eyes adjust to the dimmer light he spots a gap where the plants have been flattened, and a pair of human legs protruding from the gap. The legs are motionless, clad in black boots and mud-spattered bluejeans. Down the block, a motorcycle is parked. No lights are on in the house. Stanley can smell sweet flowers somewhere nearby, but can't see them.

I understand how you feel, Welles is saying. And why you came here. At least I think I do. I did something similar myself once, if you can believe it. Are you familiar with the work of Ezra Pound?

No sir.

You've never read Pound at all?

Does he write poems?

Yes he does.

I never read any poems, except for the ones in your book.

Really? Welles says. My goodness. Well. It's as good a place to begin as any, I suppose. But you should probably borrow a few items from my library.

A few houses away a party is winding down: Stanley can hear a tangle of raucous voices through the hedge, and a hi-fi playing a bop quartet version of "It's Only a Paper Moon." At the next intersection, the streetsign bears a name — RIALTO — that Stanley knows from Welles's book, and the sight of it raises hairs on his neck.

Welles is lengthening his stride, picking up the pace. When I was in Italy after the war, he says, I went to see Ezra Pound at the Disciplinary Training Center outside Pisa. He was imprisoned there, awaiting return to the United States to stand trial for treason. At the time there was every expectation he would be executed. Pound's work was important to me at a critical time in my life. But I found his conduct during the war to be questionable. And I suppose I went to Pisa looking for some kind of explanation. Make a right turn here.

They turn onto Grand Boulevard. The street broadens, and the sky, heavy with fog, pushes between the palmtrees.

I was never able to speak with him, Welles says. No one was allowed to do that, not even the MPs. I was only able to see him very briefly. He was kept in a cell, eight feet by six, with a wooden frame and a tarpaper roof. He wore Army fatigues. He had neither belt nor shoelaces. There were more than three thousand other men in this facility, most of them hardened criminals — thieves, murderers, rapists — and almost all of them lived in the open, in tents. There were only ten cells like Pound's. His, uniquely, was reinforced with galvanized mesh and airstrip steel. Because of the mesh walls, he was always exposed. To the sun, to the weather, to the eyes of the curious. It was always possible to see him. But no one could speak to him. In the Army's formulation, you see, language was the weapon he had used to commit his crimes. Therefore the only language permitted him in his confinement came from his own mind, from his memory. I knew when I saw him that he had been utterly vanquished. I left Pisa very disappointed and dissatisfied. But some years later — after he had been declared insane and transferred to St. Elizabeth's — I realized that that had been the ultimate acknowledgment of his power. For the Army to do that to him. I suppose in a sense I was fortunate to have been thwarted in speaking with him. More fortunate than you, I fear. We'll make a left here on Riviera.

They're nearing the oilfield now. Stanley can hear the sighs and hisses of machinery, and his sinuses churn with petroleum odors: sweet butane, bitter asphalt, fecal sulfur. In the median of a boulevard, a horsehead pump nods, throwing weird shadows under the derricks. The lights behind it wink as it rises and falls.

I was about to say, Welles says, that Pound's silence was more powerful than any words could have been. But that is not correct. His silence was worthless. Powerless. As silence always is. Rather, it was the *image* of his silence. The sight of him in that cage. *That* has stayed with me. Reshaped, no doubt, according to the dictates of my personal mythology. Because that's the trick, isn't it? Our memories of language are generally stable. But how often do we remember words? It's more often images that we recall. And images are slippery, which is why so many technologies have emerged throughout history to fix them. It's also why successful despots tend to banish poets, or to imprison them — even poets like Pound, who are great admirers of despots — and why they tend to recruit and employ painters, sculptors, filmmakers, architects. Stop for a moment, Stanley. Let's look at the moon.

They're standing on the median a few yards east of the fenced-in pumpjack. Stanley can hear the soft whir of its electric motor, the whine and howl of the working beam. A few automobiles are still on the road, mostly cop cruisers; their headlights stretch shadows from the patchy grass as they veer off and onto the boulevard. The little dog roots around with its blunt nose, turning up stripped bolts and bits of glass, but Welles is quiet, staring at the pale circle in the western sky. It dilates as it sinks toward the horizon, its perfect circle sharp-edged, even in the fog.

It's in your book a lot, Stanley says.

I'm sorry?

The moon. It's in your book a lot.

Yes, Welles says. Yes, I suppose it is.

Like that part when Crivano's on the boat. When he's escaping. He has that whole conversation with the moon.

That's right. He does.

My light conceals nothing, Stanley recites. *You are my rescue, my restoration. I seek you in constant carnival, masked Crivano, along the waterline.*

You have a good memory.

Or when he has his dream. *I labor with the blind surveyors of night, Selene, and with bricks hewn from sleep I raise your city.*

Welles shifts the leash from hand to hand. That's another one, he says. You are quite right.

There at the beginning, even. In the malediction. *The treasure he bears in his butterfly sack is none other than —*

The foremost reflector itself. Of course. The book is, after all, called *The Mirror Thief.* The mirror is not meant to be understood literally. Not exclusively so, at any rate. Crivano is an alchemist. His mode of thought is Neoplatonic, derived from the sacred texts attributed to your patron deity, the Thrice-Great Hermes. To Crivano, the world is itself a reflection, the material emanation of an idea

257

in the mind of God. We cannot know the mind of God any more than we can look directly upon the sun. We look at the moon instead, made visible to us by the sunlight that it reflects. The moon represents the Opus Magnum, the alchemist's indirect means of discovering God's thoughts in order to become like God. All mirrors contain something of this lunar essence.

Yeah, Stanley says. I got all that. It's in your book. I read it.

I — I don't think I stated it quite so explicitly in the book.

It's clear enough. You can put it all together. This equals this equals that. I'm ignorant, all right, Mister Welles. But I ain't dumb.

Welles opens his mouth, closes it, and sighs in exasperation. My apologies, he says. It is difficult to speak of these things without seeming pedantic or obscure. Especially since I've no way of knowing what you know.

Stanley shoves his hands into his jacket pockets. The fabric pulls tight across his back, pressing the blackjack against his skin. Yeah, Stanley says. Sorry. I guess the thing is, I ain't never been too good at asking questions. Thanks for being patient.

Spooked by something, a pair of gulls takes off from the crown of a derrick a block south, yelping and beating their wings, and Stanley and Welles both jump. The dog freezes, raises its head. We should move on, Welles says. The place I want to show you isn't much farther.

They cross the boulevard's eastbound lanes and pass once more into a street of battered bungalows. Derricks rise from empty lots, sometimes from lawns. The houses are dark, tumbledown, with broken windows. An abandoned Kaiser-Frazer sits on the left side of the street, perched haphazardly across the curb; it's ringed by shards of glass and crushed cigarette butts, and three of its tires are slashed. Stanley's shoreline rivals have left their marks here, painting crude snarling canines on the car's doors and hood. Dashed-off letters twist in the spaces between, advertising the illiteracy of their authors: D O G E S. Stanley smirks to himself.

We spoke earlier of wars, Welles says, and of great battlefields. I believe that battles can take a number of forms. One could even say that we are walking through a battlefield right now. Often it has occurred to me that what is being fought over in these conflicts — be they great or subtle — is the right to memory. And not only the right to remember, but the right to forget. To selectively forget.

They've come to a steep bridge over a canal. Looking down, Stanley sees the reflection of the fog-shrouded moon in the stagnant water, filtered through an iridescent glaze of oil. About fifty yards to the right, this canal joins a wider waterway that parallels the street they walk on. A block ahead is a second bridge, then a third beyond that one, and Stanley becomes aware of a network of brackish canals that runs throughout the neighborhood, scum-filmed and overgrown, a liquid shadow cast by the grid of streets. Welles and the dog walk alongside the bridge railing; Stanley follows them. As their footsteps echo below he hears the scurry of rodents, the percolating cluck of mallards roused from sleep.

The name of this place, Welles says, is not an affectation. Or not an unearned affectation, at any rate. Nearly every street that you and I walked upon this evening, and more besides, were at one time canals. The roundabout on Windward was once a lagoon. Rialto Street, Grand Boulevard, the St. Mark's Hotel: these names were originally descriptive, not merely allusive. But the city of Los Angeles filled in most of the canals in 1929 — to make the area more easily accessible by automobile, I believe — and the original character of the place has been all but lost since that time. I was quite conscious of that history while I was writing my book.

Welles takes the pipe from his teeth and thumps it against his palm, emptying the ash into the canal. His tobacco tin reappears. The intellectual tradition in which Crivano participated, he says, was syncretic, millenarian, utopian. Like all utopian traditions — think here of Plato, Augustine, More, Campanella

260

— its metaphors are inevitably urban. We find this throughout the Hermetic literature. In the *Asclepius,* for instance, we see prophesized a city founded toward the setting sun into which it is said the whole race of mortal men shall hasten by land and sea when the gods of Egypt return. In the *Picatrix,* we read of Hermes Trismegistus's city of Adocentyn, wherein the display of magical images — images, mind you! — assures the virtue and the prosperity of every inhabitant. The architecture of the city's structures reflects the architecture of the heavens. Think of the implications of this. In the perfect city, we become our perfect selves. It is literally heaven on earth.

The moon's reflection on the canal's surface is split by a swimming rat; the smooth V of its wake expands toward the banks with geometrical precision. Welles packs his pipe as he waits for it to cross. When he's finished, he lights up, then lets the burning match drop to the water. A circle of blue-green flame forms where it falls, flares for a moment, and dies out.

We think of cities as places, Welles says. They are not. Mountains are places. Deserts are places. We are, in fact, standing in a desert right now. Cities are ideas. Independent of geography. They can vanish, suddenly or gradually, and reappear thousands of miles away. Changed, perhaps. Reduced. Always

261

imperfectly realized. But still somehow the same. Retaining the essence of the idea. As above, so below, as the alchemists would say. To perfect the wonders of the One. This, for me, is the heart — the real kernel — of Crivano's story. It's what I had in mind when I wrote it, anyway. And it's why I wanted to show you this place. We should go back now.

They return to the boulevard the way they came, then make a left to pick up the boardwalk again. Stanley replays what Welles has been saying in his mind, looking for threads that might connect to the questions he wants answered. He's glad the guy's on a roll, but it's making him nervous, too. It almost seems like Welles is talking about a different book than the one he read. What was it you said a minute ago? Stanley says. About my patron? What was it you meant by that?

Hm? Oh. Yes. Hermes Trismegistus. Do you know who he is?

I know who he is in your book. He's some kind of god, or a wizard, who lived a long time ago.

He was understood by Renaissance intellectuals to be the Egyptian equivalent of Moses. He was identified with Thoth — the giver of laws, the inventor of writing — and also with the Greek Hermes, the messenger of the gods, the god of healing, of magic, and of secrets. He was an intermediary between worlds, a crosser of barriers, and as such he was regarded as the patron of thieves, scholars, alchemists, and, of course, of gamblers like yourself. That is what I meant.

So you didn't just make him up?

No! Welles says. Good lord, no. It took hundreds of people, misunderstanding one another for thousands of years, to invent the Thrice-Great Hermes. Starving poets huddled in their garrets. Drunken bards prancing around bonfires. Weary mothers luring their wee babes toward sleep. I just added my own small confusion to the end of the long and crooked column.

They're still blocks south of the arcades. The broad lots are dotted with large beachfront houses, once grand, now wind-scoured, listing on their foundations. The few that show any evidence of care only seem more decrepit for it: fresh paint coats a collapsed veranda, plaster cherubim caper on a denuded lawn, neat rows of marigolds line a path of shattered cobblestone. There's a ruined boat in the yard of the next house — long and black, a toothed iron prow, half-buried in sand — that's been turned into a flowerbox: its split hull runs over with periwinkle, coreopsis, rose mallow, the petals turned pale sepia by the streetlamps' glow.

Stanley is silent, absently counting the wide planks beneath his feet, conscious of the sandy gaps. He thinks about tightrope walkers, about how they're not supposed to look down, not supposed to think about the precariousness of what supports them. He wonders if it was a smart idea to come out here after all. What about Crivano? he says.

Crivano?

You made Crivano up. Right?

Welles sighs, looks out at the ocean. With Crivano, he says, I took a number of liberties. In the historical record he is barely a shade. I filled in the gaps as imaginatively as possible. Of course, it is precisely those lacunae that made it possible for me to write the book at all.

Stanley stops walking. Welles and the dog carry on for a couple of paces, then turn and circle to face him.

You're telling me Crivano was a real person, Stanley says.

He was a historical person, yes. I discovered a brief and rather cryptic mention of him in the letters of Suor Giustina Glissenti while I was researching an entirely unrelated matter, and I was enchanted by the metaphorical possibilities he suggested.

You're pulling my goddamn leg.

I am not, no. From Suor Giustina's account I was able to infer only that the Council of Ten issued an arrest order for a person named Vettor Crivano in the summer of 1592, accusing him of taking part in a conspiracy to steal from the craftsmen of Murano on behalf of unknown foreign entities information regarding the manufacture of flat glass mirrors. In those days, a person so accused could expect to be imprisoned or enslaved, or, if he managed somehow to escape the city, to be pursued by assassins and murdered. It was a very serious matter. As I'm sure you gathered from reading my two long poems on the commercial history of images, the Muranese greatly benefited from their virtual monopoly on flat glass mirrors well into the Eighteenth Century, so we can assume that Crivano was unsuccessful. From other sources I discovered that he was a physician and an alchemist who took his doctorate at Bologna, and I was able to trace his family origins to colonial Cyprus, prior to the Ottoman siege. The remainder of his biography I — to borrow your phraseology — made up.

So how much of what happens in the book is true?

I really prefer not to speak in such terms, Stanley. When you say *true,* I take you to mean *factual.* But there are other kinds of truth. I am an old-fashioned poet. I understand my role to be essentially that delineated by Crivano's English contemporary Sir Philip Sidney, who tells us that the poet affirms nothing, and therefore never lies. In my daily life, as I said, I am an accountant. I was employed by the Air Force for many years, and later by the aerospace industry. I admit

— in fact I insist — that genuine satisfactions are to be found in my profession's regimented artificiality. But in the hours that I call my own, during that brief plunge from work toward sleep, I choose to dabble in more ambiguous enterprises. So I hope you will understand my reticence at being pinned down on these ostensibly metaphysical issues, which at best qualify as quibbles over points of fact, and which probably ought to be regarded as no more than mere semantics.

Welles is poker-faced, pleased with himself; his demurral hangs before him like a scrim. Stanley knows there are gaps in it, but he can't see them yet. He can hear Welles's breath, his own breath too, and he's suddenly disgusted by the sound: two pairs of fleshy bellows suctioning the air while the half-dark world spins steadily beneath them.

The little dog is slobbering at his feet. Stanley closes his eyes, bunches his fists, shifts his weight to kick it. He pictures it arcing toward the sand, leash aflutter like the tail of a kite. Welles's shocked expression as the loop snaps from his yellowed fingers.

He wonders if Welles really is heeled like he says he is, and if so, what sort of gat he might be carrying. Sometimes with fat guys it can be hard to tell.

Stanley straightens up, unclenches his fingers, forces a smile. Welles eyes him expectantly. In the moonlight they look like polished marble statues of themselves.

Mister Welles, Stanley says, I would really like to know just how much of your goddamn book is true.

■ ■ ■ ■

PREPARATIO

MAY 20, 1592

■ ■ ■ ■

And seeing in the Water a shape, a shape like unto himself, in himself he loved it, and would cohabit with it; and immediately upon the resolution ensued the Operation, and brought forth the unreasonable Image or Shape.

Nature presently laying hold of what it so much loved, did wholly wrap herself about it, and they were mingled, for they loved one another.

— Pimander

23

The acolyte lights the candles as the priest opens the book. The long wicks flare, and the image of the Virgin appears in the vault above the apse, her gray form steady against the flickering screen of gold. The glass tesserae of her eyes catch the dim light, and her gaze seems to go everywhere.

The priest's hand moves across the psalter; its thick pages curl and fall. *Venite exultemus Domino iubilemus Deo salutari nostro,* he intones. *Let us come before his presence with thanksgiving, and make a joyful noise unto him with psalms.* At the priest's back are the relics of Saint Donatus, along with the bones of the dragon he slew by spitting in its mouth. Overhead, the wooden roof slopes outward like a ship's hull.

Even now, hours before dawn, the basilica is not empty. Solitary figures pass in the aisles: sleepless fishermen, glassblowers between shifts, veiled widows impatient for Christ's return. Some kneel and mutter prayers. In the narthex, at the base of a marble column, a lone drunkard snores.

At the south end of the shallow transept a man drifts along the uneven stones. His steps are cautious, slow, measured by the soft tap of his walkingstick. His downcast eyes trace images on the mosaic floor: eagles and griffins, cockerels bearing a trussed fox, peacocks eating from a chalice. Beneath the clean flames of the beeswax candles the patterned checks of porphyry and serpentine blend into a fluid surface, undulating and unfathomable. The man lifts his black morocco boots like a heron hunting frogs.

Picture him there, between the piers of the old brick church: gaunt and sinewy, around thirty-five years old, wearing the long black robe of a Bolognese doctor. His small forked beard is trimmed close, his red-blond hair cropped a bit shorter than is the current fashion. He is somewhat less filthy, less flea- and louse-ridden, than those he moves among. His velvet cap and brocade jerkin are rich but not ostentatious. His worn lopsided face suggests a difficult birth and many misfortunes suffered since. There is a strangeness to his aspect, a detachment, that those who meet him tend to ascribe to his erudition, or to his many years spent abroad, although in doing so they are mistaken.

The sea is his, and he made it, chants the priest. *His hands formed the dry land.* Mist

272

rises from the canal outside, wedding the ocean to the darkness, bearing a chill through the heavy wooden doors. The black-robed man shivers, turns to go.

Let this be him, then. Crivano, the Mirror Thief. Let him bear the name. Who else can claim it?

24

As he crosses the threshold, Crivano can hear the *Te Deum* echoing from the convent of Saint Mark and Saint Andrew, two hundred yards north. A bright halfmoon lingers in the western sky; beneath it, the Campo San Donato is all but deserted. In the distance, across the wide canal, torches light the path of a procession as it leaves the new Trevisan house. By the entrance of the baptistery just ahead, yawning linkboys trade taunts with a pair of rude commoners, watchmen of the Ministry of Night. Crivano raises his stick as he descends the church steps, and one of the boys puts a taper to his wrought-iron lantern. Here's your light, dottore, the boy says.

I'm looking for a ridotto called the Salamander.

Sure, dottore. It's across the long bridge, near San Pietro Martire. Do you want to get a boat?

I'll walk, Crivano says.

They cross the square and follow the canal

south, then turn west when it merges into a broader channel. A gap in the buildings widens toward the lagoon, and for a moment Crivano can see the lights of the city, over a mile away: weak glimmers from the Arsenal, and farther on the orange blaze atop the bell-tower in the Piazza. The sea is calm. A few boats are already on the water, bearing lanterns in their prows, and he wonders whether Obizzo's craft is among them.

The wide fondamenta grows busier as they approach the long bridge. Merchants hurry to boats moored at quayside, bearing bundles or pushing carts laden with bronzeware and majolica and spindled glass beads, eager to cross the lagoon to their booths in the Piazza San Marco before the festival crowds gather. A week ago, when Crivano last came here to Murano to meet with his co-conspirators, he found many shops along this canal closed for the Sensa, having moved their business into the city. Meanwhile, in the Rialto, the guilds had to cajole and bully their members to abandon their storefronts and show their wares in the Piazza. The guilds' case seemed difficult to make. When your whole city is a market, why bother with the fair?

From the bridge's lofty midpoint Crivano can see a tremble in the air over the buildings ahead: heat rising from glass factories. Once lit, their furnaces burn at a constant temperature for weeks on end, even months.

The boats below the bridge are stacked with hewn alderwood, soon to be unloaded.

The linkboy leads him past a church, then into a bustling campiello. The workers they pass are flush-faced and soot-blackened; their eyes are red-rimmed and hard, like they've come lately from battle. Near the campiello's wellhead a workman is beating and cursing another, pounding heavy fists on his skull and shoulders. The attacker wears a thick bandage on his forearm; the man he strikes is little more than a boy. When the young man falls, his assailant kicks him until his nose and mouth are well-bloodied. Then a pair of stout fellows steps in and halfheartedly pulls them apart.

Here, dottore, the linkboy says. The Salamander.

Crivano gives him a few copper gazettes and sends him on his way. No sign marks the building: an ordinary two-story shop, its shutters replaced by rectangles of clear aqua glass, firelight falling through the drapes behind them. There's another window set in the door, this one stained a startling orange, with a translucent red lizard wriggling at its center. The door swings open with a touch.

He's not sure what to expect inside — knife-wielding gamblers, bare-bosomed whores — but it's a quiet place: a large room lit by oil lamps with a hearth at the far end; an old woman and what must be her grown son at work behind a long wooden counter; a ceiling hung thickly with game, sausages, cured hams. In the corner a young man strums a cittern, singing wordlessly. A half-dozen or so laborers are scattered across eight tables, dining or sipping cups of wine. Crivano spots the two he's looking for right away, but stands empty-faced in the entrance until the old woman comes for his stick and robe.

Would you care for soup, dottore? We have good sausage, too. And a pheasant.

Just wine.

Crivano seats himself at an empty table. After a moment, the glassmaker Serena appears at his elbow, his hat in his hand. Dottore, he says.

Maestro. Will you join me?

Thank you, dottore. Please allow me to present my eldest son, Alexandro.

The boy is twelve or thirteen, with a serious face. He already bears small scars on his hands and forearms from the furnaces. His bow is dignified and respectful. His eyes are a man's eyes. Crivano thinks briefly of his own youth: when he and the Lark left Cyprus for Padua, they were this boy's age. He doubts greatly that either was so poised.

You help your father in the workshop? Crivano says.

Yes, dottore.

He also studies with the Augustinians, Se-

276

rena says. He's a good student.

Serena musses the boy's chestnut hair with his broad right hand. His first three fingers lack their tips; each ends abruptly with a variegated whorl of scar tissue. Crivano hadn't noticed this before. Do you enjoy your studies, Alexandro? he asks the boy.

No, dottore.

Serena laughs. He'd rather be working the glass, he says. He thinks the lessons are worthless. Sometimes I agree. The friars make him learn Latin, and the language of court. Why? Better for a tradesman to learn English, don't you think? Or Dutch.

As he says this, Serena gives Crivano a pointed look that makes him uneasy. Well, maestro, Crivano says, those are the languages of the nobility. And tradesmen want to sell to the nobility. Is this not so?

Tradesmen want to sell to those with access to money and markets, Serena says. Like the English. And the Dutch.

As Serena settles into the chair his son pulls out for him, Crivano steals a glance across the room. The silverer Verzelin hasn't moved from his spot by the fire. He's slumped forward, his head on the table. Crivano knows him by the tremors in his legs.

Serena has placed a parcel on the oak planks. Those sketches you gave me were very good, dottore, he says. Very clear and detailed.

Yes. I didn't make them.

Serena smiles. My compliments, then, to your friend's draughtsmanship, he says. He leans forward. I understand why your friend wants to remain in the shadows, he says. This kind of work — not everyone will do it. Not these days.

You don't want the job?

I'll do the job, dottore. But I'll have to choose my help with care. As you've seen, there has been — how to put it? — an increase in piety throughout the patriarchate. Piety of a particular sort. And all of us praise God for this, of course. But often we're surprised to find practices once thought merely eccentric now being decried as heresy. I see this happen in my own workshop. So I must be cautious. For this piece, of course, we also need a metalworker who can be trusted. Fortunately I know of one.

Crivano nods. He has opened his mouth to reply when a yelp comes from near the hearth; Verzelin is upright in his chair. He jerks his head left and right, barking gibberish, then slouches to the table again. The cittern player shoots a quick look at him, but never breaks time.

He's drunk? Crivano says.

He's mad.

Crivano looks at Serena, doing his best to feign surprise.

Serena shrugs. It happens to them sometimes, he says.

To whom?

To the silverers. They go mad. No one knows why. Runs in their families, I suppose.

Crivano looks at Verzelin again. He's rolling his forehead back and forth across the wood, spilling his wine. Can he still work? Crivano asks. As if this concern has only now occurred to him.

Serena is silent for a moment. Then he flips aside the folds of white cotton that envelop the parcel before him.

The gesture seems to uncover a hole cut through the tabletop. Leaning forward, Crivano expects to see Serena's legs, but his eyes find instead the exposed beams of the ceiling — and then a face, his own, with terrible clarity. He puts a hand on the table's edge to keep his balance.

Go on, dottore. Pick it up.

Crivano slips his slender fingers beneath the cloth and lifts the mirror to his face. It's about a foot long, several inches across, rounded at the corners, in precise accordance with Tristão's sketch. The glass is perfectly flat, uniformly thick and clear. Crivano tilts it toward the firelight to check the silvering and finds no blemishes. A dancing ghost-light appears across the room, on the wall above the hearth, and then vanishes when he tilts the glass back.

Verzelin made this? Crivano asks.

Serena smoothes his thick beard, watching

279

Verzelin with weary eyes. Made it, he says, or caused it to be made.

It's remarkable. Flawless.

Nearly so, yes.

Is the glass that your shop makes so clear?

Serena grunts. Even clearer, dottore, he says. If I want it to be. But if you ask me, which I admit you did not, I'd tell you that this glass is *too* clear. Your friend had better keep the damp off it, or in a year or two —

He makes a flatulent sound with his mouth.

— it's gone. Melted away like a fancy sweet. Very clear glass cannot abide moisture, dottore. Your friend should keep this wrapped in dried seaweed, always. For what he's paying he should make it last.

Crivano is barely listening, staring at his own face. Like every gentleman, he owns a small steel mirror, and over the years it has taught him to recognize himself. But this glass has made it a liar. He sees himself now as others see him, have always seen him: the shape of his head, the way his expression changes, the space his body fills in a room. He scans the map of damage written across his face and wonders how much can be deciphered: the divot in his jaw from a janissary arrow, the ear notched in Silistra by a whore's hidden razor, the front tooth chipped by the boot of a Persian onbashı in the instant before the musket went off. With a quick intake of breath Crivano replaces the cloth

280

and pushes the parcel back toward Serena. How long to attach the frame? he asks.

Not long. No more than a day.

My friend won't need it so quickly.

Once it's finished, Serena says with a sad smile, I don't want it in my shop.

He reaches into his tunic — good fabric, Crivano notices, and fairly clean — and produces a rectangle of white paper, folded and closed with a blue wax seal bearing the device of the Siren, his family's shop. Give this to your friend, he says. It's my estimate, along with a list of alterations I've made to his design. If any are unacceptable, I must be informed prior to sundown tomorrow. Otherwise I'll complete the piece.

Crivano takes the paper, tucks it into his own doublet. There's a commotion: Verzelin is on his feet, staggering. The man with the cittern angles away, ignoring him, pretending to tune his strings. *Christ!* Verzelin shouts, followed by something Crivano can't make out. A thread of phlegm dangles from his beard, golden in the firelight. Crivano sees a pair of dark stains on the table Verzelin left. The smaller is spilled wine; the larger, he realizes, is saliva.

Verzelin walks toward them, lurching spasmodically at every other step. *He walks among us, brothers!* he hisses. He's pointing at Crivano. *Promises! Promises! Promises of de-*

281

liverance!

Crivano keeps his eyes steady. The front of Verzelin's shirt is soaked with sweat and drool. Amazing, Crivano thinks: all those hours at the furnaces, and still so much phlegm. Surely he's incurable now. Still, best not to take chances.

Verzelin shapes his words with effort, seeming to gag on them. *I have called!* he says. *I am his prophet! The peacock, he's a holy bird, isn't he a holy bird? He walks our streets! Follow him, brothers!*

He's out the door, gone. Crivano tenses, tries to keep the strain off his face.

That, Serena says, is not quite the sort of piety I was talking about.

I should speak with him.

Not much of a point, dottore.

I have his payment. For the mirror.

I'll pay him for the mirror, dottore. You pay *me* for the finished piece.

Serena looks at Crivano with narrowed eyes, like he's an imbecile, but Crivano is already rising to his feet. I'll return to collect the piece in two days, he says. Send word to me in the city if the project is delayed. I'm lodged at the White Eagle.

It takes Crivano a moment to pay for his wine and to retrieve his robe and stick. By the time he's muttered his valedictions and returned to the campiello, Verzelin is nowhere to be seen. He can't have gotten far in his condition, but which way? Crivano looks for the linkboy who brought him here, but the boy has moved on. He could ask anyone else, of course, but he doesn't want to leave more of a trail than necessary.

He opts to turn right, down the Street of the Glassmakers. It's long and straight and brightly lit — by glazed lanterns hung over doors, and also from within, by the white-hot furnaces — and edged along its left-hand side by a small canal choked with boats. If Verzelin came this way, he'll be no trouble to spot.

Crivano hurries forward, his walkingstick clutched by his side. He notes the brightly colored insignia of the shops he passes: an angel, a siren, a dragon, a cockerel devouring a worm. The shutters are all opened, the wares are on display, and more than once he's startled by the image of his own anxious face.

25

A hundred yards down the fondamenta, just past a small fishmarket, Verzelin sways in front of the Motta mirrorworks, the shop that employs him, bellowing at his colleagues inside. The shop's racks and shutters are a gallery of silvered panels — ovals and circles and rectangles, pocket-size or inches across, with frames of inlaid wood or wrought metal or chalcedony glass — and they render him in fragments: his hollow chest, his twisted limbs, the silent O of his shouting mouth.

I've caught the Lord! he says. *I have, I have, we all have! But what's the good of catching if you never follow?* No one in the shop comes to the windows; passersby give him wide berth. The bricks at his feet are spritzed with white foam.

Crivano watches from a short distance up the quay. This is better, he thinks: better that he and Verzelin left the Salamander separately, and better that he's had time to think. By now Obizzo will have moored the boat; he'll be nearby, half a mile at most. The question is how to move Verzelin in the right direction. Crivano dealt with too many madmen during his years in Bologna to believe himself capable of anticipating their actions, but he has an intuition about this one, and no better ideas.

He saunters forward, giving the mirror-maker an empty stare. Verzelin goes silent, his febrile eyes returning Crivano's gaze, his lean bearded face a riot of tics and twitches. Then Crivano walks past him, carrying on down the fondamenta, the iron ferrule of his stick clicking sharply on the pavement.

Confounded, Verzelin discharges a spate of rapid gibberish, unintelligible and bestial, and Crivano picks up his pace. There's an opening on the right: the Street of the Potters. He makes the turn. Another glassworks here, along with two osterie and a lusterware factory; the other shops are dark and shuttered. Halfway down the block, Crivano steps into the recessed doorway of a mercer and waits.

Verzelin isn't far behind. With each step, his body angles left; he corrects himself like a ship beating to windward. The few people on the street hasten from his path. He murmurs as he comes. *The peacock,* he says, *he's a holy bird, a holy bird, a holy bird.*

Crivano steps into the open; the moonlight catches him. Verzelin, he says.

Verzelin blinks, squints. Dottore? he says. Dottore Crivano?

Yes. I'm here.

I conjured you, Verzelin says. I called you from the glass.

We must go, Verzelin. Do you understand? We must leave Murano tonight.

Verzelin stares without comprehension, then squeezes his eyes shut and shakes his head, like a child who's tasted raw onion.

Listen to me. The guild and the Council of Ten have learned of our intentions. The sbirri are looking for you right now. There's a boat nearby waiting to take us to Chioggia, but we must hurry.

Verzelin grimaces, stares at his shuffling feet. In his expression Crivano can see an army of fleeting impulses being enveloped by profound weariness. I will follow, Verzelin mutters. I have looked. In the glass. What I

285

have seen. And I will follow.

Crivano finds a dry spot on Verzelin's upper sleeve and tugs it to urge him along. There's a wide square ahead — early-rising merchants' wives filling pails at the well — and they angle away from it, following the curve of the street until they're parallel to the glassmakers' canal. Potters are at work nearby, singing a maudlin song about a drowned sailor, but he and Verzelin have the pavement to themselves.

Crivano speaks softly and rapidly, reminding Verzelin of what they're doing and why. From Chioggia we'll sail to Ragusa, he whispers. In Ragusa an English cog will be waiting to take us to Amsterdam. We'll be there in three weeks, God willing. And the guild's prayers to Saint Anthony will be very fervent this year, I think.

Don't want, Verzelin says, *don't want* to go to Amsterdam. Heretics! Full of heretics, it is.

Well, you'll have to convert them all, won't you, Alegreto?

Verzelin's tremors have faded, but his feet are dragging, and his voice is blunted by his dripping mouth. Can't work, he says. Lift the glass. Not anymore. *My hands,* dottore! My hands!

Crivano wraps his fingers around Verzelin's arm, glances ahead. He can see the lagoon now, and the quiet fondamenta where Obizzo is to have moored the boat. You won't have to work the glass in Amsterdam, Crivano says, pulling him forward. They've found good workers for you there. Experienced men. You need only teach them to apply the silvering.

I am afflicted, Verzelin moans. *I have seen!* There is no time, no time. Have you? Do you follow?

Of course, maestro, Crivano says. Of course I do.

Shutters open on a shop to the left, but Crivano doesn't look back. *I have caught him!* Verzelin whispers, clutching Crivano's hand. In my glass! I *have*, I have caught. Hold a mirror up to Christ, dottore! Is that not the Second Coming? Have you seen, dottore? Have you? What good is it to witness, if you never tell?

They've reached the fondamenta. The lagoon is before them, black and limitless, with a scattering of lanterns across its surface, a careful thread of light that joins the mainland to the Grand Canal. From nearby buildings issue snores, muffled voices, the sound of a couple fucking, but no one is afoot. A hundred yards south along the quay is a stand of holly-oaks; Crivano spots a white rag draped over one of the lower limbs. Come on, he whispers, pulling Verzelin's arm. Quickly.

I worked so hard, Verzelin says. So hard.

Now I see. The peacock, he's a holy bird, dottore. Just count the eyes on his tail.

Crivano takes a moment to scan windows and balconies, but no one seems to be watching them. They're almost to the trees. On the quay before them, two kittens are picking at the discarded head of a shad; aside from them and the water, nothing moves. Crivano lets Verzelin step ahead, then puts a gentle hand on his back.

The draped branch points to a palina where Obizzo's small black sandolo is moored. Obizzo has removed the passengers' chairs from his boat; there's a wadded sheet of sackcloth in the bare hull, partly covering a coil of hemp cord and an irregular block of limestone. Obizzo himself is hunched in the stern, hidden under a broad-brimmed hat and a shabby greatcoat. As Crivano and Verzelin draw even with the bow, he stands and scrambles forward.

Verzelin gasps, stops in his tracks. Even in his blighted state he recognizes Obizzo at once. *You,* he says.

Crivano lifts his walkingstick crosswise in both hands and drives it against the base of Verzelin's skull. Verzelin's head pops forward, he staggers, and Crivano slips the stick under his chin, laying it across his neck just above the thyroid cartilage. Then he tucks the right end of the stick behind his own head, levers it back with his left arm, and crushes Verzelin's larynx.

Verzelin struggles, clawing the air, and Crivano catches his right wrist with his free hand to wrench it immobile. Obizzo has Verzelin's legs; he twists them, grimacing fiercely, as if Verzelin is a forked green sapling he's trying to snap in two. Held off the ground, Verzelin writhes, grasping at nothing with his unbound left arm. There's a dull pop — a femoral head dislocating from an acetabulum — and Verzelin's body goes heavy and slack.

Like Antaeus, Crivano thinks. He holds on awhile longer, certain that the stick is tight across the carotid artery. Many years have passed since he last did this. He thinks about those other men — the touch and the smell of them, the sound of their interrupted breath — as he waits for Verzelin to die.

Come on, come on, damn it! Obizzo whispers. His hat has fallen; he retrieves it, puts it on backward, turns it around, watching the lights in the nearby buildings with stray-dog eyes. Every soul in Murano would know him at a glance.

All right, Crivano says. Take his legs.

They put Verzelin's body in the bottom of the hull and hide it with sackcloth. Crivano wraps the cord around the torso — both legs, both shoulders, a double-loop at the waist — and ties it with a surgeon's knot.

Obizzo is in the stern, his long oar at the ready. That's enough, dottore, he says. Get out and cast me off.

Crivano springs to the quay and plucks at the dockline. Be certain to put him in the water at San Nicolò, he says. Sink him in the channel. If the cord breaks, he should float out to sea.

When will I hear from you?

Crivano loops the line and drops it into the sandolo's bow. I'll find you in the Rialto, he says.

When?

Crivano doesn't answer. He watches Obizzo bring the small boat about. The sleeves of Obizzo's coat slide back when he lifts his oar, baring his thick forearms, and Crivano wonders what wild canards he tells his passengers to explain the burns that mottle his furnace-roasted skin. After a few long strokes and an angry backward glare, Obizzo fades into the dark.

The insipid honking of geese comes from somewhere overhead. Crivano looks for the pale undersides of wings, but finds none. When the sky grows quiet again, he pulls the white linen from the holly-oak branch, wipes Verzelin's spittle from his gown and stick, and throws the damp cloth into the lagoon. Then he rounds the point and returns to the Street of the Glassmakers, following it back across the long bridge, studying the shop windows along the way.

His locanda is on the Ruga San Bernardo:

lively by day, quiet at night, with no lock on its outer door and stairs to the lodgers' rooms directly off the foyer. The widow who runs the place will hear him come in, but she won't remember the hour. He bolts his door and rests his head against its wood and breathes deeply, conscious of the gallop of his pulse. Then he lights the clay lamp on the little table, hangs his clothes on the pegs beside the bed, and unties his purse.

Two pinches of basil snuff cool his blood, but he'll stay awake until he returns to the Rialto. He performs a few stretches that he remembers from the palace school at Topkapı, then sits and breaks the blue wax on Serena's letter to Tristão. Unfolded, the outer layer of rag paper reveals a second document with an identical seal; Crivano sets this aside. Then he flattens the sheet that enclosed it, holds it over the lamp's flame, and waits for the hidden writing to appear.

26

A cool wind leavens the fog over the lagoon, and the belltower of San Michele floats into view off the traghetto's bow. Aside from Crivano, the boat's only passengers are two tightlipped Tyrolean merchants, bundles clasped between their knees. The gondolier has no songs; he pauses often in his rowing to blow his nose and tighten his greatcoat against the morning chill.

Crivano is suffering a bit of rhinitis himself, along with a tightness in his throat, probably from the sleepless night. His has been a year of many such nights: recent episodes of hard travel, and prior to those long hours spent reading for his disputation, preparing to argue Galen with puffed-up chancellors who knew the *Qanun* of Ibn Sina only in translation, who'd never read al-Razi at all. Many a dawn found Crivano awake at his cluttered desk, or completing a difficult alchemical process in his tiny laboratory, and he'd rub his eyes and don his cloak and step out to wander the breezy colonnades of Bologna, feeling a melancholy thrill of inviolability, as if by waiting out the night he'd found a way to stop time, to free himself from human concerns. What pleased him most was that no one could see what he'd done, could know that he still had use of the day they'd discarded. And this, of course, echoed other secrets. Eyeing the smooth faces of students half his age as they shook off sleep and hurried to their lectures, Crivano would bite his inner cheek and marvel at his own lethal strangeness: the spider in the flower, the cuckoo in the nest.

A white pulse flashes through the mist off starboard, the wings of an egret, and now Crivano sees scores of them, nested in a bend of willows at the eastern edge of San Cristofero della Pace. The tide is low, coming in: rocks slimed with eelgrass lie exposed in the shallows, and sea-smell fouls the air. Crivano presses a scented cloth to his face and watches a distant pair of fishermen work in their cut-reed weir. When he turns forward again, the square flanking towers of the Arsenal are before him.

The traghetto puts out its fares. The Tyroleans hurry off to the south, shouldering identical burdens with identical hunches. Crivano stands aside to watch them go as the sniffling gondolier takes on more passengers. Behind him the mist has lifted, and a few Alpine snowcaps hang above the horizon, like chips in an old fresco.

The smell of boiling pitch from the Arsenal has scoured away the tideland miasma, and Crivano tucks his sudarium back into his doublet. Columns of black and white smoke rise in ghostly parallel to the new belltower at San Francesco della Vigna, a near twin of the one in the Piazza: leaner, nearly as tall, its steep pyramidal crown already crazed by lightning-strikes. Crivano shades his eyes and notes that the side of the belfry overlooking the Arsenal has been bricked up. To spoil the vantage of spies, he imagines. Crivano and his fellows are hardly the only foreign agents intriguing against the Council of Ten.

As he starts his long trek back to the Rialto, he tries to walk slowly — to be calm and alert, to abandon himself to the currents of the streets — but his head and neck ache, faces turn monstrous in his sight, and he finds himself rushing, heedless of what he passes. As he's crossing the Calle Zon bridge a sluggish exhalation of bubbles breaks the canal's surface, and he stops, overcome by nausea, to lean against the stone balustrade. Black silt rises from the bottom, corrupting the emerald water, and Crivano imagines Verzelin somewhere in the lagoon, tethered to his stone block. At peace at last. The only physic for him.

He claps the sudarium to his face, breathes through it, and the spearmint helps to focus his thoughts. He has failed to anticipate how exhausting this would be: the need to keep a scrupulous interior tally of crimes committed, of lies told. The mildest contradiction or the most innocuous statement of fact might suffice to doom him if spoken within range of the wrong ear.

Still worse: in his constant braiding of the strands of his conspiracy, Crivano finds himself inclined toward stasis, estranged from the objective that actually brought him here. When it came, the behest of the haseki sultan seemed straightforward enough: locate craftsmen adept at fashioning the flawless mirrors for which every civilized land celebrates the isle of Murano, and return with those craftsmen to the Ottoman court, so that the industry might become established there. But Crivano soon learned — to his dismay, if not his surprise — that the fabrication of mirrors is a complex undertaking, one that requires the labor of at least two specialists: a glass-maker conversant with formulae and techniques to yield a crystalline substance of near-perfect transparency, along with a silverer able to shape that material into flat sheets backed with a reflective alloy. With Muranese mirrors increasingly craved in every European court, those who possess such skills might reasonably expect incomes to shame the most prosperous pasha. Convincing such men to quit the island of their birth — an island upon which watercraft converge daily from every compass-point, delivering a particular inventory of raw materials to the factories wherein these men and their fathers and the fathers of their fathers learned and refined their methods — persuading such men to forego such advantages in order to set up operations ex nihilo in a Muhammadan land where their language and customs will be utterly alien: this seemed to Crivano to present a grave rhetorical challenge.

And so Crivano lied. Based on his accrued understanding of the industry, he guessed that Amsterdam — another city of canals, one with its own nascent glassworks — might present itself to the Muranese as a tempting destination. Whatever his reasons, the glass-maker Serena concurred readily enough. Ver-zelin did as well — or so it seemed, until Crivano was forced to conclude that the silverer's own reasoning was not so much oc-cluded as lost, annihilated by whatever afflic-tion had come to sap his brain. Disaster! The fool was too erratic to be of use in the haseki sultan's project, yet still coherent enough that any ravings about an imminent flight to the north might not have been dismissed by the authorities. In the end, there was only one option. The man murdered himself.

This Obizzo, on the other hand, is perfect. For the hundredth time Crivano wonders how Narkis was able to find him: an expert silverer, a reasonable man, a fugitive with eighty ducats on his head. Now, after last night, his fortunes are wedded irrevocably to Crivano's own. Of course, like all glassmak-ers, his disposition is somewhat choleric — Crivano dreads the task of pacifying him when he crosses the gangway and finds himself trapped in a city very different from the Amsterdam he has been expecting — but this is a trifle. The man is a godsend. Whose god sent him, of course, remains unresolved.

Laughter and a filthy song carry down the canal. Crivano turns to see a group of young nobles — drunk, garbed as Chinamen, joined by a pair of masked whores — cross the bridge to the old Zon house and pound on its heavy wooden door. The men must have been set upon lately by a mattacino: he can smell musk even over his spearmint oil. One of the false Chinamen gapes at him with kohl-slanted eyes. Crivano turns, crossing the bridge back the way he came.

In the Campo Santa Giustina he stops to seek out a monument to the Battle of Lepanto, certain he'll find one, but there's nothing. The church itself is cracked and sagging: he peeks through the entrance to see a pair of rock-doves waddling across the narthex, pale light dappling the flagstone floor from holes in the roof. He forces a sour smile, turns south again. How quickly times change. How sweet to forget.

Tomorrow is the last night of the fair. Two weeks ago, on Ascension Day, Crivano was the guest of honor on the Contarini family galley: he stood on the garlanded quarterdeck next to Giacomo Contarini himself and lent the old man a steady shoulder as they approached the mouth of the lagoon. He watched Doge Cicogna teeter aboard his Bucintoro, heard his clear voice carry across the waves — *we espouse thee, O sea, as a sign of true and perpetual dominion* — even as his councilors scrambled to keep him upright long enough to toss the ring over the side. Later that afternoon, on the Lido, Crivano took communion not far from the firing range where he and the Lark proved themselves as

297

bowmen twenty-two years before. Then he sat through an interminable banquet in order to receive a fleeting audience with Cicogna himself. *The Republic thanks you, my son, for your heroic efforts in her service.* The shrunken old doge clearly had no notion of who Crivano was, or of what his heroism consisted; he dozed off even as the words left his tongue, and Crivano was whisked away as fireworks bloomed over the distant roofs of the city. Probably just as well.

He was content then to miss the revels in the Piazza — that odd mélange of depravity and tradecraft — but now he finds himself eager to see them before they end, to lose himself in their crush and spectacle. After three wrong turns down three dead-end streets he picks up the canal again just past the apse of San Lorenzo — he can hear workers stacking tile and singing on its roof, though they're too high to be seen — and shoulders his way across a bridge through a crowd of violet-capped Greeks to the fondamenta on the opposite side. He crosses again a bit farther on, passes the plain façade of San Antonin, the gothic palaces of the Campo della Bràgora, and just as he's certain he's lost his way he emerges onto the Riva degli Schiavoni to find the Bacino of San Marco arrayed before him, shimmering like a curtain of cut-glass beads.

He steps from the flow of traffic to look

across the water. The monumental church of San Giorgio Maggiore that dominates the view was barely begun when he and the Lark first came here. Farther west on the Giudecca, the cool and stately Redeemer is entirely new to him. Both façades are pure white Istrian stone, blinding in the sun. Impossible structures in an impossible city. They remind him of Greek ruins he saw in Efes, but that doesn't diminish their strangeness. Their massive doors seem poised to open on a world never seen by human eyes.

A peote flashes past, on its way to meet an incoming carrack; its keel and oars barely disturb the water's surface. Crivano suddenly wishes he could forget his first glimpse of the city — wrestling with the Lark over the best spot on the rail as the Molo came into view — so that he might now see it fresh, weigh it fairly against other miracles he's witnessed in the intervening years: the labyrinthine medina of Tunis, the pyramids of the Giza Plateau, the living rock temples of Wadi Araba. He leans against a palina at the quay's edge, closes his eyes, and tries to retrieve the feeling of the days spent waiting out the quarantine in Malamocco, the memory of standing on a rock wall at the lagoon's edge as a storm came in. The Lark was somewhere behind him, singing and clowning for some peasant girls — *My noble friend and I are going to Padua to become physicians. Come, let me examine you!* — while he leaned into the wind, trying to sort the shapes of belltowers from the distant scud.

Sleep is stalking him: he jolts awake to find himself tipping forward, seizes hold of the palina to keep from toppling into the waves, and his walkingstick clatters to the ground. Crivano stops it with his foot, stoops to pick it up.

A group of merchants has gathered nearby on the quay. They're watching the approaching carrack; he follows their eyes. The ship's mainmast is gone — partly splintered, partly hacked through at shoulder-height, as if someone took an axe to it while the ship ran before the wind — and as it draws closer he sees that its hull is bristling with arrows, pocked with lead shot, stained rust-brown under the scuppers.

Christ have mercy, one of the merchants mutters. The pirates are at it again.

The uskoks, you think? his fellow asks.

Who else, fool? Look at the blood! That craft played host to a cannibal feast, of that you can be certain. The merchant spits into the waves. Someone should tell limp-pricked old Cicogna that his new bride cuckolds him with the Devil himself, he says. And their bastard whelps now have the run of our waters.

Crivano turns to go. Ahead, just off the Riva, a troupe of gypsy acrobats performs

300

somersaults on the foundations of what's to be the new prison. Crivano pushes through the crowd across the bridge to the Molo, passing the arcades of the Doge's Palace as he makes his way to the twin columns. Five long tables stretch between them, manned by masked attendants shaking bone dice in clay cups. Behind each table a long queue of merchants and farmers snakes toward the artisans' booths. The new wing of the Library boxes in the Piazzetta like a canyon; two rows of wooden stalls run its full length, into the Piazza itself. A disordered throng moves from exhibit to exhibit — sturdy peasant women from the Terrafirma, German pilgrims provisioning for the Holy Land, silver-veiled brides in damask gowns — and Crivano takes a deep breath and steps forward to join it.

Grotesque profusion! Engraved boxes and majolica vessels. Sachets and vials and pomanders of scents. Octavo breviaries and pornographic woodcuts. Trellises draped with chaplets and fake pearls. Shelves bowed by the weight of shoes, combs, caps, hose, needles. Pigment-vendors grinding their products into careful mounds. Goldsmiths, coppersmiths, and tinsmiths twisting chimeras from wire and foil. Empty-eyed bravi fingering knifetips. Greeks peddling leather, Lombards peddling linens, Slavs peddling wool.

As he moves among the displays, Crivano

realizes that he has managed to forget his entanglements, to loose his mind's grip on the intrigues that lend purpose to his days, to become for a moment exactly what he seems: an idle man engaged in the survey of merchandise. Some weeks ago, when he arrived in the city, moments such as these came upon him only rarely; he'd emerge from them with a start, like one who remembers he's left a coin-purse unattended. Now Crivano has come to suspect that he is safest at these times: browsing for goods, entertaining his Contarini patrons, debating learned citizens about trivia of mutual interest. Dissembly can hardly fail him when he does not dissemble. He wonders whether he might one day succeed so completely in forgetting himself — his whole occult catalogue of betrayal and deceit — that he's able to meet the evidence of his corruption with sincere bafflement.

A pair of mattacini rushes from the steps of the Basilica, launching from their plaited slings blown-out eggs stuffed with musky rags, and the shouting and shrieking crowd parts before them. Crivano steps through the gap, around the loggetta of the belltower into the Piazza itself. The shapes and textures of this place have been so vivid to him during the twenty-odd years he's been away that he tends to forget how few days he and the Lark actually spent here. His recollections have served as a kind of beacon in times of confusion and difficulty, a means of tracking his passage through the world. But now that he's come back, he's been surprised to discover how much his mind altered during his absence: how much it augmented or elided or rearranged to suit the dictates of his imagination. He feels himself moving not through the city that has haunted him for so long, but through a city that is itself haunted by that city.

He's made nearly a full circuit of the Piazza before he notices that it's grown larger. The old pilgrims' hostel has been demolished — replaced by a new Procuracy, maybe half-finished, in a fussy classical style — and the square's trapezium broadened. This space holds the fair's most elaborate installations: here the glassmakers' tables display leaping dolphins, reared dragons, winding serpents, a glass armada under full sail. Crivano draws closer to admire a miniature castle with scarlet banners, edged by a bosk of frothy trees and a moat bubbling with citrine wine.

But this all pales beside the mirrormakers' showcase. They've linked their booths with a wooden passageway of columns and rafters, like a pergola bereft of vines, and hung the inner surfaces with an assortment of flat glasses. Beneath a canvas banner at the entrance — VIRTUTUM SYDERA MICANT — five strapping guildsmen beckon to passersby, doffing their caps and singing in rough harmony. Their tune is borrowed from an old frottola, one the Lark used to perform, though Crivano can't recall its true words.

A simple art, ladies! If everyone knew it,
then every globe-blowing jackass would do
    it.
Demonstrate here? Do you take us for
    fools?
Come visit Murano! We'll show you our
    tools!

As Crivano elbows his way across their threshold, his halfsize image slides into view around him — to his right, to his left, over-head — while others, smaller still, appear alongside those, ricocheted from the mirrors opposite. Every glass surface he passes shows a procession of windowed chambers, end-lessly iterated, with Crivano the living void at its center. He reaches for his sudarium, hur-ries to the other side.

The costumed crowds, the shiny heaps of luxuries: it all might have been pleasant had Crivano arrived well-rested, but in his cur-rent state it's unsettling, a parade of morbid compulsions, and suddenly he's sorry he came. Near the clock tower he buys a pastry — a fritter studded with almonds, dusted with fine white sugar — and he eats it as he strolls along the basilica's façade, assaying the gold and the marble, the cool serpentine and carnal porphyry, the encrustation of ancient spoils. Over the northernmost vault a mosaic depicts the theft of the corpse of Mark the Evangelist from infidel Alexandria; this image triggers a quick flood of memories: his first meeting with Narkis, nearly thirteen years ago, roused from sleep in his quarters in the Divan Meydanı. *I have come to you, Tarjuman effendi, on behalf of the haseki sultan. She has made an interesting suggestion.* A week later, waiting by the obelisk in the old Roman hippodrome. Strange men hidden in the shadows, their breath clouding the moon-lit air. *Run, messer! The devils are at my heels!* Plucking the bundle from Polidoro's trembling fingers — miserable Polidoro, the thief, the slave, the dupe — as the guards' shouts rang out.

Then, later that night, the embassy in Galata, holding his breath while the bailo unwrapped it: a packet of human skin, neatly folded, its tanned surface fuzzed with short red hair. The old bailo green-gilled, unsteady, choosing his words with caution. *Rest assured, messer, that you will be duly rewarded for recovering the remains of this great hero of Christendom.* Well, they were somebody's remains, anyway. Within the month he'd sailed through the Golden Horn aboard a Lucchese galley, bound for Ravenna, his

University of Bologna matriculation certificate safe inside his doublet. Wearing, for the first time in his life, the black robes of a citizen of the Republic. Another metamorphosis accomplished.

Crivano had planned to return to the White Eagle through the Mercerie — he wants to have a look at the new bridge over the Grand Canal — but the crowds will be worse that way, and he's grown impatient with crowds. He passes under the old Procuracy and follows the long Street of the Blacksmiths, where he'll be able to hire a gondola. Walking quickly against the flow of traffic, he lowers his head and sweeps his stick to fend off the provincial whores gathered along every route, two or three deep. By the time he reaches Magazine Street the mobs have thinned, and he moves with little effort.

In the Campo San Luca he allows himself to be distracted by a band of wandering performers as they improvise a satire about a mountebank alchemist. It's clear soon enough that these are not ordinary clowns: no urchins ply the audience on their behalf, the actor playing the charlatan shows some real knowledge of Latin and alchemy, and their jokes — sharp gibes at Philip of Spain and the Holy See among them — gild the edges of a substantive argument, one that might cause them trouble if aired in the Piazza.

Every lesser metal, the sham alchemist

lectures, *aspires toward gold, just as every acorn would fain become an oak.*

Speak to the point! a player masked as a clever Jew demands. *I would follow to the tree you speak of, dottore, but you cut a crooked path through the bush!*

The alchemist feigns irritation. *These circumlocutions protect secret knowledge, my simple friend,* he explains, *just as the finest berries are hid by leaf and thorn.*

For all this fellow's shrubby words, the masked Jew shouts, *I'd think an alchemist naught but a learned squirrel!*

Crivano laughs at this exchange, winces at a sharp lampoon of Bolognese rhetoric that finds its mark, and applauds as the performance ends and the alchemist is chased away, running toward Campo San Paternian, counterfeit nuggets dribbling from his robe. Crivano is about to follow, to discover who these educated pranksters really are, when a gasp runs through the square behind him, and a woman shrieks.

In the campo near the mouth of Oven Street a dark form has appeared. Like nearly everyone else, the figure is disguised, but its costume is hardly festive: it wears a wide-brimmed black hat, a long black robe of waxed linen, and the dull bronze mask of a plaguedoctor, beaked like the head of a monstrous tropical bird. Townsfolk scatter and cross themselves as it moves through the square; a few curse it, but none stands in its way. The few unhidden faces in the crowd are convulsed with anguish, an inventory of recalled suffering inscribed in their expressions.

Seventeen years have passed since plague last came to the city. Although he was in Constantinople at the time, Crivano knows the last one was very bad: a quarter of the population dead, including what remained of his own family, those lucky few who escaped Cyprus ahead of the sultan's troops. The memory of pestilence still lies across every street and every campo here like an unseen scar. At carnival time, when order is suspended, this fellow's costume might simply be in horrific taste; during the Sensa it's unthinkable. Or perhaps this is yet another theatrical provocation. Crivano scans the crowd, alert for the arrival of more players, but nothing moves: everyone else in the campo is frozen in place, shrunken into themselves like sea anemones at low tide.

When he turns forward again, the plague-doctor is almost upon him. Crivano sidesteps to clear the figure's path, but the figure tracks him, closing the distance with slow steady paces like a terror in a dream. Wisps of burning asafetida rise from its vented beak; a slim ash wand dangles from its gloved right hand. Its robe is splashed with dark fluids, dried in the creases: what might be bile, what might be blood.

A few feet from him the figure stops abruptly, silent and statue-still. Crivano stares hard at the beaked mask's eyeholes, but they're unscryable, capped by blown-glass hemispheres. His worn nerves tighten like a springline in a gale.

He's about to issue a challenge when, with a liquid motion swifter than a blink, the figure lays its wand alongside his neck. The tip rests against Crivano's bare skin just above his ruff, as if to measure his pulse. He springs back, swats the wand away with his own stick, then slides his fingers down its shaft and swings it hard with both hands, axing the heavy silver knob downward at the figure's clavicle.

The walkingstick bites only air; Crivano stumbles to keep his feet. As he's rising again, the wand flicks his wrist, and his stick falls to the pavement. Crivano's hands are up instantly, guarding his face. He's calm, almost relieved to be in proper combat again. Flattening his gaze to hide his intentions. Figuring distances: the stick on the pavement, the stiletto in his boot. *Kill the bastard, dottore!* hisses a voice from the crowd. The plaguedoctor faces him, open-armed, motionless.

Crivano moves. He lunges, feigns a jab, rolls the stick behind him with the ball of his foot. Then he steps back, gets his toe under the rolling knob, and pops it into his hand. It's a beautiful move — he's very pleased with it — and when he lifts the stick to try another strike, the plaguedoctor is gone.

Its black shape is already halfway to the Street of the Casters, in no evident hurry, making easy strides. So quick it seemed weightless. Its turn like the pivot of a bird-rattle on the wind. Still in his attack stance, his walkingstick aloft and at the ready, Crivano looks, he realizes, somewhat ridiculous. He straightens up, adjusts his garments, plants his ferrule on the stones with a decisive click.

The campo is emptying. People avoid his eyes, embarrassed for him, or for themselves, he can't be sure which. A water-vendor appears at his side with a ladle; Crivano gratefully drinks. That whoreson was smart to run off when he did, dottore, the man says without conviction. You'd have thrashed him.

Do you know who that was? Crivano asks between gulps.

The water-vendor shrugs, eager to move along. Someone with no goddamned decency, I suppose, he says. Probably from the mainland.

Crivano hands back the scoop. I'm a stranger to your city, my friend, he says. Tell me, the costume that blackguard was wearing. Is it commonly seen here?

Not lately, dottore, the water-vendor says, and crosses himself. Not lately.

27

A shaft of orange sunlight splits the room like a blade, and a noise that Crivano takes at first for hoofbeats resolves into a steady pounding at the door. He springs naked from bed and has his hand on the bolt before he remembers the regimental emblems that mark his skin. Yes, he calls. I'll be with you in a moment.

The knocking stops. He unhooks his shirt from its peg, shrugs into it, and surveys the room as he pulls on his hose. Before lying down — just for a moment, to rest his eyes — he'd been working at the table; the report to Narkis is still there, along with the polished wooden grille which encoded it. Crivano hides the grille under the paper, then opens the door.

Anzolo, the proprietor of the White Eagle, waits in the hallway, studying the framed woodcut on the opposite wall. He turns with a ready expression, as if mildly surprised, as if Crivano has emerged quite by chance. Ah, he says. Good day, dottore.

What is it, Anzolo?

I'm sorry to disturb you, dottore. Dottore Tristão de Nis is downstairs, and he wishes to speak with you. He says that you are expecting him.

Anzolo is a very good innkeeper — he has an imperturbable ease any courtier would admire — but now a shade of doubt haunts his manner, an uncertainty regarding protocol. Doubts of this sort follow Tristão as birds follow cattle.

Yes, Crivano says. I'll be a short while. Please give Dottore de Nis my apologies for the delay, and see to his comfort. We'll take supper in the parlor.

When Anzolo is gone, Crivano bolts the door again and takes a moment to collect his thoughts. He'd been enmeshed in vivid dreams, and they slip from him now in an indistinct rush: fragments in the midst of fragments, like the mirrored passage in the Piazza. His mother and young sister on the Redeemer's white steps, milk-eyed and smiling, dead of the plague. His father and older brothers, bloodied and proud at the Famagusta Gate, offering him a robe fashioned from his own skin. Crivano wonders what these dreams augur for the success of his mission, and why they fail to disturb him.

He retrieves the wooden grille from the table and tips back the lid of his massive walnut trunk. Jostling items aside — spare shirts and hose, heavy boots and rainwear, his rapier and the new snaplock pistol he purchased in Ravenna — he uncovers his books. Beneath these is a spring-loaded panel

312

that conceals a shallow compartment, and Crivano opens this to put the grille inside. Then he replaces his belongings and closes the trunk. The brass key scrapes between the wards; the lock clicks.

As he's draping the key from his neck by its leather thong, he remembers the plaguedoctor. He lowers his wrist into the sunbeam to inspect the skin where the ash wand struck it, but he finds no rawness there, no bruise. The inevitable notion arises — was that too a dream? — but Crivano swiftly stifles it. He flexes his fingers, noting the smooth glide of tendons under skin, and returns to his task.

On the floor beside the trunk is his box of physic; from it, he withdraws a square of white linen, and a narrow ceramic jar stoppered by a wide cork. The jar is half-full of dried ragwort root; Crivano shakes this onto the linen, ties it into a bundle, and puts the bundle back in the box. Then he rolls his report to Narkis into a narrow tube, drops the tube into the jar, and stoppers it again.

The bells of San Aponal are ringing the hour, a few long breaths out of phase with the bells of San Silvestro farther south: Crivano counts twenty-three. He combs his hair, slicks the prongs of his beard, and dons his boots and doublet and black robe. A corner of curtain is trapped in the double window in the eastern wall; Crivano opens the sash for an instant to let the curtain fall

313

plumb, and the ray of sunlight vanishes. Then he takes up his jar and Serena's sealed letter, lifts his stick from its corner, and walks downstairs.

The White Eagle is quieter this evening than he'd anticipated. Most locande in the Rialto are double- or triple-booked for the duration of the Sensa, but Anzolo has been cautious not to let occupancy exceed what his eight servants can manage. The inn is expensive, especially for a room to oneself, but worth it. Narkis suggested the place. Crivano wonders how he learned of it, since the law forbids him from ever spending a night here.

Nearly all the tables in the parlor are occupied. Crivano recognizes most of the lodgers from previous meals: two fat merchants from Frankfurt struggling to parse the mumblings of a one-eyed galley captain, Bohemian pilgrims studying a map of Jerusalem with madness simmering in their eyes, a pair of shabby young nobles from Savoy pointedly ignoring a second pair of shabby young nobles from Milan.

In the middle of the room sits Tristão. He's absorbed in an octavo that he holds in his left palm; his right hand makes an automatic circuit — flipping a page, plucking a nut from a dish, bringing wine to his lips, flipping another page — as if it's a separate creature, a helpful imp. Crivano approaches, hesitates, clears his throat.

Tristão blinks and shakes his head, his eyes unfocused, as if the book won't relinquish its hold on him. Then he looks up with a broad smile and a sigh of pleasure. Doctor Crivanus, he says, rising for an embrace. You demonstrate great kindness by your willingness to see me.

They speak Latin, as is their custom. Tristão's speech is by turns stilted and poetic and urbane, a Latin learned from books, far removed from the bland efficiency of Crivano's university argot. Of the three languages they share, it's the one in which Tristão is most comfortable. In this room it also affords a measure of privacy.

May I ask how fares Senator Contarini? Tristão says, sinking into his chair. Does insomnia still prolong his nights?

I haven't spoken with the senator of late. I'm to call on him tomorrow. I'll pass along your good wishes.

I am grateful for your doing so. You prescribed him cowslip, I suppose?

Cowslip wine, Crivano says. Given his age and his temperament, I thought it best. What's that you're reading, Tristão?

Tristão averts his eyes, flashes a sheepish grin. His teeth are lead-white, improbably straight. Oh, this? he says, caressing the octavo. This is the Nolan.

The Nolan?

Tristão opens his mouth, looks up, and

315

closes it again, pushing the book across the tabletop instead.

One of Anzolo's Friulian serving-girls has emerged from the kitchen, bearing sweet white wine from Sopron. Before Crivano's cup is full, a second girl arrives with food: tiny artichokes, rice porridge, Lombardy quail stuffed with mincemeat. The girls giggle and blush whenever they meet Tristão's gaze, then hasten away. Oh! Tristão says, fanning steam toward his face with dove-wing hands. Oh oh oh!

Crivano smiles. Tristão is a caricature of masculine beauty: ample curly hair, dark eyes with feathery lashes, smooth skin the color of old brandy. A skilled physician much favored by the city's patricians, he'd long since have married into the nobility were it not for his peculiar circumstances. *He's a converso,* Contarini explained. *From Portugal. Like all Portuguese, he's assumed at best to be a hypocrite Jew, at worst an atheist and a spy for the Sultan. I will introduce you to him, of course — no doubt you share many interests — but I must urge you to be cautious in your dealings with him. He is an ingenious man, and kind, but not always prudent.*

They say a brief prayer and cross themselves. As Tristão pulls apart his bird, Crivano opens the book to the title page. *de triplici minimo et mensura,* it reads. Flipping ahead reveals a long philosophical poem — an imitation of Lucretius, inventive if lacking in grace — and then a page of geometric figures: circles and stars ornamented by flowers and leaves and honeycombs, obvious magical sigils. Crivano shuts the book hurriedly, slides it back to Tristão. So, he says. The Nolan.

A Dominican friar, Tristão says between bites, dabbing his mouth with a napkin. Long since expelled by his order. For intemperance, and for promulgating heterodox notions.

Such as?

Anti-Aristotelian notions. Heliocentricity. The wisdom of the antique Egyptians. The existence of infinite worlds. It is perhaps best not to speak of these matters here.

Tristão puts a bit of quail in his mouth, moves his jaw, puts his fingers to his lips and withdraws a pair of clean bones. The Nolan, he says, has been for many years peregrine in the courts of Christendom. Prague with Rudolf II, England with Elizabeth, Paris with unlucky Henri III. Searching for a philosopher-king. A monarch receptive to his instruction.

Where is he now?

He is here. He is a guest in the house of Lord Iovanus Mocenigus, where he has undertaken to teach Lord Mocenigus the art of memory, as practiced by the learned orators of the ancient world. That is why I am reading his book.

So this Nolan is a rhetorician as well?

Oh no, Tristão says, arranging bones on his plate. Not a rhetorician. He follows Thomas Aquinas in prescribing the art as a tool for reminiscence and devotion. But he goes much further, I think, than Aquinas would countenance.

Crivano furrows his brow, sips his wine. Mocenigo, he says. Zuanne Mocenigo? He's with the Doge's faction, isn't he?

As I understand it, Lord Mocenigus does tend to favor Spain and the pope in matters of state.

But if the Nolan is, as you say, involved in the pursuit of secret knowledge, isn't he unwise to have commerce with such a man?

Tristão shrugs. I would think so, he says. But perhaps what you or I regard as unwise the Nolan understands as fundamental to his project. Perhaps the Nolan believes that the new pope will be receptive to his teachings. And perhaps this is not impossible. After all, Picus Mirandulanus himself enjoyed the patronage of a pope.

Pico had the patronage of Alexander VI, Crivano says. Hardly a representative case. Is that what the Nolan advocates? A return to the age of the Borgias?

You can ask him yourself, if you like. Tomorrow evening he is to address the assembly of the Uranian Academy, and, as always, my patrons the Lords Morosini are to play host to the proceedings. They have asked me to extend to you an invitation on their behalf. These Uranici are powerful men, Vettor. Your presence among them would be greatly valued. I believe they hold the future of the Republic in their hands.

Crivano takes a spoonful of rice porridge — rich with beef broth and mushrooms — and chews it slowly, trying to imagine what Narkis would have him do. Recalling Ravenna, five months ago, the last time they spoke freely in person. *The best way to conceal a conspiracy, Tarjuman effendi, is to cloak it in a lesser conspiracy.* They met in a quiet tavern down the street from the old Arian cathedral. Narkis looked strong and self-satisfied, anything but diminished in his turban and simple caftan. *Place yourself in danger. Give the authorities something to discover. You become like the gecko who drops his tail.*

This, he gathers, is why Narkis directed him to seek out Tristão in the first place: to find a lesser conspiracy in which to cloak himself. And true enough, Tristão has been conveniently swift to enlist Crivano as his respectable envoy to the Murano glassworkers. His peculiar commission — suspect enough to interest the Inquisition, but far milder than the unambiguous treason of Crivano's actual

319

undertaking — has been a perfect blind, supplying a tailored pretext for furtive encounters with Verzelin and Serena. So perfect, in fact, that Crivano doubts Fortune delivered it without earthly assistance. He still has no sense of how much Tristão knows of his real purpose here.

I am greatly honored to accept your hosts' invitation, Crivano says.

One of the Friulian girls arrives with a dish of candied lemonpeel and clears away their tableware; Tristão stops her with a light touch, leans close, and praises the meal in a heartfelt whisper. The girl's lips purse, her eyelids flutter, and Crivano notices the plate in her white-knuckled hand: in it, the re-assembled skeleton of Tristão's devoured quail, a split artichoke scale substituted for its absent skull.

Oh, Vettor, Tristão says as they rise to leave — as if he's just now remembered this, as if it were not the very purpose of their meeting today — how went your visit to Murano?

It was fruitful, Crivano says. I met with the glassmaker, who is prepared to begin work on the frame.

And what of the mirror itself?

Crivano keeps his eyes low — his walking-stick, his jar — betraying nothing. I saw the mirrormaker briefly, he says. The mirror is finished. The glassmaker has it now.

How does it look?

The question carries an undertone of anxiety, audible though unvoiced, like the drone-strings of a robab. Crivano smiles evenly. It's perfect, he says.

He slips Serena's sealed message to Tristão as they pass through the White Eagle's foyer onto the darkening street. Perfect? Tristão says, tucking it into his own doublet. You are quite certain of this?

The glassmaker said it might be too perfect.

I do not think I understand you, Vettor. What does this mean, too perfect?

He says clear glass is susceptible to moisture. It might not last long.

Tristão's face clouds. Its expression is nearer to confusion than distress, as if it meets impediments so rarely that it's slow to recognize them. Then it breaks into its customary radiant grin. Ah, my friend, Tristão says. This is no great concern. After all, what lasts long in this world?

They embrace. Their cloaks are a momentary blot against the bustle of the crowd, black drupes amid wind-tossed bramble leaves. Tomorrow evening! Tristão shouts as he steps away. A banquet at sundown, and then the symposium! Be prompt!

Tomorrow evening, Crivano calls after him.

On his way toward the Street of the Coopers, Tristão stops to tweak the chin and inspect the décolletage of a fleshy harlot, then again to exchange familiar greetings with three yellow-turbaned Levantine Jews. The fearlessness that enlivens his movements seems born not of self-confidence, but rather absolute certainty regarding the ultimate fate of his soul. Looking on, Crivano considers that certain damnation could engender such boldness as easily as certain salvation. All too clearly he can see the light Tristão sheds, but as yet he has no way to guess its fuel.

Tristão vanishes around the corner to the north. The street is in deep shadow, and up and down its length most shops are closed, or closing. Crivano loiters for a moment, watching traffic pass before him until it becomes abstract and depthless in his sight: a chaos of colors, fabrics, gestures, faces. Then a gap opens and he steps into it, walking to the corner, following the Street of the Coopers south.

The apothecary's shop is a short distance away, in the Campiello Carampane: the latest location on a coded list of rendezvous points that Narkis gave him in Ravenna before they parted ways. Crivano prays that Narkis — or one of his agents; surely he has other agents — noticed the curtain that he left trapped between his sashes as he slept. Henceforth their enterprise must move ahead quickly.

San Aponal's last daylight bells are dying away as the shop comes into view. Through its lowered shutters Crivano sees the apothecary tidying his boxes and jars and posies, preparing to close up. He stops across the street to wait, examining the tongs and pliers in an ironworker's bins as the craftsman hauls his wares indoors. There's no sign of Narkis yet, but of course there wouldn't be.

A footman from a nearby palace ducks into the apothecary's shop, and Crivano follows him inside, then browses heaped bouquets and bundled roots as the apothecary fills the footman's order for vervain. As the servant departs Crivano steps to the counter, leaving his stoppered jar behind, nestled amid the herbs. Good day to you, maestro, he says. Have you any biennial henbane of quality?

Before the words have left his mouth Crivano feels a slight contraction of the air, a dimming of the light, and he knows that Narkis has entered the shop behind him, though he dares not turn to look.

The apothecary is a compact and fastidious Slovene wearing thick spectacles of Flemish glass; he speaks with urgency as he unlocks one of his many strongboxes. This very power, what I give you, he says. Must not use in tight-closed room. Must not open jar, even. You feel sleepy? You see strange sights, like dreaming? You must cover up, you must open window, you must go outside. Very very very caution. Yes?

Of course, maestro, of course, Crivano says.

The apothecary draws a wide glass cylinder from his box, lifts its tight-fitting lid — he and Crivano both grimace at the cloying stench — and reaches under the counter for an empty container. Oh, I brought my own jar, maestro, Crivano says, then tenses in feigned surprise, patting his belt and his purse, looking up and down the counter.

A voice from behind him: Forgive me, dottore, but is this what you seek?

In thirteen years, this is the first time Crivano has heard his own native language issued from Narkis's tongue. Narkis pronounces the words roughly, with effort, and the sound is eerie and grotesque, like hearing an animal speak.

Crivano turns — allowing himself only the briefest glance at the hairless face, the white turban — and plucks the empty jar from Narkis's fingers. Yes, he snaps. It is. My thanks to you.

The apothecary shakes a pile of leaves onto his scale, scrapes a few back into the cylinder to reach the proper weight, and quotes Crivano an astronomical price, which he pays without protest. The leaves fall into the jar; the cork is replaced and hammered tight. Very great power, the apothecary says, waggling a finger. Not for play.

With no second glance at Narkis, Crivano quits the shop and hastens toward the White Eagle again, eager to put distance between them. He reckons his report will be read within the hour — the wooden grilles decode more swiftly than they encode — but he can't begin to guess how long Narkis will take to formulate a response. In the meantime, the thousand surrogate eyes of the Council of Ten watch from every balcony and every window. Somewhere in the lagoon, Verzelin's gassy corpse strains surfaceward against its decaying fetters.

As he walks, Crivano is attentive to faces, alert for any he recognizes. He's fairly certain that sbirri followed him during his first days in the city — an understandable precaution, given what the authorities know of him — but he doesn't think he's being shadowed any longer. No doubt informants still track his movements, but they won't have noticed anything suspicious today. Crivano is a physician; physicians frequent apothecaries. Nothing unusual in that.

He's nearly back to his locanda when a figure catches his eye: a rustic girl of perhaps twenty years, leaning against the cracked stucco of a joiner's shop. She bends forward to study her black-soled foot, her right leg folded at the knee; a boot sags empty on the pavement below. The girl's hands are stained brown to their wrists from some recent labor: tanning, dyeing, packing fabrics. Her drooping headscarf reveals cropped russet hair, shaved and partly grown back, as if she's lately been treated for ringworm, or run afoul of the Inquisitor. She prods the filthy ball of her foot with brown thumbs, heedless of passersby, appearing and disappearing as they cross before her.

Something about her is familiar, though Crivano doesn't think he's seen her before. He watches for a moment, then draws closer and watches for a moment more. Well-muscled arms extend from her sleeveless blouse, sun-cooked nearly to match the stains. The angles of her face are boyish and hard. The small toes of her bare foot curl inward, the large one tips back, and Crivano discerns the irregular ellipse of a verruca in the pad beneath it. Does that give you pain? he asks.

For a long moment she doesn't look up. It feels strange to walk, she says.

There's physic for it. You should seek it out before you ask a barber to cut.

Her eyes are angry, but the anger doesn't seem to be for him. And what does a girl pay for that? she asks.

Crivano gives her a warm smile, and opens his palms.

She stares at him. Then her face sags, and she looks back to her foot. The hour grows late, dottore, she says. You name a price for your physic, and I'll name a price for my cunt. And then perhaps we'll make a bargain.

Crivano's mouth drops open. He closes it, and grinds his teeth. The girl brings her fingers to her lips, spits on them, and wipes them across the wart. It clarifies against the damp whorls of her calloused skin.

So, wench, Crivano says, his voice ugly in his own ears, does the entire city take to whoring for the Sensa? Or do all you slatterns come here from abroad? Good christ, every brothel from here to Munich must be shuttered.

I guess someone can answer that for you, dottore, she says. But not I. Ask a Bavarian pimp if you meet one. Will you lend an arm?

She's looking up again. For an instant he's inclined to strike her, to break her lean mannish jaw with the knob of his stick. But he gives her his arm, and she pulls her boot on. Thanks, she says. And a good day to you.

He stands by the wall to watch her limp away, her kerchiefed head bobbing among the crowds bound for the Mercerie. He half-expects to see her stop — to pitch a lewd proposition to a pack of merchants or pilgrims or sailors, to detour with one or several of them to a sidestreet or sottoportego or darkened doorway, to offer up her lean flesh for their abuse — but the girl moves ahead steadily until she's gone from sight.

And then, at the White Eagle, on his way upstairs to his room and his books, he remembers a long-ago morning out riding with his brothers south of Nicosia on the Larnaca Road. Their party came upon a procession of Cypriot girls with an ass-drawn cart, bringing baled henna to market. The girls were all bent double under their heavy packs, even the youngest; all stared fiercely at the pitted surface of the old Roman road. Maffeo spat at them as they passed, and Dolfin stood in his saddle to display his cock. Those girls are probably all dead now, Crivano figures: killed during the invasion by the troops of Lala Mustafa. Or they're in harems, or they're rearing Turkish bastards, or they're living now just as they were living then. The distant cedars of the Troödos formed a green shadow in the west that morning; he recalls watching them with unblinking attention after he turned his head away.

The girls' strong arms were dyed brown to the elbows, their legs dyed brown to the knees. Every nail on every finger was a ghostly pink oval, edged by a sepia ring, and that, Crivano thinks, must be why the insolent slut seemed so familiar.

28

The late morning arrives harsh and white: a veil of smoke traps light in the thick air above the tiled rooftops, and the Grand Canal is a listless river of quicksilver. The sun presses gently on Crivano's black robes, warming him from the core, and he feels himself grow weightless, on the verge of being borne aloft, like a Chinese sky-lantern. The thousandth year of the Hijra is only months away, and it's suddenly easy to imagine the Prophet stirring in his tomb. This is a day to herald the end of the world.

He shades his eyes to find an idle traghetto. A grizzled boatman beckons with a brusque wave, and Crivano steps aboard his tidy black-hulled sandolo. The Contarini house, he says. In San Samuele.

In reply he gets only a flash of raised fingers and a bestial bleat: the boatman has no tongue. Crivano counts him out a palmful of gazettes, then sits in the shade of the canopy. Looking over his shoulder as the long oar chews the water, he can make out the hazy shape of the new bridge, its single span arching like the brow of a submerged leviathan eye. It slips from sight as the sandolo's bow swings west.

The broad highway of the canal is paved with broken bits of sun, reflections that outshine the sky itself. The windowsills and balustrades that edge the water are draped with bright patterned carpets from Cairo and Herat and Kashan, but the rows of windows behind them are impenetrable voids. The shouts of the Riva del Vin are fading, and from time to time Crivano can hear the laughter and soft voices of unseen daughters of the Republic, bleaching their frizzed coiffures on hidden terraces somewhere high above.

Heavy-lidded from the rolling boat, he keeps himself awake by pondering what blasphemy a gondolier might pronounce, or to whom he might pronounce it, that would oblige him to forfeit his tongue. In this city blasphemy is the gondolier's cant and his lingua franca, as indispensable as his oar; it seems more likely that this rough fellow is a slanderer, or was. This comforts Crivano: the reminder that denunciation can also impose a cost on its utterer. He smiles to himself, tilts his face to catch the sun.

He's not certain Narkis would endorse his expenditure of the better part of a day in Senator Contarini's court — this excursion will do nothing to advance their plot — but Crivano feels justified nonetheless in making the visit. The Senator is his sole legitimate connection here, the authority that has established him as a person of substance and introduced him to the circles in which Narkis requires him to move; the association must therefore be cultivated. If Crivano displays something beyond dutiful resignation at the prospect of acquainting himself over extravagant meals with the most distinguished minds in Christendom, well, Narkis can hardly object, can he? Besides, how otherwise might Crivano spend the afternoon? Sequestered in his rented room, awaiting a response from Narkis that might not materialize for weeks?

The Contarini palace rises on the intrados

of the Grand Canal's southward bend, its imposing façade flush with those of its neighbors. As they approach, a sleek gondola rowed by a tall Ethiope in rich livery pulls away from the water-gate, and Crivano wonders how many others have been invited to dine.

Marco, the senator's youngest son, greets him with an embrace beneath the gate's broad tympanum. We're honored that you've come, dottore, the young man says, guiding him to the stairs. We're blessed with fine weather today, so my father has chosen to hold the banquet in the garden.

One of Marco's nephews, a chubby boy of around seven, takes Crivano's hand and leads him up two flights to the great hall on the piano nobile. The furnishings he knows from previous visits — suits of armor, shields and bucklers, sunbursts of swords and spears, all framed by tattered banners bearing emblems and devices he recalls from his childhood — are now clustered at the hall's far end, and the nearby walls are lined with folded wooden screens, rolled black curtains, and partly assembled scaffolding. Before he can make a closer inspection, the boy tugs him into the blazing atrium.

A long table shaded with parasols stretches between two neat rows of almond trees, their branches already sagging with green fruit. A dozen or so servants — twice the usual retinue, temporary help hired for the Sensa — set places across its oaken expanse with goblets and flatware. Crivano recognizes a few of the milling guests from state banquets and earlier introductions, but most faces are strange to him.

The senator himself stands at the edge of the grass, looking well-rested and magnificent in a lynx-trimmed velvet robe. He claps his big hands warmly on Crivano's shoulders. I am gratified to find you well, senator, Crivano says.

Contarini's response is spoken in the language of court, not that of the Republic; foreign visitors must be present. I give credit to you and to your physic, dottore, he says. It has restored me so completely that I am scarcely able to recognize myself.

The senator turns to the man on his right, a gaunt and balding Neapolitan of sallow complexion. This is the heroic personage of whom I spoke, my friend, he says. Dottore Vettor Crivano, a child of Cyprus like myself, who suffered years in infidel bondage, who made a daring escape from Constantinople and helped restore the remains of the valiant Marcantonio Bragadin to the hands of the Republic. Devoted in equal measure to wisdom and to brave deeds, he graduated from Bologna with distinction, and has come to our city to commence his career as a physician. Dottore Crivano, I don't believe you've met Signore della Porta.

Crivano and the Neapolitan exchange polite bows.

Dottore Crivano's father, Contarini continues, was chief secretary to my kinsman Lord Pietro Glissenti, the last chamberlain of Cyprus, and served him faithfully until they were both massacred at Famagusta. Were that sacrifice insufficient to place the Contarini family in his debt, Dottore Crivano has recently cured me of a sleeplessness that has troubled me since well before Lent. You really should seek his council about your own ailments, Giovan. He is the best man to help you.

You are unwell, signore? Crivano asks.

The Neapolitan's voice is quiet and crisp, like a shuffle of documents. It's nothing at all, he says. I'm fine.

Contarini leans toward Crivano, lowers his voice. He coughs, he says. At times I imagine his heart will leap from his jaws like a toad, he coughs so much. It's worse after he eats, which is why he refuses to dine with us. One hesitates to believe, dottore, that such terrible noises can come from the lungs of such a small man.

I pray you will forgive my discourtesy, senator, the Neapolitan says, but as you have no doubt noticed, the sun nears its zenith. With your permission, I will see to the children.

Della Porta takes his leave across the

333

peristyle, entering the great hall. Contarini claps Crivano on the arm with a conspiratorial wink and turns to greet another guest. Momentarily at a loss, Crivano fades into the crowd, seeking faces he knows, pondering the Neapolitan. Della Porta, he thinks. From Naples. Why is this familiar?

The servants have begun to seat the guests. Crivano winds up between a sullen and heavily veiled maiden and an elderly gentleman called Barbaro — a procurator of San Marco, quite deaf — who loudly denigrates the glassmakers' guild until the first course arrives. The glassworks of the Medici, old Barbaro shouts, makes lenses of quality, but it has no prayer of competing with the factories of Holland. And where do their finest craftsmen come from? They come from here! We treat our guildsmen like merchant princes, and they conduct themselves like roundheeled whores!

Crivano wants to raise a polite dissent — a pointless impulse, since the procurator is certain not to hear him — and he's sifting his brain for what little he knows of optics when recollection comes. I beg your pardon, lady, he whispers to the veiled girl. The Neapolitan gentleman who was here a short time ago, the one called della Porta — is he not Giambattista della Porta, the author of *Magiae Naturalis,* and the famous book on physiognomy?

334

Beneath clouds of gray lace the girl's eyes are riveted to his own, but she makes no reply.

Or perhaps, Crivano says, you know him as a playwright, and not as an eminent scholar? As the author of the popular comedies *Penelope,* and *The Maid,* and *Olympia*?

The girl's voice is a contralto murmur, each word precisely formed. I grant that Signore della Porta is eminent, she says. And he is certainly a scholar. I suppose we may therefore speak of him with justification as an eminent scholar.

You question Signore della Porta's scholarship, lady?

Oh, no, dottore. As one who read *Magiae Naturalis* with great zeal in both its editions, I dare not raise any such protest. Besides, the little instruction I receive in the convent school hardly qualifies me to speak on this matter. I can only parrot what I have gleaned from overhearing the discussions of my erudite cousins.

And what is that, if I may ask?

She looks at the tabletop, and her voice sinks further toward silence. If the great community of scholars can be likened to the family of musical instruments, she says, then Giambattista della Porta can be likened to a churchbell. His work is distinguished by its enviable clarity, but not by its subtlety or its scope.

Crivano laughs, drawing an irritated glare from the old procurator. As he gropes for a clever rejoinder — a pun, perhaps, about how her observation has the ring of truth — servants arrive with enormous platters: cured ham simmered with capers in wine, pork tongue and fresh grapes, marzipan and spice-cake. Crivano is rubbing his palms together, turning to the girl with some comment about the feast, when she lifts her veils.

It is as if he has been plunging like Icarus toward the sea — falling for such a long time and from such a terrible height that he has forgotten himself to be falling — and now has struck the water at last. His lungs refuse air; his jellied limbs seem to fly from him. He feels himself rise for the prayer and for Contarini's toast, raise his goblet of Moselle wine, but his ears perceive nothing but the interior churn of his own humors.

He cannot imagine why this ictus has come upon him. He has never met this girl before; he has no notion of who she is. Cream-skinned and sharp-faced, with obstinate eyes, she is not beautiful except in the ways that youth and vivacity are always beautiful. There is, perhaps, a scent. He is less entranced than terrified. He cannot bear to look upon her face. His eyes fix instead upon the grain of the tabletop, their focus as hot and relentless as Archimedes' terrible glass. Yet the only clear image in his head is that of the Lark's demolished body, its pink meat cannonball-scattered across the quarterdeck of the *Gold and Black Eagle.* Why this memory now?

The old procurator has resumed his ranting; a line of brown sauce bisects his chin. Our glassmakers lack loyalty and direction! he thunders. They could crush Florence and Amsterdam with ease, but they won't learn, they won't change, they lack science. Look here: why is the city of Saint Mark superior to the city of Saint Peter? Because it has no pagan past! This is why glassmaking is our great art: in no discipline but this do modern artisans surpass their pagan predecessors. The shops of Murano should be crowded with painters and engineers and architects, learned men seeking to emulate their example. But what do they sell instead? Mirrors! Nice flat mirrors for ladies and sodomites!

The guests empty the platters and more platters appear: roast quail with eggplant, fried sweetbreads with lemon, a soup of songbirds and almond-paste. As each majolica dish is cleared, bare-breasted images of Annona and Felicitas and Juno Moneta emerge from the crumbs and sauces, offering mute blessings to the Contarini line. Now comes a boiled calf and a pair of stuffed geese, here are chicken pies and pigs' feet, here is a pigeon stew with mortadella and translucent whole onions, sightless eyes rolling in the dark broth. Crivano eats almost nothing. The girl, nearly motionless in the margin of his sight, seems to eat even less.

Contarini rises at the head of the table, his hand in the air, his strong fingers imperiously curled. It is the height of rudeness, he says, to hasten one's guests through their meals. Thus I offer my apologies. But my esteemed colleague Signore della Porta informs me that our entertainments must commence immediately if we are to have them at all. It seems that our revels depend — as I suppose all things depend — on the advantage conveyed by the rays of the noonday sun. More than that I shall not say, for fear of evoking the voluminous wrath of the little Neapolitan. Enough! Let us recess through the peristyle, where seats await us!

Crivano mumbles a quick courtesy to the maiden, pushes to his feet, and hurries from the courtyard, seizing the chance to escape and collect himself. His pulse hammers in his temples and his gut, muffled and out of phase, like laborers sinking a pile through thick clay. He is simply ill, he thinks: stricken by some mundane lagoon miasma. It's coincidence, nothing to do with the girl. But even as he thinks these things he imagines himself as an under-rehearsed player, declaiming them to an unseen audience in the dark theater of his own mind. Already some secret part of him must know.

With nothing in his belly to slow its progress the wine is rampant in his blood, making his footfalls heavy and loose as he steps indoors. The great hall has been cleared of its clutter; the stacked screens and folded curtains are assembled and hung, occluding the windows that open to the courtyard. The only visible daylight rises through the loggia at the opposite end: a liquid shimmer on the frescoed ceiling, the oscillating echo of the Grand Canal's surface, just out of sight below. Somewhere nearby — he can't say where — he hears a soft clang of metal brushing metal, and the muted laughter of a child.

Crivano blinks, unsteady in the abrupt darkness. A servant with a lamp appears at his side to convey him to an adjacent room. Here too the windows are blocked by curtains, and before the curtains stands an upright polyptych of blank canvases. By the wan yellow light of candelabra Crivano finds four rows of campaign chairs facing the canvas screen; a wide aisle runs down their center, and he follows it to a seat near the front. As he lowers himself into his chair, he notes a small lectern standing to one side of the easels, and a long wooden trunk on the floor beneath them, one end hidden by the curtains. He's puzzling over this as the other guests file in, and suddenly the seat to his right is occupied. He knows without looking that it's the girl.

Contarini reappears, sweeping majestically into a chair, and now della Porta stands at the lectern. Senator Contarini, he says, most eminent ladies and gentlemen, my esteemed friends, I thank you for your indulgence in permitting me the opportunity to demonstrate this afternoon some principles of *scientia* that have been of enduring interest to me. I should say before we begin that the images you are about to witness may be shocking to some of you, and that any women present, or persons of delicate constitution or infirm mentality, may wish to absent themselves. I can assure you, however, that everything you see here today is produced by only the most virtuous application of natural magic, and brought about by my own reverential understanding of the hidden processes of the Divine Soul of the World. At this time I will offer no further explanation beyond referring interested parties to the expanded edition of my book *Magiae Naturalis,* widely available from your fair city's superior booksellers. The text from which I read is a verse narrative of my own composition. Extinguish the lights, please.

Della Porta begins to orate a self-important prologue concerning the past glories of the Republic, and Crivano's attention is snuffed out with the candles, wandering to the girl, to Contarini, to the other guests, to the gilt splendor of the room, to the odd trunk on the floor, back to the girl again, until a sudden thump issues from the cloaked windows and a weird panorama materializes across the canvas screen.

Gasps rise from the nearby seats, along with a few muttered curses; the girl seems to tense, to draw somewhat closer. It is as if the wall before them has dissolved to reveal a shadowy landscape: a glade ringed by misshapen trees under a sunless sky. The image is so clear and so dynamic in its color and detail as to make the best efforts of the most adroit trompe-l'oeil painters seem like the scribbles of feebleminded children. And now the leaves of the phantom trees are indeed moving, rustled by a slight breeze. The audience's gasps are renewed.

After the initial shock, Crivano thinks of a chapter in della Porta's book — and also a similar, greatly superior discussion of the same topic in the writings of Ibn al-Haitham — and he grins, pleased with himself. It's a camera obscura, he whispers. That box on the floor. It is merely the courtyard beyond the wall that we see.

For a long time the girl does not reply. *Thereafter spake wise Dandolo,* della Porta drones, *his fervor undiminished by his years.*

But we're facing the courtyard, the girl whispers. And the image is not upsidedown, as it should be.

Shhhh, Contarini hisses over his shoulder.

341

The girl is correct: this is no camera obscura, or at least not simply that. Crivano reviews his knowledge of optics and finds it wanting. A second lens? he wonders. A convex mirror?

A crash of cymbals and the eerie bray of a shawm banish these thoughts. Two parties of armored men come into view, their broadswords and bright helmets strafing the room with fantastic flashes. They take positions on either side of a rampart that emerges from the murk — Byzantines to the left, Crusaders to the right — and shake their weapons fiercely at each other.

The Neapolitan continues his labored narration of the familiar tale: the blind doge's fanatic assault on the walls of Constantinople. *And lo, the other princes looked, and saw the courage of this ancient man, and greatly were they shamed, for he whose deeds they witnessed had no sight.* Despite the inept verse and the fanciful images, Crivano finds himself less amused than disturbed. Something in the dreamlike aspect of della Porta's projection spawns in him clouds of violent memories, unmoored to anything but one another, which reach his mind's eye from nowhere and fade as quickly as they come. The Gulf of Patras red with blood, its surface aflame, choked with arrows and shields and hacked-off limbs and white turbans. A barn in Tiflis filled with corpses, steaming in the cold. The Lark reloading on the quarterdeck, singing a rude song, and then the thunderclap, and the smoke, and gone forever. Captain Bua lashed to a post in the Lepanto town square, screaming, flensed to his shoulder. The tanned hide of Bragadin upon the bailo's desk. Verzelin's white hand poking from under the sackcloth. The Lark again, unfolding his battered matriculation certificate in the firelight. *My mother will never believe I'm dead. If you give her this, then maybe she'll know.*

The rampart splits, the Crusaders overwhelm the Greeks, and the audience cheers and applauds. Della Porta steps forward with a smug bow, bends over the wooden trunk — his spindly hand aglow for an instant amid a swarm of motes, its shadow huge across the canvas backdrop — and shuts its angled lid. The panorama goes dark.

The girl is murmuring something about apertures, biconvex lenses, mirrored bowls, but Crivano excuses himself and stumbles from the room. In the great hall, the servants are removing the curtains and panels from the windows, letting the light through. The children pour in from the courtyard, laughing and shouting, wearing bits of their fathers' armor, waving their dull swords. Crivano sweeps between them to the peristyle, stepping over their sham plaster rampart, filling his lungs with warm air.

More servants are clearing away the banquet table; he passes them on his way to the courtyard's far end, where low box-hedges form concentric rings. An oval sundial stands at their center, polished broccatello on a gray limestone base; its iron gnomon, set near the analemma's top, puts the hour near the twenty-first bell. The breeze has picked up and the haze has dissipated; a few scraps of high cloud fleck the sky, moving toward the horizon with surprising swiftness. Crivano is suddenly weary. He seats himself on a curved bench and watches the gnomon's shadow creep across the glittering marble until the girl finds him again.

She's watching from outside the hedges, her face veiled, her nervous fingers bunched before her. Crivano comes to his feet, removes his cap, and stares evenly at her until she joins him. They sit for a while in uneasy silence. She's older than he thought; probably past twenty. Something about her reminds him of Cyprus, although he can't say what. Who are you? he asks.

I'm called Perina, she says. I am Senator Contarini's cousin.

Who is your father?

My parents are not living. I never knew my father. I grew up in this house.

Bells ring the hour all over the city: a bright throbbing drone, like the sound of heavy rain on a roof. Crivano's hands have begun to tremble; he clamps them on his knees to still

344

them. So, he says, you're a nun.

She makes a sour face. I'm an educant, she says. At the convent school of Santa Caterina. I have taken no vows.

They must expect that you will do so. Or you would not have liberty to come and go as you please.

Through the years, Perina says, the sisters of Santa Caterina have benefited greatly from the bequests of the Contarini family. This conveys advantages.

I see.

Near the banquet table, a child charging blind beneath his enormous bronze helmet has collided with the trunk of an almond tree. He lands on his back in the grass; his helmet clatters away. After a moment he sits up and begins to wail. Crivano smiles.

I am told, Perina says, that you fought the Turks at Lepanto. Is this true?

Other boys are laughing at the sobbing child. An older girl shushes them, stoops to tend his bloodied nose. *You fought the Turks at Lepanto,* Crivano thinks. Not simply: *You fought at Lepanto.* An interesting specificity. Yes, Crivano says. It is true.

I should like very much to hear about your role in the battle, Dottore Crivano, if you are willing to speak of it.

A flurry of black-and-yellow tits flaps into view over the roof, hunting treetops for cankerworms. They weave and dive acrobatically over the children's heads, paying them no mind, and are paid no mind in return.

That was very long ago, Crivano says, and I fear the passage of years has put my memories at some variance. No doubt you have read them already, but I must say you'll be better served by the famous accounts previously set down by veterans of the battle, if only because those men took up their quills so soon after laying down their swords.

Of course, Perina says. Still, I am greatly interested in the particularities of your experience. If you can bring yourself to share them with me, I would be grateful.

You would even, Crivano continues, find more clarity and better understanding in the writings of recent historians of the Republic who were *not* there, who have never been to war at all, who have no direct knowledge of any territory save that of their studious libraries. The ultimate import of such an event, lady, can least be discerned in the unformed chaos of its midst. My memories of Lepanto are spun mostly from smoke, and noise, and the dead and dying bodies of men. I am sure that many brave acts occurred on that grave day, but I took part in none, nor did I witness any. For myself and my fellows it amounted to a long inglorious clamber to keep our lives, one our majority prosecuted without success. Do not lament the loss of such chronicles, lady. And do not believe that the stories of these fallen men are interred with them. They are in fact the very soil that vanishes their bones.

By the time Crivano has finished speaking, his own voice sounds distant, as if reaching him from a nearby room. His vision has tunneled to exclude all but fragments of the girl: her folded hands, her powdered breasts, her veiled face.

But don't you see, dottore? the girl says, and grips his forearm with a steady hand. It is precisely this chaos, precisely this derangement, that I seek knowledge of!

He can't be certain through the veil, but it looks as if her eyes are bright with tears. Aware of her cool fingers on his wrist and of a sudden lurching grind in his belly, he shuts his own eyes and clenches his jaw. Why? he asks.

Her fingers uncurl; he feels her shift on the bench. Because, she says, I have come to believe that in such disarray resides the truth.

The tits flutter overhead. *Eee-cha,* they say. *Eee-cha, eee-cha.*

My sincerest apologies, Crivano says. I wish to continue this discussion, lady, and I have no desire to be rude, but is there by chance a nearby privy to which you can direct me? I fear that I have become ill.

The girl is on her feet, agitated, tugging his arm; he permits her to lead him into the back half of the palace, down a long corridor. From among her apologies and offers of aid and expressions of concern he gleans directions to the privy, and hurriedly takes his leave.

He's able to avoid soiling himself, but only narrowly. With his citizen's robe hung on a peg, his hose around his boot-tops, he sits over the aperture in the worn wood and rests his head on the brick wall and voids himself, sweating and shivering by turns. He feels restored almost instantly, and then foolish, and then, as he's tidying up, he's struck by the sudden desire to simply remain forever in this small reeking room, hiding from the eyes of others, estranged even from his own machinations. He draws long breaths and closes his eyes and imagines himself as a pupa, secreted in the fecund soil while the busy insect world swarms on around him.

When at last he emerges the girl has gone, but young Marco Contarini is standing in the hallway. Are you well enough to see my father, dottore? he asks. He had hoped for a few minutes of your time.

29

The senator's private apartments are on a mezzanine below the piano nobile, on the side of the house that looks out on the Grand Canal. Waiting in the anteroom while Marco consults with his father, flipping through an octavo edition of Cardano's *De Varietate Rerum* that he finds open on a table, Crivano is aware of the insistent clap of waves against the palace walls, the faint song of a boatman rowing by. A song he knows, or once knew in his youth.

Then a bolt clicks, the heavy inner door swings open, and it's Verzelin, stumbling forward on dead legs, his sackcloth shroud overgrown by eelgrass, his eyesockets picked clean by crabs. His accusing mouth spills a torrent of black mud down his chest, the mud alive with ghost-white wriggling things.

Crivano recoils — his scapulae gouge the wall, the octavo slides to the floor — but it's not Verzelin, of course it's not, only young Marco, emerging from his father's library. By the blessed virgin, dottore, he says. What on earth is the matter?

Nothing! Crivano sputters. Not a thing. The lingering effect of a minor sickness, that is all. I ate a poisonous fragment of quail at my locanda last night, and it has been slow to vacate. My apologies. There is no cause for concern.

That's unfortunate, dottore. You have my sympathy. You're at the White Eagle, aren't you? They're quite reputable, but no inn is altogether safe, particularly during the Sensa. You should reconsider my father's offer to stay here with us.

You're very kind, Crivano says, bending to fetch the dropped book. But the White Eagle is ideal for my purposes, and I wouldn't think of imposing on your busy household. After all, bad quail can turn up any locanda.

Marco narrows his eyes, cocks his head. I hope, he says, that my foolish cousin said nothing to upset or offend you.

A host of twitches convenes beneath Crivano's skin. Who? he says.

My cousin. Perina. The girl with whom —

Oh yes, of course! But no, not at all! She's a delight. Very poised. Clever.

Indeed, Marco says. Well, then. My father has asked me to apologize for the delay. He'll receive you shortly, if you have no objections to awaiting him here.

Crivano has no objections. Marco departs, and after a moment spent refocusing his faculties, Crivano continues his exploration of the room. In scholarly circles these chambers are among the most renowned in Christendom, whispered of in covetous tones from Warsaw to Lisbon. Many men would hazard propriety or commit grave offense for a passing glimpse of what he now dawdles among. Even the richness of the room's furnishings — the fireplace of serpentine and marble, the gilt frieze of allegories rendered in oils — pales beside what litters the tabletops and hangs from the walls. Glazed shards of Greek vases. Fragments of Roman sculpture.

Wooden cases filled with rare minerals, curious crystals, hides of strange beasts. A bewildering array of mechanisms for measurement and calculation. Scale models of siege engines and galleasses. Painted panels and canvases of great virtuosity and inventiveness.

Hesitant to touch anything, Crivano gravitates toward the last of these. A portrait of a bearded patrician, shunted into a dim corner by its larger neighbors, is the first to catch his eye. Cracked with age, its surface bears an image so precise in its detail as to be mistakable for a window, or a mirror. Impressive though it is, a chill lifelessness inheres in it — the antiseptic vacuity of a specimen — which might account for the prominence it cedes to other works.

The prime spot on the longest wall is occupied by something quite different, a jewel-toned scene from Ovid: bare-bosomed blond Europa, reclining on her garlanded white bull. More bovines appear in nearby frames, and one of these in particular captures Crivano's attention: a bucolic tableau of the autumn harvest. When Crivano weighs the busy composition against his own memories of a year on an Anatolian farm — his fourteenth year, the year after Lepanto, the year before the janissaries claimed him — it seems absurd, sketched after the fancy of a painter lacking aptitude for or interest in any accurate depiction of the practicalities of agriculture. The undifferentiated farmers, their wobbly stack of crated apples, the array of irrelevant tools: despite their silliness, they transfix him. Every detail seems designed to repudiate his own experience, to displace his faded memories with an abstract truth to which the painter alone controls access. The craftsman's bold hand has even hung a centaur in the distant clouds — clouds of tenebrous green that can't help but echo the spectral landscape conjured by della Porta's device.

The senator's gentle basso reaches him from across the room, like a hand laid upon his shoulder. Whatever its faults, he says, that canvas is my favorite. It pains me to no end, what has become of that man.

Crivano turns with a measured bow. The painter? he says. I don't know of him.

Senator Contarini has changed from his velvet robe into a black tunic of fine damask; he crosses the room to Crivano's side and leans against the edge of a table. The painter, he says, comes from Bassano del Grappa. He rose to prominence in the studio of his father Jacopo, who made great success with rustic scenes such as this. Many of our most ancient families delight in evocations of their distant holdings on the mainland, the source of so much of their wealth. If you have visited a noble house in this city, then I'll wager you have seen old Jacopo's work.

352

The senator reaches into a muddle of instruments and withdraws a magnifying lens, which he lifts to the painting's surface to examine the cloud-borne centaur. After the great fire in the doge's palace, he continues, Francesco — for Francesco is the given name of the one who painted this — moved his household to our city, in order to open a workshop of his own. The Great Council had entrusted to me the restoration of the palace, and I awarded Francesco a number of commissions. I believed that I saw in his work the promise of greatness. Greatness of a sort not witnessed in this city since the plague took Titian from us. That potential no longer has any hope of being realized. But who can say with certainty that I was wrong? Or am I no more than a mooncalf for concerning myself with idle matters such as these, instead of with galleys, armaments, fortifications, the various blunt cudgels of republic?

Crivano shifts his weight, watches the crystal lens roam the painted surface. If one is to wield power, he says, then one must control the image of power. Or so a certain clerk of Florence would have us believe.

Contarini chuckles. I tell myself as much, he says. Often I do. Of course, that same clever Florentine also warns us of men who dream about ideal republics that have never existed. These fools — how does he put it? — are so tormented by the notion that how we live is very distant from how we *ought* to live, that they disregard what *is* done in favor of what *should* be done. Thus do they invite ruin upon themselves, their realms, their families. I sometimes suspect that I should count myself among these dreaming fools. But this suspicion always fails to shame me.

The glass glides across the canvas: green clouds, red apples, tranquil brown cows. What became of him? Crivano says.

Of whom?

Of the painter, senator.

Contarini straightens, and his hand falls away, polishing the lens on his sleeve. Against his father's counsel, he says, Francesco began to associate with a group of learned young nobles. Politically aggressive, impatient with the Pope's dictates, involved with the search for secret knowledge. These were hardly the same nobles who had made his family wealthy. This conflicted allegiance made Francesco anxious, and his was not a temperament well-suited to anxiety. It seems clear in retrospect that he suffered from a certain infirmity of the mind. According to his poor wife, he became convinced that the sbirri of the Council of Ten were hounding him, and intended to do him harm. He believed that they attacked him with demoniacal magic while he slept, expunging and altering his memories. Or so has his wife testified. To me it seems equally likely that he simply sought release from the world, as some men do, and always have done. In any case, some six months ago he leapt from the highest window of his rented home. The fall did not kill him, but it broke him quite badly, and despite the exertions of our friend Dottore de Nis he remains bedridden today, unable to perform for himself even the most mundane of tasks. In his infinite mercy, God did not permit the natural progression to be upended in this instance: he granted heartbroken old Jacopo eternal rest in February. And any day now, I imagine, Francesco will follow his father to the grave.

Crivano furrows his brow and studies the canvas, as if it might disclose some hint of its maker's madness, but it remains as it was. I don't suppose, he says, the painter's fears could have had any substance?

His fears about the sbirri, you mean? Contarini says with a macabre smile. Or those concerning demonic assaults upon his sleeping mind?

About the sbirri.

The senator arches his eyebrows, shakes his head, looks away. I made inquiries, he says. I suppose as the man's chief patron I felt responsible to some degree. The wife's allegations seemed unlikely, but — owing to the peculiar activities of some of Francesco's young friends — not quite out of the question. The Inquisition claimed to know noth-

355

ing of him. The Ministry of Night pled ignorance as well.

And what of the Council of Ten?

Contarini claps his hands softly, cupping his palms as if to trap a fly, then flattens them, rubbing them slowly together. From the Ten, he says, I received only the routine obfuscation. They never deny anything, you know. Their potency rests on the common perception that their eyes and ears are everywhere. A denial might suggest that they don't know what you're talking about. Thus the truth of the matter must remain sealed in their leonine jaws, just as the secret of Francesco's spoilt memory can be known only —

Contarini breaks off with a laugh, claps Crivano on the arm. I was about to say that it's known only to Somnus and his three silent sons, he finishes. But you're on fine terms with dewy-winged Somnus, aren't you, dottore? You must be, given how swiftly you have reinstated me to his good graces.

This is an obvious ploy to abandon the subject — a clumsy one by the senator's standards — but Crivano can't thwart it gracefully. Instead, he forces a courteous chuckle. I'm pleased to hear this, senator, he says. I'm honored to have been of service in this small matter.

Hardly small when you're the sleepless one, dottore, Contarini says. He gestures toward the door in the corner, the door from which he emerged. Will you join me in my library? he says. It's in shameful disarray at the moment, but I'll give you a brief tour. If anything you find there will be of use in your studies, then we shall make arrangements.

You're far too kind, Senator, Crivano says. I dare not impose —

But the senator is already gone, leaving Crivano little choice but to follow him. As he steps to the library door, the old man's voice carries from inside. Here's an odd thing, it says. I know not — perhaps you will — whether this might be some lingering echo of the cowslip wine, or simply the consequence of prior deficiency, but for the past few nights, dottore, my dreams have been all but overwhelming in their intensity.

For an instant Crivano stands paralyzed at the library's threshold, stunned at the plentitude before him, before he manages to venture inside. Rather larger than the anteroom he just quit, this chamber is so loaded with treasure as to seem smaller, little more than a closet. Its walls appear at first to be constructed entirely from paper and leather: new octavos, old quartos, ancient codices, some piled flat, some with their banded edges showing, others spine-out in the modern style, and none of them chained. Only after a hard blinking glance do slivers of oak begin to materialize: a right-angled grid of shelves and cubbyholes that undergirds everything, keeping it in place. What meager territory remains unclaimed by bookcases is given over to diagrams, schematics, the sketches of engineers and architects, displayed in simple wooden frames. Crivano's vision flits between them — real and imagined structures exploded by eye and pencil onto featureless landscapes of white — until it locates a familiar image: the clean symmetrical façade of the new Church of the Redeemer.

This recognition comes with vertiginous dizziness. That unearthly white temple on the Giudecca, he thinks, was once no more than this: a few lines on paper, a notion blooming in a man's skull. Just so this palace in which he now stands, all the volumes bowing the shelves around him, the black boat that brought him here — indeed, the entire city: all of it precipitated from thousands of skulls over the course of long centuries. Just so the mirror-thieving scheme that now carries him in its wake: hatched by the fertile intellect of the haseki sultan. Just so the death of poor Verzelin: the rank issue of his own conspiring brain. Just so every subtle or sensible thing beneath the sun: once only an idea in the mind of God.

A heavy walnut chair stands a few inches from Crivano, its back and arms worked with elaborate designs, and he puts a hand on it to buttress himself, then steps forward and sinks into it. Already seated at his massive desk,

Contarini arranges and rearranges the chaos of documents on its surface as he speaks.

These dreams of mine, he says, are no mundane sifting of the day's affairs. They are eruptions from the depths of my most secret heart. Faces that death shrouded long ago from my eyes, faces I recall only from inferior portraits I've passed for years without regard — my mother, my father, my brothers and sisters, my own lost children, even the wet-nurses and the favored stewards of my infant home — these faces haunt me in sleep, appearing as vividly to me as you do now. They have led me along corridors of reminiscence to times and localities I had utterly forgotten, where I have spent whole nights feasting on details I never remarked upon my initial visitations. What is most confounding of all, Vettor, is the haste by which these dream-shades are queered and dispersed by the first morning rays that penetrate my feeble old eyes. What in sleep was pure becomes base and ridiculous. Please understand that I have no wish to avoid these dreams. On the contrary, I find myself rising from them with calm suffusing my spirit, with fervor quickening my steps. I simply regard them with wonderment, as one might a new comet or a chimeric beast, and I seek to understand them. Have you any advice to share with an inquisitive old man on such a trifling matter?

Crivano has been only half-listening; he

shifts slightly in his seat. There is a substantial corpus of literature on dreams, he says, but my own expertise in the area is far from complete. Perhaps you will permit me to study the issue further, to meditate on it for a few days, before I conceive a diagnosis. There may well be physic to help clarify these phantasms.

Of course, dottore. My curiosity is inflamed, but my urgency is not great. And I shall myself seek out the writings you've mentioned. I must confess that I have already been lured into the pages of the *Oneirocritica* of Ephesius, a book whose utility in these chambers until recently consisted of flattening curled paper on humid afternoons. It is a strange and wonderful thing, dottore, for a man of my age to awaken feeling younger, with the sense that the daylit world has grown sharper and more vivid before his eyes. It is surprising, too, to find the invigorating agent linked so closely to memories of the past, changed though those memories might be by the lens of the dreaming mind. It is not generally a tonic for old men, this act of remembering. Don't you agree?

Crivano notes the trenchant cast of the senator's white eyebrows, and he takes a moment to respond. I suppose, he says, that that depends on what is being remembered. Dottore de Nis has spoken to me of one you might consult on this matter. An expert on the art of memory, hailing from Nola, who is currently a guest in the home of Lord Zuanne Mocenigo.

Contarini spits out a rough laugh. Yes, he says. I've met the Nolan of whom you speak. An interesting fellow. Disagreeable. Quite deluded, I think. I understand from my colleagues at Padua that he has applied for their vacant chair in mathematics, which, from what I can follow of this man's thinking, seems somewhat akin to the Turkish sultan's chief astrologer seeking to become the next pope. I have begun writing letters in support of one of his competitors — the son of the famed lutenist Vincenzo Galilei, lately resident in Pisa — who seems rather promising despite his relative youth. You learned of the Nolan from Tristão, you say?

That's correct, senator.

I see, Contarini says. I hope you will forgive an old man his harangues, Vettor, if I remind you to exercise caution with Dottore de Nis.

Crivano gives the senator a broad, empty smile. As always, I receive your advice with gratitude, he says, but I have seen nothing at all in Dottore de Nis's conduct worthy of censure.

You would not. Nor would I. In fact, I would trust — I have trusted — Tristão de Nis with my life. The pressing issue is not what we see, but what the Inquisition sees.

Crivano smoothes his beard, runs a thumb

across his pursed lips. I am told, he says, that the Inquisition is weak in the territories of the Republic. Is this not so?

It is indeed so. And it is aware of its weakness. And like a starving animal, it now hungers after anything more vulnerable than itself. Jews and Turks are now entirely safe within our city, provided they identify themselves and keep to their approved areas. Likewise, all established Christian families have little to fear. But for new Christians like Tristão — for any person who navigates the boundaries between the discrete communities of our polis — dangers do remain. Because the conversions of the Jews of Portugal were coerced by King Manuel, the sincerity of Portuguese Christians is always suspect here. Dottore de Nis has many friends among the learned men of the Ghetto, including several widely reputed to be alchemists and magi. I also know him to be acquainted with Turkish scholars. The great affection he engenders among noble families — members of this household foremost among them — has thusfar kept him above reproach. But if the wrong person were to denounce him, it could be very bad.

Do you believe Tristão to be sincere in his profession of faith, Senator?

In the end, what you or I or anyone else believes will not matter.

Of course, Crivano says. I understand

362

completely. But I humbly put the question to you again. Do you believe that Dottore de Nis is sincere?

A flash of irritation clouds Contarini's face, then dissipates. He reaches across the desk to lift a large hexagonal crystal — perfectly clear but for a few fine capillaries of gold — that weights a stack of his correspondence. He shifts the crystal absently from palm to palm. Do you read Boccaccio, Vettor? he asks.

Not in a great number of years.

Perhaps you will recall a story that Boccaccio puts in the mouth of Melchizedek the Jew. Melchizedek tells the sultan the tale of an exceedingly wealthy old man, whose family passes to its most favored son of each generation a ring of great antiquity. When the time comes for this old man to write his will, he is unable to choose between his three equally virtuous sons, and instead hires a skilled jeweler to fashion two copies of the ring. So exact are these replicas that after the old man's death, no one, not even the jeweler, can tell which is the original. So it is, Melchizedek declares, with the Christians, the Muhammadans, the Jews. How is one to resolve this puzzle? If the three rings are truly identical, is it blasphemous to wonder whether this should be a concern for mortal men? Whether it matters at all?

Tongue-tied like a schoolboy, Crivano stares at the insignia carved into the senator's desk, unable to think of any response but one: *the old man is dead.* He opts to keep his silence.

The senator places the rock-crystal in a sunbeam, rotating it on its point. Colored rays sweep the desk like spokes of an invisible wheel. On its smooth sides Crivano can make out the iridescent whorls of Contarini's fingerprints.

This afternoon, Contarini says, you met my young cousin.

Perina. Yes.

She had questions for you.

Yes. She did.

Contarini draws a deep breath and lets it out. For the first time today, he looks old. I had asked Perina, he says, to be delicate and respectful, in a manner befitting a young lady of her station. But I fear that her youth in this house suffered a lack of womanly paragons for such behavior, and thus her tread is often heavier than it should be. For this you have my apologies.

No apology is needed, Senator. I enjoyed speaking with —

Contarini quiets him with a raised palm. Please, he says. Grant an old diplomat a few frank words to ease his guilty conscience. Perina sought to interrogate you about the Battle of Lepanto, for reasons you have perhaps by now ascertained. I indulged her, not only by arranging today's encounter, but also by withholding from you my knowledge of her intentions. I allowed you to be ambushed. I had imagined this to be a thing of small consequence — an amusing stratagem to disrupt your usual reserve, to encourage you to speak freely of your past deeds — but I see now that I was presumptuous.

He lays his heavy crystal down, angling a thin rainbow smear across the desktop, over the white surface of an unfinished epistle. On it, Crivano can make out a careful sketch of the Piazza, an inverted salutation written in French. The sun is dropping over the canal, lengthening Contarini's shadow. The cast spectrum has already begun to fade.

I never went to war, Contarini says. Like many of my fellow senators, I came of age during a peaceful era in our Republic's history. I and my colleagues should be grateful for this. Instead, we are envious. We see these younger men, our sons and our cousins, who tasted firsthand the victory at Lepanto, who can always respond to our pretense of aged wisdom by saying: *But I was there!* And we sigh, and we dream of the fame we might have won if only Fortune had smiled upon us as she did upon them. In short, we imagine war to be a crucible for forging glory. It is not. It is a waste and a horror — the product of the worst failures of velvety statesmen like myself — and to envy any man a brush with it is an impious folly.

Senator, Crivano says, you prosecute this suit against yourself with too much zeal. Were there no glories to be found in wars, they would have ceased long ago.

Oh, glories can indeed be found in them. And where they are lacking, there they can be placed. The installation of glory after the fact is a trade, like any other. If you have seen the new paintings in the doge's palace — miserable Francesco himself supplied one — then you know that I have participated in this unlovely business. Simply the price of governance, as the Florentine clerk said: the maintenance of the *imago urbis.* But as I sat in that dark room today, listening to Signore della Porta's absurd encomium, I realized how noxious his words must seem to one who has seen battle with his own eyes, and not through a glass, darkly. Great God, that poem! Is it not startling, the way we still laud the old blind doge after all these centuries? A crusader who made war on Christians, whose ghost has all but escorted the infidel to our gates? But our poets and our painters cut him from the tapestry of his times, they push him ever forward through our history, until he comes to signify nothing but the valor of the Republic. Thus is he emptied: a perfect surface to reflect our greatness back to us. This will happen with Bragadin, too, in time. And with Lepanto. Perhaps it is already happening.

In Bologna, Crivano says, I heard those two names fall often from thoughtless lips. But in this city they seem subjects wreathed always with silence, best not raised at all. I confess that this has been a source of confusion for me.

The senator nods. I had hoped that the city would welcome you more warmly, Vettor, he says. That they would be more overt in their expressions of gratitude. But it was difficult for me to arrange even the few paltry gestures you have seen.

I am hardly disappointed by my reception here, senator. I meant only —

That you were surprised. That is understandable. But the explanation is simple. Had your galley not been captured by the Turks — or had you somehow returned with the relics of Bragadin in hand only a year after Lepanto — then today you would probably be married into a great family, grooming your sons for their eventual dogeship. As it is, the Republic quietly made a separate peace with the sultan during your long confinement, renouncing all claims to Cyprus. Then that sultan died, and a new sultan took his place, one who is friendly to us in matters of trade. Today, the relics of valiant Bragadin that you so bravely recovered serve only to remind us that he suffered and died for nothing. Furthermore, to diplomats like myself Lepanto has become an inconvenience best abandoned to the past. So far as the history of the Republic is concerned, the battle yielded naught but glory and corpses, and may as well not have happened at all. Let the poets and the painters take care of it. You heard about Polidoro, I suppose. Do you remember Polidoro?

This is a name Crivano has not heard spoken in years, one that his sinews recall more than his brain: in the instant it takes him to place it, his limbs have already grown stiff with fear. Of course, he says. The man who stole Bragadin's remains from the Turkish arsenal. He gave them to me, and when I escaped, I gave them to the bailo in Galata.

Polidoro also escaped. Did you know that? The Turks recaptured him, and they tortured him most foully, but some weeks later he was somehow free again. He now resides in Verona, the city of his birth. A few years ago he petitioned the senate for a monthly pension of sixteen ducats, citing his heroism in the Republic's service. The senate granted him five.

Contarini is watching Crivano closely. Crivano shrugs. I knew Polidoro only as a pair of hands in the darkness, he says.

Just as well, Contarini says. The man is a simple thief. Thieving put him at the oars of one of our galleys. That galley was taken at sea, so he came to row for the Turks. Winter brought him to the arsenal, where Bragadin's relics were kept. Then thieving brought him back to the Republic again. I confess my own vote was to give the man nothing. Why should the Republic reward a thief for being a thief? Last week, an asp bit my enemy. This week, it has appeared in my garden. Do I offer it food on a dish of gold? No. I reach for my stick.

Some of the silk has gone from Contarini's voice; weariness is gathering, settling in. There will be no tour of the library today. Crivano studies the dry lines in the man's face, the slight tremor in his strong left hand. What grand dreams must visit that snowy head, he thinks.

I have a small favor to ask, the senator says.

Of course.

Tomorrow, my family and I are to depart the city. The summer is upon us, and the warm weeks ahead are to be spent in the more pleasant air of our mainland villa. This evening, my vulgar young cousin is to return to the convent school of Santa Caterina. It would mean a great deal to me, and a great deal more to her, if you can spare a few idle hours to call on her while we are away. I suspect that she was a bit of an affliction upon you this afternoon, but I give you my word that she can at times be charming. Whether you choose to visit her or not, I hope you'll make use of the library here while I am gone. Rigi, the porter, will grant you entry.

The sun breaks under the window's upper arch, and the senator's features vanish into silhouette. Crivano squints and looks down at the desktop. Of the spectrum the crystal cast only an orange sliver remains at the desk's dentiled edge. Crivano's chest feels as if it has shrunk and tightened, like the wrinkled skin of a dry fruit.

You are very generous, Senator. I shall comply happily with your request. May I also ask a question of you?

You may.

Why did Perina wish to speak with me about Lepanto?

The senator's shadowed form is very still for a long time. She didn't tell you? he finally says.

No, Senator.

I had thought she would have.

A brightly festooned galley passes on the canal outside, on its way to the Bacino. Young men in bright stockings sing and caper on its quarterdeck. The last night of the Sensa, Crivano remembers.

Perina, the senator says, had a brother who was killed at Lepanto. A brother she never knew. She was too young, you see. Did she tell you — who she is?

Crivano tries to moderate his breathing, the tone of his voice. Through the window, the blazing sun seems to spend all its dying light on him. She said she is your cousin, he says. She told me only that.

Yes. She is the youngest daughter of my kinsman Pietro Glissenti, whom I am certain you remember from your youth in Cyprus. Your father was his chief secretary.

My God.

Pardon me?

Her brother —

Was named Gabriel, I believe. He was quite young when he died. About your own age, I should guess.

That is not possible.

I'm sorry?

Lord Glissenti's daughter died in the plague. She and her mother fled Cyprus before the invasion, and they came here, and they both died in the plague, seventeen years ago. So I was told.

And that is all quite correct, dottore. But you are speaking, I believe, of Lord Glissenti's elder daughter. Perina left Cyprus in her mother's womb. She was born here. When her mother and sister died, she was five years old. Her father and her two eldest brothers were slain at Famagusta. And as I said, her youngest brother, Gabriel, died at Lepanto. She never knew those men. But you knew Gabriel quite well, didn't you?

Crivano realizes with a start that he's been staring at the setting sun: when he turns toward the senator, the man's face is blotted by a drifting gobbet of green. Gabriel was my

371

dearest friend in my boyhood, Crivano says. We came here together from Cyprus to enroll at Padua, and we both signed on as bowmen when we heard that Nicosia had fallen. I was next to him when he died. He was blown to bits by a cannonball.

I see. When you narrate your experiences to Perina, dottore, you might consider the omission of that last detail.

I don't believe it, Crivano says. I cannot believe it.

But Crivano does believe it. He knows it to be true. Or true enough.

Perhaps now, Contarini says, you can see why I was eager for you to make Perina's acquaintance, even if my coordination of the event was shamefully inept. You are for her the only tangible connection to her family's past, about which she is quite curious. And — if you will forgive me once again for speaking frankly — I think it's clear that a close friendship with Perina could be a substantial boon to you, as well. I am an old man, with few years remaining on this earth, so I shall come to my point. Perina is my charge, and I have great fondness for her, but she is not my child. The dowry I am reasonably able to supply for her is insufficient to attract a noble husband, and until now I have been at a loss to find a suitable match for her among the citizenry. As I said, her dowry will not be that of a Contarini daughter, but it will be a

considerable sum, particularly for a gentleman like yourself: not old, but no longer
young, and seeking to become established in
short order. Keep in mind, too, that she is
the last of the Glissenti, a noble line. Her
children will sit in the Great Council. But,
enough! I have said enough. Visit her. Speak
with her. Consider.

Everywhere Crivano looks he sees pulsing
green shapes — ghost-images of the sun,
obliterating everything. The floor beneath the
chair seems to move, as if the palace has
slipped off its piling and now floats freely on
the waves. A sound fills his ears like someone
blowing softly into them.

But, Senator, Crivano whispers, the young
lady is wedded to Christ. Is she not?

She is not. She is *betrothed* to Christ. And I
am not at all certain that he is the best
husband for her. No man could be more
constant, of course, but it is not difficult to
imagine others who might be more attentive.
Are you feeling all right, Vettor? In this light
you look quite pale.

30

By the time Crivano is on his feet again —
roused from his faint by a pinch of sal volatile
from the senator's laboratory, fortified with a
glass of strong brandy — the sun has nearly
set, and he's late for the Uranici banquet. He

makes his apologies, says his farewells, and pulls on his cloak, stepping through a side entrance off the courtyard, where the grizzled porter packs crates for the trip to the mainland. Old Rigi trains a skeptical eye on Crivano as he rushes past.

The Morosini palace is halfway back to the Riva del Vin, on this same bank of the Grand Canal. The fastest way to reach it is by boat, but Crivano feels like walking, so he walks. He needs to think, to clear his head, to situate himself. If that means he must miss the banquet as a result, well, at the moment he's not particularly hungry.

The Sensa is approaching its frenzied end. Every palace spills its inhabitants into the dusk: greasy boys with skintight hose stretched across their buttocks, plump girls divulging their breasts' upper hemispheres to the cooling air. Crowds of them teeter into boats, parade through secluded alleyways. All wear masks. Soon the night's first bell will ring, linkboys will emerge to sculpt the darkness with their lanterns, and the city will begin to play at forgetfulness once more: what is permitted, what is forbidden. In the milling street Crivano feels invisible again, a tessera blended into a mosaic.

His feet move him at the pace of his thoughts, carrying him past glazed windows, frescoed walls, the opened and closing shutters of unfamiliar thoroughfares. No matter which way it roams or how far, his mind returns always to the same location: the girl Perina, the question that her existence poses. *How is it possible? How is it possible? How is it possible?*

He and the Lark left Nicosia some nine months before it fell, almost two years before their fathers and brothers died at Famagusta. The news came while the fleet was at anchor at Guiscardo, about to sail inland for fresh water. The Lark had been scraping the pan of his arquebus, blowing down its barrel. *We have just gotten word, my boys, that Famagusta has fallen.* Captain Bua on the quarterdeck, his voice quaking with rage. *General Bragadin, God rest his soul, surrendered to Lala Mustafa with honor. And that son of a whore, he cut off his nose and his ears. The infidel savages flayed him alive, they stuffed his skin with straw, they paraded it through the streets on the back of a cow. And they will suffer heartily, my boys, for what they have done.* The expression on the Lark's face — anguished, frightened, furious, thrilled — echoed the contents of his own heart. Fatherless now. The last of their clans. Both thirteen years old.

Until today he has never once tried to imagine what it must have been like for the women: searching the harbor at Kyrenia for some Genoese or Ragusan captain willing to make arrangements, then crushed in the dark hold of a rolling ship among splintered crates and bolts of cloth, palms clamped over their children's wet faces, because what if the Turks were to hear? During the sack of Tunis in 1574, word got round to Crivano's orta that the wife of a Spanish officer had barricaded herself and her five daughters in a house on the harbor's edge. The taunting janissaries took an hour to break her door, by which time the wife had smashed each young skull with a belaying pin and slit her own throat. What stories did young Perina hear from the downturned mouths of her mother and sister before the plague came for them? What might she remember of those stories now? How is it possible?

Could Narkis know about her? It seems unlikely. If he did, why would he care? A pure product of the Ottoman boy-tribute system, he's always seemed perplexed by the tangle of agnatic bonds that defines the Frankish world. *I come from Macedonia, from high in the mountains. Before the Ottomans took me, I had never seen a church, or a mosque. I had seen no writing of any kind. I had not seen gold, or glass. Now I have traveled to Mecca, to Punjab, to Kathmandu, to China. I do not think of my family. If they ever try to think of me, then they have no way of understanding what it is I have become.* Likewise, Narkis could hardly understand what Perina signifies to Crivano. But what *does* Perina signify? If none but Crivano himself can say, can she be made to mean whatever he wishes? Can she be said to mean anything at all?

What if the haseki sultan knows? The idea stops him in his tracks, as if the wall he walks beside has just collapsed to reveal an unsuspected maze of hidden passageways; for an instant he's lost, dislodged from whatever current has been guiding his mindless path through the streets. A short while ago he crossed a bridge. Was it the bridge behind the house of the Garzoni, or the one behind the Corner palace? He dithers for a moment at a constricted junction until a pack of revelers — four wigged and rouged young men wearing ladies' gowns, in pursuit of a plump fifth diapered like a baby and otherwise nude — charges around the north fork and scrambles past him. Crivano spits a curse at their backs, continues the way they came.

He met the haseki sultan only once. Her summons arrived some months prior to his first encounter with Narkis, and Crivano thought nothing of it at the time: she was negotiating with a group of Genoese bankers and needed an interpreter's services. *I have heard favorable reports about you, Messer Crivano.* The sound of that old name on the air — not *Tarjuman,* the name the viziers had given him — raised gooseflesh under his fine

377

new caftan. *You were born in Cyprus, yes? Tell me about that.*

Even in middle age she was relentlessly beautiful, nestled like a jewel among her cushions. Her scarlet entari worked with gold thread, the gömlek that billowed from her sleeves sheer as spidersilk. Terrifying. Grotesque. Like anything made beautiful by pure necessity must be. *And after the fleet returned from Tunis, your orta went east to fight the Safavids, is that so?* A full hour of questions, each one put to him in his native tongue. Her speech inelegant and tedious, but clear, and free from errors. The Genoese bankers never arrived; in time, Crivano was dismissed. Practice, he assumed. Although he never could decide whether the haseki sultan was practicing a language new to her, or one from years before that she'd forgotten. He'd heard the rumors, of course: the sultan's favorite concubine was the daughter of one of the Republic's most ancient families, installed in the harem after being abducted by pirates from a family galley when she was little more than a child. Crivano had always found the tale difficult to believe. Having now spoken with her, he figured her more plausibly as the issue of Dalmatian fisherfolk than any sort of displaced Frankish noble. Still, it was remarkable, wasn't it, how rapidly the sultan's favor turned toward the Republic after this girl bore him a healthy son?

So the rumors persisted. And always at their margins, in whispers that were not even whispers, a more profound fantasy lurked. If this haseki sultan truly was a child of the Republic, wasn't it possible — however remotely — that her supposed abduction had been orchestrated from the outset by the Council of Ten? That an unlikely ploy to place one of their operatives inside the harem had succeeded beyond their wildest hopes? That their girlish spy had risen to become the Turks' de facto empress, and had birthed the sultan his heir? It was marvelous and perverse to imagine: where for centuries all the armies of Christendom had been thwarted, this once-nubile creature had prevailed. Small wonder Lepanto could be so easily forgotten.

A ridiculous scenario. But like a weaving drunkard measuring his steps, the more Crivano tries to steer his mind away, the more insistently it returns. If it were so — and it couldn't be — what would it mean for him? If the long puppet-strings that guide his movements do not terminate in Constantinople, but merely round the pulley of the haseki sultan to end somewhere in the darkening streets he now treads, how would that change the nature of his mission? Where might the unknown architect of this peculiar conspiracy have placed Perina in its structure? How is it possible?

However Crivano tries to conceive the plot, it refuses to hold a shape, and remains formless as a gob of spit. What preoccupies him in these speculations about the haseki sultan — in these conjectures about a woman who, so far as he can judge, simply hungers after flat mirrors and intends to see them manufactured by her subjects — are the echoes of his own story he hears in them. A child of the Republic sails the pirate-haunted seas, there to be redirected and transformed. A Christian child bows toward Mecca; who can say what is in that child's heart? When, after many years, the child encounters a face from home, what recognitions occur? Which are disallowed? Which can be evaded?

How is it possible? It's a stupid question. The girl's existence seems improbable only because he's never considered that it could be the case. He went so long without news of home or family, without giving them a thought. He had to. His eventual freedom depended on it, on his seeming indifference. When he needed signposts and antecedents, he never sought them in the world, but only in myths and fancies half-remembered from his childhood, refashioned according to his momentary need. He always found them. Was his indifference only seeming? If so, what did it conceal? These are better questions, but they slide from his attention like quicksilver on an ointment slab, and he's disinclined to pursue them.

Shouts from the campo ahead: a group of portly nobles costumed as New World savages — wooden clubs, fur loincloths, twigs and dry leaves in their hair — chasing after a gang of common boys, hollering propositions. *Show us that downy-wreathed cock of yours, you young devil!* The boys laugh and run toward Crivano; the handsome one in the lead kicks a leather ball before him with unworried ease. Firelight through a casino window brushes the boy's face, and for an instant he's the Lark — pausing to catch his breath in a football game, plucking ripe medlars from a fruit stall in the Rialto, dancing a galliard across the deck of the *Gold and Black Eagle.*

Then the boy skids to a halt, stops the ball with his toe, takes a few limping sidelong steps while beckoning to his comrades, and he's no longer the Lark, no longer a boy at all, but the crop-headed whore from last night, the one with the warty foot and the dye-stained hands. As they rush by, he sees that each of her companions is also a young woman, a whore attired as a boy, no doubt to tempt rarefied fancies.

As the last of them passes, Crivano's gaze returns to the first, to her smirking face. A fine evening to you, dottore, she says, and doffs her cap with a stifled giggle. Then she gives the ball a mighty kick, and is gone.

In the next moment the sham savages are upon him, slowed hopelessly by their rope-and-wood sandals, hooting like jungle apes as they shoulder past. One of their number — bald and squat, with the face of a cruel idiot child — takes a halfhearted swing at Crivano's head with his cudgel; Crivano ducks, and cracks the man across the ribs with his own stick. The blow echoes with a hollow meaty sound, but the man lumbers on, unperturbed, after the fleeing whores. Too drunk to notice pain. Tomorrow he'll have a pretty bruise he won't recall receiving, at the very least. Crivano half-hopes the cur will black out unnoticed in a sottoportego somewhere, drown in the night on his own blood.

Here's your light, dottore!

A torch bobs toward him, sweating fiery beads of pitch that vanish as they strike the pavement, clutched in the hand of a linkboy of about seven years. On the opposite side of the campo, under the star-sifted indigo sky, Crivano can make out the orange lights of more mooncursers, probably the elder brothers of this one.

I'm looking for the Morosini house, Crivano says.

It's nearby, the linkboy says, then narrows his soot-rimmed little eyes. But it's not easy to find, he says. I could show you.

Crivano sighs. He's late, tired, suddenly famished, and he dips into his coin-purse to sprinkle dull green copper into the urchin's upraised palm.

31 .

The Morosini house is on the Riva del Carbon, just north of the church of San Luca; it's small, or seems so in the shadow of the looming Grimani palace two doors down. Candlelight pours from every window of every floor. Watching the bright and dark shapes that pass before those portals, listening the many-tongued chatter within, Crivano recalls a wicker cage of colored birds he once saw offered for sale by a wild-eyed Somali boatman, somewhere near Heliopolis on the delta of the Nile.

Two torches blaze in sconces at the open landward door, and Crivano brushes past the linkboy to walk inside. He wonders how he'll manage even rudimentary exchanges with his learned peers given the disturbance he's just suffered. Were it not for Tristão he would not have come tonight — yet even as he thinks this, he can feel his body disentangling from its shock, comforted by rote performances of salutation and gratitude.

A footman hastens from the water-gate to greet him, then disappears and returns with the steward, a muscular Provençal with a neat black beard and a stoical expression. Good evening, dottore, he says with a deep bow.

The Brothers Morosini welcome you.

I apologize for my tardiness, Crivano says as he surrenders his stick and his robe. Has the banquet concluded?

With the sweep of an arm, the steward invites him upstairs. The staff is clearing the table now, he says. Tonight's address is soon to begin.

A muffled catlike yowl issues from Crivano's empty stomach. I see, he says. If there is any way I might be granted access to whatever esculents remain, I'd be grateful. I'm afraid unforeseen circumstances prevented me from taking a meal prior to —

Of course, the steward says as they emerge onto the piano nobile. I'm sure we can make some arrangement. Forgive me, dottore, but may I ask your name?

Crivano, Crivano says. Vettor Crivano.

The man snaps to a halt, clears his throat, inhales deeply, and his stentorian voice echoes from the beamed ceiling. *Gentlemen!* he says. *Dottore Vettor Crivano!*

There are nearly two dozen men in the great hall, divided into shifting groups of twos and threes and fours. A few look his way and nod. Crivano sees nobles and citizens, lawyers and physicians, scholars and friars; he overhears discussions in German, French, English, Latin, and the language of court, along with the Republic's own tongue. Under the hum of voices he can hear a soft chime of plucked strings, but his sight finds no players. Neither does it locate Dottore de Nis.

Nearby, a pair of young patricians argues spiritedly with a third: slightly older, with an absurd plume of hair, attired in a busked and bombasted Spanish doublet that even Crivano can recognize as outmoded. But Lord Mocenigo, one of the pair says, the ships of the Turk suffer worse than do our own the assaults of the uskok pirates. Surely blame must lie with the Hapsburg princes who ply them with weapons and gold?

So, Crivano thinks, this buffoon is Zuanne Mocenigo: the Nolan's patron and host. He casts his eyes about the hall, trying to guess who the Nolan himself might be, until the elder of Mocenigo's interlocutors disengages and walks toward him. Greetings, dottore! the man says, seizing Crivano's arm. I must say, Tristão described you perfectly. I knew you at once.

If he erred at all, signore, Crivano says, it was no doubt from generosity. You, I gather, are one of my noble hosts, although I confess I know not which.

I'm Andrea Morosini. That's my brother Nicolò there, in debate with Lord Mocenigo. Come, I'll introduce you.

Milord, the steward says, forgive my intrusion, but the dottore has not yet taken his supper. If you'll permit me, I'll take him to the pantry now, and return him to you in a

385

moment.

Yes. Of course. Go with Hugo, dottore. He'll see you fed. Our Nolan friend is about to begin his lecture, but with any luck I can delay him. Oh, dottore?

Andrea takes Crivano's elbow as he's moving away. He's somewhat shorter than Crivano. Athletic, poised like an acrobat, but soft. He leans in close and speaks.

You did a brave thing at Constantinople, he says. No one can dispute that. My brother and I are proud to have you in our house.

Before Crivano can consider what might have prompted this commendation, the steward is leading him through the huge room, past the long banquet table, now almost bare. The dark terrazzo floor is flecked by stone chips of mossy gray and blackbird-beak orange; its polished surface — like that of an underground pool — returns Crivano's blurred image. As he walks, slow fireflies swarm before his drowned phantom self: the reflection of the candles on the brass chandeliers overhead.

To his right, through the door of a day-room, he glimpses the musicians: a sturdy black-beaded man with a lute and a Servite friar wrestling with a massive theorbo. They've paused in their playing for a good-humored squabble. No, the one with the lute says, plucking a repeated note. Down, he says. Tune down.

Crivano has passed the dayroom by the time he hears the Servite's response. Down? the friar says, twanging a bass string. You're deaf. Listen to that buzz!

The voice is familiar. Why? Crivano pauses, turns back, and meets the eye of a second friar just outside the dayroom door. This one is dressed in a tunic and scapular of matching bole: the habit of no order Crivano can name. Sharp-featured. Splenetic. A patchy chestnut beard, and the frail physique of a sickly boy. He's been conversing in Latin with a Hungarian baron while a bookish German youth looks on. Noting Crivano's gaze, the friar's eyes flash, his weak jaw snaps shut, and he counters with an insolent glower of his own.

Hunger has turned Crivano's temper foul; he's about to square his shoulders and call the man out when the steward takes hold of his elbow. Here, dottore, he says. This way. Before our hired girls depart with all the food.

Crivano permits himself to be led, and as they resume their course, realization dawns. The lean and quarrelsome friar, he thinks: that pompous little ass must be the Nolan.

The hirelings have removed the banquet to a storeroom off a nearby corridor; the steward dismisses them with handclaps and a few brusque words in Friulian. Let me set a place for you, dottore.

That's hardly necessary, Crivano says,

387

unsheathing the knife on his belt. You may leave me. I'll only be a moment.

He sets in immediately on the hindquarters of a jointed hare, then moves on to a flaky piece of mullet in a black-pepper glaze. Consumed, these somehow leave him more famished, and he steps up and broadens his assault: a wedge of pigeon pie, a salad of rocket and purslane, a bowl of noodles with cinnamon and shaved cheese, the ruined donjon of a sugar castle, the thigh of a roast peacock. Across the room, a rawboned Moorish girl who's stayed behind to dump bones into a stockpot eyes his progress nervously. After a moment she wipes her greasy hands on her apron and tiptoes away, leaving Crivano alone.

He presses on. The skin of his belly grows tight, so he limits himself to single bites as he moves from dish to dish, searching the cluttered table for whatever taste will collapse the void gnawing in his gut. Walnuts. Boiled squid. A soft yellow cheese. Poached quince. A purple candied rose. Fish jelly. A white-stalked herb he can't even identify. He recalls the siege of Tunis: the door-to-door hunt through the medina for escaped Spaniards. Numbing, desperate, faintly ridiculous. What within himself wants so badly to be fed?

He's attacking a cured Milanese sausage when Tristão bursts in, a wary and determined cast on his comely face, as if he half-

expects the room to be filled with cloaked assassins. Not atypically, his mien is that of a
man in the midst of a great and nebulous
adventure. Vettor! he says. Here you are! You
are here.

Crivano's knife saws through the mold-
dusted sausage casing; he speaks through a
mouth only partly empty. I am indeed, he
says. Where in God's name have you been? I
don't know any of these Uranici. How do you
expect —

Come with me, Tristão says. We must be
swift. The Nolan is soon to speak.

A moment, please. I'm eating.

Come! Tristão says, grabbing Crivano's
sleeve with one hand, beckoning with the
other. Come come come come come!

Crivano folds the thin sausage slices into a
scrap of bread and follows Tristão into the
corridor. They turn not toward the great hall,
but deeper into the house. As he walks,
Tristão fishes a folded sheet of paper from
his doublet, flattens it, and hands it to
Crivano. Here, he says. Look.

Penciled off-center on the yellow sheet is
an oblong shape, pinched at one end like a
deformed pear, or a long-stemmed fig.
Crivano stares the drawing, rotates it, but
can make nothing of it.

This, Tristão says, will work. Don't you
think so?

Crivano looks at Tristão, flummoxed.

Tristão looks back. He seems intent on resuming a discussion Crivano doesn't recall having had in the first place. Don't I think what will work? Crivano says.

Tristão flicks the paper with a long middle finger. *This,* he says.

What is it supposed to be? A uterus?

Tristão stops, gives Crivano an icy glare, and plucks the drawing from his hand. He slaps it flat against the wall, produces a pencil from his robe, licks the tip, and scrapes it across the paper, darkening the lines on either side of the shape's broad end, as if to thicken the womb's endometrium. Your man on Murano, he says. Your mirrormaker. He will do this for me. With — I don't remember how to say it.

Silvering, Crivano says. You want to make an alembic.

Yes! An alembic. What else would it be?

A mirrored alembic. An alembic lined with silvering.

No, Tristão says. Not lined. Coated. On the outside. A clear glass alembic. To trap the light within. Do you see? Do you not believe that this method will work?

Tristão has never discussed alchemical practice openly with Crivano before. If the wrong person — Mocenigo, or a pious servant — were to overhear, they likely would find themselves facing the Inquisition. Tristão could be tortured and expelled. Crivano gapes in disbelief, but Tristão's face shows no concern: impatient, but otherwise calm.

I — I don't know, Crivano says. I have not had access to a laboratory in some months. And I have never considered —

He looks past Tristão to the drawing, still held against the wall, and squints at it. Is light produced during the Great Work? he says. I've never heard such a thing.

I don't know if light is produced, Tristão says, exasperated. I think perhaps that no one knows this. I could find nothing conclusive in the literature. For that reason, if no other, this approach must be attempted. If the sun never set, Vettor, would we know that there are stars? No. We would not.

Crivano is at a loss. He looks at Tristão, then back at the drawing, then down at the bread and sausage wadded in his hand. He lifts them, takes a small sheepish bite.

Tristão's nostrils flare; he stuffs the pencil and the drawing back into his doublet. When he speaks again he takes the tone of a beleaguered schoolmaster, his voice soft and sharp. How do we judge the progress of the Great Work? he says.

Crivano shrugs, chews, swallows. By the colors it takes, of course.

Yes. We speak of blackening, of whitening, of the tail of the peacock, of the final redness that yields the elixir that we seek. They agree on little else, but all sources agree on this.

The colors are important. Perhaps they are more important than we know.

I don't see what you're getting at, my friend.

Perhaps, Tristão says, the colors are not merely qualities, but products. Perhaps the key to a successful operation is to feed not the alchemist's vision with their display, but the chemical engine itself. To *hold* the color, undevoured by the human eye. And what holds color, as liquid is held by clay, or hard wood, or metal, or glass?

A mirror.

Only that. Nothing else. Scholars of optics and of perspective describe the mirror as a device to assist our vision, but it is not. Or it is so only accidentally. The mirror is an invisible object. It is a machine for unseeing. And I believe it is the hidden heart of the processes to which we devote our efforts.

Crivano knits his brow, puts a thumb across his lips. Interesting, he says. A fresh approach to the problem, without question. And yet I must confess, Tristão, that I can think of nothing in the alchemical literature to ratify your claim.

Tristão elevates his eyebrows mildly. No? he says. Permit me to refer you to the foundational text of our art, the *Tabula Smaragdina* of Hermes the Thrice-Great.

Crivano stifles a laugh. The *Emerald Tablet*? he says, louder than he means to. He looks both ways down the corridor, steps closer, whispers. You can't be serious, he says. To what passage do you refer?

Its very name, Vettor. The word *emerald.* The Greeks of antiquity used the same word to name any polished green stone, as did the Romans after them. Emeralds, jaspers, certain granites. In Pliny we read of the Emperor Nero, weak of sight, who viewed the deeds of his gladiators with the aid of an emerald. Our historians always identify this object as a lens, but I believe it to have been a curved jasper mirror. Furthermore, I believe it likely that the original text of the *Emerald Tablet* was etched upon a mirror of similar design, no doubt mislaid in the chaos of passing centuries. Mirroring is, after all, what it prescribes — *as above, so below* — and mirroring is its intended function.

Tristão has advanced this case with waning fervor: not as though beset by doubt, but rather as though unable to maintain his interest in prosecuting a line of reasoning he regards as self-evident. Crivano gapes in disbelief. Every educated man — from Suez to Stockholm, from Lisbon to Lahore — has at least a passing knowledge of the *Emerald Tablet,* even if only as an ungodly thing to be eschewed and condemned. Any scholar concerned with the pursuit of secret knowledge knows its thirteen enigmatic sentences by memory. Yet in a lifetime of study — in *two* lifetimes, Ottoman and Frankish — Crivano has never encountered the notion that Tristão so blithely puts forth, nor any notion that might be its parent, or its sibling. For the first time he finds himself considering the possibility that his handsome friend may not be merely eccentric, or imprudent, but genuinely mad. He wonders whether Narkis knows this, wonders again why Narkis directed him to make Tristão's acquaintance in the first place.

Tristão seems lost in thought; Crivano clears his throat softly to reclaim his attention. So, Crivano says, that's what you wanted to show me?

No, Tristão says. This.

He steps forward, opening a door to another storeroom, this one filled with dusty crates and casks. A lamp burns on a table in the room's center, illuminating a small beechwood strongbox. Tristão pulls a key from around his neck, unlocks it, and opens the lid.

It's full of coins: silver ducats and gold sequins. Well over a thousand, to judge by its dimensions. Tristão closes it, locks it, hands the key to Crivano. For the glassmaker, he says. Give it to him, please, and bring my mirror to me.

Crivano sets his half-eaten bread and sausage on the table, takes the key, and drapes it around his own neck. Then he takes hold of the box's handles and tries to lift it. It won't budge.

Tonight, Tristão says, when you depart, you will have the assistance of Hugo and the footman. About my project they know nothing of import, and they can be trusted to be silent. I am very grateful to you for this errand, Vettor.

He bends, blows out the lamp.

Crivano gulps the last of his food as they hurry down the corridor. The lute and the theorbo are playing again; the candles in the great hall are being snuffed, and the Uranici are congregating in the dayroom. Come quickly, Tristão says. There is a fellow here tonight to whom I have pledged to introduce you.

Most of the guests have gathered around the two musicians; they clap and shout encouragement as the players embark upon a fantasia that grows increasingly complex and harmonically improbable. The lutenist plays as if he has surplus fingers. Crivano can see the long neck of the theorbo nod with the rhythm, but the musicians themselves are hidden by the crowd.

Tristão walks to the chamber's opposite end, toward the row of breeze-sieving windows that opens onto the Grand Canal. Two men converse there; Crivano notes with displeasure that one is Lord Mocenigo. As they draw near, the noble's vaguely cretinous face clarifies in the dim light, its expression aggrieved and conspiratorial. *You now tell me,* Crivano overhears him say, *that you met no one in all of Frankfurt who successfully learned the Nolan's so-called art of memory?*

The other man, a tall and burly Sienese, seems unfazed by Mocenigo's question, but he smiles with relief and gratitude when Tristão and Crivano approach. Dottore de Nis! he says. As always, your arrival makes the rest of us seem even uglier than we are.

Mocenigo emits an irritated puff, stalks away. Messer Ciotti, Tristão says, allow me to present Dottore Vettor Crivano, who has come recently from Bologna. Dottore Crivano, this is Messer Giovanni Battista Ciotti, who may be known to you already as the proprietor of Minerva, our city's finest bookshop.

They exchange bows. Crivano has been in Ciotti's shop; he heard of it even before he left Bologna, and made a point of visiting soon after he arrived. It's very good, stocking many titles concerning secret knowledge that he'd hesitate to carry openly in the street. I'm pleased and honored to make your acquaintance, Crivano says.

Ciotti's smiling response is lost in cheers. The lutenist has doubled time against the bass thrum of the theorbo, executing runs along his fretboard that Crivano's ears can barely sort out. The end arrives with a daring flourish, and applause fills the room. As it fades, a distant *bravo!* sounds from a boat passing on the canal, and everyone laughs.

Guests stoop to congratulate the players, the crowd begins to part, and Crivano catches a glimpse of the lutenist, sheepishly eyeing his calloused fingers. Extraordinary, Crivano says. Who is he?

I have not seen him before, Tristão says. He is quite adroit.

He's a scholar from Pisa, Ciotti says. I imagine he learned to play from his famous father, who recently died, I'm sorry to say. He, good sirs, was a fine lutenist.

The Nolan is standing near the hearth now, conversing with the Paduan scholar who's to introduce him; the German boy hovers nearby. Messer Ciotti, Tristão breaks in, at our last encounter, I believe you mentioned to me your need for the services of a person able to read and understand the writing of the Arabs. Someone also capable of discretion. Do you still suffer from such a lack?

Ciotti seems surprised for a moment. I do, he says. An Arabic document has come into my possession, an esoteric manuscript, and I've recently had it translated. I would like to have this Latin rendering authenticated before I pay my translator the balance of what he is owed.

This man, Tristão says, placing a hand on Crivano's shoulder, speaks and writes the Arabic tongue with great proficiency. Also

397

the languages of the Greeks and the Persians and the Ottoman Turks, the last of whom kept him prisoner for many years and came to rely upon his skills and experience as an interpreter. I think that perhaps, if he is willing, Dottore Crivano could be of great help to you in this matter.

Crivano and Ciotti look at each other. Then both speak at once, fall silent again, and smile awkwardly. I would consider it a privilege to assist, Crivano says. May I ask how lengthy is the manuscript in question?

Not long. Scarcely ten thousand Latin words.

Crivano nods, suddenly wary, as if he's stepped among slip-nooses. It might require several hours, he says. I don't suppose you'd permit me to remove the translation and the original manuscript from your shop?

Ciotti smiles. I might, he says, if I were the manuscript's owner. But I am not.

He turns to Tristão. Dottore de Nis, he says, when last we spoke, you suggested to me that this task might be compassed most quickly by a pair of translators working in concert. Do either of you know another scholar with a facility in Arabic?

Crivano looks at Ciotti, then at Tristão, who's watching them both intently, like a child who's trapped a pair of scorpions in a jar. In fact, Tristão says, I may know of such a man.

Gentlemen! A voice rises from beside the hearth, speaking a clear and reedy Latin. Members of the Uranian Academy! it says. Distinguished guests! On behalf of our hosts, the generous Andreas and Nicolaus Morosini, I thank you for your attention. As always, I am Fabius Paolini, and tonight I am pleased to welcome Philotheus Iordanus Brunus Nolanus to the convocation of this assembly. This is not the first time that Doctor Brunus has addressed us. This chamber was full on the occasion of his previous visit, and all those who were here surely recall as vividly as do I the spirited debate that arose. I shall therefore assume that our speaker is known to most of you — from your familiarity with his famous publications on philosophy, cosmology, memory, and magic, if not from my earlier long-winded introduction — and I shall therefore forego a second one. Tonight Doctor Brunus will, I believe, lecture us on the art of memory, a subject of considerable interest to many in this room. Doctor, I gratefully surrender the floor to you.

The Nolan moves into the space that Paolini has vacated; he makes a slow circle, as if testing the soundness of the floor. His gait is feline, or viverrine, not quite human. He walks with bent knees, on the balls of his feet; his small deep-set eyes scour the room with raw contempt. Crivano recalls a torch-bearing dervish in Tiflis who made a run at

399

their powder store; the janissary archers shot him so full of arrows that when he finally died their shafts kept his limp corpse off the dirt. The dervish's face as he charged bore an expression identical to the one the Nolan wears now. The world, Crivano thinks, is a poor container for such men.

When at last he speaks, the friar's voice is rough and shrill, as though coarsened by frequent shouting. My thanks, Doctor Paolini, he says. In fact, I will *not* be speaking on memory tonight. I have done so before in this room, and to raise the subject here again would cheapen it. Those still unconvinced will remain so, regardless of how I argue. Tonight, rather than lecturing on the art of memory, I will demonstrate it. Perhaps this exercise will quiet those who say that the art is a sham, a waste, a fancy. Gentlemen, I invite you to name my topic for me. We are all learned men, are we not? Choose whatever subject pleases you, and I, extempore, shall engage it.

A startled silence ensues. The Nolan faces his audience with a cool sneer. The quiet collapses into soft grumbles, a few snickers, the shuffle of nervous feet. Paolini clears his throat.

Oh, come now, audience! the Nolan says. Wherefore this reluctance? Choose! Be bold! You are scholars, are you not? Each of you has a favored subject, held always close to heart. Name it! I may not match the erudition you command while ensconced in your bookish chambers, but note that I will speak with recourse to no library save that resident within my own mind. Doctor Paolini, you have written knowledgably on occult themes in Virgil, have you not? Shall I speak on that? Or mathematics, perhaps? Have we a geometer among us who will demonstrate his acumen?

The Nolan shoots a pointed glace at the lutenist, and receives a melancholy smile in response. The derision rustling through the crowd grows louder, the embarrassed tension more palpable. The German boy crosses his pale arms and takes a protective step toward the friar. Crivano and Ciotti swap bemused shrugs.

But no, the Nolan continues. All too easily I could have prepared myself in advance to confront those subjects. My desire is only to be challenged, for it is by such challenges that truth becomes clear. Stipulate, someone, beyond these suggestions of mine! If the Nolan is to be taken, it must be by surprise!

The mirror, Tristão says. Address the issue of the mirror.

His smooth limpid voice bears a sudden edge that silences the room. The Nolan seems confused: he squints, his eyes spring from face to face. Who speaks? he says. Who has spoken?

Tristão doesn't respond. His face is blank, dispassionate; his attitude that of a gambler who has placed his wager and now awaits the revelation of the dice. Every eye present has unmoored itself from the Nolan and drifted to him.

After a long moment, Ciotti answers on his behalf. My friend Dottore de Nis, he says, has asked that you discourse upon the mirror.

The Nolan scowls. The mirror, he says. I must confess that this request leaves me somewhat at a loss. At a loss, that is, to judge why your friend would ask a scholar like myself to address that topic, and not seek the expertise of an unlettered tradesman. I had understood this forum to be concerned with higher things.

A familiar voice rises from the room's opposite end: that of the second musician, the Servite friar. Crivano suddenly remembers where he's heard it before: it's the voice of the mountebank alchemist he saw yesterday in Campo San Luca, shortly before the plaguedoctor appeared. But this can hardly be. Friars donning masks to play satire in the streets?

Hold, please, the Servite says. I beg your pardon, Doctor Brunus, but if you will dismiss the mirror — its construction and its function — as a subject devoid of science, suitable only for debate by the guilds, then I grant you will find many who agree with you, but I cannot place myself among them. Philosophers may long for a world in which the artifex's technique proceeds always from the application of reason, but more often we find that methods simply arise, and it falls to us thinkers to scurry after them, to wring significance from industry and accident. The flat mirrors lately turned out by the Murano craftsmen may indeed present such a case. Who among us has gazed into one of these without the symptoms of wonderment and disturbance?

Now Paolini speaks, his voice quickened with zeal. In the *Phaedrus* of Plato, he says, as I'm sure Doctor Brunus recalls, we read King Thamus's remark to the god Thoth: the parent of an art is not always the best judge of its utility. As Brother Sarpi has just suggested, with the mirror this may well be so. Thamus refers, of course, to Thoth's invention of writing — so this strikes close to your own scholarship, Doctor Brunus, for Thamus's complaint is that the invention of letters aids not the memory of the Egyptians, but instead causes it to atrophy. Writing promotes not recollection, but reminiscence; it delivers not truth, but only a semblance of truth. In your previous lecture to us, you described the picture-writing of the Egyptians as superior to the alphabets of the Greeks, the Romans, and the Hebrews, for it evokes pure sense, not mere sound. You delineated for us your system of memory based on figures and patterns, which you say will enable the disciplined magus to assemble in his imagination a picture of the universe entire, thereby to gain power over its most hidden correspondences. And now Dottore de Nis has raised the issue of a simple invention which precisely, if fleetingly, captures the images of particular objects placed before it. Should we fear the ubiquity of this device in our dwelling-chambers? Will the image-making capacity of our imaginations sicken in its presence? Surely these are not inconsequential concerns for a philosopher.

A general murmur of assent follows, then builds in volume. *Until this academy refuses to suffer such frauds,* Crivano hears someone say, *we hardly deserve to be taken seriously. How has this self-important clown been twice invited? It's the fault of that idiot Mocenigo, I think.*

The Nolan flushes a deep red, casts his eyes down, squeezes them shut. After a moment he turns out his palms, looks heavenward, and begins to rise on tiptoe. As if rehearsing his eventual deliverance from the base ignorance of his earthly tormentors. His face grows calm, he sinks back to the floor, and he fixes the room with the sad and sickly smile of a martyr.

For a moment, his lean features are half-lit by pink flares launched from a passing galley, but no one seems to pay these small fraudulent comets any mind. They trace fiery arcs across the night sky, then perish with a hiss on the surface of the canal.

Very well, my friends, the Nolan shouts. As promised, I shall grant your request. Let us now consider the mirror.

■ ■ ■ ■

SVBLIMATIO

MARCH 16, 2003

■ ■ ■ ■

I speak of the American deserts and of the cities which are not cities. No oases, no monuments; infinite panning shots over mineral landscapes and freeways. Everywhere: Los Angeles or Twenty-Nine Palms, Las Vegas or Borrego Springs . . .

— JEAN BAUDRILLARD, *America*

32

In Curtis's dream his head is bandaged, his eyes taped over with balls of white gauze, and somehow he can see right through them.

He's walking away from his overturned Humvee, cracked and hissing on the cobblestone street — although the crash really happened on a dirt road south of Gnjilane, not anyplace that looked like this. Italian marines from the San Marco Battalion squat in the shade of a row of palmtrees, watching him with grim sympathy. Curtis raises a hand to them, and now he knows this place: Split, in Croatia, where he came ashore during Dynamic Response back in '98, three years before the accident.

The blue harbor is stretched behind him. The blue sky is punctuated by a line of Sea Stallions, their rotors muttering in the breeze. Green mountains to the north. A couple of belltowers poking over tiled rooftops. Ahead, the Iron Gate of Diocletian's palace, framed by low arches. The pavingstones are slick

409

beneath his slippered feet, worn down by centuries of passage.

Someone is on his left, leading him, someone he can't see. At first it's Danielle; then he remembers that he can't have met Danielle yet, that he's still months and miles away from Bethesda, and the realization thrills him: he's moving under his own power, safe and unafraid, gliding through the wide and shifting world. The person leading him speaks low, at the threshold of his hearing. He can't make anything out. The voice guides him like a silver thread in a labyrinth.

They're moving quickly through twisting streets, past the Byzantine arches of a Gothic loggia, beneath a boxy white belltower, through an ancient peristyle. Twinned stone lions. A granite sphinx. The passageways narrowing. The walls filmed with shimmering esophageal ooze. Everywhere now the tang of the sea.

The crown of a second tower — brick, square, topped by a steep pyramid — appears and disappears in the spaces between rooftops. As they draw close, it seems to grow taller, thicker, greener at its tip. They cross jade canals, slosh through puddled corridors, and emerge into a colonnaded square swarming with white doves. Startled into flight, the birds ripple like foam across the gray sky. The great belltower catches their shadows. Curtis knows this place, too.

He's alone now, moving forward between the tower and the domes of a gilded basilica, rounding the corner of a grand hall and looking out at the churning sea beyond. There's a small group of ragged gamblers on the quay up ahead, gathered between two marble columns, throwing dice below the stinking corpses of hanged men. As he approaches, Curtis sees Stanley crouched over the tumbling cubes. Stanley looks up and smiles, and Curtis can see that he's dead: his flesh sagging, his eyesockets black voids. He offers Curtis the dice with a withered hand, and Curtis declines. The dead Stanley turns and hurls them with tremendous force, aiming at an island on the lagoon's distant edge. If they hit the water, Curtis doesn't see the splash.

The gamblers are gone. Curtis pushes through crowds of camera-slung tourists, self-conscious in his hospital gown; he crosses a bridge to the entrance of the Doge's Palace, and he's in the casino again, just left of the high-limit slots. He works his way toward the elevators, eager to get back to his bed. As he passes the Oculus Lounge he scans the tables for Veronica, then for Stanley, and finally for the kid he chased last night. Thinking back, replaying it in his head, Curtis is embarrassed for both of them. The Whistler with his little mirror, Curtis with his fumbling pursuit. Grown men playing at being detectives, spies, criminals. Damon too, with his scheming and his faxes. And Stanley. Stanley with his whole life. But Curtis — who has seen misery and death in seven countries, who has been broken and imperfectly rebuilt, who should at this point know better — Curtis worst of all.

33

He's awake now.

It takes him a minute to find the book in the sheets. He spent most of last night reading it: in Veronica's room, after she fell asleep on the couch, then here, until he dozed off himself. He wipes his eyelids, reaches to turn off the lamp on the nightstand.

The Mirror Thief. Curtis can't make heads or tails of it. So far as he can tell, it's mostly about a guy named Crivano who's some kind of wizard. Other people are in it, too: somebody called Hermes, somebody called the Nolan. The moon has a speaking part. Sometimes it seems like a plot is coming together, but then a six- or seven-page poem comes along — about the business of alchemy, or the technology of glassmaking, or the relationship of metals to planets — and the story gets put on hold. It's all supposed to be very smart and serious, but at the same time there's something goofy and *Dungeons-&-Dragons* about it, too.

Lust and war! The Gorgon's stony gaze
masks the inner limit of the body —

adulterers ensnared by such silk thread
as spiders hoist upon the rafter-beam.

Web-spinners, mirror-makers, Athena
Parthenos and her ill-shaped sibling

shield the lexicon of craft and trick:
the redirecting flash, the circle-step

made sideways on back-turned feet, as
the logarithmic nautilus records.

Crivano, too, moves along such spirals.

Curtis is sure there are clues that he's missing. At the beginning, for instance, a page
has been razored out — the second printed
page, the title page, with publication data on
the back — cut evenly, close to the spine, so
just a sliver of paper remains. Tomorrow,
when the libraries are open, he'll call around,
see if he can't scare up an intact copy.

He throws off the covers, makes the rack.
No faxes, no messages. He opens the curtains, drops to the deck, and does two minutes each of pushups and situps. Fast, not
counting. Timing himself off the little clock
on the CNN crawl. Onscreen, Chinese people
in surgical masks. Girl run down by a bull-

413

dozer in Palestine. Still no war. Curtis sits up, cycles through channels: BET, USA, Disney, PAX, History, Travel, TV Land.

He showers, shaves, gets dressed — gray slacks, brown crewneck pull-over — and checks himself in the mirror in the sunken livingroom. He remembers the weird hallucination from last night, then thinks of the dead Stanley in his dream. Curtis steps closer, watches his own reflection for a long time. As if expecting it to offer him advice. The sky over the Strip is deep ultramarine with a dusting of high cirrus, and the shallow crescent scar to the left of his nose is prominent in the sidelong morning light. He slips on his glasses and it vanishes under their slender black rims.

Curtis steps into the bedroom, strips down the rack, makes it again. Stretching the sheets tighter this time. Bouncing a Louisiana statehood quarter off it when he's done. He sits in the chair by the window to think, spinning the coin on the wooden table. At first he's doing this to keep his hands busy; then he's just doing it. He flips the quarter off his thumbnail, tries to follow the arc, to catch it in the air. Listening to its fluttering chime: a perfect sound when he connects just right. It comes down with a slap in his cupped palm: heads or tails. It'd be nice if there was something he could decide this way. *He comes up with these new systems that don't* make any sense at all, that have nothing whatsoever to do with probability. A coin toss is fifty-fifty; the odds of a natural twenty-one are — what? Five percent? Curtis can't remember. *In Stanley's mind, about the least interesting thing you can do at a blackjack table is win money.* Curtis's attention wavers; the coin drops, he stoops to pick it up. Running the pad of his thumb over the outlines of its little pelican, its tiny trumpet. He thinks about phoning his dad, but then doesn't.

At ten o'clock the maid knocks on the door. Curtis puts his blazer on and lets her in, chatting a little in Spanish. She's quiet, her gaze tightly policed. If she's surprised at the tidy rack it doesn't register. When she disappears into the head, Curtis clips his revolver onto his belt, closes the safe, and goes below to look for Stanley.

He buys coins from a change dispenser in the slot area, not far from where he spotted the Whistler, then exits through the Doge's Palace to catch the trolley south. He swaps his glasses for shades as he hits the sidewalk, surprised by the coolness of the outside air. The pedestrian overpass takes him across to the Treasure Island side, where he passes the two frigates becalmed in Buccaneer Bay, the dormant volcano fountain. The massive right-angled façade of the Mirage doubles itself in its mirrored windows, and Curtis stops under

415

its covered entrance to wait. The sun is still climbing. The sky below is flat, muzzy, lemondrop-yellow, a screen behind the mountains. Duststorms somewhere to the east. Curtis thinks of the painting in his room: its muted colors and indistinct shapes. Across the Strip, through the palmtrees and the fountain-spray, his hotel's grooved brick belltower is frontlit by the Mirage's reflective glass; he watches the golden light play across it. The trolley pulls up to the curb, then pulls away, and Curtis is still standing there, jangling coins in his closed fist.

He had the right idea in choosing his hotel. Everything he's done since then has been wrong. There's not an inch of sidewalk here Stanley hasn't stepped on, not a single table he hasn't taken money from. Every time Curtis wakes up in this town, he walks out into Stanley's head. He's got to start hearing the echoes, seeing the ghosts.

But this isn't Stanley's Vegas anymore. The old city is masked, vanished into itself. Curtis remembers the old guys bitching about it: a smoky circle of them in his dad's Irving Street walkup. Carlos Huerta, Jim Press, Cadillac LaSalle. *Goddamn developers gonna kill that town, with their palm trees and their goddamn volcanoes.* Henry Tsai, once dealt five consecutive aces out of a six-deck shoe at the Hacienda. Won six thousand dollars on the hand. Walked away, never cracked a smile.

You can't hardly find a decent table no more. Hell, most people ain't even looking. Slow Tony Miczek, who gave up a thumb in '66 rather than pay his stake back to a loanshark. Turned around and quadrupled it at the Sands in sixteen hours of continuous play, same day he left the hospital. Detouring to the washroom every couple of hours with fresh bandages and a bottle of Bactine. Settled his debt. No hard feelings. *College students. People with kids. Squares and light-weights.* Stanley staring out the grimy window at the university clocktower, the Capitol dome and the white obelisk beyond. Silent, then speaking. *There's no way to get in the game anymore, because it's all a game.* His dry clucking laugh. *They do all the dreaming for us now. Nothing's left to chance.*

Augustus Caesar is coming up on Curtis's right, his plaster gaze fixed on the Flamingo across the street. The old hotel seems demure in the light of day. Some of those neon tubes have hung there for thirty years. The feathered pastel frontispiece is shaded, cool and blank as the face of a sarcophagus. Curtis keeps walking.

He was sore yesterday after the long hump from Fremont, but today he feels good, glad to be on foot. The docs cleared him to drive over a year ago provided he'd install a collision alarm and some extra mirrors, but he

417

hasn't been behind the wheel since the crash. He's not scared — a little nervous, maybe — and he could get comfortable again with some practice. He's just not ready yet. What's funny is that he hasn't missed it. It's been good, satisfying, to do without a car. His new slowness has shown him a hidden world he'd ignored, that he's only now begun to discover. He'd never admit it, but he's grateful for the enforced patience, the fresh awareness of distance and spaces between.

The Eiffel Tower pokes up from the middle of the next block, beyond the telescoping entrance to Bally's. The last time Curtis came to town it was still brand new, and he and Damon and a bunch of other guys took cabs from the North Strip to check it out. Very weird place. Lots of fake trees and blurry Monet carpet, and everything smelled like baguettes. Standard-issue fake casino sky everywhere, even over the gaming floor: it felt strange to be gambling out in the open, even though it wasn't really the open. They hit the bars and rode the elevator to the top of the tower, swaying on drunken legs, watching the Valley fill up with lights. The younger jarheads were horsing around, doing imitations of Pepe Le Pew. Damon was staring at the runty Arc de Triomphe down below. *Napoleon, man!* he kept saying. *Fucking Napoleon!*

418

Crossing Harmon now. New York ahead on the right. Stanley grew up in the shadow of those buildings: AT&T, Century, Chrysler, Seagram, Empire State. What does he think of when he sees them? What does he remember?

Passing this way on Friday Curtis met a bartender — a dayshifter about to clock out — who knew Stanley's name right away, who'd seen him in the last week or so. Dayshift doesn't start for another hour, but Curtis figures he can wait.

At the entrance, a close-up of a billowing flag is playing on the scaldingly bright LED readerboard, UNITED WE STAND overlaid in yellow, and Curtis wonders again what's happening with the war. He makes his clockwise round of the gaming area — done up like Central Park, without the typical fake sky — and when he sees no familiar faces, he climbs the stairs to the mezzanine. He gets a couple of hotdogs from Nathan's in the Coney Island Pavilion, eats one while listening to the shrieks and rattles of the rollercoaster overhead, and finishes the other afoot, strolling Bleecker and Hudson and Broadway, taking in the sight of fire escapes and steam-venting manholes and graffiti-tagged phonebooths and brownstones draped in ivy.

When he stops at the piano bar in Times Square, she's there behind the counter: redheaded, matronly, maybe five years older than Curtis. In good shape. Talking to a couple of conventioneers in a rich Staten Island accent that probably landed her this job. She doesn't recognize him when he sits down. Then she does. He's close enough to see the dark flash of her expanding pupils: he's come to the right place.

She's smiling at him, putting down a napkin. Hey, pal, she says. How's business?

Tough to say. It's been a weird couple of days.

Tell me about it. What can I get you, hon?

Just an orange juice, please. You seen Stanley?

She stops, half-turned to the bar, looking away. No sign of him, she says. He's been a popular boy this weekend.

I'm not the only one looking?

She laughs, shrugs. Like it's a joke. Pours the juice.

Has Veronica been here?

She sets the plastic cup down, takes the ten from his fingers, moves toward the register. Doesn't respond. She's not smiling anymore.

What about a little guy with a gap between his front teeth? You seen anybody like that?

When she comes back she still has his ten, and she places it on the bar with a battered twenty on top of it. You loaned me a double the other day, she says. I'm paying you back. Thanks. Your drink's on the house.

That twenty was a toke, not a loan.

420

I don't mix 'em that good, bub.

She leans in close, looks him in the eye. If this was a movie, she says, I would take money from the whole bunch of you. Play you off each other and get rich doing it. But this ain't no movie. I'm gonna say something, and then somebody's gonna get hurt, and I don't want that on my conscience. You seem like a nice guy, and I wanna keep thinking you're a nice guy. So I'm not gonna talk to you about this anymore. *Capice?*

I'm not going to hurt anybody.

It ain't you that I'm worried about doing the hurting.

She's smiling again, somewhat sadly. No fear in her eyes, just concern. She's been living out here a long time. Who's been coming around? he asks.

She takes a breath, lets it out. The little guy with the teeth, she says. Another one, too. Tall. From the South someplace. The little guy's from out of town, but the big guy's local. I seen him around. He's bad news.

And Veronica? She's been here?

She looks down, closes her eyes. Nods.

Curtis takes a sip of his juice. Swills it in his cup. Were they looking for each other? he asks.

What do you mean?

Did all of them just ask you about Stanley? Or did they ask about each other, too?

She thinks for a second. The big guy asked

421

me about both of the others, she says. About Veronica, and about the little guy. The little guy asked me about Veronica. Veronica and the little guy both asked me about you.

Curtis smiles. What'd you say about me?

That I'd seen you in here Friday night, at the end of my shift. That's all.

Did you give anybody my number?

No. I didn't have it with me.

But you've still got it someplace.

Yeah. Yeah, I still got it.

If Stanley shows up here, Curtis says, don't call me. It's not safe. Give him my number if he wants it. Tell him about everybody who's looking for him. Tell him everything you told me.

He's in some trouble, huh?

I think so, yeah.

Curtis lifts the two bills off the bar, looks up at her, and folds them into his wallet. Absolving her. He is on his own.

If anybody asks you about me, he says, just tell them the truth. I'm not going to bother you anymore.

He stands, turns to go. Turns back. How did he look?

Who? she asks.

But she knows who. Not too good, she says after a while. Not good at all.

34

Walking out of the bar, Curtis comes across a little indoor brook that flows into the fake Greenwich Village from the fake Central Park, and he follows it upstream toward the gaming tables. He's moving slowly, unsure of where he's going, turning what the bartender said over in his mind, when he feels eyes on him. He stops, looks up. Turning automatically to his left.

And there's Albedo, grinning, watching him from a craps table a few yards away. Skywriting illegibly with the cigarette in his beckoning fingers.

Curtis freezes for a moment. Albedo shifts in his seat, tokes his dealer, stands up. Draining his plastic cup, leaving it on the baize. Hey, man, he says, sauntering over, his big soft hand coming out. Curtis blinks, shakes himself, takes it. Thinking. Trying to make himself think.

You have a good talk with ol' Red in there? Albedo says.

Curtis just looks at him.

She's a classy lady, that Red. I know her real well. Albedo returns his cigarette to his thin lips. Say, man, you're not headed back to the North Strip, are you? I got a pickup at the Sahara in another hour, a two-girl deal. I can give you a lift.

No thanks. I've got some errands to run

down here.

Albedo looks back toward the piano bar, steps in closer. Curtis smells patchouli and brine. Listen, Albedo says, I got a message for you. From Damon. I talked to him this morning. Things are getting all manner of fucked-up back in AC, man. We need to talk. C'mon, walk with me.

You talked to Damon? On the phone?

Albedo's bloodshot eyes swing his way. No, Curtis, he says. With the telepathic powers of my mind. Yes, on the damn phone. What're you talking about?

What's the message?

Hey, can we walk? I gotta get rolling here.

Curtis gives him a hard look. Albedo is sporting a sleeveless Metallica T-shirt today, sunglasses weighting down the droopy neck. No jacket. Jeans too tight to hide anything except maybe a knife. Okay, Curtis says. Let's go.

They cut through the slots on the way to the main entrance, Curtis doubletiming it to keep up with Albedo's long stride. Damon just wanted me to tell you that he's gonna be out of touch for a few days, Albedo's saying. Hard to reach. That you just oughta hang tight in the meantime and be cool.

A few days? How many days?

I dunno, man. A few days. He'll let you know.

And he told you that this morning?

Yeah. It was about ten a.m., I think. Woke my ass up.

That doesn't make any sense. This thing I'm doing out here, it's time-sensitive.

Yeah, Damon told me all about that, Albedo says, then checks his enormous wristwatch. Sixty hours, right? A little under that, now. Look, here's what you do. You keep looking for Stanley, just like you been doing. When you get a line on him, you call me. I'll put him in touch with Damon. No cause for concern.

Curtis is shaking his head. This is no good, he says. Why doesn't Damon call me himself? What's going on in Atlantic City?

Things are hairy out there, man. Ownership at the Point's gone completely Joe McCarthy over this cardcounting shit. They're looking to tar and feather. Damon's got to watch his ass, be careful about who he talks to. That includes you.

But not you?

Albedo laughs. Aw, don't be jealous, man, he says. It's unbecoming.

They're walking under the porte-cochère, headed for the valet station. Albedo flicks away his cigarette, gives the Vietnamese boy standing there a folded bill and a quick and elaborate handshake. He jaws with the kid while the car comes around. Curtis fumes silently, staring at the battlements and parapets of the Excalibur across the street, until

425

he hears the kid yell *holy shit.*

The car coming up the drive is massive, gleaming, thunderously loud. Black and silver and chrome. Boxy, with a few grooved recesses near the tail, like a block of balsa attacked halfheartedly with a router. Four headlights. A bumper that looks like it weighs more than Danielle's Saturn. A steeply angled windshield that seems to jump forward ahead of the rest of the car. The silver hood-ornament a bold right-angled V inscribed in a circle. Ain't she a beaut? Albedo's saying.

The valet looks on, popeyed. What the fuck is that, man?

Mercury Montclair Phaeton sedan, my young friend. Manufactured in the year of our lord nineteen hundred and fifty-eight.

Is it real rare?

Naw, Albedo says. You see 'em around sometimes.

He tips the kid who's stepping out of the car, slides the seat all the way back, leans in and unlocks the door on Curtis's side. You restore it yourself? the kid asks.

Hell no, son, Albedo says, settling into his seat, flashing his yellow teeth. I don't know shit about cars. I hit the progressive at Caesars last June, and I went a little crazy. Bought the whole thing as-is on eBay.

Curtis pops the door, sits down, and Albedo puts the machine in gear, pulls into the stream of traffic. Curtis reaches to fasten his seatbelt and finds that there isn't one. Yeah, sorry, man, Albedo says. I never bothered to put a harness on yours. The girls always ride in the back.

Curtis cranes his neck to the left, and sure enough, Albedo is wearing both a standard lap belt and an aviator's double-strap shoulder harness, bolted onto the back of his seat. No sweat, though, he's saying, plucking the sunglasses from his T-shirt, sliding them onto his face. I promise I won't wreck us. We going back to your hotel?

Curtis has been trying to come up with a gambit — a wild-goose chase he can lead Albedo on to take control of the situation, to trick him into revealing what he knows — but he's got nothing. Yeah, he says at last. I'm staying at the —

I know where you're staying, man. Damon told me.

Most of the traffic coming off the freeway is turning onto the Strip, and their pace picks up after they get through the light. Curtis tries to settle in his seat, feeling naked without a belt. The Merc's interior is cluttered and filthy, M&M wrappers and paper cups and empty In-N-Out bags on every flat surface. Curtis kicks aside a set of jumper cables, a slim attaché case, and a folded-over and underscored copy of *Soldier of Fortune* before his feet find solid purchase on the sticky floorboard.

Something else, Albedo says. Damon wants us to start leaning on Veronica.

Curtis blinks. What? he says.

Veronica, man. That skinny little bitch Stanley runs around with.

I know who Veronica is.

Well, Damon thinks we need to sweat her a little. The girl is weak, man. After a few days with Stanley being UA, she's apt to be freaking out. Apply a little pressure, and she's gonna roll.

Curtis stares at Albedo: his beaked nose, his slit of a mouth. Yeah? he says. And what the fuck does Damon know about it? I'm not gonna go around town extorting people just because — look, this is bullshit. Damon wants to keep playing, he's got to show some cards. There's shit going on that he's not telling me about.

Albedo snickers, punches the cigarette lighter on the dash. You got that right, man, he says. And you are way better off without the details, believe me. I mean, jesus christ, Curtis, what's with this wanting to know everything all of a sudden? I thought you were a marine, man.

That was very different from this, Curtis says.

Was it? Was the Desert very different from this? Isn't it always about taking care of your buddies, and fuck the big picture? You know the answer, man.

428

The lighter pops up. Curtis jumps a little, but he doesn't think Albedo notices. Albedo pulls it out, holds the orange coil to his cigarette, and smoke swirls between the half-open windows. Curtis turns away, looks outside. They're at the light at Koval, on the edge of McCarran: Boeings and Airbuses are queuing up for takeoff, the heat from their engines bending the light, deforming the air.

You been checking out NA meetings? Albedo says.

Say again?

NA meetings, man. Miss Veronica used to have herself a little coke problem back before Stanley straightened her out. If he's not around, she might start going to meetings. It's worth a shot. But, hey, you know what? Let me handle that angle. I'm connected pretty good with that crowd. You just keep doing what you're doing. And if she turns up again, you call me. I'll take care of it.

Albedo makes a sharp left, heading north. The decorations hanging from his rearview mirror jangle and sway, and Curtis turns to get a better look: a strand of green Mardi Gras beads from the Orleans, a mini-discoball, a set of dogtags on a beaded steel chain. Curtis reaches up to look at the tags, thinking he'll get the proper spelling of Albedo, but they're made out for a marine named L. ALLODOLA, O-positive, who wears a medium gas-mask and has no religious preference. Curtis lets them drop.

Hey, you wanna see something real cool? Albedo's saying. Pick up that case there at your feet. Pop that sucker open.

Curtis picks it up. From the weight he can guess what's going to be inside, but he opens it anyway, just enough to see. A submachine-gun, nine-millimeter, about a foot and a half long, nested in a foam lining. It's supposed to look slick, very James Bond, but the case's shell is cracked, duct-taped in a couple of places, and the foam lining is yellow and uneven, like it was ripped out of an old couch. The gun looks like all guns look: scary and stupid, like a wasp trapped in a room. A suppressor and a couple of extra clips sit next to it, and they slide around whenever Albedo jostles the steering wheel, which is often. The suppressor looks like it could have been some junior-high-school kid's shop class project. Curtis shuts the case.

Sweet, huh? Albedo says. Bet that brings back some memories.

Not for me.

No? Oh, wait — it was Damon who worked embassy security, right? Not you. I get y'all mixed up. I tell you, though, that little darlin' sure brings back the old Force-Recon days for me. I know this dude who's got a little shooting range set up outside of Searchlight. Sub rosa. Strictly off the books. I'm gonna take it down there in a couple of weeks, tear shit up a little. You ought to tag along if you're still in town.

I'm not gonna be, Curtis says. He steals a glance over at Albedo. Sure, he thinks. This guy was Force-Recon. Just like I was Secret Service.

So what *you* got under that jacket, man? Albedo asks. Curtis doesn't answer. What's the matter, you shy? C'mon, what're you carrying?

.357 snub, Curtis says.

Magnum? Holy shit, man. You came out here to do business.

I'm using hot thirtyeights, Curtis says. You get better control.

Albedo looks over at him, eyebrows arched behind his shades, and then laughs. That is exactly like you, my brother, he says. If I may say so. Little dude, big gun, medium-size bang. That's real cute. Yeah, man, I got your number.

Laugh all you want, Curtis says, scowling. You ever shoot a magnum cartridge in a closed-in space, like a hotel room? You wanna go blind and deaf in the middle of a firefight, knock yourself out. I don't go for that Schwarzenegger shit.

I ain't arguing, man, I ain't arguing. Can I take a look?

Huh?

Lemme see your little gun, man. C'mon.

They're pulling up to the stoplight at Koval

431

and Flamingo, cattycornered from the Westin. Curtis looks hard at Albedo, trying to see his eyes through the shades. No way could he pull anything now. Not while he's driving. And Curtis is sure he cleared the backseat before he sat down. Almost completely sure.

He looks around sheepishly at the nearby drivers, all of whom seem to be gaping at Albedo's car, not at its occupants. He leans forward and draws the revolver from his waist, keeping it low, near his thighs. Curtis swings open the cylinder, works the ejector rod, and dumps the five oily bullets in his right palm.

He gives the gun to Albedo. Albedo takes it, looks it over. It all but vanishes in his big hand. Smith, right? he says. Pretty nice. That's a Speer cartridge you're loading? Gold Dot?

I guess, Curtis says. It was on sale.

The light changes. Albedo hands the revolver back, puts his palm on the wheel. So what do you think I should do with that thing on the deck, man? he asks. You think I can get two grand for it?

I wouldn't know, Curtis says. He's reloading, slipping the pistol back in its holster. The convention center is coming up on the left, the rear entrance to Curtis's hotel just beyond it.

I'm thinking about just hanging onto it, Albedo's saying. I know these guys in North

432

Cackalack — buddies of mine from the Desert — who're looking for a few good men right about now. Once boots start hitting the ground over in Iraq, and ol' Saddam gets himself deleted, it's gonna be the Gold Rush over there. See, Dick fucking Cheney's privatized the whole deal. The occupation, the rebuilding, the policing, the oil-stealing: that's all gonna be private, run by these private corporations.

Is that so.

And the thing is, these beancounting cocksuckers don't much like getting shot at. So they're looking for guys like us to provide security, run counterinsurgency ops, shit like that. And they're really writing the checks, man. *Huge* money. I mean, don't get me wrong, I didn't enjoy the fucking shit out of the Corps or anything — I left for a reason — but it would've been a hell of a lot more tolerable if they'd been paying me a hundred-fifty grand a year to do it. See what I'm saying? Plus with these guys there ain't all the hierarchical, shit-floats-to-the-top, byzantine-ass bureaucracy we had in the USMC. Not much in the way of government oversight, neither. Yeah, sure, you gotta put up with a bunch of fat guys from Halliburton, but fuck it, man. Just keep those checks coming.

They're pulling into the porte-cochère now. The valets crane their necks to get a good look at the ugly gleaming ride. I can absolutely put you in touch with these fellas, Albedo says. You got just the stuff they're looking for. You say the word, man. Pronounce the syllables.

Thanks for the ride, Curtis says, and pops the door. An empty Styrofoam cup and a battered and accordion-folded color brochure drop onto the pavement.

I'm serious, man. The next couple years are gonna be for private paramilitaries what the day after Thanksgiving is for Wal-Mart. You mark my fucking words.

Curtis lets the big door slam, picks up the cup and the brochure, and starts toward the hotel entrance. Hey, Curtis! Albedo shouts.

What?

This thing you got going? With Damon, with the Spectacular? It's maybe not gonna work out the way you're hoping it's gonna, partner. I'm real sorry to tell you. It's gonna turn out bad, or it's not gonna turn out at all. You know it, and I know it, and baby makes three. You might oughta start making other plans. Okay? Peace.

Albedo flashes two fingers, pushes his shades up the bridge of his nose, and puts the Mercury in gear. Curtis stands there with Albedo's trash in his hand, watching him roll away. The brochure is sticky. Looking down, Curtis sees the words SIN CITY ESCORTS, a pair of lipsticked mouths pouting beneath them.

He finds a trashbin near the automatic doors, then walks into the lobby. His fingers stick to the button when he summons the elevator, cling again to his thumb when he tries to wipe them off. He struggles for a minute in front of his room, fishing out his wallet, removing the keycard, and opening the door without touching anything with his right hand. In the midst of his contortions, a white guy about his own age passes in the hall. Fat, balding, sunburnt, in baggy swimtrunks. He's carrying goggles and a tiny underwater digital camera. He and Curtis eye each other uneasily. What happens here stays here, Curtis thinks.

By the time he gets inside, his skin is crawling. He shrugs out of his clothes and climbs into the shower, turning it up as hot as he can stand, then hotter once his skin gets used to it. He scrubs fiercely, systematically — scalp and face, rinse, left arm, rinse, right arm, rinse, just like they taught in boot camp — until he reaches the soles of his feet. Then he starts over. By the time he's done, the room is thick with swirling mist. Little drops bead the marble tiles, inch down the mirrors.

He puts on a robe and steps into the entryway, and steam spills around him like aspic from a mold. A slim white envelope is at his feet, an inch inside the door, and he stoops to pick it up. CURTIS is printed on it in a familiar spiky hand. Inside is a ticket to

435

the museum down below — ART THROUGH THE AGES, it says: *Masterpieces of Painting from Titian to Picasso* — and a note written on Quicksilver hotel stationery.

Meet here @ 3
Keep it quiet
V

Curtis has walked by the museum at least twice a day since he checked in; he's never really paid it any mind. It seemed to have nothing to do with Stanley — to be the kind of thing he'd write off as theme-park bullshit, a waste of floorspace, a consolation prize for uptight spouses of gamblers and convention-eers — but maybe Curtis has missed some-thing. Didn't Veronica say that Stanley had gotten interested in art? Maybe it was his-tory; Curtis can't remember. It may not mat-ter anyway. Veronica doesn't seem to under-stand Stanley a whole lot better than he does himself.

The book is on the nightstand where Cur-tis left it this morning. He picks it up, carries it to the table by the window. He was half asleep when he read through it last night, still a little buzzed from Veronica's bourbon, and not much stayed with him. He thinks he remembers a poem about a painter, or about art — at least he thought that's what it was about — but flipping around now, he can't find it. It seems unlikely that he could miss it in a book with under eighty pages, and he wonders if it was in his head: if a line he read just reminded him of something that Veronica told him, or that Stanley said long ago, or even something he saw himself in some museum while he was on leave in Europe. He can't be sure.

The maid of Corinth runs
her knife across the bricks,
    fixing the shadow
    of her errant love.

If a mirror should possess a soul
it would perceive the image it holds.

As songbirds fly
at Zeuxis' grapes
    Parrhasius gestures
    toward the curtain.

If a mirror should possess a soul
it would perceive the image it holds.

In Murano's furnaces
glass-workers drizzle
    liquid mercury
    on quickened tin.

If a mirror should possess a soul
it would perceive the image it holds.

> Here is true alchemy: the curtain
>   conceals only itself
> and the maid loves the shadow
>   more than the soldier.

Soon Curtis isn't reading anymore, just thinking, staring at the framed print over the couch: the tiny masts of tall ships poking from a yellow-brown chaos of sky and sea. Something scary about that painting. He hasn't really noticed that before.

He checks his cell display: 2:15. Plenty of time to scope the museum in advance. He shuts the book, stands up, and is turning toward the steps when he notices a fax in the machine.

Damon, from four hours ago. A full-page sketch of a giant phallus bent into a graceful question mark. A pair of shaggy testes dangling where the point should be. WHUT DA FUUUK??? written in heavy letters inside its interior curve.

Curtis flattens the fax on the desk. He shreds it into neat ribbons across the diagonal, making straight tears with the sharp beveled edge of the desk. Then he stacks the ribbons and tears them again, making a palmful of black-and-white confetti. Each tear makes a good sound, a certain sound. It's nice to feel certain about something.

On his way out the door, he scatters the

confetti in the toilet, pisses on it, and flushes it down.

35

The museum is a dark steel box that runs between the lobby and the casino floor. After a counterclockwise turn around the armillary sphere, Curtis shows his ticket at the entrance. He does a cursory walkthrough to make sure Veronica's not already here. The place is small; it doesn't take him long. Three bulkheads divide the gallery into four rooms, with about ten paintings in each room. The rusted-steel walls seem to float in midair, not quite touching the deck or the ceiling; Curtis sees shadows and feet pass by through the gaps at the bottom. He brushes a stealthy finger across the surface of one to see if it really is steel: it's chocolate-brown, glazed to look moist and oily. He feels like he's inside a fancy leather handbag, or a healthy kidney.

Afternoon sun trickles through slots in the outer wall, augmenting tracklights hung along the maple overhead. Outside, the morning's clear blue has gone dull and planar, a yellow pall across the sky. Only a couple of dozen people wander around; a few more are in the gift shop. None of them is Veronica. Curtis works his way back through the exhibit, dividing his attention between the art and the crowd, keeping himself alert. He'll spot

Veronica with no trouble, but he's worried that the Whistler might be lurking some-where. He doubts he'd recognize the kid right away, if at all.

The exhibit is chronological, ending with a growling cartoon dog from 1965. Curtis is walking through it in reverse, moving back-ward in time. Barely looking at the paintings. He's never thought much of modern art, with its drips and splats and big monochrome squares. At one piece, a plain black box on a plain white background, he has to stop and shake his head.

Years ago, during one of his surprise re-appearances in Curtis's boyhood, Curtis's dad spent an afternoon lecturing him about black painters — Raymond Saunders, Frank Bowling, Beauford Delaney, Alma Thomas — and about how Picasso stole his best ideas from African masks he'd seen in the Musée de l'Homme. The next Saturday Curtis rode his secondhand Schwinn the two fast down-hill miles to the new MLK Library and sat and flipped through massive hardbound books for hours, befuddled by bright blotches and smears. And then months later, when his father visited again, the sermon was about how black abstractionists were just aping the white man, how they didn't challenge the sensibilities of white culture, and how jazz was the only revolutionary Afro-American artform. Curtis smiles, wondering what his father would be saying were he here today. Probably something about how Islam forbids image-making. *The Holy Prophet, peace be upon him, teaches that on the Day of Resurrection, all the artists will be commanded to give life to the stuff that they created. And when they can't do it, they'll be punished. Think about it, Little Man. It makes sense. Every living thing comes from God. God made us all in his image. And it ain't right to make images of God.*

When Curtis comes to a torpid bare-breasted Venus that resembles nothing so much as a Playboy centerfold from the late Fifties, he starts paying closer attention to the art. He's in the 1700s now — older than America — and the paintings are more realistic, more precise. An angel with a flaming sword. A pale creepy infant prince. A baleful wolfhound with intelligent orange eyes. Curtis leans in to get a close look at the hound, the detail in its fur, its chain, its collar. He and Danielle always talked about getting a dog once they moved out to East Lansdowne. A big dog. They've been there almost four months now and still haven't done it. Curtis would feel better about being away if he knew Danielle had a big dog around.

As he nears the museum entrance he's back in the Renaissance, spotting names he remembers from Mediterranean shoreleaves: Lotto, Tintoretto, Titian. One big canvas

441

looks familiar, although the artist's name — FRANCESCO BASSANO, 1549–1592 — doesn't ring any bells. *AUTUMN,* it's called: a group of rustics harvesting apples and stomping grapes beneath the eerie green light of an overcast sky. Curtis isn't sure what about it caught his attention, unless maybe it's the thunderbolt-brandishing centaur bounding through the distant clouds, which reminds him a little of the bearded gods on the map in the lobby. Studying the canvas, he spends a moment trying to figure out whether he saw the real one in Italy before he remembers that this *is* the real one.

He's looking at the exhibit's oldest piece, a portrait of an unsmiling merchant from 1436, when Veronica breezes in. Just the sight of her puts him on edge. The shuteye she caught on the couch last night hasn't done much for her: even from across the room her eyes are hooded in blue. Her movements seem loose, marionettelike, as if she's held up by something invisible outside herself, as if each step she takes is an arrested collapse. Her feet brush the blond parquet as she glides toward him.

Veronica's decked out in white running shoes and a lavender jenny-from-the-block tracksuit that she doesn't quite have the body to pull off; the outfit is at serious odds with her teased-out hair and insomniac pallor. Her wide smile is probably intended to be disarming, but it's straying into cymbal-playing-monkey territory and has pretty much the opposite effect.

She nods at the portrait of the merchant as she strolls up. They don't make 'em like that no more, eh? she says.

Curtis glances back at the painting. The merchant's eyes are sharp in its smoky half-light, staring at him across five and a half centuries. That's the truth, he says. Looks like it could've been taken with a camera.

It was, Veronica says.

Curtis blinks, looks at her, tracks her eyes back to the oak panel. There are small cracks in the paint on the merchant's nose and forehead. Say again? he says.

It *was* taken with a camera. As in camera obscura, as in a darkened room for the projection of images. I mean, it *is* a painting, obviously. In the Fifteenth Century, there was no way to chemically fix an image. Van Eyck projected the sitter onto the panel with some kind of optical device, and then he painted over the projection.

Veronica brushes past Curtis toward the wall, sweeping her hand over the portrait's face like she's tagging it with an invisible spraycan. Look how he's framed, she says. Look how he's lit. Look at that softness, those shadows. You see that in Leonardo's *sfumato,* then later in Giorgione, Hals, Rembrandt. Canaletto and Vermeer, too, but those guys

443

came later; they had fancy glass lenses. Van Eyck had to make do with a concave mirror. But the basic approach is the same. You see how the tonal grading opens the figure's dimensions and gives the painting depth? That's a total giveaway. You take a look at a Spanish or Sienese painting from the same period, it'll be as flat and closed-off as the king of clubs.

What, Curtis says, are you talking about?

You haven't heard about this? All the big guys, all the marquee names — van Eyck, Leonardo, Giorgione, Raphael, Holbein, Caravaggio — they all used optical devices. This is old news, man. This was on *60 Minutes* like a year ago.

Curtis looks at her, irritated, and then looks at the merchant again. The portrait's eyes seem to follow him through the room.

Veronica is backing into the gallery, turning girlishly on the ball of her foot. No optics in Titian or Tintoretto, she says, gesturing at the walls. But you can still see the influence of the optical style. Dark backgrounds? That's from optics. Images projected in a camera obscura always have dark backgrounds. But holy shit, the van Dyck? The ruffles on that collar, are you kidding? Definitely optics. The Lotto, too, although he hides it pretty well. And check out the Pontormo. Look how fucked his proportions are. He used the camera obscura to nail down Mary's face and

444

hands, the baby Jesus' head and arm. The rest of the painting's on a different planet. The hands and the faces don't fit the bodies. If that Mary were to crawl down from the canvas she'd look like a power forward for the NBA. Those arms are like four feet long.

She grabs Curtis's elbow and tugs him into the next room, talking loud, pointing. A young couple in matching sweatshirts and khakis is standing next to the wolfhound as they round the corner. Their brows are furrowed in disapproval, like this is the Sistine Chapel or something. Curtis gives them a mind-your-own-business glare.

Let me see if I'm getting this, he says. You're telling me all this stuff was —

Don't say *traced*. *Traced* sounds dismissive. There's a lot more to it than that. You've got to get the tonal values right, and the colors. It's not easy. It's not like these guys were cheating. You gotta remember, we're talking about the Dark Ages here. Painting didn't exist as some kind of noble alternative to photography like it does today, expressive of some ineffable human truth or whatever. It was just the only means these people had of recording images. Nobody cared whether van Eyck captured his subject's individual essence: they had no concept of individual essences. They just wanted to know if the fucking thing looked like Uncle Hubrecht or not.

445

Veronica slows her stride. Her eyes pass from painting to painting. I will never understand, she says, why people lose their shit over this. I mean, so what if they used optics? Why do we have to make these guys out to be superheroes? I was at Columbia when Hockney first started talking about this stuff, and believe me, *nobody* wanted to hear it. They were all about pure theory: Bataille, Derrida, Lacan. Nobody cared how paintings were actually done. You'd make an argument based on science, on methods, on empirical observations, and they'd look at you like you'd just come to fix the color copier or something. It's not that they didn't believe it. They just didn't see the point.

She's losing steam, getting distracted. Tension steals back into her shoulders, her face. I forgot that, Curtis says. That you studied art.

Art history, she says. Not art. Completely different. As I quickly found out.

They walk a few paces in silence. Veronica stares at the parquet, lost in thought. Curtis walks beside her, eyeing the walls. He'd been imagining the paintings talking to her, pouring out their secrets in a language he couldn't understand, or even hear. Now that she's not looking, they seem to go dark one by one, like tenement windows.

You come down here a lot? he says. To the museum?

She laughs, looks up. I've been in the casino

every night for a week, she says. Six hours a night, hundred bucks a hand minimum. I've racked up so many comps that they're about to name one of the towers after me. I'm getting sick from eating ossobuco and foie gras at every meal. So I figure, free museum tickets? Sure, why not? I like it here. It's quiet. It's a nice place to hide.

Hide from who?

She smiles at that, shakes her head. I just remembered, she says. I haven't eaten anything since this morning. You want lunch? I got vouchers out the wazoo.

I ate, but I'll tag along. You feel safe walking around out there?

She grins — a little crazy — and eases closer as they walk. She's maybe a half-inch taller than he is. Well, she says, you're gonna protect me. Right?

He stops. She steps around, turns to face him. He searches her expression for a tell — a clue that she's just opening up to reel him in — but even as he does it he knows that it's hopeless, that he's outclassed. If she's playing him, then he's going to get played. It's the only move he's got.

Look, he says. You asked me before if I'm the only one Damon sent out here to find Stanley. I told you yes. That's what I thought at the time. I was wrong. There's another guy. Local. Tall white guy. Sort of a dirtbag. Calls himself Albedo. You know him?

Her face turns sour. She shakes her head no. She's telling the truth.

Well, Curtis says, you probably ought to keep an eye out, and steer clear. He wants to make some trouble for you.

Damon sent this guy?

Yeah.

And Damon sent you.

The muscles are tight in her jaw and forehead. There's way more rage in her face than fear. For a second he thinks she might bite him. He looks away.

Then what the fuck are you telling me about him for, Curtis, if you guys are on the same team?

I want to do this my way, Curtis says. That's all I want.

She wheels and takes a few steps in silence, then stops again. Staring at the floor. After a while she looks up, past him, at the canvases to his right. Calm now, one hand on her cocked hip. Her posture reminds him of an explorer surveying a treacherous valley, and also of a white girl from Santa Barbara that he dated for a few weeks during his one semester at Cal Lutheran.

Look what happens after 1839, she says.

He tracks her gaze past the bare-breasted Venus he ogled earlier to a couple of later canvasses: a haystack and a field of flowers; a pond glimpsed between trees. Brightly daubed mosaics of color. Curtis looks at them for a second, trying to see what she's seeing, before his eye slides back across the rusted steel to the Venus. Her piled hair and small white breasts. Her sleepy smile. A ray of late-morning light falls on her from somewhere, and she's stretching, waking up. Her face half-hidden by her plump raised arm. Her single visible eye watching him with undis-guised lust.

1865 and 1880, Veronica's saying. Corot and Monet. For the first time in four hundred years paintings are flattening out. Chemical photography begins in 1839. All of a sudden the replication of projected images by hand isn't such a neat trick anymore. The chal-lenge from here is to paint the world the way the mind sees it, not the eye. Not to capture external objects but the act of perception itself. The monocular tradition — the thumb and the eyeball, the picture plane and the camera lens, the illusion of depth — that's over. Now it's all about two eyes and a brain in between. Flat retinas and flat canvases. The eye that tricks itself. This is the beginning of modern art.

Curtis shoots her an uneasy glance, but she's not looking at him. Her eyes are shift-ing up and down the walls, chasing a thought, following a story written there. She's talking to herself. It's impossible to tell how much she knows about him, how much she might have forgotten.

Eventually her attention lands on the Venus, and she flashes a lupine grin. She's a real creampuff, isn't she? she says. Even a hundred years before photography, you can tell people are getting bored. Everybody knows the game. You look at her, she looks at you. Trying to get under your skin through your eyeballs. All the old tricks are almost embarrassing. Joshua Reynolds owned a camera obscura that folded into a book.

Curtis and Veronica stand side by side, very still, for a long time. He can almost feel her quick and steady pulse through the sanitized air.

The Venus's single eye is all pupil, wide and bottomless. The red curtains painted behind her are billowy, frozen, with a pool of dark tangled in their folds. The position she's in — right elbow above her head — doesn't look very comfortable. The blond Cupid that tugs at her sash will never untie it. The hand that hides her face will never fall away.

C'mon, Veronica says after a while. Let's go upstairs. I'll buy you a doughnut.

36

The area between the slots and the Doge's Palace is swarmed by packs of middle-aged white guys wearing golf shirts and identical red-and-white Ace Hardware caps. Some are wheeling luggage, some have the blush of afternoon drunkenness on their cheeks, and all shout back and forth in thick-necked last-day-of-school bonhomie. Curtis and Veronica weave between them, Veronica walking a little in front, alert and unhurried, head sweeping from side to side like a prowling lion's. Curtis notes the efficient shuttle of her calves and shoulders, and he thinks back to Friday night, watching her at the blackjack table. Her spine tilted like an antenna toward the cards.

They step onto the escalator. Veronica leans on the rubber handrail, looking up at the vast oval canvas on the ceiling: a sturdy blond queen enthroned on a cloud, a levitating angel crowning her from above. Two steps down, his head level with her ribs, Curtis sees that Veronica's vinyl handbag is two-thirds unzipped, and he remembers the little SIG that she pulled on him last night. It should make him nervous, the fact that she's carrying, and he wonders why it doesn't, why he feels relieved. Then, for a sudden sick instant, he's sure he's never going to see Stanley Glass alive in this world again. The feeling thins out like smoke, and he follows Veronica into the Great Hall.

On their way toward the fake sky they pass another living statue, or maybe it's the one Curtis saw last night; he can't tell. Same whiteface, same robes, same roundlet cap. Ringed by a marble railing topped with crumpled dollar bills. Veronica doesn't give it a second glance.

At the Krispy Kreme in the Food Court she swaps a voucher for a half-dozen glazed, and they carry them back to the Grand Canal to walk along the railing and listen to the shouts and songs of gondoliers plying the chlorinated water below. How much to ride the boats? Curtis asks.

Like fifteen bucks, I think. In Italy, the real thing would set you back a C-note.

A commedia dell'arte troupe is headed their way — a courtesan and a masked scaramouche harassing what looks like Napoleon — and Veronica makes a swift evasive left onto a bridge, surprising an older couple cuddling over the canal. The permed-and-dyed wife looks at Curtis, then at Veronica, then back at Curtis. Her eyes narrow. The husband — tan, silverhaired, crew sweater around his neck — puts a hand on her back and steers her away.

Whoops, Veronica says. Did we just walk into a Viagra ad?

She takes a doughnut from the box and leans to eat it, her elbows propped on the marble rail. Sugar flakes fall from her fingers, vanishing as they hit the water. There's a tattoo, a big one, across the base of her spine; Curtis looks at it for a second, looks away, looks back. It's a tree with seven branches, each labeled with a symbol: sun and moon, male and female, something that looks like a four, or maybe a two, and something that looks like a flat, or a lower-case b. They're familiar, but Curtis can't place them. The highest branch, the seventh, is hidden by Veronica's top. Two figures are under the tree; Curtis can just see their heads over her waistband. The design is inked in black, like an old woodcut. Thinking of his own tats — bird-ball-and-chain on his right deltoid, devil dog on his left pec — and the way they've softened over time, he figures hers as eight or nine years old, minimum.

Look at that shit, Veronica says. She's nodding at the old couple, now strolling the arcade hand in hand. It's so middlebrow I could shoot somebody. Come to the themed city! Experience the themed culture! Purchase and consume your own reified emotions! Huzzah! Another loveless marriage preserved! I guaran-goddamn-tee you when that guy comes back for COMDEX in November the first thing he'll do is put on his fuzzy white robe and order himself a nineteen-year-old callgirl for a leisurely half-and-half. He'll come back to this hotel because he had such a great time here with the wife. He won't see any contradiction in what he's doing. And he'll be right.

She finishes her doughnut, sucks the tips of her fingers. I hate this place, Curtis, she says. I hate the good things about it most of all. I hate that I like it sometimes. It's such a relief to outsource your thoughts and feelings. You don't have to worry about making an original gesture because original gestures are impossible. You just stick to the script. It's like senior prom with gambling and shopping.

Hey, Curtis says. Can I ask you a question?

Sure.

Did you ask to meet for a specific reason, or did you just want to talk? Either's fine with me. But if we need to do some business, I'd just as soon get it out of the way.

She laughs silently, straightens up. The tattoo disappears. I did invite you for a specific reason, she says. Which was, in fact, to talk. This morning I made a few calls to people in Philly and D.C., and I checked you out. Everybody told me basically the same shit. Stand-up guy. A little square. Not mixed up in anything heavy. Nobody in Atlantic City seemed to know you at all, which I took to be a good sign. But I wanted to feel you out myself. Without pulling a gun on you first.

I appreciate that. How am I doing?

Not bad. You're a good listener. If we can improve on *great sense of humor,* I think you'll be all squared away. You're gonna make some young lady very happy.

Thanks. You mind if I ask who you talked to in Philly and D.C.?

No, I don't mind, she says. But I'm not going to tell you, either.

She grins at him, but she won't hold his gaze, and he starts watching her carefully, sure he's close to something. Curtis hasn't been part of her world in years. There's only one person she could've talked to this morning.

Veronica turns away, crosses the bridge, walks back the way they came along the opposite side of the canal. He falls into step on her left. Somewhere behind them Napoleon and the courtesan are singing a hammy duet for the sidewalk diners; their harmonies blend and clash with the piped-in Vivaldi on the sound system, the murmured conversations of passersby, the low hum of air conditioners underneath everything. Just ahead there's a German family — *ein Papa, eine Mama und zwei Kinder* — studying a lightbox map of the shopping area, their sharp angelic features gilt from below, like they're peering into a sanctum sanctorum.

I think you should go home, Curtis, Veronica says. Right now. You've got no good reason to be out here. Don't get mixed up in this.

I'm not mixed up in anything. I'm just looking for Stanley. Just trying to help.

She gives him an irritated look, the same look he often draws from Danielle when he's being stubborn, and it makes him stifle a smile. Curtis, she says. C'mon. Damon Blackburn? Seriously? I know he's your old war buddy or whatever. But you've *got* to know the guy's shady.

No, I don't know that. Why don't you tell me about that.

Veronica draws a breath, opens her mouth to speak, then exhales quietly. She does this a couple of times. She's slowing down; her neck and shoulders droop. For a second he's afraid she'll fall asleep right there on the pavement.

I would like to know, she says, *exactly* what Damon told you. About the marker he gave Stanley, and about the counters who hit the Point. I'd like to know exactly what he wants you to do for him, and why.

Curtis thinks about how best to respond. He's not holding much, and he figures he'll just lay it out. Damon told me he loaned Stanley ten grand, he says. Not long after, the counters hit the Point, and those other places. Stanley stopped returning Damon's calls. Damon's afraid that if Stanley defaults, Spectacular management will think he had something to do with the counters, and they'll fire Damon for approving the loan. So he asked me to find Stanley, and to report back. That's all he wants.

And you believed that.

Not really, no.

Why not?

Curtis is cautious with his answer. Damon and Stanley are friends, he says. I've never known Stanley to borrow money from a friend.

Veronica closes her eyes, smiles. That was the right answer, and he waits for the coins to drop. She's still creeping forward, listing from side to side. Curtis thinks of spinal patients he met in physical therapy, and also some Japanese dancers he saw one time in Okinawa.

The marker for ten grand wasn't a favor, Veronica says. It was to cover expenses while Stanley was putting the team together.

Curtis blinks. Shit, he says.

Stanley and I did all the legwork, but Damon helped with recruitment. He also brought in most of the money. Nobody but Stanley was supposed to know that Damon was involved, but of course Stanley told me, just in case anything happened.

Veronica's tone is flat and tired, precise but unrehearsed. Listening, Curtis gets a quivery rollercoaster feeling; his pulse shifts into lower gear. He hadn't expected this, but he's not really surprised by it, either. It fits.

There were a dozen of us, Veronica says. Working in two teams. Big casinos have gotten good at spotting teams, but with us they never had a chance. We were like amoebas oozing through the tables. Transparent. Whenever a pit boss would start getting wise, we'd change shape. The bosses knew something was up, but every time they'd pin one of us down, they'd just create an opening someplace else. Pushing on a balloon. On top of that, the bankroll Damon put together was enormous. I personally started the day with two hundred grand in a Betsey Johnson bag. And I was one of the lightweights.

Hold up, Curtis says. You're telling me Damon helped put this team together. Why did he think it'd be a good idea to hit his own place? That makes no sense to me.

We didn't hit the Spectacular.

Curtis shakes his head to clear it. But the Point lost more money than —

Listen to me. We didn't make a dime off the Point. They knew we were coming, and they immediately shut us down. They had security all over us from the moment we stepped through the door. Every time a count would go up they'd lower the table limit, drop the minimum to bring in the grinds. Every time we'd ID a weak dealer he'd disappear. It was like playing tick-tack-toe: it was obvious we were gonna spend the whole night fighting to break even. We left after an hour. The shift boss was waiting for us at the exit, handing us these cheap-ass gift baskets full of shampoo and lotion and shit. Big grin on his face. Better luck next time, assholes.

But —

Just listen. That was the agreement we had with Damon. Get it? We'd make the Point our last stop, we'd go in, and we'd get cut off at the knees. Damon would show up to work earlier in the day with screen-capture photos of all of us, he'd give a we-happy-few-we-band-of-brothers speech to his security detail, and he'd be a hero. Immediate induction into the casino-management hall of fame. *The Spectacular: The One They Couldn't Break!* You see the picture? Remember, Stanley and I were the only ones who knew Damon was in on the deal. The rest of the team was bouncing around the tables with steam coming out of their ears, trying to figure out how we got burned so fast. Not a lot of acting was required.

Veronica, Curtis says, the Spectacular got *slaughtered* at the tables that night.

Not by us.

Well, then what the hell happened?

She shrugs theatrically. Last I heard from AC, she says, management at the Point's brought in the cops. You know as well as I do how casinos like to avoid doing that, so they must be pretty sure they've got a serious problem on the inside. How is Damon explaining all this?

I couldn't tell you. Whatever he's saying, he's not saying it to me.

When was the last time you talked to him?

Not since I left Philly. Damon's not real big on using the phone. He likes to keep in touch by fax. Which is funny, because he's about as

459

dyslexic as they come. Can't spell worth a damn.

Curtis's forehead is starting to ache from furrowing his brow. He pushes his glasses down his nose to massage his temples, trying to loosen himself up. Even if it *was* an inside job, he says, somebody on your team had to have known about it. It must've been co-ordinated. You said your team was in the Point for an hour before you gave up. Can you account for everybody during that time? Do you know where everybody was?

She takes a long while to answer. He's given up on her, is trying to come up with another way of asking the question, when she finally speaks.

The team was divided into two groups, she says. I led one. The other group was led by a guy who calls himself Graham Argos. He isn't somebody I knew beforehand, and I don't think Stanley knew him well, either. But he was good, really good. One of these MIT hotshots, or so he said. Excellent counter, great actor. Totally nondescript. I had five or six conversations with him — long conversations, one on one — and I'm still not sure I could pick him out of a lineup. He looked a little different each time I saw him.

Veronica glances at Curtis's face, but her eyes don't quite focus, and he can tell she's seeing somebody else, remembering. Maybe fifteen minutes after we walked into the

Point, she says, Graham disappeared. We didn't see him again until we got back to our suite at Resorts to split the take. He met us there. He told us some story about how Spectacular security was up in his face, making threats, and how he got scared and left. I didn't believe it at the time. I just figured he'd given up early on making any money and didn't feel like waiting around for the rest of us. Now I'm not so sure.

Are you still in touch with him? Have you talked to him lately?

No, she says. I haven't. But you have.

The Whistler. The guy with the teeth.

Veronica nods. He's got some caps that he wears sometimes, she says. Dental veneers, I guess they're called. So don't lean too hard on the gap as a way to spot him.

Curtis's mind is clicking, rolling over like the board at 30th Street Station, sorting through everything the guy — Argos — said on the phone last night. The same phrases keep shuffling to the top: *I know what happened in AC. Lay the fuck off me. I'm the guy you're really looking for.* Veronica, Curtis asks, if you and Stanley didn't know Argos beforehand, how did you get partnered up with him?

She's smiling as she replies, but her voice is angry, brittle. Damon spotted Graham at the Point maybe six months ago, she says. Graham was working with a weak partner. That's

461

the only reason Damon burned him. He could tell Graham was good. Instead of running him out, Damon put him on the payroll as a position player. And then one night, a few months later, Damon asked Stanley if he'd be into putting together a blackjack team. For old times' sake. Because he'd met this kid — you can guess the rest.

Fuck, Curtis says.

He's reaching way back now, through years of memories. Damon at Leonard Wood, at Twentynine Palms. Things he did and said coming back in snatches. The expression on his face at certain moments. The way he always seemed to stand a little apart, winding everybody up, watching them run themselves down. Patterns are forming that Curtis has never noticed before, or never wanted to.

Curtis, Veronica says. Seriously. You should go home.

And at this point that's pretty much what Curtis wants to do. His nose tickles, his face grows hot, and he's blindsided by a memory, something he hasn't thought of in twenty years or more: a trip he took to the shore with his dad and Stanley and some gambler friends. Curtis couldn't have been more than six or seven. Somebody told him a story about pirate treasure; he found a corroded can, picked out a spot on the beach, and spent the afternoon slinging sand while everyone else horsed around in the surf. When his hole got hip-deep he ran to show Stanley, but by the time they made it back, it had filled with seawater. *Knock it off with the whining, kid. This is no good. You gotta find a map. Take it from me, kid: a story is not the same as a map.* Curtis has no map. After all these years, he still hasn't learned. Tell him the right story and he'll start digging.

He blinks, looks up. They're coming to the end of the fake sky. He thinks of the gun on his belt, of the wedding ring locked up topside, of Albedo cruising the Strip in his big black car. He's been lucky. There are worse ways this could have gone.

But he's still not quite finished. Where was Stanley? he asks.

Huh?

While your team was in the Spectacular. Where was he?

She looks confused for a second. He was back at the hotel, she says. At Resorts. Graham and I ran the team in the field. Stanley was with us at the beginning, at the first couple of places we hit, but that's all. He got too tired.

She grimaces, then looks away, pretending to check out a mannequin in a shop window. Stanley doesn't get around like he used to, she says. To function in a team like ours, you have to move quickly. Stanley can't.

He's pretty sick, isn't he?

I don't know. He won't see doctors. I kept telling him to go. I kept saying that I was just going to call a fucking ambulance. I guess I should have. And now —

Her voice is steady, but she's still looking away. Her hands are balled into fists. The fake sky is falling away behind them. Ahead, the living statue stands in its marble circle, a daub of pure white, a lone candle in the gloom.

I think maybe he's just bored, Veronica says. He wants a challenge that's worthy of him. He's afraid he's wasted his one real gift.

He nods, half-listening, distracted by what he's still puzzling through. Then he notices her scowl.

I don't mean gambling, she says. I mean looking.

She's quiet for a second. Do you know Frank Stella? she asks.

He's a gambler?

He's a painter. A post-painterly abstractionist. I heard a story once about Frank Stella from one of my professors. Stella thought that Ted Williams — the Hall of Fame hitter for the Red Sox? — he thought Ted Williams was the greatest living American. He thought Ted Williams was a genius because Williams could *see* faster than anybody else alive. He could count the stitches on a ninety-mile-an-hour fastball as it was coming across the plate. Frank Stella would have *loved* Stanley Glass.

For Stanley, vision *is* action. It's a pure, discarnate thing. The swing and the hit aren't even necessary. The look itself is the home run.

They're back in the Great Hall. Veronica's eyes are aimed at the ceiling: the fleshy queen and her allegorical court, afloat above awed onlookers. Armored horsemen on rearing stallions. Heralds and angels blowing trumpets. A winged lion statue. Gray cumulous hung between white spiral columns. Curtis walks quietly beside her, following her eyes, half-aware of the big painting. Thinking instead of a trick Stanley used to do: Curtis's dad would throw a deck of cards across the room — *let's play fifty-two pickup* — and Stanley would collect them, naming every facedown card before he turned it over.

They're on the escalators now. Down below sunlight blazes orange through the doors of the Doge's Palace. The Ace Hardware guys have thinned out; the hallway is less crowded. A masked mattacino is performing there, comparing his flexed biceps with a security officer's.

Veronica is still looking up. Veronese, she says, pointing. Did that dude have some balls, or what? Check out that forced perspective. Look how beefy those guys at the bottom are. I'll bet when they unveiled the real one in the Hall of the Great Council people were afraid to stand under it. Have you ever seen it?

465

The real one? Curtis says. I think so, yeah. Couple of years back, when I was on leave in Italy. Does Stanley still talk about going over there?

Just about all the time, yeah.

Why doesn't he? Short of funds?

No. Money is never an issue with him. He just never had a passport.

Veronica steps off the escalator and moves fast toward the exit. Curtis follows her, not sure where she's going. The mattacino spots her as she walks by, doffing his feathered cap — *Come sta, bella?* — and she sidesteps him without breaking stride, flips him off without bothering to look at him. A second later she's out the door.

Curtis catches up with her against the railing of the outdoor canal. The sun is sliding toward the mountains — big and soft, a yolk on a tilted frypan — and the sky is a yellow muddle interrupted by pink flares of contrails. She's chewing on a thumbnail, arms crossed tight on her chest. Looking at the moored gondolas without really seeing them. Jesus, I fucking hate those guys, she says. People in masks creep me out.

Curtis frowns, then grins, studying her profile. Except when it's you wearing one, he says. Then it's okay. I got that right?

She nods. Used to be, she says, when I was a kid, I'd wear a mask the whole week of Halloween. I'd never take it off, not even in the bathtub. My mom would bring home these blue gel-masks from the spa where she worked, and I'd sleep in 'em. It was the only way I *could* sleep. Otherwise I'd just lie there all night. Wondering how I could ever be sure that anybody was anybody. Or that I was myself, even. My poor mom had me in counseling like you would not believe. I probably took the MMPI six times before I so much as heard of the SAT.

Curtis leans on the rail to Veronica's left, looking down at the water. A guy with a net on a long aluminum pole is fishing trash off the surface, sweeping it back and forth. He looks like a gondolier without a boat.

Veronica shifts her weight, moves closer. She must have showered abovedecks before she cleared out this morning: she smells like the hotel soap. What about you? she says. What were you for Halloween, back in the day?

Curtis doesn't look at her. My grandparents were Jehovah's Witnesses, he says. I never got to do all that much for Halloween.

But as he says it, he's remembering a party he went to once in Springfield with some of the guys from Leonard Wood. Black shades. The charcoal suit he wore to his grandmother's funeral. A piece of coiled handset cord snaking from his ear to his jacket. Damon was there too, in a regimental tailcoat and a bicorn hat, no telling where he found them. Stupid, the things we want. Stupid to want anything.

What are you gonna do now? Curtis says.

Right now? I'm gonna hit some tables. Get paid. My bankroll's getting —

Not right now. I mean in general.

She fakes a laugh, tosses her hair. Honestly? she says. I have no idea. How 'bout you?

He smiles softly. I was hoping Damon would get me on with security at the Spectacular, he says. But that's starting to look pretty unlikely.

You still in the Marines?

I retired in January. Got my twenty, got out.

Twenty years? she says. Christ. What did you do?

In the Corps? I was an MP. Military policeman.

No shit?

No shit.

Wow, she says. So you're not just playing around with this detective business.

Curtis laughs, shakes his head. I didn't really do anything like that in the Corps, he says. I was more about security. Guard duty. Stuff like that.

She's looking at him again, sizing him up. You were a security guard for twenty years? she says.

Base security, rear-area security on the battlefield, processing prisoners of war. I did other stuff, too. But security's what I liked.

468

That's some pretty glamorous shit, Curtis.

Curtis just smiles, lets that pass. Below, the canal-cleaner has caught a bunch of red carnations; they drip over the edge of his broad flat net.

What did you like about it? Veronica says.

Curtis thinks about that. He opens his mouth a couple of times to answer, closes it again. I like getting in the way of stuff, he says after a while. I guess I just like being in the way.

She laughs, shakes her head. That's it? she says.

Basically, yeah.

That's bullshit.

Curtis sighs, straightens up, sighs again. Back in '81, he says, when Reagan got shot, I was about two miles away, in high school, at football practice. They pulled us all off the field. And then they kept showing it on TV. You remember that?

I was in — let me think — third grade.

That guy Tim McCarthy, Curtis says. The Secret Service agent, the one who caught the fourth bullet. He jumped right in front of it. I remember it just blew my mind that somebody could do that.

She's giving him a strange look. Skeptical. He can see it at the edge of his vision. He's not sure why he's telling her this. He keeps his eyes trained on the water.

You played football in high school? Veronica says.

I did. I was on the offensive line.

You were not.

I was. I was a guard.

You went to high school in D.C., right?

Dunbar, all four years.

She's studying him closely. How tall are you, Curtis? she says. If you don't mind my asking?

I don't mind. I'm five-seven.

Five-seven. And the other kids were —

All about eleven feet tall, yeah.

That cracks her up. Okay, she says. Cool. And after you got out of the hospital? After all the gnarly physical therapy? What did you do then?

Curtis laughs too. I went to college, he says. For about a minute. Then I went into the Marine Corps.

They're quiet for a while. She looks to the right, past the façade of the Ca' d'Oro, toward the clocktower — twenty-four-hour dial, gold zodiac loop — and the pulsing readerboard above it. She shifts her weight as she turns. Her hip comes to rest against Curtis's leg: scrawny and sharp, fever-warm. He looks down. There's the tattoo again, more of it this time. The two figures under the tree are a bearded old man and a young man with a sword. Two triangles are superimposed over the scene: one pointed up, one pointed down.

Veronica's skin is dark, tanning-bed tan.

You ever think about going back to school, Curtis?

That's pretty much what my wife wants me to do.

I'll bet she's real excited about you being out here, isn't she?

Yeah. We weren't exactly on speaking terms when I left. She's pretty upset.

Veronica's hair is sliding off her back, across her left shoulder. She drops her head forward and the rest of it comes down. Behind her, the hotel readerboard is playing video of a juggler next to flashing blue text: A PEACOCK WITH A THOUSAND EYES!

Curtis, she says, how come you're not wearing a wedding ring?

He takes a long breath, moves away a little.

Is that a bad question?

No, he says. It's a good question. I'll give you an honest answer.

She straightens up, looks at him.

When I was stationed overseas, he says, every so often I would run into these intelligence guys. Interrogators. Sometimes military, sometimes not. I never got to know any of them personally. But a few I met, they liked to talk about their work. What they did. And what I found out was, there's a certain kind of person who's good at that job. I got a sense of how these guys operate, how they see the world. Now, to people like you and me, a ring on my finger just says *I love my wife.* But to these guys, a ring on my finger says *this is how you can hurt me.* I always liked to think these guys were few and far between. But once you learn to spot them, what to look for, then you start seeing them all the time. Anyway, coming out here, not knowing what I was getting into, I figured that's something I better not broadcast. That's all.

She nods. I understand, she says. You're smart to be careful.

Curtis smiles, shrugs.

Well, she says. I should go. I'm getting light on walking-around money.

You headed back inside?

No, she says, I can't win here. If you win big or lose big, people start to notice. They're paid to pay attention. I don't want anybody to ever remember seeing me here.

Present company excluded, of course.

Of course. Anyway, the fucking smell in this joint is killing me.

Smell? Curtis says. I guess I stopped noticing it.

They pipe it through the vents. All the Strip joints do it, but this one is by far the worst. It's like ferrets fucking in a potpourri bowl.

Curtis laughs. Veronica smiles, looks away.

Hey, Curtis says. Thanks for talking to me. Seriously. Thank you.

No sweat, she says. It was my pleasure. I hope all this shit works out.

She offers her hand, and he takes it. Then she steps behind him and heads toward the bridge to the Boulevard.

Hey, Veronica?

She stops, half-turned.

Is Stanley gonna talk to me?

Veronica looks at him for a second, squinting against the sun. Then she opens her mouth to speak.

I know you talked to him last night, Curtis says. You don't have to tell me where he is. I'm not even gonna ask. Do you think he'll talk to me?

A challenge appears in her eyes, then fades, replaced by something closer to pity. I think so, she says. But not now. He's not ready yet.

She turns again to walk away, then turns back. You shouldn't wait around for him, Curtis, she says. You should just go home.

Her long shadow slices between the balusters on the bridge, a moving beam of dark. Curtis watches her go. He could head over to McCarran first thing in the morning. Get on standby. He ought to call Danielle, let her know.

He hears a rush of wings: a flock of snow-white pigeons billows from the parking garage, pouring around the belltower in a formless spume. The shimmering cloud thins out over the city, banking across the sun; the white wings go black in silhouette. Curtis looks for Mount Charleston in the distance,

473

but with the sun behind them the mountains are indistinguishable, shrunken, and he can't make out its shape.

On his way topside Curtis digs out his cell to call his wife, but he winds up phoning Walter Kagami instead.

37

The Strip gets shabbier north of the New Frontier, but Curtis opts to walk it anyway, to give himself time and space to think.

The block ahead is Old Vegas: the neon clowns of Circus Circus, the Stardust's psychedelic mushroom cloud, the flashing incandescent egg-beaters of the Westward Ho. Jarhead joints: places Curtis knows. Half the properties are boarded up, waiting for the wreckingball. The equilateral A-frame of the Guardian Angel Cathedral overlooks the droning gorge of the superarterial, the blue mosaic on its western face lit weakly from below, its sleek freestanding spire echoing the distant tower of the Stratosphere.

The night is cool, maybe fifty degrees, and ambivalent breezes rustle palmfronds, spread exhaust. Curtis sticks close to the curb on the boulevard's east side, nothing to his left but eight lanes of traffic. He walks quickly, although he's not in any hurry: Kagami won't be able to meet until late. He pushes forward, lengthening his stride. As if trying to gain ground on a thought he should be having. He's pissed off, mostly at himself, and ready to be gone.

What little Curtis knows about playing blackjack he learned in joints like these — Slots A Fun, the Riv, the Ho — after years of fruitless lessons from Stanley and his father. *Pit bosses don't believe black folks can count, so they'll never catch you. I'm giving you the keys to the kingdom, Little Man. You won't have to work a day in your life.* But blackjack with his dad was like driver's ed with Richard Petty: Curtis had no point of entry. And even back then Stanley was playing an entirely different game.

It was Damon who finally taught him basic strategy: mornings spent sobering up at the two-buck tables at Slots. By the time Curtis rotated back to Lejeune, he'd worked his way through all the North Strip casinos, figured out how to stay afloat for hours of free drinks. He even grossed a little, although his take came out way under minimum wage. Still, he went back to North Carolina with a new understanding of what his dad and Stanley actually did, even if he was still foggy on exactly how they did it. He owes Damon for that, at least. Doesn't he?

It was two weeks ago today that the call came. As Curtis rode the Broad Street Line south to Marconi Plaza, as he walked the half-mile past the bocce courts and the

475

Quartermaster Depot to the Penrose Diner, his head was buzzing with questions he'd been afraid to ask himself, questions he knew Damon would understand, would maybe even have some answers to. What should he be doing? Should he go back to school? With Curtis's employment handicap and thirty-percent disability, Voc Rehab would pay tuition, would maybe even offer subsistence allowance, but is it worth the trouble? Was it dumb for him to get married so soon after getting hurt? With marines mounting up for the Desert again, would it be crazy to think about reenlisting?

Curtis never got to ask Damon those questions. It's starting to look like he never will. At no point did he believe the story Damon told him, not for a second. But he didn't exactly disbelieve it, either. Damon has talked him into plenty of questionable shit over the years, but Curtis has never felt suckered or used. Not till now.

The Riviera's seething façade and the pink parabolas of the La Concha are behind him now. He passes gas stations and fast food joints done up in stuttering neon, new condos where old casinos used to be. SOUVENIRS T-SHIRTS GIFTS INDIAN JEWELRY MOCCASINS LIQUOR. Coming up on the Wet 'n Wild: dark and quiet, strange silhouettes against the Sahara towers. The onion dome of the casino just ahead, less Egyptian than Persian, less

476

Persian than Byzantine. The boulevard's west side is mostly empty lots, hibernating till the next boom. It's dark enough here to see a few stars, Jupiter high in the southeast. Curtis feels vulnerable without his gun. He doesn't like the feeling, or the fact that he's feeling it.

The few people on the sidewalk are gathered in nervous packs, and Curtis scopes them in his periph, catching bits of conversation as they pass. Winsome Scientologist types shilling for timeshares. A clutch of staggering Ace caps, maybe the same guys from before. *What asshole hits a hard twelve against a six? That clown cost me a hundred bucks!* A sandwich-boarded street preacher screaming apocalypse at two hard-eyed motorcycle cops. A wedding party in full finery: mulleted groomsmen, plump bridesmaids in seafoam organza, the bride's arm held aloft by balloons that catch headlights in their Mylar skin, a cluster of rolling eyes. Four Japanese girls with pink hair and funky glasses, bright-eyed and laughing, huddled like trick-or-treaters. A sunburnt panhandler, cane in one hand, coinpail in the other, and wraparound shades identical to Curtis's own. IF YOU ARE MEAN ENOUGH TO STEAL FROM THE BLIND, HELP YOURSELF. A black kid who looks about thirteen, handing out leaflets for escort services. *Azar é palavra que não existe no meu*

477

dicionário, y'know what I'm saying? A drunk in a rumpled seersucker suit who's just pissed on a palmtree, pale dick still peeking from his trousers, foxtrotting an invisible partner across a parking lot, singing "It's Only a Paper Moon" in a deep steady voice.

At the Holy Cow Curtis crosses to the opposite side and continues north. When the wind is right he can hear the rumble of the Big Shot and the High Roller up ahead, the screams of their riders. He's too close to the tower now to take it all in at once: the inverted-lampshade crown, the spotlit tripod base. He tries to ID the international flags outlined in neon above the marquee, then remembers that they're all fake. Imaginary countries. *All countries are imaginary,* Stanley would say. That reminds Curtis of something else, something Veronica said, about why Stanley's never been to Italy. *He just never had a passport.* Why *never had?* Why not *doesn't have?*

A working girl is jogging down the sidewalk toward him — red wig, black fishnets, six-three in four-inch heels, probably trannie — trying to pull on a coat and hail a cab at the same time. She keeps looking over her shoulder at the Aztec Inn like she expects somebody to be after her, like maybe her trick just went apeshit, or she lifted his wallet, or his heart exploded while she was blowing him and she needs to make herself scarce. The

478

look on her face says things are only going to get worse for her. Curtis steps out of her way, avoids eye contact.

A steady stream of taxis picks up and drops off at the casino's porte-cochère: UNLV kids on double dates, Midwesterners in windbreakers and running shoes. The cabs all turn south when they hit the Strip again. Curtis slips off his ballcap as he steps through the entrance, tucks it in his waistband where the revolver ought to be, letting the brim dangle over his tailbone.

Ten bucks buys him a ticket for the elevators. It takes him a while to figure out where to go next, but once he does the wait's not long. A walk-through metal detector — a new Garrett machine — sits at the head of the line, just as Kagami said it would. Security officers hand-search bags and fannypacks, but this doesn't slow things down as much as the photographer who's snapping digital photos of everybody who's headed topside. The guy in front of Curtis — drunk and swaying, handlebar moustache and BUCK FUSH T-shirt, cringing wife and two silent kids — won't stop bitching about it. Typical Vegas, brother, he says to Curtis. They always gotta be selling you something.

They take the photos, Curtis says, so they have a record of who goes up to the tower. If one of us turns out to be loaded with Semtex and blows the joint up, it'll make our remains easier to identify. If they can earn a few extra bucks selling the pictures as souvenirs, then I guess they might as well.

The guy laughs and looks at Curtis, but Curtis doesn't laugh, doesn't smile, and the guy looks away and quiets down.

The observation deck is on the hundred-and-eighth floor, eight hundred feet up. The elevator takes under a minute to get there. Curtis is still early for Kagami, so he does two laps of the observation deck, clockwise and counterclockwise, yawning hard to pop his ears. The valley glitters to the mountains in every direction, sodium orange and mercury blue, crystals scattered in a pit.

He finds an empty bench between two coin-operated telescopes and sits down and tries to think. Out of habit he wonders where Stanley is, but he knows now that that's the wrong question, has been the wrong question all along. Better to ask why he's been so hard to find — or even better, why Damon wants so badly to find him. If Veronica is telling the truth, and Curtis thinks she is, then the number of likely answers to that last question are relatively few, and Curtis doesn't like the looks of any of them.

He keeps getting distracted by the city, by landmarks translating out of the grid. From this height, the cleared lot where the Desert Inn used to be gaps like a knocked-out tooth. He spots his hotel where the Strip bends due south, its belltower a pale finger laid across Caesars' brilliant reader-board. Flying in Thursday morning, Curtis was able to catch glimpses of the Luxor, New York, Mandalay Bay, but he couldn't make out much on the north end; the drop was too quick.

Curtis hadn't been on a plane since they medevaced him home from Germany a year and a half ago; he was too doped up on Demerol then to register much. For the flight to Vegas Damon had booked him an aisle seat on the 757's port side, but Curtis checked in early enough to swap it for a starboard window. As the plane gathered altitude in its wide takeoff loop he looked down on acres of cranberry bogs in the woods southeast of Evesham, pools of spilt mercury ricocheting the sunrise, as if the earth were bursting with inner fire. Alone in his seat, watching the continent scroll below, a cool thrill stole over him, a calm like nothing he'd known in years — and it didn't go away when the plane touched down. The whole time he's been out here he's felt like this: alert but detached, not quite involved or implicated, like he's watching everything through a screen from a tremendous distance. It's not a bad feeling, but he's starting to mistrust it.

The night sky is busy with helicopters, mostly charter flights buzzing the glowing corridor from here to McCarran. One flies low to the southwest, an LVMPD chopper, and Curtis watches it aim a searchlight into Naked City, the residential blocks between here and Sahara Ave, at a spot where the blue-and-red pulses of police cruisers have congregated. The old neighborhood buildings multiply and divide the swirling lights like a kaleidoscope, and the noise of the sirens is muted by distance and thick glass. Curtis checks his watch, then heads below into the lounge and orders himself an Irish coffee, watching the restaurant, one deck lower, rotate glacially while the bartender pours the Bushmills. On the little stage, a jazz trio is playing Jobim to the disinterested room: "Inútil Paisagem," the singer's clear and icy delivery closer to Gilberto than Wanda Sá. She talks to the bassist and the piano player with shifts of her weight, small movements of her hands. The three of them seem content to be ignored.

Curtis snags a small table on the lounge's southern side and looks down at the Strip as he waits for Kagami, sometimes redirecting his focus to his own dim reflection. Remembering things about Damon: stories he's heard, and told, and retold. Seeing shadows in them that he'd always ignored. The time Damon commandeered a brand-new Z3 from some Simi Valley fucknut — just took the keys right out of the guy's hand — so he could use it to pick up a girl he'd met at Mandalay Bay. Or the time he roped Curtis into running interference on the MPs at Twentynine Palms while he smuggled some shitbird PFC offbase in a laundry truck. Or the time he backed down a halfdozen goat-ropers in the parking lot of a Waynesville bar, M9 pressed against a lean cowboy cheek, the skin around the barrel making a livid ring, and Damon stone-cold sober. Curtis feels like he's been working a crossword puzzle, staring at it for days, and he's just now seeing that the first words he filled in were all wrong. Or it's more like one of those pictures that were popular maybe ten years ago, the ones that were 3-D if you focused your eyes just right, a bunch of random dots if you didn't. Curtis feels like he's still not focusing right. He never could get those damn pictures to work for him, he recalls. And now, of course, he never will.

Kagami's image pops up in the window: a dark shape full of stars where it blocks the overhead light. The lenses of his spectacles are twinned quartermoons hung in the black. Curtis turns, offers his hand. Thanks for agreeing to meet, Walter, he says.

No sweat, kid. You're not putting me out. I just got done with an appointment down the hall. Hope you haven't been waiting long.

Just enjoying the view.

Kagami eases into a chair. He seems distracted, like he'd rather not be here. Curtis almost doesn't recognize him. His jacket and tie are gone, replaced by a purple-and-blue patterned sweater; he's removed his jewelry aside from a gold wedding band. Curtis thinks of his own ring, locked in the safe, and moves his left hand into his lap.

Meeting on a Sunday night, huh? Curtis says. You closing a big deal?

Kagami smiles. This wasn't business, he says. I was just socializing. Making some plans for next weekend.

What are you planning to do?

Oh, we're gonna walk up and down Fremont for a couple hours. Wave some homemade signs around. Yell *no blood for oil.* That sort of thing. You can come too, if you want. Bring fifty or sixty friends. It'd be great to have more ex-military.

Curtis wonders if Kagami is baiting him, like last time with Gitmo. He tells himself to keep cool, then realizes that he's not upset, then wonders whether he ought to be. I'll be in Philly next weekend, he says. But I appreciate the invite. You think you'll get a good crowd?

Kagami shrugs. We marched from Bellagio to the Trop back in January. Drew a couple hundred people for that. I hope we get at least that many this time.

I guess that's pretty good for Vegas.

There's a solid group of anti-nuke folks out here, what with the old Nevada Test Site, and now Yucca Mountain. Plus there's the university, and sometimes the unions. The Culinary got over a thousand pickets out on the sidewalk in front of your hotel when it opened back in '99. You should get off the Strip sometime, kid. There's a lot of stuff going on out here that you don't know about.

I didn't have to leave the Strip to figure that out, Walter.

Kagami grins. Still striking out on Stanley?

I'm not even swinging anymore, Curtis says. He looks evenly at Kagami for a moment, hoping to spot something in his face or his posture, some hint, but he knows that this is hopeless. Walter, he says, do you know a guy named Graham Argos?

Doesn't ring any bells. Who is he?

He was on the team of counters that hit AC over Mardi Gras. He's here in town now. I got a call from him last night on my cell.

Did he give you any leads?

No. I think he's looking for Stanley too.

Kagami chuckles, shakes his head. I hope Stanley's getting a kick out of this, he says. For years it seemed like Stanley was just part of the landscape out here. People took him for granted. Now all of a sudden everybody's looking for him, and nobody knows where the hell he is.

I think you know where he is, Walter.

Kagami's smile is steady, his expression unchanged.

I think Stanley's got a firewall set up, Curtis says, between the people who know where he is and the people who know what really happened in Atlantic City. I don't think you know what happened in Atlantic City.

Kagami remains statue-still, but his eyes flicker evenly across Curtis's face, his chest, his hands. Taking him in. Curtis feels like he's being sliced up, sorted into piles. I have to admit, Kagami says, that I am pretty curious about that.

Yeah. Me too.

Kagami shifts his weight, crosses his legs. Did you get the latest bulletin? he says. As of last night, the Casino Gaming Bureau is no longer running the show at the Spectacular. It is now a Major Crimes investigation.

Curtis blinks. What happened? he says.

Well, it seems that a couple of days ago this old geezer was out on Absecon Bay in his Boston Whaler. Trapping crabs. The old guy hauls in one of his traps —

Kagami held out his hands as if cradling a regulation football.

— and there's this enormous blue crab in it. A real monster. And the crab is gnawing on a chunk of human foot. Foot belongs to a Southeast Asian male in his late twenties or early thirties. The missing dealer from the Point is a twenty-eight-year-old Korean kid. So. Everybody say hello to the Major Crimes Division.

Curtis is aware of his pulse, an impatient

tap in his neck and temples. He looks out the window. A long way off the ground. This is fucked up, Walter, he says.

A little more than you signed on for, ain't it, kid?

Curtis stares at the table, rotates the empty mug beneath his fingers. Picturing Damon in the Penrose Diner. His red-rimmed eyes. His ripped sleeve. It was maybe a bad idea to drink the Irish coffee. He thinks he can feel the tower swaying in the wind, but there isn't any wind. Walter, Curtis says, I'm not gonna ask you where Stanley is. I will ask you this. Did you put Graham Argos onto me? Did you give him my number?

You got a reason to think I did?

He tried to make me think he got it from a bartender or a pit boss or somebody. But I think he got it from you. He knew that I'd talked to you. And he knew Damon sent me out here. Only you and Veronica knew that. He hadn't talked to Veronica.

What's your point, kid?

That was not a nice surprise for me, man. That dude makes me nervous.

Yeah? Kagami says. Well, no shit, Curtis. He makes me nervous too. I was hoping you guys would short each other out.

You could've given me a heads-up. Why didn't you call me?

Because I don't like you, kid. You give me a bad feeling.

Kagami says it softly, almost apologetically. He crosses his arms over his chest, turns to look down at the Strip.

Curtis lets that hang for a few seconds, breathing in and out. You don't even know me, man, he says.

Let's just say that what I do know does not endear you to me.

They sit in silence for a while. Curtis clenches his jaw; Kagami slumps wearily in his chair. Curtis is angry, but he can't shake the feeling that Kagami isn't entirely out of line. He's about to stand up, head for the door, when Kagami catches a passing waitress and orders a cognac. What're you drinking, Curtis? he says. You want another coffee?

No, thanks. I'm good.

C'mon, kid. Hang around for a couple minutes.

Ginger ale, Curtis says, and settles back in his seat.

The lights have stopped flashing in Naked City aside from an ambulance headed west on Sahara; they watch it until it reaches the interstate and disappears. Then their eyes drift back to the Strip. Following its blazing path south as it grows denser and purer, a tracer round fired at Los Angeles.

Put yourself in my place, kid, Kagami says. I didn't know what the hell was going on. I still don't. What would you have done?

I hear you. You just want to protect Stanley.

488

I just want to be a good goddamn citizen of the People's Republic of Clark County, Nevada. That's all I want. I want to defend Stanley's inalienable right to disappear when he wants to, and to stay disappeared for as long as he likes. I take this stuff very seriously, Curtis.

The waitress comes back with their drinks. Curtis sips his ginger ale, sips again. Kagami swirls his brandy, looks out the window. You spend a lot of time out here, kid? he says.

In Vegas? Not too much. My last trip was about three years ago.

Have you heard the CVA's new ad slogan yet? The official slogan?

What happens here stays here? Curtis smiles. Yeah. I heard it.

It's brilliant, Kagami says. It sums up everything. People call Las Vegas an oasis in the desert. *No!* It *is* the fucking desert. That's the key to the whole trick. Look down at that valley. You know what was down there a hundred years ago? Nothing. Some Mormons. A couple dozen cowboys. A few pissed-off Paiutes. The year I was born, there were ten thousand people living there. Today there's a million five. That's sixty years. Sixty years is nothing, it's a heartbeat. What's drawing all these people? Huh? *Nothing.* It's like a big blackboard, or one of those — what do you call it? — a dry-erase board. Wipe it clean. Draw in what you like. I mean, read

489

up on your history, kid. You wanna make something disappear? You wanna make it invisible? Haul it out here. The desert is the national memory hole. Manhattan Project? Never heard of it. American Indians? Hey, I don't know *where* those guys went. Gambling. Hookers. Nuclear waste. I guess you probably noticed the Desert Inn.

I noticed that it's gone, yeah.

Steve Wynn blew it up a couple years ago. October 2001. Collapsing buildings were not regarded as so much fun at the time, so he did it without the usual hoopla. But remember the party he threw back in '93, when he imploded the Dunes? Or that New Year's Eve when they brought down the Hacienda? Name me another place anywhere that routinely *blows up* its historic buildings. Las Vegas is a machine for forgetting.

Kagami sets his snifter on the table. I'm gonna smoke a cigar, he says, leaning over and reaching into his pocket. Do you want a cigar?

No, thank you.

Kagami produces a brown leather case, removes a dark panatela, and sets to work on it with a gold bulletcutter. You've been around, Curtis, he's saying. You've seen the world. Europe. Asia. Middle East. Me and my wife, we travel as much as we can. We did a fun thing last year for our tenth anniversary. We went back to Italy for two weeks. North-

490

ern Italy, where we did our honeymoon. You know what we did? We used the same guidebooks. Just to see if we could. And it worked. Same restaurants, same hotels. I remember we ate at this one place, this bacaro, that had been in business since 1462. Blew my mind.

Kagami's cigar case and cutter disappear. He takes a big naphtha lighter from his pocket and strikes it. A spritz of sparks. A two-inch tongue of flame. After a few puffs he snaps it shut with a loud clear chime, like the sound of a flipped coin.

Okay, he says. Now imagine you and your better half are tooling around Las Vegas with a guidebook from 1993. How do you think you're doing? *Ooh, honey, let's go see the Sands!* Sorry, sweetie-pie. What about the Landmark? The Landmark's a parking lot. The El Rancho? The Hacienda? You'll never see the Hacienda, it doesn't exist. The city is always changing. Always, just for the sake of doing it. And that's why it's always the same. Get it? That's its nature, its essence. Invisible. Pure. Formless. Indestructible. What do you know about roads?

Say again?

Rhodes. Island in the Aegean Sea. Used to be a colossus there, right? Okay. What about Alexandria? Had a pretty nice library, I hear. New York? Couple tall buildings. I'm talking about ruined fortresses here, kid. Collapsed empires. Places become defined by what they lose. Once it's gone, it's eternal. Everything you see down there — everything! — is on its way out. Everything self-destructs. I mean, fuck Rome. *This* is the eternal city. Pure concept.

The waitress appears again out of nowhere with an ashtray and a fresh ginger ale that Curtis doesn't really want. Kagami moves the tray a few inches closer, then takes a sip of cognac. The jazz trio is playing a sad French song that Curtis can't quite place. *Les musées, les églises, ouvrent en vain leurs portes,* it goes. *Inutile beauté devant nos yeux déçus.*

Kagami rotates his cigar slowly, deposits a tidy gray mound in the cutglass tray. I love this silly fucking town, he says. I got desert running through my veins. I was born out here. Did you know that?

Curtis shakes his head. My dad told me you knew Stanley from California, he says. I figured you were from out there.

My family's from Los Angeles. And L.A.'s where I grew up. But I was born out here. About a hundred fifty miles on the other side of those mountains.

Kagami aims a short finger in the general direction of Mount Charleston, lost somewhere in the darkness over Curtis's right shoulder, far out of sight. Curtis doesn't turn around.

You know where the Owens Valley is?

Kagami says.

Not exactly. I know it's west of Nellis, across the state line.

It's about fifteen miles outside of Death Valley National Park. That should give you an idea of the climate. I was born there at a place called Manzanar. You ever heard of Manzanar, Curtis?

Curtis gives Kagami a tight smile. Kagami's not even looking at him. Yeah, Curtis says. I've heard of it.

I was born there in 1943. I don't remember it except in little pieces. How the Army blankets smelled. Brown dust in everything. You'd fill up a pitcher with water, and before you could get it to the table there'd be dust on the surface. Little swirls of it. I remember that. My mother wouldn't talk about it, and my dad died in Italy, but over the years I've tried to educate myself a little bit. That led me to other things. If I'm remembering right, Curtis, your father spent the late Sixties and early Seventies playing clubs in Montréal. He ever tell you what I did during Vietnam, Curtis?

No, sir. He didn't.

I went to prison. I walked into the Hall of Justice with my draft card and a Zippo lighter, and I spent twenty-two months at Terminal Island. I'm not trying to be an asshole here, kid. I'm not judging you, and I'm not gonna say you should live your life any different. But if I act a little hostile to the whole idea of military police, then I got some reasons. That's all.

Kagami puts the cigar back in his mouth. A gray cloud rises toward the lights. Two thirtysomething women at the next table — flashy shoes, pricey coifs, monogrammed everything — get up and move to the other end of the room, fanning open hands before their disgusted faces. Curtis takes long breaths, counting them, until his teeth unclench.

I was an MP for twenty years, he says. No matter how hard I try, I can't get myself to feel bad or regretful about that. Maybe that means that one of these days — when I'm in a real different mood — you and I'll have to sit down and have ourselves a big old argument. That's fine. Right now, all I'm going to say is this. I'm not an MP anymore, Walter. But I am still Badrudin Hassan's son, Donald Stone's son. And I'm still Stanley Glass's friend. You and I may be at odds somewhere, but on this particular issue we want exactly the same thing. Which is to keep Stanley safe.

That may be so, kid. But we want it for completely different reasons.

I don't see how that matters.

I know you don't, Kagami snaps. That's the whole problem. At this point, Curtis, it's about the only thing that still matters.

Curtis can feel tightness in his neck and

temples: the beginnings of a headache. He can taste it on the back of his tongue. He's about ninety-eight percent sure that he's wasting his time here, but that other two percent keeps winking at him, lifting up its skirts. The jazz combo is taking a break, and somebody's forgotten to turn the piped-in music back on; it's strangely quiet in the room.

I'm sick of this shit, Curtis says. I've been jerked around now in just about every direction. I am ready to go home. There's only one thing keeping me from getting on a plane. If I leave, and later I find out that I brought something bad onto Stanley by coming out here, something that I had the power to stop, then I'm gonna feel real sorry about that. And I got enough stuff in my life to feel sorry about. So I guess what I want to hear from you is whether you think Stanley's gonna be okay.

Kagami shoots him an incredulous look. No, he says. No, Stanley's not gonna be okay. The man is dying, Curtis. Get it? It doesn't matter what you do or you don't do.

It does matter, Curtis says. It matters to me.

Kagami doesn't respond. He's staring at the night, looking very sad and very tired. Smoke rises from the ash of his cigar in a solid wavering column, like the ghost-white proboscis of butterfly, until the HVAC whisks

495

it away. Curtis is watching it snake toward the ceiling when he notices a low rumble of turbofans outside. He looks out the window, searching the sky for moving lights.

Recognize that? Kagami says.

Curtis listens hard, then shakes his head.

New stealth fighter. I'm pretty sure. Haven't seen it yet.

The sound of the engines fades. Heard any news about the war? Curtis asks.

Kagami shifts in his chair, leans forward. Curtis can see him getting comfortable, shuffling facts in his head, winding himself up for another practiced run of summary and analysis. Then he stops, like he's tapped out, like he just doesn't have it in him. Curtis, he says, when's the last time you talked to Damon?

I got a fax from him this morning. I haven't talked to him since I been out here. He's not returning my calls.

The waitress passes, and Kagami signals for the check, scribbling on an imaginary pad with the cigar. Then he lifts the panatela to his lips, takes a series of quick puffs, and crushes the stub in the cutglass tray.

Listen, kid, he says. Stanley's gone. He left town this morning, before dawn. I dropped him at McCarran myself. He didn't say where he was going, and I didn't ask, but my guess is that he went back to AC to settle with Damon. I think he's done about all the hiding out he can stand.

Veronica's still here. I just saw her.

Well, she would be, right? If Veronica and Stanley both have the goods on Damon, then they're gonna split up. They become each other's insurance.

I figured they'd be watching each other's back.

Kagami shakes his head. You got this all wrong, he says. You're still talking about Stanley and Veronica like they're regular people. They're not. Different set of rules, different set of concerns. You've put yourself in a bad spot here. You want me to believe that you're a stand-up guy, that you're not some kind of thug? Okay. Be a stand-up guy. Go home to your wife. You can't help Stanley, kid. You don't have the juice. Not here, not anywhere. And that's not something to be ashamed of, believe me. The best thing you can do for him is to forget about all of this. We're not talking about your old Uncle Stanley who used to do magic tricks. You're not in that scene anymore. I could tell you some stories. But I won't. Because he wouldn't want me to.

The check comes. Kagami lays a crisp bill in the plastic tray.

I will tell you this, he says. I heard this one maybe a year or two before I even met Stanley. Back when he was still a very young guy, he was in this poker game in Pasadena —

Stanley doesn't play poker.

497

He did back then. He was never any good at it, so he quit. To play poker you have to understand people. Stanley doesn't. It took him a while to figure that out. So. He's in this poker game in Pasadena. Underground casino, very exclusive. And he's not doing so great. The pots are bigger than he counted on. So he asks the house for a marker. And they just laugh at him. *Come back when you can afford to play here, kid.* Okay. Stanley gets up, walks over to the roulette wheel. Roulette's a pure game of chance, right? No skill involved. Stanley takes a hundred bucks — four green chips, lot of money for a young kid in those days — and as soon as the ball drops, he puts them on four numbers. Bam-bam-bam-bam. So fast you can hardly see his hands move. The numbers are all over the board — but on the wheel, they're consecutive. Right? One of his numbers hits. Now he's got eight *black* chips. Then, right after the croupier drops the ball again, Stanley splits that stack across four more numbers. Also consecutive on the wheel. And one of *those* numbers comes up. Seven thousand dollars. He asks them to double the table limit. They call the boss. Boss says okay, but we're switching croupiers. They bring in the new guy, new guy turns the ball loose, Stanley does it again. He's sitting on twenty-one grand, and he asks them again to double the limit. *Don't you want your money back?* Sure they do. And all of a sudden he's got over fifty thousand dollars in front of him. By this point the place is shut down. Nobody is playing but Stanley. Everybody in the casino — bartenders, musicians — is gathered around that table. Stanley says he wants the limit upped again, he wants to bet twenty grand. Boss thinks about it, and says okay, but you gotta move to a different table. New table, new croupier. The ball drops. Stanley puts down his four stacks of big nickels. These stacks, he can barely fit his hands around them. The place is like a church. Dead silent, except for that clicking wheel. And then it explodes. Stanley Glass has just won a little over two hundred thousand dollars in five consecutive spins. The dealers are all looking at each other, wondering if they're gonna have jobs tomorrow. It's obvious that if Stanley keeps playing he'll wind up owning the joint. Stanley collects his take, he looks up at the boss, and he says, *Do you want to keep playing here, or do you want to let me back into your fucking poker game?* This happens, I believe, in 1961. Stanley is nineteen years old.

The waitress comes back. Kagami waves away his change. He puts his elbows on the table, looks out the window.

How did he do it? Curtis says.

What do you mean?

I mean, what was the trick?

Kagami gives Curtis a smug smile, lowers his voice, leans closer. The trick was, he says, there *was* no trick. Stanley saw where the ball was going to go.

Curtis blinks. How is that possible? he says.

With an open-palmed shrug, Kagami sags back into his chair. All Stanley's abracadabra gobbledygook, he says. I used to think it was misdirection. Then I thought, maybe it's real magic — like he was trying to make impossible things happen. Now I think it's something else. Impossible stuff happens in Stanley's world all the time. It's no big deal to him. I think the magic is him trying to *make sense* of his world. Which is a very different place from the world you and I live in. And which is maybe some pretty lonely territory for a sick old man.

Curtis nods, then knocks back the last of his ginger ale. The combo is back on: Sleepy John Estes, barely recognizable. *Lord, I never will forget that floating bridge.* The piano and the bass are barely playing, setting soft suspended sevenths adrift over the clatter and murmur of the tabletops. *They tell me five minutes' time underwater I was hid.* Beneath the music, the big windows shiver with a distant afterburner growl.

It's getting late, Kagami says. Let me give you a lift back to your hotel.

38

Curtis's sleep feels nothing like sleep, only a rapid and jittery dream-ridden wakefulness. He's on a narrow cobblestone street, moonlit and shadowed, Stanley at one end, Damon at the other. There's an explosion, a pillow-muffled boom, and Curtis is in midair, suspended like one of the fake-fresco angels on the ceiling of the hotel lobby, jumping in front of the bullet. He jolts awake before it hits, not sure if he got to it in time, not sure who was shooting whom.

Still dark outside. He's pressed every button on the bedside clock-radio before he recognizes the sound of his cellphone. Throwing off the tangled sheets, he reaches for the little well of pale blue light on the dresser, picks it up before the voicemail kicks in, glances at the display — *Whistler* — and answers. Yeah, he says.

Good morning, Curtis. Hope I didn't wake you.

Curtis unplugs the charger, stumbles to the wall, finds a lightswitch. Rubbing his eye with the heel of his hand. What's up? he says.

I want to meet.

When?

Right now. I'm in the parking garage at the Flamingo. The sixth floor. I'm sitting in a Fortune Cab. The guy's got the meter running, so I'm not gonna stick around long.

You better get it in gear.

Curtis looks again at the clock, lying where he left it, upsidedown on the mattress: 4:31. Yeah, he says. Okay. I'll be right —

Listen, Curtis. Don't call anybody, and don't bring anybody with you. If you're bringing somebody else, go ahead and dial 9-1-1 before you come, because I'm gonna shoot you and everybody else I see, and I am not bull-shitting about that. Also, bring cash. At least a couple hundred dollars. Because this is going to be an expensive conversation. Got all that?

Yeah. I got it.

Say it back to me.

Curtis takes a breath. Flamingo parking lot, he says. Sixth floor. Fortune Cab. Two hundred dollars. Just me. Nobody else.

The call ends with a soft electric pop. Argos, Curtis thinks. Graham Argos. He's not calling from any cab; he wouldn't have said all that shooting-spree shit in front of a cabbie. This is some kind of setup.

He stands with the dead phone against his ear, eyeballing his reflection in the mirror over the dresser. Stubbly scalp, twisted-around skivvies. Not too suave. He takes a long moment to sort his dreams from his memories, to remember what he knows, where he stands. Stanley has left town, or so Walter says. It sounds like Damon at this point is basically toast. People have turned

502

up dead back in AC; Argos was involved somehow. Curtis has nothing to gain by meeting with him. This thought is like a weight coming off, a light from a familiar doorway: nothing to gain.

Curtis gets dressed, clips on his pistol, drops the speedloader in his jacket pocket and hits the door in a hurry, pressing the elevator callbutton in the hallway. Back in high school the coaches would rarely play him until the bleachers were emptying and the outcome of a game was no longer in doubt; it was embarrassing at first, but in time he developed a taste for it. It made everything purer, and gave him a kind of ownership of his efforts that the first-stringers could never claim. He catches something like that fourth-quarter feeling now as he waits by the sliding copper doors, tired and giddy and sure of himself. Today he is going to figure some shit out.

When the elevator hits bottom, Curtis detours to the cage on the gaming floor to cash more traveler's checks: five hundred, just to be safe. He puts the envelope of bills in his inside pocket, heads for the galleria. Along the way he passes a silent caravan of security officers moving from table to table, harvesting the drop. Something in their attitude — smooth blank faces, sharp efficient eyes — has the joyless finality of a toe-tag. None of the strung-out gamblers in the big room looks at them; they just stare at their cards like they've been enchanted, turned to stone, as their money walks slowly away.

Curtis hops a taxi in the porte-cochère and tells the cabbie to step on it; they make the Flamingo garage inside of three minutes. Curtis hands over a bill, gets out on the ground floor, and walks to the opposite end of the building to take the stairs.

On each floor he steps out of the stairwell, looking around before continuing up. The first two levels are valet spaces, mostly vacant. People and vehicles are moving on the next two decks, but they thin out as he gets higher. When he comes to Six he skips it, walking up one more floor to the roof: aside from a primer-gray Impala with a herring gull perched on its hood, it's empty. The full moon, huge and waxy, sinks toward the mountains, and the leafy Flamingo courtyard is shadowed by hotel towers. Its broad blue pool glows beneath the fronds and branches, and Curtis thinks of the display of his cellphone as it rang on the dresser. He should've called Danielle last night; he doesn't know why he didn't. He wishes he had. The gull tracks him as he passes, nervously stamping a webbed foot.

He walks down the ramp to the sixth level. It's nearly as empty as the roof: a couple of sedans, an SUV parked by the stairwell. No cabs. Curtis's attention goes to the SUV; he creeps toward it, his hand on his pistolgrip, and crouches to scan its tinted windows against the fluorescents overhead. So far as he can tell, it's clear.

A squeal of tires below. Curtis straightens his jacket, steps between the SUV and the stairwell. Ready to move in either direction. Bleary-eyed and unshowered, he feels sharp, but he can't tell if it's genuine-sharp or the kind of sharp you feel after a couple of beers. He checks his watch. 4:43.

Headlights. It's a cab: white, with black skirting and magenta fenders. It slows as it turns off the ramp, moving steadily ahead. Nobody but the cabbie is aboard that he can see. As it approaches, it angles broadside, rolls to a stop. Its flashing dorsal LED screen tells him that the NCAA first-round pairings have been announced. Its back door says FORTUNE CAB.

A quiet drone: the driver's-side window coming down. Hey, man, the cabbie says. You Curtis?

Yeah, Curtis says. Where's your fare?

You're my fare, man.

Okay. Where am I going?

The cabbie — dreadlocked hair gray at the temples, creased and sagging nut-brown skin — gives Curtis a slow once-over. I'm gonna tell you how it is, he says. And then you can decide if you want to ride or not. See, I'm not supposed to tell you where you're going.

I'm supposed to take your phone away, and I'm not supposed to talk to you once you're in the cab. How's that sound?

Curtis thinks about it. Can you tell me how long the ride's gonna be? he says.

I'll tell you what it's gonna cost. One-sixty. I take that up front.

Hundred sixty? Curtis says. That's a long ride. We crossing any state lines?

The cabbie gives him a thin crooked smile. What's it gonna be, man? he says.

Curtis peels eight twenties from the envelope in his jacket pocket and hands them over. Then he gives the cabbie his cell. The cabbie powers it down as Curtis opens the back door and sits.

They wind their way to the garage exit and turn south, passing the flashing hyperboloid of the Barbary Coast on their way to the interstate. As the cab descends the entrance ramp and merges into traffic, the driver speaks again. May as well settle in, he says. You're looking at an hour and a half, maybe an hour forty-five.

Curtis furrows his brow, calculating distance and time. Drawing blanks. We going to Indian Springs? he says.

The cabbie doesn't reply. Curtis shifts in his seat, adjusts his gun, looks out the window. Still a lot of cars on the road: after the expressway they thin out, and more vanish into North Las Vegas. The cab stays on the interstate. Soon they're passing the speedway, the airbase. The quiet radio plays Anita Baker. Hey, Curtis says. You know what's going on with the war?

The cabbie takes a long time to answer. I don't know anything, man, he says.

How about finding me some news?

The guy cranks the volume a little and punches a button until an NPR station pops up. The *Morning Edition* billboard is just starting. The U.S. has told UN inspectors to start leaving Baghdad; France says it'll veto any authorization of the war; Bush says he'll act no matter what; Americans support an invasion by a ratio of two to one.

By the time Bob Edwards comes on, Curtis has tuned the radio out. He meant to check in this morning with the concierge, try to get online, get some news from AC. If what Kagami said about the missing dealer from the Point is true, it'll be in the papers by now. He should have checked last night, should have made some calls, but he was too tired, too distracted. That would be some good dope to have for this meeting with Argos, who was right in the middle of whatever went down, or wants Curtis to think he was. *I know what happened in Atlantic City. I'm the guy you're really looking for.*

The radio fizzles as they climb into the mountains. The highway angles east; the horizon is watery blue, with a gathering band

507

of white. The desert materializes: jagged rocks, clumped white bursage and creosote-bush, the odd scarecrow silhouette of a joshua tree. Sometimes the headlights catch skunks and cottontails, soft flashes by the roadside.

When they pass a brown FHWA sign for Valley of Fire State Park the cab's turn signal clicks on. Curtis checks the exit number and the time: they're maybe thirty-five miles outside the city, still forty-five minutes from their ETA. The cabbie pulls folded sheets of paper off his dashboard and flattens them against the wheel: printed directions. Curtis can't make them out. After a few seconds, the cabbie folds them again.

The two-lane blacktop turns south, then east. The edge of the sun peeks at them between jagged ridges until they turn south again. There's nothing else on the road. By the time they hit the park boundary the radio's getting only gales of static, occasional stuttering voices: *multilateral support . . . respiratory syndrome . . . Irish-American . . . uncertain whether . . . winning the peace.* Instead of turning it off, the cabbie absently sings a Bob Marley tune over it, humming when he forgets the words, always looping back to the first lines, about being robbed and sold to slavers after emerging from a bot-tomless pit. The cabbie has a pretty good voice. Curtis likes the song, but he can't remember the words either.

Away from the road the ground is steep and broken, crowded with wind-scoured monoliths of deep orange that cast long shadows in the oblique light. The cab drives on, winding past campsites and picnic areas, past a visitor center — Curtis checks his watch again — and through the state park's exit, into the Lake Mead National Recreation Area.

The blacktop soon ends in a T-intersection: another two-lane road, this one running north-south, parallel to the lakeshore. The cabbie brakes to a gentle stop, reaches for his directions again, studies them for a long time. We lost? Curtis says.

The cabbie shuffles the pages. A whine of static comes from the stereo speakers, pulsing with the rhythms of human speech, but no speech comes through. The sun is well above the rocks now. Through the window Curtis sees blue and yellow flowers between the bursage clumps, coming up everywhere there's dirt. The cab's engine shifts into idle. No cars pull up behind them. Nothing passes on the other road.

The cabbie slides the pages back onto his dashboard, lifts his foot, and rolls straight across the intersection to the opposite side, off the blacktop and onto a dirt road that Curtis couldn't see before. When the speedometer hits about twenty the cab starts to shudder, Curtis's molars clack together, and the cabbie slows down. A cloud of pink dust rises behind them, spread by a stiff breeze. They won't be surprising anyone.

They're on the dirt road for about three miles. It ends at the lake, or a steep drop where the lake used to be. The cabbie stops. This is it, man, he says.

Curtis straightens in his seat, looks back and forth. There's a port-a-john, a wide spot to turn a car around, and not much else. Wind is coming off the lake, whipping the flowerheads and the sagebrush stems. Great, Curtis says.

He gets out of the car, leans back in. Did the guy say where he'd meet me?

You know as much as I do, the cabbie says. More, probably.

Can I have my phone back?

The cabbie gives him his phone. Curtis turns it on as the cab pulls away under the dustcloud it made. The phone can't get a signal. Curtis switches it off again.

From here he can see the water, its surface aflame with reflected light. Big birds — gulls or ducks — float across its surface like sunspots. Still a long way off. Just ahead the earth slopes down steeply; a gray stain of riversilt shows where the water used to come. It looks like it hasn't been anywhere near here in a while. There's been a long drought; Curtis remembers hearing about it. He shades his face with a cupped right hand and scans the flat expanse between the base of the slope and the waterline, but against the glare he can't make anything out.

The wind whips his ears. He turns, then turns again. Never so mindful of the limits of his vision as when he's out in the open, exposed. He draws his revolver — self-conscious, like he's just dropped trou in public — and clears the Port-a-Can with a rough yank on the door. It's empty, immaculate, reeking of solvents and perfumes.

He's beginning to worry about how he'll get back to the Strip when something catches his eye down by the water. A flash to the south. Regular, but not machine-regular. A signal. Curtis grunts, remembering the little mirror the Whistler used in the casino, and starts walking.

He has to poke around the edge of the bluff for a while before he finds a good route to the bottom, a downgrade gentle enough to avoid slips. Once the surface levels out, the trail is pretty clear. Curtis used to be good at eyeballing distances; since his accident he's not so sure. He figures the flash for two klicks away.

The lakebed is a good five degrees warmer than the bluff. Shrubs and grasses cover most of it, along with scaly saltcedars tall enough to reduce visibility. A few low spots are muddy; elsewhere the ground has cracked into irregular dinnerplate-size tiles, some

511

unsteady under Curtis's feet. The fissures between them are sometimes better than an inch across, deeper than he can see. A crunch announces his every step: a pale layer of rough alkaline crystals left by evaporated water. The trail branches, then branches again. Each time he thinks he's lost, the strobe of the little mirror comes over the brush to guide him. It's getting hot. He owns clothes that would be worse for this hike than what he's wearing, but not many. His shoe-laces bristle with needle-sharp burrs.

In time he comes upon a broad trail with no grass on it, no plants at all. So straight it could have been plotted by a surveyor. The flash comes from the end of the trail: a broad clearing there, what looks like a flat boulder. The reflected light is low to the ground, always in Curtis's eyes. If Argos wanted to shoot him he'd be shot by now. Curtis approaches slowly, his palms open, his arms out.

He notices something in the grass to his right: a hollow column of bricks, like a chimney, not quite knee-high. As he draws closer, turning his face from the mirror's glare, he sees that it is in fact the base of a chimney: part of the brick-edged foundation of what was once a small building. Soon he's able to recognize more ruins nearby: mud-crusted slabs, silted-up wells, splintered beams ghost-white with residue. This must've been a town back before they built the dam and made the lake. Underwater for decades. The drought has uncovered what's left.

Argos's voice, the whistle harmonizing with the wind: Keep coming, Curtis! he says. That's good, what you're doing with your hands. Keep 'em out, just like that.

He's seated in what looks like a cheap plastic lawnchair next to a parked dirtbike. A second chair is about ten feet in front of him. Unless somebody else is coming, Curtis figures that for his seat. Both rest on the smooth concrete foundation of an old building long since gone, rotted or floated away by rising water. Aside from a few chipped corners where rebar peeks through, the slab looks ready to build on. Curtis can barely see Argos. Beneath the blazing mirror in his upraised left hand, he's no more than a shade.

Hey, Curtis calls, Could you maybe knock that shit off?

Argos doesn't answer, and the mirror doesn't go away. Curtis takes another few paces forward. Slow and deliberate. Squinting. When he's an arm's-length from the empty chair, the light disappears, and Argos's other hand comes up.

There's a gun in it: a matte-black semi-automatic pistol. Argos holds it like he's watched a lot of movies. It makes Curtis nervous, but not too nervous. He's figured on this, more or less.

Come toward me, Argos says. Keep your

arms out. Closer. Now turn around, put your hands on your head. Spread your legs. Good.

Curtis steps onto the slab and does as he's told, letting Argos take away his pistol and ineptly pat him down. Curtis takes off his jacket, hangs it on the back of the empty chair, and sits.

Argos wears white-framed sunglasses with blue lenses, iridescent and opaque. He's dressed in a sleek padded motocross outfit, so spotless it looks like he changed into it after he got here. He sinks into his own seat, setting the two guns beside him on the closed lid of a Styrofoam cooler. Curtis can see what Veronica meant: the guy's face is totally unremarkable. He's white, but not just white. Part Asian, probably, though he could just as easily pass for Hispanic, or Middle Eastern. Staring hard, trying to see around the sunglasses to what's underneath, Curtis thinks of an illustration from an Intro Psych textbook he had at Cal Lutheran: a blurry picture of a man's face, made up of the superimposed images of dozens of faces. Curtis can't remember what the picture was supposed to be illustrating, but that's what Argos looks like, right down to the blur.

Before we get started, Argos says, I ought to tell you something.

Okay.

About three hundred yards over your right shoulder, on top of the rise, there is a little clump of creosote-bush. Don't look. Just take my word for it. Sitting in that clump of creosote-bush is a friend of mine, all decked out in camouflage. My friend has a rifle with a scope on it, and right now he's got the crosshairs of that scope glued to the back of your skull. I'm sure you know more about these things than I do, Curtis, but my friend tells me that with his rifle three hundred yards is a pretty easy shot. So just keep that in mind, please.

For an instant Curtis tenses, his skin crawling, but it doesn't last. Argos is already holding a pistol on him; why mention the rifle? It has to be bullshit: the guy's alone out here, and he's scared. Scared enough to be dangerous, maybe. But definitely alone.

You made pretty good time, Argos says.

Thanks. What do you want?

I want to make a deal. I'm sick of getting chased around. I want to get back in business, start putting teams together again. I'm not greedy, and I know where I stand. I want some specific and convincing guarantees from Damon that he'll lay off me from here on out, and let me do my thing.

What are you offering?

Argos grins. His grin is crazy, but calculatedly so: a crazy grin. I'm not offering, he says. I'm *giving*. We're having ourselves a little potlatch here.

Okay. What are you giving?

I'm giving up my memory. I'm forgetting any and all claims I have on any portion of my take from the Spectacular. Okay? I'm forgetting what happened in AC. It's entirely forgotten. Hell, I'm forgetting that Atlantic City even *exists*. I'm never setting foot there again. All this I do unilaterally. No need for reciprocal gestures. You can tell Damon that it's my gift to him.

He and Curtis look at each other. The wind hisses through the saltcedar. It makes a lot of noise, but Curtis can barely feel it.

However, Curtis says.

Argos sighs. *However,* he says, before I did all that forgetting, I wrote a few letters. I won't say how many. I sent these letters to some friends of mine. Good friends, and not-so-good friends. I told these people that if they hang onto these letters, I'll send 'em a little something every year for their trouble. Some cash. They don't have to do anything. Unless, of course, if that little something of mine *doesn't* show up one year. Then they're supposed to forward the letter to the New Jersey State Police. You know how this process generally works, Curtis, I'm sure. I don't have to spell it out.

Curtis nods. His heartbeat is gathering steam, but he tries to keep his face calm. He's getting close, but he doesn't know how to play this guy. Then something clicks, and he does. He can see himself through Argos's eyes

516

now: who and what Argos thinks he is. It's not a good feeling, but he can use it.

Well, Curtis says, Damon's gonna want to know what that letter says.

Argos makes a face. What are you talking about? he says. It's not about his techniques for cheating at the Links, Curtis. What do you think it says?

That's not good enough. Damon's gonna want to know exactly what you said, and exactly how you said it. You say you know what happened in AC. Okay, that sounds good. But what do you actually have? You need to show some cards.

What? Argos laughs. Does Damon want me to send him a copy of the letter? I hope he opens his own fucking mail.

Tell it to me, Curtis says. Right now. Tell me, like you'd tell the cops.

A weird twitch passes from Argos's nose to his lips. As if his face might be changing shape. Curtis, he says, I don't really have time —

You need to make time, Curtis says. If you want to settle this.

Argos is still for what seems like minutes. The wind ruffles his short brown hair. Okay, he says. Where do you want me to start?

Curtis thinks back to Veronica's story, trying to remember where the gaps were. Stanley and Damon put the cardcounters together, he says.

Stanley put the team together, Argos says. I knew from Damon to expect his call. But Stanley didn't know what Damon had planned for the Point. That was between me and Damon and the dealer. Though I'm sure Stanley's figured it out by now.

What happened at the Point?

Look, Argos says. Do I really —

Tell it, goddamn it. What happened at the Point?

Argos makes an irritated little puff. The team moved into the tables, he says, just like it did at all the other joints. We got into position, and the dealers started burning us, just like Damon had planned. When my team scattered, I ducked into the restroom, I changed, and I headed for the high-limit area.

His eyebrows arch over the rims of the sunglasses. As if this should be enough. Spell it out, Curtis says. What did you do?

I sat down, Argos sneers. I began to play *blackjack.* I began to bet the *table maximum,* which was ten thousand dollars a hand. I broke even for a while, and then I asked them to double the limit. They doubled the limit. Then I started winning.

How did that work?

This is ridiculous, Curtis.

How did it work?

It's fun, though, you know? I'm really enjoying it. I feel sort of like a kinky hooker right now. Can we do some more roleplay when we're done? Scoutmaster and his young Cub, maybe? How does that grab you?

Tell me how it worked, Argos.

Argos stares at Curtis for a second, slack-jawed. What did you call me? he says.

The question catches Curtis off-balance, but he keeps the doubt from his voice. That's what you go by, right? he says. Graham Argos?

Argos smirks, shifts his weight in the rickety chair. Sure, he says. If you write a check to Graham Argos, I will have no trouble cashing it. Is that the name Damon gave you for me?

Curtis leans forward, puts his elbows on his knees, and fixes Argos with a steady glare. I want you to tell me, he says, right now, how it worked.

The ensuing silence is broken by a strong warm gust that sweeps ashy powder from the old lakebed. It hisses against Argos's cooler and Curtis's shoes, and forms a brief dancing spiral in the spreadfoot foundation of a nearby ruin. A few grains ping off Curtis's safety glasses.

The dealer was crooked, Argos says. That's how it worked. It was pretty amazing, if you want to know the truth. He was as good a mechanic as I am a blackjack player, and I do not say that lightly. I knew exactly what he'd be doing — what to look for — and I still couldn't see it. That is not a skill you hear praised a lot, but it ought to be. It is a shame and a sin that that guy is no longer in the world.

How come they didn't catch you?

Like I said, the guy was good.

Bullshit, Curtis says. Doesn't matter how good he was. The casino was on high alert. They knew they had counters on the floor; they had already burned some. Who authorized increasing the limit? Why didn't anybody see the money moving your way?

They were looking in the wrong places, Argos says. Sure they knew they had counters on the floor. That was the beauty of it. I told you, I was in the *high-limit* pit. Cardcounting teams don't work high-limit tables; they'd get caught there in a fucking snap. Too much attention, not enough traffic. Damon had pulled his hotshot pit bosses and his best eye-in-the-sky guys *out* of high-limit, to the regular tables. That's where the perceived threat was. He was offering cash bounties for burning our team. Meanwhile, I've got a crooked dealer, a green pit boss scared of pissing off a whale, and a bunch of security freaking out because they're missing the real action across the room. Plus — this is key — Damon had worked up a phony credit history for me, so on paper I *looked* like a whale. I could've gone into the drop with a fucking shovel and gotten away with it.

What was your take?

Argos grins nastily. Did Damon give you

permission to ask me that?

That's between me and Damon.

Yeah, Argos says. I guess it is. Okay, Curtis. At twenty K a hand, I cleared a million and a quarter in a little under ten minutes. That's the number I took to the cage, and that's what I walked out with.

They just let you leave with over a million dollars in cash?

They didn't like it much. They tried to hold me up with bullshit excuses about filing a Form 8300, so by then they must've figured something was off. But at that point, what could they do? Again, I wasn't just some guy in a suit. I was a rated player.

Curtis looks over Argos's shoulder to the long grasses along the water, watching patterns form and vanish as the wind shakes them. Damon had you working at the Point before, he says. As a position player. After he burned you. Before any of this happened.

Did he tell you that?

Is it true?

Sure, Argos says. So what?

So you're telling me that you used to play poker at the Point on a daily basis — and then you came in with your team, ripped off a high-limit table for over a million bucks, and cashed out at the cage — and nobody recognized you?

Argos shrugs. I am good at what I do, he says.

Curtis sits back and looks him over. He could be twenty-five, thirty-five, forty-five years old. Beneath the sunglasses his skin is smooth and uniform, like plastic, or clay. Something about him is creepy, not fully human. He resembles a regular person the same way a coyote resembles a dog. Curtis isn't afraid of him at all anymore.

What happened to the dealer? he asks.

Curtis expects Argos to hesitate here, but he doesn't. This is the part he's been wanting to tell.

After I cashed out, he says, I hid my take in a deposit box and met my team up at Resorts. There was a lot of hand-wringing and confusion and cussing the Spectacular, but nobody was heartbroken, because everybody made very nice money everyplace else. Stanley, I think, knew by then that he'd been fucked at the Point, and I think he knew that I'd been in on it. But he wasn't feeling good, and he kept pretty quiet. It took us a while to work the split, then we went our separate ways. I went back to my deposit box to get the money, and then I went back to the Point.

Wait a minute. You went where?

Yeah. I wasn't too happy about it either. But that's where Damon wanted to meet to settle shares, because he and the dealer couldn't get away from work for very long. Or at least that's what he said. So I made some adjustments to my appearance, and I headed back. Very confused vibe on the gaming floor. Lots of people showing up from other casinos with congratulations, wanting to find out how the Point had burned us, while at about the same time, Spectacular management was realizing just how badly they'd been hosed. It felt like walking into a convenience store a few minutes after it's been held up. Or coming through a little town after a tornado's hit. Only nobody could see the tornado. Everybody was excited, keyed-up. I didn't hang around very long. I hustled up to the room.

What room?

Just a regular room in the tower. I knocked, some guy answered.

What guy?

I'd never seen him before. I knew right then it was a setup. The thing was done, we had the money. Why bring in somebody else?

What did he look like?

Tall. Six-four, I'd guess. One-eighty, one-ninety. Greasy. Country-boy accent. Obvious muscle: a guy who'd done time. He let me in — the dealer was already there — and then he left. He said he'd be back in a minute with Damon.

What did you do?

I got the fuck out of there. What do you think I did?

Why?

Because I'm fucking smart, is why. Look: I

show up, Damon's not there, some hardcase thug I don't know answers the door, checks to make sure I have the money, tells us to stay put, and splits. I mean, holy shit, Curtis. He might as well have spread out some plastic sheets and told us to lie down on them till he got back.

You got scared.

Maybe I wasn't a hundred percent sure at the time. I just had a bad feeling, and I went with it. But look what happened to the dealer. The dealer stuck around. Now he's a chumline in Absecon Bay.

You didn't actually see what happened to him.

No, Curtis, I didn't. I didn't hide in the bushes while Damon and his triggerman loaded the body in a trunk. I didn't follow them to the harbor like Nancy fucking Drew. You're absolutely right. I'm being silly. The Jersey cops won't give a shit about what I know. I'm sorry I wasted your time. But isn't the lake lovely? Now come get your gun and shoot me in the head.

Did you take any of the money?

No, I didn't take the fucking money! Is Damon saying I took the money?

Why not? Why'd you leave it?

Argos squirms, runs a hand through his hair. It wasn't winnings, he says. It was stolen. Which, fine. But a lot of it was new bills. I wasn't sure what to do with it. And Damon's

524

plan wasn't seeming all that clever at the time. I opted to cut and run.

What did the dealer do?

He tried to stop me. He was freaking out. I tried to explain why I was leaving, but his English wasn't too good. We got into it a little bit. I pushed him down. He probably would have chased me, but he didn't want to lock himself out of the room.

What was his name?

He never told me. I didn't see him until I sat down at his table, and then I didn't think to look at his badge. When we met up later, I wasn't there long enough to do any icebreaking activities. I found it on the internet yesterday, and wrote it down somewhere. Some Korean name.

Curtis squares his jaw, looks at the water. Grinding his teeth. He's angry, enough to scare himself. Thinking about ways to get to the guns. The sun is high now. Some of the big birds he had taken for gulls are white pelicans, gliding inches off the water, fishing the reedy shallows, pressing long bills into their breasts.

What if the other guy wasn't a hired gun? Curtis says. What if he was there to buy the cash?

What are you talking about? Argos says. But he knows what Curtis is talking about; he's been thinking it too. It's in his voice, if not his face.

You said yourself it was new bills, Curtis says. Maybe that was the other guy's job, to wash the money. Maybe he wasn't a shooter. Maybe the deal only went bad because you left, and they panicked, and they went after each other. Maybe this is all your fault, Argos. You ever think about that?

Argos smiles wanly, makes a dismissive gesture. I tend not to dwell on such stuff, he says. It makes me unhappy. This business is all about attit—

His smile evaporates. He sits up in his chair. What the fuck is that? he says.

Curtis's chin drops in disbelief. You got to be kidding, he says. I'm supposed to turn my back now, right?

Something's on the road.

Argos picks up the two pistols, puts them on the concrete, and tips back the lid of the cooler: bottles inside, along with a pair of binoculars, which Argos lifts to his face. This would be a good time to rush him, but Curtis can't psych himself up for it. Probably just your imaginary friend with the rifle, he says. Sick of waiting on you.

It's a car. Did you have anybody following you?

Nobody followed me, Curtis says. Thinking about it, though, he never really checked the cab's mirrors. Still, it doesn't seem possible.

Well, Argos says, I gotta run.

He steps to the dirtbike, throws open the

saddlebag, stuffs the binoculars inside. Keep your shit together, Argos, Curtis says. It's probably just the park ranger.

It's not the ranger.

Argos tucks his gun into his waistband, then unloads Curtis's revolver and puts it and the loose bullets in the cooler. Curtis rises from his seat. You're just gonna leave me in the desert, huh? he says. How do you recommend I get back to town? I can't use my phone out here.

Oh, you picked right up on that, didn't you? Argos laughs. Pretty sharp. You got that phone from Damon, right?

Curtis blinks. What's that got to do with anything?

He gave me one, too. Pretty nice phone. Funny thing, though. After I ducked Damon and his triggerman at the Point, for the next couple of days, I kept having these crazy close calls. I'd be sitting at a restaurant or some random place, I'd look up, and there Country Boy would be, looking around with his beady eyes. A couple of places I had to leave through kitchens and windows. But you know what? After I dumped the phone, that shit stopped. Sure, I know what you're thinking: correlation ain't causation. But if you're wondering why I wanted to meet up way out here, well, that's why.

Curtis shakes his head. You're one paranoid son of a bitch, he says.

Argos puts his pistol in the saddlebag, along with two bottles of water from the cooler. His crazy grin is back; it seems less affected this time. You think I'm paranoid, huh? he says. Okay. Let's talk about our pal Damon for a second. What did Damon do after the Gulf War, Curtis? Embassy security. Where? Bolivia. Pakistan. Who hangs out at those embassies? You're gonna tell me Damon didn't network with those guys? Damon Blackburn? C'mon, Curtis. This guy knows the secret handshake, okay? He owns the decoder ring.

Curtis laughs at that, shakes his head like it's ridiculous, but at the same time he's thinking: how did Albedo find me yesterday at New York?

Argos pulls his binoculars from the saddlebag to scan the rise again. Curtis risks a glance of his own this time. Sure enough, there's a pink column of dust there, fading in the breeze. He can't see anything moving on the ground.

A helmet hangs from the dirtbike's handlebars; Argos pulls it on, fastens the chinstrap. Then he stows the binoculars and shuts the saddlebag. Wait a minute, Curtis says. We're not done yet.

Oh, I'm afraid we are, my friend.

Curtis forces himself to think quickly, to get back in character. He still doesn't have what he needs. Not enough. Not yet. You're full of shit, man, he says. If you expect Damon to make a deal based on what you just told me, then you really are crazy. You've got nothing. Go ahead and give that story to NJSP. Damon'll say you cooked it up. He'll say you and the dealer put the scam together on your own, and that you whacked the dealer yourself. Anything you claim he did on the inside, he'll say you could have done yourself from the outside with a little fore-sight. Who can corroborate?

Argos straddles the bike, tips it, and kicks up the sidestand. Have you guys found Stanley yet? he says. No? I didn't think so. I guess I'll see you at the finish-line.

Nobody's gonna find Stanley, Argos. You know that. He's not gonna save you. You need some kind of physical evidence against Damon, and you don't have it. You're going up against a decorated ex-marine, and you don't even have a real name. All you've got are your paranoid bullshit stories.

I got a number, Argos says.

Say again?

A number. Seventeen ninety-seven.

What the hell are you talking about?

That's the room at the Point where I met the dealer and Damon's triggerman. I can't say for sure, but I got a suspicion the dealer didn't exit that room under his own power. I just hope for Damon's sake he didn't leave all the cleanup to Housekeeping.

Argos turns the bike's ignition key, shifts to neutral, squeezes the clutch, and presses the starter. The noisy little engine sputters and catches. *I'll be back in touch in a few days!* Argos shouts over the buzzsaw drone. *You better have some good news!*

He rolls forward, angles away, and opens the bike's throttle, skidding in a long arc along the old drowned road, scattering fine gravel and alkaline dust in a seething cloud. Before Curtis can get his hands up, the brunt of it catches him in the chest and face. It feels a little like being downwind from teargas. He spits and curses. Then he smiles. The whine of the bike's engine pitch-shifts and fades. Room 1797, Curtis thinks. That's good. That might do the trick.

The Styrofoam cooler still lies open on the concrete slab. Curtis stumbles to it, reaches inside. Two bottles left. He opens one, removes his glasses, fills his cupped palm, and splashes his face and scalp. He does it again, rubbing his wet hand over his neck, and drinks the rest of the water. Then he wipes his hands on his trouserlegs and puts the bullets back in his gun.

The vehicle on the dirt road must have been the park ranger. Just in case it wasn't, he'd like to get out of here soon. He ties his jacket around his waist, puts the last waterbottle in its pocket. His left eyesocket stings and tears up: something must've gotten into it around the safety glasses' lenses, or maybe while he was washing his face. He wants to rinse it again but he's dehydrated already, and can't spare the second bottle.

A short distance away, behind a waving screen of toothy grass, he spies the unbroken foundation of a house, well-made enough to trap and hold the most recent rains. It could almost be a rectangular pool in a Roman atrium but for the tumbleweeds clustered along its western edge. He makes his way to it in the hope of examining his reflection, but all he can see is the dark outline of his head. Then he kneels and closes his right eye tight, balancing blind as he lifts rainwater to his face.

It doesn't help. He can't stick around here any longer. The visitor center is ten miles back at least, part of that over rough ground. Curtis towels off with the upstretched hem of his shirt. The wind dries his scalp as he hikes the rise back to the road.

39

The clouds he saw east of town yesterday must have had rain in them, because the desert is blooming: yellow flares of sunray coreopsis, blue spires of phacelia and loco-weed, pink evening-primrose and golden poppies, and some rangy ocotillo, their coral-red flowerspikes bobbing over the orange dirt like hazard-flares. Curtis trudges past them all, head down, a salty trail on his left cheek.

When he reaches the blacktop it gets warmer, then steeper. He drains the last waterbottle. Brown lizards scurry from his path. Dead animals on the road: snakes, ground-squirrels, a ringtail cat pecked over by ravens. Curtis has a long time to think. Damon's been using him as his hunting-dog, his pointer, flushing Stanley and Argos so Albedo can shoot. Not even that. A hunting-dog at least knows what it's doing, knows how it's being used. Not a decoy, either. Decoys are fraudulent, innocuous. Curtis is more like one of those machines they used to use a hundred years ago to trap songbirds. A flashing whirligig. Wind him up and watch the fun.

Across the state park boundary he finds a turnoff to some campsites and detours to look for a spigot, to drink and to rinse his eyesocket again. Still no good. He finds a restroom and checks the mirror, pulling the lid back. He can't see anything wrong. When he gets back to the hotel, he'll have to take it out.

It's past one o'clock when he comes to the visitor center, a red-brown box skirted by a white sunshade, U.S. and NV flags flapping lazily in the traffic circle out front. The building almost disappears against the smooth elusive shapes in the ruddy sandstone: domes, columns, balanced rocks. Curtis looks up at them while double-checking that his jacket hides his gun. The formations look organic, alive somehow. Curtis sees things in them. Ghost faces. Cloacal openings. Spineless marine creatures. A human figure with a bird's beaked head. He's glad Argos wanted to meet early; he wouldn't want to be out here at night.

He drinks from the waterfountain until he's afraid he'll get sick, then refills his bottle. Inside, he bypasses the video monitors and the glass cases of samples and artifacts and heads straight for the payphone. He digs into his wallet — old prepaid calling cards he hasn't used in months, the name and number of that cabbie who drove him to meet Kagami — and he starts dialing.

Nobody picks up at the cabbie's number. A brief vague greeting — English, then Arabic, then French — followed by a beep. Hello, Saad, Curtis says. You probably don't remember me, but my name is Curtis Stone, and a couple of days ago you gave me a ride to the Quicksilver. We talked about jazz a little bit. Listen, I don't know if you're working today, but I need your help. I managed to get myself stranded out here at Valley of Fire State Park, and I could use a ride back to the Strip. I know that's probably not on your regular route, but I can make it worth your time. My phone's not getting a signal, so I guess I'll just call you back in a little while. I'm at the park visitor center. Thanks.

Curtis dials again, selects Directory Assistance, and asks for the number for Sin City Escorts in Las Vegas. He listens to sleazy music and breathy boilerplate for a minute. Then the phone rings and a woman answers. Sin City Escorts, she says. How can we make you happy today?

I'm looking for a guy who drives for you, Curtis says. A guy named Albedo. He drives —

Hold please, the woman says.

Curtis holds for a while. Wiping his cheek with some toilet paper he took from the campsite restroom. A man's voice answers. Who's it you're looking for? it says.

A guy named Albedo. He drives for you sometimes. He drives a big black car, an old car. I'm trying to get in touch —

I know the guy, yeah. But I can't put you in touch. We don't give out that kind of information. You leave me your name and number, and maybe next time I see him I'll give it to him, if I think about it.

You don't have to do that, man, Curtis says. I've got his number. I'm just trying to figure out if he's back from Atlantic City yet.

Atlantic City? the guy says. Yeah, he's back from Atlantic City. He's been back for like a week and a half. Did he go out there again?

Thanks, Curtis says, and ends the call.

He wipes his cheek and leans against the wall and thinks for a minute.

Then he calls the switchboard at the Spectacular in AC and asks for lost-and-found. Hi, he says. I was in your hotel a couple of weeks ago, and I think I might have left something in my room.

Young female voice on the line. Sure, it says. We'll check. What did you lose?

I lost a cufflink, Curtis says. Gold, with a black gemstone.

And do you remember what room you were in, and the dates of your visit?

I was in Room 1797, Curtis says. I was there for one night, on — when was it? It was over Mardi Gras weekend, I remember that.

Okay, the voice chirps. If you'll hold for a minute, we'll see what we can do.

A click. An Eagles song comes on. After a verse and a chorus, another click. I'm sorry, the same voice says. What was your name?

My name is Albedo, Curtis says. But I don't know if the reservation was made under my name. I was there with a group.

Well, I may have some good news, Mister Albedo. We did have a lost cufflink logged on March Second. I'm going to check with Risk Management now.

The Eagles come back on. Then they fade into Fleetwood Mac, and Fleetwood Mac fades into Norah Jones. Curtis is leaning his head on the wall with his eyes closed when a voice comes from behind him. Hey, it says. Are you Curtis Stone?

Curtis spins, blinks. Yeah, he says.

It's a park ranger, looking irritated. Your taxi just called, she says. He's coming. He says it'll probably be two hours before he gets here.

Okay, Curtis says. Thanks.

Do you want to talk to him?

I can't right now. Sorry. Thanks.

The ranger rolls her eyes and walks away. Curtis wipes his cheek and rests his forehead on the wall again. Thinking of Damon in the Penrose Diner. *Look, this is not dangerous. Nobody's breaking any laws.* Curtis grimaces. Norah Jones rolls over into Elton John. Then a click. Mister Albedo?

Yeah. I'm here.

The girl's voice is tense now, and Curtis knows he's getting close. I'm really sorry for the delay, she says. I've got Security Officer Ramirez on the phone now. He'll explain the situation regarding your cufflink. Okay? Officer Ramirez?

Another voice: Hello? Mister Albedo?

That's right.

I've been, ah, investigating the matter of your cufflink, and what I have basically discovered is that we do have a record of such an item being found in Room 1797 on March Second, but the item is no longer in our lost-and-found. Do you know anybody else who

536

was in the room that night who might have claimed it?

You know, Curtis says. I just might. I'll have to check. Don't you guys keep a record of what gets claimed?

We do, the guy says, but, y'know, sometimes paperwork doesn't get done. I'm really sorry about this. Um — while I've got you on the phone, Mister Albedo, do you mind if I ask you a couple of questions about some damage that was done to that room?

Curtis ends the call. He stands there holding the dead phone until it starts to buzz. Then he puts it back in the cradle. Running different formulas in his head. Weighing things against each other that he'd never really appreciated as separate before. Coming up with the same result every time.

In the end he thinks: this is how I help Stanley. This is what it comes down to.

He lifts the receiver, dials again. A few rings. His dad's voice on the answering machine. Curtis talks over it. Pop, he says. I know you're there. It's Curtis. Pick up.

A click, and his father's voice again, louder and clearer. What's up, Curtis? it says. What's wrong? You in trouble?

A tear falls from Curtis's face and makes a dark spot on his foot. His black shoes are pinkish-gray with mud and dust. Their laces are snarled with burrs. They look like some foul echinoderms that might slither along a reef. It's okay, Curtis says. I'm okay.

I didn't ask if you're okay, Little Man. I asked what's wrong.

Curtis laughs quietly. Well, he says, a lot's wrong. Nothing that can't be fixed, though. I'm sorry to put this on you, Pop, but I'm in a tricky spot out here. I can't really explain specifics right now, but I need you to do something for me that's gonna cause you some aggravation and take up a little of your time.

In the silence that follows, Curtis senses a great gathering of judgment, like the rise of water behind a dam. When his father speaks again, Curtis can hear strain in his voice from the effort of holding it back. He loves the old man for that.

Okay, his father says. What do you need?

You got something at hand to write with?

Yeah.

Okay, Curtis says. I need you to call the Jersey State Police.

40

When Saad appears — dressed in sandals, a workshirt with rolled sleeves, and khakis stained dark brown at the knees — Curtis is taken by surprise: he hasn't seen a cab pull into the visitor center lot. I am not working today, my friend, Saad says. I am in my personal vehicle. I was at home when you

538

called, working on the roof of my house. What is wrong with your eye? Do you need Visine? I have Visine.

Saad shows Curtis to a white Honda and opens the back door for him. There is no meter, of course, he says. For the distances I looked at MapQuest. It will be one hundred fifty dollars. Okay? I hope you will give me a good tip.

Sure I will. You're making me feel bad for messing up your day off.

Saad shuts Curtis's door with an indifferent wave. Bah! he says. Why do you feel bad? I told you, I was working on my roof. Now what am I doing? I am driving in the beautiful mountains. Maybe you will give me a nice tip, and then I can pay some men to fix my roof, which is what my wife always has been telling me to do. You see? I am happy you called. And soon we will be gone from the mountains, and I will find some nice jazz on the radio. Yes?

The Honda turns left on the Valley of Fire Highway, and soon crosses the park's western boundary. The radio starts to flicker and the scenery calms down. You are tired of the casinos, I see, Saad says. Your luck did not improve.

Curtis slumps in his seat. He's worn out. He doesn't want to think anymore. The early morning excitement and the long dry hike and the irritation in his eyesocket have ground him down to a nub. No, he says. It sure didn't.

So you left the city, Saad says, and came to the desert. Just like Jesus. Yes?

Exactly like Jesus, Curtis says. Or Muhammad. Muhammad went to the desert too, didn't he? After things got nasty for him in Mecca.

Or Moses! Moses led his people out of Egypt, yes? Led them into the desert. I understand this, you see. I also led my people out of Egypt. Now two of my people are at the university spending my money, and the other of my people, she asks me every day why the roof is not yet fixed. Yes, my friend. It is sometimes good to go to the desert.

Curtis smiles, wipes his cheek, leans his head back. Sleep sucks at him like quicksand; his arms and legs are already numb. I guess I'm more like Jesus than those other two guys, he says. When I went into the desert, nobody followed me.

You are wrong, my friend, Saad says. I followed you. You see? I am very loyal.

The drone of the tires works its way up Curtis's spine and expands to fill his chest, warm and liquid. He's seeing the landscape through closed eyes now. To the north, a field of pricklypear and tree-cactus, the cyclone fence of Camp Delta, the blue Caribbean beyond it. To the south, the smoke-curtain over Al Burgan, the blackened long-legged corpses of camels, the lake of burning oil. Curtis hears the crunch of gravel under the Honda's wheels, imagines it cast from the pavement into his eyes, and jerks awake. Hey, Saad, he says, can you tell me anything about that old town in the lake?

I don't know what you mean, my friend.

I was just down at the lake. The water's really low, I guess from the drought, and there's what looks like a little town that's come out of the water. You can see streets, chimneys, some of the old foundations.

Oh yes, Saad says. I saw this on the news. They built the Hoover Dam, and then the water came, and this town was covered up. Like Atlantis, yes? Now there is no rain, so it comes back. The people who made this town, they were — how do you call them? The ones who build the white temples.

Mormons?

Yes. Mormons. But there is a different name.

LDS, Curtis says. Latter-Day Saints.

Yes, Saad says. That's who. I am curious about these people. I meet them sometimes in my taxicab. The young men I see sometimes on their bicycles. Are these Christian people, these Latter-Day Saints?

Depends on who you ask, I guess. My dad's a Black Muslim and my mom was a Jehovah's Witness, so I'm not gonna talk any trash about Mormons.

Saad leans down to mess with the radio and coaxes a melody from the speakers: Sonny Rollins, "How High the Moon," a West Coast session with Barney Kessell and Leroy Vinnegar. A quick regular thrum of static cuts against the swingtime, then fades. Curtis shuts his eyelids again.

These saints, Saad says. In some way, they are like the Jews, or the Muslims, yes? They have difficulties — oppression, discrimination — and they come to the desert. They say this about themselves, maybe. *We are like the Jews!* It is not only these saints, of course. In this country, this always is possible. Enough! we say. We will go to the desert! We will make our own city. For ourselves, for our children. It will be a holy place, and just. We will know ourselves and our God by the shape it takes. So we build it. And people come, and more people. And then one day it is strange to us. No longer what we wanted. It has become, perhaps, the very thing we fled. So we go back into the desert, and we weep and pray that God or Fortune will flood the land, will bring the sea down upon the armies of Pharaoh, will erase our mistakes from the earth. But though the waters may rise, nothing is ever erased, or ever can be. The city is everywhere.

At some point Saad's voice becomes Stanley's, and Curtis knows that he's asleep again, or nearly so: one foot trailing in the current

542

of dreams. He tries to balance as best he can, so Stanley's words won't fade, and then he can see them, each word independent and alive, sprouting feather-leafed branches that bear other words, spoken in other voices. He can hear the voice of the old poet, Welles, and the voice of *The Mirror Thief.* His own father's voice. Walter Kagami's. Veronica's. Danielle's. The voice of the magician called the Nolan. The voice of the god Hermes. The clear quiet voice of the moon itself.

Then another voice, familiar. *My fellow citizens,* it says, *events in Iraq have now reached the final days of decision.*

Curtis jerks upright, claps a hand on Saad's headrest. Shit, he says.

Are you okay, my friend? You were sleeping. We are almost there.

Curtis shakes his head, squints out the window. They're downtown already, passing under the spaghetti interchange for the Vegas Expressway. A green sign has Charleston Boulevard coming up in a quarter-mile. Curtis's throat is sore; he was snoring. What's happening? he says. Did the war start?

The president speaks, Saad says. You are awake, so I will turn it up, okay?

Peaceful efforts to disarm the Iraq regime have failed again and again because we are not dealing with peaceful men, the radio says. *Intelligence gathered by this and other govern-*

ments leaves no doubt that the Iraq regime continues to possess and conceal some of the most lethal weapons ever devised.

Saad exits on Spring Mountain Road. Hey, Curtis says, can we just cruise the Strip for a little while? I'd like to hear this.

Of course, my friend. Whatever you wish. Shall we say one dollar for each five minutes?

Curtis unties the arms of his jacket from his waist, finds the envelope in the inner pocket, opens it. Why don't I just give you three hundred for the trip, he says, and you can tell me when you need to go home.

The United States and other nations did nothing to deserve or invite this threat, but we will do everything to defeat it. Instead of drifting along toward tragedy, we will set a course toward safety. Before the day of horror can come, before it is too late to act, this danger will be removed.

When it hits the Boulevard the Honda turns south, past Curtis's hotel, past the pirate ships and the volcano, past the Bellagio's dancing fountain. After all the walking Curtis has done it's nice to be on wheels, nice to see all this stuff — the neon and the incandescents, the signs and the readerboards, the grab-bag casino entrances and the mirror-glass towers behind them, shiny masks with empty eyeholes — and to know that he's not part of it. It took him a while to find the right table out here, but he figures he broke even.

All the decades of deceit and cruelty have now reached an end. Saddam Hussein and his sons must leave Iraq within forty-eight hours. Their refusal to do so will result in military conflict commenced at a time of our choosing.

Okay, Saad, Curtis says. I've heard enough. You can turn around.

Saad hangs two lefts and hits the Strip again across from the Luxor, north of the crouching Sphinx. The boulevard seems busy for Monday afternoon. As they roll through the light at Trop Ave, Curtis sees a crowd gathered on the sidewalk by the Statue of Liberty — a keening pipe-and-drum corps, shamrock-green T-shirts and plastic hats — and he remembers what day it is.

Many Iraqis can hear me tonight in a translated radio broadcast, and I have a message for them. If we must begin a military campaign, it will be directed against the lawless men who rule your country and not against you. As our coalition takes away their power, we will deliver the food and medicine you need. We will tear down the apparatus of terror and we will help you to build a new Iraq that is prosperous and free. In a free Iraq, there will be no more wars of aggression against your neighbors, no more poison factories, no more executions of dissidents, no more torture chambers and rape rooms. The tyrant will soon be gone. The day

545

of your liberation is near.

On the sidewalk south of his hotel, some motorcycle cops and security officers are arguing with five or six young LaRouche canvassers who've been hassling passersby with placards and brochures. The kids point and shout; one of the cops talks into his radio. THE METHODOLOGY OF EVIL, the kids' placards read. STOP OLIGARCHS IMPEACH DOGE BUSH! CHENEY'S NUKES OR GREENSPAN'S DOLLAR – WHICH WILL *BLOW* FIRST? Curtis imagines Walter Kagami in his Cosby sweater, chanting through a bullhorn as the police load him into a paddywagon. Curtis isn't sure yet how he feels about the war, but he doesn't envy Walter. It's got to be hard to hate something so much when you know there's no chance in hell you're ever going to stop it.

The speech hasn't ended by the time they pull into the porte-cochère, but Curtis has gotten the gist. He passes the envelope of bills over Saad's shoulder and opens the door. Your eye is okay? Saad says. You are sure? I can take you to a doctor.

It's fine, Curtis says. I'll fix it when I get topside. You working tomorrow?

Yes, Saad says. Tomorrow I will work.

You might hear from me again. I may need a ride to the airport.

You have my number. Good luck, my friend. Stay out of the casino!

Thanks! Curtis calls. Keep off your roof! But Saad is already pulling away, and can't hear him.

When he slides the keycard and opens the door, Curtis spots a steady flash on the night-stand: the phone's message-light. Jersey cops, no doubt. They've been waiting three hours, probably, for a callback. Curtis figures another few minutes won't kill them. Or anybody else.

He throws his jacket on the bed, opens his suitcase, unzips the mesh pouch on the underside of its lid and removes the Ziploc that hold his saline and peroxide and suction device. Then he carries the bag into the head and turns on the light.

He takes off his safety glasses, washes his hands, washes his face. Then he scrubs his hands again, past the elbow this time. When he's done, he unwraps a glass tumbler and spreads one of the hotel's fluffy white towels over the sink.

The spotless mirror and the bright overhead lights don't make it any easier to see where the problem is. Could be an allergic reaction, or maybe he's just dehydrated. He pulls back the lids to take a good look.

It's still amazing to him: the tiny pink fibers in the offwhite sclera, the individual cords in the mouse-gray iris. The ocularist at Bethesda did a hell of a job. Between the bumpy ride south from Gnjilane and waking up blind and terrified in Landstuhl he remembers next to nothing, certainly nothing of the accident. Things get a little clearer later: sitting on the runway at Ramstein, trying to understand through the painkiller haze why the plane wasn't taking off. *We are not flying, Gunnery Sergeant, because nothing is flying. The FAA ordered a ground stop of all flights, civilian and military, within or bound for U.S. airspace. No sir, nobody knows, because this has never happened before.* At the time it seemed like everything was wrecked, like nothing would ever be the same. And nothing has been, really. But it's been surprisingly easy to forget the specifics of what's changed, to forget exactly how he got hurt, to forget what he can and cannot see.

Curtis wets the suctioncup with a squirt of saline, pinches its rubber bulb, and presses it to his acrylic cornea. Then he pushes down his lower eyelid with his thumb, and the prosthesis drops into his damp left palm.

He puts it in the hotel's tumbler and covers it with peroxide, then parts his lids again to peek at the blank curve underneath: the orbital implant's white coral sphere, filmed with conjunctiva. On the countertop, the prosthesis stares up through the peroxide bubbles. Thin, hard, curved. Its smooth edges nearly triangular, like a worry-stone.

As he's flushing his empty socket with

saline, his cell rings. He towels his face, steps into the bedroom to pick it up. A local number, not one he knows. He thinks for a second about what Argos told him. Then he presses the green button. Yeah, he says.

Curtis, it's Veronica. Where are you right now?

A swirl of ambient noise around her voice. Nothing he recognizes. At my hotel, he says. What's up?

Listen, I just talked to Stanley. He's flying back from AC tonight.

Curtis blinks. Okay, he says.

He's been dealing with Damon. Curtis, your buddy is fucked. The Point put an exclude-eject on him, and now I'm hearing about an arrest warrant, too. I don't begin to follow what's going on, but Stanley is coming back, and he wants to meet with you.

Curtis hears a PA behind her voice: pages, security announcements. She's at the airport. At the end of the suite evening light pours through the windows, making a golden band across the final feet of the left-hand wall. Not much of it is getting to Curtis. He switches on the bedside lamp. The moment he does so, the fax machine across the room begins to hum.

Curtis? You still there?

Yeah. I'm here.

Did I catch you at a bad time?

No, Curtis says as he moves across the

549

room, reaching for the paper as the machine spits it out. No, it's fine. Hey, uh — is there any chance you could call me back on a landline? On my hotel phone?

No time. Sorry. Stanley's plane is gonna be wheels-down in like five minutes. Can you meet or not?

The paper in Curtis's hand is mostly black. Its thick border seems at first to be squiggles — like someone was trying to get a cheap inkstick started — but resolves instead into a grisly thicket of anatomy: cunts and cocks and balls, unspooled intestines, shattered skulls spilling like cornucopias. Each corner is adorned with the image of an eyeball, trailing an optic nerve like a kite's tail. In the middle of the crowded page is a message. YOUR FUCKT TRATER, it reads.

Sure, Curtis says. I can meet. When and where?

The Quicksilver. Walter hooked us up with a room. Just go to the bell-desk and give your name. They'll have a keycard for you. If we beat you there, they'll just give you the room number.

You won't beat me there, Curtis says.

He crumples the fax as he looks out the window. A plane, maybe Stanley's, is dropping toward McCarran now. On the wall by Curtis's shoulder the murky painting is bathed in amber. Most of its vague details vanish in the glow, but others emerge. In a lower corner there's a sea-monster that Curtis never noticed before.

Hey, Curtis? Veronica's saying. One more thing. Can I ask a favor?

Yeah. Sure.

Can you bring Stanley's book when you come? I think he'd like it back.

No problem, Curtis says, but Veronica is already gone. He stares at his dead phone for a few seconds, then pockets it.

The Mirror Thief sits on the circular table, inches from his hand. Although Curtis didn't get much from it aside from a headache, he somehow wishes he'd read more. As he lifts it through the sunbeam, the flecks of leftover silver on the binding flash gold.

On his way back to the head to replace his prosthesis, Curtis notices the tracks that his desert-filthy shoes have made across the carpet: pale alkaline rings for every step, like the footprints of a ghost.

■ ■ ■ ■

CALCINATIO

MARCH 1958

■ ■ ■ ■

And the waters richer than glass
Bronze gold, the blaze over the silver,
Dye-pots in the torch-light,
The flash of wave under prows,
And the silver beaks rising and crossing
    Stone trees, white and rose-white in the
        darkness,
Cypress there by the towers,
    Drift under hulls in the night.
                    — EZRA POUND, Canto XVII

41

Gulls' voices wake Stanley. His eyes open to the sight of motes adrift in the pencil-slender sunbeams that pierce the boarded-up back window of his and Claudio's lair. He wasn't dreaming about New York just now, but the light still seems wrong, like it should be coming from the other direction. He sits up, rubs his face, listens to noises from outside, sharp in the cool spring air.

On some mornings, a full understanding of the distances he's covered arrives in a rush that knocks the wind from his chest, and this is one of those mornings. He used to open Welles's book and marvel at the catalogue of faraway lands and exotic cities that Crivano passed through: Nicosia, Ragusa, Iskanderun, names that meant nothing to Stanley, that conjured nothing in his head but unfocused images of incense smoke and winding alleys and veiled faces and sharpened knives. During his long ramble across the country he'd often pretended to be retracing the steps of the Mirror Thief, and only now and then did he realize that the places he visited were no less strange to him than any named in the book, the expanses traveled no less vast. He'd sit quietly for a moment and imagine his own journey recorded in some neglected book, and he'd consider who years from now might take the time and the care to read it.

Eight full months it took to get here. His progress random and inexorable as a crack working its way across a windshield. He hitchhiked, hopped boxcars, rode buses, walked for miles in all kinds of weather. Gravel truck in Indiana. River barge in Memphis. Local accents as alien to him as other languages. He crossed from Arkansas to Oklahoma in the back of a Willys Overland among crated peaches, glued by spilt juice to the sugary truckbed, stung by ants the whole way. He slept in an Indian pueblo in New Mexico, a whorehouse in Denver, a county jail in Amarillo, a monastery in Juárez. Often as not, he slept outdoors. And one twilit evening, making camp on a cactus-clumped roadside after being dumped by a pervert, he saw the eastern sky sundered by a terrible ball of fire and watched spellbound as a cloudhead rose, lightning flickering in its dark crown, until the noise and the wind reached and flattened him, leaving crusts of salt on his cheeks where there had been tears of wonder.

Last night, after all those months and all that distance, Stanley finally found what he was looking for. He found it, and he couldn't remember a goddamn thing, not any of the things he'd planned to say: nothing to show that he'd gotten the message, that he'd understood. He just followed Welles around like a goddamn dunce while the old man ran his mouth and that nasty little dog peed on stuff.

Patches of light inch along the floor, and drifts of white powder on the concrete glitter like pixiedust in a Disney flick. Stanley hears car engines, a faraway motorcycle, the faint thud of heavy surf. The gulls sob like old women at a funeral.

Claudio doesn't stir when Stanley rises and stretches. They didn't get in last night until very late, and the kid'll probably be copping z's for hours yet. But Stanley can't sleep anymore. Too much to do.

The leg of his jeans sticks to his calf. He tugs it free, then winces, remembering the cut. He steps into the front room, pisses in a milkbottle, stoppers it to hide the smell. Then he opens the pack, drinks from the canteen, brushes his teeth.

When he's done he takes off his pants, removes the bloody bandage, and rinses the wound. It doesn't look too nice. He finds his bottle of rubbing alcohol, his spool of thread, a clean white T-shirt he can spare. Then he pours alcohol on the cut, yelping through clenched teeth at the sting. There isn't much left in the bottle, and he uses it all. He wipes his watery eyes with the T-shirt, rips it up, bandages himself again. Finding sturdy satisfaction on the other side of the pain: a pleasure at tending to himself, spiced with earned contempt for the soft squarejohn world that can't or won't do the same, that fixes everything with money. Lately it's not in daydreams but in moments like this — performing grim simple self-sufficient tasks — that he feels closest to Crivano.

Once the bandage is tied, he bites off a length of thread and sews up the tear in his jeans. Later he'll rinse off the dried blood in the ocean.

In the backroom, Claudio rolls over and says something in Spanish. Stanley leans in the doorframe to watch him sleep — a funny smooth shape under the blanket — then reaches through the hole in the gypsum-board to find what he stashed there last night.

After he and Welles finally parted company, it took Stanley a while to retrace their steps, to find his way back across cracked sidewalks and swampy lawns to the parked motorcycle, the pond curtained by bulrushes, the street he couldn't recall the name of: Navarre. The motorbike was still there, as was the pair of black boots, poking through the vegetation. After a nervous pause to make sure the coast was clear, Stanley crept to the water's edge to see. An overjolted biker, just like he'd figured: gaunt face, blue lips framed by a handlebar moustache, spike still in the vein. A strong smell of piss mixed with night-blooming jasmine. Stanley held his breath, leaned down, and jackpot: four cellophane envelopes tucked inside the stiff's denim vest.

By the time he made it back to the coffeehouse it was nearly two. People were filing out, the jazz combo was putting horns in cases, and the poets — Larry and Stuart and John — had Alex boxed in a corner, arguing about someone or something called Molloy. Stanley caught Alex's eye without even trying, like the guy could smell the junk when it walked into the room. As Stanley watched, Alex produced a pencil and a black notebook, scratched on a page, tore the page out, and passed it over his shoulder to Lyn, his black-haired girl. No pause in his monologue. *De Gaulle gave him the Croix de Guerre. But his behavior during the war was not heroism. It was simply what one did. No act that's justifiable by reason should ever be regarded as brave. His books — the fierce refusals they contain — those are his heroic acts.* The girl drifted over, wraithlike, to put the folded page in Stanley's hand. Stanley roused yawning Claudio from his seat by the door, and they walked into the night with the foreign pulse of Alex's voice at

559

their backs. *Yes, I knew him in Paris. I published him, when no one else would. In some ways he became like a father to me.*

Now Stanley pulls on his mended pants, stuffs the cellophane packets into the front pocket, and unfolds the page from Alex's notebook. 41 CLUB HOUSE AVE, it says. He moves the pinewood plank from the door, glides into the street.

Club House is seven short blocks away, north toward Ocean Park. Scant traffic on the Speedway, but Stanley opts to use the boardwalk, to see what the water's up to. Heavy surf. Uneasy blues in the waves and sky. The shoreline seems limp, collapsed, like an old helium balloon. Somewhere out there the Pacific's making plans for rain; no telling when it'll come. The mercury must be in the barometer's basement. Stanley's sinuses feel too big for his face.

The boardwalk had a rough night by the look of things: lost shoes, used rubbers, motorbike tracks on the sand. Gulls and terns fighting over choice vomit. At the corner of Westminster Stanley picks up a trail of dried blood — ruddy sunbursts, widely spaced on the planks — and he follows it for a block before it swerves away. The few faces he meets all seem sleep-starved, punch-drunk.

He doesn't like how he's feeling: rudderless, out of step. Finding Welles last night shook him up, and not in a good way, not the way he expected to be shaken. It's like the beacon he's been tracking has turned out to be only a shiny surface, reflecting something else. He needs to know what. Everything the guy said last night was guff, intended to keep the real secret hidden. There's a question Stanley needs to ask; he's running out of chances to ask it. Before he sees Welles again he needs to figure it out.

On Club House the buildings look like they started out residential, then went commercial, and are backsliding toward residential again. Number 41 is an old storefront, sign long gone, door scraped clean, black paint rolled over the windows. The insistent bark of a typewriter comes from inside. Stanley knocks. When the typing doesn't stop, he knocks again.

The typing stops. After a long silent moment, the door swings open, and Alex's sharp nose appears. Small eyes glint behind it, like mica on a cave wall. Room service, Stanley says.

Of course. Please do come in.

Alex is dressed in boxershorts and a white A-shirt; his sandaled feet scrape the smooth cement floor. He gestures toward an orange-crate draped with an Indian blanket, which Stanley sits on. The place is dark, practically bare. Not much better than the squat on Horizon. Stanley spies the typewriter in the far corner, a black lozenge perched on a rickety folding table. A forty-watt bulb hangs over it, shaded by butcher-paper screens glued to stretched wire hangers, thick with red and violet gouache. The bulb casts light on the typewriter and almost nowhere else. A pile of looseleaf notebooks sits on one side of the tabletop; a neat stack of typed pages sits on the other. As Stanley's eyes adjust to the gloom he sees more typed sheets on the floor below, arranged just as tidily, though this paper is old, well-handled, warped and cured by fingertip oil. Stanley guesses the stack on the floor would come halfway up his calf.

Alex seats himself on a second orange-crate. Behind him a door opens onto a slightly brighter room, where indirect daylight falls through a window Stanley can't see. Sheets and blankets, the edge of a mattress, a slender extended arm. The arm goes away; bare bruised legs appear. Then Lyn is backlit in the doorframe. A pale band describes her upper arm and shoulder, the sharp relief of ribs, the curve of a breast and the hollow of hips, like the hint of craters in a crescent moon.

Who is it? she says. Her alto voice is muggy with sleep.

Why, it's our new friend Stanley, Alex says. Fix us some tea, won't you?

She falls back, vanishes around the corner. What does he want? she says.

Alex has produced his kit. He unsnaps the folded leather, lays out the contents on the low table between the crates: cotton, eyedropper, needle. He wants to help us, Alex says. What have you brought for us, Stanley?

Stanley stands, pulls the bindles from his pocket, sits, drops them to the tabletop. Each hits the wood with a resonant splat. Alex tilts forward like a dowsing rod. Nothing in his face suggests excitement, but his eyes are as bright as Stanley has ever seen them. May I? he says.

Stanley nods. Alex unfolds a packet, moistens a fingertip, dips and licks. Lyn emerges again, wrapped perfunctorily in a short satin kimono, and crosses behind Alex to the sink. It's no more than a tin basin nailed to the wall, a rubber hose run into it. Her kimono falls open when she bends to turn the valve of the spigot, and she doesn't bother to fix it. She fills an electric teapot, plugs it in.

Alex cuts a strip from a dollar bill with a pair of scissors, then measures powder into a spoon. I had imagined, he says, with all the rough boys and their motorcycles, that some shit must have come into town.

Another splash from the basin, and Lyn comes back to set a pink Depression-glass tumbler on the table. Alex dips the eyedropper, fills the spoon, strikes a match. Lyn switches on an ancient Zenith console radio in the corner, and a watery classical-music broadcast seeps from the loudspeaker. The vacuum-tubes glow blue against the wall, through the tuner dial.

We've been hung up for shit for some time now, Alex says. Quite difficult to come by. Stuart and his friends can always find dolophine, paregoric, goofballs. But of course they are no real substitute.

He puts the cotton in the spoon. While the solution leaches through it, he screws the needle onto the eyedropper with the dollar-bill strip. Then he ties off his arm.

The teakettle whistles. Lyn picks it up. Stanley, she says, would you like some milk and sugar?

Her accent is Long Island Irish, though she doesn't look Irish. The single turn that holds the ends of her belt together has slipped below her navel. Stanley wonders why she even bothered to put the robe on. No thanks, he says.

Alex squashes the eyedropper's bulb, puts the needle in the cotton, and draws up the fix. Then he hits a vein in the back of his left arm. The liquid in the dropper moves up and down with his heartbeat, gradually darkening. He pumps the bulb, then loosens the belt. Stanley keeps his expression cool, bored, but he's thinking about the overjolted biker, getting ready to make tracks if Alex hits the floor.

Alex just sighs and sits back on his crate. As if the fix was of less consequence than downing a glass of icewater. He holds the rig out to Stanley, raises his eyebrows.

No thanks, Stanley says again.

Alex looks surprised, then smug. Ah, he says. I see. You prefer the rapture of your own perceptions. For one of your relative youth, that is not surprising. You've not yet been made aware of the force and the dimensions of the historical currents arrayed against you. Perhaps you've even managed a few small victories. It's possible. What separates the savagery of the juvenile delinquent from the transformative gestures of the Cabaret Voltaire is precisely that awareness. When at last it does find you, junk will begin to make sense.

Stanley gives Alex a cool once-over: his heavy brow, his sunken eyes, his sleep-tangled hair. Mister, he says, I don't have a damn clue what you're talking about.

No? Alex says with a constricted smile. My apologies. I'm afraid there's a junkie protocol to which I am not adhering. I'm supposed to say that you're wise not to have a habit, that you'd be foolish to start one. Well. That page of my script must have been left in the mimeograph.

Lyn brings mugs of tea. She knots the belt of her robe, sits on another crate, pushes up the sleeve, ties off her arm. Stanley lifts his mug, blows across it, sips.

Alex has opened his billfold; he counts out a wad, hands it over, and leans back in the shadows. His nose as sharp and protuberant as the dorsal of a shark. Stanley fans the bills, folds them, puts them in his pocket. It's more than he'd expect to get in New York, but probably less than it's worth. He doesn't know the local market, and Alex knows he doesn't know, so Stanley's not going to gripe. You're leaving town, Stanley says.

That's correct. For Las Vegas. Within the week.

Okay. What do you need?

Alex shrugs. What's your connection good for? he says.

Can't say exactly. Anything shy of an ounce should be no sweat.

Alex pinches the opened bindle, lifts it from the tabletop. It'd be the same shit as this? he says.

You bet. But he'll be shipping out soon, so we gotta move quick.

Your connection is with the motorcyclists, I suppose?

Stanley sips his tea.

Ahhh, Lyn says. The leather strap slides from her arm to the floor, and she slouches on the orange-crate with a dull bleary grin. At least her robe stays closed. Her crate is topped with a cushion, not a blanket, and Stanley sees a logo upsidedown on one end: the same company that bought the harvest that he and Claudio worked in Riverside.

A quarter-ounce should suffice, Alex says.

Two yards I'll need for that. Up front.

Alex purses his thin lips. I can manage one-fifty now, he says.

Stanley pretends to think about that for a second, then nods.

I'll have it for you tonight, Alex says. Some of the resident shoreline poets — Stuart and John and a few others — are fêting me. A bon-voyage of a sort. You should come. We're to meet here at ten. Bring along a pail, and your dark handsome friend. We'll all catch ourselves some fish.

Alex stirs his tea. The spoon makes lazy peals against the sides of the mug, like a windchime signaling a storm's approach. Lyn wipes away a daub of blood with a paper napkin. Good clear veins in the crook of her arm: she hasn't been using long. Alex tells me you're from Brooklyn, she says.

That's right.

I'm from Hicksville. You know where that is?

I know where it is, Stanley says. I never been there.

Don't bother, she says. It's the absolute *pits.*

She spreads the napkin, lifts it before her face. Red dots of various sizes appear between its folds. Alex is the greatest writer of his generation, she says. You may not care about that, but I think you should know.

Stanley does not care, Alex says. He is not sentimental. And what is writing if not

567

sentimentality? Unless it's the dropping of a few slick turds to mark one's passage. I'm not certain that I care myself.

Don't say that, Lyn says.

Stanley takes another sip, then swallows. I heard you typing, he says.

Yes. I was. I like that: *typing*. Much better than *writing*. And I'm very glad you didn't say *working*. That's what Stuart and his friends always call it. They imagine themselves to be in sympathy with the proletariat. The truth is that they want their labor to be acknowledged by the marketplace, no matter how they pretend otherwise. That's a difficult thing not to want. So let us not condemn them. But neither let us call it *work*. It's play, or it's nothing. Minstrelsy at best.

Okay, Stanley says. So what are you typing?

I'm not sure, to be honest. I'm trying to remain unsure. What was it Antonin Artaud said? We spend our days fretting over forms, when we should be like heretics at the stake, gesticulating as the flames engulf us.

Stanley nods toward the tall stack of papers on the floor. It looks like you got a bunch of it, he says. Whatever it is.

Alex frowns, then considers the stack with narrowed eyes. The way somebody might look at a strange animal they've taken in, uncertain about what to feed it, how big it might grow.

It's not poetry, he says. Nor is it a novel,

though I have written novels, and published them. It is not artful in any way. During my time in Paris, I became involved with a group of young — how shall I describe them? Revolutionaries? Avant-gardistes? Criminals? To be any one of those, you must exert a plausible claim on the other two. My young friends were convinced that art in all its forms is counter-revolutionary. So-called avant-garde art most of all. Thirty years ago, the Dadaists called it the safety-valve of culture: it eases internal pressure, averts the transformative explosion. Instead of demanding adventure and beauty in our own lives, we seek their simulacra in films and cheap paperbacks. Instead of doing battle with cops and their finks, we sit home and recite our slogans into mirrors. The most skilled evocation of the most perfect society may help us to imagine it, but it brings it no closer to fruition. Quite the opposite. It's a substitute. It makes our dissatisfactions tolerable, when they must *not* be tolerable. We rejected all that. We practiced a kind of auto-terrorism. We took as our main objective the construction of situations, and we walked the streets of the city with the demand that they reshape themselves according to our desires. Sometimes — very rarely — they did.

Stanley looks up, interested. How did that work? he says.

Alex doesn't answer. The three of them sit

in silence. The air grows thick with steam from their mugs and the electric kettle.

Stanley's about to ask again when footsteps scrape the sidewalk outside. The door lurches in its frame; the deadbolt stops it with a clunk. A rapid knock follows. Stanley tenses, turns. The shadow of someone's elbow appears and disappears at the edge of the painted-over glass.

Stanley looks at Alex, then at Lyn. Lyn is examining the veins in her arm. Alex lights a cigarette, shakes out the match. After a moment, without knocking again, the person at the door goes away. Muttering unintelligibly to himself. The voice is one that Stanley knows: the poet, the ad man, the drunk.

Lyn looks up with a sad smile. Charlie, she says.

Yes, Alex says. I suppose he's forgotten again.

He leans forward, like a tree bent by ice-caked branches, and slides a mayonnaise-jar lid closer on the tabletop.

Perhaps, he says, it's only a diary that I'm writing. A catalogue of impressions. A psychogeographical atlas. A rutter of drift. It's the thread that I've unwound through the invisible labyrinth, in case anyone should care to retrace my steps. Such reports are not without value. Often I have relied upon them myself. The explorer who reaches a summit and curses to find another's ice-axe already there is no explorer at all, but only a conqueror and a thug. Every worthwhile initiative is a collaboration, a conspiracy, a series of coded messages passed across the years from hand to anonymous hand. Such was the nature of our endeavor in Paris.

Stanley can't tell if that was intended as an answer to his question. A long curl of sour smoke rises from Alex's cigarette; he draws on it just enough to keep it lit, tips the ash into the mayonnaise lid. The passage of time inside the room seems keyed somehow to that cigarette: like Alex has smoked the clock down to a crawl. Stanley fidgets on his crate. He's forgotten how much he hates junkies.

As concerns method, Alex says, we simply took to the streets. With no intended destination, no expectation of what we might find. Accident and chance were our means of clearing the slate. We sought out signals and traces with the unerring antennae of our desires. If this sounds effortless I promise that it was not. It required dedication and tremendous fortitude, because the enemy was always present within us. Desire is treacherous, it wants only to be satisfied, and thus it is always ready to accept ruinous compromises. We hoarded our dreams like pirate treasure, and like all proper treasures, they generated maps. In those days we spoke often of a city — imaginary, but still realizable — that would be built with no objective beyond the facilitation of play. The chief obstacle, of course, was architecture. Desire is fleeting; architecture is not. So desire learns to accommodate itself to architecture. Play becomes professionalized. Pleasure becomes rote. We had no solution for this. We believed that in the city of our dreams, every man would inhabit his own cathedral. But through the years the best I've ever been able to manage —

Alex puts the cigarette in his mouth, lifts the needle and the eyedropper from the table, shifts them into his left hand, and plucks the cigarette from his lips again.

— is a fortress, he says. A citadel. You see, the best thing about having a habit is that you always know what your desire is, and that it is your own. It's not like wanting a new Oldsmobile. It seals those other lesser desires in amber, so you can look upon them with a cool eye. I have not forgotten the city that we sought. I once walked its streets, and I believe that one day I will do so again. I must confess that I have very high hopes for Las Vegas. They are certain to be disappointed.

Lyn sighs, leans forward, opens the pack of Luckies on the low table, lights one. She rolls her head as she exhales her first puff, like a gangster's moll in a movie. Then she picks up a book from the floor — *Listen, Little Man!* it says on the spine — and returns to the bedroom, untying her silk belt as she goes.

As she turns the corner, the kimono slips from her shoulders to the floor. Alex doesn't look at her, or at anything else. He puts the cigarette to his lips, and its tip glows. It's not yet a third gone.

Say, Alex? Stanley says. I don't suppose I could borrow your john for a minute?

The lightsocket hung over the commode is empty. Stanley finds a box of matches and a votive candle on the toilet tank, then shuts the door. Almost before he's dropped his pants the typing has resumed: a quick initial burst, followed by sporadic chatter, and the occasional hiss of the carriage return. Long silences creep in. Soon Stanley can count the letters of each word so easily that he's tempted to guess what they are. He thinks of Welles, picturing the fat man seated at his own desk. The triangle formed by his eyes, his fingers, the shuttling page. Stanley closes his eyes, stretches out his arched fingers over an imagined keyboard.

When he's done he flushes, removes his jacket and his shirts, and washes his face and neck and arms and chest in the bathroom sink. The mirror on the medicine-cabinet is streaked; he's about to wipe it with a towel when he sees that the streaks are letters, written in grease-pencil, now almost erased. He lifts the candle, looks closer. The hasty serrated writing is distinctive, familiar: a match with the slogans he read last night on the coffeehouse walls. THIS IS THE FACE OF GOD YOU SEE, it says.

Stanley dries himself and dresses, then waits till the typewriter is going at a good clip again before blowing out the candle and opening the door. In the rectangle of light that leads to the bedroom he can see Lyn's pale feet, their toes angled down at the edge of the mattress. The right foot is still; the left rises and falls, like the pumpjacks by the canals. Alex doesn't look up at Stanley, not even when he stops typing. The forgotten Lucky Strike droops between his lips, burnt gray to its filter. Before the ash falls, Stanley shows himself out.

42

On his way back to Horizon Court Stanley passes a small department store as it opens for the day: the manager props the door, then walks to the back and steps into the stockroom to retrieve merchandise. The woman at the register flips through a catalogue. Stanley crouches between racks and tables; no one sees him come in or go out. He leaves with a new pair of bluejeans, a new shirt, some brown gabardine slacks that caught his eye. Two doors down he steals a bottle of rubbing alcohol from a druggist who's on the phone with his bookie. Why does anybody ever pay for anything? Stanley wonders.

He raps on the door of the squat in the pattern that he and Claudio rehearsed — the kid had better not still be asleep — then walks to the corner. When he's sure the street is clear he walks back, taps twice, and the door swings open.

Claudio hides behind the doorframe, still in his jockeyshorts. Where have you been? he says. I have been very concerned.

You coulda asked me where I was going.

I was asleep.

Stanley sets his bundle of clothes on the glass-topped counter. You weren't that asleep, he says. Hey, take a look at this stuff I picked up. You like these pants?

This is where you have been for these hours? Finding pants?

Cool it a minute, kid. I was doing some business. We got money coming tonight.

Money? What money?

Big money. A hundred and fifty clams.

Claudio's eyes widen; his mouth forms an O. What? he says. Is this true? From where will this money come?

From that guy Alex. Remember him? He was at the joint last night. From England or someplace. Great big nose.

Yes, Claudio says, knitting his brow. I do remember. I talked to him. I thought something was not right about him and his wife. They seemed strange.

They seem like a couple of junkies and

grifters, which is what they are. That's what makes 'em good for a touch. They're giving us cash for junk.

Stanley removes his shoes, then unzips his dirty jeans and pulls them off. He puts them on the counter and unrolls the gabardine slacks.

Sorry, Claudio says. They will give us cash for what? Junk?

Junk, Stanley says, pulling on the trousers. Hop. Shit. Dope. Get with the program, kid.

Narcotics?

What, are you the Kefauver Commission all of a sudden? What do you think of these pants? Pretty swank, huh? Do they go with the shirt?

Stanley, Claudio says, what are you talking about? Where will you get this junk?

Goddammit, would you relax? I got it already. I took it off a dead guy last night.

A dead guy? Where is this dead guy? Where is your junk? Is it here? If the police —

Shhhh, Stanley says, putting his hands on Claudio's jaw, his thumbs on his lips. Just listen, he says. The junk I found, I already sold it to Alex. That's the grift. I sold him a few buck's worth, and I told him I'd get some more. He's giving me the cash for it tonight. He's leaving town in a week.

We will keep his money, Claudio says, and give him no junk. That is your plan? This will not cause problems for us?

I been thinking about that, Stanley says, and at first that's how I had it figured. Now I got a better idea. If we rip him off the way you're saying, we get the hundred-fifty, and maybe some bad feelings. But if we deliver the goods, we could net at least that much, or more. I think it's worth looking into.

But how? Where will you get such a quantity of narcotics? We know no one here whom this Alex does not know also.

The hell we don't, kid, Stanley says. What about the Shoreline Dogs?

Claudio's eyes narrow; he takes Stanley's arms by the wrists, gently removes them from his face. What in hell are you talking about? he murmurs.

This is genius, kid, Stanley says. It solves all our problems. We get a nice chunk of cash, and we get those clowns off our backs. We'll have ourselves a little powwow, pass the peace pipe around, and we'll make a deal. Everybody'll go home happy.

But the Dogs hate us. They want to kill us. We humiliated them.

Stanley steps back, unbuttons his shirt. You don't understand these chumps like I do, he says. All hoods are the same, the whole world over. They're all looking for the big score, but they got no imagination. I guarantee you they know somebody who'll get us what we need, and they'll be happy with whatever cut we give 'em. I'll talk to that guy, I'll set this thing

up, and bygones'll be bygones. Him and me'll
be pals for life.

What guy is this you will talk to?

You know, Stanley says. The guy. The boss.
That greaser I kicked in the nuts. The rest of
that crew I wouldn't trust to make me a
sandwich, but that guy I can work with. He's
smart enough to know he's dumb.

Stanley slides into the new shirt, tucks in
the tail: a cream-yellow rayon blend, ochre
inset stripes running alongside its shiny shell
buttons. It's fancy — just the thing for the
next time he sees Welles — but he'll have to
be careful about wearing it on the street. Any
smart cop will know at a glance how he came
by it.

Claudio stands aside, his arms crossed, his
thumb across his lips. Is there another way?
he says. Another way to get money?

Whaddya mean? There's lots of other ways.
But this is what came along, so this is what
we're doing. It's a fast pitch, sure, but it's in
the strike zone. So we gotta take a swing.
How do I look?

Stanley smoothes the shirt's fabric, holds
out his arms, pivots. Claudio gives him a
quick worried glance. You look nice, he says.

If you like these duds, I can get you some,
too. Those jokers in the shop —

Your idea, Claudio says. It has many dangers. The hoods. The police. We do not know
if this Alex is to be trusted. It is a serious

crime we will do, Stanley.

Would you quit bellyaching? Look, it's no different from crossing a city street. Maybe a runaway cement truck'll smash you dead. It could happen to anybody. But you cross anyway, right? It's just like that. Kid, you have got to get tougher if you're gonna make the grade out here. You can't go around scared all the time.

What about your man? Claudio says. Your poet?

What about him?

Can your man help us get what we want? In a way that does not break any law?

Stanley thinks about that. Then he steps forward, pinches the elastic of Claudio's shorts, and gives it a gentle snap. No dice, he says. From that guy, there's something else I want.

Later, when Stanley's new clothes are draped on the clothesline, when he's watching the shallow curves of Claudio's back sway beneath the pencils of light, he remembers something.

I changed my name again last night, he says.

Claudio makes a soft quizzical sound, his voice sleepy and thick.

I said I changed my name. It's Stanley Glass now.

Why?

Stanley puts his nose between the boy's smooth shoulder-blades and breathes in. It

579

was time, he says.

Mmmm. I only will call you Stanley.

That's fine. Oh, we need to steal a bucket, too.

A bucket?

Yeah, Stanley says, spitting on his fingertips. You know, a bucket. For fish.

43

The illuminated dial at the hardware store on Windward gives them the time: a little before nine o'clock. For an hour now it's been raining hard, with no sign that it'll stop. The sweep of headlights through the distant traffic circle makes it look like a dull carnival ride: the slow kind, for old people and little kids. From time to time a car rolls by, big drops streaking the air before it like scratches on a reel of dark celluloid.

Stanley and Claudio huddle under the colonnade between the Forty-Niner and Semper's Men's Wear, stepping to the wall whenever the wind gusts, watching water ripple over the laughing faces on the cast-iron columns. It's about time Stanley stole himself a watch: he's been telling time by daylight, but tonight's sunset got snuffed by the incoming storm and put them out in the rain an hour too early. Claudio's quiet, like he's frosted about something. So long as they're already soaked, Stanley figures, they

580

might as well head over to Alex's pad. Somebody'll probably be around.

The boardwalk arcades keep them more or less dry till they're halfway to Club House; after that, they scurry between canvas awnings and pinch their collars shut. As they make the turn they see three figures pass through the bright cone of a streetlamp, pails dangling from their fists, newspapers draped over their heads. The figures shout and pound at the door of Alex's apartment, and after a moment they're admitted.

Stanley hunches his shoulders, doubletimes down the sidewalk. Claudio's right behind him; Stanley can hear raindrops ping off the tin bucket in the kid's hand. Ahead, flecks of red and orange light escape the apartment's blacked windows where the paint is chipped, then vanish when shadows pass over them. Soon Stanley and Claudio are close enough to hear laughter, voices.

A knock opens the door right away. A face appears: bespectacled and goateed, backlit and unintelligible. Not a face Stanley knows. Can I help you, man? it says.

Stanley wipes rainwater from his nostrils and lips. Alex around? he says.

Another shape steps into the doorframe, peeking over the goateed guy's shoulder: Stuart, the bearded poet from the coffeehouse. He was among the three who just arrived: his shirt is soaked, translucent, and droplets glint in his black hair. Hey, he says, I recognize these two drowned rats.

Now Alex's voice: Is that young Stanley already? he shouts. Don't stand there in the bloody entrance, Tony. Let him in.

Swinging back, the door pushes aside stacks of buckets: they scrape against each other, against the concrete floor. Stanley shrugs off his dripping jacket; Claudio shakes rain from their upended pail and steps inside. I see you brought the items I requested, Alex says. But you've come a bit early, haven't you?

Me and my buddy started Daylight Saving Time a month ahead, Stanley says. Trying to get a jump on the competition.

Alex and Stuart chuckle, and Stanley scans the hazy room. The orange-crates are all occupied; more young men sit Indian-style on the floor, skunky smoke rising from their cupped hands. A sharp-looking Negro is in the chair behind the typewriter; when his eyes meet Stanley's, the guy gives him a cautious smile. From everybody else, suspicious stares: their gazes move from Stanley to Claudio to Alex and back again.

Fellas, Alex says, I'd like you to meet — if you have not yet met — Claudio and Stanley, two criminal toughs of my recent acquaintance with a burgeoning interest in art and poetry and other fine things. It falls to us, gentlemen, to see that these lads are not lost to the felonious abyss.

A voice from the corner: Maybe these two can save the rest of us from art and poetry, it says. Make us into honest crooks.

It's Charlie. Stanley almost doesn't recognize him: he looks sober, or nearly so. He's giving them a tight smile and a narrow knowing glare, but it's not convincing. It's a look that says *I had the goods on you, buddy, but then I forgot.* Stanley plays it cool, laughs a little at Charlie's joke. Nobody else does.

Clockwise from left, Alex says, meet Bob, Bruce, Milton, Saul, Maurice, Jimmy, Charlie, Stuart whom you know, and Tony, our doorman. Now take your friend's jacket, Stanley, and come with me.

In the bedroom — sheets haphazard on the bare mattress, drooping indecipherable paintings tacked to the walls — Alex takes the jackets and hands Stanley a wad of bills. Count it, he says, and Stanley does: one-fifty. He nods, and Alex whisks him back to the main room.

Stuart and a couple of other guys have restarted what seems to be a favorite argument. One of the new faces — fleshy, fake-professorial, probably queer, sipping red wine from a coffeemug — has the floor now. Of *course* poems should be like paintings! the guy's saying. Why wouldn't they be? I mean, *ut pictura poesis,* man: that's the whole history of the form in a phrase. It's right there in Horace — and Horace was just quoting

Simonides. The instant impact of the image, the negative space of the blank page, the depth of potential detail. That's what we all want, right?

I'm not sold on that, the colored guy — Milton — says. How many of the poets in this room are painters, too? Just about all, unless I'm mistaken. If you're satisfied with one, why bother with the other?

Tony, still standing by the door, motions Alex over, speaks quietly in his ear. He keeps looking at Stanley and Claudio, unhappy about something. Stanley can't hear what he's saying.

Stuart's arguing with the tubby professor. You missed the scene at the *Coastlines* reading, Bruce, he says. If you'd caught it, there's no way you'd still be trying to shovel this shit. Ginsberg ain't no painter, man. You take the most massive painting you can think of — take the Sistine Chapel ceiling, for chrissakes — and you're still nowhere near the thing he read. You're hung up on some kind of museum-academy trip, man. You're filling little jars with formaldehyde. I love paintings, but they don't exist *in time*. Poems don't happen on the page. They're made from living breath.

Ginsberg? somebody says. He's the strip-tease star, right?

— *just theater,* someone else mutters under his breath.

584

So what's the matter with theater? Stuart says. Poetry needs more theater! It needs more music! Get it off the page, man, and onto the stage! Get some red blood pumping in those paper veins!

Oh, christ, Bruce says, refilling his cup from a gallon jug on the floor. Here we go again with the jazz canto jive.

Across the room, Alex has an avuncular hand on Tony's shoulder, a raised finger in his face. Tony isn't talking anymore.

Poets and painters gotta quit shadowboxing each other, Stuart says, and start aping jazz. Free up the forms! Smash the phony barriers between art and life! That's how we'll reach people, man. It's guerrilla warfare. Nowadays everybody's an image junkie, everybody's hypnotized. The frontal attack is no good. You gotta get in through the ear, you gotta communicate with the inner eye, the eye that won't be tricked by some subliminal projection.

Charlie speaks up, his voice a little too loud in the small room. Whoa, Trigger! he says. Now you've got me confused. Are we talking about poetry or advertising?

Stuart and Bruce shoot glares at him, exasperated, at a loss, knocked off their rhythm. In the sudden quiet, Tony's low voice comes through the room: *on top of being dope-peddling JDs,* he says, *they're an illegal*

585

sex, to boot.

Let me let you guys in on a little trade secret, Charlie says. This is my area of expertise, dig? You know what's even better than subliminal projections for selling stuff? *Super*-liminal projections, man! Just put it out there! You guys talk about people like they're sheep, like they can't think for themselves, like if they weren't all such saps they'd be right here at the oceanfront with us, painting pictures, writing poems, sleeping on the sand, living off horsemeat from the pet shop. Truth is, they *love* to be fooled. They want to be told what to do, what to want, what to like. They love their illusions. Just like us, right? But we think our illusions are *better.* If you guys want to change the world, start paying attention to your Starch Ratings. Just like we used to say around the office: *you can't sell a man who isn't listening!*

A tide of grumbles wells up around Charlie; he's smirking, pleased with himself. That's a bunch of cynical crap, man, Milton says quietly.

C'mon, Charlie says. Just 'cause I don't buy my own BS, that makes me a cynic? I'd love to be wrong about this, believe me. Am I wrong, Alex? What's it that your left-wing deviationist friends say? Give people the choice between love and a garbage disposal, most of them choose the garbage disposal. Right?

Alex half-turns from Tony with a wan

patronizing smile. I think you've made your point, Charlie, he says.

I'm not trying to make a *point,* Charlie says. Shrillness creeps into his voice, and he lifts his hands to his face: a little like Jack Benny, a little like a mortified child. His hands are trembling. I just want to know what I should *do,* he says. What I should *write.* I want to be honest, I want to renounce Moloch and all his works, I want to not make the world any worse. How do I go *about* that, Alex?

Alex leans against the wall, his arms crossed, his head cocked. Everybody looks at him except Claudio, who looks at Stanley. The people here all treat Alex like he's famous or something, Stanley realizes. Maybe he is.

When Alex speaks, it's less to Charlie than to the rest of the room. The writer's task, he says, is to make a record of his times. To stand apart, and to bear witness.

Oh! Charlie says, snapping his fingers, then slapping his knees, rising to his feet. Well, *that* sure clears it up! Boy, do I feel like a dunce! All this time, I've been trying to *create* something. I guess I ought to take up painting if I want to do that. Huh, Stuart? Or maybe just go back to the ad firm. I could be *very* creative there. Hey, Alex, can I borrow my old john back for a minute? I need to take a crap.

I trust you remember where it is, Alex says.

And how it works.

Charlie moves through the room, tiptoeing between orange-crates and the mugs of wine. I sure wish you'd caught that *Coastlines* thing, Charlie, Stuart says as he passes. That cat Ginsberg, he used to write ads too, y'know.

Ginsberg *still* writes ads, Charlie snaps. You guys are always talking down Larry Lipton for selling the Beat Generation like soap, but your real gripe is that he's not *cool* enough about it. *The poet always stands naked before the world!* Great. Hey, Alex, I just took some Polaroids of my crotch. You think *Evergreen Review*'ll publish 'em?

Charlie steps through the bathroom door, shuts it, curses, opens it again to find the matchbox and the candle. I don't know what the hell you want, Charlie, Bruce shouts.

I want a fucking drink, Charlie mumbles, and closes the door again.

Everybody stares into space, avoids eye contact. The room is starting to smell bad, like too many bodies and too few baths. It's quiet except for the sound of Charlie pissing, and then it's just quiet. Two hands reach for the wine-jug at once; both withdraw awkwardly. Somebody — Maurice? Bob? — moves toward the old Zenith, but Milton intercepts him with an upraised palm. Listen, he says. I think the rain stopped.

In a rush the men are on their feet, slipping into their jackets, passing the buckets around. Stanley and Claudio stick close together, drift with the pack back onto the street. A sticky mist still billows, everywhere at once. The dense fast-moving clouds are lichen-green with moonlight, but Stanley can't make out any moon.

Charlie catches up, still buttoning his pants, as Alex is closing the door. You didn't erase the mirror! he says, clapping a hand on Alex's shoulder. Then he runs ahead, his voice breaking with sounds like joy. Stuart! he shouts. He didn't erase it! The thing that you wrote for me is still on the mirror!

They move to the boardwalk in a ragged column, two and three abreast, buckets swinging jauntily. Streetlamps and patches of sky flash around their feet from deep puddles in the potholed pavement. Stanley can see small bonfires on the beach, shadows passing between them.

He and Claudio walk in silence, bringing up the rear. Claudio has no clue what they're doing. It's not that he didn't understand what Stanley told him; the kid follows well enough. He's just dead set on being behind Stanley no matter what, never mind what the reasons are. Stanley should be grateful for that, he figures, but instead it annoys him a little.

So the pad was that of Alex, Claudio says after a while, but was once the pad of Charlie? Is that right?

Beats the hell outta me, kid.

They trudge along for a few more paces. The head of the line has reached the boardwalk, is crossing onto the sand.

Claudio tries again. Charlie was unhappy, he says. Do you know why?

He's afraid he's a joke and a phony, I guess.

But why is he afraid of that?

I dunno. Maybe 'cause he is one. Look, why don't you run ahead and ask him?

He does not want to hurt the world, Claudio says. But how can a poem hurt the world? How can it do anything? I do not understand this.

The column loses shape when it hits the dark beach, jumbling like a dropped rope. People walk by: a woman and two younger guys, all three nude, on their way to the water. Nobody looks at them twice. In the ring of light cast by the farthest bonfire, a bare-chested man in sunglasses plays a pair of high-pitched Cuban drums, not very well. The drums look and sound like toys. A rhythm rises against the crash of waves, then gutters, then starts up again.

Milton checks his watch. High tide in ten minutes, he says.

These knuckleheads better put out their lights, Stuart says, or else they're gonna spook all the fish.

A motorcycle sputters along the Speedway,

turning toward the traffic circle. From somewhere near the oilfield comes a series of loud pops that could be backfires, could be pistolshots.

Ten minutes, then? Alex says, digging through the pockets of his denim overalls. Anyone fancy a round of pinball before the arcades close?

Stanley grins; he feels like his mind's been read. Lead the way, pal, he says. That's my meat and potatoes.

They step onto the wooden planks again. Claudio and Charlie and one of the others — Jimmy? Saul? — break off to follow. Stuart calls to them as they go. *We're headed south,* he says, *where it's darker!* Alex lifts a hand in vague acknowledgment, doesn't turn around. Charlie has vanished before they've crossed the boardwalk: off to find a bottle, Stanley figures.

The penny-arcade is an old Bridgo parlor, small and seedy and full of machines that look like they fell off a truck. The sign hung on the colonnade was new maybe ten years ago, which puts it ahead of the sign on the boarded-up building next door, which was new in maybe 1930. The interior is about a quarter whitewashed, like somebody stopped in mid-brushstroke partway along the left-hand wall when they ran out of paint and money, or maybe just realized that nobody cared. A shrill wash of noise spills from the windows and bounces off the bricks: bells and thumps, mechanical whistles, sickly celesta melodies.

It's the usual crowd inside: soldiers, sailors, laborers, pachucos, thugs. A few sorry-looking hookers loiter at the door and windows, asking passersby for dimes. The Dogs are here too, though not in force: three of them, manhandling a Daisy May machine in the corner, their backs to the door, Whitey among them.

Stanley drops some coins into Claudio's palm, parks him at an ancient wobbly Bingo Bango. Back in a minute, he says. Just sit tight.

He crosses the room and taps Whitey on the shoulder before anyone sees him coming. It isn't hard. Stanley keeps his weight back, his stance open, in case somebody takes a swing.

Whitey turns, does a doubletake. For an instant, alarm flickers in his eyes; then he plasters on a hyena sneer. Well, whaddya know, he says. We may get some blowjobs tonight aft—

Can it, meathead. I'm looking for your boss.

Whitey squares his shoulders and juts his jaw, puffed up like a peacock, but his voice is clear, and he's breathing through his nose: he's not going to pull anything. For my *what*? he says.

You heard me. Where is he?

Probably still at the last job I quit, asshole. I ain't got no boss.

Okay, smart guy. Then where's the joker does your thinking for you? You know who I'm talking about. Don't act like a putz.

It ain't my week to watch him, nosebleed. You think I'm his secretary?

I don't think about you at all, chum. When you see him, you tell him that me and my buddy are about to do some business on the waterfront. If he wants a cut, he better let me know pronto. I'm not gonna track him down.

Whitey's sneer sags, like his face is getting tired; he sifts the contents of his brain for a sharp response. Stanley fades back slowly until Whitey open his mouth again. Then he spins on his heel and walks.

Claudio's watching with panicked eyes; he steps forward, meets Stanley halfway. What are you doing? he whispers. Why do you go to the hoods?

You know why, kid, Stanley says. Look, we can't talk about it now. I need you to hold onto something.

He pulls Alex's wad of bills from his pocket and presses it into Claudio's hand. Claudio's eyes get wider; his jaw drops. Stop it, Stanley says. Look at me. If you see those punks make a move — I mean if they come over here, understand? — then you let me know right off. If anybody throws a punch, then you scram the hell outta here. I'll meet you at the hideout.

Alex and his buddy are playing adjacent machines at the room's far end, a Shoot The Moon and a Mercury, their mist-damp heads silhouetted against the sleek painted rockets of the glowing backglasses. Alex is good: he tilts his machine with subtlety and skill, lecturing as he plays. Pinball's true appeal, he's saying, resides in its embodiment of the stiff social mechanisms that ensnare us. To play is to strike at them in effigy. Pinball and jazz are the two finest things your country has given the world, and they arise from the same spirit of opposition.

Stanley moves past them to an Arabian Nights machine. He drops a dime and the backglass lights up: a veiled bellydancer, a turbaned sultan ringed by busty harem girls. The sultan is smug, portly, reading aloud from a massive book; Stanley thinks of Welles and grins. He figures he doesn't have much time, so he draws back the plunger, launches the first ball, and lets it drain. He does the same with the second, and the third. Then he starts to play for real, racking up points in a hurry, slowing down when he feels Alex loom behind him. Not bad, Alex tells him when the game ends.

Thanks. Not too shabby yourself.

I used to play quite a lot in Paris. I've rusted a bit, I'm afraid.

Stanley puts his hand in his pocket, comes

out with another coin. Time for one more game? he says.

Why not? The fish will wait, I suspect.

You wanna win back some of your cash?

As Alex plays — warping the cabinet with the pressure of his knees and elbows, deforming the course of the little silver balls — Whitey and his hammerhead sidekicks exit, flipping Stanley the bird as they go. Claudio seems to relax a little. A light breeze filters through the windows, and Stanley can see moonlight on the waves; the rainclouds must be blowing through. The pinball cabinet groans against Alex's weight. Score lights climb the backglass; the machine clunks and dings.

Soon it's Stanley's turn. He doesn't even look at Alex's score. Moments after he's launched his first ball Alex begins to laugh; he takes a fin from his billfold, creases it down its middle, lays it across the lockdown bar. Ah, but you're a good fucking con, Stanley, he says. Go as long as you can, now. It's worth five just to see you play, you magnificent bugger.

Stanley never tilts; he's never tried, isn't really sure how. He touches nothing but the flipper-buttons. The left is a little tacky; sometimes he can see where the ball's going but can't do much about it, and that gets on his nerves. His eyes track the streak of silver as it ricochets between bumpers. The trap-holes light; the machine vomits replays. Three million points. Four million. Five. Claudio, bored, taps out a mambo rhythm on the tin bucket with his fingertips. Stanley's still on his first ball. Sweet christ, Alex whispers to Claudio. I've not seen anything like it.

Eventually the machine maxes out. Stanley pockets the fin, then tears off the replays and hands them to Alex. So, he says, who's ready to go fish?

They find Stuart and the others near the entrance channel to the new marina. Stuart and Milton are at the water's edge, staring into the swash, outlined against the emergent moon. The others sit farther back on the dry sand, beside empty buckets and scattered shoes. The group has grown: Lyn's here, with three other women, faces Stanley recalls from the coffeehouse. One of them plays a soft melody on a guitar. Charlie's nearby too, a little apart, nursing a bottle from a paper bag.

One of the women greets Claudio by name; he must've met her last night, while Stanley was with Welles. While Claudio talks to her, Stanley slips off his shoes to join Milton and Stuart. As he approaches, Stuart signals caution with a raised hand, and hisses for silence, although Stanley isn't making any noise.

Stanley crouches between them, watching the surf. A couple of slender silver fish — maybe six inches long — swim in the backwash of the last wave, there for an instant, then gone. Hey, Stanley whispers. What're we looking for?

Stuart squints at the ocean, his heavy features fierce and alert. Fish, he says.

Another silver fish zips through the shallows, furrowing the water with its smooth back. Stanley looks at Stuart, then at Milton. What do we do when we see 'em? he says.

Catch 'em, Stuart says.

With what? We got nets?

Don't need nets, Milton says. Just use your hands. You grab 'em, you drop 'em in the bucket. They come right out of the water.

Stuart's still wearing his purposeful Bomba-the-Jungle-Boy expression, scanning the white foam. Stanley looks past him. Probably twenty or thirty small fish cruise along the water's edge between here and the stones of the half-finished jetty. Turning north, he spots even more. What are they supposed to look like? he says.

Like big sardines, Milton says. Five, six inches. Skinny and silver. You'll see a few males at first: those are the scouts. They case the beach, make sure everything's a-okay. Then the ladies make the scene, to lay the eggs.

Stanley points. Are those the scouts? he says.

Milton and Stuart hunch forward. Each presses a palm to the wet sand, balancing on it, and shades his eyes from the moonlight with the other. In this position they look like a couple of gargoyles, or stone lions. Well, I'll be damned, Milton says.

Stuart looks over his shoulder. Get ready! he barks. Here they come.

Within minutes the sand swarms with writhing fish. The crowd on the beach rolls their trousercuffs, rushes forward with whoops and cheers; Claudio hits the cold ocean with a gasp, then wades forward to fill his pail with seawater. The first wave that sweeps Stanley's bare ankles numbs his skin, seizes his shivering body. He can hardly put a foot down without something squirming under it. Saltwater soaks through his bandage, stings his cut. He stoops, clasps slick scales between his stiff blue fingers, lifts and drops his catch into Claudio's waiting bucket.

More fish sweep in on each wave, flipping and thrashing, burrowing tail-first into the sand. Patches of beach all along the waterline glitter in the moonlight, as if mirrors have shattered there, their shards come to wriggling liquid life. Stuart and his friends splash past, laughing through chattering teeth. *Don't take more than you'll eat,* Milton says. *Leave some for the next new moon.* Alex has a small fish cradled in his palm, its head clamped in the crook of his thumb; he whispers something to it, then puts it back into the waves.

The buckets fill, and people amble back to

the dry sand. Someone's playing a blues shuffle on the guitar: *I wish I was a grunion, swimming in a cold deep sea,* she sings. *I'd have all you pretty people fishing after me.* Stuart chases one of the women through the knee-deep water, trying to slip a fish down her blouse. Charlie has stolen Alex's shoes and slipped them on; they're too small for him. He dances on tiptoe, waving his bottle in the air, shaking his hips and bellowing in an unsteady Scottish burr. *Iamb trochee!* he shouts. Dig my metrical feet, man! They're longfellows!

Stanley's half out of breath — from the cold, from the effort of scrambling after the fish, and also from something else: an unfamiliar feeling that's hard to name. A wakeful amazement. A sad fragile sense of presentness, of moments passing. The low moon breaks through the clouds for a second, and Stanley thinks of the fireball he saw that time in the desert, and how he felt when he saw it. He thinks of *The Mirror Thief,* too — thinks of it in a way that he used to think of it all the time, but hasn't really been able to since he made it out here, since he got close to Welles, as if Welles has been blocking it somehow. Now Stanley remembers. There are certain moments that open onto another world, onto the world that Stanley's sure he belongs in. The book is a map that will take him there, a password that will unfasten the locks.

He walks back onto the beach for a moment and sits. Claudio rests the bucket on the sand and crouches next to him. Stanley? he says. Are you okay? Are you sick?

Stanley looks at him. Then he looks away. He watches the moon multiplied in the water, the silent buildings along the boardwalk. Streetlamps and the lights of oil-derricks have reshaped the inhabited ruin of the waterfront into a maze of shadows, a hidden web that links a set of illuminated stages. Each empty stage glows like a diorama viewed through a peephole, the scene of a cancelled performance, and hints at something that this place once tried to be. Stanley can feel it reverberate around him, as if he's inside a struck bell. I'm great, he whispers. I'm doing great.

After a while he rises again. By now they've crowded Claudio's pail with as many fish as seems reasonable, but the bucket that Charlie brought is lying nearby, forgotten on the sand, so Stanley picks it up, and he and Claudio fill it too. What will we do with so many? Claudio asks.

We're gonna eat 'em. Whaddya think, we're gonna train 'em to do tricks, like in a flea circus?

How will we do this? We have no place to cook.

Leave that to me, kid. I got a place in mind.

The pulsing silver carpet keeps coming, but soon everybody's done, loaded with all they can carry. Alex and Lyn have become fidgety, eager to get indoors. They dust themselves off and drift toward town, and the crowd follows them, angling first one direction, then another, pausing sometimes for no reason Stanley can see. The stops and starts spook the captured fish; they ping their snouts against the tin sides of the bucket.

Stuart and the woman he chased hang back, arguing quietly. At Windward they split: Stuart stops to light a cigarette under the Center Drug portico; she continues down the boardwalk with their bucket. Except for Lyn all of the women go with her, and most of the fish go with the women. The men stand around, hands in pockets, watching them walk away. Everything cool, Stuart? one of the guys asks.

Stuart shakes out his match like a movie tough, draws deeply, exhales a volcanic plume through his nose. Can we go someplace, he says, where I can just cool out and *think* for a goddamn change?

They wind up at somebody's pad: the upper floor of a rickety old house, now subdivided into a triplex, in the neighborhood that Welles and Stanley walked through last night. The buckets are lined up on the landing, their silvery surfaces broken now and then by a

601

tiny fin or a gasping mouth. Inside, a new bop record rotates on the hi-fi, and the sleeve gets passed around: a photo of a white altoist posed with his horn in the shade of trees, cool and blank-faced, eyeing something offstage right that could be the setting sun, could be approaching doom, it's all the same to this cat. Stuart and Tony sit on the floor by a cinderblock bookcase, smoking and complaining. *I go home, and it's the kids, the bills, the rent. How am I supposed to get any serious work done? Women don't understand how hard it is to keep an idea in your head, especially when it's a dangerous idea, one that nobody wants you to be having.* At the kitchen table Alex has settled in: matches, dropper, spoon, needle, the dead biker's junk. Some of the guys are rolling up their sleeves. Lyn drifts from room to room like a shade, ignored by everyone. Charlie's propped in a corner, trying to open a bottle of beer, talking loud in his radio voice: *Are you risking your life — or the life of your child — by using dirty syringes?*

Stanley aches all over, in his leg most of all, and his skin is raw and filmy from the sea. He can't stop thinking about the fish outside, tapping their noses against the sides of the pails, sucking air off the top. Whatever moment he felt passing before has now definitely passed. He and Claudio slip outside as the

602

moon sets, saying goodnight to no one, lugging their heavy buckets home.

44

Adrian Welles lives in a clapboard bungalow on Wave Crest, a big house for the neighborhood: two stories, custard-yellow eaves and siding newly painted, long second-floor deck ringed by a wrist-thick wisteria vine. The slab has settled unevenly over the years; from the street, the front door seems slightly off plumb, tilted at a funhouse angle. The house sits on its wide sandy lot like a lunatic on a parkbench, tricked out in his best suit, with nowhere to go and nothing to do but fix passersby with a silent crooked smile.

Stanley and Claudio have spent the day in a frenzy of primping, hauling their filthy clothes to the coin laundry, then hiking north along the beach into Santa Monica to shower and shave at the communal washroom there. By the time they got back to Horizon Court, the wrinkles had fallen from Stanley's stolen clothes; Claudio slicked his hair back and donned a loud rayon shirt. Then they crowded together as Stanley held out his steel pocket mirror in an outstretched hand. The two of them could pass for horn-players in a hot hotel combo — or film stars, Claudio insisted. We are like two young stars of film.

They headed up Pacific as the sun began to

603

sink, moving through the shadowed mercantile valley of liquor stores and shuttered warehouses and careworn Jewish bakeries, slowed by the weight of the buckets they bore and the risk of splashing seawater on their clean trousers. Stanley's greatest fear — an encounter with the Dogs that would end, at best, with their catch spilled — did not come to pass, and as they made the corner onto Welles's street they paused for a moment to relax, to flex their cramped fingers, to feed the gathering neighborhood cats with the handful of fish that died in the night.

Now they've come to the house. At this hour the light is exactly wrong for peeking in the windows: each pane is a mute sheet of reflected sun, shaded here and there by pale green clusters of unopened wisteria blooms. Beyond the low wooden gate, the flagstone path is edged with winter-green, infiltrating the patchy grass. Tall hibiscus grows beneath the windows, and a pair of fuchsias hangs in baskets over the stoop. On the left side of the lawn is a shallow birdbath; on the right is a sundial set on a concrete pedestal, its rusty iron blade adorned with a round laughing face. Text curves around the pedestal's edge: *but a name I snatched,* it says. Stanley can't read the rest. Somewhere inside the house a hi-fi plays a string-orchestra record; it's hard to hear at first, but when it crescendos, it's loud enough to rattle the windows in their frames. The music is discordant, keening, like nothing Stanley has heard. He has a hard time imagining why anybody would listen to it on purpose.

Stanley, Claudio says. Will we go in?

Stanley feels a gentle pressure on his ankle. He looks down. One of the bag-of-bones stray cats is rubbing the dome of its skull against his leg; another rears on its hind feet to tap the rim of his bucket with a cautious paw. Claudio is fending off three more.

The volume of the music increases; the front door has opened. A peal of laughter comes from the stoop, and then a woman's voice. What on earth? it says.

Stanley and Claudio look up. The woman at the door is slender and very tall, dressed in a long flowered dress that looks homemade. Her winged wire-rimmed glasses and her long straight ponytail make her seem younger, and at the same time older, than she probably is. She wears no makeup, and her bronze hair is streaked with gray. Stanley figures her for about forty. Good afternoon, ma'am, he says, putting on his best little-boy-lost front. Is Mister Welles at home?

Yes, he's here. Are you Stanley? You must be Stanley.

She swoops down the steps, along the path. Her gait is quick and athletic; it's easy to imagine her playing tennis, or golf. She's barefoot, and her tan forearms are speckled

605

with what looks like white paint. She's carrying a steaming cup of tea, and as she reaches the fence she shifts it to her left hand to shake with her right.

I'm Synnøve, she says. I'm Adrian's wife. He was so happy to meet you! He couldn't stop talking about you. Now, who is this?

I am called Claudio, Claudio says. I am greatly honored, *señora*.

Sorry for the mess on my hands. I've been all morning in the studio. My word, look at all these cats! What on earth are you carrying?

My friend and I, Stanley says, we went fishing last night, and —

Are those grunion? So early?

Yes ma'am. We wound up with more than we know what to do with, so we thought that maybe you and Mister Welles —

Well, aren't you both dear! You've come at the perfect time, too. I hadn't a notion of what to do for dinner tonight, and we simply adore grunion. Now, you must both come in at once, before these furry bandits devour you. Come, come! I still have hot water for tea.

Mrs. Welles — Synnøve? — has a funny accent: Scandinavian maybe, or German, or Dutch. She speaks English like she learned it in England. *Adrian!* she calls over the music as she opens the front door again. *Stanley and Claudio are here! They've brought us fish for dinner!*

If Welles responds, Stanley can't hear him over the shrieking hi-fi. He and Claudio set their buckets on the kitchen floor — the fish make shadowy airfoils under the ceiling fixture's light — and while Synnøve fixes the tea and chats with Claudio, Stanley takes a look around. The walls and the tabletops are cluttered with weird art: old planks splashed with hot lead, driftwood snared with yarn, burst ceramic eggs that something hatched from in a hurry. As Stanley pokes around, he hears a quiet precise male voice filter from the next room; at first he thinks it's Welles. Then a second voice joins in, just as Stanley's noticing the tinniness of the sound: it's a radio program, coming through a loudspeaker. Why the radio and the hi-fi would be on at the same time he can't begin to guess. From upstairs comes a creak of floorboards, a scrape of wood: someone moving just overhead.

Stanley, Synnøve calls, Adrian told me that you've come all the way from New York, and that you found his book of poems there. Is that true?

Yes, ma'am, Stanley says. I'm from Brooklyn. I picked it up in Manhattan.

Wonderful! I think it's what every poet dreams of, in a way. It's like putting notes into bottles and throwing them into the ocean. I am an artist — when I make some-

607

thing, I know where it goes — so I don't really understand. Adrian says I don't. But I must tell you this. Yesterday? When he came home from his office? He went upstairs to his study, and he closed the door. Now? Tonight? It is just the same. He has not written like this in years. Years! It is because of you. He will not tell you this, so *I'm* telling you. Would you like some milk in your tea? Or sugar?

No ma'am. Just plain. Thanks.

A pale light flickers in the next room — Stanley sees its reflection in the windowglass, and on the glazed curve of a lamp's base — and he realizes that the quiet voices are coming not from a radio but a television set. He steps across the threshold for a closer look. It's around the corner to the left: a Philco model, with a twentyone-inch tube in a mahogany console. Stanley's been around TVs before, plenty of times, but it's mostly been in shops, not people's houses. This one's playing newsreels — old ones, he's guessing, unless the Nazis are back in power somewhere and Roosevelt's risen from the grave. Just like always, Stanley has a hard time focusing on the picture: he keeps getting distracted by the texture of the screen, staring until the image disintegrates into a mosaic of tiny pulsing lights. He blinks hard, shakes his head, turns away in sudden revulsion.

When his vision settles again, it finds another pair of eyes staring back at him from

608

near the floor. He jumps, makes a startled sound.

It's the dirty-blond girl from the coffeehouse: the one he saw kissing Welles's cheek. She's seated on the thick patterned rug — her back pressed against a footstool, a multi-colored afghan draped over her shoulders — and she blends smoothly into the furnishings. Stanley can't remember the last time he walked into a room and didn't notice somebody. He thinks maybe he never has. The girl's eyes track him; her body doesn't move at all. Her expression is relaxed, alert, leonine. It says *you're still alive because I'm not hungry.*

Synnøve comes up behind him, hands him a cup and saucer. Oh! she says. Cynthia! I thought you'd gone out.

Something in Synnøve's voice is uneasy, like she's as startled as Stanley to find the girl here, and not quite happy about it. The girl's eyes shift from Stanley to Synnøve, then back to Stanley again. She blinks once, slowly, and says nothing.

Cynthia, Synnøve says, meet Stanley and Claudio. They're friends of —

She breaks off abruptly, like she's forgotten what she was saying, or thought better of it. They are our friends, she finishes. Would you like tea?

Yes please, the girl says.

Her voice is plummy: a fat girl's voice,

609

Stanley thinks, though she's hardly fat. He makes her for seventeen, eighteen tops. She's got nice curves for her age, but it's a figure with a sell-by date: in ten years she'll be fighting the weight off. Most guys won't see that now, of course, or won't care. If her outfit's not the same one she wore two days ago — bulky black scoop-neck sweater over a black leotard, gossamer crimson kerchief knotted at her neck — then it's identical. I saw you at the coffee joint, Stanley says.

Cwoffee, huh? she says, copping his accent with a raised eyebrow. Solid, pops. I hear you cats knocked us some fish.

You heard right.

Groovy, the girl says. A slow smile creeps across her face like a dropped egg.

Synnøve reappears, bearing another teacup and saucer; Cynthia stands up slowly, stretches — twisting her arms above her head till her spine pops — and takes them. Stanley can't decide if this girl is movie-star gorgeous or slightly grotesque, which he guesses must mean she's gorgeous. Stacked sugarcubes ring her cup; she spoons a few into the liquid, then eats the rest, crunching as she stirs. The milky tea is exactly the color of her eyes, and a whole lot warmer. Stanley can already tell that he and this skirt are not going to be pals.

Claudio shoulders past him into the room. Cynthia! he says.

Hey, gatemouth, the girl says. Slip me some skin.

I have some skin for you, *mija,* Claudio laughs, and gives her a warm careful hug. Their teacups rattle on their saucers. I did not expect to see you, he says. What are you doing here?

This is my lilypad, froggy. This is where I catch my cups.

Stanley looks rapidly between the two of them. You know this chick? he says.

This is Cynthia, Claudio says, looking at Stanley like he's gone simple. My friend from the café. I told you.

Stanley furrows his brow. Maybe Claudio did tell him; he doesn't listen to half of what the kid says. He watches the two of them chat — naming people he's never heard of, who he never cares to meet — until he notices the large canvas hung on the wall behind them. Amid rough splashes of flung color and glued-on dried flowers and lumps of paint-soaked fabric, Stanley gradually discerns the shape of a tree. Sigils cut from silver foil scatter in its gnarled bare branches. Two shadowy human shapes huddle by its trunk.

From the kitchen comes Synnøve's voice, calling over the sound of the running faucet. I just remembered, she says. The bakery closes early today, and I want a loaf of challah bread for dinner. Cynthia, will you entertain our guests while I'm out? I'm afraid

611

I can't guess when Adrian will emerge from his lair. Boys, if I give you my good knife, would you clean the fish you brought?

I'll clean the fish, Cynthia says.

As Synnøve pulls the front door shut behind her, Stanley and Claudio carry the buckets to a sunny spot on the covered side porch. Cynthia gathers equipment — brown paper bag, vegetable scraper, eyelash-thin fillet knife, beachtowels to sit on, old copies of the *Mirror-News* — and follows them outside. The porch is bordered by plank benches, and she spreads newspaper over these, then pours water from one of the buckets onto the lawn, crowding the fish down, making them easier to grab. The salt will probably kill the grass, but Stanley doesn't say anything.

Cynthia hands the scraper to Claudio. You're doing the scales, she says.

Then she dips her hand into the bucket, comes out with a squirming fish, slaps it on the paper, and opens its belly from its anus to its throat. Her small thumb slips inside to push out the little lump of guts. Then she chops off its head just behind its pectoral fins, and she hands the body to Claudio. The tiny downturned mouth is still gasping as she tosses it, trailing intestines, into the paper bag.

Claudio sets to work on the headless fish without asking Cynthia any questions, without even seeming to think, and soon the newspaper is showered with silver flecks. Cynthia has the head off another fish and is starting on a third. The one she just finished twitches a little on the paper. Her knife reminds Stanley of one he had for a while back home: he taped the handle of his, wore it on his calf. Then he used it and had to get rid of it. He begins to feel lightheaded from watching her work. He stands up, crosses the backyard to where a rambling rose pushes through the fence, and breathes deeply over its waxy white blossoms.

Soon a ragged calico cat is walking toward him across the toprail, sniffing the air; a second cat meows from somewhere below. Back on the porch, Claudio has fired up his customary jag, talking about movies, movie stars. The chick has no problem keeping up: she chimes in with her own material — foreign-sounding names that Stanley's never heard in his life, strung together with obscure hepcat jive that he can't make heads or tails of — as she slaughters her way through the twin buckets. Looking past them to the house, Stanley sees Synnøve in the kitchen, home from the bakery. He figures he probably ought to go in and talk to her about art or something, but he doesn't. Instead he just moves back and forth along the fence, stopping sometimes to scratch the stray cats on their matted necks, sometimes to catch them as they make beelines for the bag of heads and plop them back over the fence. Just once, he thinks, just one goddamn time, he'd like something to work out like he expects it to. That might be nice for a switch.

After a while the girl takes the cleaned fish into the kitchen, and Claudio crosses the yard. Stanley? he says. Are you okay?

Stanley keeps his eyes on the cats. Don't come near me with that shit on your hands, he says.

In a moment I will wash them. Are you feeling sick? You seem strange.

I'm doing great, Stanley says. I just got a lot on my mind.

Claudio's quiet for a second. He's doing that nervous thing he does with his fingers: Stanley can hear soft smacks as their tips stick and unstick from his slimy thumb. Cynthia is my friend, Claudio says. I like to make friends. I believe it is a natural thing to do. You left me in the café alone. You did not say you were going. Stanley, you don't think —

The screen door slams: the girl is back. She does a ballet move off the porch, then pounces on Claudio, mussing his hair. Watching Stanley the whole time.

Stanley, Claudio says, Cynthia and I are going to see a film tonight after dinner. Will you come along with us?

Stanley gives them both a frosty look. Sorry, he says. I gotta have a word with your pops tonight, sweetheart. Man to man. But thanks for the ask-along.

A funny expression crosses the girl's face — irritated and embarrassed, a little panicked too, like Stanley just interrupted her graduation speech to tell her her slip is showing — but then that's whisked aside by a wiseacre grin. Wow, she says. It's a little early to be asking for my hand, don't you think? We haven't even had our first date.

Yeah, Stanley says. Well, I move pretty quick. Hope that trousseau's coming along okay.

She throws her head back with a showy, throaty laugh. Then she smacks Claudio on the side of his head. Go inside and rinse your dukes, you savages, she says. We'll see if Mommy needs any help with the chow.

They start toward the porch. So, Stanley asks, what's the movie?

Bonjour Tristesse, Claudio says.

Buh-huh buh what?

Bonjour Tristesse. The new film of Otto Preminger, starring David Niven, and the young actress Jean Seberg. In *Saint Joan* she was not so good, I think. But maybe for her this role will be better.

Is this some kinda frog flick?

Ribbet-ribbet, Cynthia says.

The door swings open, and Adrian Welles is standing in the kitchen, resting an affectionate hand on Synnøve's back. He turns to them with an impish grin.

615

He's an inch or two shorter than his wife. Not quite as thick around the middle as Stanley had thought: broad, sure, but more brawny than soft. He must've been wearing a bunch of layers the other night. The snuffling dog is with him; it charges the open door, yapping its monstrous little head off. Cynthia catches it by the collar and hauls it inside, its white-rimmed popeyes rolling.

The air in the kitchen is thick with the smells of hot oil and celery and garlic and fish. Welles's powder-blue eyes have taken on a bright sheen beneath his spectacles, like pebbles of quartz washed by unaccustomed rain. He calls to Stanley and Claudio over the skillet's hiss. Greetings, my young friends! he says. Such unexpected pleasure you have brought us!

45

The fish get plated alongside scoops of green-bean casserole and hunks of fresh bread. Synnøve pulls an extra folding chair from a hallway closet, passes some cucumber salad around. Stanley watches carefully before he takes a bite of anything.

Everyone eats the fish whole — bones and all, like sardines — but they don't taste like sardines. Stanley remembers small fish that his Italian neighbors cooked around Christmastime, in those years when his father was away and his mother wasn't speaking and he had to take meals wherever he could find them: these taste a little like those did. As he chews he thinks of the seething silver carpet on the moonlit sand, and also of the bag of heads by the backdoor — the tangle of guts, the little mouths working, the cloudy unblinking eyes — *making* himself think these things. But they don't really bother him. The fish taste good. He's hungry. He hasn't had a proper kitchen-table meal in months.

Welles keeps standing up and sitting down, splashing pale gold wine into half-empty glasses. *Soave classico,* he says. I've had these bottles for more than a year. It's lucky I saved them! For this meal it's just right. Fish on Friday! My god, are you angling to re-Catholicize me? Well, it may be working, damn it all, it may be working.

The guy is keyed up, on a roll; nobody makes much effort to share the stage. Synnøve and Cynthia each get in some good licks, and Claudio slow-pitches a few earnest questions, but mostly they just let Welles wind himself down. Stanley feels like he's watching a swordfight in an old movie where the hero — Errol Flynn, maybe, or Tyrone Power — holds off a dozen guys at once, only none of them seem to be trying very hard to scratch him. Cynthia keeps raising her eyebrows, smirking. Welles talks with his hands, barely touches his food. Stanley finds it all sort of depressing.

Speaking of Catholicism, Welles says, and then recites part of a poem, something he just wrote. Stanley clenches his jaw, stares at his plate, pushes a french-cut greenbean around with a tightly gripped fork. *Thus does faith fold distance!* Welles says. *So bend the Ptolemaic rays! And Poor Clare perceives, ether-borne, the priest's vestmented image on the wall.* Please stop, Stanley thinks. Stop spoiling it. Stop talking.

I suppose you've heard, Welles says, that the pope just named Clare of Assisi the patron saint of television. Two or three weeks ago, I think. Rather more inventive than declaring the Archangel Gabriel to be the patron of radio, wouldn't you say? But then the church has always been quite comfortable with the concept of the discarnate word propagated through space. Less so with the discarnate image. The pope had to work a little harder to locate divine precedent. Lately, as I write, I'm finding myself drawn to stories such as these. It seems that this is what the new work will be *about.* The power of the image. The image of power.

Cripes! Cynthia says. Get a load of the clock! We better cut out, kemosabe. The curtain goes up at tick sixteen.

She and Claudio retreat to the entryway, Claudio clasping hands and murmuring thanks as Cynthia passes him his jacket. Stanley gets up, catches Claudio in the hallway, hands him some folded bills. For the movie, he says.

Claudio palms them with a guilty look that quickly passes. You will be here when I return? he says.

Here, or at the squat.

You should stay here, Claudio says. I like it here.

Synnøve is clearing the dishes; Welles moves through the living-room — still eating from the plate in his hand — to put an LP on the turntable. Cynthia glides over to the two of them in turn, planting kisses behind their ears. Claudio and I had better trilly, she says. Don't wait up for us.

Take it slow, Stanley tells Claudio as he steps outside. Keep your eyes peeled.

We will not go to the Fox, Claudio says with an irritated backward glance. We will go to a nice place.

The door closes. Stanley watches them through the window as they chase a couple of cats off the lawn. He feels a funny prickle in his sinuses, a sore tremble in his throat. He wonders what his goddamn problem is all of a sudden.

Music crashes from the hi-fi: a crazy choir chanting in some weird language while woodwinds and tympani toot and boom behind them. Welles leans into the entryway, shouting over the racket: Synnøve and I will do the washing-up, he says. You should go upstairs and poke through my library. Borrow something you think you might like. I'll be up in a minute with a couple of beers. Does that sound good?

On the narrow staircase Stanley feels dizzy, slows down. He rarely drinks, doesn't much care for the drowsy off-balance feeling he gets. He lifts his feet, plants them again. His pulse throbs in his wounded leg.

As he comes to the top the air changes, becoming dry and close and old. There's a strong odor of pipesmoke, and another smell beneath it: paper, fabric, glue, the invisible insects that eat such things. Even before Stanley finds the switch on the table lamp, he *feels* the books. With every step he takes across the creaking floor the whole house seems to shift, the contents of the cases to strain against each other on their shelves.

In the weak yellow lamplight, Welles's offer becomes ridiculous: Stanley could search this room for hours and find nothing to interest him. Books on economics and nuclear energy and the history of Italy, books about metallurgy and glassmaking and electronics, books in other languages. A lot of them remind Stanley of *The Mirror Thief,* but not of anything that he likes about it. After a few minutes of browsing he loses interest, shifts his focus to the room itself.

The study takes up nearly half the floor. On the west wall a french door between two curtained windows opens onto the moonlit deck. In the middle of the opposite wall there's a heavy black portal with a regular deadbolt plus a massive external sliding bolt, like something out of a medieval fortress. Curious, Stanley throws the big bolt — the loud hi-fi downstairs swallows the noise — and tugs on the knob, but the door is locked. He puts the slider back the way he found it, transfers his attention to Welles's desk.

It's immense: polished teak, ornately carved. Several peculiar paperweights — a bronze pelican, a clear glass hemisphere with colors swirled inside it, a jagged hunk of metal that looks like part of an exploded shell — are clustered at the lower right corner, probably to catch rollaway pens and pencils, since that's the way the floor slopes. A few sheets of rose-white paper sit on the blotter, crowded with handwriting, steeply slanted and illegible. Next to them is a letter, still in its ripped-open envelope, from someone in a hospital in Washington, D.C. Stanley pays these little mind. With one ear cocked toward the stairs he begins to open the drawers, to scan their contents.

They all have fancy brass locks, but none is locked. The first one he opens — the long shallow one in the middle — contains a pistol: a .45 automatic, 1911 model. Stanley guesses it's got a round already chambered, but opts not to touch it to learn for sure. Seated in the swivel chair behind the desk, Welles could get to it in a hurry. Two drawers down on the right Stanley finds a second pistol, a Wehrmacht P38. If Welles keeps this stuff stashed in his study, what's hidden in his sock-drawer? A greasegun, maybe. Or a bazooka. The guy probably drives to work in a tank.

On the wall behind the desk hangs a framed map. Stanley figures it for a map, anyway: it shows a club-shaped island city the way it might look from a plane flying by, though not directly overhead. The perspective strikes Stanley as strange, because the style of the map makes him think it was made a long time before there were any such things as airplanes — like whoever drew it had to close his eyes and project himself into space, and then to hold the picture of the city in his head while he nailed down the streets and canals and houses on paper. Remembering all he could. Imagining the rest.

Welles is on the stairs, singing in a deep buttery voice as he climbs. *O Fortuna,* he chants, *velut luna statu variabilis. Semper crescis aut decrescis, vita detestabilis —*

Stanley keeps his eyes on the framed map, hunting out details: domes and belltowers, plazas and sailing ships. A couple of smaller outlying islands are labeled; their names are almost familiar. IVDECA, one says. MVRAN, reads another.

Welles's voice. Recognize it? he says.

Sure. It's the city in your book.

That's right. I don't suppose you've ever been there?

Stanley squints, leans closer. His nose nearly touches the paper. I don't think so, he says. Where is it?

It's in Italy. On the Adriatic Sea. If you had been there, I suspect you would remember.

Italy, Stanley says. That's in Europe. Right?

Yes. Europe. Correct.

No, Stanley says. I never been to Europe.

Welles steps forward, puts a cold bottle in Stanley's hand: a Goebel. You should go when you can, Welles says. You would find it intriguing. If nothing else, my modest lecture on local history of two nights ago would accrue broader resonance. The city — the original, I mean — is built on the water. Directly on it. There is no earth to speak of, not really. It sits in the midst of a lagoon. Do you know what a lagoon is?

Sure. My dad was at Eniwetok.

Then of course you do. Our word *lagoon* comes from the Latin root *lacuna,* which refers to a gap, an absence, an interruption. Which may explain why this city throughout the years has become a locus of such diverse and vigorous species of desire. It has deliberately situated itself in a void.

Stanley steps back from the wall. A beer is about the last thing he wants right now, but he sips the Goebel anyway. It's a nice place you got here, he says.

Thank you. At this point, I suppose, Synnøve and I can afford to move up in the world, as they say. But this feels like home. Along the waterfront, we are left to our own peculiar devices. And frankly I can't abide the thought of moving all these books.

Stanley nods toward the bolted door. What's in there? he asks.

That, Welles says. He takes a long sip of beer. That is Cynthia's room, he says.

Stanley looks at Welles with upraised eyebrows. Then he takes a long stagy glance at the sliding bolt, and looks at Welles again. You scared maybe she'll get loose while you're sleeping? he says.

Welles forces a laugh. *Ah ha ha!* he says. It looks a bit eccentric, I know. Often I have wondered why the previous occupants saw fit to install such a door. The realtor claimed total ignorance. I used to imagine all sorts of things. A bootlegger's storeroom. A white-slave dungeon. The asylum of some grown idiot son. All plausible in this neighborhood. Nowadays I hardly think of it at all. Shall we have a seat on the lanai?

The what?

The lanai, Welles says, opening the french door to the deck. I was afraid that we'd have rain again tonight, but for now it looks to be lovely. We'll come back in if we get chilled, of course.

Outside there's a stumpy wooden table ringed by folding canvas chairs, the kind of chairs that Claudio's screen magazines always show movie-stars and famous directors sitting in. The deck doesn't afford a view of much except the side of the neighboring house, but Stanley still has a sense of the ocean's closeness. An armada of small dense clouds sweeps across the dusk-blue sky, and the moon hangs among them like a bruised apple, its perfect circle on the wane.

Welles gives Stanley the chair with the best west-facing vista. Stanley doesn't want it — it'll put Welles in silhouette; he'd rather to be able to read his face — but he takes it anyway, because it seems rude to decline. So, Welles says, getting comfortable in the creaking chair. You have some questions for me.

Yeah, Stanley says.

They sit in silence for a while. The hi-fi downstairs must have played through the LP's side. Overhead, the buzz of an airplane grows and fades.

Well, Welles says, there's no rush. Take whatever time you —

I want to know about magic, Stanley says.

All right. What can I tell you?

You can tell me how to do it. How to get it to work.

Welles is quiet. Then he chuckles. The sound is smug, patronizing — and fake, too. You're asking the wrong fellow, I'm afraid, he says.

Whaddya mean?

I don't know anything about magic, Stanley. I learned a few card tricks in the Army, but I've forgotten even those. I'm sorry.

Stanley shifts his beer from hand to hand. Crivano knows about magic, he says. You wrote about him. So you must know something.

Welles seems to think about the question for a while, but Stanley can tell he's not really thinking. It courts banality to make the point, I suppose, Welles says. But I am hardly Crivano.

Like hell you're not. C'mon, Mister Welles. I'm not talking here about the real, historic Crivano. I ain't interested in that. I'm talking about *your* guy.

Welles opens his mouth to reply, then closes it again. He leans forward in his seat, puts his beer on the table, steeples his fingers across his lips. He seems irritated, but also — somewhere deeper — nervous. Stanley takes long breaths. He's closing in, but this next turn will be tough to make.

Is that really what you wanted to ask me? Welles says. You want to become a magus. An alchemist. A magician. Is that right?

That's pretty much it, yeah.

I can't tell you how to do that, Stanley.

Stanley nods, sips his beer. I don't believe you, he says.

Welles is blinking fast, trying to work himself up, to maintain his front. This is fantasy, Stanley, he sputters. I mean, come now. You are not a child. These are not things that happen in the world. They exist in our imaginations.

Bullshit, Stanley says.

Stanley.

Bullshit. That is bullshit. I'm sorry, Mister Welles, excuse me, but it is. I know. I have read your goddamn book many, many times, and I know what is real and what is not real, and I know that that is bullshit. I know magic ain't about sawing ladies in half, or telling the future, or changing Coca-Cola into 7-Up. I know it's about seeing a pattern in everything. I want you to show me how.

Welles stares at him. There's a flat warning in his eyes, one Stanley hasn't seen since those first moments when they met on the beach. Here at last is the Welles he's wanted to talk to: the Welles with barred doors in his house, the Welles who keeps guns in his desk-drawers.

Their eyes remain locked for what seems like a long time. Then, without blinking, Welles flops back in his deckchair and sighs heavily. He puts his hands behind his head, interlacing their fingers. You have my apolo-

627

gies, he says. Indeed, you are *not* a child. Childhood's end arrives when we realize that the world is unacceptable. Am I right? It's unacceptable! It's corrupt! It is a vale of sorrows, a kitchen full of smoke, a perpetual travail. What can we do? We can capitulate. We can give up our expectations, and accept what is the case. Or, we can fight. We can resist. Here, I think, is where the desire to create originates: from this great visceral disgust with the world, and with the experience of living in it. I'm not speaking of a desire to reform or reshape the world, mind you. I'm talking about the desire to negate it entirely, to replace it with something better, more suited to ourselves. In recognizing this desire, of course, we find ourselves in the company of our two friends, the poet and the magus.

Welles stands, lifts his beer from the tabletop, walks to the deck's wooden railing to gaze toward the sea. When I was a young man, he says, I admit I entertained the notion that the poet and the magus are somehow unified by this refusal. That they are, in fact, identical. I thought that a poem, properly made, can become a magic spell, and can transform the world. I have matured somewhat, and I now see that I was mistaken. The poet changes nothing. He creates palatable alternate worlds, and he invites others to take refuge in them. From such vantage we can

628

sometimes look upon our own base and quotidian existence and see it with a clearer eye, but this is accidental, and beside the point. The poet's trade is illusion. I am a poet.

Why not be a magician, then?

Because it doesn't work, Stanley. It's a pointless waste of time. Worse! It's like the child who ties a blanket around his neck and jumps through a window, convinced by his television that he can fly. It's choosing to live in a poem that has become invisible to you *as* a poem. It's not magic, it's madness.

I don't accept that.

At your age, Welles says, I suppose you probably shouldn't. At my age it's hard enough. Listen, I don't wish to seem glib, or disrespectful, or to suggest that your question isn't a good one. I have given this a great deal of thought — I still do — and that is my honest answer. The world simply does not work that way.

Welles peers down at his backyard. His elbows are locked; his hands are widely spaced on the wooden rail. The thick outline of his body looks like some kind of glyph.

But what if it's like you said the other night? Stanley whispers. What if all this —

He moves his beerbottle in a wide circle, indicating every solid thing surrounding him. Welles's back is still turned; he doesn't see.

— what if it isn't real? What if it's just a reflection of something else? What if there's another world?

Welles doesn't answer at first. He sags forward a little, like he's tired. Can you think of any reason, he says, to believe that that might be the case?

It feels right, Stanley says. It feels possible.

It does, doesn't it? But then it would. Of course it would. I will say this: if you choose to believe it, then you are in very distinguished company. After all, that was the charge that Plato levied against us poets, wasn't it? That we are pretenders of wisdom, copiers of copies. Perhaps we are. Who can say? Perhaps we're wasting our time on fancies, while the real conquest of the invisible world is being carried out by modern-day alchemists, wearing the white smocks of atomic scientists and aerospace engineers. Perhaps we're being sentimental: we cannot bear very much reality. We say we long for it, but when it finally emerges and fails to present us with our own pretty reflections, we recoil. We retreat to our islands in the river, and we pine away like the Lady of Shalott.

Have you ever killed anybody, Mister Welles?

Stanley catches his breath, blinks in surprise. He hadn't intended to ask the question, wasn't even thinking it. Was he?

At the edge of the deck, Welles is motionless and silent. Almost invisibly, the stiffness has moved from his elbows to his back.

Stanley's breathing fast, scared at first that he's said a bad thing — and then he's just scared, he's not sure of what. Somewhere below a treefrog has started to chirp. Now Stanley can hear dozens of them, all over the neighborhood, that he hadn't noticed before.

No, Welles says. No, I have not.

Stanley has a fast out-of-control feeling, like he's going to vomit. I have, he says.

Welles is half-turned, still facing away. You have, he says. I see.

Probably a lot of guys would tell you something like that just to impress you, Stanley hears himself say. And maybe that's partly why I'm telling you. But what I'm saying is true. When I was thirt—

His voice catches and breaks. He clears his throat, starts again.

When I was thirteen, he says, this Puerto Rican kid tried to stab me. And I broke his arm with an iron pipe, and I took his knife away, and I cut his throat.

Stanley's face is hot; his cheeks are dripping. He has no idea where this is coming from. All of a sudden it's like he's been carrying another person inside him without knowing it: some pansy little kid, curled in his guts like a worm in a fruit.

Welles has turned around to look at him; he's inching closer across the deck, with the moon in his hair. You had no choice, he says. You were defending yourself.

631

Sure, Stanley says. I guess. I guess anybody who ever kills anybody thinks he's defending himself from something. Last year I threw a guy off a roof. That's the two I know about. There's other guys I hurt real bad in fights who maybe died and I don't know. Last year I was on this burglary where this cop got shot, so according to the law I killed him too. That's mostly the reason I had to leave New York.

Welles steps over the little table, then sits on it, facing Stanley. Stanley doesn't look up. Why do you want me to know these things? Welles says. Why are you telling me this?

You probably think, Stanley says, that I'm just a smart kid who liked your book, and who maybe got some funny ideas from it. I don't blame you for thinking that. In your shoes, it's what I'd think, too. But what I want you to understand, I guess, is that I have seen and done some pretty fucked-up stuff in my life, excuse me, and I have been through a hell of a lot to get out here, and there are some questions that I would really like to get some answers to, Mister Welles. Now, maybe you don't know the answers. Or maybe you knew 'em once, and then you forgot. But I been thinking a lot about something you said the other night, about how a book can know more than whoever wrote it. Because I think your book knows, Mister Welles. I think it

632

knows that this kind of magic is really possible.

Welles looks at him for a long time, leaning close. For a while Stanley thinks Welles is going to touch him, put a hand on his leg, and he wonders how he'll handle that. Then Welles speaks.

That book, he says, is now entirely perplexing to me. It took me ten years to write it. Did I tell you that? I started it in Italy, during the war, when I was still relatively young. At the time I had — or I thought I had — a clear sense of how to proceed, of what form it would take. I felt as though I were standing on a mountaintop, looking down on the valleys and forests through which I would pass in the days to come. Straightforward enough, it seemed. But of course it's very different when you're *inside* the dark wood, beset by briars and quicksand, distracted by meanders, fearful of wolves and brigands and god knows what else, unable at any given moment to see more than a few feet ahead. By the time I finished it I had forgotten largely why I'd begun, what I had wanted it to be in the first place, why I'd been interested in it at all. I don't mean to be evasive, or to flatter you, when I say that you have a better sense than I do of what it's about.

Stanley opens his mouth to reply, but Welles is off again, speaking in a torrent, rising from his seat, leaving his empty beerbottle on the table. He seems eager to forget what Stanley just confessed. The whole house shifts and groans as he crosses the deck.

It wasn't just my conception of the book that changed, he says. It was my belief about writing itself, about what it means to write. As I said before, I abandoned early on the notion of poem-as-incantation. I adopted instead a scarcely less romantic theory that poetry is a sort of lovemaking — a series of gestures designed to produce in another a release, an orgasm, an egoless rapture — and hopefully also some corresponding pleasure in oneself. But I eventually came to realize that this analogy is not apt. Because the pleasure of the other is deferred, you see. And because it happens at a distance. The experience is not shared. You evidently derived some pleasure from my book, and I am gratified by that. But by the time it found you, I had moved on to other concerns. So I am forced to conclude, with Flaubert, that the urge to write is essentially masturbatory. Onanistic. These are hardly new metaphors, of course, but they are rich, and worthy of contemplation.

Welles is at the rail again, leaning on his elbows. His slippered foot taps the base of the woodstained slats. Stanley can tell that he's not done yet, so he waits, drying his face with the yellow sleeve of his new shirt.

For me, Welles says, it's like shitting. It

really is. To pretend otherwise is stupid. Shit is fertilizer, of course. And shit is *prima materia*. But to the shitter, it is simply shit. Properly construed, the distance of which I spoke between the writer and the reader — the deferred pleasure — is no impediment to the success of a poem. The poem depends on it, in fact. I imagine, to my great chagrin, that you are learning this even now. You read my book, and in some way it excited your imagination. But when you found its author, you discovered him to be a fat bourgeois, a pompous blowhard, and you realized that he is — as the expression goes — full of shit. The book cannot help but be diminished by this encounter. How much happier for you if I had remained a mystery! How much better if the book could go on existing only as you'd imagined it! Isn't it the case that the works which most move and inspire us are the most formless — the most irredeemably fecal — that we stumble upon? Because they leave to us the task of completing them, of wringing meaning from them. Because, in so doing, we always encounter ourselves. Their degraded chaos resolves gradually into our own image, projected and made strange. It is ever thus. The reader — not the poet — is the alchemist.

Stanley's nose and throat are clear now. The night smells sweeter and sharper. He can't remember the last time he cried like that.

Not when his father died, or his grandfather. Maybe when his dad left for Korea. Even then it was only later, alone, when nobody could see. What I want, Stanley says, is to get inside your book. All the way in. I want to tear it apart. I want to know everything Crivano knows, whether you know it yourself or not. I want you to tell me how to figure it out. Where to get started.

Welles turns around, folds his arms, leans back on the rail; it creaks and bows with his weight. For a second Stanley thinks he'll fall through, but he doesn't. Welles fixes his eyes on the deck, creases his brow in half-interested concentration, like he's trying to recall the names of old friends from grade-school.

Then he slips a hand inside his cardigan, into his shirt's breast pocket, and comes out with his pipe. You'll have to do a lot of reading, he says. The *Corpus Hermeticum,* of course, in its entirety. Also the *Picatrix,* and the *Tabula Smaragdina.* Plato and Plotinus, in order to situate the tradition in proper context: Crivano certainly would have read both of them. Marsilio Ficino and Pico della Mirandola are major figures. Who else? Abulafia, I suppose. Llull. Reuchlin. Trithemius. Agrippa. Cardano. Paracelsus, certainly. You may wish to explore John Dee and Robert Fludd, as well, although they were contemporaneous with Crivano, and he would not have been aware of them.

All that stuff is old, Stanley says. Right?

Quite. Crivano, remember, was active in the waning years of the Sixteenth Century. I should warn you that many of the key writings I mentioned may not be available in reliable English translation, but only in Latin, or in various German and Italian dialects. Some may not be widely available at all.

Is there anybody who does this sort of stuff now? Magic, I mean?

Welles has withdrawn his tobacco tin from his trouser pocket; he's slowly packing the bowl of his pipe. When he's finished, he lights it, tamps it out, and packs it again, aerating it with a needlelike tool.

Oh yes, he says. People still do it.

Stanley stares hard at his face. The treefrogs are almost deafening; they sound like the string-orchestra piece that was playing downstairs when he and Claudio first arrived. Who? he asks. Who does it?

Another match flares, tripled in Welles's spectacles, and a stinking cloud rises over his head. Here in Southern California, he says, you can locate them without a great deal of effort. You can readily find Theosophists and Rosicrucians, as well — along with adherents of Dianetics, and the New Thought, and the Science of Mind — although I do not recommend that you do so. In fact, seeking out contemporary practitioners of magic is probably unnecessary. As I discovered when I began my own research, they will find you soon enough.

But talking to 'em is a waste of time, you're saying?

Once you have a sense of the tradition, Welles says, it will be easy for you to tell who is a charlatan, who is simply insane. There are some who are knowledgeable and serious, I suppose, but they tend to keep to themselves. Also, their interests seem to accrue around industrial abstracts and pulp science fiction, rather than musty alchemical treatises left over from the Renaissance. I worked with one of these fellows at the Aerojet Corporation, believe it or not. Jack Parsons was his name. I had no idea what sort of strange mischief he'd been engaged in until 1952, when he somewhat carelessly blew himself to kingdom come with a large quantity of fulminate of mercury. Evidently Jack spent years of evenings and weekends performing magical rites, literally trying to summon the Whore of Babylon and spawn the Antichrist. This gentleman was one of the founders of the Jet Propulsion Laboratory, mind you. So, yes. People still do it.

There's a strain in Welles's voice, a false note, but Stanley can't think of the right question to ask to decipher it. He's still feeling shaky, pissed off at himself for cracking up. That list of names you just gave me, he says. I'm not gonna remember it. Could I maybe get you to write 'em down?

But of course. Of course. It would be my pleasure.

Stanley picks up his beer and finishes it. His gut turns queasy as the last of it goes down. You probably think I'm a damn fool, he says. Don't you? For wanting to do this.

Welles takes the pipestem from his mouth, slowly shakes his head. Not at all, he says. Quite the opposite, in fact. This is a difficult time for you, I can see that. I don't know you well. But I have confidence in you. I believe in you. And I — Synnøve and I — would like to help in any way we can.

Stanley's tearing up again, though he's not sure why, not sure if it's real or fake. He thinks of an armed robbery he was on a couple years ago where he and his team all wore gauze Halloween masks: he remembers how it felt to hold a pistol on the humiliated nightwatchman, to look him straight in the eye and know that he could see nothing but the crude face of a weeping clown. Stanley feels that same way now — powerful and ashamed — only this time the mask is inside him, and he can't control it.

I gotta be straight with you, Mister Welles, he says. I don't think about myself the way you think about yourself. About the reasons why I do things, I mean. There's never really been a time when I didn't know what to do,

639

or at least have some idea. So I've never had to stop and just think. Sometimes I feel like it wouldn't be bad for me to do that once in a while, but I'm not even sure how. And it's starting to scare me. Because lately I feel like I'm turning into something, and I don't know what.

Welles is silent, puffing rapidly. Soon the pipe has burned to ash. For what it's worth, he says, I am not worried about you.

It ain't specifically me I'm worried about, Mister Welles. It's everything else. I just don't always feel like I belong in this world.

A deep chuckle rises from Welles's gut. I daresay I know that feeling, he says.

I guess you're about to tell me that I'm gonna grow out of it.

You might. Though I sincerely hope that you do not.

He steps forward slowly, then grips Stanley's shoulder in his thick-fingered hand. It's a cheap and stupid little world, the one we're given, he says. Don't fucking *settle* for it. Go out and make your own.

He straightens, puts the pipe back in his teeth. Now, he says. Did you remember to bring the book?

Yes sir. Downstairs, in my coat.

Well, run and get it. I'll be writing out that list I promised you.

As he descends, Stanley can hear Synnøve somewhere nearby, singing wordlessly to herself, but he doesn't look around. He opens the hall closet, pulls *The Mirror Thief* from his pocket, mounts the stairs again.

Welles has turned on the desklamp; it glows under its opaque green shade. As Stanley approaches, Welles lifts with a flourish the page he's written and hands it over. This will keep you busy for a while, I'll wager, he says. May I?

Stanley gives him the book, takes the page. He looks it over in the dim light: a long column of strange names, uniform and equidistant, as if plotted with a ruler. The handwriting is neat, but cramped and peculiar, and he knows he's going to have a hell of a time making sense of it.

When Stanley looks up again Welles has the book open on his desk, a fountain-pen in his hand. He's motionless, wearing a confused expression. Oh yeah, Stanley says. I guess I forgot to tell you. Somebody already wrote in my copy. Like I said, I got it second-hand. I never been able to read the message.

Welles begins to laugh. It's a funny laugh: a little hysterical, then joyless and forced. Ah, he says. This is beginning to make sense. Where did you say you found this, again?

The Lower East Side. It belonged to a thief who got sent off to Rikers.

What was his name? Do you know?

Stanley shrugs. Everybody called him Hunky, he says. I never met him.

Hmm, Welles says. Then I suppose you got it — let's see — third-hand, at the very least. Here, I'll read it to you. *Dear Alan* — ah, good, I see I misspelled that — *I salute your naked courage. Yours respectfully, Adrian Welles.*

Oh, Stanley says.

I gave it to a poet who came through town two summers ago. A young self-styled visionary. Blake, by way of Whitman. Larry Lipton, I think, had invited him to come down from San Francisco. During the reading he had an altercation with someone from the crowd, and to demonstrate — *something,* his sincerity, his commitment, I don't know what — he disrobed completely. It struck me at the time as a rather impressive gesture.

Welles closes the book, sits to open a drawer. You know, he says, this copy is rather the worse for wear. I've got one here in my desk that's essentially untouched. Let me replace —

Stanley puts a quick protective hand on the book. If it's all the same to you, he says, I'd just as soon keep the one I got.

Welles's eyes track up Stanley's arm to his face. Something in them seems slightly wounded. Then he smiles.

When he rises, he's holding a metal ruler. He sets it down, fishes a razorblade from the top drawer. Opening the book again, he slips the ruler inside and cuts out the inscribed

642

page with a single swift motion. Stanley tenses for an instant, about to spring, to seize Welles's arm. Then he realizes that he doesn't care. He'd rather be rid of it.

Welles flips to the preceding page, uncaps his pen again. As the nib scrapes the paper, Stanley's eyes drift across the room: the mountains of books, the arsenal desk, the great barred door. After a moment Welles blows across the ink to dry it and puts the open book in Stanley's hand. I tried to be more forgiving with my penmanship this time, he says. Can you read it?

Sure, Stanley says. Most of it.

It's a quotation from Roger Bacon, the Thirteenth-Century English magus.

Okay. What's it mean?

Welles caps the pen, turns off the lamp. It means I'm glad I met you, he says. Very glad indeed.

Welles picks up his pipe and steps toward the french door again, but Stanley doesn't follow him. He stands next to the desk, holding the book, staring into space. Thanks for everything, Mister Welles, he says. Really. But it's time for me to go.

Back downstairs, as he's pulling on his jacket, Synnøve does her best to get him to stay — there's a murphy bed in my studio, she says; I promise it's quite comfortable — but he exits as quickly as he can, accepting a peck on the cheek, giving her an awkward hug. Wait! she says. Did you want to take your fish-buckets?

Oh, Stanley says, those aren't actually mine.

Welles walks him down the path to the gate. What shall I tell your friend when he and Cynthia return? he says.

He'll know where I am. You don't need to worry yourself.

Welles offers his hand. Stanley takes it, and Welles pulls him into an embrace. Stanley is suspended for a moment, his ear against the man's chest, breathing in his spicy smoke, hearing the roar and rumble of his chambered interior. Then Welles releases him.

As he steps from the curb, Stanley turns. Oh, Mister Welles? he calls.

Yes?

When we first met on the beach, a couple nights ago, you said something to me. What was it?

Welles walks away slowly until he reaches the stoop. Then he turns and leans against a wooden column. I don't think I recall, he says.

It was in another language, Stanley says. You said it twice.

Welles is a featureless silhouette against the open door. His wife stands behind him, looking sleepy and sad. Two points of light appear in his spectacles. Stanley can't tell where that light is coming from.

I'm sorry, Welles says. I must have enunciated so poorly that whatever I said sounded foreign. I'm sure I spoke only English. And that badly, it seems. My apologies.

Stanley nods. Okay, he says. Goodnight, Mister Welles.

Goodnight, Stanley.

On the way to the boardwalk, maybe two lots down, Stanley passes an overgrown yard with a cat in it. The cat has something in its mouth: a sandy fishhead, trailing scraps of viscera. It watches him with glassy green eyes.

Stanley clenches his jaw, aims a kick at the cat's skull, then pulls it at the last second. The cat hunches, flattens its ears, and tears off through the grass, darting under the porch. Stanley's vision is blurring again; a tremor gathers in his throat, and his breath comes heavily.

He looks over his shoulder at Welles's deck, just visible through a spearpoint row of juniper trees. There's a dark shape on the rail that must be Welles, though Stanley can't tell if he's watching or not.

You're a lying sack of shit, Stanley hisses through his teeth.

46

When Stanley wakes the next morning in the squat on Horizon Court, Claudio isn't there. Stanley sits up, wipes his eyes, looks around. Wondering if maybe the kid knocked at some point and he didn't hear it. Then he remembers last night — Cynthia and her frog flick, Synnøve and her murphy bed — and he knows exactly where the kid is.

He flops down again, pulls up the blanket. Trying to get mad, not quite managing it. The kid is soft; of course he'd take the bed. Can't blame him for that. Stanley's not even sure why he was in such a hurry to leave Welles's place himself. Partly because he was embarrassed by his waterworks performance, sure. And partly because the talk had quit paying off. But there was something else: an uneasiness he can't name, a sense of something compromised or put at risk. Trying to pin it down just makes Stanley sad, and being sad always makes him tired.

It's late morning before he wakes again; he's not sure how late. Still no Claudio. He's starting to feel like he's made a bad bet: bankroll too small, number taking too long to come up. He shoves away the blanket, brushes his teeth, drinks from his father's canteen. The list of names Welles gave him is still in the breast pocket of his new shirt; he finds it and flattens it on the counter in the front room, then looks at it from time to time while he gets dressed. It may as well be in Chinese. Sometimes it's hard for Stanley to say just what he crossed the country to find, but it goddamn sure wasn't this. Welles has ducked him again, shifting shape like some wiggly undersea thing, leaving Stanley in the usual cloud of ink.

He thinks of the long walk he took with Welles the night they met, and all the gobble-dygook the guy spouted along the way. What if it was all intended to put Stanley off the scent? What if the secret wasn't in Welles's speech, but in his steps, in the path he took over the filled-in canals? Stanley thinks of a word he saw on a streetsign that night, a word he keeps seeing: RIALTO. What does it mean? In *The Mirror Thief* it's a place, a neighbor-hood in the book's haunted city — not the same as this city, but not completely differ-ent, either. The word points toward some-thing. What?

It could be something from history, but Stanley doesn't think so. History is just more books; the secret he's after has nothing to do with books. It's either in the world — hidden there somewhere — or it's not worth know-ing. The closest Stanley's come to it was on that walk: the way the old man, caught off-guard, pointed to the city to explain himself. Welles wrote the book, sure, but he didn't build the city. The city is the key. Stanley needs to get outside, to take another look around.

He laces up his Pedwins, slides quietly to the street. Part of what's put him in a sorry mood is the air pressure: he can feel more rain coming in, though the sky's clear. As he turns onto the boardwalk he catches a sour sickly smell — bad familiar, rhyming some-how with the odors from the oil-field — and he remembers that he forgot to change the dressing on his leg. Thinking about it brings back the ache; he feels woozy, slows down. The last time he cleaned the wound was yesterday afternoon, at the showers in Santa Monica. It looked all right then; now he's not so sure. He thinks about going back to the squat, but then figures it'll keep for a couple hours.

He picks out a spot by the water to sit and watch the boardwalk and think. After a while, when the streets and buildings haven't dis-closed anything, he turns around and looks out to sea instead. The sun is just overhead; the waves are dark translucent blue. Some-times at the limits of his vision he can see the flash of a garibaldi among the rocks on the bottom, like a ripe Riverside tangerine lost in the waves.

Stanley pulls Welles's list from the pocket of his jeans and goes through it again, one name at a time, puzzling over each slip of a letter in turn. One name he knows from the book — Hermes Trismegistus, of course — but the rest are gibberish. He stares at them, half hoping they'll wriggle to life on the page like millipedes and spell out something other than what they say. Before long Stanley has a fierce headache, and they're no different than they were.

He folds the page, pockets it, and walks north, shoeless along the sand where the ocean breaks. The tide is out. The beach is long and flat and smooth, specked at odd intervals by flotsam that leaves straight comet-trail paths to the water: scattered moon-jellies and by-the-wind sailors, the shells of periwinkles and jackknife clams, the creepy fudge-brown egg-cases of skates, lengths of yellow kelp bowed seaward by the tug of waves. As Stanley looks inland toward the arcades — a couple of shiftless drunks by the Fortune Bridgo, a well-dressed old Jew with a violin case, a woman pushing a baby-carriage and towing a kid with a white balloon — his foot finds something hard buried in the sand, and he stops to uncover it.

It's the skull of some crazy bird: a light-brown beak, forearm-long, and huge hollow orbits where eyes once were. Beach-grains have pitted and polished the beak, and a single barnacle adorns its blade near the midpoint. Stanley studies it, then looks down at the cavity it left in the sand. Bulbous at one end, tapering to a point, it looks like a letter from some archaic alphabet. The wave-graded sand around it is blank and uniform, seemingly empty, though there's no telling what else it might hide.

Stanley stoops to the smooth beach-surface and makes a deep slash with the beak's downturned tip. Then he makes another one — longer, curving — next to it. The three marks look like they might spell something in some language, though Stanley doesn't know what language, or what it might mean. In *The Mirror Thief* Crivano writes on the beach to summon the moon, which rises and talks to him. The book never says what marks he makes. Welles probably doesn't even know. But the book knows.

Stanley bends again, slicing long furrows through the sand. He thinks of the old apartment on Division: the white wall across from his pallet, the first thing his eyes met every morning. How he hated that fucking wall. He begged his mother to ask his grandfather for permission to hang something there — a hamsa, a painting, anything — but she never would. The wall always seemed to be watching, although it would never acknowledge him. Eventually he had enough. He considered wrecking its pure surface with the letters of his name, but even then he was trying to detach himself from it, to leave it behind. Instead he wrote SHIT, the most powerful word he knew. To blind the wall. To keep it from judging. Thinking of it now, he remembers the handprints and footprints in the forecourt of Grauman's Chinese, and the memory makes him smile. He straightens, stretches, sidearms the bird-skull back to the sea.

For a long time he walks the wet sand, eye-ing the boardwalk, eyeing the water. His shadow precedes him as he goes. To the east almost everything he sees was made or placed by human hands; to the west almost nothing was. The pale void of the beach stretches between. A gull flies by with a dead grunion curved in its beak. Stanley thinks of the fish swarming in the waves, and wonders what switch the moon flips to summon them to the land — whether they're aware of it in themselves, whether any among them ever opt out, want no part of it, choose to remain below, lurking and lonesome and proud.

As he nears the quiet amusement pier at Ocean Park he spots Charlie ambling along the beach. Charlie's wearing tatty business attire — white shirt, silk tie, jacket and slacks, fedora — but he has no shoes or socks, and his pants are rolled to his knees. He holds a tube of paper in one hand, a bottle in the other, and he cuts a crooked path across the sand. Hey! he shouts. Hey, Stanley! Bwana Lawrence was just asking about you!

Hey, Stanley says, raising an open palm. Who?

Bwana Lawrence. Lawrence Lipton. Lipton teabags. Hip, fun glad-rags. You know who I mean, man. He said he met you the other night, at the jazz canto.

Stanley squints, shades his eyes. He an older guy? he asks.

An aged man! That's right. But not a paltry thing. Larry's the chief cantilever of the canto, in fact. He's the most load-bearing, soul-clapping old coot you'll likely find here along the mackerel-crowded sea. And he wants to meet you.

How come?

Because of his book. You've heard about his *youth book,* right? His monument of unaging intellect?

Stanley shakes his head.

He's tape-recording us, Charlie says. All of us. He's writing a book about what's going on here.

Stanley looks at Charlie, then pivots on his ankles, trying to put his own face in shadow. It must be past three by now. Okay, he says. What *is* going on here?

Oh, disaffiliation and reaffiliation. Dedicated poverty. The last outpost against the approach of Moloch. Lots of stinkweed, and not too many baths. An entirely new way of life. Depends on who you ask. Larry wants to ask *you.*

Why me?

Charlie sips from his bottle with a sly wiseacre smile. Bwana Lawrence is interested in your unique perspective, he says. *Id est,* why would a hardnosed juvenile delinquent travel clear across the country to meet an unknown poet. *Id est,* word has gotten around about your visit to good Doctor What's-His-

Name. I think Larry's jealous, to tell you the truth.

Yeah? Stanley says. Do I get anything out of this deal?

From the *deal,* Charlie says, you get a *meal* you don't have to *steal.* Probably half the guys who talk to Larry just do it for the chow. Then they badmouth him behind his back. It makes me sort of sick, honestly. I always tell them: stow your romantic bullshit, because that is what a real writer looks like. Larry's published novels. He's written for the movies, and for TV. I have to admit, it's not always pretty. It's not always subtle. But he *chose* to be here. He didn't just wash ashore, like the rest of us. He believes in the reality of Moloch, and he came here to resist him.

A thin shrill sound comes from the boardwalk — a child crying — and a small spherical shadow sweeps over the sand. Stanley glances up in time to see a white helium balloon pass overhead; then he loses it in the sun. By the arcades the woman with the baby-carriage is stooped, talking to her bawling kid. He can't hear what she's saying. The kid wails louder. Well, Stanley says, thanks for letting me know. I'll look him up.

Charlie's demeanor has shifted. His mouth works like a rabbit's; he seems sickly-pale beneath his tan. Larry *gets* Moloch, he says. He understands how he works, what he wants. Larry thinks you can steal the language

653

back from Moloch and use it against him. I'm not so sure. I think it might be spoiled for good. Because I've *seen* Moloch, you know? I've seen him in the world. It isn't hard, once you know how. I saw him when I was just a child, in the library in Boston. Bullhorned. Furnace-fisted. As in the gold mosaic of a wall. Later I saw him in Europe, too. I'd look down from the ballturret, and there he'd be. Lit by hellfire. Accepting his sacrifices. I think he comes to eliminate the surplus children, and that means he'll be everywhere soon. Trot out all the sociology you like: I'm talking about a *literal demon.* A demon that lives off complacency and fear.

The kid on the boardwalk is stamping its feet in a tantrum, screaming like it's being murdered; the kid in the carriage has started to cry, too. Stanley shifts his weight, impatient and uncomfortable. So, he says, pointing to the tube of paper in Charlie's hand. What's that you got there, Charlie?

Charlie's confused for a second. Then he brightens, passing his bottle to Stanley, unrolling the tube. A going-away present for Alex, he says. See?

It's a promotional notice for a movie called *Cowboy,* starring Glenn Ford and Jack Lemmon. The long yellow poster shows the two men in their cowboy duds, one huge in the foreground, the other tiny in the background; Stanley can't remember which actor is which.

He has a hard time believing anybody would make a movie with a title as boring as *Cowboy*. The poster's tagline reads, *It's really the best because it's really the West!*

Nice, Stanley says. Alex likes horse operas, huh?

Charlie rolls up the poster, takes the bottle back, and grins. No, man, he says. I don't think he gives a damn about them one way or another.

He takes another sip. The woman with the baby-carriage slaps her screaming kid across the face, and it shuts up. Stanley's aware of the waves at his back; they sound like distant fireworks. Well, he says, I better move along. I'll see you later, Charlie.

Be sure to visit Larry Lipton! Charlie calls after him. Get your free meal!

Stanley doesn't turn around. He makes his way to the boardwalk, angling toward the penny-arcade where he played pinball two nights ago while waiting for the fish. He wonders for a second if Claudio's made it back to the hideout yet — if he's wondering where Stanley is, if he's been having a great goddamn time — but then he puts it out of his mind. By now the boardwalk has filled with slumming weekenders: beachcombers with metal-detectors, respectable Lawrence Welk fans, junior-grade officers and their girls. In another few hours the sun will drop and the moon will rise, these people will disappear, and all the usual werewolves will come out.

The penny-arcade is bustling, but nowhere near packed. Stanley hopes the Dogs will be around — he wants to get moving on the junk for Alex — but it's all flattops and crewcuts inside, nary a duck's-ass or a dollop of grease to be seen. Funny, he thinks. They'll probably turn up later.

He walks around to look at the machines — Domino, Hayburners, Meat Ball, Dreamy — but nothing grabs him. Then, in the corner, he finds a row of ancient nickel-vend Mutoscope peepshows, with FOR GROWN ADULTS ONLY – NO KIDS stenciled on the wall above them, a few degrees off parallel with the layered bricks. Stanley isn't normally interested in peepshows, but he also doesn't like being told that something's off-limits. He saunters over, drops a coin.

It's pretty standard fare, maybe a little sleazier than average: AN ARTIST IN HIS STUDIO, the title card says. Stanley puts his face to the viewer — rising a little on his toes — and turns the crank. It rotates, with each turn making a steady clunk at about six o'clock, and pictures flicker into view: the bearded bohemian artist dabbing from his palette to his canvas, and his nude model wrapped in a strategically placed white drape. Dab-dab, dab-dab; this goes on for a while. The model is flush-cheeked, curly-headed, maybe twenty years old. She'd be — what? — fifty now, at the very least. She stands still, blinking, clutching the flimsy drape to her chest. Suddenly the painter drops his brush and his palette and rushes to embrace her, and the door behind him bursts open as the girl's fiancé barges in. For an instant, the drape falls below her nipples. The reel ends with a thump. Beginning to end, the thing lasted about a minute.

Stanley leans back, sinks to the floor, looks around. Nobody seems to give much of a damn that he's using the machines. Maybe they figure him for older than he is, but he guesses he could put a toddler in a highchair in front of one of these and get the same amount of guff: the sign is for cops, not customers. With boredom already tugging at his sleeve, he moves to the next viewer.

THE PRINCESS RAJAH, this one says: it's an Arabian "princess" in an outlandish outfit, doing a wriggly belly-dance, then picking up a wooden chair with her teeth. Stanley's no expert on Arabian princesses, or on their dancing, but the whole production strikes him as phony and laughable.

The next Mutoscope asks a dime, not a nickel; Stanley's inclined to skip it, but then he notices the title card: THE BATHING GODDESS, it says. IN COLOR!

His dime drops with a soft click onto a hidden mound of other dimes. The picture starts: a smooth-faced young guy in a toga peeks through a bush; a woman swims around in a pool, her coiffed head above water, her white body a shapeshifting blur underneath. The images have been laboriously hand-tinted: pink cheeks, green leaves, blue water. The goddess rises dripping from the pool, showing her bare ass for a moment, and then turns forward, plucking a towel from a branch to dry her chest. The guy in the bushes gasps and trembles in open-mouthed ecstasy. The goddess hears him; her face twists in shock and rage. She aims an angry gesture his way, and he explodes in a cloud of yellow smoke. Thump: the end.

Stanley drops a second dime, then a third. The photo-cards inside the machine turn on their spool; some arrangement of lights and mirrors carries each picture to the viewer, then in an instant the turning crank whisks it away. Stanley becomes aware of the separateness of the individual images, each one a small colored jewel in the interior light. He tries to crank slower — to see between the cards, to cancel the trick his eyes are playing — but past a certain point the viewer just goes black. He drops a fourth dime. The naked goddess's image is doubled, cut to pieces on the rippling surface of the pool. The toga-clad watcher vanishes, replaced by the plume of smoke. The branches around him disappear, then reappear with a jerk a half-inch from where they were.

The machine won't take nickels; Stanley's out of dimes. In a minute he'll have the attendant break a dollar, but in the meantime there's one last nickel show left.

The label has worn away, or been removed. The title card just says JULY 4, 1905. Stanley's nickel falls with a hollow lonely clank.

The first thing he sees is a long black boat, making its way down a broad canal, a massive rollercoaster in the background. That image is quickly replaced by others: camels and pachyderms, a miniature railroad, bathing beauties in bizarre swimsuits, bowler-hatted men and their corseted wives strolling through shaded arcades. Then Stanley spots a familiar sign: ST. MARK'S HOTEL.

His hand freezes on the crank; the viewer goes dark. He starts it again, and soon other familiar sights emerge: buildings along Windward and the boardwalk, though the names of just about all the shops — Harry A. Hull Billiards, H. C. Burmister Grocery, Frasinelli Fruit Co. — are strange to him. Most disorienting of all, in this film Windward doesn't stop at the boardwalk: it crosses the beach to become the midway of a thronged amusement pier, with bathhouses and dancehalls and lit-up carnival rides. When the spool ends he feeds the machine more nickels. Eventually he spots the building that will one day become the Fortune Bridgo parlor, and then, a few doors down, the building he's standing in right now. He presses his face to the brass viewer, inches the crank forward. Tiny silent figures march erratically along the pier, black-garbed and plume-hatted, flickering like the ghosts they are.

A moment of panic seizes Stanley: the sensation of being watched. He straightens up and turns to scan the room, but he meets no eyes. The air has changed, grown heavy. Beyond the open windows, the sky over the ocean has gone gray and solid. He has a creepy Rip-Van-Winkle feeling, like something just slipped past him. He stands stock-still, eyeing the boardwalk and the shore, waiting for whatever's coming.

Soon he sees it. Charlie again, slouching across the beach, his expression sober and serious. He has an arm around somebody's waist, somebody he's helping to walk. Their approach through the clotted air is nightmare-slow.

Stanley dashes out the door, onto the boardwalk. Wanting to see, though by now he knows. The figure with Charlie stumbles forward as if half-blind; his eyes, Stanley sees, are swollen nearly shut. He cradles his right hand against his chest as if it's a bird stunned by a flight into a windowpane; Stanley can tell right off that the hand is broken. As messed-up as he is, the figure measures his steps, keeps his chin high, and it's mostly from that — and from the blue rayon shirt he wears, now flecked down the front with rusty dried blood — that Stanley is able to recognize him as Claudio.

47

At a luncheonette on Market they get Claudio a glass of water and an icepack for his hand. Claudio sips the water through a drinking-straw. Stanley's worried at first that his jaw is broken, but when he finally speaks his voice is clear enough. Thank you, he tells Charlie. It is okay for you to go. I will be fine.

Charlie's nearly in tears as they walk away, kneading his hands in the middle of the boardwalk, as if Claudio were his own wounded son. Stanley clenches his teeth, holding something in, though he's not sure what: curses maybe, or puke. His stomach feels like it's dropped into his thigh.

They're no more than a hundred yards from the hideout, but Claudio won't go there. It takes them just about forever to pass the four blocks of boardwalk to Wave Crest. The crowd parts around them, passing on both sides. Stanley watches the faces light up as they draw close and see Claudio: startled, sympathetic, disgusted, amused. A few servicemen on dates stop to offer help, but Stanley waves them off. At the corner of Club House a beat cop detains them for a couple of minutes with questions. My buddy just had a bicycle accident, officer, Stanley says. He ran into a telephone pole. No, nobody else got hurt. He's gonna be okay.

Yes, Claudio's split lips corroborate. It is just as my friend has told you. A telephone pole.

All along the walk, Claudio whispers, then falls silent. Relentlessly repeating himself. I looked every place for you, he says. All the morning I looked for you, and all the afternoon. I had so many things I wished to tell you. I had so many ways I had learned to make our lives better. And I could not find you. Where were you?

Stanley clenches his teeth, says nothing.

The first round of knocks brings no one to Welles's door. A second round — hard and protracted — also dies away with no results, and Stanley is about to jump from the stoop and try the side door when the lace curtain swings aside to reveal Synnøve's face, her pale paint-smeared hand over her horrified mouth.

She wraps Claudio in an afghan — the same one Cynthia used last night — then makes another icepack, and hurries from the room to the telephone. Stanley holds the new pack to Claudio's face; Claudio keeps the freeze on his cracked hand with the other one. His forehead is corpse-pale; he's bruising quickly under both eyes. Where were you,

Stanley? he says. I looked every, every, everywhere.

Listen, Stanley says. Shut up a minute. Tell
me who did this.

The hoods.

No shit it was the hoods. What hoods?

Claudio's mouth goes sour. It doesn't matter, he says.

It does matter, kid. Who was it? I gotta —

Where were you? Claudio says. A sharp
note creeps into his voice, sad and dangerous.

Kid, Stanley says. You need to tell me, right
now, who did this. Because if you don't, then
I'm gonna have to guess. And I'm gonna
guess whoever it was had a lot of help, and
I'm gonna wind up making a bigger mess
than I need to. Now. Who? Whitey, right?
How many more?

Why did you want to make any deal with
them? Claudio says. Why did you think it
could be any good?

Who else? Stanley says, moving the icepack
to Claudio's opposite temple, coming around
the chair to face him. The boss? If you don't
tell me, then I'm gonna think yes. Got it? You
understand what that means?

Claudio's slotted lids blink at Stanley. Then
he looks away. His lips open and close. It was
the one you guessed, he says. The white one.

Okay. Who else? The boss?

Claudio shakes his head, winces.

663

What about those other two? The ones we saw with Whitey at the penny-arcade?

Yes. Those. No more.

Stanley lifts the icepack to move strands of hair from Claudio's eyes. His brow is clammy. What happened, kid? he says.

I do not wish to talk about this with you.

Goddamnit, kid. Why didn't you fight 'em off like I taught you? Why didn't —

Claudio reaches up with his icepack, bats Stanley's arms away. I fought them, he hisses. I fought them like you said. And look.

He tries to lift his broken hand; grimaces. Skin's missing from the knuckles; Stanley hadn't noticed that before.

I fought them, Claudio says. I tried to go with no fighting, but they would not permit me. They would make me do a thing that I did not want to do. They tried to make me, but I fought them. In the way that you said. I kicked them, and I hit them with my hand, and when I hurt my hand, I kicked them again. I hurt them. I made them go.

Stanley nods. Okay, he says, touching Claudio's hair. Okay. That's good. It's good that you tried. But, kid, if you'd done like I told you — exactly like I told you — then you wouldn't have a busted hand, and we wouldn't be in this fix. You got a lot of heart, chum. But we still got some work to do toughening you up. Next time —

No, Claudio says. He cocks his head under

664

Stanley's hand, looks him in the eye. Then he lifts his left fist and punches Stanley in the forearm, hard. It's a glancing blow, but it hurts. Stanley takes a step back. Claudio sits up just enough to hit him again, in the shoulder, moving him farther away. Whoa, Stanley says. Take it easy, kid.

Why do I have to do these things? Claudio says. Why, Stanley? I do not want these things. *You* want them. *Tough?* God damn you and your *tough.* I do not want to be tough. I want to be brave. I want to be beautiful. I want to be famous.

Stanley rocks back on his heels in the little kitchen, rubbing his arm with his thumb where Claudio struck it. Tomorrow he'll have a bruise there. Okay, he hears himself saying. That's fine. We can do that. I'm sure there's ways we can do that.

Claudio settles in his chair, picks up the icepack, puts it on his hand again. There are one million ways we can do it, he says. One million times did I try to tell you. But you did not listen. You did not listen.

In the next room the phone returns to its cradle with a soft chime, and Synnøve rushes back into the kitchen, opening cabinets and closing them. I reached Adrian at the office, she says. He's leaving work early. He'll be home soon, and then he'll drive you to the hospital. For now, let's keep the ice on your hand. And — here, Stanley, here's a bottle of

Tylenol. Get Claudio some water, and have him take two. I'm sorry, I'd do it myself, but I'm filthy from the studio. I have to clean up before Adrian gets here.

Where's Cynthia? Stanley asks, but Synnøve's gone from the room before she hears him. As he opens the bottle and shakes the white pills onto his palm, Stanley hears her move through the house: running water, opening drawers.

He puts the Tylenol and the dripping glass on the tabletop next to Claudio's hand. Claudio's fingers release the icepack, pinch each pill in turn, bring them to his lips. Then he washes them down with sips of water. He moves very slowly. His eyes are closed.

Not talking to me, huh? Stanley says.

Claudio slouches in his seat. His lips and eyelids are bluish. A vein flutters in his forehead, shrinking and growing like the belly of a snake. His bloody inflated face hangs on his skull, and for a second Stanley can't remember what he really looks like.

I had so many things to tell you, Claudio mumbles. But you never listen.

For a long time Stanley watches him like that: sipping from the crystal glass, fighting to keep his head up. He's sideswiped by a memory of the long rainy days that closed out their February: the kid reading his stolen screen magazines while Stanley read *The Mirror Thief*. Stanley was combing his book for clues; Claudio was just killing time. That's what Stanley thought, anyway. In Claudio's head, of course, it was the other way around. Stanley's known this before; maybe he's always known it. Now he understands it differently — harder, colder, more serious — and it feels like he's met a high wall, or a fork in the road. This kid has his own warm body, living and dying, and a black-box mind that cannot be seen: just the same as Stanley, or anyone. And Stanley can't know him; he can barely know himself. There are many questions that Welles's book can aim him toward the answers to, but this is not one of them. The best it can do is convince him that questions like these don't matter, and Stanley hopes one day it will.

He stands behind Claudio and stares at the back of his skull until he can't take it anymore. Then he steps to the side door — his rubber soles soundless on the linoleum — unlatches it, and slips onto the porch. He does this without so much as creaking a plank, but Claudio must feel the air change when the door swings open. Stanley? he says.

Stanley leaves the door ajar behind him. He's pretty sure that Synnøve's in the bathroom, not anyplace where she'll see him leave, but he rushes across the yard anyway, vaults the fence, jogs the half-block to Pacific Avenue. He's breathing hard now. His own pulse hammers his eardrums like the footfalls of pursuers.

By the time he makes it back to the squat the wind has picked up, levitating loose papers from ashcans, rocking streetlamps into herky-jerky pendulums. Below the wall of incoming clouds a sliver of red sun has dipped into the ocean. Stanley glimpses it for a second as he passes Horizon Ave; when he turns onto Horizon Court he loses it again.

Before he left this morning he put his things away with care, just like always; it doesn't take him long to find the items he needs. After a minute of packing up Claudio's stuff he's on the street again, dodging oncoming cars on the Speedway, moving with tunnel-visioned ease, like he's lived in this neighborhood for years. Even with the sun gone and bad weather coming, the world feels disenchanted, shrunken. Stanley's on familiar ground now, comfortable and sad.

The first big drops catch him on the boardwalk, as he's settling onto a bench; they flash under the streetlamps, leave jagged silver-dollar-size sunbursts on the wooden planks. When they strike his skin they're heavy and cold, like shoulder-taps from a ghost.

He watches the windows of the penny-arcade — still a block away — until he's good and soaked, and his wet shirtsleeves have become loose reptile-skin on his arms. At this distance he can just make out faces: Whitey with a fat lip and a swollen eye, his two junior punks with minor scratches. All three look sullen, unhappy with each other and with themselves.

People pass between Stanley and the arcade in a steady stream, moving quickly in the rain: some share umbrellas, some huddle under newspapers. Their silhouettes pulse across the windows like gaps between cards on a Mutoscope spool. From time to time someone joins Stanley on his bench — a drunk, a grifter, a pervert — but Stanley won't look and won't say a word, and eventually they all go away.

Stanley thinks of Welles's list of names in his pocket. He should have left it at the squat; the ink will run when it gets wet. Not much to be done about it at this point. It was probably bullshit anyway. It was a bad move, trying to play the game on Welles's terms instead of his own. He can see that well enough now.

One of the two punk Dogs — the one farthest from the door — finally steps away from his machine, headed for the john. Stanley rises from his bench. He closes the distance in a hurry without breaking into a run, and he takes deep breaths as he goes. A couple of the people he passes must be able to read the intention in his face; they avert their nervous eyes, give him a wide berth. Soon he's standing in the door, puddling the concrete with the rain he's accrued. The punk is just a few feet ahead, his back turned.

Whitey's clear across the room, facing Stanley, blinded by the game he plays, or by whatever he's thinking about. For a flickering instant Stanley thinks what he always thinks at these times: *You don't have to do this. You can walk away.* The idea slows him up more than he's used to. He feels like he's at the first tall drop of a rollercoaster track; his eyes are squeezed tight with the effort of imagining himself elsewhere. But of course he is not elsewhere. He is here.

He takes a few quick steps, passes behind the first punk, stops, and elbows him in the kidney. A half-human moan bursts from the guy's lips as his knees fold. Stanley drops with him, fingers tangled in his greasy hair, to drive his face into the steel coinbox.

Stanley scrambles on all fours to the corner, past the row of machines, then stands up as he circles around to Whitey. A couple of people are staring at the fallen punk; a few more hotfoot to the exit, but Whitey plays on without looking up. Stanley is close enough now to see his score: two million points, one ball left to play. The guy isn't bad; he knows what he's doing.

As Stanley comes up behind Whitey he peeks over his shoulder for a second at the bubbling seahorses and topless mermaids of the playfield, the flash of the silver ball. He lets Whitey keep playing until the guy feels eyes on his back, realizes that something is wrong. His concentration wavers. The ball drains.

Stanley pulps Whitey's right hand against the cabinet's edge with the swung blackjack. Then he hits him again on the side of the head, and keeps hitting him until he's motionless on the concrete. A girl a few machines down screams.

The third Dog isn't yet finished in the john, so Stanley goes in after him, kicking his stall door open, bringing the blackjack down until it connects with his face. The Dog balls up, sags against the spattered wooden panel. Through a small glory-hole over the roll of paper Stanley sees someone cringing in the next stall. Oh god, a voice says. Oh my god.

On his way back to the boardwalk, Stanley pauses to club Whitey one more time, taking care not to step in the slick of blood that spreads from his body toward the ocean, carried by the downgrade of the concrete floor.

48

It takes no more than a minute to clean out the squat. Soon Stanley's on the street again, his dad's fieldpack on his back, Claudio's duffel slung over his shoulder, walking through wind-driven rain as the crack-bulbed streetlamp overhead creaks and thrashes on its black cables. He'd planned on using the Speedway, but flashing lights of squadcars and ambulances — he can't tell how many — have congregated at Westminster, a block from the penny-arcade. He stops under a leaky canvas awning to watch as red pulses from their gumball beacons throw the gigantic shadows of rainslickered cops against the sides of buildings. Stanley thinks of black scorpions attacking Mexico City.

He doubles back to Market and heads inland, into town, taking Cabrillo to Aragon to Abbot Kinney, taking Abbot Kinney west again. As he's making the left on Main an ambulance rockets through the intersection behind him, siren keening, and this makes Stanley feel a little better: if the guy inside was dead, nobody'd bother with the siren. At least that's what people used to say back in the neighborhood.

Wave Crest comes up in a few blocks. As he's crossing Pacific the clouds open up, the wind sweeps the rain into a solid-seeming wall, and he hastens to the doorway of a bakery for shelter, already firehose-drenched. This is probably where Synnøve bought last night's bread; today it's closed for Shabbos, its carefully labeled window racks — TEIGLACH רעטלגייט – HALVAH הבלח – HAMANTASH שאָט־ומה — bare and swept of crumbs. Stanley puts his wet nose to the glass and inhales, but it just smells like glass, like nothing.

Welles and Synnøve must have taken Clau-

672

dio to the hospital by now; nobody seems to be home, which is what Stanley's counting on. To be certain, he bangs on their front door, leaves the two packs on the stoop, and waits in the yard, crouched between the sundial and the row of dark hibiscus, out of sight from the street. Nobody answers. Stanley stands up, knocks again, hides again. To kill time, he reads the brass letters set along the sundial's circumference. It takes him a second to figure out where to start. *I snatched the sun's eternal ray,* they say, *and wrote till earth was but a name.* Raindrops drum against Stanley's back as he bends to read.

He makes a quick circuit of the house to look for lights in windows and finds none. Under the shelter of the deck he crosses the side porch to the kitchen door. A burbling drainpipe pukes dark water onto the pavement; a prefab concrete channel aims the flow into the flowerbed, where it forms a puddle. The knife-edge of the peaked roof appears in the puddle's rippling surface, black against the moon-green sky.

Stanley pulls an old roll of maskingtape from a jacket pocket; it's swollen now at its edges from the damp. He tears off strips and tapes over the door's lower right-hand windowpane, the one closest to the knob, until it's covered entirely. He overlaps the strips so

673

everything will stick. His hands are cold and stiff and badly puckered from the rain, and it takes him a while to do it. When he's done, he puts the tape-roll back in his pocket, takes off his jacket, folds it in two, and presses it against the taped-up window with his left hand. Then he punches it with his right fist: a hard, glancing blow. The pane breaks with a flat crunch. A few slivers, smaller than rock-salt, sprinkle the porch and glitter around Stanley's feet. He shakes out his jacket, drapes it over his shoulder, peels up the layer of tape. Almost all the broken glass comes away with it; he sets this aside. Then he reaches through the window and lets himself in.

The air inside is dry and warm and full of strange smells that Stanley hasn't noticed before, or that weren't here. He feels like an archaeologist who's just unsealed a tomb. He moves quickly through the house to the front door, hangs his dripping jacket over the banister, and hauls the two packs in from the stoop.

In the john just off the staircase he finds a towel, dries his hair and hands. Then he opens his pack and comes out with the thick wad of cash — Alex's junk money, the take from the boardwalk con — that he's amassed over recent weeks. He combines this with what little he has in his pockets now, counts the total, and divides it in half, as well as he can with the bills he's got. It's even within a few bucks. Stanley puts the smaller half back in his fieldpack, tucks the larger half into Claudio's duffel.

Then he searches the house. He grants cursory attention to the ground floor — pump shotgun under a dust-ruffle in the tidy master bedroom; weird sculptures in Synnøve's cluttered studio, adipose blobs, skinless and shapeless, like organs without bodies — but Stanley already knows what he really wants to see.

Upstairs in Welles's study, he throws the bolt on the big barred door but finds the internal deadbolt still locked. He steps back to look at it. There's probably something downstairs in Synnøve's workroom that'll knock the lock off or pry it open, but that seems inelegant, amateurish, and Stanley isn't sure he has time for it anyway. Besides, he has a feeling Welles keeps a key stashed close by.

He checks the obvious places first: the undersides of the desk and the swivel chair, the drawers and the backs of the drawers. The desk is still unlocked, the two pistols within easy reach. Welles doesn't lock up his guns, but he keeps that big black door locked. *Cynthia's room,* he called it. Bullshit.

Stanley opens drawers and closes them. Every time he bends down he smells the bandage on his leg; he still hasn't taken the

675

time to change it. Every time he sits up his vision swims, he gets lightheaded. He feels like he's running a fever. Outside, the wind gusts; cold rain hisses against the windows and the french door.

After a while Stanley sits in the swivel chair and leans back and thinks. Trying to imagine his way into Welles's big pipesmoked body, into his swelled head. He's not having much luck. He runs his fingers along the edge of the desk, lingering in the spots where the wood is worn, the finish faded. The letter he found last night — the one from the hospital in Washington — lies open on the desktop, and it looks as though Welles has started to draft a response:

Naturellement any man possessed of a modicum of reason and intellectual courage is compelled to be anti-Jew, and anti-Christian as well —— hardly the greatest but surely neither the least of the Nazi errors manifested itself in superficial Wotanism and a lack of serious understanding of their Germanic forebears' pagan wisdom.

In the brass wastebasket next to the desk Stanley finds five or six crumpled pages that bear minute variations of the same sentence. He crumples them again, slowly, and places them back in the basket. Then he sags into the chair again, scanning the room.

The key is in a goddamn *book;* it's got to be. Probably a book by one of the goddamn names on the fucking list in his pocket, the list that Welles made, the list that's smeared now, turned to mush by the rain. He wonders if he can spot the key just by looking — there'll be a gap in the right book's pages, or between its pages and its cover — but most of the spined-out volumes have others laid flat atop them; plus the bookcases all go clear to the ceiling, and Stanley isn't tall enough to see the upper shelves. His eyes crawl along the spines, up and down the walls. Thousands of books. Which one?

He sits up. Then he rotates the chair, all the way around, and rises to his feet.

As soon as his fingers touch the frame of the old map he can feel it: the long sheet of glass that shields the yellow paper pivots on a small bump somewhere near its midpoint. Stanley lifts the frame, slips a hand under its lower edge, and finds the key hung in a little leather sheath just below what looks to be the island-city's main plaza. He tugs it free, settles the frame in place. On the map's surface an ornamental drawing of a muscle-bound god — nude, armed with a trident, mounted on a grotesque sea-monster — stares up at the spot where the key was, like he'd been trying all along to tip Stanley off, to give the game away. Thanks a ton, jack,

Stanley whispers. Now you tell me.

At first he's afraid the key won't fit the lock. Then, of course, it does. The deadbolt slides with a low click.

Black curtains fill the doorway, flush with the inner wall. Stanley finds a gap, and parts them: abyssal darkness beyond, blacker than the curtains themselves. The weak green light cast by the desklamp seems unable or unwilling to cross the doorframe. Stanley can see an inch or two of wooden floor on the other side — same as the floor he now stands on — but nothing else.

He slips through. The curtains fall shut behind him. The room he's entered sounds empty and big, much larger than Welles's study. He waits for his eyes to adjust to the dark, and when they do, he still can't see anything. He runs fingers under the drapes on both sides of the door but finds no light-switch. Strange smells: sharp, sweet, cloying. Wrong somehow. Gooseflesh rises on his fore-arms.

He retreats to the study, finds a box of matches in the desk, strikes three on the doorjamb on his way back through. The pale flare of ignition barely reaches the walls: the room takes up the entire remainder of the floor. Stanley can make out low wooden benches a few paces ahead, a chandelier just past them, hung at his eye-level. Something big and shapeless beyond that, hung with colored drapes. White lines across the floor-boards. Black curtains on the walls, all the way around. The ceiling is painted uniformly dark. Everything seems designed to devour light.

The matches burn down to his fingertips; he hurries to light more off their dying flames. The chandelier ahead is a real chandelier, not electric; Stanley passes between the two benches, stretches to light a candle, uses that one to light others. The rain is quieter, muted by the curtains, and by what must be an attic overhead. He wonders if he'll be able to hear if someone comes through the front door downstairs.

Circles of yellow light appear on the ceiling, and the shape of the chandelier casts a fluttering web across them. The room's furnishings all look antique, vulgar, made by hand. Stanley feels as if he's slipped back in time, out of history, or into a history that nobody knows. Whenever he moves, the polished boards creak underfoot, singing like cricket-legs.

The shapeless thing at the room's distant end is a massive canopy bed, its posts coiled and draped with sheer silks of red and black and gold. Fancy cushions litter the thick mattress; a pair of dark chifforobes towers behind. Stanley can't look at it. He isn't ready to think about what it is, or what it means. This has been a big mistake; he's not sure yet how big. By now he knows he won't find anything he's been looking for in this room. But he needs to see it anyway. To get past it. To kill off something in himself that's been hindering him, making him weak. Like yanking out a rotten tooth.

He looks down at the white lines under his feet, stoops to bring his light closer. Three triangles point toward him, away from a stepped wooden platform in the room's right-hand corner. Small draped tables sit at the triangles' tips, and each has something on it: a basin of water, vented metal cubes bristling with stick-incense, an upright black coffer covered by a veil. The platform and triangles are set at an odd angle to the walls, as if oriented by compass, not the slant of the shoreline. Everything seems precisely placed: distances calculated by ritual formulae. To the left is a small podium, set at the midpoint of concentric circles inscribed in concentric squares; the empty spaces between the orderly lines are crowded with writing in an alphabet Stanley doesn't know: not Hebrew, or Russian, or Arabic, or Greek. He thinks of Welles on the beach, intoning that foreign phrase. A secret language. Something creepy little kids might make up.

Stanley sinks onto one of the benches. He's dizzy; his breath sounds ragged in his ears. The candle in his hand tips as he leans forward, and drops of liquid wax spatter the floor: clear, then white. He counts the steady splashes, then loses count.

The platform in the corner has objects on it — red candles, brass dishes, dried flowers, a book, a painting of a black tree with runes labeling its branches — but Stanley can't get interested in any of it. It's too obvious a trap: not a trap that Welles has set for him, but a trap that Welles has fallen into. The book does not lead here. It's time to get this over with.

Stanley comes to his feet, staggers a little, crosses the big room. A sour tightness rises from his belly — he tastes it at the back of his throat — but he keeps moving forward. The canopy bed looms plushly, flanked by two ankle-thick candles on huge brass sticks; behind it, between the two chifforobes, Stanley spots a low dainty vanity backed with a tarnished mirror. He sniffs the air, prods the red velvet comforter with a fingertip. Suspended over the mattress is a second mirror, bigger and newer than the first, parallel to the floor, hung from the bedposts by four even chains. Stanley's own upturned face greets him there, childlike and frightened; he looks away, then spots himself again afloat above the dresser, a dim ghost wasted by the smudged and blistered silver.

His foot bumps something under the dustruffle and he stoops to pick it up: a hospital bedpan. He sets it on the comforter, opens one of the chifforobes. A few weird costumes hang inside — outlandish, almost obscene — along with ordinary blouses and sweaters and skirts, nylon stockings and black leotards, faded summer dresses, girlish brassieres and briefs. Cynthia's room.

Stanley reaches in, pinches the sleeve of a sweater, pulls it and lets it drop. He stands staring for a moment. Then his stomach flops — like something's hatched inside him — and he turns and vomits into the pale granitewear bedpan. He gasps, seizes the pan, carries it down as he sinks to his knees. On the floor he catches the sour smell of his bandaged leg and vomits again. He hasn't eaten since the fish last night, so nothing comes up but clear liquid and a few celery veins. His diaphragm pistons; he can't breathe. He feels transformed: a fleshy cannon, a debased crawling thing. As if he's expelling every human feature of himself.

Eventually he rocks back on his haunches, clears his throat and spits, cleans tears and acid and mucus from his face with a pair of Cynthia's underdrawers. He should torch this place, he thinks. Plenty of stuff in Synnøve's workroom'll burn. Turpentine. A flaming trail of it up the stairs, out the side door. Once those books catch this place will be cinders right down to the slab. But then where will he stash Claudio's stuff?

A door slams downstairs; a faint voice calls. *Hello?* it says.

Stanley stiffens — a jolt like a plunge into cold water — and then forces himself to relax, to listen. Once his pulse has steadied he puts his palms on the floor and pushes, rising like a puff of smoke to his feet, weightless and smooth. As he crosses the big room back to the study he tries to stay close to the walls, to step on spots where the floor is firm and feet have rarely fallen. A few planks squeal — it can't be helped — but he keeps calm and breathes easily. Fighting the urge to run like he'd fight off a sneeze. The intruder is a relief, actually. Seconds ago Stanley was lost, a stranger to himself. Now he's on familiar ground: the burglar who didn't get out in time.

Welles's desk is finely made; its drawers open and close with no sound. Stanley figures the Wehrmacht pistol for war booty Welles never bothered to register, so that's the gat he picks; the .45's too big for his hand anyway. He puts his blackjack in his front pocket, lets his belt out a notch, and tucks the pistol into it where the blackjack was, at the small of his back. It's not comfortable, but he doesn't need it to be. He's pretty confident the safety's on, pretty sure he won't shoot himself in the ass by mistake.

At the top of the stairs he pauses, listens. No noises in the house. The staircase is a dark empty tunnel with a splash of light at its bottom, fallen from the entryway window. Stanley glances at his feet for an instant as he starts his descent, fitting his steps to the stairs' rhythm, and when he looks up again the girl is standing right there in front of him, hardly more than an arm's-length away.

He freezes, knees bent, hand on the wall for balance. Cynthia's shapely white fingers rest on the banister — his jacket hung a few feet behind — and her sandal-clad foot perches on the next step. Her sharp chin is tilted, her spine and shoulders beauty-pageant straight. She doesn't look surprised to see him, or worried, either. Her caramel-cream eyes are bright, like they're caught in a moonbeam, though no moonbeam reaches them here. She and Stanley stare at each other for a long time. Rainwater is dripping from Stanley's jacket: a quiet tap counting the moment down.

The girl speaks. So, Betty Crocker, she half-whispers. What cooks?

Stanley opens his mouth to reply, but all that comes from his vomit-scoured throat is a mute rasp. He swallows, tries again. What, he says, the *fuck* goes on up here?

A wild ugliness flashes across Cynthia's face, like she's inhaled a wasp. Then she goes blank. It's a blood-drained, million-watt blankness, a blankness like the downriver side of a hydroelectric dam. Stanley has seen this once or twice before: on a woman about to jump off the Williamsburg Bridge, on a guy about to shoot three people in an Alphabet City snackbar. A face turned to a burnt-out mask, no longer broadcasting, overloaded by something it can find no right expression for. Often Stanley has imagined himself to be alone in the world, but this is what alone really looks like, and it scares him. He takes an even breath, keeps his knees bent, adjusts his footing, moves his free hand a little closer to the grip of the pistol.

Have you been in my room? Cynthia says.

Stanley doesn't answer. He could put his shoulder down and run her over — grab his pack and his jacket and scram — but now the house seems to be shrinking to trap him, or else the girl is expanding, swelling like a white balloon to fill the stairwell. Part of him wants to just shoot her. He imagines the jerk of the pistol, pictures her vanishing with a moist elastic pop.

But he's out of danger now, or nearly so. Her eyes flit everywhere, everywhere but his face, and the color creeps back to her cheeks like schoolchildren returning after a bomb scare. She's a little shaky; she keeps fidgeting to hide her jitters. Her tone, too, is shifty when she speaks again: apologetic at first, then accusatory. I guess you probably think, she says, and trails off. Listen, she snaps, don't think for one hot minute you understand —

Trust me, Stanley says. I don't.

Cynthia cops a coltish Audrey Hepburn pose on the banister, getting back her cool by acting cool. Her voice is bright and thick and unconvincing, maple syrup dripped over spun glass. They're not my parents, you know, she says. Claudio told you, right? I've just been shacking here for a couple months. I met Adrian on the beach, just like you did. They're nice people, no matter what you think. Anybody who asks, we just tell 'em I'm Synnøve's niece. Around here, nobody asks.

She's staring hard now at nothing; her fingers fiddle with a phantom cigarette while her eyes dice up the empty space before her. Nobody *makes* me do anything, she says. I don't get what's wrong. There's not any harm in it. Just because somebody says. It's just different, dig? Like you and Claudio.

You don't know shit about me and him.

She blinks. Then her eyes sweep the stairway — mechanical and eerie, like the eyes of an old porcelain doll — and they settle on his face. She fixes him with a watery sneer. You're a child, she says. I don't care where you've been, or what you've done. To me you're just a kid.

She holds his gaze for a couple of breaths, then looks away again. Almost like she's bored. There's plenty of space now between her and the wall, enough to push through. It's stupid for him to stay here any longer.

So, Stanley says. What's with upstairs? The

furniture. The marks on the floor.

Her sneer gets sharper, crueler. What do *you* think it is? she says.

He shuffles his feet. Magic shit, he mumbles. An altar.

I bet, Cynthia says, that you would just *love* to see what goes on up there. Wouldn't you? To be a little fly on the wall. I'll bet you'd sit there on the bench, and fold your hands in your lap, and you'd never make one single peep.

For a second — just a second — Stanley's face feels hot.

I don't *believe* a word of it, she says. Just so you know. All the mumbo-jumbo's lost on me, dad. It's all pretty silly, I think. Juvenile. All that time and effort, trying to catch ghosts. There aren't any *ghosts.* It's weak-minded and sad, thinking like that. You read that book *Atlas Shrugged*? That's where *I'm* coming from, man.

Stanley leans against the wall, crosses his arms to hide the shake. Well, he says. I guess that pretty much makes you a goddamn whore, then. If you don't believe it.

Her mouth falls open with a tiny gasp. Not shocked: surprised. Like he's just handed her a flower that he'd kept hidden behind his back.

Then she throws her head back and laughs. It's not a fake laugh, either. It sounds a little relieved, a little insane. Stanley's mother laughed that way when his grandfather died, for hours and hours. It was about the last sound Stanley ever heard her make.

It's a while before Cynthia can breathe well enough to speak. Poor Adrian! she wheezes. He thinks he *conjured* me. Did Claudio tell you that? No joke. It's *pathetic,* dig? Wanting to *see*! Wanting to *know*! I don't get it. I mean, it's not like I *enjoy* what we do. It can be kind of a drag, honestly. But I get home-cooked chow, I get a nice place to sleep, I get some extra pocket change. I make choices, just like anybody. This is a whole lot better than where I came from, believe me.

Yeah? Stanley says. Where *did* you come from?

The question snuffs what's left of her smile; a flicker of the blankness returns. Then she grins: a broad bottomless grin. She looks like a kid who's figured out how to burn ants with a magnifying glass. Hell, she says. I came from hell.

That brings on a fresh round of sniggering. Soon she's doubled over, wracked by hiccups, wiping her watery eyes. *A whore!* she says. That's *perfect,* Clyde. And not just *any* old whore, either! Oh, no! Man, that's really good. That's a regular scream.

Yeah, Stanley says. Hilarious.

He draws the pistol from his belt and tips up the safety-lever and points the slim round barrel at her face. Cynthia looks at it, confused. Her wide mouth closes; her full pink lips curdle into a frown. She doesn't seem scared. The two of them stare at each other. She hiccups again: a soft fleshy cluck in the dim quiet.

Get up here, Stanley says.

He marches her into the study, then across it, to the black door. Where are we going? she says. What are you gonna do?

We're not going anywhere, toots. I'm dusting out. First I gotta lock you up.

Where is everybody? Did you kill them?

She asks the question in the same mildly curious tone that she might ask *Have you heard the new Johnnie Ray album?* or *Is that a new Van Heusen shirt you're wearing?* It wrongfoots Stanley for a second. My buddy got hurt, he says. Synnøve and Adrian took him to see a doctor. I got cops looking for me. A lot of cops. I don't want to be around when people get home.

As Cynthia draws the black curtain aside, she stops and turns to face him with a toss of her hair. Her eyes are wide, thrilled. The boardwalk? she says. That was you?

What? Did you see something?

I saw cops. Some ambulances. They said it was a gang brawl, that three guys got hurt real bad. Was one Claudio?

No. The kid's fine. Just a little knocked-around is all. Did they say — did you hear if anybody died?

She pivots on her heels, still hiccupping quietly. The curtain's draped like a toga over her shoulder, her left breast. She shakes her head no.

Stanley looks at her. Then he looks at the floor. Then he sighs. Okay, he says. Step back. I'm gonna shut the door.

They want me to have a kid, Cynthia says. Did Claudio tell you?

Stanley stops. His left hand rests on the smooth black wood near the doorknob. The heavy door sways easily with his touch. Is that a fact, he says.

If I do it, she says, they'll get me my own pad. They'll pay the rent, for six whole years. They'll pay my tuition to UCLA if I want to go. I just have to have the kid, and give it to them. Do you think I should do it?

Stanley feels dizzy again, feverish. His vision is tunneling. What the hell do they want a kid for? he says.

Beats me, man. You're asking the wrong chick. I don't know what *anybody* would want a kid for. But I guess it's all part of their —

She waggles her fingers in the air, jerks her head toward the candlelit room over her shoulder. You know, she says. She hiccups again.

Cold sweat drips down Stanley's temple, along his stubbly jaw. What are they gonna do with it? he says.

Cynthia shrugs. She fans the black curtain before her like a lacy petticoat, or a Dracula cape. Her huge-pupiled eyes lock on his. Do you think I should do it? she says.

Stanley looks at her. Then he looks at his hand, pale against the door's black edge, its veins too clear under the skin. It seems detached, lifeless. Nothing to do with him. Surfaces seem flat and static, equidistant. Like this room is just a painting of a room. He's getting sick again, passing out.

So, he says — his voice hollow in his ears, too loud — who's the proud poppa gonna be? Your dear old Daddy Warbucks, right?

Now she has the curtains pulled tight against both sides of her face, bunched in her hidden hands. She's a talking mask, afloat in a void. I guess that depends on who you ask, she says. And what you believe.

Stanley blinks hard, shaking his head, trying to regain his bearings. Cynthia's disembodied face seems to rise, to advance toward him, a cold moon in starless dark. The sight of it already feels like a bad dream, one that he'll have many more times.

Well, Stanley says, good luck to you, Cynthia.

He swings the door shut on her cute button nose and slides the big bolt home. Then he sinks to the floor — gulping air, trying to get blood back to his brain — and presses his forehead to the smooth wood.

From the other side comes the girl's muffled voice. *Hey,* she shouts. *My name isn't really Cynthia, you know.*

Stanley swallows, moving a trickle of spit around his cottony throat. Yeah? he says. Well, get a load of this. My name ain't Stanley, neither.

A few seconds of silence. Outside, the rain has stopped, or nearly stopped. She speaks again, quieter. *Okay,* she says. *I guess I'm pleased not to meet you, then.*

Stanley closes his eyes, smiles. His lips feel numb and rubbery, like he's drunk. He presses his nose to the crack between the door and the jamb. Sweetheart, he hisses, I couldn't even tell you that I'm pleased.

He grabs the doorknob, hoists himself to his feet. The room disappears. He sees red, then white, then wild explosions of color, then black, and he grips the knob and grits his teeth and doesn't move and waits for the vertigo to pass.

Eventually it does. The first thing that comes into focus is *The Mirror Thief.* It sits on an eye-level shelf an inch from his nose, as if Welles set it down while unlocking the door and forgot about it. Stanley puts out a hand to touch it, then stops.

It's identical, of course, to the beat-up book that he's toted around the county. But this copy looks like it's never been touched, or hardly touched. Its pages are flat and compact, its flaps uncreased, the silvered letters of its cover unpitted. It could have been printed yesterday. This is his book, but it is also *not* his book — and the fact of its barely read existence seems to mean that the copy he found in Manhattan, the copy he's been carrying, isn't entirely his either. *Anybody* could pick this thing up. Stanley remembers what Welles said that first night — *three hundred copies, a hundred of those still sitting in my attic* — and he pictures that latent automaton army crated overhead. For the second time today he wants to burn this fucking house to the ground.

He rushes downstairs instead. In the john off the master bedroom he finds what he needs to remake himself: iodine, rubbing alcohol, fresh clean gauze. He rolls up the waterlogged cuff of his jeans, peels away the reeking bandage. The barbed-wire wound looks bad: slimy, edged with pus. He retches over the commode a couple of times as he cleans it, but nothing comes up, not even liquid. From the mirror above the sink a wasted stranger watches: blue lips, waxy skin, skull-sunk eyes. *This is the face of God you see.*

On the laminate countertop sits a pair of cheap ceramic mugs in the shapes of animal heads: a white cat, a black dog. Stanley fills the dog-head from the tap and drinks from it. Then he pukes in the sink. Then he fills it and drinks again. In a lower cabinet he finds a bristly wicker basket full of old medicine-bottles; some of them look like they might be sulfa drugs. He swallows a few, pockets the rest.

When he's done he stands in the entryway and listens to the hiss of cars along the wet pavement, the impatient pacing of the girl upstairs. He tries to think of what else he might need. There's probably some cash lying around — maybe some jewelry, too, or a nice watch — but at the moment he's pretty flush. He could take some canned goods from the pantry but they're probably not worth the extra weight. He turns in a slow circle, scanning the walls and the furnishings. Around him the house rises like a dead thing, an emptied-out shell repurposed by the girl: she occupies it like a hermit-crab.

He came too late. That's the goddamn problem. Maybe if he'd gotten here a few months ago, before she came, it would have made a difference. Probably not, though. Probably by the time he picked up *The Mirror Thief* in that Lower East Side dive the game was already over: Welles had already given up, lost his nerve. He'd swapped whatever led him to write the book for desires that were easier to keep straight in his head: a home, a wife, a family. He'd made peace with his own wild strangeness, found a way to tame it with magic circles and black curtains and barred doors. He no longer understands his own book. But Stanley understands it. To follow where it leads he'll have to go alone — at least as alone as Welles was when he wrote it. Maybe as alone as the girl is now. A day may come when that seems like a hardship, but at the moment Stanley couldn't care less.

Beside the front door is a coat-rack crowned by upcurved horns; hats hang from the horns. Among them is the tweed driver's cap that Welles wore the night Stanley first met him. Stanley takes it, puts it on his own head. It fits better than he expected.

He pulls on his wet jacket and takes up his father's fieldpack and leaves the house through the side door in the kitchen. He stands in the yard with mist slicking his bare neck and imagines the car pulling up: Welles and Synnøve on the walk, their dear boy Claudio between them, hand in a plaster cast, a grin splitting his battered handsome face. The three of them sweep to the porch, eager to get indoors, to free imprisoned Cynthia, to chant their spells and bare their bodies and commence their beautiful life together: the perfect family in a perfect world. Stanley pictures himself, too: creeping after them, toward the creaking bedsprings and the moans and the laughter, the black pistol heavy in his hand, and every whispering shoreline ghost gathered at his back.

He's fleetingly aware of who he is at this moment: distinct from people he used to be, people he'll one day become. In times past he would have torched this house with no second thought. Most of his future selves would do it, too; even now he understands that about himself. Years from tonight — in idle moments, half-asleep — he'll imagine the blaze he could have made, the ending he might have written. Picturing it as seen from the sea, or from a passing plane: the house a bright unsteady flare on the dark shoreline, throwing shadows in every direction. The girl the raw fuel hidden at its heart. Hell, he'll think, looking back on this moment. I could have showed you hell.

But not him. Not tonight. No such luck.

When after a few minutes the car hasn't appeared, Stanley adjusts the pack on his shoulder, unlatches the gate, and walks into the wet narrow street.

REDVCTIO

MAY 22, 1592

■ ■ ■ ■

Thus in the end we find all divine nature reduced to one source, even as all light reduces to that first self-lit brightness, and images in mirrors as numerous and varied as there are particular substances reduce to one ideal and formative principle, which is their source.

— GIORDANO BRUNO, from
The Expulsion of the Triumphant Beast

49

With a short laugh Crivano wakes himself, then sits open-eyed in the breath-warm darkness, trying to recall what in his dream so amused him.

It was quite late last night when he left the Morosini house. Still, he now he feels entirely restored, scornful of more slumber. He kicks his blankets aside, rises to stretch, withdraws the chamberpot from beneath the bed.

As he's pissing, he notes a dim indigo sliver of sky between the closed shutters and wonders at the hour. In his memory the Nolan's voice persists — odd, since Crivano granted the lecture but a modicum of attention. *In Cecco's commentary on Sacrobosco, we read of the demon Floron, who can be apprehended in a steel mirror by means of certain invocations.* So spoke the Nolan. Or did he? Could this still be the dream-voice of Crivano's imagination, limpeting fast to whatever daylit surface will hold it? He can't be sure.

Ten bells ring from San Aponal as he lights

the lamp, fills the basin, splashes his face and neck. In half an hour the sun will be up. He's to present himself at Ciotti's shop by the stroke of twelve: plenty of time for a stroll through the Rialto, an inspection of the new bridge. Last night his passage into sleep was hampered by anxieties over the day's strange events — Tristão's insistent introduction to Ciotti, and the unexpected emergence of the girl Perina before that — but this morning these concerns seem distant, as if stifled by some antic reassurance received in his dreams. Crivano feels vigorous and reckless, like a vessel running before the wind.

Among the wise Egyptians, the mirror evokes Hathor the Cow, she who rings the sky as the Milky Way, the Earth as the Nile. The comparable Greek figure, of course, is Amphitrite. The Nolan spoke last night for perhaps two-thirds of an hour. It seemed longer. Crivano might have followed more closely had he not been so unnerved by Tristão's conduct: his indiscreet mention of the silvered alembic, his suggestion of the mirror as the Nolan's topic. This, surely, is why Narkis directed him to associate with Tristão in the first place — the man's imprudent dabbling in secret knowledge is the thrashing shark that will feed the swift remora of their own conspiracy — but Crivano can't help but feel exposed, compromised, by such rash gestures. Last night Tristão retired from the chamber only minutes after giving the Nolan his subject: a whisper to Ciotti, and he was gone. While no doubt eccentric, it's unlike Tristão to be rude, even to a popinjay like the Nolan.

Hathor is the wife of Ra, who is the Sun. So too, as Isis, is she the wife of Osiris. So too, as Seshat, is she the wife of Thoth. Crivano hears a buzz of snores as he makes his way through the corridor. No other lodgers seem to be astir. In the parlor downstairs, a yawning Friulian girl in a nightshirt feeds the fireplace with split wood. Good day, young woman, Crivano says. Has Anzolo yet risen?

The girl turns, startled, then averts her eyes. Not yet, dottore, she says. Shall I fetch him?

He takes a moment to look her over: limp hair, wide hips, fourteen or fifteen years old. They always seem a bit frightened of him, these girls. Never charmed or smitten, as they are with Tristão. Stupid to be envious, of course. No need, Crivano says. Give him a message. Last night he helped me carry a small strongbox, which we locked away in a closet. I am going out now; I plan to return to the White Eagle by the fourteenth bell. At that time I will need a dependable and able-bodied gondolier to take me to Murano with that box. I trust that Anzolo will be able to make such arrangements.

I'm sure he will, dottore. I'll see that he gets your instructions.

Outside, the sky has ripened to a yellow-tinged blue. Shutters open, carpets drape sills, and the smell of leavened dough trails from the baskets of women on their way to the fornaio. Crivano idles under the White Eagle's sign to formulate his route to the Mercerie — closing his eyes to assemble the city's image in his head, imagining himself afloat above it — and as he sets off, the sun's first rays flare across the belltower of San Cassian.

Halfway along the Street of the Coopers a blue-flowered bunch of pennyroyal in an apothecary's window distracts him, and he misses the turn onto Swordsmen's Street. Not till he smells the fishmarket ahead does he realize his error, by which time he's disinclined to turn back. He can see bright air over the canal, a wall of light where the buildings fall away, and he continues toward it. Suspending his purpose for a moment. Luxuriating in the ravel of possibilities, the sensation of being neither lost nor certain.

The Babylonians speak of Hathor as Ishtar. The Hebrews call her Astarte. The Greeks also know her as Io, beloved of Zeus, guarded by a giant with one hundred eyes who is, of course, slain by Hermes. Crivano steps over puddled seawater and piles of offal, moving among the fishmongers' stalls to see what the ocean has divulged. Much is familiar from his visits to the Balık Pazarı during his years at court, but much is also new, or forgotten. Gangly spidercrabs. Coral-hued langoustines. Frogmouthed monkfish. Razor clams in neat rows, like the spines of books. A tangle of octopodes, their purple arms pocked with white suckers. Mullet and seabream stiffening in the warm air, their eyes gone foggy, like inferior glass. Behind the booths the water is a weave of pulsing lozenges, borrowing blue from the sky, orange from the palaces along the Grand Canal. A bragozzo moored at the white limestone quay is emptying its hold, spilling out sardines in a slick mirrored torrent.

Crivano passes by the moneychangers and bankers at their benches under the colonnades, then proceeds south through the Rialto, pausing to examine red chicory from Treviso, wheels of cheese from Asiago, sheaves of asparagus from Bassano del Grappa. He finds bright-skinned lemons and bitter oranges from the Terrafirma, including the fragrant teardrop fruit from Bergamo, but the handful of sweet citrus available is absurdly expensive, and he asks a vendor why this is so. Uskoks, the man says with a shrug.

The pungent hemp and pitch in the Ropemakers' Square are pleasing to his nose, but Crivano has no interest in this merchandise. He turns down the narrow Street of the Insurers, passes through a sottoportego into the Campo San Giacometto, and emerges near the Proclamation Column, surprised to find himself in the spot where twenty years ago he and the Lark heard the news that Nicosia, city of their birth, had fallen. They'd been crossing the square to the Pisani bank to redeem more of his father's letters of advice: two doe-eyed street wanderers, eager to be corrupted. Those boys seem entirely strange to him now: anxious, smooth-cheeked, full of foolish notions. They stood open-mouthed, their hearts striking the anvils of their ribs, as they struggled to parse the dialect of the comandador atop the porphyry column. In the general uproar they made their way south to the Molo and stood weeping and howling with rage under the arcades of the Doge's Palace as the clerk copied their names — *Gabriel Glissenti, Vettor Crivano* — into the register of the *Gold and Black Eagle* of Corfu. Ravenous as only the young and privileged can be for their own annihilation. It was a clear day in September; they'd been planning a visit to a bookshop. That much, at least, has not changed.

The Rialto too seems much the same. Crivano crosses the pavement to read the notices posted around the hunchbacked statue at the column's base. *When trading with Dalmatia, captains of state-auctioned galleys must henceforth make port at Spalato. The Serene Republic encourages the Hapsburgs*

*and the Sultan to resolve without warfare their
ongoing dispute in Croatia. Uskok pirates have
intercepted three merchant vessels of late,
murdering the crews and eating the hearts of
their captains, as is their custom.*

Not till Crivano turns to check the clock
on the façade of San Giacometto does he
glimpse the new stone bridge. Its stepped
incline rises from the Street of the Goldsmiths
and arcs across the Grand Canal in a single
broad span, fed from the Treasury and the
Riva del Vin by a pair of steeper staircases. A
moment ago Crivano had forgotten it; now
he hurries toward it as if expecting it to dis-
solve into air.

When he and the Lark first came to the city
they often heard discussion of the need for
such a bridge — a permanent link between
the Rialto and the Piazza befitting a great
Christian power — but they gathered that
such debates had been ongoing for fifty years
or more, and it seemed that plagues, fires,
war, and the opposition of foot-dragging
reactionaries on the Great Council would
delay its construction forever. Now, here it is.
Ascending along the south balustrade,
Crivano surveys burci and trabacoli unloading their cargo below: iron and coal on the
left bank, wine-casks on the right. He stands
in the apex of the pavilion and looks down at
the Grand Canal, watching its dark surface

play tricks with the rising sun. When the breeze shifts, he can make out the sharp tang of fresh-cut limestone through the water's briny stench.

On his way down, he moves into the double row of shops in the broad central passage to browse the offerings of jewelers and gold-smiths. Toward the bottom he finds a glass vendor displaying beads made in imitation of fine pearls — better than perfect, in gorgeous and improbable colors — and as he looks up from them he's startled to meet his own gaze in a flat mirror hung on the side wall. It's a rectangular Del Gallo glass of very high quality, only a few inches long, set in a swirling calcedonio frame; Crivano would swear it to be a window were his own face not watching from the midst of it. He recoils, looks again. His lined skin, his jagged teeth, his jackal eyes. Reminded once more of who and what he is.

He locates Ciotti's shop near the Campo San Salvator: the small wooden sign that announces it as MINERVA appears and disappears behind billowing red silks displayed by the mercer next door. Ciotti himself stands in the entrance, consulting in easy German with a man whom Crivano takes to be his printer. When Crivano approaches, Ciotti claps him on the shoulder and waves him inside with a broad smile.

A fine-boned boy of about thirteen stands

in the front room; he greets Crivano warily. Behind him, over a low partition, two bespectacled proofreaders sit at a table by a widow, bent over a stack of unbound pages. One reads aloud almost inaudibly as the other checks the text. Both move their lips; Crivano can't tell which one speaks.

He peruses the octavos displayed in the front room as he waits. Fifty or so titles stacked on two narrow tables: histories and biographies and volumes of verse. Most are printed in vulgar tongues, mostly local and Tuscan; a sizable minority are in Latin. The books in the tallest stack — an anthology of missionary correspondence from China and Japan — bear the shop's own imprint. At the edge of the far table, Crivano finds two books by the Nolan. One is the octavo that Tristão showed him over supper at the White Eagle; the other is a philosophical dialogue written in Tuscan, in the style of Lucian. Its front matter states that it was published here in the city, and this amuses Crivano: it was obviously bound by an English printer, perhaps jealous of the Aldine pedigree. He wonders if this deception was made at the Nolan's request.

As Ciotti steps through the door, Crivano leans down to feign a close examination of the stacked books. I was just admiring the craftsmanship of this table, he says. It supports both these Jesuit letters and the works of the Nolan without tipping discernibly in the direction of either.

Ciotti laughs. I appreciate your attentiveness, he says. It is not always easy to strike such a balance. Especially in this neighborhood, where the very ground beneath our feet fairly often seems to shift.

Crivano rises to exchange bows and clasp hands with the Sienese. Were it not for the thick-lensed spectacles hanging by a chain around his neck, Ciotti might be mistaken for a prosperous artisan: a baker, perhaps, or a carpenter.

I was surprised to see your own device on the frontispiece of the Jesuit anthology, Crivano says. Your friend Lord Mocenigo must be quite pleased with that undertaking.

The bookseller's smile cools into a perspicacious smirk. Judge not, my friend, he says. I'm sure you'll agree that as narrators of voyages, the foot-soldiers of the Pope are unsurpassed. My favored customers are always eager to learn of the customs of distant lands. Of course, all of our Republic's citizens are interested to read news of Spanish activity at the far corners of the earth. And, naturally, those among us who hold with the Curia in matters temporal and spiritual are delighted to find printed accounts of the Society of Jesus available at this emporium. Yet you will note, Dottore Crivano — as I myself note with displeasure each time I open or close my shop's shutters — that this stack remains quite tall, even as those around it diminish. Would you care to join me in my workroom? Dottore de Nis's friend should be with us shortly.

Ciotti leads Crivano to a small cluttered office near the back of the shop, then closes the heavy door behind them. Crivano takes a seat beside a table awash in loose charts and unbound proofs; Ciotti sits opposite. The brick walls are laddered with oak bookshelves, each stacked to the base of the next.

I just crossed the stone bridge, Crivano says. Quite impressive.

Ciotti seems pleased and proud, as if he built it himself. Yes, he says. It was completed quite recently.

A single span, Crivano says. Surprising. Not very classical.

Ciotti shoots him a pointed glance. Not very Roman, I believe you mean, he says.

Who was the architect?

Antonio da Ponte. Aptly named.

Crivano shakes his head. I don't know of him, he says.

He's an engineer. Formerly head of the Magistracy of Salt. Not until now known as a builder. That grandiloquent fool Marcantonio Barbaro did all within his power to bestow the project on Vincenzo Scamozzi, but the grace of God spared us another of that peacock's theoretical demonstrations.

709

He's done enough harm in the Piazza as it is. Signore da Ponte was barely able to persuade the Senate to prevent him from adding a third floor to the Library. Can you imagine? The Lords Morosini showed me some of Scamozzi's sketches for the Rialto project. Disgusting. Relentlessly geometrical. Absurd ornamentation. I ask you, is a bridge a temple? No. It is a bridge.

Crivano smiles. I met Lord Barbaro just yesterday afternoon, he says, at a banquet in the house of Giacomo Contarini. He seemed eager to convey to us that the glassmakers of Murano have compromised the Republic's future by concentrating their efforts on the manufacture of mirrors, instead of lenses, as the Florentines do.

Yes. That's a favorite subject of his.

After dinner, his argument was dissolved by a famed Neapolitan scholar who inadvertently demonstrated that lenses can produce spectacles to match or exceed in frivolity any yet conjured by silvery glass.

Well, I can only pray that our mirror-mad friend Tristão de Nis was present to see that demonstration, Ciotti says, and narrows his eyes appraisingly. If I may ask, he says, what did you make of the Nolan's performance last night?

Crivano shrugs. If his intent was to demonstrate his prodigious memory, he says, then I suppose he succeeded. If he sought to impart some definitive judgment on the subject at hand, then I confess I came away unenlightened.

Ciotti leans back in his chair; his right hand comes to rest atop a shallow wooden tray on the table beside him. It is a rare rhetorical gift, he says, that permits a man to speak knowledgeably about a topic and still deliver his audience into a state of enriched confusion. At times I think this skill chiefly defines the profession of magus. The Nolan has it, I think you'll agree. That said, I cannot dismiss him as a charlatan.

From what Tristão had told me of the fellow, Crivano says, I expected either a trickster or a madman. As if these categories must be exclusive.

Ciotti nods; the wooden tray clicks beneath his fingers. It's divided by slats into square compartments, and each compartment is filled with short slender pieces of dull metal. Their sound recalls the rattle of bone dice in a cup. Tracking Crivano's gaze, Ciotti scoops a few metal bits from the tray and offers them with a pinched, beaklike hand. Here, he says. Have you seen these before?

Crivano takes them. They slide on the ridges of his creased and calloused palm. Each is cuboid, smaller than a newborn's finger, cast from a lead alloy. Each has a Greek letter — Λ Η Θ Η — in low relief on one of its smallest ends. Movable type,

Crivano says. I saw a printing press once in Bologna. But I've never seen loose pieces like these.

We call these *sorts,* Ciotti says. They're bound together into a *forme,* from which a page is printed. That work is not done here. I pay a printer to do it, and he generally casts his own type. He's discreet and reliable, but he lacks facility in Greek. I recently took a commission to print the *Enneads* of Plotinus, so for that I had to have my own type made. When I first began, all I ever used was the Latin alphabet. But after the Brucioli had such success with their Hebrew books, such trade became difficult to ignore. Some of my guildsmen — I refrain from naming them — have even secured the privilege to print in Arabic, and now turn profits by selling Muhammadan holy books to the Turks.

A hopeful gleam appears in Ciotti's eye — an invitation, perhaps — and Crivano suppresses a wince. He saw Frankish Qurans from time to time in Constantinople: inert, graceless, full of shocking errors. Their shoddiness didn't scandalize the muftis so much as the very fact of their existence: the idea of God's final message propagated not by the living breath of the Prophet and his companions, nor by the motions of a calligrapher's hand, but by the uncanny iteration of soulless machinery. Crivano opts not to explain this to Ciotti. He stretches forward, dumps

712

the sorts back into the Sienese's cupped palm.

Ciotti looks at them himself, prodding them with his forefinger, like a farmer evaluating a handful of seed. I thought of these last night, he says. Something the Nolan said reminded me. He spoke of the world shown by the mirror, and how it differs from this world. How did he put it, exactly? Do you recall?

Crivano does not. He's opening his mouth to reply when a soft knock comes at the door. Ciotti rises to pull it open, and the pale boy's face appears in the gap. A Turk is here to see you, maestro, the boy says.

Very good. Please show Messer bin Silen in.

Sweat beads in Crivano's armpits when Ciotti pronounces the name, his heartbeat quickens, but his face remains placid, his posture relaxed. He's wary, but not afraid. Some part of him has expected this.

Ciotti isn't looking at him anyway. He's pushed the door shut, and now stands facing it, his nose a palms'-breadth from its knobby wood. The metal sorts are still trapped in his left fist; he shakes them absently. Their soft chime fills the room like the sound of a distant riqq, muffled by palace walls.

The man who originated this way of printing, Ciotti says, was a mirrormaker first. Or so the story goes. Did you know that? This was many years ago. He was a German

713

goldsmith, and he made small mirrors for pilgrims visiting the chapel at Aachen. It was thought by simple folk that these mirrors could catch and contain the invisible blessings that emanated from the relics there. By the standards of Murano they were unimpressive, I'm sure. Made of lead and tin. Similar to my sorts, in fact, in their composition. But they were flat, and therefore whatever images they caught would have been reversed. I like to imagine that this is what gave the German goldsmith the idea for typesetting: tiny backward letters, lined up in rows. The mirror-image of the page-to-be. The reflection never shows the world as it is, as the Nolan told us. But it does show us things about the world. In this way, too, perhaps it is not unlike a book.

A second knock at the door. Ciotti tugs the wrought-iron handle. Messer bin Silen, he says. Thank you for the loan of your expertise. I am Giovanni Battista Ciotti. Welcome to my modest enterprise.

50

Entering the room, Narkis seems stiff and weightless, propelled by a force outside himself, like a straw man at a fair. He's wearing blue trousers and an embroidered caftan the color of boiled quince. Even in his turban he's barely taller than the boy who escorts him. His large eyes are focused on a point on the floor about six feet ahead: the signature attitude of an expatriate Turk in an unfriendly city. He speaks softly in his bestial croak. Good day to you, Messer Ciotti, he says. I thank you for your hospitality.

Ciotti maintains his warm smile, but he seems uncomfortable, anxious to take his leave. He keeps glancing toward the shop's front room to see who might be there, might have seen Narkis come in. Concerned, no doubt, about appearances.

Allow me to introduce Vettor Crivano, he says, who is to be your collaborator on this morning's errand. Dottore Crivano is from Cyprus, and lived for a number of years among your people. Dottore Crivano, this is Narkis bin Silen, who joins us today from the Turkish fondaco.

Crivano and Narkis exchange stiff bows.

My eminent friends, Ciotti says, I have no wish to detain you today longer than is necessary. My request is simple. A young gentleman of my acquaintance has recruited me to publish — in limited circulation — a Latin rendering of a brief practical work by the Muhammadan alchemist Geber. The work has come into this gentleman's possession in its original Arab script, and I have retained a scholar from Padua to execute a translation. My concerns, and those of my patron, center on the accuracy of this translation. I gather

715

that our scholar is a very learned man, but also a bit of a poet, and somewhat given to ornament at the expense of clarity. You both have the advantage of knowing the great Geber's original tongue, and you share an understanding of the practical considerations of a working alchemist. I ask merely that you examine the Latin against the original and evaluate its suitability with these concerns in mind. I can compensate you in coin, or in merchandise. Although, he smiles, I strongly encourage you to take the merchandise.

Ciotti chases the two proofreaders from the shop, sending them off with fistfuls of copper gazettes to a casino on the opposite side of the block, then lays the manuscripts on the thick table. The sun is high enough that it misses the window, but it bounces from the fresh-plastered wall across the alley, giving them plenty of light to work.

Ciotti returns to his office, but leaves his door open. Crivano searches Narkis's face for a sign of how to proceed, but the look he gets back is so bereft of recognition that he wonders for a moment, against all reason, whether this can be Narkis at all, and not some never-suspected identical twin. The little Macedonian seems to assess him with an equal measure of curiosity and revulsion, as one might inspect a strange songbird found dead beneath a newly glazed palace window.

They seat themselves. With a flicker of his eyes, Narkis indicates that Crivano should take the original document. Crivano settles in his chair and begins to read from it aloud. It's a brief text; he reads slowly. Narkis moves an inkwell within his reach and stares down at the Latin translation with steady half-lidded eyes.

The text is a treatise on the transmutation of metals, fairly unremarkable in its content had it not been written by the great Abu Musa Jabir Ibn Hayyan, known to the Franks as Geber. As Ciotti no doubt knows, it's almost certainly a fake — a latter-day imitator or, worse, a translation into Arabic of an original Latin forgery. But this is not the issue Ciotti has asked them to address.

Crivano steals a glance at Narkis from time to time as he reads. Their encounter in the apothecary's shop was fleeting by design; this is the first close look Crivano has managed since their appointment months ago in Ravenna. Narkis's face is smooth, unfurrowed, almost a child's face, fairer than Crivano's and Ciotti's both. Even here he retains his stork-like sense of enclosed calm. The hand which travels to and from the inkwell has a black bird emblazoned on its skin, the emblem of his orta, and Crivano considers how different his own fate would have been had Fortune seen him marked thusly, rather than on his chest and his leg, under his clothes.

For half an hour they work through the text. Narkis sometimes interrupts with a question, sometimes makes a notation in his margins. The tension is almost unbearable. Crivano begins to wonder if Narkis is waiting for some signal from him, but can't imagine what that might be. He becomes sloppy in his recitation, repeating some lines while skipping others, and Narkis gently corrects him.

Then, without looking up, Narkis makes a swift gesture with his right hand and touches his fingers to his lips. This is işaret, the language of deaf-mutes, known by all who have served in the sultan's silent inner court. Crivano never managed to learn it well; much of what he once knew he's forgotten. But he understands well enough now. *Speak,* Narkis says. *Tell me.*

Take any portion of the stone with its mixture, Crivano reads, *and grind it with copperas and sal ammoniac and water until it becomes black.* The glassmaker and the mirrormaker are both committed, and are ready to depart upon a few hours' notice. We await your instructions. *Then subject it to very slight heat until it takes on the odor of a man's ejaculate.*

Crivano keeps his voice flat, his inflection uniform. His stomach tightens as he makes his report, though he knows no one within earshot but Narkis can understand his Arabic

718

words; they hear only his ongoing recitation.

Narkis's hands speak again: *What of the dead man?*

He's in the lagoon. No one will find him. I have heard of no disturbance related to his vanishing. *When it has that smell, remove it and wash it gently with pure water, then roast it with low heat until you perceive a visible vapor.*

Narkis nods. Then he speaks aloud, also in Arabic. The glassmaker's refusal to leave Murano without his wife and sons is very bad, he says. The risk is unreasonable. Can he be dissuaded? Can you convince him that they will be delivered to him in time?

This was the principal demand in Serena's hidden message, the chief feature of Crivano's encoded report. He'd hoped that it wouldn't present any great difficulty — once Narkis has arranged an escape for three men, what trouble is the addition of two boys and a woman? — but evidently his hope was misplaced. The glassmaker is no fool, Crivano says. We have to do what he asks. Don't worry about the family. I'll find a way to include them without compromising our project. *In this fashion the water will be driven off, and the weight of the stone will be reduced, yet without the loss of its essence.*

I have found a ship, Narkis says. It departs from Spalato in three weeks' time.

It's now Crivano's turn to be vexed. From

Spalato? he says. Why not from here? *Remove it and submerge it again in water, and make a powder of it under water, and roast it again as before. Its blackness now diminishes.*

Too dangerous, Narkis says with his hands. *The journey must begin by road.*

He's worried about the uskoks, Crivano realizes. *Take off the dry stone when the water has been absorbed,* he says. This is certain to create difficulties. The craftsmen still believe they're being taken to Amsterdam, not Constantinople. The mirrormaker in particular is very desperate, and will not be easy to control. I fear he'll try to escape to the Netherlands on his own if he reaches the mainland. *Grind it in pure water and roast it again. It becomes green, and the blackness vanishes.*

Persuade him to cooperate, Narkis's hands say. Then his voice. I will take my payment today in coin, he says. You will take yours in books. I will hide the information you need inside the Latin *Kitab-al-Manazir* on our host's front table. The second book in the stack. You and the craftsmen must be prepared to embark at Cannaregio for the mainland in three days.

Narkis looks up from the manuscript to meet Crivano's eyes. He holds them for a moment, then looks down, and does not speak again.

Within the hour the text is finished. The two of them browse the books in the front room in silence as Ciotti fetches Narkis's payment from his strongbox: a small stack of soldi. Crivano presents Ciotti with his selections — a new translation of Galen, one of the Nolan's works, the *Kitab-al-Manazir* — and by the time Ciotti has deducted them from his inventory, Narkis has gone.

The midmorning light casts strange shadows down the Mercerie as the textiles billow in the late-spring breeze. Underfoot are traces of last night's revels: spilled wine, soiled ribbon, fragments of eggshell. Looking south toward the Piazza, Crivano thinks he can make out Narkis's turban, slipping in and out of sight like a moon among clouds, but he can't be sure. A couple of laborers from a coal ship pass by, laughing boisterously, their eyes clamshell-white in their blackened faces. A group of bravi loiters at the corner of a sidestreet, watching the workmen, watching Crivano too. One of the ruffians, probably late of the wars in France, has a face so mutilated it hardly can be called a face: a slash of a mouth and one glaring eye emerge from a welter of scars. Crivano shudders, walks the other way.

This Spalato development is no good. He'll need to find Obizzo soon, give him the news, but first he'll have to settle on the best way to tell the story. He can't imagine how he'll keep Obizzo contained once they're on the mainland. He knows very little about the man. Four years ago Obizzo was sentenced to the galleys for assisting his elder brother's flight from Murano; he's been hiding ever since. His brother now runs a prosperous glassworks in Amsterdam, a city for which Obizzo expects to be bound soon himself. In this belief, of course, he is mistaken. Crivano knows these things, and also that Obizzo is willing to murder. He and Obizzo know that about one another now.

He leaves the Mercerie, continuing down a wide straight thoroughfare toward the Grand Canal, where the crowds move more quickly. He's eager to return to the White Eagle, where he hopes to have time enough to open his new books — to place the wooden grille over the coded message, to see what Narkis has planned for him — before he has to depart for Murano. But then, on the Riva del Ferro, he stops.

The bridge again. With most of the boats now loaded and unloaded and sailing for the Terrafirma, it's unobstructed, clearly visible from the quay. Colors reflected from the surrounding façades turn its white limestone surfaces slightly golden, like the seared flesh of a scallop, and snakes of light play along the underside of its grand arch. Crivano imagines what might have been built instead — the mock-Roman temples that Ciotti described — and smiles. The new bridge is breathtaking in its practicality, so well-matched to the hidden rhythms and textures of the Rialto that it almost vanishes.

In the city that can build this, he thinks, great deeds are surely possible.

51

Despite, or because of, their obvious drunkenness, the two gondoliers Anzolo has found are resolute and quick: they slide a beechwood oar through the iron rings of Tristão's strongbox and lift it aboard their batela as if it's a stag they've poached. Then they seat Crivano on a bench with the box between his boots and row hard toward the Cannaregio Canal, trading verses of a strange barcarolle about a doomed lady who weaves an enchanted web. Soon they've passed beneath the Bridge of Spires — another new construction, another single span — and through the muddy encrusted layers of the city's newer neighborhoods to meet the open waters of the lagoon. The bow swings north, then east. Crivano breathes through his sudarium and crouches over the strongbox, his stomach clenching each time the keel tilts on an errant wave.

A flat crack comes across the water, and a white cloud rises from a sandolo off the bow: a pair of hunters shooting diving ducks. A second plume appears in the farther distance, at the marshy edge of San Cristofero della Pace, and the sound of the shot arrives a heartbeat later. Off starboard a crew of shouting laborers is clustered around a barge, now stranded by low tide; they're driving piles in the muck, turning shallow water into solid earth, extending the city outward.

The batela angles north again, aimed at the mouth of the Glassmakers' Canal, a smudge of furnace smoke on the vacant sky. Crivano can make out a green shadow at the island's edge: the stand of holly-oaks where he crushed Verzelin's throat. He wonders in passing whether the mirrormaker's absence has been widely noted or commented upon, but this speculation fails to hold his interest, and he turns his eyes toward the city again. The boatmen's oars slash the water, the pale willows of the nearby islands slide across the unearthly obelisk of San Francesco della Vigna, and Crivano feels a rush of astonishment, a sudden recollection of what it was like to see the city for the first time. Two days ago on the Molo it eluded him: clear in his mind but lifeless, a picture of itself. He's able to reach it now only by way of a memory from years later: he was traveling the King's Highway in the caravan of an adventurous young vizier, and they made a detour to al-Bitrā, the ruined capital of the Nabataeans, south of the Dead Sea. As he walked among the empty temples, rosy monoliths carved into the canyon walls, he could think of nothing but the moment when he and the Lark first glimpsed the Basilica's domes: built on nothing solid, every constituent substance estranged from its origin. The impossible city of their ancestors, precipitated from the mist.

The gondoliers moor their boat in a vacant berth next to another batela, this one riding quite low, filled to the gunwales with split alder. The fragrant fresh-cut wood is a garish orange in the sun. As the boatmen lash their lines to a palina and ready an oar to lift the strongbox, Crivano springs to the quay and enters a door bearing the device of the siren — a stained-glass chimera with shapely bare breasts and the claws of a raptor — hung in a frame of dark wood. The shop's shelves are crowded with the output of the attached factory: great crystal pitchers in the shapes of sailing ships, wide shallow goblets for red wine, carafes so thin and so clear as to be visible only by their filigree, interspersed with urns and plates and dishes of calcedonio glass in odd and startling hues. The shopgirl behind the counter listens meekly to a plump woman in an elegant saffron zimarra; as Crivano enters, they both turn and curtsy. The older woman's eyes flash when she notes his black physician's robes; her mouth tightens. Serena's wife. She knows who he is, why he's here. Good day, Crivano says. I'm looking for Maestro Serena.

As he speaks, the thin goblets along the walls shiver with the sound of his voice; their high chime gilds its roughness, rings into the stillness that follows. The woman's reply is a low murmur to which the glass does not react. Yes, dottore, she says. You will find four men here who answer to that name.

Crivano smiles. This is good: the woman knows who he's looking for, but she's clever enough not to give that fact away. She'll be no trouble in the escape: an asset, even. Narkis has nothing to fear. My business is with Boetio Serena, Crivano says. I have payment for him, and I would like to collect an item that he has crafted for me.

Mona Serena turns to the girl. Show the dottore to the workroom, she says.

The girl leads him through a side door, down a hallway, and then asks him to wait. She tugs open a thick portal banded with iron — heat billows through the gap, along with the smell of scorched air — and vanishes to the other side. In a moment she returns with young Alexandro in tow, the boy whom Crivano met at the Salamander. Ash dusts Alexandro's face and hair, paints the edge of his jaw where sweat has smeared it. He wipes his hands on a linen rag with the air of a man eager to get back to his business. Dottore Crivano, he says with a bow. Your visit honors us.

Crivano returns the greeting. Young maestro, he says, I need to have a word with your father.

He's mixing the batch now, but he'll be done soon. I can show you to our parlor if you'd like to wait there. Or may I address your concern?

The look on the boy's face makes it evident that his question is no question: his purview extends to all that occurs here. Crivano assesses his cool eyes and easy bearing — so like the Lark's — and realizes that this is why Serena chose to join Crivano's conspiracy, to remove his family from Murano. The glassmaker, he recalls, has two elder brothers; those brothers have many sons of their own. Alexandro practices his family trade not only as if he's studied it diligently, which no doubt he has, but as if he has an inborn genius for it. Yet he will not run this shop in his lifetime.

On the pavement outside, Crivano says, are two gondoliers. You will find them in song, I imagine, asway with drink, and bearing between them a strongbox heavy with coin. This is payment for a piece your shop has made. Collect it from them with my thanks — but do not trouble yourself to fetch the item I've purchased. I'll wait for your father. I have an unrelated matter to discuss with him.

As you wish, dottore. I'll show you to the parlor.

Is there a chance, Crivano says, that I might linger in your workroom instead? I'm curious to witness the exercise of your craft. Or would my presence compromise confidential procedures?

Alexandro considers this, then smiles. It would, he says, if you are able to scry the insides of our skulls, to see the secrets hidden there. Otherwise there is no danger. I'll grant you access, but keep well clear of the furnaces and the hot glass. Unless you're prepared to spend your physic on yourself, dottore.

A nervous grin: for an instant, the boy seems his true age. But this passes, and he leads Crivano through the heavy door.

Crivano wonders whether he shouldn't have waited in the parlor after all: the air stings his eyes and nose, all but cancels the aroma of his sudarium. The space before him swarms with frenzied scrambling men, silhouetted by the hard coppery light cast by two furnaces that blaze at the workroom's far end like the infernal tombs of arch-heretics. Alexandro aims him toward a stack of crates in the corner, directs him to take a seat. My father will be with you shortly, he says.

Serena himself works nearby, ladling water into a tub of white batter as a laborer stirs it. Behind them another workman shapes paste from a second tub into small white cakes, sets these cakes to dry on a rack near the smaller furnace. Now Serena laughs; he

728

musses the stirrer's filthy hair and crosses the factory floor, past rag-draped wooden trays where fused lumps of frit are cooling, to meet the sweat-drenched drudge who breaks the snowy frit with an iron maul. Serena stops him for a moment, bends to pick up a shard, studies it, drops it again. Then he moves to the larger furnace, checking the work of the man who loads the broken frit into crucibles, the man who stirs and skims the molten glass, the man who pours the melt into steaming pans of clean water. Here again Serena stoops, fishes a blob of cool glass from a pan, and holds it to the light that pours through the furnace's glory-holes.

Crivano makes a quick count of the laborers and arrives at ten: young men, a few boys, mixing the batch, working the glass and the frit, feeding the furnaces, splitting wood. And these are only preparatory gestures: no one has yet begun to work the glass into finished shapes. This task, he guesses, will fall to Serena's older brothers and their favored sons; in Constantinople it will be Obizzo's charge. But who will keep the furnaces burning steadily, and how will he know what temperature is right? Who will choose the wood to fire them, the stones to build them, the clay to seal them? The man who skims the crucibles in the long furnace is using a metal scoop with a long handle; Crivano has never seen the likes of it for sale in any tinsmith's

729

shop. Will such tools have to be made? Who will know how to make them? Has the haseki sultan any notion of what will be required for production to begin?

Serena's insistence on bringing his family looks less and less like selfishness or sentiment, more and more like the wise recognition of necessity. No doubt the glassmaker has already considered how he'll find his materials once he's relocated to Amsterdam — but he isn't going to Amsterdam. Has Narkis considered this? If Serena isn't able to begin work quickly he'll grow frustrated, restive, tempted to a second betrayal, one that the Spanish and Genoese spies in Galata will be eager to assist. And Obizzo! Obizzo will become a rampaging beast.

Narkis needs to address this: these issues of tools, facilities, raw materials. Spiriting the craftsmen out of the Republic's hands will be wasted if their skills can't be put to use. What preparations are being made for Serena's and Obizzo's arrival? Does Narkis know anything about making glass, really? What should Crivano tell him?

He begins a clumsy impromptu survey of the crates and sacks he sits among. Some of the containers are open, half-full; most contain a glittering powder with the texture of coarse flour. Crivano takes this for crushed quartz: extraordinarily pure, more uniform even than the whitest beach-sands of Egypt.

Sacks of magnesia alba, too, and various salts, none in great quantity. More white powder, even finer than the quartz. Some sort of flux, probably. He wets a fingertip in his mouth — the dry air drinking the moisture from the whorls of skin — and dredges it through the powder to taste it. Cool and sharp and bitter. Slick on his tongue. He tastes it again.

I'll have my niece fetch you a sweet, dottore, if you're hungry.

Serena strolls up beside him, wiping his forehead with a cotton cloth. He still holds the lump of raw glass in his left hand, kneading it like a worry-stone. Crivano rises and returns Serena's bow. I was just examining your materials, maestro, he says. This is potash, I suppose?

Soda ash, Serena says. From the Levant. The guild buys it through a syndicate with the soapmakers and the majolica makers, who also use it. I'm told it's made from the ash of a plant that drinks saltwater like the freshest rain, that can uproot itself and move about on the wind to spread its seed, although whether this is true I cannot say.

It's true enough: Crivano remembers seeing wagons laden with the dry round shrubs along the Syrian coast, and more blowing free along the roadsides. In Tripoli he saw laborers burning it, packing it for shipment to the West — al-qaly, it was called. What of the crushed quartz? he asks. Where does that come from?

The riverbeds of the Ticino and the Adige. The magnesia is from Piedmont. There are other sources, of course, but these —

Alexandro's angry voice cuts through the shop: he's just returned from leading Crivano's gondoliers to the storeroom, and now stops to berate the man who rakes the contents of the smaller furnace. The workman had become inattentive, probably watching Serena with Crivano; now he blanches, refocuses his attention.

Serena grins. We calcine the batch in the small furnace for five hours, he says. It must be raked all the time, so it will heat uniformly, and fuse into frit without melting. If it melts it becomes worthless. It can even destroy the furnace. Every man you see here, dottore, has the capacity to ruin us all at any moment. This is why you often find glassmakers with black eyes, bloody knuckles, absent teeth.

I fear I have become a spectacle in this room.

Serena's damaged right hand makes a dismissive gesture, but his expression is not so cavalier. Don't worry yourself, dottore, he says. All the same, perhaps you'll indulge me in a respite from the heat. Let us retire to my counting room, where I'll show you what your friend has purchased.

He leads Crivano to a side door bearing an impressive German lock, which opens with a heavy key. The room beyond is small, neat, lit from beside the desk by a window of modest size; Crivano is seated and leaning toward it for a breath of fresh air before he realizes that it's glazed. Uniform and colorless, the panes appear in the fog of his breath, then vanish again as he moves away.

On the floor behind the desk Serena casts open more bolts, these on a massive strongbox that looks as if the entire building must have been fashioned around it. After a moment he rises, lifts the lid, and reaches inside.

When he turns, the sun blazes out of his broad chest. Crivano lifts his hands to shield his eyes, then lowers them when the brightness fades, only to meet his own wincing face suspended between Serena's rag-bundled fingers.

Serena sets the mirror on the table. Crivano leans to inspect it, blocking the sight of himself with an open palm. Verzelin's glass is even larger and clearer than he remembered it, and Serena's artfully affixed frame hides little of its surface. The frame is crafted from three braided strands of chalcedony glass, perfectly symmetrical, with seven wire threads wound around them. The glass strands, cream-white and identical on their surfaces, flare like opals when caught by the sunlight, disclosing veiled interior colors: fiery red, near-black indigo, the variegated blue-green of a peacock's tail. The frame must be shaped around a hidden armature of some kind, because it also supports a series of medallions, each about the size of a gold sequin, that float along its outer edge. Crivano notes the designs struck on them — a naked archer, two fighting dogs, a man mounted on a lion, a woman being beaten — and he knows without counting that there are thirty-six. Serena is right to want this out of his shop.

Will this satisfy your friend's expectations, dottore?

Yes, Crivano says. I'm certain that it will.

Turning again, Serena closes the strongbox lid and begins assembling items on it: twine, thick paper, raw cotton, slats of wood, dry gray-green leaves. I am not a pious man, dottore, he says. As you have probably gathered. But now that this is done, I'm going to make a very sincere confession, and I'm going to give Saint Donatus a few of your friend's coins. With this item under my roof I have slept not well at all.

I hope for my sake, maestro, that you will keep your confession brief, vague, and tightly focused on the topic at hand.

Serena turns with a wink and a grin. And not mention my impending travels, you mean? he says. No, dottore, I'll confess those sins after I've committed them. I'm sure Amsterdam contains priests of some variety.

Crivano's expression must betray fear; Serena laughs as he whisks the mirror away and turns back to the strongbox. It's safe to speak in this room, dottore. No one will hear us over the workshop's racket. Now, tell me of your plans.

Crivano frowns at Serena's broad back. Well, he says, you might consider spending what coins you don't give to Saint Donatus on jewels for your esteemed wife. Diamonds, rubies, emeralds. Anything lighter than gold. Something that will travel.

She and my sons are guaranteed passage?

Of course.

When?

In three days, you and your family are to travel into the city and lodge for the night at a locanda called Cerberus. You'll find it on the Fondamenta de Cannaregio. I will come for you, and together we'll make a night-crossing to a trabacolo anchored in the lagoon. The trabacolo will take us to Trieste.

Trieste? Why Trieste?

We're going overland. To Spalato. We'll board a Dutch ship there.

I'm not sure I understand, dottore. As long as we're going overland, why not go to Trent? Why not go the right direction?

For the first time, Crivano detects a trace of anxiety in Serena's voice, and tension in his posture. Murano is a comfortable cage for him; he's probably never set foot on the mainland, may only have crossed the lagoon to the city a few dozen times in his life. He is not Obizzo. He has a great deal to lose.

Every inn, Crivano says, in every town we'd pass, on any road we'd choose, would contain informants for the Council of Ten. The Terrafirma is the Council's web, as strong and invisible as that of Vulcan, and those roads are its strands. If we touch them, they will know. The sbirri would have us before sundown.

We can't sail to Ragusa? Find a Dutch ship there?

Due to the uskoks, the only vessels safely able to sail the Dalmatian coast are galleys owned and armed by the Republic. Which, clearly, would not be safe for us.

Crivano hears the scrape and the stretch of rough twine, and Serena turns to lay the finished parcel on the table before him. The knots that bind the heavy paper are scarcely less artful than the mirror they enclose. I've packed it in seaweed, Serena says, to prevent damage from moisture. As I mentioned, I suggest that your friend make a habit of this also. Any good apothecary will stock it. Brandy, dottore?

Crivano nods. Serena withdraws a bluish wide-bellied carafe from a cabinet, along with two simple crystal cups of surpassing clarity and grace. He unstoppers the carafe and fills the glasses, then sits and raises his. To Trieste, then, I suppose, he says.

Trieste, Crivano repeats. Their cups meet

with a soft reverberant peal.

Crivano nearly chokes on his first sip: he can taste the volatilized liquor in the air above the glass. From Trieste, he says, clearing his throat, we'll proceed to Fiume, then to Karlstad, and then through the mountains to the coast of Dalmatia. We must be in Spalato before the Feast of Saint Anthony. Do you foresee any complications? Can your wife and boys travel such distances?

Serena sips, nods, sips again. He doesn't look at Crivano.

Crivano studies the cup in his hand, rotating it slowly in the sun. Is there any way, he asks, that your boys can be kept clear of the furnaces until our flight commences?

Probably. Why?

We have days of hard travel ahead of us. Some of it on disused thoroughfares. In my experience — I'm speaking now as a physician — young men with fresh burns do not easily suffer prolonged exposure to the elements.

In Serena's eyes is a flicker of something like anguish. Yes, he says. I see your concern.

He drains his cup and refills it, swilling the liquid inside. It coats the glass's edges like oil. Mirrors, he says. We'll be making mirrors, you say?

You'll make mirrors in the spring, Crivano says, and then whatever you like the rest of the year. Those are our terms.

I don't know how to silver mirrors. Or to flatten glass.

Yes. We know that.

Serena rolls the base of the carafe back and forth along the desktop. Drunkenness has begun to inhabit his eyes. So, he says, you must have someone else, as well.

That's correct. We do.

Dottore, Serena says, were you ever able to locate Verzelin the other night?

Crivano looks at Serena, but Serena still won't meet his gaze: he watches the rolling carafe with a sly half-smile. Crivano takes a sip of brandy before he replies. His pulse thuds patiently in his throat. Oh yes, he says. I found him.

I thought you might have, Serena says. No one on Murano has seen him since. When the men from the Motta mirrorworks came and asked me about him, I told them that you'd gone out looking for him.

The brandy is inching back up Crivano's throat.

I'm sure they'd already heard as much from the old woman at the Salamander, Serena continues. I also took the liberty of telling them that I met you in the Campo San Stefano later that night, and that you told me you never found him. I had a hunch that I should tell them that. I hope you don't mind, dottore.

Crivano lets out a long sigh that becomes a

nervous laugh, a giggle, at the end. He holds his cup out to Serena wordlessly, and the chime sounds again. They drink in silence for a while.

Say, dottore, Serena says, what do you make of this?

He passes Crivano the carafe. It's well-made, if uninspired. The glass could be clearer, whiter. Still a better piece than anything he ever saw in the sultan's palace. He shrugs approval, passes it back.

I made it when I was twelve, Serena says. My first carafe. That's a glassmaker's daily bread, carafes. This one wasn't good enough to qualify me as a journeyman. But I was still young then.

Crivano nods, drains the last of his brandy. He examines his cup again in the light from the window. Tipping it. Holding it close to his face.

Can you see it? Serena asks.

He looks again. There, in the base: a tiny line of bubbles, smaller than an eyelash. The bubbles themselves visible only as a group. This blemish, you mean? Crivano says. This is why it's not for sale?

Of course. You think I'd sell a piece with such an obvious flaw? Still, the shape of these was pleasing to me. And I needed a pair of cups.

Crivano sets the glass down. Serena fills it again. Crivano's cheeks are warm, like he's been near a very hot fire. Which, in fact, he has. You make very beautiful things, maestro, he says.

Serena gives him a strange look as he stoppers the carafe, sets it aside. No, dottore, he says. I do not. I make this.

His hand plucks something from the desktop and tosses it to Crivano; Crivano's caught it almost before he realizes it's been thrown. It's the lump of raw glass Serena took from the cooling pan in the workshop: smooth, oblong, flatter on one side, a pointed lobe opposite, pitted here and there by delicate bubbles. It's greenish and frosted, but it lets light through. Its shape recalls something; Crivano can't say what.

Other men in this shop make beautiful things, Serena says. One day, when they are older, perhaps my boys will do so as well. But me? I make this.

He leans forward and takes the raw glass from Crivano's hand, then sits back in his chair. The blob sits in his right palm like a wet frog, sheltered under the branches of his three scarred tipless fingers.

I make it so it melts evenly, he says. So it can be worked. I make it strong and pliable. I make it clear, when clarity is called for. When mystery is desired, I make it play games with the light. I hope very much that others are able to make it beautiful, dottore. But that is their responsibility. It is not mine.

52

As the traghetto draws near San Cristofero della Pace, disturbing a group of avocets and black-winged stilts in the shallows, Crivano vomits most of Serena's liquor over the gunwale and begins to feel better. He rinses his mouth from the gondolier's flask, settles in the shade of the canopy, and rests his head on one of the posts, watching the birds along the bank, the fishermen's nets drying in the afternoon sun. So heavy, his teeming skull. He imagines it filling like the bottom bulb of an hourglass, every grain a thought, a memory, a secret.

The gondolier moors his craft. Crivano pays him and disembarks onto the fondamenta, clutching his parcel tight against his chest, so intent on keeping it safe that he leaves his walkingstick behind. The gondolier runs after him, catches him when he's nearly to the Campo Santa Giustina; Crivano thanks him, pays him again.

He has no intention of stopping in the church but somehow winds up there anyway, weaving from sunbeam to mote-dusted sunbeam across the broken floor of the nave, thinking of Lepanto. Captain Bua in his breastplate and helmet: *Santa Giustina, we pray that on this, your feast day, you will intercede on our behalf, and secure for us the blessings of God as we fight to defend the chastity of our great Republic from savages.* Clutching the Lark's spray-slick hand as the fleets closed: the last good moment, before the drums and cymbals crashed over the waves to be answered by horns from the Christian galleys, before the line dispersed and the real horror began. The first man he killed: turbaned head blown off and scattered on the water as he jumped from the oven platform. Slipping on the blood-brown deck, ankles tangled in viscera. The Lark clubbing a dead janissary with someone's severed forearm while keening cannonballs tore the air overhead. The thunderclap when the *Christ over the World* lit its powder magazine, shattering the Ottoman galleys around it, bits of wood and iron and flesh raining through the smoke. The gulf aflame with burning wrecks, drifting into clusters like petals on a pond, lodestones on quicksilver. Fumbling in the tear-blurred darkness for the Lark's matriculation certificate as the Turks stormed the decks overhead.

He needs to eat something. Outside, behind the cracked apse, he finds a small casino serving spit-roasted kid along with chewy bread and an unimpressive red wine. The only other customers are four hard-faced Arsenal workers with scavenged wood shavings bundled at their feet; they cease their dice-game when he walks in, unhurriedly hiding their cup and coins, glaring in silence. With so many ridotti springing up around the city, Crivano's surprised to see them gaming in public; their flagrancy speaks to the decline of the campo. The stares don't abate, so Crivano makes short work of his meal, rises, and — feeling restored by the food, emboldened by the wine — approaches them. Will you good fellows take a physician's wager? he says.

After permitting them to cheat him out of a small sum, Crivano orders wine for the table, and inquires about the state of the church. It's shameful, they agree; no fit memorial for Lepanto's honored dead. One of the four was in the battle himself, or says he was: at the oars of Vincenzo Quirini's flagship, jabbing his pike through Turkish ribcages. He came home with his freedom, a few ducats' worth of loot, a few stories no one wants to hear. Only fools boast of fighting for nothing, he says, so I never boast. The diplomats, they never intended to retake Cyprus. That's clear enough now, isn't it? They were making their deal with the sultan even as we sailed into battle. But I defended the lives of my bench-mates, I sent a lot of Turks to hell, I didn't shame myself through cowardice. I'm satisfied. If anything else matters, I don't see how.

The sun is low by the time Crivano is on the street again. Beside the church's steps he meets a young priest with a taper, drunker than he is, skulking inside to light the few remaining candles. The sallow skin of the

743

man's neck is inflamed by traces of the Spanish disease. For a moment Crivano wants to pursue this wretch, to thrash him with his stick, but he thinks better of it. His anger surprises him. Why should he be troubled that Lepanto is forgotten? Hasn't he tried to forget it himself?

He thinks of Perina: her urgent questions, her wide searching eyes. What convent is she in? Santa Caterina, isn't it? Nearby, past Zanipolo, not far from the Crucifers' church. What was it she said? *It is precisely this chaos I seek knowledge of, for in such disarray resides the truth!* Ah, youth's sincere conviction when it speaks such words! Amusing, disquieting, embarrassing. Like watching children at play with their fathers' swords. He wants to see her, to speak to her. And the fact that he's about to commit an act of treason shouldn't preclude him from keeping his promise to the senator, should it?

A busy salizzada takes him to Campo San Zanipolo, where he steps between the peddlers' carts by the mounted bronze of Colleoni to pause in front of the Scuola of Saint Mark and regain his bearings. The odd trompe-l'oeil façade with its pelicans and phoenixes and winged lions only serves to confuse him further, so he rejoins the crowd, moving west. At first he's able to plot his route by the ancient squat belltower of the Crucifers and the slender onion-domed campanile of the Apostles' church, but he's soon among the high walls of hospitals and new palaces and has only the sun to locate him. He's all but given up hope of finding his way when he crosses a broad canal to see the long latticed façade of the Zen palace, and Santa Caterina just beyond.

A lamp burns by the convent's outer door, though the sun has not yet set. Crivano tries the handle, finds it locked, and raps with the head of his stick. His parcel grows heavy; he sets it down, then picks it up again, swaying on the stone steps. After a moment he resumes his knocking.

A bolt slams, and the door opens to reveal a sliver of nun: downturned mouth, wrinkled cheek, patient eye. I'm sorry, dottore, the nun says. Visitors are not permitted in the parlor after sundown. I hope you will come again tomorrow.

Crivano's words emerge somewhat slurred; he tries to polish his elocution. The sun, good sister, is anything but down, he says. Even now its fiery orb cleaves my eyes. I have come a great distance to see Signorina Perina Glissenti, who is an educant in your care. Admit me, please.

The eye narrows, but the voice remains courteous. Again, it says, I'm very sorry, dottore, but that's simply not possible. Even in daylit hours only the educants' close relations may enter the parlor. And under no

745

circumstances can inebriated persons be admitted. Good night, dottore.

Crivano places his left hand in the door as she closes it. The wooden edge presses against his fingers: it's quite smooth. As if he might be only the latest player in a scene repeated many times at this portal. Inebriated? he scoffs, pressing his nose to the crack. Sister, I am a physician; I will thank you to leave such diagnoses to me. Open now, and fetch the signorina. It is very important that I speak with her at once. It concerns an exceedingly vital matter of state security.

The nun gives the door a careful shove to indicate her conviction, and Crivano winces. He can feel eyes from the campo on his back. We'd like to assist you, dottore, the muffled voice says. Simply return tomorrow with a relative, or a written directive from the Council. Good night.

I am a relative, Crivano shouts. I am. I am the young lady's brother.

The pressure on his hand lessens a bit. As I understand it, the nun says, the signorina's siblings are all deceased.

Yes, Crivano says. That's right. As you can very plainly see, I am dead. I have come back tonight from my sailor's grave to visit my young sister, and would fain be admitted to your parlor at once.

Again, I bid you good night, dottore.

Now see here, good sister, Crivano says,

moderating his tone. I have been asked to visit the signorina by her cousin, Senator Giacomo Contarini, whose name I'm sure is familiar to you. This was a special request put to me by the senator himself. I believe he gave authorization for my visit. Consult with your abbess if you must, and supply her with another name: I am called Vettor Crivano.

After a lengthy silence, the door swings slowly inward.

Without bothering to take his robe, the nun directs Crivano to a pair of high-backed caquetoires, lights an oil lamp on the candlestand between them, and stalks away down a dim corridor, leaving him alone. Aside from scattered chairs and endtables the large room is bare. Over the cold hearth hangs a painting of Catherine of Alexandria in the antique style: gilt aureole shimmering in the lamplight, spiked wheel demolished by a touch. Crivano seats himself, resting Tristão's wrapped mirror across his knees, resting his stick atop the mirror.

He falls asleep immediately, then jolts awake again, uncertain of where he is. Overhead and across the city, bells toll once for sundown; vespers echo through the wall from the adjacent sanctuary. A commotion in the corridor: footfalls and whispers. Then Perina, with the nun at her heels. She sweeps forward with a long unladylike stride; the nun's white

747

hands flutter about her face, trying to fix her veil.

When her eyes find his black shape in the lamplight, they burst with gleeful surprise; her mouth forms a word that her breath never catches. Now she's made out his face. Her expression becomes confused, alarmed. Dottore Crivano? she says.

His stick slides to the floor as he rises. He bows deeply, steadying himself on the backrest. Signorina, he says, it is I.

This is an unanticipated pleasure, she says, and I am glad that you have come. But what urgent matter brings you here at such an odd hour?

Pious lady, I must confess: I have dissembled. For this I beg your pardon. The exigency that impels me to your parlor can claim as its ambit naught save the animal confines of my own person. It is perhaps a priest's sanctuary I should seek, but my feet led me here, in hope of opening my mouth to evacuate my brain. Fair Perina, I have come lately upon a man who fought at Lepanto, and the reminiscence thusly prompted made me long for your ready ear and kind attention. Will you sit with me?

They sit. With great effort Crivano retrieves his stick from the floor. Be brief, the nun says. Perina, I trust you know the rules that govern proper conduct in the parlor, and I trust you will keep the dottore cognizant of them.

The nun crosses the room, lights a second lamp, sits, and takes up a drop-spindle and a basket of wool. Her unblinking eyes prick him through the shadows as she spins.

After our last meeting, Perina says, I felt certain that thereafter you would seek to avoid me. I feared that my many questions had given offense. So I am very happy to see you now, dottore. Though I do wish I had known to expect you.

He smiles, looks at her. Disgusted with himself for having been even a bit surprised when the senator told him who she is. So much Cyprus in her — though she's never set foot there and never will. So many echoes that she herself cannot hear. Being near her carries an illicit thrill of invisibility, a thrill compounded by her appearance: dark wool frock and swiftly donned veil, accidental and ingenuous, unornamented for the eyes of men. This pleases him. He could tell her anything.

The senator explained to me who you are, he says.

She swallows. Shadows appear and disappear along her throat.

I will speak to you of Lepanto, he says, though there will be little you do not already know. Your brother and I were on our way to Padua when news came to us of the fall of Nicosia. We elected to sign onto a galley as bowmen. We were young, younger than you are now, and no warriors, to be sure. The only galley that would take us was a Corfiot ship called the *Gold and Black Eagle.* The *Eagle* met the Holy League in Messina, and on the day of the battle we were in the right wing. The fighting was all in our favor at first, but when the Turkish flank came fully into view our maneuvers became confused. Our admirals doubted one another, our line broke, and we lost sight of the other Christian galleys. We prevailed in a few close exchanges — alas, your brother perished in one of these — but we soon found ourselves entirely surrounded. Our captain, a man called Pietro Bua, chose to surrender, and the retreating Turks towed us to the harbor of Lepanto and assembled us in the town square. They were very angry at their defeat, and greatly sorrowed by the loss of so many men. All Christians of noble birth were divided from the rest. To be ransomed, we thought. But the Turks beheaded these gentlemen, and they flayed Captain Bua alive. The survivors passed into slavery.

How did my brother die?

He was struck by a cannonball. A ball from the centerline pedrero of an Ottoman galley. Quite a large stone: at least fifty pounds, I should think. The ball must have cracked when it was fired, for I found a scattering of limestone chips where it had passed. Had the enemy been in a trough between waves and not riding a crest, the shot would have sundered the deck, and I and many others would have died as well. As it was, it went high. Your brother stood beside me, then he did not.

Were you able to see to his remains before you were overrun?

I tried, lady. But there were no remains to speak of. I am deeply sorry.

She nods. Her posture suggests grief, but there is no grief in her face, only excitement, and exhaustion. Everyone of noble birth was executed, she says. So Gabriel would have died anyway.

Yes. I sometimes comfort myself with that thought. The cannonball spared him agony and indignity alike.

She's silent now, rubbing her hands in her lap as if to warm them, although it is not cold in this room. Or is it? It's hard for him to say. He stares openly at her, sorting her into pieces to memorize every detail — her lips, her feet, her brow — but everything his stare gathers slides swiftly toward oblivion, warm rain striking bare rock. It's rarely the eye, he knows, that best serves the recollecting mind. He fights the urge to press his nose to her scalp, to take hold of her soft palms, to see what he can untangle from the webwork of lined skin there. After tonight he does not plan to see this girl again.

What happened to you? she says. After the

Turks captured you?

Crivano shrugs. I was fortunate, he says. I was not put to the oars, as many of my shipmates were. Owing to my youth, I was given to the janissaries, and with them I encountered hardship and adventure in strange lands I had never dreamed of. I learned their language, and the language of the Arabs, and in time I became an interpreter.

And then you escaped.

Yes. I betrayed the trust that I had earned, and I fled. I wish I could declare my choice to have been an easy one, but it was not. Almost half my life had been spent among the Turks. My boyhood home was lost, my family gone. The lands where I was to seek my freedom were alien to me. The world into which I had been born no longer had any means of recognizing me, nor I it.

With no family, Perina says, you are no one here. Worse than no one. You are a corpse. An effigy. A ghost.

Her expression remains placid, her voice reserved, but Crivano senses a whisper of rage in her, so pure as to be invisible, like a very hot flame. Yes, he says. I'm sure you understand.

Why did you come back?

Crivano looks at his lap, at the floor. His drunkenness is abandoning him, leaving him sluggish and stupid, in peril of forgetting that

752

his lies are lies. As we grow older, he says, we sometimes find that our most momentous decisions are unseen by us as we make them. We perceive only a confusion of paltry choices, like the tesserae of a mosaic. Only with distance do prevailing images become clear. A man came to me in the night and said he had stolen the skin of Marcantonio Bragadin, the hero of Famagusta. He asked me to help him, and I said I would. All else has issued from that.

They sit in silence for a while. The sound of voices singing the *Magnificat* echoes from the corridor. Across the parlor, the nun pulls and winds her thread. Her impatience settles over them like a fog.

I must make a momentous decision soon, Perina says.

To take your vows?

She nods. I am twenty years old, she says. I have been an educant here since I was eight. Most of us are married or clothed as nuns prior to our sixteenth year. I fear I am becoming a source of anxiety to the abbess. She informs me that she has already selected my new name, and looks forward to bestowing it upon me soon. She has been informing me of this on a regular basis for more than a year now, and her considerable patience is on the wane. I have no words to tell you, dottore, how fervently I seek to quit this barren harem of Christ. There is nothing —

753

Her eyes are riveted now to his own, glinting like obsidian under her veil.

— *nothing* that I would not do to leave this place. Nothing.

Crivano casts a nervous glance at the nun, but her beleaguered expression remains unaltered.

Don't be overly concerned about Sister Perpetua, dottore, Perina says. She's very devout, but also somewhat deaf. We prisoners of Santa Caterina are fortunate to have her as our gatekeeper.

I gather, Crivano says, that you sense no vocation toward the veil.

If you search this edifice brick by brick, dottore, you will find herein perhaps a dozen genuine vocations. Mostly we are the surplus daughters of the Republic's great families, married off to Christ without indignity or excessive expense, and we spend that portion of our day unallocated to prayer enacting doll-game renditions of the rivalries that engage our families in the outside world — only with no real consequence, of course. The few among us with any brains avoid those of our own rank and consort instead with the repentant harlots, who know something of life's complexities, who know the best songs and the best stories, who offer explicit instruction on how we can best entertain our husbands and lovers as we seek our ultimate stations in the world.

Crivano realizes that his jaw is agape, and shuts it.

I, naturally, have little stake in such talk, she continues. I spend my days with whatever books come to me, and in shameful reveries. Would you like to hear the most shameful, dottore? The daydream which has most pre-occupied me in recent days, which I would confess to no one but you, is this: I imagine that the ship that carried my mother and my sister from Cyprus never did find the lagoon safely, but instead was set upon by Ottoman corsairs. I imagine that I was born not in the comfortable lair of the Contarini, but in Constantinople, where I became an odalisque in the seraglio. And then of course I imagine a young sultan who values the small wit I do possess over the great beauty I do not, and takes me for his favorite. You blush to hear these things, dottore, and yet I do not blush to speak them. Would it be somehow less shameful for me to make one small addition to my fantasy, and wish that I had been born into the seraglio a boy? To wish, in short, for a life like the one you yourself have led? Odd as it may be, I cannot.

Crivano holds her gaze as best he can. His arms are wet-wool heavy; he's not sure his legs will carry him when the time comes to rise. We can hardly choose our dreams, lady, he says.

Can you help me escape this place? Only

escape. Nothing more.

He shakes his head slowly. A mistake: when he stops, the room spins on. You don't understand what you ask, he says. Where would you go?

There are places, she says. And people. Please, dottore.

The revolving walls make him nauseous, so he closes his eyes. Breathing deeply. Laughing under his breath. It is very easy, at this moment, for him to imagine himself as dreamed into being by this girl. As a shadow cast by her childish hands before an as-yet-unseen light.

Dottore? she says. Are you again unwell?

Your new name, Crivano says. Do you know yet what it is to be?

No. I could guess, I suppose.

He opens his eyes. It thrills the blood, doesn't it? he says. The thought of casting aside an old name. But it is not a thing to do casually. Lest you find yourself with no name at all.

Perina, the nun says. It's time. Show your guest to the door.

Perina rises, tugs gently on his wrist; he's grateful for her help. I want to tell you more about your brother, he says.

I have many questions. You'll come again soon, won't you?

He was greatly loved by everyone who knew him, Crivano says. He gave all of us courage until the moment he died. To this day he remains for me a paragon of grace and boldness.

A shadow passes across Perina's face; her gaze drops to the floor. Then she folds her arm into his and eases him toward the exit. I have been told, she says, that in his boyhood my brother was greatly inclined to solitude and melancholy. And that you were much to thank for lightening his disposition.

There's a note of uncertainty in her voice: a concern she's eager to dismiss. It sobers him like packed snow against his neck. I must confess, he says, that the years of struggle and sorrow have added weight to my own temperament. I can scarcely recall the playful youth you describe. But if I did anything to ease your brother's brief bright path through the world, then I am honored to have done so.

She smiles under her veil. Moving him forward. Her eyes fixed on the stone floor. The nun, on her feet again, hovers behind them.

Perina gives his forearm a surreptitious squeeze. You'll help me, she whispers.

I — will try.

The door swings open and the night comes in, airy and echoless. Belltowers and chimney-funnels and the edges of tiled rooftops cast black outlines against the western sky, while shadows rise in the streets below. The canal's

757

surface shuffles the left-behind light — blue heavens, orange lanterns — and Crivano slouches toward it, descending the convent steps. Halfway down he sags against the rail and turns back. Perina still stands in the door. Your cousin, he says. The senator. What did he say about me?

She's surprised by his question, at a loss for an answer. Very little, she says. Nothing, really.

He only arranged our meeting.

Yes, she says. I asked him to do so.

The nun is behind her, one hand on her shoulder, the other on the doorframe. Perina's veiled eyes are lost in the dusk.

Then how, Crivano says, did you first learn that I knew your brother? That I fought at Lepanto?

There's a lengthy silence. A breeze rustles the crowns of the sea-pines in the churchyard. Dottore de Nis, she says at last. Dottore de Nis told me.

Good night, dottore, the gatekeeper nun shouts as she shuts the door. Do be vigilant in the dark.

53

The bolt slides home with an emphatic boom. In the ensuing silence, Crivano stares at the gray oak planks of the convent door until lamplight vanishes from the gaps be-

758

tween them. Then he takes a swift weary inventory — his parcel, his stick — and turns south, toward the church of the Apostles and the Rialto beyond. In the distance the bell-tower in the Piazza glows like a hot iron against the starry sky; Crivano can see pale flashes of night-birds around it, feasting on insects summoned by the fire.

When he comes to the Saint Sophia Canal he takes a few unsteady paces to the water's edge, sets his burdens down, and parts his robes to piss, splashing the quay, tracing crazy patterns across the surface, nearly wetting himself. He wants to dwell on what he's just heard but cannot: he needs to find Obizzo, to give him the news. He never should have come here. What perversity impelled him? Was it engendered in himself, or — somehow — by the crooked city streets, which seem willfully to frustrate his errands, to distract him with queer spectacles, strange musings, unfamiliar impulses? Even now each shuffling step toward the Rialto brings him no closer: he sees the Grand Canal flash between palace walls but finds no path that leads there.

In the campo of Saint John the Golden-Tongued he finally gives up, chooses a street he's certain will connect him to the Mercerie, and emerges instead behind the German fondaco, at the Grand Canal at last, near the very spot where the new bridge spans it. Crivano hurries to the Riva del Carbon, searching the face of every idle gondolier in the hope of glimpsing Obizzo. When he's nearly reached the Morosini house — where last night he half-listened to the Nolan's lecture — he turns around again. The bridge is a needle-fanged maw over the water, its broad philtrum lit with torches; their phantom twins gambol in the waves below.

In the works of Thrice-Great Hermes, we read of the double essence of Divine Man, of how He looked down from the armature of the spheres and fell in love with Nature when He saw His reflection upon Her waters. Climbing the bridge's sloped central pathway, Crivano spots a figure he recognizes leaning against the marble balustrade: the wart-footed streetwalker, alone, tired, probably hungry, but not in any visible distress. She's looking down at the city: rows of inscrutable palaces, lanterns winking from black outlines of boats. The expression she wears is familiar from his janissary years; he saw it sometimes, albeit rarely, in the faces of peasants displaced by the sweep of armies. How wondrous, it seems to say, is this thing that destroys me.

Crivano slips from the waning procession to stand undetected behind her, close enough to study the sinews in her neck and shoulders, to smell the many days of peppery sweat her skin has accrued. The brown dye on her hands and forearms has faded somewhat.

When she stirs, adjusting her weight, Crivano
hastens away.

*The Universe, in all its disorder and variety, is
the mirror which captured Divine Man's as-yet-
unseen reflection. But its seeming chaos masks
a unity: Amphitrite, the Ocean, who also cor-
responds to the waters wherein naked Diana
bathes when she is glimpsed by Actaeon, the
Intellect.* Crivano wanders south to the limit
of the Riva del Vin, north to the fishmarket,
long vacant at this hour, though still reeking.
Boatman after boatman after boatman, solic-
iting fares, awaiting their masters, laughing
and cursing with their fellows. Obizzo is
nowhere to be found. On his way through
the Ropemakers' Square Crivano realizes that
the image he's fixed in his brain — the lens
through which his mind's eye has been scanning the canal-sides — is not Obizzo's broad
countenance but the lean face of dead Verzelin. He's confused the features of a man he
murdered. He could have passed Obizzo a
dozen times tonight and never known.

He slumps against a pillar in the colonnade
of the Treasury and closes his eyes, breathing
through his sudarium. Sober now, but ach-
ing, exhausted. The White Eagle seems very
far to go. A baffled heaviness that's stalked
him all day has at last overtaken him; he still
cannot fathom its source. The aim of all his
intrigues is now practically within his grasp:

761

in mere days his work will be done. So wherefore this misdirection, these impediments, that seem to bubble from the ferment of his own brain? Even now, as he tries to retrieve Obizzo's visage, the only image that appears is Perina's veiled face, her beseeching eyes. *Only escape,* she said. *Nothing more.*

There is another course that Crivano could take. The thought rattles his heart. How easily Obizzo could join Verzelin on the lagoon's floor: a fugitive, he's practically dead already. Then a private word to the senator — *I have recognized one of the Turks at the fondaco as the chief tormentor of my days in bondage, and I must be revenged* — to protect him from the sultan's agents. A meeting with Narkis in a secluded spot; a stiletto between his ribs. Serena would say nothing; what could he say? In two decisive sweeps, the conspiracy would be erased. Here, then, is the ultimate perversion: Crivano could abandon the betrayal masked by his current respectability and *become* respectable. The gecko who drops his tail.

He has the senator's blessing. He *could* wed the foolish lovely girl. What would prevent it? Who would object? He could forsake his current treachery for a treachery altogether more loathsome and more profound, a treachery unknown to every other living soul. The idea is not without its appeal: to become, at last, the perfect impostor.

Someone is watching. Crivano opens his eyes.

It's the whore. She's only steps away, standing with her back to the canal. Her expression empty, or emptied. Here I am, it says.

Until now he has taken her for a provincial girl, selling herself during the Sensa for extra coins; in doing so, he may have been too hasty. She's chosen this moment with care. She seems certain of what he'll do; more certain than he is himself. He wonders how that could be possible.

He tucks away his sudarium and steps toward her; she greets him politely. He inquires after her foot, and she says that it still troubles her. He asks if she has a bed for the night, and she says that she does not, not yet, but that she's sure she'll manage. Then he asks her price.

Back at the White Eagle, he interrupts Anzolo's supper to give him Serena's parcel. This must be delivered to Dottore Tristão de Nis before dawn, he says. You will find him at the house of Andrea and Nicolò Morosini. The men who carry it should be well-armed, entirely trustworthy, and lacking any formal affiliation with this locanda. Its contents are of incalculable worth, and uncertain legitimacy. I intend now to retire, and I should not like to be troubled prior to the fourteenth bell. Oh — have a chambermaid bring a large washbasin, a clean flesh-brush, and a spare pitcher of water to my room. An extra lamp, as well. Immediately, please.

The whore is stepping from her skirts when the knock comes. Crivano opens the door wide enough to gather in what the maid has brought, then shuts and bolts it with muttered thanks. He fills the basin, lights the lamp, and hangs up his own garments while she washes herself. Her eyes linger on the two emblems that mark his skin — the key on his chest, the Sword of the Prophet on his calf — but she asks no questions. Her long shadow stretches over the walls, dulling and sharpening in the erratic light.

When she's done, he grips her by the neck and washes her again, scrubbing hard until her flesh turns rosy beneath its sun-darkened brown. She makes no protest. He wipes her dry, directs her to the bed, moves the lamps closer. Then he begins to inspect her, minutely, for condylomata and chancres. His eyes are dry and tired. She's immobile, silent, watching the ceiling. Soft voices rise from the street outside. From somewhere more distant comes the low liquid whistle of a scops-owl.

He stands, washes his own arms past the elbow, and directs her to sit up. Then he tilts her head toward the light and puts his fingers in her mouth. Her tongue, her cheeks, her throat are free from signs of disease. He tips her back onto the wool-stuffed mattress, folds the hinges of her knees, and applies his spit-slick fingers to her anus and vulva. He intends this as a prudent preliminary to copulation, but it soon becomes an end in itself: it is what he wants, what he is doing, why he brought her here. He recalls the invasion of Georgia: lovely young corpses stacked in a barn in Tiflis, the stench of death arrested by the brutal cold. Extraordinary machines! More perfect with their souls gone. He could have spent hours exploring them, days cutting them to pieces.

The hair on her body is curiously fine, the same russet hue as her cropped scalp. On her shins it's nearly blond. A thin hooked scar, well-healed, traces the lower edge of her left scapula. He pulls her toes, probes the hollows of her armpits, drags his knuckles across the rough verruca on her foot. Pinching her lips, her nipples, her earlobes: the flesh blushes and puffs. His thumbs smooth her brows, brush her closed lids. When her eyes open — their pupils shrinking — he looks at them for a long time. Peculiar colors. Greens and grays and browns. A deep swift stream, churned by the boots of soldiers.

Gradually she becomes impatient, unnerved, uncertain of how this use of her will end. She begins to reach for him, to redirect his actions into something intelligible. Each time she does so he stops her hands: gently at first, then more forcefully, if only to feel

765

the occult architecture of muscle and sinew straining against his own. This is a new invisibility, blood-warm and mindless, hidden under skin. Nothing like the one sought by the alchemists. Every discovery is instantly forgotten.

This continues across what seems like many hours, although Crivano recalls hearing no bells. Only when they're both clumsy, fumbling, all but asleep, does he let her touch him. She settles an arm around his waist; her hand makes a few perfunctory strokes. He rises to clean himself.

Sometime during the night her snores wake him; he's uncertain of the hour. Dark. The lamp on the table has burned itself out; the fresher one in the corner still flickers. He slides from bed, refills the new lamp's reservoir, shapes its wick with a needle until he's built a steady flame. Then he unlocks his box of physic.

He places his square marble slab on the tabletop, along with a pair of small tin spatulas and a sealed jar of beeswax, and turns to inspect his herbs. Birchbark. Fig-leaf resin. Celandine. The biennial henbane he bought from the apothecary, moments before he met this girl for the first time. Why did he purchase so much of it? Enough to kill everyone in the White Eagle, and many more besides. Might not the sale raise suspicion?

He puts that concern aside, makes his selections, measures them onto the slab. Then he gathers beeswax on a spatula, softens it over the lamp-flame, smears it across the scattered herbs, stirring and scraping them into an ointment. Once he's gathered it in a vial, he returns to his box, fishes out a long slim razor, and rouses the girl.

She recoils when she sees the blade. He claps a hand over her mouth before she can scream, pinching her nose, pressing her skull downward until the bed-ropes groan. Then he begins to whisper in her ear, and he keeps whispering until her struggles cease, until she understands and accedes to what he's about to do.

He releases her, then takes hold of her thigh and rolls her quickly over on her stomach. He straddles her, rests his buttocks against her own, bends her back leg. As if she's a horse he's shoeing. He tilts the pad of her foot toward the lamp until the wart is clearly visible. Then he begins to cut.

He draws no blood, or very little. As the shaved-away callus litters the sheets, he sweeps it to the floor with the back of his hand. When the area of the verruca is cleared, he applies the poultice, then dresses it with a snug bandage. Clean this every night, he says. Put ointment on it every morning. Don't walk unless you must. If you do these things, within a month it will cease to trouble you.

He stands, freeing her. She he rolls onto

her side, then cocks her leg, prods the bandage. Looks at him. Dottore, she says.

She says nothing else. After a moment, she rolls onto her belly and draws in her limbs, rising sphinx-like on her knees and elbows, swaying sleepily in the lamp's flame. Crivano watches her for some time. A sound escapes his throat: a wet exhalation, like a small beast dying or being born. Then he climbs across the mattress and commences to use her in the manner of the Greeks, in the same manner the janissaries would sometimes use him, in same the manner he'd sometimes put the Lark to use during the long slow dream of their boyhood, those unspoiled days when nothing was different and nothing would ever change.

54

When he wakes, sunlight is pressing through the curtains, and the girl still sleeps beside him.

When he wakes again, the sunlight has shifted, grown softer, and the girl is gone. He tries with some success to sink back into slumber, but recollections of the night before — along with concerns about what the girl may have stolen, and the desire to void his bladder — finally rouse him.

Stool and urine in the chamberpot already. Enough water in the pitcher to clean himself.

The stack of coins that he left for her is gone, of course, but his own purse still jingles when he lifts it. The ample sheaf of papers in his trunk's false bottom — letters of advice from a bank in Genoa, an account Narkis established for him — has led him to be somewhat careless with his funds; he turns out the purse on the tabletop to take stock of its contents. Gold sequins, silver ducats, silver soldi, copper gazettes. A few lire and grossi. One scarred and flattened giustina, MEMOR ERO TUI IVSTINA VIRGO visible on its reverse. Coins from other lands: a papal scudi, an English half-groat, a quart d'ecu bearing the device of Henri IV. One blue-green piece he can't identify. He opens the curtains, winces, holds it to the light. A ducat. A coin of necessity, struck during a siege by a local treasurer from whatever metal could be spared. One side is illegible, worn smooth; the other bears a winged lion, and the year the coin was minted: 1570.

Crivano's arm spasms and goes numb as if struck on the ulnar nerve; the ducat clatters to the floor, rolls to a corner. Crivano, trembling, stoops to retrieve it. He sits naked at the table, reading the coin's relief with his fingertips as his eyes grow wet. Thinking of his father. *I demand that you end this fatuous sulk at once. I have made my decision. Maffeo and Dolfin will stay here with me. What you say is true: if we defeat the Turks, my estate will pass to them. But we will not defeat the Turks. Don't you see? The sultan's victory may come this year, or next year, or ten years from now. But it will come. There is no one who does not know this. To Maffeo and Dolfin, I bequeath my lands and my properties, which are worth nothing, which are in fact a curse that dooms them. To you I give my name, my seat on the Great Council. I am sending you and the Lark to Padua not because you have no legacy in Cyprus, but because the only legacy for you here is death.* Crivano wipes his cheeks, dries his face on his peg-hung shirt, dresses himself. Wishing for an instant that he still had Tristão's mirror: wanting to read the history in his face, history he's labored greatly to conceal, to forget. History no other living soul could recognize.

Bells are ringing; he loses count. It must be quite late in the day. Obizzo, he thinks. There isn't much time left.

On his way out, he ducks into the parlor — unusually crowded — and finds Anzolo by the door to the kitchen. Good day, messer, he says. Did the item —

Ah! Good day, dottore!

Anzolo sweeps forward with a theatrical solicitousness that's entirely unlike him, and claps Crivano on the shoulders. I am greatly pleased to see you, dottore, he says. But I confess I'd hoped you'd arise a bit later.

770

Knowing of your fondness for lamprey, I had intended to send my girl to the fishmarket this morning, but in my carelessness I forgot until only now.

Crivano is nonplussed: he detests lamprey. I beg your pardon, he says. I don't believe I requested —

Dottore, a valued guest like yourself should not have to make such requests. You have my apologies. We shall have lamprey for you tomorrow, I hope. Today a very fine turbot will emerge soon from our oven, and I hope you will flatter me by eating some of it before you depart.

Anzolo has a tight grip on his upper arms, restraining him from turning toward the exit. Crivano feels his skin flush, his lip curl with displeasure. A moment ago he'd simply sought to inquire after the parcel he sent to Tristão; now reflex moves his fingers along his walkingstick's shaft, preparing to thump this fool in the sternum. He opens his mouth again to protest.

Please, dottore, Anzolo says. I insist.

The innkeeper's face is garlanded with a beatific smile, but his eyes are fierce — and, Crivano now sees, frightened. The color that rushed to Crivano's cheek an instant ago now flees; hairs stiffen on his arms and his nape. Of course, he says. Thank you.

A new voice comes from behind him, not a voice he knows: Will you join me, dottore?

Anzolo's fingers loosen and fall away. Crivano turns.

A compact and sinewy man has risen from his seat at the corner table; he salutes with a raised hand. His garments are simple, grays and blacks, but of good fabric. His several rings and silver pendant put him at the uneasy margin of the sumptuary laws — unless he's a citizen, or a noble, which Crivano very much doubts. The cut of his hair and beard suggests Spain. His loose bearing recalls the battlefield.

I have just finished my own meal, the man says, and now find that I have nothing better to do on this fine summer day than to sit in this parlor and broaden my association. Shameful to be so idle, I suppose. But gregariousness can be its own species of industry, don't you agree, dottore? Please. Sit.

His jeweled hand drops to indicate the chair before him. The lace curtains behind him move in a breeze — swaying in unison as if linked by a thread of spidersilk — then sag again, inert. Through the windows, under the awning of a joiner's shop across the street, Crivano spots two loitering figures; both wear new cloaks of like provenance, though of differing hue. The man at the corner table also wears such a cloak, and has opted not to surrender it to the parlor closet, although the weather is quite warm. As Crivano watches, one of the men across the street shifts and turns, revealing a single rolling eye, a dark hole of a mouth, a confusion of scars from chin to forehead, ear to ear. It's the bravo he saw yesterday morning on the Mercerie, by Ciotti's shop. Crivano takes a long slow breath, tightens his sphincter so as not to shit himself.

I don't believe I know you, sir, he says.

As yet, the man replies with a bow, you do not. I'm called Lunardo.

Vettor Crivano, Crivano says.

Yes, dottore. I know.

Lunardo points to the chair again, raising his eyebrows good-humoredly. Crivano smiles. He has his walkingstick, and the stiletto in his boot. There will be more of these men — outside, and also in here, at other tables. If the White Eagle has a rear entrance he doesn't know where it is; he should have checked.

He steps forward and sits. Lunardo settles into his own chair. The three men at the next table aren't wearing cloaks, but Crivano can feel their eyes follow him. Six bravi, then. More?

Who are you? Crivano says. What do you want?

I am only a proud resident of the Rialto, Lunardo says, concerned for the security of my neighborhood. I have a few questions for you, dottore. Very simple questions.

Sbirri, Crivano thinks. In the employ of the

773

Council of Ten. That's good. Were they assassins, they probably would have cut him down last night in the streets. How long have they been watching him? How much have they seen? The girl he brought here? Perina at the convent? Serena at his factory? When he first saw these men on the Mercerie, were they following him, or Narkis? What snares does he now step among?

Ask what you will, Crivano says.

I shall. Where is your home, dottore?

I have come only recently to the city from Bologna. Until I establish myself, this locanda is my home.

You were a student in Bologna?

That's right.

And before Bologna, Lunardo says, where was your home?

Surely you know all of this. Come to your point, please.

Lunardo smiles. Where do you hear the Mass?

Crivano furrows his brow. San Cassian, most recently, he says. Also San Aponal. Why?

Do you know Lord Andrea Morosini? Or his brother, Lord Nicolò? They keep a house on the right bank of the Grand Canal.

Crivano scans Lunardo's face before he answers. The man's eyes are bright and quick, his mien that of a cunning animal, inventive at feeding itself.

The Morosini house, Crivano says, is on

774

the *left* bank. I was there two nights ago. I met both brothers at that time.

Anzolo is moving across the room, a full plate in one hand, a goblet in the other. His Friulian serving-girls stand awkwardly aside. Are you good sirs quite content? he asks two men seated at the parlor's opposite end. And *you,* sirs? Is everything to your liking? This latter query is directed to the three men at the next table: he's showing Crivano where the sbirri are. Eight, then. The plate appears before him. Enjoy, dottore, Anzolo says. Be cautious of the little bones.

Lunardo waits for Crivano to begin eating. Crivano has no appetite, but lifts his spoon anyway, feigning as much hunger as he can manage. Baked turbot, with a crust of crumbs and cheese. Rice porridge dotted with small grapes.

If you did not know the brothers Morosini prior to two nights ago, Lunardo asks, what brought you to their home?

Crivano chews very slowly before answering. I believe the Morosini often host scholars, he says. I am a scholar.

They invited you?

I was invited, yes.

Lunardo seems amused by this — by everything under the sun. The ill-matched rings on his fingers, Crivano now understands, once belonged to other men: men who now rot in prisons, or fill ossuaries, or pollute the lagoon with their corpses. The heavy silver pendant around his neck is in the shape of a key. Not functional, probably. No way to know what it means, if anything. Crivano recalls the key inked on his own chest, the emblem of his orta. The girl saw it last night. Has she told anyone?

What went on at the Morosini house two nights ago, dottore?

You know this already, I'm sure.

I do, Lunardo says. But I would like you to tell me.

A lecture. By a friar from Campania.

What was the friar's name?

I don't remember his name. He is called — and calls himself — the Nolan.

What did he speak of in this lecture?

A bone pricks Crivano's gums. He scrapes it along his teeth with his tongue to strip the sweet white flesh, then pushes it between his pursed lips, plucks it away with his fingers. Mirrors, he says. He spoke of mirrors.

And what did this Nolan have to say about mirrors, dottore?

Crivano lifts his goblet and sips. What little I do recall, he says, you could not possibly comprehend.

Lunardo laughs, shaking his head ruefully. Then he leans forward. Last night, he says, Brother Giordano Bruno, known to you as the Nolan, was taken into custody by the local tribunal of the Inquisition, and detained in order to answer very serious charges of heresy. If you are unable to explain to me what the Nolan said, dottore, then you had best prepare yourself to relate it to the tribunal, because you are all but certain to be called before them. Until then, you are not to leave the city under any circumstances. Do you understand?

For a moment Crivano is bewildered. Then he struggles mightily to keep the relief from his face. The Inquisition? he says. They arrested the Nolan?

That is what I said, dottore.

Crivano's eyes water; his diaphragm quakes. Subtly he pricks the heel of his right hand with his knife to distract himself, to stave off the gathering hilarity. Heresy! he thinks. The overbearing little fool must be ecstatic!

But surely this is a trap. It must be, even if what this man says is true. Eight sbirri to question a solitary witness in such a trifling matter? Some other unspoken concern is afoot. Good fellow, Crivano says, I assure you I can report no heresy committed by the Nolan. Obscurity? Yes. Fallacy? Again, guilty. But not heresy.

Lunardo nods. I see, he says. Tell me about his lecture, dottore.

It was, as I said, obscure. And, at times, false.

You have a particular interest in mirrors, don't you?

Crivano forces anger into his eyes to blot out the fear, willing his gallbladder to spill forth its contents. I would not say so, he says. I don't believe I have a great number of *particular* interests. My interests, like those of any true scholar, are universal.

You were in Murano yesterday, Lunardo says. In the Serena family glassworks.

Crivano takes a bite of fish, an impatient sip of wine.

What were you doing there?

What does one do in a glassworks, sirrah? I was buying glass.

Glass, dottore? Or a mirror?

Mirrors, as you may have noted, are often made of glass.

The Serena family made a mirror for you?

Crivano's pulse flutters in his neck, like a small bird trapped in a flue; he hopes his ruff is high enough to hide it. He shifts in his chair and opens his legs, intending to avoid hitting his knee on the underside of the table when he lifts his ankle to draw the stiletto. No, he says. The Serena family made the frame. A craftsman at the Motta shop made the mirror. Alegreto Verzelin, he's called.

Describe this man to me, dottore. This Verzelin.

Tall, Crivano says. Slight. Unkempt. Quite mad, I should judge. A sickness is upon him which causes him to produce a great deal of phlegm, much as a rabid animal does. In my

778

time as a physician I have never before seen its likeness. Why do you ask?

When did you last see Maestro Verzelin?

Crivano looks at the tabletop, tapping the wood with his fingertips, counting backward. Four nights ago, it was, he says. I approved the work he'd done, and I gave it to the Serena craftsmen to be completed.

You haven't spoken with Maestro Verzelin since then?

I didn't speak with him then. I only saw him. He seemed badly troubled by the symptoms of his sickness. When I tried to engage him he hastened away. When I sought him in the streets I did not find him.

I should very much like to see the mirror these craftsmen made for you, dottore.

I suppose you would, Crivano says. But you will not do so. It is halfway to Padua by now, I imagine. On its way to Bologna.

Bologna?

Indeed. A colleague of mine at the university asked me to have it made.

Who?

I will not tell you that.

Can you describe the mirror to me?

I can, Crivano says. But I will not.

Lunardo smiles, as if this genuinely pleases him. He reaches into his doublet, withdraws a rumpled wad, smoothes it on the tabletop: a pair of well-worn chamois gloves, flesh-colored, very finely made. I urge you to reconsider your reluctance, dottore, he says. I will not insist that you speak, but the tribunal will do so, I fear.

The tribunal? Or the Council of Ten?

Lunardo doesn't respond. He begins to pull on a glove, sliding his fingers inside with great care and patience; against his skin the chamois all but vanishes. So, dottore, he says, was your little entertainment last night quite to your liking? I can't remember if I've tried that particular girl. There are, after all, so very many.

Our dialogue is concluded, Crivano says, pushing back his chair. Good day, sir. To you, and to your fellows.

She's hardly the one I would have picked for you, dottore, I confess. But there is a certain satisfaction, I suppose, in a really cheap whore when you know you can afford better. So long as she knows it too. Right, dottore? Such enthusiasm!

You are a dog, sirrah. I will not speak to you again. Tell your masters that they may find me here at the White Eagle if they have further business with me. And when next you plan to cross my path, wear those distasteful gloves, and look to your life.

As Crivano turns, his eyes make a slow sweep of the room and the street outside, taking in every face he sees: he needs to be able to recognize them again. The few innocent patrons here all inch their chairs out of his way, huddle over their plates in a pantomime of disinterest.

Lunardo raises his voice as Crivano departs. I can certainly understand, he says, why you were so quick to hire a girl last night. I can hardly walk past a convent without *my* prick turning to stone. And most of them are practically brothels anyway. Aren't they, dottore?

Crivano is hesitant to expose his back to Lunardo, but he doubts the man will strike. If the sbirri were ready to do him harm, they would have done it. They want something from him, for him to give something away. What?

He meets Anzolo's eyes as he crosses the parlor. I'll be in my room, he says.

Lunardo comes to his feet now, too, but he's in no hurry. Weren't you going out, dottore? he shouts.

I was, Crivano says. I am no longer.

He's in the corridor, on the stairs, inside his room, bolting the door. He paces the empty area between the bed and the wall — clutching his head in his hands, unable to think of anything — until Anzolo's knock comes. I'm sorry, dottore, Anzolo says as he hurries inside. I tried to warn you.

You did warn me. I thank you. And I pray your interference with these knaves will not bring any great misery upon you.

Anzolo grimaces, waves an impatient hand.

All innkeepers are outlaws, dottore, he says. We must be. It is my pleasure to oppose the sbirri. I hate them! Everyone in the Rialto hates them. But poor and desperate people sometimes sell them their eyes and their ears. When you go out again, assume that you are everywhere observed.

Crivano resumes his pacing. I've done nothing wrong, he says. Believe me.

It doesn't matter, dottore.

I have to go out, Crivano mutters, half to Anzolo, half to himself. There are errands I must attend. But how? How am I to move freely through the streets?

Anzolo shifts his weight, angles his shoulders toward the door: sympathetic, but eager to distance himself. Crivano can hardly blame him. I'll send word to Rigi, Anzolo says. The porter at the Contarini house in San Samuele. I recall correctly, do I not, that you are acquainted with Senator Giacomo Contarini? That's very good. That will help you. Rigi can collect your things and lodge you until this matter is resolved. You'll be safer there than here in the Rialto, dottore. Far safer.

Crivano nods. Yes, he says. That's wise. But don't send for him until I've gone out again. Between myself and my equipage, I'd like to divide the sbirri's attention.

As you wish, dottore. They'll search your room once you leave, of course. I won't be able to stop them. I will try to prevent them from ruining or stealing your possessions, but the best I may manage is to keep tally of what's lost.

Crivano steps to the window, parts the drapes to look down on the Street of the Coopers. Leisurely crowds move from storefront to storefront. The Jews' Sabbath: no red hats or yellow turbans in sight. A cloaked figure watches from across the street; he looks young and sturdy, but also stupid and feckless. Crivano lets the curtain fall.

Do you think the girl told them about me? he says.

Anzolo is silent for a while. I spoke to her this morning, he says. I gave her a meal. She was in fair spirits, and she said you were generous. If she tells them anything, I think she'll wait until she's certain it won't make any difference. No one hates a sbirro more than a whore, dottore. And she's a good girl.

I'm sorry that I brought her here, Anzolo.

Tell your priest, dottore, not me. If I forbade such women in my rooms, my enterprise would collapse. I therefore cast no stones. I should go, dottore. They will be waiting for me.

Crivano bolts the door behind Anzolo, listens to his footfalls recede down the corridor. The muted voices from downstairs are soon drowned out by churchbells; it's later than he thought.

Could it be that the sbirri he saw near Minerva were following neither him nor Narkis, but Ciotti? After all, Ciotti sells the Nolan's books; the Inquisition is bound to be suspicious of him. But this can't all be about the Nolan, can it? Crivano's plot with the mirrormakers and the Nolan's heresy are linked only by pure accident: his attendance of the friar's lecture, coupled with its unfortunate topic. Whatever demoniac impulse could have prompted Tristão to suggest it?

That clever sbirro downstairs seemed very interested in the mirror that Serena and Verzelin made. He wanted Crivano to describe it. Why? Could he have deduced its purpose? Perhaps this is about heresy after all — or about secret knowledge, at least. Just another skirmish between the Republic and the Pope: the Council of Ten seeking to keep account of the city's magi in advance of renewed meddling by the Inquisition. Perhaps no one yet suspects the glassmakers' pending flight.

Obizzo still doesn't know of their plans. How to tell him, without leading the sbirri to him?

Crivano opens his trunk and withdraws items from it: a quill, two jars of ink, a sheet of foolscap. He sits and stares at the blank page for a long time. Then he stands to resume his pacing.

The sunbeams under the window inch across the floor. Crivano pulls the curtains open, flooding the room with light, and returns to his trunk. He removes the letters of advice and the wooden grille from its false bottom, tucks them into his doublet, and replaces them with his esoteric books. The sbirri will surely discover these; let them think they've found something. The gecko who drops his tail.

Crivano removes the snaplock pistol from its case and holds it to the light. He wishes he'd taken it to the Lido and fired it sometime over the past few days; he'd meant to. Now he'll have to make guesses.

He draws back the cock — his thumb straining mightily against the spring — until it catches, then fixes a fresh flint in its clasp. He pulls the trigger: a shower of sparks, and a loud snap that makes him blink. The sharp smell tickles his nose.

Crivano wipes down the mechanism, cleans the barrel, clears the touchhole with a needle and a puff of air. Then he shakes grains of black powder into the flashpan, closes it, and pours more down the barrel. Unsure of proper quantities. Erring toward excess. He cuts a strip of wadding, rests a heavy lead ball in it, pushes it into the barrel with the ramrod. Then he loosens his belt and tucks in the pistol, aligning its grip with a slash in his robe, within reach of his right hand. The afternoon sun casts his silhouette against the floor; he inspects it, watching for the pistol's telltale bulge, until he's satisfied.

He sits again. Taking up the foolscap, he tears it neatly across the edge of the table, then tears it again until it's quite small. He dips his quill into the first jar — the ink colorless as water — and writes. He blows across the paper until the liquid has vanished, then cleans his quill, opens the second jar, and writes again, this time in deep black. A brief message; a few simple instructions. Tiny letters in neat rows.

He rolls the paper into a tight tube, ties it with a bit of gauze from his box of physic. Then he approaches the window — climbing across the bed to the corner, keeping his head down, so no one who watches from the street can see — and pins the rolled paper into a fold of the curtains, on the backside of the fabric, where it overlaps the wall.

Now, perhaps, he is ready.

On his way out, he leaves keys in the locks of his trunk and his box of physic. They're good locks, expensive; it seems a pity to have them broken.

55

The world outside greets Crivano with the fierce clarity of a nightmare. The sun crawls down the firmament; a pale daub of moon lingers at the horizon. Rough breezes lurk between buildings, pouncing at odd intervals, and delicate changeable clouds rush like vengeful angels to the east. The ultramarine field they cross could herald any weather. Everything arrayed beneath it appears fleeting, provisional, doomed.

Each passing face seems glimpsed through a lens, so acutely does it prick him; the texture of every surface looms so sharp in his vision that it seems to chafe his skin. Many years have gone by since terror last awakened him like this. What most troubles him is how little mind he's paid by the city's innocuous inhabitants: they obstruct his path like sleepwalkers. Among them he is insubstantial, a miasma.

His antagonists, however, find him often enough. Sometimes it's the sbirri themselves, brazen in their matching cloaks. Sometimes it's a lingering stare — a beggar, a watervendor, a whore — that's withdrawn the instant he returns it. Sometimes he simply feels eyes follow him, or senses that a street is too quiet. Has this watch been kept over him since he arrived? Is he only now able to perceive it?

He strides purposefully, his stick's ferrule ringing the flagstones and thumping the dirt, but in fact he has no purpose save to frustrate the sbirri and ascertain their tactics. His boots dissect the Rialto, tramp its every street at least twice, step into shops and churches, turn corners so capriciously that he surprises himself. Once he's begun to intuit the sbirri's methods — one will follow him for a block's length, then vanish as another takes his place — he crosses the new bridge to the Mercerie and treads its busy thoroughfares until he hears work-bells herald the day's approaching end. Then he boards a traghetto and crosses the Grand Canal again. This is the long afternoon's one moment of repose: kneading his sore shins under the boat's canopy while accidental gusts crease the water in vague patterns and the sbirri track him along the banks.

By now they will have guessed that he's waiting for darkness. In this they are nearly correct. The innumerate moments before the single bell announces sundown contain his final chance to contact Obizzo; he's resolved not to let it escape him.

Shutters close in the Rialto, pushcarts rattle home, carpets slide from windowsills. Crivano stops in a cutler's shop, drinks a cup of wine in a casino. Waiting for the light to turn gold. They're following more closely now: almost always, it's the men in cloaks. Eventually they'll lose patience — sure that they've either missed the crucial gesture, or that he's withholding it — and they'll fall on him. He has no good lies to tell under torture, no time to invent or rehearse them. If they take him, he'll say what he knows.

There: a glow on the belltower of the Frari.

He hurries into the street, zigzagging toward the great confluence at Campo San Aponal. A glance over his shoulder reveals two cloaks, both close behind.

In the campo he mixes with the milling crowd, holding his breath until he sees them: linkboys, gathered with their lanterns on the church steps, laughing and tussling at rough plebeian games while they wait for the darkness to come. Crivano sweeps toward them. Holla, mooncursers! he shouts, rubbing his palms together. Who would earn a bit of silver before the sun has gone?

The boys swarm. Crivano squats on his haunches, opens his purse to remove a bright ducat. Their unblinking eyes converge on it, aligned like compass-needles. This coin is more than any of their fathers will earn in a week — if indeed any of them have fathers. The youngest among them doesn't even know what it is; another boy's terse whisper puts an explanation in his small ear.

So, Crivano says, who among you rabble knows the Contarini house, in San Samuele?

A shrill chorus of affirmation follows.

Be at ease, whelps! Crivano says, and passes the coin to a tall harelipped boy. I have silver enough for all. You, varlet, to earn your coin, will deliver a message to Rigi, the Contarini porter. Now — who knows the Morosini house, in San Luca?

Crivano produces another ducat to more

agitated yelps, more grasping fingers. The harelipped boy is half-turned, half-crouched, ready to run; his hiss-honking voice cuts through the din. What's your message, dottore? he asks.

Be patient, my pup: you shall have it soon enough. You there! Here's a coin for you. Your task is to seek out Hugo, the Morosini porter.

For hours now Crivano has recited these instructions in his head, memorizing them like an incantation, like a magic spell — which they might as well be. He dispatches a third boy to Ciotti at Minerva, a fourth to the gatekeeper-nun at Santa Caterina, a fifth to the small casino near Santa Giustina where he spoke drunkenly of Lepanto. He has more ducats in his purse than there are linkboys. He directs another to the apothecary who sold him the henbane, another to the gondolier who last ferried him from Murano, another to the proprietor of the glass shop on the new Rialto bridge. In his mind he has assembled a map of the city: the city not as it is, but as he has encountered it these past few weeks; a map constellated from his movements and memories, congruent with tangible marble and brick, but submerged beneath the visible surfaces. Now each set of directions aims a lowly urchin down these imaginary thoroughfares.

The most vital errand he delegates to a boy who's a bit quieter than the rest, who meets his eye coolly, who listens and thinks. He's neither the youngest nor the oldest among them. He won't be a linkboy for very long. You, Crivano says, laying the ducat in the boy's palm, will go to Anzolo at the White Eagle. Do you know the place?

Soon every mooncurser has a coin. Crivano stretches from his crouch to peek over their heads; the two cloaked sbirri watch from the crowd, twenty paces off. Crivano motions the boys near, then whispers. To all, he entrusts the same message: *Look behind the curtain.*

What curtain do you mean, dottore?

The men whom you seek, Crivano says, will know what curtain. Or they will not. It doesn't matter.

Who do we say the message is from?

Say only what you know: that you were sent by a dottore, with light hair and a forked beard. That will suffice. And be nimble and clever, lads, for sbirri are about who would deter you. All go together now, on my command! Ready?

A loud handclap sends them charging like unleashed hounds. The sbirri have anticipated Crivano's stratagem, but they're at a loss for a response; they make half-hearted grabs for the nearest passing boys, then turn back to Crivano with incensed expressions. Crivano scans the crowd — four more cloaks dispersed at the edges of the campo, some now flying in pursuit of his little messengers —

then bolts to the right, around the belltower and behind the apse, doubling back toward Campo San Silvestro. *Dottore!* a voice calls. He ignores it.

The sun is down. The first bell rings at the Frari to the west and San Marco to the south; then the sound spreads to San Polo and San Aponal and San Silvestro like ripples over water. Crivano loops back again, without intention or direction. He passes the sbirro with the mutilated face who a moment ago was following him. In a gap between shops he sees one of his linkboys scurry by; he's unable to recall where he sent that one. He's very tired now. He wants to return to the White Eagle, but he can't. Not yet.

The crowds thin as the sky grows dark; soon, Crivano fears, he and the sbirri will be the streets' only occupants. He begins to seek the shortest and narrowest passages, where he can disrupt his pursuers' view. Once the second bell has rung, he thinks, I'll go back to the locanda and sleep. Not till then.

As he's navigating a constricted bend, looking over his shoulder, a strong arm snakes from a doorway and clamps hold of his elbow. He pulls away, fights to raise his stick, then notes the turban and caftan. Stop, Narkis says. Come this way. Quickly.

Algae-slick steps fall away to the right. Crivano has passed them six times today, probably. He failed to remark them at all until nearly sundown, and even then he took them for an ancient water-gate which once opened onto a canal long since filled with mud and silt. Now, as he struggles to retain his balance against Narkis's impatient tug, he sees that it's the entrance to a sottoportego, leading to a small high-walled corte. At bright noonday this passage would be dim; at dusk it's midnight-black for most of its length. On the lowest step, some small creature has left a lump of feces, now crowded with glossy black flies; they scatter as Narkis and Crivano rush by, shooting straight up, slowing as they rise, fading in all directions like sparks from a fire.

Narkis whispers as he hurries Crivano forward, speaking Turkish with his old elegance and felicity. You have been discovered, Tarjuman effendi, he says.

Crivano's sputtered response is in the local tongue; his agitated brain won't find the Turkish words. I know that, damn you, he says. I've had sbirri at my heels since the morning. I've only just now managed to get word to Obizzo.

Obizzo?

The mirrormaker.

Narkis freezes, as if turned to stone. Then he claps a hand to Crivano's chest. That business at the church with the linkboys? he says. That is what that was? That is how you sent your message? Are you mad? What if the constables intercept them?

Crivano closes his eyes, takes a long breath — remembering his other life: the view of the sultan's palace from Galata, laughing janissary faces around a campfire, the texture of a silk caftan against his skin, a cradlesong an Albanian girl once sang for him — and when he speaks again, the old language comes. Do you take me for a fool? he says. I was careful. The boys know nothing. One will set the true messenger in motion.

Whom?

My innkeeper.

This man can be trusted? You're sure? How do you know?

Of course I'm sure, Crivano says, but now he doesn't feel sure. Could Anzolo's performance this morning have been for his benefit, not Lunardo's? But no: an innkeeper who cooperated with sbirri couldn't stay in business very long. Could he?

I left a note in my room, Crivano continues, where it won't be found. The note tells the innkeeper how to find Obizzo.

How?

Obizzo is a gondolier in the Rialto. He has scars on his arms from the furnaces. The gondoliers all know one another. You can always find one, if he wants to be found.

What message did you send?

The one you told me to send, Narkis. In two days, he's to row to the lagoon west of San Giacomo en Palude under cover of darkness, and look for an anchored trabacolo showing two red lanterns. That is all.

Crivano can barely make out the shape of Narkis's head against the blue light from the corte; it's motionless for a long time. Loud muffled voices come from behind them, but no boots scuffle on the steps, not yet. Come, Narkis says, and presses on.

Crivano's boot drags through a puddle; the odor of the sea rises with the splash. You have done well, Narkis says. Our project may not be completely destroyed.

I don't know how the sbirri discovered me. They want me to think it has to do with a heretic who's been arrested, but I don't believe that.

It is the mirrormaker, Narkis says. The one you killed.

Verzelin?

They have found his remains. They washed up on the Lido yesterday morning. He must have drifted quite far. The gulls showed where his body had come to rest. The flesh had been badly disturbed by various creatures, but the constables knew who it had been in life from a ring that it wore: a glass ring, bearing a false black pearl. You should have removed that, I suppose.

Crivano stops. The skin of his face is numb, as if blasted by an icy wind. He shakes his head. Verzelin wore no rings; Crivano would have noticed them as he bound the dead man's hands. Surely he would have. You're quite certain, he says, that the corpse is Verzelin's?

I can only repeat what I have heard. The mirrormakers' guild has declared that the corpse belongs to the man you murdered. Prevalent opinion is that he suffered despair due to his sickness and drowned himself. Although there is some doubt that, in his infirm condition, he could have tied certain knots. Also, no boats are missing from Murano. This is difficult to explain.

They're going to accuse me.

I think it is likely that they will do so, yes. They suspect a larger conspiracy.

What should I do?

You should stay away from the glassmaker and the mirrormaker whom you have recruited until they have safely escaped. You should avoid arrest until they are gone. If the constables arrest you, they will torture you, and you will confess. Everyone does.

But *what* —

Crivano's voice is suddenly harsh in the tight space: a stranger's voice. His clawed hands gather the folds of Narkis's caftan.

— should I *do*?

Narkis is still for a moment. Then he sighs. I do not know, Tarjuman effendi, he says. They are hunting me as well. The constables came to the fondaco this afternoon. I fled through a window and escaped along the rooftops.

Crivano's grip loosens. The sbirri saw them both at Ciotti's shop; of course they'd be looking for Narkis too. Is all lost, then? he says. Who will arrange the escape of the craftsmen? We ourselves can do nothing now.

Rest assured, Tarjuman effendi, that others can accomplish these things.

Narkis's cryptic tone is ugly to Crivano's ear; it flavors his restrained panic with a new disquiet. If that's so, he says, then perhaps we might now consider how best to save ourselves. What if we leave for the mainland tonight? With a few days' advance travel we can meet the ship in Trieste, and then go with them to Spalato.

Our party may not be going to Spalato after all, Tarjuman effendi.

Or, Crivano says, we could risk the uskoks, and sail directly for Constantinople.

They will not be going to Constantinople, either.

Crivano's teeth chatter; he's suddenly cold. So damp: he feels as if he's been ingested by some leviathan. What, he says, are you talking about?

Narkis doesn't answer. He begins to walk toward the corte again; Crivano stumbles after him. In the opening he can see a small carved wellhead, and fallen tiles littering the pavement. Old friend, Crivano asks again, what do you mean?

797

In arranging the passage of the two craftsmen, Narkis says, I have had assistance from other interested parties. These parties have made suggestions that may alter aspects of our scheme.

Who? What parties?

I am speaking of certain instruments of the Mughal Empire.

Crivano stops again. Narkis walks ahead for several paces, then slows and turns back. Somewhat sheepishly, it seems. Tarjuman effendi, he says. Come along.

What in the name of God did you just say?

The Mughals. They have been lately challenging our Safavid enemy along his eastern borders, and have conquered Gujarat and Bengal. It seems —

Do I understand correctly, Crivano says, that you intend to take the craftsmen not to Constantinople, but halfway across the world, to Hindustan? To install them among savages, where not a single soul can speak or comprehend their language? Is this what you mean, Narkis? Because, if so, you are insane.

Speak low, Tarjuman effendi. Please.

Crivano's voice is shot through with hot veins of hysteria; it trembles and cracks like a fuzzy-cheeked boy's, but he does not hold his tongue. How in the name of the Holy Prophet, he says, can the Mughals assist us? They're separated from Frankish lands by the breadth of our own empire, and another

798

empire besides. Between us and them lies not only a continent, but an unceasing bloody war. What can they do?

They have arranged to escort us through the lands of the Tatars and the Turkmen, across the Caspian Sea, up the valley of the Amu Darya, to Kabul. We need never enter Safavid territory.

Ah! Crivano half-shrieks. Splendid! I wonder, though, if you have considered how the emperor of Japan might also help us? Now, there is a resource we have not yet exploited! And neither must we ignore the New World, of course. Perhaps we can hitch our craftsmen to a team of parrots and fly them to safety! Oh, it sounds mad, sure. But is it really?

Narkis steps forward and slaps him. Crivano recoils, then raises his stick; it strikes the low ceiling and clatters from his hands. Trembling, he sags against the slimy wall, his eyes full, his breath coming in rapid gasps. After a moment he feels Narkis's gentle hand on his head. Calm, Tarjuman effendi, he says. I am truly sorry for this. It is not what was intended.

Crivano gulps air, hiccups, picks up his stick. They continue together toward the corte. What do you expect of the craftsmen? Crivano says, when he can speak again.

They will be angry. That is inevitable. But this cannot be avoided. After all, they already believe they're going to Amsterdam. Is Lahore a much greater deception than Constantinople?

I'd say so, yes. What will you do? Cage them like beasts bound for a menagerie?

If I must, yes.

As they approach the end of the sottoportego, Narkis's features come gradually into view: first his eyes, reflecting blue light from the corte, followed by his pale face, the fabric of his caftan. A black ribbon runs from the edge of his turban down his cheek and onto his shoulder. Crivano remarks it vaguely; he's not seen Narkis wear such an ornament before.

I'm not going to Lahore, Narkis, Crivano says. I won't.

Yes. I expected that you would not.

What, then, should I do?

Sequester yourself for a few days. Once the craftsmen have escaped, come forth and cooperate with the constables. They will be lenient; you can tell them much that will be of value to them. You can continue your life here. Have you a place you can go now? A safe place?

I think so. The Contarini house.

Yes. The senator will protect you. The Morosini, also. These men are powerful, and opposed to the faction that now controls the Council of Ten. You will survive.

Could I return to Constantinople?

Narkis is silent for a long time. That would be difficult, he says.

They enter the corte, stepping around debris to lean against the wellhead. Its hexagonal base bears the emblem of an ancient family, disgraced or devastated by the accident of history. Crivano pays it little mind. Overhead, coppery Mars shines, along with a few bright stars, dulled by the glow of the waxing gibbous moon. Dense scattered clouds still rake the sky, slate-gray against the deep blue.

What are we, Narkis? Crivano asks. Whom have we betrayed, and on whose behalf? Of whom are we agents?

Narkis's chin is tucked against his chest; he pushes a chip of terracotta back and forth with his boot's toe. We are agents of the haseki sultan, he says. And agents of the Mughal emperor. We are agents of no one. We are agents of ourselves. And, as we are both scholars, I believe us to be agents of the truth. I truly believe this, Tarjuman effendi.

Crivano now sees that the dark ribbon that runs down Narkis's face is a column of blood, spilled from a gash on his forehead, an inch forward of his temple. It's clear in the moonlight against the yellow silk of his caftan; it stains his shoulder, then vanishes into his armpit.

When I was a young man, Narkis says, the grand vizier chose me from among the sultan's guard to join an expedition to the court of Akbar, the Mughal emperor, who was then still quite young. The journey was difficult. Many of us were killed by sickness and cold, by packs of wolves, by Safavids and Cossacks. Some fell into ravines. Some were struck by lightning. One man was devoured by a tiger: a terrible sight, glorious in its way, and one I will never forget. When finally we presented ourselves to the emperor in Delhi, we were greatly depleted. He welcomed us with pity and wonder. A remarkable man! Entirely illiterate, but with a flawless memory. Moderate in his diet. Subsisting from fruits, and very little meat. Intensely curious. Capable of extraordinary sympathy. A Muslim, but friendly toward Christians and Hindus, and those of less common faiths. He suspects, as we do, that diverse beliefs and practices have as their common basis a single truth, and he devotes himself and the vast resources of his empire to uncovering it. Most remarkable. I stayed with him for a number of years.

You became his agent.

I became an agent of the truth. As I have said.

Crivano looks at the walls that edge the corte. He can see dim lamplight in some windows. What does your emperor want with our craftsmen? he says.

He is interested in mirrors. He keeps a sizable collection of them. The ones he showed me were quite old, and inferior to what Murano now produces. He confided to me that he dreams of building a mirrored palace, where everyone can be seen always, where everyone can always see himself. Everything is always clear. The emperor's grand unlettered mind is itself like a mirror, Tarjuman effendi. Its surface can hold anything, and yet remains unscarred by error and falsehood. I believe him to be the perfect sovereign. The Guided One foretold by the hadith.

A long silence. Then more muffled shouts from the street, and a flash of lantern-light down the sottoportego. Crivano tenses in fear, but Narkis doesn't react. After a moment the light moves away, and the voices cease.

They will return soon, Narkis says. With more men. They know that we have come here.

Is there another way out?

There is. A moment, please.

Narkis's face is slack with weariness, or disappointment, or grief. Crivano has never learned how old he is; at this moment he looks very old. What about you? Crivano says. Where can you go?

Vacant buildings, Narkis says. Since I do not speak the local language well, it will be difficult for me to arrange passage from the city. Perhaps I will hide myself among the Greeks and escape to Dalmatia on one of their boats.

What happened to your head, Narkis?

Narkis looks up, touches his cheek, looks at his fingers. This? he says. This is nothing. A group of boys throwing stones. They were trying to knock off my turban, I think. It happens often enough. They meant no real harm.

Crivano watches him with a mixture of sorrow and revulsion. Millennial fervor abounds in Muslim lands this year, the thousandth year of the Hegira, but it has never occurred to Crivano that Narkis might be susceptible to it. He remembers something Tristão said about the Nolan, about how he'd been searching the courts of Christendom for a philosopher-king to instruct. Perhaps he should have traveled farther east. What produces credulous fools like these?

He remembers something else. Might not Tristão be in danger? he says.

Who?

Dottore de Nis. How much does he know of our plot?

Narkis's eyes narrow in the dark; the hint of a furrow appears on his smooth brow. I know of no one by that name, he says.

Of course you do. The Portuguese alchemist. The converso. When you and I met in Ravenna, you instructed me specifically to seek him out. You said that his activities could serve as a blind for our own conspiracy. Like the gecko who drops his tail, you said. You must remember.

Narkis offers a tentative nod. Yes, he says. I suppose I do. His name came to me from the haseki sultan, by way of her lady-in-waiting. My recollection is faint, I confess. My attention has since been directed to other matters.

But you must know him, Crivano persists. He arranged our meeting at the bookshop. He introduced me to Ciotti. He suggested you as a translator. I'm sure I saw sbirri watching us when we left Minerva, so I thought that surely —

Crivano's voice trails off. The crease in Narkis's brow deepens, stretching his skin, reopening his cut, but now his eyes are wide. My summons came from the bookseller himself, he says. I have never met the person of whom you speak.

The scrape of a boot echoes from the far terminus of the sottoportego; a half-hooded lantern glints along its slick wall. Crivano can hear gruff whispers. They're coming, he says.

Narkis has moved to the corner of the corte almost before Crivano has turned around. A thick piece of pinewood is propped against the wall there; Narkis climbs it to grab a loop of rope that dangles from a narrow window, then squeezes inside as Crivano pushes his feet from below. Crivano hands Narkis his walkingstick and ascends, planting a toe on the cracked dentil molding long enough to kick the wood aside, dragging himself through the window as Narkis pulls him by the arms. Shouts from the sottoportego, and a bobbing light: the sbirri must have heard the pinewood fall. Crivano pulls up the loop of rope after himself.

They're in a dark and musty storeroom, cluttered with empty and broken crates; many are rotten, fuzzed with moss. Soft footfalls come from overhead. Someone is upstairs, Crivano whispers.

Narkis waves a hand, as if this is no concern, and steps out of the moonlight. Crivano takes hold of his sleeve to follow him. They emerge in a hallway, which leads in turn to an ancient staircase; as they descend, it groans menacingly under their weight. Narkis leads him to a heavy door, then stops, his hand on the bolt. They must be near the street now; Crivano hears strident commands, heavy boots on pavingstones.

Beyond this door, Narkis says, is a storefront. The shopkeeper and his family are upstairs; they will be down soon when they hear it open, so you must be quick.

You aren't coming with me?

Narkis shakes his head with grim impatience. Walk through, he says, and then unbolt the door to the street. Go back to your inn, collect your possessions, and go to the senator's house.

Where will I be when I come out?

In the Campiello del Sale. Do you know

where that is?

Of course. Where are you going to go? You can't stay here.

Narkis doesn't answer. With some effort, he throws the bolt and casts the large door open. The storefront is lit through its slatted shutters by the lantern of the locanda next door. For an instant, Crivano can see Narkis's face: haggard with anguish, his eyes brightened by tears. Then Narkis shoves him through, and the door slams behind him.

Loud voices from above, and rapid steps: soft at first, then, after a pause, boot-shod. Crivano vaults the counter, crosses the room, unbolts the door. He peeks through the crack — the campiello looks clear — and slips out. But the moment his feet touch the flagstones, a pair of sbirri enter from the north, on the very street he'd planned to take; he turns left, makes the corner before they spot him. Something different about these two. Walking together. Both wearing sidearms. Hunting, not following.

He's soon in the Campo San Aponal again — a group of young nobles is gathered before the church, grousing about the lack of linkboys — and from there he takes a back route to the White Eagle over the Slaughterhouse Bridge Canal. Along the way, he passes a pair of watchmen from the Ministry of Night, drinking cups of wine in a casino with its shutters still open. They don't seem intent on resuming their rounds anytime soon. Tonight they've ceded their streets to the sbirri.

He expects cloaked swordsmen at the locanda's door, or in the parlor, but there's no one to be seen aside from one of the Friulian girls, who scurries away in evident terror as soon as Crivano appears. He pays her no mind, rushes upstairs, bursts into his room, bolts the door. Then he turns to survey the damage done to his things.

His things are gone. The sbirri must have confiscated them. The message pinned to the curtain is gone, too. Who found it first?

He nearly collides with Anzolo on his way to the street. Dottore! Anzolo hisses, and shoves him backward, down a corridor, into the kitchen, out of sight. They're out there now, Anzolo says. It's very bad, dottore. They're everywhere, and they're all armed. Wait here until the street clears, then go to the Contarini house at once.

Did the boy find you?

Yes, dottore. He did.

And the gondolier, did you find him?

I did. I gave him your message. Let me check the street for you. I'll tell you when it's safe.

Yes. Thank you, Anzolo. Oh — my items: my box and my trunk. Do you know where they took them?

Anzolo stops in the doorframe. Where who took them, dottore?

The sbirri. Didn't the sbirri seize them?

Bafflement settles on Anzolo's face. I thought you took them, he says. I thought you had them sent to the Contarini house.

But I've just now come for them. I didn't send for them. Who took them away?

I — I wasn't here at the time. I was on the Riva del Fabbriche, seeking out your gondolier. Agnesina was here. Agnesina!

He calls the girl's name several times, but she does not appear. They find her in a storeroom, hidden behind a stack of boxes: the one who fled when Crivano arrived.

Agnesina! What's the matter? What's come over you?

Young woman, Crivano says, what became of my trunk, and my box?

The girl recoils into the corner, making an elaborate gesture with her hands. The gesture is familiar, though Crivano can't place it. Her eyes are vast and terrified. Hairs bristle on Crivano's neck.

Agnesina! Anzolo thunders. Answer the dottore! Who took his things?

When she finally speaks, her voice quakes as if she's freezing. It was him, she says. He took them himself.

Her unsteady finger is aimed at Crivano's chest.

Agnesina, Anzolo says, that is not possible. He is here now to collect them. The man who came earlier: what did he look like? How

809

many were with him?

No one was with him, she says. No one.

Are you sure? The dottore's trunk is far too heavy for a single man to move.

What did he look like? Crivano says. His voice seems to come from outside himself.

You, she says, weeping now. Like you. But also not. And with different — garments. Garments like — a doctor — like during —

Leave her be, Crivano says. It doesn't matter. Leave her be.

He waits in the corridor, listening through the door as Anzolo alternately upbraids and consoles the girl. His heart thuds in his chest like a separate creature, like it knows of terrors as yet unsuspected by the rest of his body. In a moment, Anzolo emerges from the room, but he won't meet Crivano's eyes. You should hurry, he says. I'll check the street.

What was that gesture that the girl made?

It's nothing, dottore. She's very excited, with all the sbirri. I'll talk to her when she's calm, and we'll make arrangements for your things.

Anzolo, Crivano says. What was the gesture?

Nothing. As I said. Something superstitious peasants do.

Why? Why do they do it?

I don't know, dottore. I'm a city man, myself.

Anzolo attempts a smile, but can't sustain it. Crivano fixes him with a flat stare.

They do it to ward off evil, I suppose, Anzolo says. Evil spirits.

Evil spirits? Crivano says. Are you sure?

For a long time Anzolo says nothing. He stands in the corridor with one hand on the wall, facing the door to the street. He's shivering too; Crivano can see that now.

The plague, he answers at last. They do it to protect themselves from the plague.

Crivano takes a deep breath, releases it slowly. His lungs fill and empty; blood thickens in his brain. He can feel parts of himself awakening that have been dormant for years, while everything within him that has been awake now seems to grow dull and indifferent: pale worms in winter mud.

Yes, he says. I thought that might be the case. Thank you, Anzolo.

56

A pair of sbirri passes, Anzolo gives the signal, and Crivano steps from the White Eagle's door. It closes behind him with a quiet brush of wood on wood: a final sound. He is alone. He has always been alone — since the Lark died, at least — but his isolation can no longer be hidden. Like a splinter of steel lodged in a muscle, he is no longer part of what he moves among.

He turns right to return the way he came, but immediately spots two more sbirri at the casino down the street; they've stopped to argue with the nightwatchmen he saw earlier. Crivano detours into a dark doorway and waits for them to move on. Instead, one of them enters the casino — *I'll chase this heretic dog down with ease, I promise you, once I've taken a nice shit* — and leaves the other behind. Crivano recognizes the remaining sbirro as the feckless youth who watched his room all afternoon. The boy puffs out his chest, fingers the pommel of his rapier like it's a new toy. Crivano counts his pulse, giving the young sbirro's partner time enough to reach the privy and pull down his hose. Then he hurries along the street — stepping from shadow to shadow — and clubs the boy in the face with the iron head of his walking-stick.

The young sbirro shrieks, drops to the packed dirt. The watchmen rise in half-crouches, looking at Crivano, looking at each other. Crivano raises his stick again, and they both sink to their seats. The sbirro moans, clutching his wrecked face, retching blood and mucus. Crivano keeps steady eyes on the seated watchmen as he relieves the wounded boy of his sword and scabbard.

They shout and scramble to fetch the second sbirro from the privy once Crivano's out of sight, but he's a safe distance away now, moving west, out of the Rialto. The wind has lessened, the sky is cloudless, and the air has grown dense, unseasonably cold. The warm canal waters send up tendrils of mist; he sees them as he crosses the little bridge. The moon is low, but there's still plenty of light. Too much light.

By now the sbirri will have rounded up all his linkboys; they will have found the recipients of his message, and all will have professed ignorance of its meaning. Those are the places the sbirri will congregate, in hopes of his reappearance. Crivano therefore opts to propel himself into quarters as yet unknown: toward San Polo and the Frari. As usual the streets conspire to steer him elsewhere: north instead, approaching the upper bend of the Grand Canal. Crivano makes no real effort to resist their redirection. At this point it doesn't much matter where he goes.

What is he? Whose agent? What has he become?

Only with effort can he now recall the two boys who stood on the deck of the *Gold and Black Eagle* — the boys who both died there, and were there reborn. He kept himself alive for years with promises of eventual vengeance, with the dream that the Turks would one day pay in blood for what they had done to his home, to his family, to the Lark. He so cherished the dream of retribution that he concealed it in a treasure-box within himself, and locked that box inside other boxes, until finally — after the campaigns in Africa and

Persia, after the camaraderie with the men who shared his cookpot, after the failures and successes along every frontier of the sultan's empire — Narkis's proposal arrived, and Crivano thought: *this is the time, if ever the time is to come.* By then, of course, the vengeful boy was nowhere within himself to be found. As he departed Constantinople he consoled himself with the thought that he'd simply mislaid whatever keys would open those old boxes, that they'd reemerge with time. Now he knows that the compartments are empty, and always were. His cold ferocious heart is no more than a corridor lined with mirrors, a procession of ghosts and absences, haunting one another and themselves.

He's passed the lengths of a half-dozen streets and seen no sbirri. A few watchmen make their rounds — these haven't been relieved of their duties — and Crivano steps from view whenever they appear. Somewhere behind him the sbirri are tending to their wounded boy, widening their patrols. They'll catch up soon enough. He'd planned to circle south, to cross the Grand Canal to the Contarini house, but he can just as easily hire a boat on the upper bend, by the Cannaregio Canal. That could be better, in fact: the sbirri won't find him under the canopy of a sandolo. And it would be pleasant to float free through the heart of the city one last time, to watch the moonlight play on the palace façades. A good way to bid this place farewell. He'll hide at the Contarini house for a few days, then find a ship to Constantinople. Or Ragusa. Or Tunis. Any port will do. Crivano is a physician, after all, and disease is everywhere.

On the Street of the Dyers he evades two approaching watchmen, then notices that they're inattentive, deep in discussion. He sits in a doorway to eavesdrop.

So this all has to do with that heretic they've arrested? the first says. Some sort of plot, I suppose?

Damned if I can say, comes the reply. The heretic was denounced by his patron, Zuanne Mocenigo, who's widely known to be a fool and a two-faced coward. They say he's mixed up with sorcerers, those who conjure demons. Earlier tonight, some villain painted a vile curse in Latin across Mocenigo's palace gate; now a half-dozen bravi guard his doors, and every candle, lamp, and lantern he owns is ablaze. He's terrified.

And the two men that the sbirri hunt —

Only one, now. The physician. They found the Turk a short while ago, afloat in the Madonnetta Canal.

Dead?

Of course, dead. You think he was swimming? As far as who killed him — the sbirri, or the Turk's own accomplices, or perhaps he

815

died by his own hand —

Shush! *Who goes there?*

They've seen him. The tired muscles of Crivano's legs and back protest as he rises from his seat on the steps, ambles forward.

Good Christ. That's him.

Their light falls on his face; he squints. These look like ordinary city commoners: sleepy unskilled tradesmen carrying clubs and a lantern through the streets for a few extra coins. Men with debts and families. The three of them exchange bleak looks, trapped in a moment that none has wished for. Then Crivano shifts his walkingstick to his left hand, and begins to draw the rapier.

Run! the first watchman barks, but the other is already running: orange sparks fly from his clattering lantern as he stuffs a wooden whistle between his lips. Thin harsh notes pierce the cooling air. Crivano hears people in adjacent houses stir.

He lets the watchmen go. By now the sbirri must be close; these two will find them soon enough. The campo of San Giacomo dall'Orio is but a short distance away, the Grand Canal not much farther on: Crivano could be safely aboard a boat within minutes. But he's going to wait in the campo instead. He's not quite satisfied, not quite finished. Behind him the dark streets scroll like pages in an old codex, one he's struggled for years to parse. He feels as if he's reached the end

816

only to discover that he's been misreading it all along — taking for literal truth what was meant as allegory, or vice versa. He wants to flip back to the beginning, to start over with fresh eyes. Even if doing so means he can never be free of it. Even if it's too late now for understanding anyway.

A few paces ahead, at the next intersection — a narrow street branching to the west — a chill settles over him, and he stops, aware that he's being watched. For a long time he remains motionless. Knowing already. Not wanting to see it. Finally, with effort, he twists his stiff neck to the left.

It's perhaps a hundred feet away, down the sidestreet, backlit by a fat yellow moon. Blocking the light. Crivano can see the outlines of its wide-brimmed hat, its ash wand, its beaked mask. He can't smell the asafetida, but he can see the smoke: little wisps adrift before its glinting glassy eyes.

He wants to go to it. To kill it. To come to the end. But as he's drawing his sword he hears a shout from somewhere behind him, and another answering it: the spread of the watchmen's alarms. He looks away for an instant, and when he glances down the side-street again, the fiend is gone.

He isn't ready for this. He hurries forward on clumsy legs, tingling like he's been still for too long, like he's exchanged his body for another's. In the campo torches blaze at the church's side door; strange shadows waver under trees. The thing is everywhere now: always at the corner of his eye. He turns, turns again. Sniffing the air.

The church door opens with the pressure of his shoulder; Crivano steps into candle-light. No priest inside. No one here at all. As if the city belongs only to him and the demons he's conjured. He walks to the west end of the nave, dips his fingers in the font and crosses himself, feeling foolish for doing so. Along the walls, from chapel to chapel, he takes long breaths to cool his blood and brain. Looking at everything. The ship's-keel roof. Fossil snails in the floor. A green marble column taken during the Crusades. Paintings of saints and the Virgin. One shadowy canvas — John the Baptist preaching to a rapt and reverent crowd — seizes and won't relinquish his attention, and he steps forward to examine it.

This is surely the hand of the mad crafts-man of whom the senator spoke: the one who believed himself hounded by sbirri and magi-cians, the one who cast himself from a window toward his death. Crivano manages an ironic smirk, but it falters. It's all too easy to imagine: the painter's confident departure from Bassano del Grappa. The thrill he must have felt when the city first met his eyes. The heavy charge given by his patron: to maintain the *imago urbis,* to distill and sublime eight

818

quicksilver centuries with a few daubs of pig-
ment, a few brushstrokes. The vision of
beauty and order that burned in him; the
anguish he felt when, from within and without, that vision was betrayed. It's all there on
the great canvas, rendered clearly enough: in
the rapturous upturned eyes of a woman in
the audience, in the sourceless darkness that
weights everything from above. Crivano
clenches his teeth and thinks of reckless
Tristão in his laboratory, of Narkis dead in
the warm filthy water, of the Nolan rotting in
his long-coveted cell. *The pathetic example of
Narcissus warns us against a direct approach
to the mirror, for then our eyes meet only our
own image. In such a closed circle, no good
can result. The example to emulate is that of
noble Actaeon, who entered the grotto of the
Moon by accident, who cast his slanted gaze
toward the pool's silvered surface, and who
glimpsed there, half-submerged, the goddess's
unclothed form.* Fools, Crivano thinks. All of
them. To want what they wanted. To seek
what they sought.

The side door opens. A man steps through
it. He wears a rapier and the cloak of a sbirro.
He and Crivano look at each other without
expression for several long breaths. Then the
man opens the door again, and steps outside.

Crivano's tread is well-practiced; the soles
of his boots are soft. He catches the door

819

before it has fully closed. The sbirro is a few paces ahead, beckoning to his two fellows in the campo; he turns as the door opens, and Crivano drives the ferrule of his stick into the side of the sbirro's head, just above the ear.

The two sbirri in the campo draw their rapiers and charge. Crivano steps over the fallen man, unsheathes his own blade, waits for them to close the distance. As he's anticipated, they're fierce and ruthless, but not skilled swordsmen. He stabs the first in the kidney, the second in the eye.

The second sbirro screams, throws down his sword, hides his face in his hands, and screams again. Then he bolts, runs headlong into the trunk of an old bay laurel, and collapses in mute convulsions. The kidney-hit sbirro sinks to the packed earth — slowly, like a sick drunk — and begins to weep and moan. Crivano kicks him twice at the base of his skull to silence him.

More shouts: someone has heard. Looking down the Street of the Dyers and the Ruga Bella, Crivano sees lanternlight in the distance, lending color to the brick walls, shaping buildings from the blackness. He falls back and rounds the church's corner, passing the twin hemispheres of the apse, dashing through the Campiello of the Dead.

He's about to follow Broad Street north — the Grand Canal two hundred yards away, not yet visible — when something draws his eye. Shadows on the base of the old bell-tower. Two silhouettes cast by a pair of torches, identical and overlapping, as though seen through crossed eyes. The torchlight emanates from a gap between buildings, a gap he hasn't noticed till now. Crivano stares at the oscillating shadows until he sorts out details: the curve of a beak, the ellipse of a hat-brim, a long slim wand aslant a wrist.

He tiptoes to the gap, pressing his shoulder to the bricks, then circles wide as he turns the corner, his rapier at the ready, his stick high to ward off attack. But nothing's there — no figure to block the light, no torches to cast it — only a dark and narrow street edged by modest shops, moonlit at its midpoint by the transit of a canal. The air over the tiny bridge swirls with rising mist. Crivano moves steadily forward, his sword's blood-streaked tip an antenna in the dark.

On the other side of the canal, beyond the curtain of fog, the street changes. Quiet before, it's now entirely silent: devoid of tittering rats, soft human snores, the lap of water. Here the storefronts seem implausibly perfect: no brick chipped, no wood rotten, every window tidily glazed. It seems like a backdrop for an elaborate intermedio, or some similar spectacle. As if it might topple backward at any slight touch.

The street bends left, then right, and terminates in a cramped campiello. One end leads to a private bridge and a bolted palace gate. The other end abuts the Saint John Beheaded Canal. Crivano is trapped. He has trapped himself.

He can hear the deliberate approach of the sbirri: they call to one another and stamp their booted feet. They must know where he is, and that he's cornered; they hope he'll hear them and rush forward again, racing them to the bridge. They want to catch him with the canal at his back, to overwhelm him with their superior numbers.

Crivano opts not to disappoint them. He hides the bright blade of his sword in its scabbard and creeps through the darker shadows on the street's right side, hunched like a subhuman, inching toward the canal. The sbirri have left their lanterns behind; he can barely see them on the opposite side: two in the vanguard, at least two more behind those. Preparing nervously to cross. When the first pair reaches the bridge — squinting through the mist, their shapes edged by moonlight — he springs.

They fall back immediately, intent on drawing him forward — opening space to flank him, forcing him to engage three or four abreast — but Crivano keeps a foot planted at all times on the bridge's wooden planks, and fends them off with deep lunges. He counts five here, more on the way: torches by the base of the distant belltower, sparking and guttering as their bearers charge forward. Crivano's stick and rapier make slow theatrical sweeps, beating the blades of the sbirri, offering them a simulacrum of real battle. Then, after clumsy parries and a brief stumble, he retreats onto the bridge.

No! Fall back! shouts a stern voice from farther up the street, but the sbirri don't listen: the first one lurches after him, the second queues behind, and the three others who'd been shuffling eagerly in the background press forward as well, sensing weakness, smelling blood, covetous of the chance to do harm. Crivano scrambles backward, gasping in feigned distress, until three of the five have followed him onto the bridge, and he feels pavement beneath his heels again.

Then he starts killing them. The first man becomes an impromptu barricade, crumpled on the planks with wounded knees and punctured lungs; the second loses his footing as he steps over his comrade, falls into the canal when Crivano's blade finds his femoral artery. The third jumps back in a panicked rout, collides with the man behind him, plunges uninjured into the water. The last two retreat to await their fellows' arrival.

The clangor of clapped steel echoes in Crivano's ears, but for a moment the air is still: he hears only the quick rough breathing of his adversaries, the gurgling wheeze of the dying man at his feet, the splashes of the fallen sbirro as he swims east in search of a quay, the approaching footfalls of the next wave. It has been a long time since Crivano last fought for his life. He is no longer young. Cold sweat soaks his shirt and streaks his face. The tibialis anterior of his right leg aches and burns from lunging.

Five more sbirri appear at the opposite end of the bridge. The clever one from the White Eagle, Lunardo, is among them. He dismisses two of the others immediately, sending them for reinforcements. Good evening, dottore! he calls, raising an arm. I've worn my gloves, you see! Just as you asked. Now, come across the bridge!

Lunardo wears a rapier and an offhand dagger, and two of his men — one is the scarfaced ruffian — wield cudgels. A defense against such variety will be difficult to maintain. Crivano floods his lungs with air, shakes out his legs. His wrists are trembling.

I should tell you, Lunardo shouts, that many more of us are on the way. Some will come on boats, and will moor in the campiello behind you, thus to envelop you. These men will not kill you, dottore. They will be armed with clubs, and they will beat you, and break your hands and feet, and they will deliver you to the Council of Ten. The Council will have you tortured, and strangled, and put in the lagoon. Much as you put that mirrormaker in the lagoon, isn't that so? Hardly a death a man would choose, dottore. But you have other choices, don't you? I think you do. So, then. Shall we wait? Or shall we pass the time by killing one another? Come across the bridge, dottore.

Crivano doesn't reply. He measures the space he stands in, pacing the width of the planks between the smooth wooden cart-curbs, the distance from the fallen man to the pavement. The light dims suddenly in the west, then turns orange: a boat is passing the canal's terminus, eclipsing the reflection of the moon on the water; someone aboard bears a blazing torch. After a moment the boat slips from view, and the light is as it was.

Lunardo squats on his haunches at the canal's edge, smiling, bobbing to stretch his legs. Crivano cleans the gore from his blade, then steps onto the bridge, over the dying sbirro. He will go no farther. Lunardo salutes as he comes forward, but Crivano doesn't reciprocate. Beneath their feet, the planks are daubed with dark medallions.

They begin. The walkingstick fouls Lunardo's sword with semicircular parries; soon Crivano opens small cuts on the sbirro's thighs and arms and cheek. Lunardo is an adequate swordsman, but no master, and although the stick grows heavy in Crivano's weaker left hand, it gives him the advantage of reach. He presses his attacks, wanting to finish this man quickly.

Again and again Lunardo falls back to the pavement; Crivano takes these opportunities to catch his breath, measure his steps. He finds these attempts to lure him over the bridge insulting. Lunardo must know by now that he won't prevail without bringing his men into the fight; Crivano can read calculation in his stoat-like eyes.

Just as Crivano's decided that his opponent lacks the courage to make the charge, it comes: Lunardo hurls his main-gauche over the canal and lunges with a cry, sprawling forward, scrambling on his knees and emptied hand, slashing wildly with his rapier. Crivano glances the crown of the man's skull with his stick, but he's forced to fall back; he steps over the dying sbirro, onto the end of the bridge. Lunardo keeps coming, as he surely knows he must, accepting a hard blow to the right shoulder to block Crivano's final desperate riposte: it opens a gash on his side, but his ribs turn the point away. The men collide with an ugly sound of jarred bone, and when they return to their feet, they're both standing on the pavement.

Another sbirro is already across the bridge, swinging his cudgel; in the time it takes Crivano to parry him, Lunardo has retrieved his thrown dagger. Soon Crivano is fighting a third man as well, a wild-eyed Genoese with a rapier, and the faceless cyclops is not far behind, at the bridge's midpoint, awaiting his opening. Crivano can do nothing but hold his ground, and that only poorly. The snaplock pistol still hangs in his belt, but he'll have no chance to withdraw it. He tries to keep calm, to encourage their confidence. He fights like an automaton, distributing his attention to the periphery of his vision. Watching for a mistake. He needs to kill someone very soon.

But now he sees lights flicker in the glazed windows around him: torches coming at his back. The sbirri's reinforcements have arrived. Crivano is beaten. He hopes he can fight hard enough to die here, to avoid capture. He gauges the approach of the sbirri behind him by the spread of the lupine grins on his adversaries' faces. He keeps his stance forward, waiting until the last moment, hoping to gut at least one before their bludgeons pulverize him. He and his opponents have all grown shadows: the fires are close. Then, as Crivano readies himself to drop and pivot, he registers a flicker of confusion in Lunardo's eyes, and stops.

A diminutive figure darts past, a torch in its outstretched left hand, and sets the Genoese's hair on fire. Then a belaying pin smashes the Genoese's foot. Lunardo's mouth falls open in alarm, and Crivano lunges: the rapier's tip is stopped by the man's breastbone, but Crivano passes forward and redoubles and lands the stick's ferrule on the bridge of his nose. Lunardo drops with a cry.

Crivano turns and kills the panicked Genoese, then looks over his shoulder for more attackers, but no one else is behind him. The sbirro with the cudgel is swinging at the torchbearer, who ducks, throws the belaying pin, ducks again, and catches a blow in the side. *Narkis!* Crivano thinks — the torchbearer is similarly slight — but it isn't Narkis: the yelp of pain is high-pitched, childish. Somehow familiar. One of the linkboys?

Crivano hears a distant twang, and a loud crack nearby: someone has fired a crossbow. He spins, searching the surrounding windows and rooftops, but they're all clear. The sbirro raises his club to strike the torchbearer again; Crivano sweeps forward and stabs him in the chest. The blade reemerges from the man's back, below the inner edge of his right scapula, then snaps inches above its hilt as he stumbles and falls. The torchbearer is curled on the pavement, moaning through clenched teeth, clutching his ribs. The torch lies beside him, sputtering and hissing.

Lunardo has shaken off Crivano's blows, returned to his stance. His face is livid, his left eye dark with blood. In the unsteady footlight cast by the dropped torch, Crivano searches for the Genoese's fallen rapier, and spots it at the canal's edge.

The one-eyed mutilated sbirro is coming over the bridge, his cudgel at his side. As his boots touch the flagstones, he drops the truncheon with a clatter. Then he begins to speak in a deep resonant voice. *Toute leur vie estoit employée non par loix, statuz ou reigles, mais selon leur vouloir et franc arbitre,* he says. *Se levoient du lict quand bon leur sembloit, beuvoient, mangeoient, travailloient, dormoient quand le desir leur venoit; nul ne les esveilloit, nul ne les parforceoit ny à boyre, ny à manger, ny à faire chose aultre quelconques.*

Lunardo and Crivano look at each other. Then they both look at the scar-faced sbirro. He passes between them, swaying like a drunk, still speaking slowly and very clearly. *Ainsi l'avoit estably Gargantua,* he says. *En leur reigle n'estoit que ceste clause: fay ce que vouldras.* The fletched shaft of a crossbow bolt protrudes from the left side of his skull. After a few steps, he bumps into the closed shutters of a shop, turns, and slides down the wall to sit on the pavement. He's whispering now, a great sadness in his voice.

For an instant, Crivano and Lunardo meet each other's eyes again. Then Crivano throws his broken rapier at Lunardo's head and dives for the fallen sword of the Genoese. Lunardo ducks, intercepts him, slices him across the left biceps. Crivano pauses, his stick held high, his empty right hand hovering over the weapon on the pavement. Then he feints, parries Lunardo's thrust downward with his stick, draws the stiletto from his boot, and punches it through Lunardo's chest, a half-inch to the left of his sternum. Lunardo rises from his crouched stance. A look of mild irritation passes over his face, and he falls backward into the canal.

The splash echoes and fades. *Car nous entreprenons tousjours choses defendues et convoitons ce que nous est denié,* whispers the scar-faced sbirro.

Dottore, groans the torchbearer. Help me up. We must go.

Crivano's hands spasm, his legs cramp. He can barely hold the walkingstick. He leans down, offers the boy his arm. The dirty face is known to him, intimately so, but Crivano can't place it. Like a dream-face that belongs to someone dear, that speaks with the same voice, but resembles the person not at all. Could this be the Lark?

Who are you? Crivano says.

It's me, dottore. It's Perina. I came as quickly as I could.

Crivano blinks, shakes his head, looks again. The small nose, the full mouth, the obstinate eyes. He touches her cropped scalp with his trembling hand. What became of your hair? he says.

I took my vows.

What?

I took my vows. I didn't know what else to do. Don't be angry, dottore. I couldn't find you unless I could move through the streets at night, and I couldn't do that unless I could pass as a boy. You see? I couldn't pass as a boy without short hair, and the nuns wouldn't cut my hair except for my profession. So I took my vows. I simulated a sudden mania of piety, and I wept and begged until the abbess included me in tonight's clothing ceremony. Then I fled. The linkboy you sent sold me his garments.

Crivano stares at her, gape-mouthed. A tremor gathers in his belly: the beginning of laughter, or tears. He's very tired. The cyclopean sbirro with the bolt in his brain has fallen silent, his chin on his chest. The one lying on the bridge no longer breathes. Dottore, Perina says, seizing his hand. We should hurry. Others will be here soon.

So, he says with an antic smile — one he suspects of containing more than a hint of madness — what is your new name, then?

Her eyes flash. Perina, she says. It's Perina. As always.

She pulls him away from the bridge, toward the campiello, but he resists. There's no way out there, he says. We must cross the canal.

No, dottore. Your friend is here, with his boat. He'll meet us this way.

My friend? What friend?

The gondolier. The one you sent to Santa Caterina to meet me when I escaped. He didn't say his name.

The one I sent? What are you talking about?

Your message, dottore. You said to flee the convent by the third bell, and to meet the gondolier on the Misericordia Canal.

Who told you this?

The linkboy told me. Dottore, we must go!

She's tugging his arm like the bridle of a recalcitrant mule. Her skin is blotchy with pink, her face rived with terror. The cool air has grown much colder. The torch on the pavement goes out abruptly, as though it's been dipped in a bucket. A thick rope of smoke rises from it. There is no wind.

Did he tell you to look behind the curtain? Crivano says.

Who?

The linkboy. The messenger.

Perina relaxes her grip on his hand. Her expression is baffled, exasperated. What curtain? she says.

Over her shoulder, the twisting street that leads to the campiello has gone entirely black at its center. As if the night itself has gathered there, clotted like a wound. Crivano looks up from Perina's face. Merciful Christ, he whispers.

Listen, dottore. We must —

Crivano drops his stick, seizes Perina by the collar, and pulls her against his chest. She lets out a startled squeak as her face strikes his ribs. His fingers scurry along the fabric of his robe until they find the slit, then search inside for the smooth grip of the snap-lock pistol. He's vaguely aware of the sound of his own chattering teeth.

Already the fiend is almost upon them, gliding with the silent speed of a diving owl. It seems to hang on the air, not to move at all. As if the space between it and them is simply vanishing, shrinking like the foot of a snail. Crivano's hand has found the pistol. As he draws it, the cock catches the fabric of his robe. The fabric rips.

Perina pushes away from him; he claps his hand on the base of her fuzzed skull and pulls her back with a thump. The pistol is free. He thrusts out his arm. The demon is yards away now. Its ash wand held high. Smoke streaming from its beak. Perina turns her head to protect her mashed nose, and Crivano moves his left palm over her exposed ear. Then he wrenches back the cock — opening a bloody furrow across his thumb's first joint — and pulls the trigger.

A white flare as the pan ignites, and a breathy whoosh. Then nothing. His vision wrecked by the flash, Crivano stares into the blackened street, his lips twisted in a rictus of idiot horror. His eyes can discern nothing but the twin glassy spheres that move toward him through the void, aglow like glory-holes. They are coming. They have always been coming. Now they are here.

The pistol fires. From its muzzle emerges a

globe of flame that erases everything and vanishes, leaving only a pulsing afterimage on Crivano's seared eyes. But the roar of the blast remains, a howling hiss, an undiminishing echo that runs circuits of the street until he can hear nothing else. Perina has broken away; she's looking at him, gesturing, screaming. Her voice reaches him not as sound, but as a gentle pressure on his face. She grabs his left hand, pulls. His right arm, the arm with the pistol, is over his head. He lowers it gingerly. He's aware of sharp pain in his bludgeoned ears: a lacerating high-pitched chime that, he realizes, is the sound of broken glass striking the pavement under every window on the street.

The plaguedoctor is gone. Crivano's eyes rake the smoke-shrouded air, and the pavement where the monster stood, but they find nothing: no pink mist, no pooled blood, no beaked mask, no ash wand. Blown to bits, he thinks. As if the pistol were a cannon. Blown to bits. Blown to bits. Blown to bits.

The cloud of smoke from the blast is rising, signaling their location. Perina's face is streaked with angry tears; she twists his arm, looks over his shoulder. Crivano searches the ground around his feet for his dropped walkingstick, then sees that Perina is holding it. He tries to put the pistol back in his belt, but his arm won't move as it should. His hearing is returning, heralded by a dull ache;

he can make out Perina's urgent whisper, shouts from the Campiello of the Dead. Sbirri are coming over the bridge: three that he can see, more lights behind them. The first freezes when he sees Crivano, fear animating his dull eyes, and the second stumbles to avoid a collision. They huddle together on the bridge, scuffling their feet like tethered dogs.

Perina and Crivano turn and run. She's fast, he's tired and old, and he can't keep up. Fallen glass splinters and cracks beneath the sbirri's feet: they're gaining on him. By the time he turns into the campiello they're on his heels. One brushes a hand against his shoulder, then collapses with a thud and a gasp, tripping up the man behind him. Crivano sees the sandolo now, Obizzo outlined against the setting moon, lowering his crossbow to stand in its stirrup, a fresh bolt clamped between his teeth.

Perina has already cast the boat off. Crivano catches a foot on the gunwale as he jumps, lands facedown in the hull. Dozens of dry bouquets are crushed under his chest; the odor of lavender fills his sinuses, followed by the ferrous tang of blood. The sandolo rocks but doesn't capsize. Crivano rises with effort, wipes his injured nose.

Obizzo fires again, catching a sbirro in midair as he vaults from the quay; the man drops with a splash. More rush into the campiello, but caution slows them. Obizzo passes the crossbow and quiver to Crivano and takes up his oar; Crivano steps in the stirrup and fixes the string to the nut, then levers it back while he gropes for a bolt. By the time it's loaded, they're a safe distance from the sbirri's angry cudgels, but Crivano fires and wounds one anyway out of spite.

Damn you, dottore! Obizzo growls. Save your bolts. A caorlina crowded with these devils still awaits us on the Grand Canal.

Crivano blows his nose into his palms, shakes the mess overboard. The scent of lavender reaches him again. How did you find me? he says.

With difficulty, thank you. Your messages were a lot of bilgewater. I had to row along till I heard the hue and cry, then follow the noise. What in God's name was meant by that nonsense about the curtain?

Messages? Crivano says. How many —

Obizzo shushes him. Torches have appeared on the bridge ahead. Crivano loads another bolt, takes Perina's position in the bow. A quick brightness in the west: at first Crivano takes it for a casino's hearth-lit door, but it's what remains of the vanishing moon, peeking at them from a dead-end street. Good luck, it seems to say. I can do nothing more for you tonight.

The torches on the bridge have been smothered; dark shapes now crouch where they shone. Crivano snorts, swallows blood and phlegm, and nestles the crossbow's buttstock against his shoulder. The sandolo's black keel slices the mist-veiled water, heading north along the Saint John Beheaded Canal.

■ ■ ■ ■

COAGVLATIO

■ ■ ■ ■

It is pictures rather than propositions, metaphors rather than statements, which determine most of our philosophical convictions. The picture which holds traditional philosophy captive is that of the mind as a great mirror, containing various representations — some accurate, some not — and capable of being studied by pure, nonempirical methods. Without the notion of the mind as mirror, the notion of knowledge as accuracy of representation would not have suggested itself.

— RICHARD RORTY,
Philosophy and the Mirror of Nature

57

Two packed charter buses are unloading in
the porte-cochère as Curtis enters the lobby
of his hotel: conventioneers with rolling
suitcases and sheathed laptops sweep through
the glass doors, an unbroken column from
the sidewalk to the registration desk. Curtis
isn't quick enough to find a gap; he stops
under the armillary sphere to wait them out.
They collect their keycards, break away,
recombine in cheery clumps, crushing hands
and clapping shoulders, calling back and
forth in sportscaster voices, shooting each
other with finger-guns. Somebody passes
bearing a huge foamcore placard —

    9:00 a.m. — The Three Most Powerful
              Skills For Success In
              Sales
    9:45 a.m. — How To Achieve Your
              Personal Best In Times
              Of Turmoil

— and Curtis can see nothing of the person who carries it aside from a pair of white sneakers and eight curled fingertips.

Another big fake painting stretches overhead; Veronica, no doubt, could tell him what it's a copy of. A hero on a winged horse, about to harpoon a fire-breathing monster. A man with chains drooping from his mouth. A guy with a broken-stringed violin, his arm around a naked lady. Another guy who plucks a lyre in front of a thick city wall while stone blocks levitate all around him. Curtis gets that the lyre music is lifting the stones, but he can't tell if it's supposed to be building the wall or taking it apart. The painting's midpoint is a field of blue sky. A pair of gods floats there: Mercury with his snake-twisted staff, Minerva with her gorgon-faced shield.

The crowd of conventioneers thins and Curtis moves forward, then gets snared by a plainclothes security guard blocking the exit. The guard holds the door for a tall silver-haired man in a black bomber jacket who looks exactly like Jay Leno, and it takes Curtis a second to realize that it's Jay Leno. Then he realizes that he's standing in Leno's path.

842

Curtis's hand is still extended from where he'd been about to push through the door, and Leno grabs it and shakes it. Hi! he says with a broad grin.

You're Jay Leno, Curtis says.

Yeah, Leno says. Have a great conference!

He passes Curtis on the left. The security guard is right beside him, and gently eases Curtis out of the way. Leno and his small entourage pass through the lobby — Leno waving, shaking more hands, walking the same way every famous person Curtis has ever met has walked, quick and restless, like if they stop moving they'll die — and then they all disappear through a passage to the left of the registration desk. Curtis watches them go. More people with luggage push past him into the lobby, chattering excitedly. *Jay Leno!* most of them seem to be saying.

Outside, Curtis climbs into the first idling taxi. It's another Fortune Cab, black and white and magenta, and Curtis wonders if it'll be the same cabbie who took him to the lake this morning. But when he sits down and sees the eyes in the rearview mirror, they're Saad's. Saad? Curtis says.

I'm sorry?

It's not Saad: this guy is younger, less relaxed, not Arabic. Bangladeshi, maybe. But the white hair is the same, and the wrinkles. Can you take me to the Quicksilver, please? Curtis says.

In Henderson?

No, Curtis says. In the hills east of here, the edge of the valley. It's a new place. A few blocks off North Hollywood, above the Mormon Tem—

Yes, the guy says. Now I know. Thank you.

He makes good time to the freeway and Lake Mead Boulevard, using the same route Saad took. He doesn't try to make conversation, and Curtis appreciates that. In the fast-failing light, Curtis opens *The Mirror Thief* one last time, wanting to read a little more before Stanley takes it back. Curtis isn't thrilled about how things have gone out here, but he figures at this point he ought to be satisfied. He's not satisfied, though. Not even close. Maybe once he sees Stanley he will be.

Be secret, Crivano! This poisoned world,
blown out like an egg, hides nothing.
No cross for you, no Campo de' Fiori —
be not covetous of such monuments,
sad fictions of kingdoms deferred. Nothing
here is saved, nothing worthy of saving.
     Evaporation is your legacy,
your ecstasy, your escape. All matter
is mere shadow, swept over dark glass.
Your moment, Crivano, is done: a bubble
hung in history's slow amber, a seed
in silica suspended, then fed back
to the furnace. Burn, thief of images,
on the amnesic sea!

844

As Curtis reads, he tries to imagine finding the book the way Stanley found it, to guess what strange pull it could have exerted on a fifteen-year-old Brooklyn kid with a dead father and a crazy mother and a fifth-grade education. Curtis can't fathom it. He thinks of his dad's stories about growing up in Shaw in the Fifties, then of his own fifteenth year — what it felt like, what went on in his head — but he can barely recall, and the memories suggest no new route into the book. Instead Curtis just winds up thinking about Jay Leno: how friendly and cheerful he seemed. How that friendliness and cheer seemed to close him off like a stone wall, and how that wall could have been hiding anything. Or nothing. He thinks about the conventioneers performing for each other in the hotel lobby, and of the cocktail waitresses performing for the well-heeled grinds in the Oculus Lounge. He thinks about the bartender at New York with the Staten Island accent, and about Saad — *you do this rap for all your fares?* — and about Argos's blanked-out features, shifting in the hot light off the lake surface. He thinks of himself in high school, practicing his game-face in his grandparents' bathroom mirror. Trying to be convincing. Trying to convince himself.

Every substance, Hermes says,
must fashion its own reasons.

845

Even now, oligarchy's thugs
unmuzzled stalk Rialto's corridors.
To hide what can't be seen, Crivano,
install it in plain sight, everywhere.
Invisible commonplace! Machine
for unseeing! Submerge your name,
weighted with your past. Wall-hung,
neglected, the moon-skin lies in ambush.
And then, one unexpected day, you meet
the stranger you have always been.

A couple of UNLV co-eds dressed as leprechauns are stationed between the Quicksilver's riverstone columns; they grin and wave
as Curtis's cab pulls up, bend to pin plastic
shamrocks to the cardigans of wheelchair-
bound gamblers. Curtis pays his cabbie, steps
onto the rubbery sidewalk. At the valley's opposite edge, Mount Charleston is a blue
shadow on the purple dusk. The setting sun
lights its snowcap like a brand.

Welcome to the Quicksilver! one of the
leprechauns says. Need some luck?

No thanks, Curtis says. I'm not playing
tonight.

The PA in the lobby has swapped its New
Age flutes and rainsticks for New Age
bodhráns and uilleann pipes. The kid behind
the counter wears a green plastic bowler hat,
keeps himself busy by adding links to a six-
foot paperclip chain. Hello, Curtis says. I'm
Curtis Stone. Walter Kagami is holding a

room for me.

The kid hands over a keycard in a small paper envelope. Top floor, he says. First door on the right. It's a suite.

The elevators are on the far side of the gaming floor. There's not much traffic at the tables or the slots, but what traffic there is moves awfully slowly, and Curtis doesn't feel like navigating it. He tracks the right-hand wall to the bow windows that overlook the sunken courtyard, then follows them across the length of the casino. Lights are coming on below: in the palmtrees, under the recirculating fountain and the waterfall. The guineafowl that he saw last time are not to be found — gone wherever they go at night — but a peacock has climbed atop one of the stone picnic tables, and as Curtis passes, he spreads and shakes his tailfeathers into an oscillating iridescent screen.

When Curtis reaches the corner he immediately tenses, feeling a bad closeness, something wrong, but it's already too late: a heavy plastic coin-pail bumps his ribs and a smooth voice murmurs in his ear. You ain't wearing anything green, my man, it says. Somebody's liable to pinch you.

Curtis jerks to a halt. Albedo shoves the pail against his side again; something in it is heavy and solid. Keep on marching, my brother, Albedo says.

A flood of adrenaline sweeps through Curtis's limbs into his groin; he shudders with the need to piss. Takes a deep trembling breath, lets it out. Walks on.

Albedo came up on Curtis's left, from slightly behind: exactly the spot where Curtis's nose blocks his peripheral vision. He knows about Curtis's eye; Damon must have told him. When Curtis first met him in the Hard Rock the other night, Albedo kept leaning back in his chair: he was testing Curtis, feeling out the limits of his sight. This has been the plan all along. Albedo knows that Stanley's on his way.

There's no surveillance by the windows, probably. Cameras watch the elevators for sure — but when he and Albedo reach the elevators, Albedo falls back, giving Curtis plenty of room. Even if Kagami is watching, he won't see anything.

Curtis doesn't press the callbutton. He hopes Albedo will talk to him — ordering him to do it, giving himself away — but Albedo just moves past him and presses it himself. A car opens at once, empty, and they step into it. Don't talk to me, Albedo whispers as he crosses the threshold.

There's a small lens behind the tinted glass of the instrument panel; maybe a mic somewhere, too. They rise to the top floor, the sixth, in sullen silence, sunset streaming through the glass at their backs. Curtis studies Albedo closely. Albedo doesn't meet his gaze. He has a cool dead-eyed aspect like some guys get when they're drunk, but Curtis doesn't think he's drunk. He wears a bright-green T-shirt under his motorcycle jacket. His boots and bluejeans are dusty, snarled with burrs and what look like tiny pricklypear needles. Through the frayed fabric at Albedo's knees Curtis glimpses bloody skin. The handle on the coinpail is stretched slightly by whatever weight it contains, and a plastic bag spread over the top hides its contents. The big hand that holds the pail is raw, scored all over by scrapes and scratches. FIGHT ME — I'M IRISH! Albedo's T-shirt says.

On Five the door slides open with a low chime, and a turkey-necked old codger with a glossy toupee, a bolo tie, and a poof-banged, decades-younger date on his arm tries to step in. Albedo moves into his path. You goin' up? he asks.

Goin' down, the old dude says.

Albedo pushes the guy backward lightly with the fingertips of his right hand. Well, sir, he says, y'all might oughta give that little down-arrow button a tap.

Albedo's outstretched hand looks like it was worked over with a potato peeler. The old guy stares at it openmouthed. The door slides shut again.

I believe I went to high school with that girl, Albedo says.

As soon as Curtis exits on the next floor, Albedo draws a pistol from the pail, spread-eagles him against the wall, takes away his revolver, and pats him down. Albedo is fast, looking for nothing but wires and weapons. When he's done he tugs Curtis upright by his collar, aims him down the hall. Open the door, he says.

Curtis fumbles a little at the keycard slot. When the green light clicks on and the handle turns, Albedo lunges forward and slams his shoulder into Curtis's upper back. Curtis sprawls through the door, face-plants on the carpet. Albedo is right behind him, kicking him in the side, stepping over him, keeping him covered with the little Smith revolver as he clears the suite with his own pistol. Curtis sucks air through his clenched teeth. *The Mirror Thief* is on the floor, a few inches from his chin. Albedo's plastic bucket hangs from Curtis's upraised left foot.

Albedo disappears into the bedroom for a second. Then he reappears, both pistols leveled at Curtis's face. Albedo's gun has a thick blunt taped-up suppressor on its barrel that looks like it might have been made from a can of beans. The gun is a matte-black semiautomatic, similar to the one that Argos had this morning. Curtis thinks of the pink column of dust he saw on the lakeside road, and then he thinks: no, not similar, the same. The thought makes him feel sick, and scared, and angry. Angry most of all.

So, Albedo says, another twenty, thirty minutes, you reckon?

Fuck you, man, Curtis says.

Albedo laughs quietly. He seems tired, strung-out. Yeah, he says. I reckon maybe twenty, maybe thirty minutes.

Curtis kicks the pail off his foot, rolls over, sits with his back against the wall. You're playing this wrong, he says. You're too late. Killing Stanley and Veronica is not gonna fix anything for Damon. NJSP has issued warrants based on physical evid—

Not for *my* ass, they ain't, Albedo says. C'mon, Curtis, don't act like a retard. I ain't looking to fix shit for Damon. That boy's gone and fucked hisself. Which is his prerogative, but he's damn near gone and fucked me, too. Soon as I clean up here, I'm getting on a damn airplane. And ol' Damon better be a-wishin' and a-hopin' that the Jersey cops get hold of him 'fore I do.

That's a bad plan, Curtis says. You don't think —

Lemme give you some advice, Albedo says. Shut your fucking mouth. While you're at it, start thinking about how I'm gonna round Damon up when I get back to AC. You come up with a fool-fucking-proof plan of which you are an indispensable goddamn component, and you don't say another word till you got one. Because right about now, Curtis,

851

you are looking mostly like a problem to me.

Albedo slides a chair away from the table with the toe of his boot. Then he sits, puts the two guns on the tabletop — their barrels parallel, aimed at Curtis — and begins to examine his damaged hands, plucking at cactus-spines with his long fingernails. I told Damon, he says. I told him *on numerous occasions* that bringing you in on this would be a dumbass move of pretty much the highest order. And I bet you wish more than just about anybody — don't you, Curtis? — that he'd paid me a little more attention on that point. Well, nobody ever listens to my fucking advice. I mean, I told *you,* didn't I, that this shit was gonna go wrong, and to make some other plans. Did you listen? Hell, no. I told Damon that he had only one advantage, only *one thing* working for him in this whole ugly shitstorm, which was that nobody he'd got crosswise with was apt to talk to the cops. And what's the *first thing* that ingenious motherfucker does? He brings in a cop.

Albedo glances up, warming to his subject, then jerks and freezes. He's staring slack-jawed at the wall to Curtis's left; his widened eyes are all pupil. He spasms, blinks hard, gives his head a violent shake. Then he snatches Argos's pistol from the tabletop. Waving it around as if targeting a phantom housefly. *Fuck,* he says. He turns back to the wall, sights along the pistol's slide. No, he says. No way. Fuck.

He fires. Then he fires again. The suppressor swallows the muzzle-blasts, but not the cracks — loud, like a yardstick slapping a table — of the bullets going supersonic. A cloud of pulverized drywall bursts over Curtis's head, and then the air is full of glitter: sharp stinging grains that strike his scalp. He curses, shields his eyes. Whoa, he says.

A high-pitched cacophany fills his left ear: glass breaking and falling. Albedo has just shot out the big mirror that hung over the room's dressing table; Curtis couldn't see it from where he sits. Jesus, Curtis says. What the fuck, man.

Albedo's laughing silently, trembling, shaking his head. Oh, buddy, he says. Holy shit. I am tweaking for sure. I coulda just sworn —

The phone rings. Albedo jumps, puts a third bullet in the wall; Curtis's hands go to his face again. On the second ring, Albedo sighs — a little sheepishly — and points to the phone with the pistol's fattened barrel. I'm guessing that's gonna be for you, he says.

Curtis rises to his feet. His knees are wobbly; he stumbles on his way to the desk. He reaches the phone on the fourth ring, lifts the handset. This is Curtis, he says.

Curtis, it's Veronica.

He's badly shaken: he has to fight hard to steady his voice, to pay attention. A lot is riding on the next few seconds. Behind Veronica's voice he can hear more crowd noise and PA pages: the airport again. She sounds tense — irritated and fatigued — but not scared. Listen, she says, Stanley's jerking us around. He wasn't on the flight.

Curtis blinks. Say again? he says.

Stanley wasn't on the plane he said he'd be on. He called while I was at baggage-claim. You're not gonna believe this, but he's in — He's gone. He's long gone.

Curtis feels as though he's just stepped off a cliff, he's hanging in midair like a cartoon coyote. Then a crazy thrill creeps up his spine to his throat, and he fights to keep a smile off his lips. Okay, he says. Go on.

He wanted me to be at the airport, Veronica says, because he's got me booked on a flight out. It's boarding in like five minutes. I still have to put some stuff in a locker and go through security, so I don't have much time.

Curtis closes his eyes, puts a hand on the desktop to steady himself. Through the tangle of white noise on the telephone line he imagines he can hear Stanley laughing, shouting coded numbers like a quarterback.

Don't ask me to explain what he's doing, Veronica says, because I have no idea. But I wanted to call, to let you and Walter know what's up. Now I better —

Curtis opens his eyes. Walter? he says. Walter's coming?

Yeah. I figured he'd be there by now. He's

854

usually off-duty by — oh, shit, I gotta run. Listen, Curtis, I'm really sorry. And thanks. I'll be in touch.

The phone clicks, goes dead. Albedo's watching him, a furrow deepening on his brow. Curtis lets his focus go soft on the desktop, studies Albedo's face in his periph. Fumble recovery, he thinks. The ball is lying at his feet.

Sure, Curtis tells the dead phone. I guess that works. What's the arrival time?

Ghostly clicks from the earpiece, like pebbles dropped in a dry well.

Got it, Curtis says. Look for me at baggage-claim. Don't leave. I may be a couple minutes late.

He hangs up the phone. Change of plan, he says. Stanley's flight was delayed. They're not coming here. I'm supposed to meet them at McCarran.

Albedo stares at him. Then he stands up. How is *that* gonna work? he says.

Look, man, I didn't know what else to do.

Albedo still seems dazed, but he's snapping out of it. How 'bout you get 'em the fuck over here, he says. That's what. Or you send 'em someplace else. *Anyplace* else. A goddamn police station'd be an improvement. Jesus, Curtis, the fucking *airport*? Exactly how many people are you gonna make me have to shoot?

Curtis swallows hard. I think Stanley's

855

spooked, he says. He knows something's off. Veronica wasn't sure where they were going after they picked up his bags. I don't even know if he's gonna wait for his bags, man. I think he might bolt.

Albedo's face clouds; his jaw sets. That'd be kinda bad for you, he says.

Yeah? Curtis says, forcing a panicked shrillness into his voice. So let's get rolling, all right?

Albedo drops Argos's pistol back in the coinpail, then tucks Curtis's revolver into his belt, covering it with his motorcycle jacket. On their way out of the room they both step over *The Mirror Thief,* a dark window in the neutral beige carpet. Curtis hopes that whoever finds it will know what to do with it. Know better than he did, anyway.

He's scared the elevator will slide open to reveal Walter's surprised face — that after their week of butting heads, he and the old man will each wind up being the last thing the other sees — but when the car arrives, it's empty. They don't meet him on their way out either, only a prim pink-haired old lady in a gold lamé jacket, balancing on an aluminum-frame walker. Her blue eyes are big and damp; her pupils frosted with blindness. She smiles sweetly as they rush past.

Curtis keeps hoping that Kagami's gotten wind of what's up — that he'll have LVMPD waiting at the exit — but everything looks

856

routine on the gaming floor. On the way to the lobby Curtis spots a couple of security officers among the tables, but none who's likely to be armed. He doubts Albedo would think twice about shooting in here, so he keeps his eyes forward, doesn't try anything. He's still jittery from the gunshots, but his legs are firming up fast, his mind is humming. All week long he's just been playing around; now he's in real trouble. It still doesn't *feel* real, though. Stanley wouldn't have put him in this spot unless he was sure Curtis could find a way out. Would he?

G Seventeen, says a clear amplified voice from the bingo room. *G Seventeen.*

Outside the western sky is dark except for a blue rind at the horizon. The black field is vented all over by starlight, gritty and diamond-hard, except for a few spots where invisible clouds block it. Albedo wraps his parking ticket in a twenty, passes it to the valet, tells the kid to fucking step on it. Then he turns to face the leprechauns. You Irish, sweetheart? he says. You don't look Irish. But green is definitely your color.

The girl flashes a grin which immediately turns queasy when she notices Albedo's bloody hands and ripped knees and the dead-fish look in his eyes. She shrinks back, lifts her basket of plastic shamrocks in both hands like a flimsy shield. Her partner — a little older, a little more assured — glances at Curtis. She looks worried, which must mean that Curtis looks scared. *What's wrong?* her eyes say. *Can I help?* Curtis tries to smile.

Soon he hears the monstrous engine of Albedo's car; he still can't see it. The valet parking lot is underground, off the building's north side; Curtis hadn't noticed it before. The big black Merc makes the corner, rolls up the drive. Its weak yellow headlamps sweep them: searchlights in search of something else. Curtis still doesn't know how he's going to sidestep whatever's coming. Then, suddenly, he does. He knows exactly.

As the car pulls to the curb, Curtis glances through the windows. The usual junk inside — magazines and newspapers, paper bags and plastic cups — plus some interesting new hardware in the backseat: what looks like a tablet PC with a GPS attachment, what looks like a handheld police scanner. Interesting, but not surprising.

The valet opens the Merc's door, then steps hurriedly aside. His expression is disgusted, freaked-out. Your chariot stands at the ready, my brother, Albedo tells Curtis. You may take up the reins.

Hey, Curtis says. Guess what? I can't drive.

Albedo gives him a fierce look. Then he steps forward. Hey, he says. Guess what? Fuck you. I known me a whole shitload of one-eyed dudes in my time. All of them motor around just fine.

Too bad none of them are here, Curtis says. Because I don't.

Albedo has already opened the passenger door. Look, he says. Don't smartmouth me, Curtis. Get in the fucking car.

Curtis gets in the car. He has to slide the seat forward a good six inches to get his feet comfortable on the accelerator and clutch. The shoulder-straps bolted to the seatback are too high for him; he doesn't even try to put them on. Something somewhere in the car smells like piss and shit and worse things, and Curtis starts to breathe fast and feel sick. He fastens his lap belt. Then he fusses with the mirrors.

Oh come the fuck *on,* Albedo says.

You're gonna have to help me watch to my left, man. I can't see there at all.

Albedo puts the pail with Argos's pistol on the Merc's cluttered floor. Curtis's revolver is in his right hand. There ain't nothing to your left, he says. There ain't nothing nowhere. Now get this bitch in gear and drive.

Curtis puts the car in gear. It rolls gently from the curb. The downgrade carries it past the limestone QUICKSILVER sign to the narrow roadcut of the exit-ramp. Curtis brakes to a stop and sits there for a long time with the Merc's left-turn indicator clicking and flashing. No traffic comes from either direction. Over the mutter of the big engine, Curtis hears a jet pass overhead.

You're clear, Curtis, Albedo says. You are completely, totally clear, my man.

Once he's made the left turn, Curtis eases toward the flashing red light, coasting in neutral as the incline grows steeper, stopping well before the white band painted on the blacktop. It's easy, driving. He's not sure why he expected it to be hard.

Okay, Curtis says. You gotta help me out here.

A long line of headlights is coming from the right: cars hung up behind some kind of heavy truck, maybe a dumptruck. Vehicles on the left, too, in the distance: the blurry lump of Curtis's nose is edged by the glow of approaching halogen. On the other side of the road there's a wide shoulder and a guardrail, then nothing: the ground plunges away into what must be a deep wash. Traffic on the through-street seems to be doing about fifty as it passes beneath the two flashing yellows. Tilted on the downgrade, the Merc's weight strains against its brakes.

You can turn now, Albedo says.

This is not gonna work, man.

Quit acting like a little girl, Curtis. You just missed your shot. Ooch up a little so's I can see, and put your signal on.

Curtis flips on the right-turn signal, eases up very slightly on the brake. The Merc jerks forward a few inches. To the right, the big truck labors on the upgrade; cars cluster

860

impatiently behind it. More vehicles pass from the left, lit by the Merc's headlamps: an SUV, two sedans. Soft underwater whooshes as they go by. Am I clear? Curtis says.

Not yet, Albedo says, leaning forward in his seat. Almost. Hang on.

The big truck — it's a cement-mixer — is gathering speed, puffing black smoke from its exhaust. Behind the smoke, the stars and valley lights mute and flicker. Curtis can't watch it anymore. He looks ahead, measuring his breaths. The rearview is still tilted wrong, angled so that he sees the stubbly dome of his own head whenever the red light flashes. He's not sure what he should be thinking right now, what he wants to be thinking. About Danielle, probably. He tries to put his mind on her, but he can't do it. Instead he just keeps staring at the shape of his skull in the tilted rearview mirror. There I am, he thinks. That's me.

Two more cars speed by from the left, startling him. Okay, Albedo says. You're good. Let's go.

That truck's over the line, Curtis says. It's too tight to turn. I can't see distances, man. I got no depth perception.

Albedo looks to the right. It ain't over the line, he says. You got scads of room.

I'm gonna wait, Curtis says.

He moves his right hand to six o'clock on the steering wheel, closer to his seatbelt

861

buckle. Then he takes a deep breath, relaxes, and pisses himself.

Look, dumbass, Albedo says, turning to face left again. Next time I tell you to go, you fucking go. See, now you got another bunch of cars —

Curtis releases the buckle, lifts his foot from the brakepedal, pulls the handle to open the door. The Merc lurches forward, rolling into the intersection, under the flashing lights; Curtis's wet warm boxers scrape his thighs. As his left foot swings over the pavement he hears Albedo's strangled scream, the squeal of brakes, the low blast of the cement-mixer's airhorn, and then every sound is swallowed by the roar of the gun. Albedo's first shot tugs Curtis's jacket-sleeve and smacks into the door — Curtis hears it ping between layers of steel — and then Curtis slips from the seat onto the moving blacktop, showered by glass as Albedo fires again, bluegreen tesserae pricking his face and hands as he falls, mixing with bits of silver from the exploded side mirror, all lit up by oncoming headlamps and hanging in the dusty air. Curtis slams to the ground, rolls away from the Merc's rear tire, and is scrambling to his feet — has raised himself to a half-crouch — when an oncoming Toyota truck hits him.

He folds over the hood and slides. Everything is silent. His arms and legs are heavy, stretching in opposite directions, wringing him in the middle like a wet towel. Albedo is still shooting; the air contracts as each bullet passes. The pickup's windshield spiderwebs under Curtis and he's in the air again, wobbling like a poorly tossed football. Three shots. Four. Curtis's left hand closes on something hard and smooth. He comes down in the truck's bed, slamming into the gate. He caught the last bullet. Everything spins, then settles. Curtis sprawls splaylegged on the polyurethane bedliner, looking at the road. Broken again. Still alive. The blob of lead cooling in his palm.

The screech of metal tearing metal wounds Curtis's ears, and for an instant the cement truck eclipses his sight. Once it's passed, the Mercury appears before him, spinning like a dreidel on its front bumper, its tail end bent where the mixer hit it: a dancing question-mark. It rotates slowly, drifting toward the edge of the road; then its deformed trunk falls open and Argos emerges, dead, his bloody plastic shroud unfurling like a scroll as he drops to the pavement. The Merc brushes the guardrail, tips, and now here comes Albedo, sliding turdlike through the shattered windshield, a befuddled expression on his pale torn-up face. The Merc is falling, he's rolling down the hood like a gymnastic toddler, and as the car vanishes into the wash he slides over the silver V of the hood-ornament and plops onto the blacktop, slumped against the damaged barrier, his legs crossed almost casually atop the roadstripe. His right hand still curls around Curtis's empty revolver; he's breathing, but a lot of fluid issues from his ears and nose, and Curtis can tell he's done.

Curtis doesn't hear the crash when the car hits the ground, but after a minute black smoke rises from the wash, blotting out the valley, and it's followed by a few tongues of flame. Curtis tries to shift his weight but can't move; now he knows that he's hurt badly, which is fine. He's on home turf now, for the first time in years. Bones broken. Spine probably okay: he can feel pain coming in a hurry, getting decoded by his brain. It's going to be bad, but he thinks he can pass out soon. Unconsciousness is teasing him; he tries to remember it like an old phone number.

He caught the last bullet: the one that would've been Stanley's. This is what he wanted. It's big and glassy in his hand, and he uncurls his fingers to look at it. It hurts to move them, but he does it, slowly, and then he smiles. His own unblinking gray eye stares from the bowl of his palm.

By the time the flames find the Merc's tank and the orange rose blooms over the desert Curtis isn't seeing anything anymore, but he feels the heat on his closed eyelids, and he imagines the flower rising, going black. The warmth is a comfort to him. He follows it into sleep.

58

Stanley would like to go back to the board-walk, to see it one last time before he splits, but he thinks better of it. Cops will still be out in force — hunting for him, cleaning up the mess he made — and he has no special desire to shoot a cop tonight. Besides, in some ways he feels like he'll know the water-front better once it's out of sight for good, once his memory has begun to take it apart.

He heads through the neighborhood, paral-leling the shoreline, through the traffic circle and into the streets that he and Welles walked through. Almost no one is afoot, which makes Stanley look suspicious; he zigzags a lot, doubles back often. Somewhere in the city Welles and his wife are seated in a waiting room while some doctor patches Claudio up — or else they're on their way home by now, headed back to rescue the girl. Stanley has no picture of it; can't get himself to care. The thought of them won't stay in his head: it's shoved out, as if by the wrong pole of a magnet.

Cop cruisers sweep the streets, but plenty of other cars are out too: the traffic on the main thoroughfares and the pattern of one-way streets makes it tough for them to follow a pedestrian. Sometimes squads pass him and U-turn suddenly, or speed up to make a block, but Stanley's always able to cut across a yard and disappear, or to lie low in a flowerbed while they circle. The bright rows their headlights carve across the wet pavement remind Stanley of the twin furrows of Sonja Heine's skates in the forecourt of Grauman's Chinese.

By the time he's reached the oilfield and the first of the old canals, his duck-and-cover routine has grown tiresome: he's feverish again, wracked by chills, ready to get off the street. He crosses his arms, hugs himself, lowers his head and quickens his step, muttering curses through chattering teeth. Cursing himself and the world. Cursing Welles most of all. Maybe you conjured *me*, Stanley seethes. You ever think of that, you fat son of a bitch? Maybe it was me all along you conjured. Maybe you conjured me.

For a long time he walks without being aware of walking. His mind is elsewhere, or nowhere; his feet advance mechanically, of their own accord. When he snaps back to attention with the sensation of waking up, he's surprised to find himself still in motion, and uncertain of where he is. He stops by a parked car, puts down his pack, unsheaths the canteen and drinks. The taste of the water is sharp on his tongue, flavored by the old tin; he thinks of his father in Leyte and Okinawa, deadened and enlivened by hours of fighting, tasting the same tinny water. He remembers struggling to lift the fieldpack the day his father gave it to him: it was bigger than he was then. *If I don't get into this war, I'll go nuts. I don't understand nothing about peace. That may be fucked up, but it's true. People don't want me around, and I don't want to be around. In peace I'm nobody. I don't even recognize myself.*

The rain has stopped but the clouds are low; they push against the rooftops. Stanley is still among the canals. Mist rises from them like curtains, sealing each block of houses in a gauzy box. Just ahead there's a bridge; beyond it, a pair of derricks burns off natural gas, their crowns lit by slow-moving pillars of clean flame. Their unsteady lights throw two faint shadows behind every solid thing within reach.

Figures on the bridge: a large man, and a small crawling child. The man leans against the rail; the child huddles at his feet. Both peer at the oily water below. Stanley shoulders his pack, moves closer. The child is no child at all, but a stocky dog; Stanley can hear the hoarse rasp of its panting. One of the burning derricks is directly behind the man, and it puts his head in silhouette. Stanley can make out the edge of his face, the tiny flames reiterated in his spectacle lenses. Smoke

867

swirls around his fleshy chin; a pipe dangles from his mouth. He wears a tweed driver's cap identical to the one that now sits atop Stanley's head.

It's Welles and his little dog, out for their nightly walk. It has to be. But then, as Stanley approaches, he sees that it's not. Exactly what it is about this guy that fails to match with Welles Stanley can't say, but he's certain this isn't Welles at all. Something is off. This guy's dog looks a little bigger. Or — Stanley draws closer — a little smaller. He still can't see the man's face.

Stanley steps onto the bridge. He's tiptoeing now; he's not sure why. The low roar of burning gas sounds like flags blown flat and straight by a steady gale. This has *got* to be Welles: it looks just like him. Stanley tries to rationalize it, though he knows it isn't true. Could he be back already from the hospital? If so, why didn't he stop at home? Maybe Synnøve drove Claudio to the hospital on her own, and Welles stayed behind. But this is *not Welles.* It's definitely not. Could Stanley's eyes be playing tricks? Could Welles have a twin? Or could *this* be the real Adrian Welles at last, and the other one — the one Stanley met, the one who signed his book — be the counterfeit?

The figure lowers the briarwood pipe. His hand comes to rest on the railing. Something about the sight of that hand freezes Stanley in his tracks, raises the fine hairs on his neck. It looks just like Welles's hand: a normal human hand. But it is not.

The dog plants its front paws on the railing's lower crosspiece. Then it tips back on its hind legs and walks, tottering like a wind-up soldier. It rotates slowly to look at Stanley. The furry bug-eyed face beneath its long velvet ears is human, or not inhuman. It grins at him with drool-glazed rows of white baby-teeth.

Then it speaks. It calls to Stanley in a low croaking voice. It calls him by his name, his birth name, the name he buried with his dreadful grandfather, the name no living soul but his mute lunatic mother knows.

Or at least, many years from now, this is how you will remember it.

Stanley stumbles backward. The little dog stomps gracelessly toward him. The figure on the rail is turning around. If Stanley meets its gaze, everything that he is will disappear. This is what he came here for. This is what the book has tried to tell him. Some dark thing in this world shares his face.

He reaches for the pistol but the pistol is gone. He dropped it, lost it, never had it, put it in the fieldpack and then forgot. The thing on the rail speaks in its unearthly made-up language; this time, some part of Stanley understands. Now: its face. Its spectacle-lenses are lit by unborrowed interior fire.

Stanley turns and runs. He runs until his infected leg screams with pain, and he keeps running until the pain goes away. He runs until he can hear nothing but the muffled beat of his own shoes on the pavement. He runs until he can't see straight. He runs away from the ocean and away from the moon that pulls it, from street to unfamiliar street through the mess of the centerless city, until he has no notion of where he is or how he came to be there, until he's shaken every memory of the shoreline loose from every route that might lead back to it, until those memories connect to nothing but themselves and the book: an island of narrow tangled passageways, suspended in a void.

59

The water must be near. Each time Crivano wakes, he's aware of gusting wind, small waves striking the base of the wall behind his head. The sound is a pleasant muddle at first — a confusion of bright splashes — but when he concentrates he can hear patterns in it, or almost-patterns: regular pulses, slightly out of phase, recalling elaborate handclap games that idle children play.

It occurs to Crivano that these unmatched pulses might conceal a larger design — one that, properly discerned, might give clues about the dimensions of the building he's in.

But it is, of course, in his temperament to think such things. He smiles, then winces as pain runs laps between his nose and chin.

He has no recollection of coming here. Most of last night is spilt quicksilver in his fingers. He can remember wielding arms in fear and anger, maiming and killing many men, fools who took courage from wine and ignorance and superior numbers and who were poorly suited to oppose a real soldier, a janissary, even an aged one like Crivano. His memories of violence are always unsettling, because in them he is never himself. The animal that looks through his eyes and moves his limbs in combat seems not to possess a memory of its own — which, he supposes, is how it comes to kill so well. The thing in him that fights is like the thing in him that fucks, or shits: he shares a body with it, but it is not *he.* So he tells himself.

He thinks again of Lepanto, of the Lark. His friend was never so ardent of spirit as in the weeks before the battle, never so full of song. As the fleets massed in the Gulf of Patras, every eye on the *Gold and Black Eagle* was upon him; every face grinned and every heart gladdened at his valor. But when the fighting began, the Lark would not shoot. He never retreated from his position on the quarterdeck, never wavered when the Turks swarmed: he pushed them back tirelessly until the moment the cannonball took him.

871

But his arquebus went unfired till Crivano — blood-spray hissing on the overheated barrel of his own weapon — took it up. The Lark was a fine soldier, and had he survived to matriculate at Padua he would have made a marvelous physician, far better than the one Crivano has become. But he was no killer.

Crivano tries to sit up; his sore body refuses. Beneath the sheets his legs twist in inert agony, wrenched by swordsman-footwork, cramped by hours folded in Obizzo's boat. His arms are no less distressed. He manages to drink a clay cup of water he finds beside the bed, but hasn't enough strength to lift the pitcher and refill it. He sleeps again.

At some point a girl enters the room: a Jewess, bearing a steaming bowl of soup and a small chunk of bread. She sets these beside the pitcher, refills the cup, and departs, making no attempt to rouse Crivano. He rises to eat and drink — the soup is rich, mild, thick with goosefat — then lies down again. Nearby, perhaps in the next room, he hears a woman in the throes of carnal ecstasy and wonders if this place might be a bawdyhouse. If so, the whore on the other side of the wall is very enthusiastic, or very convincing.

When next he wakes, the light through the room's small window has acquired the first blush of evening. He feels stronger. He sits up, drinks again — the soup-bowl has gone — and throws off the covers to stand on his trembling legs. He's naked, bandaged extensively; he loosens his dressings to examine the wounds. Scraped right thumb. Short deep cut on his left arm. Crescent gash on his left side, haloed by a yellow-edged bruise. His ears still hiss and whine with the echo of last night's pistolshot; his right hand and forearm ache from the jolt of the wooden grip. On the table where the soup was, Crivano finds a steel shaving-mirror — similar to his own — which he uses to check his face: blood crusted in his nostrils, a sooty bruise on his chin. The mirror shows his face in patches, blurry around the rim; it feels familiar in his hand. He realizes that it is indeed his own mirror: one his father gave him years ago, shortly before he left Cyprus. The mirror was packed in Crivano's walnut trunk, the one that vanished from the White Eagle. How has it come to be here?

He steps to the open window, cautious to avoid unfriendly eyes. As he draws near, a gust further disorders his sleep-mussed hair.

Below is an unfamiliar junction of broad canals. Across the water, rosy sunlight strikes the unadorned façades of a row of buildings, much taller than anything around them: on one, Crivano counts eight rows of small windows between the roof and the waterline. No quay edges the buildings; no water-gate offers access. The walls look as impermeable as those of a fortress or prison. To the left,

Crivano spots the onion-dome that crowns the Madonna dell'Orto belltower. That, along with the cast of the sunlight behind him, locates him north and east of the Cannaregio Canal. He's looking at the walls of the Ghetto.

He becomes aware of a sound: a soft chirp emanating from a nearby chamber, sluggish and monotonous, like a locust's mating-call. He turns toward the room's exit. A set of clothes — not his own — hangs from pegs by the door: fresh garments of a sort that might befit a prosperous tradesman. The fabric feels rough and heavy against his skin. Crivano dresses slowly, with effort, then steps through the doorway into the corridor beyond.

He comes to a cluttered kitchen, where a serving-girl hurries to set out a simple meal of bread and cheese and green apples. At the end of the room is a table, Obizzo seated there, crossbow leaned in the corner behind him. The mirrormaker's big hands are busy at some task, issuing the noise that Crivano has followed here.

He glances up disinterestedly as Crivano limps into view. Good evening, dottore, he says. I see you've chosen to go on living.

Crivano opens his mouth, then closes it, unwilling to spend vitality on a reply. He crosses the room to the table. The serving-girl ignores him.

Obizzo has a leather-fletched bolt in his

scarred left hand; he scrapes an iron file along its heavy pyramidal tip. Black powder falls with each pass, sprinkling the tabletop, dusting the thick hair on Obizzo's wrists, sticking to the underside of the file itself, drawn by some weak force hidden in the metal. Crivano leans on a chairback; he's afraid he'll be unable to rise again if he sits. Then, after a moment, he sits. Where are we? he says.

South of Saint Jerome. Outside the New Ghetto. Not far from the Cerberus, the locanda where we'll meet tomorrow night. Your friend brought us here. You remember?

My friend?

Your friend. The physician. The hypocrite Jew.

Crivano nods. Tristão, he says.

If he gave his name, Obizzo says, I don't remember it.

He stops filing, tests the quarrel's point with a broad thumb. Then he puts the bolt down and leans forward. Listen, dottore, he says. What about this new plan? I like it, but I don't trust it. It's too simple. What do you think?

Crivano squints. New plan? he says.

Your friend hasn't told you, then. He fears the sbirri may have learned of our arrangements. About the trabacolo we're to meet in the lagoon, I mean. He says that I should row our party — Serena and his family, the young fugitive nun, and you, and him, which is to

875

say your Jew doctor friend — to the trabacolo just as we've planned. Only there we'll
play a trick. We'll pretend a loading and
unloading of passengers. All will get off my
boat, then come aboard again, in different
garb. I'll row us to Mestre. From there we'll
go overland to Treviso, to Bassano del
Grappa, to Trento, and across the mountains
into Tyrol.

As Obizzo is speaking, Crivano looks down
at his own raw and bandaged hands on the
tabletop. Then he closes his eyes. Recalling
Narkis's tearful face in the darkness off the
corte, then imagining that face lifeless, breaking the moon-silvered surface of a canal: a
dark oval interrupting the film of light. The
last time Crivano sat with Narkis in Constantinople — it was the afternoon before he met
Polidoro in the hippodrome, before he delivered the hide of Bragadin to the bailo of the
Republic and passed unsuspected into Christendom again — they drank a pot of sweet
kahve together at a quiet kıraathane in Eyüp,
and Narkis explained the haseki sultan's plan,
and what would be in store for them. Thirteen
years of Crivano's life were contained in that
conversation: thirteen years that ended
yesterday. When they finished, Narkis upended Crivano's cup, removed the brass zarf,
and lifted it to reveal the pattern left by the
dregs. Turning the copper dish with a pale
hand, he spoke earnestly of what the leavings

portended. *Each fleeting moment, Tarjuman effendi, contains every moment. The result of our most mundane act is full of messages that tell us what Fortune wills.* Crivano peered at the black-brown circle of sludge — two curved slits in its midst, dark liquid bleeding from its edges, a muddy blot eclipsing the bright metal — and tried not to laugh.

Well, dottore? Obizzo says. What do you think?

Crivano opens his eyes, doesn't look up. It's a good plan, he says.

You think so? What if the sbirri are waiting in the lagoon to intercept us? What if informants on the Terrafirma spot us on the road, and send word to the Council of Ten? What then?

If they intercept us, Crivano says with a sigh, we will kill them, just as we killed them last night. If they find us on the road, we'll take another road. On the Terrafirma we can hide ourselves. On the sea we cannot.

Obizzo frowns. He takes up his file again. This is a new song for you, dottore, he says. I hope you've learned all the verses.

They sit wordless for a while, the file buzzing across the bolt's corners. A pale ghost sweeps through the kitchen: the serving-girl affixing her backspread yellow veil. When it's pinned, she opens a door and rushes down the steps without a glance. The food she's prepared sits covered on the counter.

Curfew, Obizzo says. In the Ghetto by sundown, or she'll have trouble. She's bold to be working in a Christian house at all, isn't she? If that's what this is.

Crivano pushes back from the table, sags in his chair. It shifts and groans, but it holds together. Not unlike Crivano himself. Where's Tristão? he says.

With a flick of the bolt, the mirrormaker indicates a corridor to his right. In his workshop, he says. I think it's a workshop. That heavy door at the end of the hall.

Crivano nods. Then he puts his palms on the chair-seat and forces himself up. His legs are stronger, but still unsteady. His hands no longer return automatically to the shapes of the walkingstick and the rapier-grip; he can almost straighten his fingers.

The door in the hallway is broad enough to permit the passage of a large handcart. A chaos of sharp smells seeps from behind it, most of them mysterious, some familiar from Bologna and the secret processes Crivano studied there: the sour tang of dissolution and separation, the acrid torment of materials sublimed and calcined, the unsettling sweetness of reductions and coagulates. He lifts his fist — the tendons in his forearm still disordered by the pistolshot — and raps the hard black wood. After a moment, he knocks again. Then he tries the latch.

The door opens easily, sucked forth by a gust of wind, to reveal an airy room. Windows line two walls, giving a view of the apse of Saint Jerome, the lagoon beyond, the snow-capped ridges of the distant Dolomites, the red sun over the edge of the world. The space before is crowded with apparatus: jars and bottles of colored and crystalline glass, tongs and long spoons, mortars and pestles, complex networks of alembics and cucurbits and retorts, a delicate many-bulbed pelican, low shelves crowded with books and herbs and phials of colored powders, clay crucibles and leather bellows like those in Serena's factory. In the middle of the room, between a long reverberatory furnace and an iron brazier burning with a smokeless fire, is a cylindrical clay athanor of the traditional type. Behind it, propped on a wooden easel, is the glass-framed talisman that Serena crafted from Verzelin's mirror. The dark room that the mirror shows moves whenever Crivano moves; after a few steps, his own white hands appear in the glass. Anxious, he looks away.

Tristão is nowhere to be seen. Crivano stops, calls to him. Tristão? he says.

From the corner opposite the windows, behind an inlaid-wood screen of which Crivano had taken no notice, a soft commotion arises, followed by Tristão's voice. Ah! it says. Forgive me my neglectful inattention, Vettor. Even now I emerge to greet you. And let me add that I am greatly relieved to be once more in your waking presence. I have been most concerned. Tell me, how do you feel?

Crivano is slow to answer, disinclined to converse with one he cannot see. I feel bad, he says. I'm slow and sore. Too old for fighting.

You battled admirably last night, the screen says. So Perina's report informs me.

Perina, Crivano says. How is she? She took a hard blow from a sbirro's cudgel.

Bruised. Not badly. She will soon recover. I am tending to her.

Crivano grunts, nods, looks at the screen. It's open at the bottom; he can see Tristão's slippered feet. Tristão, he says, what are you doing?

Tristão doesn't answer. After a moment, he steps into view. He's attired casually in a belted tunic and hose; he looks well-rested, alert. In his outstretched hands he carries a large brass chamberpot, and as he crosses the room, Crivano catches the odor of feces. Oh, Crivano says. I see.

Perina and I bandaged your injuries, Tristão says. She has, I believe, a genuine gift for the treatment of wounds. If you have been able to review our work, I hope you have found it to be adequate.

I have, Crivano says. And I have. For that I thank you. I suppose I should thank you, too, for engineering my rescue last night. Before I do so, I should like to determine if it was you who put me in danger in the first place.

Tristão stops at a high wooden counter, sets the chamberpot down. He stands with his back turned, his eyes on the distant mountains. A difficult question, he says at last. I do not believe that I placed you in danger. Partly Narkis bin Silen did this. Partly you did it yourself. Also, as always, we must blame Fortune. It is true that I might have helped you more, and sooner. I might have informed better, or explained more. But in so doing I greatly would have endangered myself and my own project. Therefore, I did not. It burdens my heart to confess this, but it is indeed so.

Against the windows, his slender black form is edged by fire. He does not move except to speak. A pair of flies has come upon the chamberpot; they float above it in tight spirals, fighting the changeable breeze.

Tristão, Crivano says, what in God's name has transpired?

Tristão turns. His face appears and disappears in the scarlet sunset. The events of the past week, he says, are perhaps best likened to an obscure codex with a broken spine, the contents of which have been scattered everywhere. All interested parties possess a few pages, but only the book's author knows the whole. Indeed, even the author himself may have forgotten.

Who is the author?

I do not know.

Crivano frowns, crosses his arms. Pain shoots down the length of his right ulna, and he uncrosses them again. Very well, he says. Tell me this. What is your interest? How did you come by your pages?

At first Tristão doesn't answer. He lifts a touchwood from the counter behind him, ignites it in the brazier, and puts it to the wicks of several candles around the room. The high ceiling begins to catch their light. In both Ghettos, he says, I am acquainted with many learned men. Among the so-called German Jews of the New Ghetto, and also in the Old Ghetto, where my own people live. Through these men I have come to correspond with scholars in many cities, Constantinople perhaps foremost among them. Generally our correspondence consists of discussion about our mutual pursuit of secret knowledge, but sometimes we share news, or ask of each other simple favors. This is how I came by my pages.

Someone in Constantinople told you about me. Someone told you that I'm a spy for the haseki sultan.

I have learned that you believed yourself to be so, yes.

And you knew of the plot with the mirror-makers.

I knew what you knew of it, Tristão says. I also knew that Narkis bin Silen had made other arrangements for their removal. Please understand that this, to me, was only trivia. It remained so until I became aware that your enterprise was ruined. At that time I perceived a means of helping you, and of helping myself also. Only then did I interfere.

You arranged my meeting with Narkis at Ciotti's shop. You knew it to be watched by sbirri. You wanted us to be seen by them. To be seen together.

What you have spoken, Tristão says, is indeed so.

Why?

Tristão lights the last of the candles, throws the slender brand into the brazier. Then he gathers handfuls of firewood chips from a bin and drops them in, as well. They flare and blacken on the white-hot coals, and for a moment the round brazier seems to recapitulate the setting sun.

The sbirri were following you already, Tristão says. I suspect they had already gleaned the crude outlines of your plot. I reasoned that if I could induce you to associate openly with the Minerva bookshop, with the Uranici, with reputed magi like myself, then the dimensions of your conspiracy might seem larger than they were, and the Council of Ten might postpone your arrest until more could be learned. Had not Lord Mocenigus's unexpected denunciation of the Nolan spurred the Ten to swifter action, you and the mirrormakers might have escaped the city with minimal bloodshed. Narkis bin Silen, of course, had doomed himself from the outset. I had been informed of his intention to remove the mirrormakers to the territories of the Mughals, and I knew this to be hopeless and ridiculous, but I saw no reason why his careful preparations could not be redirected toward practical ends. I lured him to the bookshop to make him known to the sbirri, in the hope that they would eliminate him before his foolishness ruined your entire project.

Crivano purses his lips. He supposes he should be angry, but he is not. When you speak of practical ends, he says, I assume you're referring —

I mean only that the mirrormakers and their party are now to be taken not to faraway Lahore, nor even to Constantinople, but to Amsterdam, exactly as they have been promised all along.

The expression on Tristão's face is so sincere, so devoid of irony, that Crivano can't help but laugh and shake his head. Let me ask once more, Crivano says, for I still lack understanding: what is your interest in this matter? On this you have yet to speak.

Tristão looks at him appraisingly. His eyes seem dimmed by regret, or sadness. In his hesitation Crivano perceives no fear. Almost everyone whom Crivano has met since he came here, even Senator Contarini himself, has seemed wary of him — everyone but Tristão, whose ambitions are even grander than his own, who has even less to lose.

After a moment, Tristão lifts a long metal spoon from the countertop. and dips it into the chamberpot. He scoops up a quantity of feces — the stench intensifies in the fire-warmed air — and transfers it to a thick-walled beaker, scraping the spoon clean with a polished wooden rod. Then he adds water from a pitcher, stirs, and turns to the rows of jars and phials in the cabinet behind him. I have, he says, two principal interests. I have pursued both in this city with zeal and considerable satisfaction, but in both I have now reached an impasse. While your recent misfortunes sadden me, they have also provided me with a solution that is, I believe, comprehensive.

You're going to Amsterdam, Crivano says. With my mirrormakers.

That is my intent, yes.

Crivano shifts his weight, smoothes his matted hair with an absent left hand: the right one hurts too much to lift. He needs a chair. He finds one against the wall by the door, turns it around, drags it noisily across the floorplanks. Then he slumps into it to watch Tristão add blue and green salts to the beaker's vile contents.

You're performing the first operation, Crivano says.

I am, yes.

You're beginning the Great Work with shit.

It is perhaps not the only way, Tristão says, but I think it best. I have been cautious with my diet since the fine meal you and I shared at the White Eagle, eating only what is mercurial, martial, and venereal, according to the classifications of Marsilius Ficinus. It would have been better had I fasted through the previous week, but of course much has arisen that was unforeseen.

You hold with those who believe the *prima materia* to be excrement.

I believe that excrement can serve as such, if one makes certain preparations. In the works of Rupescissa we find the *prima materia* described as a worthless thing, found easily anywhere. Morienus tells us that all men, highborn and low, regard the *prima materia* with contempt, and that the vulgar sell it like mud. To what sort of matter might these descriptions apply, besides dung?

Most alchemists regard those descriptions as allegorical, Tristão.

Yes, Tristão says. In doing so, I believe they are mistaken.

He measures a quantity of red crystals — Crivano can't tell what — onto a scale until it balances against a five-grain weight. Then he pours them into the beaker, and stirs with a sheepish grin. Of course, he says, all we alchemists regard our rivals as deluded fools. In this I typify my species.

The wooden rod swirls the brown liquid, chimes against the beaker's edge. It sounds like a churchbell heard on a warm day across miles of calm ocean.

A moment ago, Crivano prompts, you were speaking of your two interests.

Tristão sets the wooden rod on the countertop with a heavy sigh. I hope you will forgive my clumsy reticence, he says. Often I find myself at a loss when compelled to speak of things that are perfectly natural. Of perfectly ordinary human concerns.

You're referring to Perina, I suppose.

Tristão glances up, his expression bashful, his eyes bright and relieved. Ah! he says. I envy your intuition, Vettor, and am grateful for it. She is, as you have discerned, my love. Because she is a daughter of nobility, and because I am what I am, our union will never be permitted in the Republic's territories. Thus we have chosen to depart.

Amsterdam will be more accepting, you think?

It scarcely could be less so, my friend.

A set of iron firetools hangs from the brazier's rim; Tristão reaches for a poker, stirs the blaze, uses a small spade to load the lower chamber of the athanor. Slow squeezes of a bellows coax a steady glow from the coals; Tristão takes up a stout crystal cucurbit on the counter. His firelit face appears fleetingly in the surface of the mirror-talisman; Crivano starts when he sees it, as if it might be a conjured demon wearing the face of its impious summoner. Outside, behind the dark form of the church, the lights of linkboys move down the fondamenta that abuts the canal.

What of your second interest? Crivano says. What is that?

Tristão shrugs, pours ordure from the beaker into the cucurbit. My continued studies, he says. When last we spoke in the Morosini house, I told you I intend to explore optical phenomena associated with the Great Work. I now lack resources to do this; in this city I have no reasonable expectation that my lack will be remedied. I require unfettered access to mirrormakers. In Amsterdam I will have it.

Crivano watches Tristão fasten an alembic to the cucurbit, a glass bulb to the alembic's downsloping neck. The devices are so well-made and well-cleaned as to be invisible but for the candleflames they reflect. The shape of the alembic echoes the beaked mask of the plaguedoctor. Crivano smiles; his eyelids sag with sleep.

Obizzo told me of your new plans for

escape, he says. Rowing to the trabacolo. Feigning an embarkation. Do you really believe this will succeed?

Do you see reason to doubt?

If the Council of Ten knows what ship you intend to use, the sbirri will meet you in the lagoon. Or they'll already be aboard when you arrive.

They do not know what ship, Tristão says. Aside from the sailors themselves, who have been told nothing of their expected passengers, no soul in this city aside from myself knows the name of the vessel that is to bear us.

Narkis knew, Crivano says. So did the Mughal spies with whom he collaborated.

Tristão busies himself in the athanor's upper enclosure. He fixes the cucurbit in a sandbath, balances the glass apparatus on a rack above the coals' rising heat. Narkis bin Silen was alone, he says. Even his fellow residents at the fondaco had no knowledge of his activities. And his Mughal friends are not here. They await him in Trieste, I believe.

You're sure he confessed nothing prior to his death?

I am, yes.

Wherefore this certainty, Tristão?

I was present when Narkis bin Silen died.

Tristão moves his hands away from the arrangement of glass atop the athanor. It retains its position. Then he adjusts the height of the

889

platform that bears the coals below. He does not look at Crivano.

I did not kill him, Tristão says. I certainly would have done so, had that been necessary. But he knew what was possible, and what was not. I told him who I was. He understood. He put a cord around his neck, and he hanged himself from the Madonnetta Bridge. I cut his body down and let him drift in the canal. It was not a happy end, Vettor. Not at all. But for him no better end would have come.

Crivano watches his friend's smooth face, intent in the orange light. He isn't sure he believes Tristão. He isn't sure it matters anymore.

If the Council of Ten doesn't know what ship you'll use, Crivano says, why bother with the simulation of boarding? None will be watching to be deceived.

Tristão's hands fidget around the clay cylinder, although there is nothing more to arrange, no task left to accomplish. An additional precaution, he says. Sbirri will patrol the lagoon, and may see our lights. They will also be keeping careful record of vessels passing through the channel at San Nicolò. Once they learn the glassmakers have gone, they and the guild are likely to send assassins. I much prefer that those assassins be sent to Constantinople, not to Amsterdam.

Crivano is silent. Tristão continues to bustle

890

around his apparatus until this demonstration can't help but seem asinine. Then he straightens, sighs, turns to meet Crivano's gaze.

You're lying, Crivano says.

Tristão looks wounded. Not at all, he says. Why do you accuse me of this?

It's a foolish risk you've planned, to no certain profit. As you've said, the sbirri are patrolling the lagoon. Why tarry, then, with elaborate charades that no one may see? Why not row headlong for Mestre?

Tristão remains silent, moistens his lips with his tongue.

It's not a charade you need, Crivano says. It's a diversion. You need the Council of Ten to *know* what ship we'll use. To have good reason to believe we've sailed on it.

The trabacolo, Tristão says, is called the *Lynceus.* Its crew expects to sail for Trieste, of course, but for the right sum, I imagine they will go anywhere in the Adriatic. Any port you might wish.

Crivano stares at Tristão. Then his eyes sink to the rush-strewn laboratory floor, tracing patterns in the matted carpet of dry stalks and coarse sand. A few specks move there: weevils, beetles, fleas, the tiny spiders that hunt them. Impossible from this height to tell which are which. Crivano could slide from his chair and come to rest among them, could spend the rest of his life watching their microscopic intrigues. In his very vastness he would be invisible: a peculiar new mountain.

The Church of Saint Jeremy rings the first bell; Saint Jerome echoes it a moment later, along with others. Crivano rises, walks past Tristão to look out the west-facing windows. The sun-absented sky has turned an angry violet.

Even now, Crivano says, sbirri comb the streets for me. But the Council of Ten is ignorant of your involvement. Am I not right?

You are correct.

It knows nothing of Serena and his family? Nor of Obizzo?

The Council now seeks to arrest Serena. He is known to have had dealings with you. But he and his family are already in hiding — I sent them an alarm — and I believe they will reach the Cerberus safely. The Council knows of Obizzo, of course; it has sought him for years, due to his collusion in his brother's escape. But it does not suspect that he works the canals of the city as a boatman.

And what of Perina? Do they know of Perina?

They do not.

You're sure? I visited her at the convent. Perhaps they saw me.

You visited her at the senator's behest. It is not suspicious.

I sent a linkboy to her last night, bearing a cryptic message.

I intercepted that linkboy. I replaced him

with one in my own service. Your message will lead no one to her. Rest assured, Vettor, that among our present company you alone are hotly pursued.

Crivano falls silent. A solitary blue cloud darkens the air over the mountains, rushing forward on a terrible wind, changing shape as it approaches. For a moment it resembles a crawling thing crushed on a pane of dark glass; then it becomes a gob of spit, dripping from fine dyed satin. Then it simply looks like a cloud. Crivano is weary; he wants to sleep, ungoaded by dreams. I have no wish to go to Amsterdam, he says.

I thought not. We can put you aboard the *Lynceus* on our way to Mestre. You have money left from the haseki sultan?

Oh yes. Letters of advice.

If you like, Tristão says, I can send my servants into the Ghetto to redeem them for precious stones. Jewels are safer, perhaps, than are your letters. And prices here are reasonably good.

You still haven't answered my question. How can we be sure that the sbirri will follow me, and not you?

Tristão steps closer, puts a warm hand on Crivano's upper arm. This is difficult, my friend, he says. Circumstance compels me to charge you with a heavy task.

You're going to tell them that I'm on the *Lynceus.*

They will not learn this, Tristão whispers, until we are all aboard Obizzo's boat. I know of informants whose eyes watch the Cannaregio Canal. As we depart, we shall take pains to ensure that those eyes fall upon us. After last night's escapades, you surely will be recognized at once. Yet even with the most fleet of messengers at their disposal, even with the sturdiest of oarsmen, the sbirri will be unable to intercept us until we've reached the *Lynceus,* whereupon they will find our red-lanterned trabacolo racing for the open sea, and Obizzo's sandolo cast adrift.

You're exchanging boats, as well?

Of course. The *Lynceus* will have a shallow-drafted riverboat — a topo, this type is called — roped to its north side. If Fortune smiles, we will cross the lagoon at peak tide, passing over sandbars that will obstruct any who would apprehend us. But I do not think we will be pursued.

Because the sbirri will be chasing the *Lynceus.* They'll be chasing me.

They will try to board you in the lagoon. Likely they will try to blockade you at San Nicolò. They may fire on you from the Lido, as well. The crew of the *Lynceus* is well-armed and lawless, disinclined to surrender. I think you will escape.

The sbirri will see me on the quarterdeck. They'll know I'm aboard, and they'll infer the presence of the mirrormakers. Thereafter, the spies of the Council of Ten will track me wherever I go. Their assassins will seek my trail in every Mediterranean port.

Tristão moves his hand from Crivano's arm to the back of his neck. The skin of his palm is dry and smooth. If you can leave Christian lands entirely, he says, it would be better for you, I think.

I may not be welcome in Constantinople any longer.

It is a large world, my friend. With many places in it, and great empty distances for vanishing. You could sail for Alexandria, for instance. Or Tripoli.

Or Cyprus.

Yes. There is always Cyprus.

Crivano shrugs off Tristão's hand, moves along the counter to examine the athanor. The fluid in the cucurbit is motionless, its color unaltered, but liquid is beading in the alembic above. How long does it take? he asks. Your method?

The time varies. No less than three weeks. Often a month or more.

And yet you intend to depart tomorrow night?

Yes, Tristão says. This process yields reductions and coagulates that are stable and portable after sixteen hours. I intend to collect them before we go. Also, if sbirri crash through our doors tonight, I want to be able to show them this, and to say: *No, of course I am not planning to flee your city! Look here — I have just begun a complex operation that is to last a full month!*

Crivano manages a sour smile. He presses a knuckle to the cucurbit's warm glass, then withdraws it. Lowering his eyes, he scans the assemblies of vessels and devices, the use-disordered rows of chemicals and herbs. Though his limbs remain still, his muscles flex and extend, recalling the automatic gestures of a working magus. To open a window onto a world of ideal forms, to know the mind of God: these are the goals of his art. But Crivano is surprised at how many of his fond memories of the laboratory are bodily — akin to his recollections of janissary calisthenics, or of kickball games he learned as a boy. The rules were arbitrary; you practiced until you moved without thought. Those were ideal worlds, too, weren't they?

I've been thinking of your mirrored alembic, Crivano says. And also of a passage in the *Corpus Hermeticum* that the Nolan saw fit to cite, about the instance of reflection that induces Man to descend from Heaven and inhabit the Earth. He looks down; He sees His own perfect shape reflected in Her waters. So arises our double nature: mortal flesh, housing immortal souls.

Tristão nods, but seems distracted. He reaches for the water-pitcher and empties it into the chamberpot, rinsing the wooden rod and the long spoon as he pours. When the water is gone, he sets the pitcher on the counter. Then he lifts the chamberpot, swirling it in his right hand.

Indeed, he says. But here we should be cautious. Often we are told, and rightly so, that we can know God by knowing ourselves, for we are made in His image. We are not base, it is said, but divine. Yet this, perhaps, is saying too much. For even in our baseness — in our excrement — we might discern the work of our Creator.

All things come from God, Crivano says. Even shit can be sublimed.

But should it be?

Tristão fixes Crivano with a fierce glare. Then he steps to the windows, and with a smooth sudden motion slings the chamberpot's contents into the canal below. The liquid strikes the surface with a weak slap.

Should it be sublimed? Tristão says. Should it be transcended? When we seek to do this, is our desire truly to know God? Or is it to know that God truly is as we always have imagined him: the perfect distillate of our corrupt selves? So — we are made in the image of God. Have we considered what this might mean? *Innumerable are the egos in man,* Paracelsus writes, *and in him are angels and devils, heaven and hell.* Perhaps God too is like this. Pure and impure. Is it so difficult to imagine? A God of flesh and bone? A God that shits?

His voice chokes off, as if overwhelmed by some passion: rage, sorrow, Crivano can't guess which. Tristão drifts away, toward his own approaching form in the mirror-talisman; the image of his torso gradually fills the glass. With the silver window eclipsed the room seems to grow smaller; Crivano shuffles his feet to keep his balance.

I want to know, Tristão says, how God is *unlike* us. I want to know how our eyes become traitors. To know what they refuse to see. I no longer seek to transcend, nor even to understand. I want only to dirty my hands. To smell. To feel. Like a child who plays with mud. I believe the key is here —

His fingers brush the flat glass before him; they're met by fingers from the opposite side.

— but not in the way that others have said. The Nolan warned us of this. Do you remember? He said the image in the mirror is like the image in a dream: only fools and infants mistake it for the true likeness of the world, but likewise it is foolish to ignore what it shows us. Therein lies the danger. Do we look upon these reflections without delusion, like bold Actaeon? Or, like Narcissus, do we see only what we wish to see? How can we be certain? With love in our hearts, we creep toward each shining surface, but we are all haunted, always, by ourselves.

Tristão raises his other hand to the braided-glass border of the mirror. Then he lifts it from its easel and turns, bearing it before him like a platter. Crivano glimpses the top of his own head just inside its frame; he backs away in alarm.

I would like you to have this, Tristão says.

Crivano grimaces. No, he says. You are — you are far too generous, my friend. You paid so much.

I have no further use for it. I needed it to arrange my mind for the challenges I am soon to face, but now I am ready. And I cannot travel with it. Our passage through the Alps is it certain to result in its breakage. And if someone were to find it — the risk is too great, you see. Shipboard, however, it may travel safely. Take it, Vettor. Or tomorrow night I must cast it into the lagoon.

The talisman's tilting plane catches the cracked stucco of the ceiling; the cracks sweep and jerk across its surface. Crivano shuts his eyes and pictures the strongbox of coins that paid for it: the bend in the drunken gondoliers' oar. Very well, he says. I thank you.

He makes no move to take it. Tristão holds it, a bemused look on his face, then sets it on the countertop. The mirror's retreat feels like the snuffing of a light, the closing of a door: Crivano is both relieved and diminished by its departure. I shall have this wrapped securely for you, Tristão says.

Yes, Crivano whispers. You're very kind.

Are you all right, my friend?

Crivano's arms shiver, as if he's cold, though he is not cold. He sighs. I'm quite tired, he says. I should rest.

That is wise. Tomorrow will be difficult. And the many days to follow.

I would like to see Perina.

The words rise to Crivano's throat with the timbre of a challenge — which, he supposes, they are. He and Tristão watch each other in the darkening room. Firelight glints in their eyes. Their shadows move with the wind.

No doubt she is eager for your visit, Tristão says. She has been concerned for your well-being, but unwilling to disturb your sleep.

If Tristão knows the rest — the last secret, the one that would unravel Crivano completely — he gives no sign. Perhaps he has judged Crivano unraveled enough.

You will find her in the room beside your own, Tristão says. Go to her now, my friend. Then sleep. Sleep soundly, with all my gratitude.

Crivano nods. He raises his left hand in salute, and turns toward the exit.

Tristão's voice comes again as he opens the door. Oh, Vettor, it calls. I took the liberty of extracting a tincture from your henbane.

Crivano stops, half-turned in the doorframe. My henbane, he says.

Yes. In your box of physic you had a very

large quantity of what appeared to be biennial henbane. An alarming quantity. I think it
is better not to travel with so great a measure
of the raw plant, so I have made from it a
tincture, which will be much easier to trans-
port. When the extraction is complete, I will
bottle it and put it among your things.

My things?

Your box of physic. Also, your trunk. If you
need them, you will find them in the storeroom below. If you like, I can have them
brought to your room.

A fresh chill settles on Crivano's neck.
When did my things arrive? he says.

I cannot be certain. A footman found them
inside the water-gate last night, just after
sundown. I assumed that you had them sent.

Crivano's brow furrows, but the muscles of
his face are too weak to hold the expression.
Instead he smiles: an airy drunken smile, with
no mirth in it. Yes, he says. Yes, I suppose I
did.

In the darkening kitchen Crivano finds a
tallow candle, lights it with a brand from the
hearth: the mutton-fat smokes and sputters
as a glow fills the room. The cheese and bread
and apples the Jewess set out are greatly
diminished; Obizzo must have eaten and
retired. A pile of iron filings still blots the
tabletop, casting a small shadow on the wood.

Three soft knocks bring Perina's voice from
behind her door: a vague sound, either an

invitation to enter or a request to keep out. Crivano tries the latch. The portal swings open.

The air in the room is thick, trapped by shuttered windows, heavy with long-forgotten smells of home. Crivano stands in the entrance with his eyes closed — his mind reassembling the rooms and corridors of the great house in Nicosia, the house this girl was born too late to know — until he has adjusted to the darkness within.

Perina emerges from her blankets like a part-risen shade: a bare white arm from the brown wool, then a tonsured head. The girl watches Crivano as he closes the door, lights two candles atop a low trunk with the wick of his own. She does not speak.

A chair sits beside her bed; Crivano eases into it, puts his candle on a shelf fixed to the bedpost. Perina slides backward, sits up, takes hold of his hand. You are well? she says. Her voice is coarsened by snores. The rough tick of her mattress has left a gridded imprint on her cheek.

I survive, lady, Crivano says.

She smiles.

I am greatly in your debt, he tells her. You must know that. I endangered myself foolishly, and in the course of my rescue you were injured. That fact rests like a capstone upon me.

I was not so badly hurt, dottore. Tristão

902

must have told you.

Yes, Crivano says. He did. May I look?

Her large eyes grow larger in the dim. She does not answer, and she does not move. Wind rattles the shutters. The light falters as the candleflames dance.

Crivano grips the blanket's edge. You were struck on this side, he says. Were you not?

She nods.

He lifts the cover just enough to examine the pale band of flesh beneath it. A violet quarter-moon darkens Perina's swollen skin a palm's-breadth below her half-hidden breast. Had the blow been lower, had it landed more squarely, she might be dead. As it is, she likely won't think of the wound at all by the time another Sunday has passed. For once, Fortune has smiled.

He lifts the blanket higher, slides the candle closer on its shelf, squints. With a tinge of impatience, she plucks the fabric from his still-weak fingers and draws it aside, baring her body to the knees.

Crivano blinks. His ears fill with too-sharp sounds — the wind, the water, distant voices, the creaks and pops of the settling building — as if he's about to faint. Take a deep breath, he says: to the girl, to himself. Breathe in as deeply as you are able.

She breathes, wincing as her lungs swell, but neither coughs nor cries out: her ribs remain unbroken. Her strong shoulders angle back: they're Dolfin's shoulders, almost exactly. Aren't they? After so many years of careful forgetting, it's difficult to be sure. The girl's oblong areolae wrinkle in the cool air; her nipples grow stiff. Cutis anserina appears on her forearms. Crivano reaches across her lap to replace her blanket. In Dottore de Nis's care, he says, you will heal very rapidly. Of this I am certain.

Perina looks down, smoothing the blanket to the contours of her hips. We are leaving the city, she says. Going to Amsterdam. We're to depart tomorrow night. Did Tristão tell you?

We spoke of it, yes.

Her hand closes on his once more. One of them is trembling; he can't tell which. Perhaps both. You're coming with us, she says. Are you not?

Crivano looks at the shuttered windows. Of course I am, he says.

You can't remain here. Every villain in the lagoon now stalks you.

He pulls his hand away, rests it on the black fuzz of her cropped head. I will come to Amsterdam, he says. I will. Of course I will.

She's weeping now, quietly; her voice remains steady. There are many things I would ask you, she says. So many things. About Gabriel. About my lost brother.

I will tell you, Crivano whispers. I will tell you many things.

He smoothes the short hair at the base of her skull. Then he lowers his heavy head onto her shoulder and closes his eyes. For once — for the last time — permitting himself to remember. How he snatched the slow match from the blood-slimed deck where Captain Bua threw it. How he leapt into the hold as the Turks pushed past the pikemen. How he turned not toward the powder magazine, as ordered, but toward his own hammock, and that of the Lark. Tears inch down his nose, land with heavy taps in the folds of the blanket. After a moment, he feels Perina's hand on his neck.

They sit together for a long time, both of them near sleep, half-dreaming.

What was your name? Perina says. The name they called you?

Crivano doesn't answer. He lifts his head, sits up. Keeping his eyes shut. His damp cheeks are cool in the open air.

The things I recall, Perina says, the things told me by my mother and my sister before the plague took them, it all slips away now. I write down as much as I can, of course. But memories do not simply vanish, do they? They alter. They become something else. And there is naught to take bearings against save the shifting memories of other minds. Thus it becomes difficult to know what is true.

Yes, Crivano says. You have spoken fairly.

He's thinking now of the lies he's told

through the years: to others, to himself. Clearly enough he remembers what he did that day on the *Gold and Black Eagle,* but he cannot remember why. His mind in those frightful hours was twisted by grief and panic, filled with misshapen fragments, wriggling like grubs churned from the earth by a spade. *My mother will never believe I'm dead. If you give her this, then maybe she'll know.* He feared being ransomed; he feared being butchered. He wanted to go home to his family; he wanted to vanish forever. He wanted to live; he wanted to die. But none among those reasons seems adequate to what he did. Something else inhabited him. In that moment, who did he become?

With the Turks howling victory, with cannonballs plucking at the cordage, with his shipmates abovedecks screaming in despair, he ransacked the darkness, the match smoking in his teeth, until his fingers found them: two certificates of matriculation, for Gabriel Glissenti and Vettor Crivano. He tucked his dead friend's document into his shirt. Then he touched the tip of the slow match to his own, pressing it against the careful letters of his name — the name his father gave him — until the parchment blackened, and the flames took it away.

It was because of your voice, Perina says. You had such a beautiful voice, and you knew every lovely song. My mother spoke of this often, with great affection. What was the nickname they gave you? Until I recall it I'll be rendered sleepless, even in my great exhaustion. Won't you take pity on me, dottore?

Crivano opens his eyes. His face is wet, but his vision is clear. Across the room, another gust pushes against the shutters; the candle-flames tip away from the windows, and the candles' shadows stretch toward them.

The Lark, Crivano says. Your family called me the Lark.

With a broad melancholic smile, Perina slides supine on the mattress. Her eyelids droop, as if in a rush to meet the blanket that she draws to her chin. In the morning, she says, our faculties will be restored. Then we shall speak pleasantly and at our leisure of the happy past, and what warm recollections we share will bring us both solace. Now, we want for sleep. Will I be judged greedy, dottore, if I beg you to lull me in the old manner of your boyhood? This small favor, I promise, will discharge any debt you may imagine you accrued last night, and will tilt the balance toward me.

Her blanket-hooded face smiles up at him. Her eyes are squeezed shut against encroaching disappointments. He watches her closely. Much has been lost; much more will be: among those casualties, an ancient name is hardly foremost. But the courage of his forefathers — the fatal courage that Fortune spared him — still persists on the undeserving earth. This brave girl has made him proud.

His throat tightens. He clears it, then leans forward to blow out the candle on the bedpost. The second bell moves across the city, measuring the sun's retreat; the gaps between the shutters have gone black. Crivano draws a steady breath and tries, as sweetly as he is able, to sing.

The Shroudy Stranger's reft of realms.
Abhorred he sits upon the city dump.
His broken heart's a bag of shit.
The vast rainfall, an empty mirror.

— ALLEN GINSBERG,
"The Shrouded Stranger"

60

Curtis wakes to white light, black dark, a cop's voice. It's Coach Banner's voice from high school, Colonel Gandy's from Kosovo; he can't understand anything it says, but he knows exactly what it's saying. *You did okay, Stone, but you screwed up, too.* Curtis doesn't need to be told. His eyes roll back; he's out again.

Time passes: a slideshow flashed on a flapping white sheet. Doctors and nurses in masks and gowns. The bright OR; the dim recovery room. Interchangeable LVMPD badges. At first there's no sequence — everything happening all at once — but then events line up, and Curtis starts to make memories again. Albedo rode in the ambulance with him, he's pretty sure of that, but never made it to the ICU.

Curtis wakes again, realizing that he's already awake. Taking inventory. Adding up limbs, losing count. He feels like something's missing, or something extra's been added.

He must've twisted left when the headlights came at him: his right wrist is in a cast. A figure-eight sling pins his shoulders back; that means *collarbone*. Foam boots on both feet, pendent weights hung from the bed's edge: traction to keep his legs straight. That means *both hips broken.*

Curtis takes a breath, lets it out. His throat hurts; his arm itches where the IV needle's taped. He's going to bounce back from this. Probably not all the way back, and that's fine. Nobody ever bounces all the way back. Not from anything. That's the way it goes, bouncing.

He's on a bunch of pretty heavy drugs. Even as he thinks this, he can feel them fade: a cold dead tide going out. That's probably why his eyes are open. Somebody must want to talk to him.

Mister Stone?

A tall thin Hispanic guy, in a steel-tube chair beside Curtis's motorized rack. Curtis's age, or a little younger. Patient. Not fed up, or put-upon. Not like most cops Curtis has known. Federal, probably. Somebody in Jersey got his message.

Curtis? the guy says, like he's trying different frequencies. Mister Stone? Master Sergeant Stone?

Yeah, Curtis says. I'm here.

His own voice sounds harsh and loud, although he knows it can't really be loud. His throat feels like it's tearing. He clears it, coughs. His right side aches.

The Hispanic guy gives Curtis his name — Agent Something — then starts with the customary spiel. LVMPD wants to bring serious charges against you, Mister Stone, he says. I asked them for some time with you first. There's a bigger picture here that I don't think anybody has seen yet.

Yeah, Curtis says. You got that right.

You want to tell me about it?

Curtis licks his lips. Flecks of dry skin scrape his tongue. There's a lot of pain inside him someplace; he glimpses it now and again, like a lantern moving through the windows of an old house. The traction on his legs means the docs haven't cut there yet. Maybe he hasn't been out so long. I want to talk to my wife, Curtis says.

The agent smiles. Danielle's on her way, he says. She's in the air now. Metro's sending a car for her. Of course, we don't know yet when they'll clear you to see her.

I'm under arrest?

You haven't been arrested. I understand you used to be a military policeman, so you know how this works. I should tell you, though, before we say anything else, that you have the right to remain silent, and to have an attorney present for any discussion with me. You can get an attorney, and I can get a tape-recorder, and we can do this more

913

formally. Do you want to do that, Curtis?

Curtis closes his eyes, toggles his head back and forth. I'm sky-high, man, he says. No judge'll let you use any of this.

The guy shrugs. He already has an inkstick out; now he flips open a spiral notebook, stuffs his tie in his breast pocket. You want to wait? he says. Sober up?

Curtis shakes his head. No, he says. I want to tell it now.

He tells it as well as he can. It's hard to keep it all straight. He gets confused, makes mistakes, goes back to correct himself. Even uninjured, unmedicated, he never had a handle on a lot of it. But he does his best.

He tells about the call he got from Damon, about meeting him in Philly at the Penrose Diner, and also about Stanley, and about the cardcounters at the Spectacular. He tells about Albedo, and about Argos, and about the missing dealer, and about what Argos said in the desert, and he tells about the call he had his dad make to the Jersey cops. For the most part he keeps Veronica out of it. He's not entirely sure why. It's what Stanley would want him to do, he figures, and she never seemed like that big a part of it anyway. She was about as far outside as Curtis was himself.

Hang on, the Hispanic guy says, scribbling. Wait up a second. What's the point?

Curtis blinks. Say again? he says. What do

914

you mean, what's the point? You asked me to tell it, so I'm telling it, goddamnit.

No no no, the guy says. You keep talking about *the Point*. Like, the cardcounters hit *the Point*. You wanted to get a job at *the Point*. I don't know what that means.

The Spectacular, Curtis says. The Spectacular is the Point. The name's got an exclamation mark after it. In its logo. The official name. Exclamation *point,* I mean to say. Before they even opened, this story went around — I don't know if it's true — that a PR guy got fired because he forgot to put the explanation point, the *exclamation* point, on the end of the name. People working there started calling it the Point. As a joke. And it spread. Most people who say it now, they don't even know how it got started. But that's how I heard it from Damon.

Okay, the guy says. Got it.

His pen scratches across the little notebook; Curtis reads upsidedown. POINT = SPEC-TACULAR, the guy writes.

Later he holds a cup of water for Curtis; Curtis sips, keeps talking. As he gets tired and hurts worse he starts to explain things that probably don't matter, to repeat whatever details stick in his brain. The ripped-up faxes on *SPECTACULAR!* letterhead. The machine-gun in Albedo's car. The cellphone Damon gave him. The calls he made from the visitor center at the state park. The cufflink torn

915

from Damon's sleeve. Jay Leno in the hotel lobby. *The Mirror Thief* left in the Quicksilver suite. Did anybody pick that book up? Curtis asks. Somebody should go over there and pick that book up.

By now the agent has all but stopped scribbling; the look on his face says he's waiting for something. Curtis tries to think of what that might be, to think of questions he's been ready for that the guy hasn't asked yet. He comes up with quite a few. One big one. Where's Damon now? Curtis says.

The agent doesn't answer. He leans back slowly in the steel-tube chair, retracts the point of his rollerball with a soft click.

You don't know, Curtis says.

The guy smiles. It's not a happy smile. For the first time Curtis can tell that he's operating on not much sleep. Do you have any thoughts, the agent says, as to where we might find him?

Curtis squints, shakes his head. Shaking it makes him dizzy. I figured NJSP'd have him by now, he says.

The guy stares evenly, his eyes expressionless. Monday afternoon, he says, two NJSP detectives met Damon at his townhouse. Follow-up visit. They'd interviewed him before; he'd been cooperative. Damon invited them in, put on some coffee, shot them both in the face. One died at the scene, the other's on life-support. Probably not coming off it.

Local uniformed patrol found them within the half-hour — somebody must have known something was wrong — but by then Damon had already cleared out.

Curtis tries to take a deep breath but chokes on it, and for a second he's afraid he'll puke. The room spins, like the restaurant at the Stratosphere, and he shuts his eyes to make it stop. He's thinking back, trying to recall: what time he phoned his dad, what time Damon's last fax came. What he might have caused, or failed to stop.

Damon hadn't shown up for work that day, the agent says. Risk Management conducted a search of his office. The story is, they found nothing on his computer but porn videos, and nothing in his filing cabinets except dirty cartoons. Pretty disturbing stuff, from what I hear. People are wondering why it took so long to realize he was a problem. He must be a real charming guy.

Curtis hears a rustle as the agent flips through his notebook, maybe looking over what he's just written. Do you have any thoughts, he says again, as to where we might find him?

Curtis keeps his eyes shut, steadies his breath.

I have to say, the agent goes on, he picked a pretty good time to be a fugitive. As of Monday night, law enforcement nationwide is on orange alert. That's because of the war.

With everybody on defensive footing, investigations are going to slow down. An elevated alert can make it harder to hide a vehicle, though. Damon probably knew that. His Audi turned up a few hours ago, at a park-and-ride in Maryland.

Curtis opens his eyes. Maryland where? he says.

College Park. We've got CCTV of Damon boarding the inbound Green Line. I know what you're thinking, and don't worry: your dad and his wife are safe. We've got them in a hotel. Their home is under surveillance. If Damon shows up there —

He won't, Curtis says. He's gone. If Damon went to D.C., it was to get help traveling. Visas, passports. People there would do that for him.

The agent doesn't like that answer: he looks irritated, confused. He opens his mouth, but Curtis cuts him off. You understand who we're talking about here, right? Have you pulled his DD 214?

His what?

His service record. You ought to look at that. Look at what he's done, where he's been. He's not in D.C., man. He went to BWI, or to National. He got on a plane. He could be anywhere by now. South America. Asia.

The guy is about to argue the point, but then gives up, deflates. His mouth hangs open for a second; he shuts it, rubs his face. Curtis feels bad for him, feels bad generally. He doesn't want to believe what he's just heard — habit works his brain hard, plugging in scenarios and explanations that put Damon in a better light — but he knows it's true. His whole life he's never understood anybody, not even himself. Himself maybe least of all. He wants to go to back to sleep, to slip out of a world where shit like this can happen.

Wait a minute, Curtis says. What about Stanley Glass?

The agent's eyes open; his inkstick clicks again. Stanley Glass, he says.

Where is he?

The agent shrugs. Still in Atlantic City, he says. Last I heard, NJSP was looking to bring him in. They didn't have him yet, but they were getting close. I understand he's seriously ill. His mobility's restricted.

Curtis shakes his head. If Stanley's still breathing, he says, then NJSP is not as close to him as they think they are. And I highly doubt that he's still in AC.

Okay. Where do you think he is?

He's wherever Damon is. And vice versa.

The agent makes a skeptical face. I know it doesn't make much sense, Curtis says. But that's how it is with those guys. They've got the goods on each other. They've got something to settle, and they're gonna settle it. The question is where.

The guy's rollerball hasn't touched his notebook. So your advice on how to find Damon Blackburn, he says, is basically to find Stanley Glass. And vice versa. Have I got that right?

My advice, Curtis says, is that I hope you have better luck than I did. That is pretty much my entire advice.

The agent pulls his tie from his pocket, smoothes it across his breastbone, replaces it with the inkstick. Mister Stone, he says, I should let you know that I am not anywhere close to being done with you. But I do wish you a speedy recovery, and I thank you for your cooperation today.

No problem, Curtis says. Hey, do me a favor, though. I'm starting to hurt pretty bad here. If we're done for now —

Sure thing, the agent says. I'll get the nurse.

The nurse comes, messes with Curtis's IV, and soon everything's flattening out, becoming dull and vague. For a second, he has an answer to the agent's question — it's obvious: he pictures *The Mirror Thief* lying on Veronica's coffeetable, dropped on the Quicksilver carpet — but then the drug snatches it away, and he lets it go. He wants to quit thinking very soon.

A warm swell of tears fills his half-empty eyes. He waits quietly and thinks of Damon until the medicine finally finds his brain, until he can't remember anything anymore except

920

the weightless surge of planes taking off —
out of Ramstein, out of Philly — until he
knows nothing of his own past, until time
seems to have stopped and he feels like he is
no one at all.

Curtis. Add up the letters of the name, they
come to four hundred eighty-two. *Autumn
leaves,* it means. Or, believe it or not, *glass.*
Add those three numbers — four plus eight
plus two — you get fourteen. *A gift,* or *a
sacrifice. To glitter,* or *to shine.*

Sometime later — minutes or hours, it's
hard to know for sure — a telephone somewhere nearby will start to ring.

When the cops and nurses burst into his
room, Curtis won't even be aware of the
sound. He'll wake grudgingly, blinking at the
overhead lights as cops gather: whispering
into cellphones, setting up a recorder, stretching the cord of the hospital phone until the
base rests next to Curtis on the mattress.
He'll watch their busy mouths as they talk to
him, and he'll nod, although he'll understand
nothing they say. And then, as someone's
finger mashes the phone's SPEAKER button,
he'll angle his head, and he'll try to listen.

Somehow he'll know right away. He'll hear
the ghostly whine and hiss — long distances,
strange satellites — and know exactly who's
calling, and from where, and why.

But he'll ask anyway. He can't help himself.

Stanley? he'll say. Is that you?

And then, after a long moment, you will answer him.

Good morning, kid, you'll say. Or good evening I guess it still is, where you are. Been a long goddamn time, hasn't it? I'm glad to hear your voice.

You won't keep Curtis long. Not because of the cops — what can cops do to you now? — but because there isn't much to say. Or there's too much. Anyway, you'll keep it simple. You'll say thank you. Then you'll say you're sorry. Then you'll say goodbye.

Another gust: the hotel window rattles. You hear churchbells ring, the scream of a gull. You draw the blankets tight around your chin.

In another minute or two you'll get up, make the call. You put the kid in a bad spot, so it's the least you can do. You should phone Veronica, too, while you're at it. See if she found what you left her in the airport locker. Her inheritance. That'll be a tough goddamn conversation. But you guess it ought to be done.

Veronica. Three hundred eighty-eight. A hard stone, like flint, or quartz. To veil. To conceal. To spread out. To be set free.

First things first: you should go to the window. Slide your feet to the slick hotel floor, grip your cane, rise. Somewhere down there — among the fruit- and flower-vendors in the Campo San Cassiano, the bundled old women on the bridge's dainty steps, the black gondolas that slide down the mucus-gray canal — Damon is hunting you. He must know he's running out of chances to do this his way: with each passing minute you slip farther from him. So you expect him soon. When he turns up, you want to be ready.

He's an annoyance more than anything else. A distraction. You had big plans for coming here, but you waited too long. You'd hoped to make a last trip to the Bibiloteca. The lady librarians are probably relieved today to get a break from your questions. *What's this mean in English? How do I locate that?*

You'd like to have seen more of the city, too, of course. So far it's been mostly Disneyland bullshit: cameras and fannypacks, glossy maps and flapping pigeons. But every so often there's a moment — a name on a sign that you know from Welles's book; columns and windows that echo buildings on Windward and the boardwalk — that'll freeze you in midstep: trying to peek through the gap before it closes again, trying to see past overlapping screens of truth and fiction to Crivano. But it's hard to catch these moments, hard to keep yourself loose and open to them when you're looking over your shoulder all the time. Damon has spoiled this for you, too. You tell yourself it doesn't matter, but it does.

In your younger days — not so long ago — you'd have fixed this by now. Sipped espresso at the Caffè Florian till you picked him from the crowd. Tracked him till the sun went down. Plenty of secluded spots. Bricks fall in this city all the time.

The strange thing is, part of you is glad to see him. Glad he's here. The parting fuck-you that you delivered in AC on Sunday afternoon — *I'd like to tell you gentlemen a funny story about your shift boss, Mr. Blackburn* — seemed cheap, inadequate, like a copout. But this feels right, feels earned.

Besides, you've found a few safe places where you don't have to think of him, where you can seek what you came here to find. The closest you've come to Crivano was yesterday, on the powerboat you hired to get a look at the city from the lagoon: belltowers emerging from late-winter mist, just as he might have seen them. Well, maybe not quite: in his day San Michele wasn't yet a graveyard; the Fondamenta Nuove hadn't been built. More of your cash sent the boat around Santa Élena into the Canale di San Marco, and there you saw Crivano's city at last — somewhat sunken, with a few extra buildings, but otherwise much the same. The driver killed the engine, the boat began to drift, and as the fog and sea-smell settled around you a memory came, as clear as a punch to the forehead: playing cards with your dad on the

Staten Island Ferry, looking up as the skyline of Lower Manhattan appeared through the clouds. Nothing natural in sight but water and gulls. Pure invention, imagined into being.

You stayed out on the lagoon too long, caught a chill, needed to piss. Pushing yourself to your feet, you leaned on the gunwale, unzipped, tugged your diaper down. The driver rose from his seat in alarm — *Ao!* he barked — but he shut up in a hurry when he saw the hot stream you splashed across the sea's surface turn from yellow to red.

He dropped you on the Riva degli Schiavoni, and you wobbled toward the twin columns, your balance still troubled by the memory of waves. Lying here now, you can almost feel them again, an echo of the ebb and flow of your own sluggish blood.

Sniff the air: you've shit yourself. You'd like to change before Damon comes. It won't be messy; you hardly eat anymore. Not being in control used to upset you; these days, not so much. You can get used to anything, or stop caring. As you've gotten sicker you've grown almost to enjoy it: it feels good, the warmth and the weight. Alive. More alive than you feel. You're always a little surprised to find that something so strange and vital can still come from what remains of you.

In another minute, you'll get up. You'll go to the window. You'll make the two calls. In just another minute.

It might have been nice to find a table somewhere. But of course that's the first place Damon would look, and anyway you've had enough of that scene. You're sick of gamblers, with their systems and their percentages. *Blackjack is the only table game with a memory.* Walter Kagami — still a kid, black-haired and skinny, in his guayabera shirt — explaining it to you for the hundredth time. *Cards get dealt, they're out of play till the cut-card comes up. That's why cardcounting works. Get it?* But you never understood, not really. That wasn't the world you lived in, or wanted to. Now the very thought of them — fixed to their tables like assembly-line robots, tethered to machines by frequent-player cards, that sorry bunch that fancies itself most free — turns your stomach. Wrong to call it play. *Chance is not what makes gambling possible,* Walter says. *It's limits. Fifty-two cards in the deck. Six sides to the dice. Limits are what gambling's about.* You're done with limits. Limits are bullshit. A bunch of fairy-stories, dreamed up to ease us toward sleep.

The casino on the Lido is closed anyway — for the winter, maybe for good. Another's supposed to be nearby, on the Grand Canal. You must have passed it your first morning in town, on your €250 gondola ride: the thug-beautiful boatman singing his guts out, the colorful competing palace façades like low-tech precursors to the joints on the Strip. But what's the point? You've already been to the Piazzetta, already stood between the famous twin columns: brought to the city from the Holy Land, along with the plague. That's where it really started, right? Dice-tables pitched on the execution ground.

After the hike from the Riva where the powerboat dropped you, you found yourself lightheaded and nauseous, overwhelmed by the grandeur of that space, by all the history that built and shaped it. The feeling came upon you so fast that you thought: *this is it.* And what a way to go that would have been! What a spot for an exit!

But it wasn't. When you came to, you were kneeling on the dark trachyte tiles like you'd stopped there to pray. People were starting to gather. Kids at first, their expressions thrilled and scared. A few mommies and daddies following after. A lot of years gone since you last made a scene like that, since you last felt so *visible.* Something about the looks you got — wide eyes peering down from lovely foreign faces, worried murmurs in a dozen tongues — put a goddamn lump in your throat. You wanted to hold those eyes forever.

So you did the first thing that popped into your head: you dug a pack of cards from your jacket pocket. Right away your body remembered the posture, retrieved the feel of pavement beneath your knees, put your hands into automatic motion. The king of hearts, the seven of hearts, the seven of diamonds. Each card creased up the middle, lifted and dropped, rising and falling, dancing in midair. Forty-five goddamn years since you last worked a crowd like that. Not since that night on the boardwalk with Claudio.

Claudio. Two hundred eighty-seven. *To be fragrant.* Or seventeen. *Fortunate. To dream.* Or eight. *To breathe after. To long for.*

You've seen him every now and then: small speaking parts in movies and TV shows, a face in the corner of a soap-opera magazine. A different name, of course, which makes it hard to be sure. But the sightings have been steady through the years, so you figure he's doing all right. He could be famous, even; you wouldn't necessarily know. You hope he's happy, wherever he is. You hope he got those long brown fingers around some of what he wanted.

It's all good and scattered now: every piece of those days. If the whole scene had passed out in the sand, been carried off by the tide, you wouldn't have been surprised. But that's not what happened: it blew up instead. Larry Lipton's youth book came out in '59, and against all expectations it was a big hit. Every poet and painter from Santa Monica to the Marina del Rey became famous for a while, mostly as somebody else's punchline, and right away the fame started killing them: dope, disease, murder, suicide. Charlie drowned himself in '67; cancer took Stuart in '74. Alex published his own book in '61 and never wrote another. Somehow he kept his junk habit going for another twenty-odd years. His real life's work.

Welles checked out in '63, the same week as Jack Kennedy. You didn't hear about it till months later, passing through L.A. after wearing out your welcome in Palm Springs. You sent Synnøve flowers anyway; Walter helped you figure out how to do it. She sent a nice card back, brief and vague, snapshots from the funeral enclosed. No familiar faces. The girl nowhere to be seen.

Welles's death sent you back to the book, which for a few years you'd put aside. You half-expected the spell to be broken, but it wasn't — though the book had changed, shifted along invisible faultlines. Or maybe you'd grown into it, in ways he'd surely predicted. *You're a gambler! You live by skill and fortune.* By then it was true. Even today the old bastard finds ways to poke at you, to jerk your strings. He must've known you'd find your way here eventually. The city's been waiting — a trap he baited — and you've waltzed right into it.

Just how much of your life has he scripted? That scene yesterday between the columns was pure Welles: probably playing in his head the first night you met him. *You were running a card game on the boardwalk. I won a dollar from you.* Still, kneeling there with the sea at your back, you never felt like a sucker or a patsy — and it was hard not to take satisfaction from it: moving the cards with your old fleet hands, working the switch, there at the very center of the web you've been walking.

Maybe that's why you weren't too surprised when you looked up to find Damon watching you: leaning against the marble railing of the loggetta, eating gelato with a plastic spoon, appearing and disappearing in a line of tourists queued behind an upraised umbrella. He wore a new linen suit, a new wool overcoat, and a deeply pissed-off expression: the ensemble of a traveler who's left someplace in a hurry, who had time to pack nothing but cash. A battered leather shoulderbag hung at his side, flap unbuckled, within easy reach of his right hand. You grinned at him, but you're not sure he saw it. You have no idea, really, what other people can see.

For another ten minutes or so you kept the cards going while Damon finished his ice cream, started drifting closer. Just as you began to think about how best to get away, a cop showed up — lithe, poised, runway-model handsome, state-funeral tidy — and answered the question for you, helping you stand, gently shooing you away. *Oh, thank you, signore,* you said, plenty loud enough for Damon to hear. *I'm sorry, but I'm not feeling well. And this city is so confusing! I'm staying at the Aquila Bianca in San Polo. Can you tell me how to get there?*

So now you wait. Damon's probably bivouacked this very minute at the bacaro across the street, flipping through a magazine, wondering when you'll come down, or when he should go up. Odds are the bacaro closes for a couple of hours after lunch; most of them do, it seems. It's getting late. You have a clear picture of what comes next: Damon will knock back the last of his wine as the proprietor motions to the exit, he'll rub his sleepless eyes and adjust his coat as the door locks behind him, and then, with a few easy steps, he'll cross the gray flagstone street.

You won't be making it back to the Biblioteca Marciana. Probably just as well. You've seen what you came to see, well past the point of diminishing returns. The library girls brought them to you on platters, helped you tug on the white gloves that protect their frail pages: the collected correspondence of Suor Giustina Glissenti. You understood hardly any of it, but you knew the one word you were looking for, and you were certain your eyes wouldn't miss it.

It wasn't there. You flipped through again to be sure: backward this time, slower, your nose an inch off the paper. The result was the same: no mention anywhere of anyone named Crivano. Why would Welles lie? Did he lie? Even at this dead end you turned up clues, or what might be clues. The nun's letters stopped after 1592, the same year Crivano supposedly fled the city. Suor Giustina's name doesn't appear in her convent's records after that date — but it isn't listed before that date, either, although you did find a record of another Glissenti girl: a cousin, maybe. To make matters worse, some letters that were supposed to be in the box were missing. Why? How long have they been gone?

It felt something like cardcounting: filling in gaps based on what little you can see. Walter and Donald could probably figure it out in a heartbeat — but they're not around, and your head doesn't work like that: if you can't see it, then you're at a loss. But you can almost always see it. Almost always.

Patterns: that's what you're best at. Seeing the figure in the tealeaves. You could spot it — you're sure you could — if you had a little more to go on, a few more dots to connect. Vettor Crivano flees this city one thousand lunar years after Muhammad leaves Medina: some kind of echo there. Ezra Pound is released from St. Elizabeth's Hospital a few weeks after you depart the shoreline; he dies and is buried half a mile from here, at San Michele, the same year Veronica is born. John

Hinckley, Jr. watches a movie, shoots a president — launching Curtis on his own funny trajectory — and then gets locked up at St. Elizabeth's. All of this must add up to something, must spell something out. You're running out of chances to put it all together, to see it whole.

Or maybe soon you'll see everything.

At the desk downstairs there's only the proprietor, visible through the window from the street; Damon shouldn't find it hard to get around him. You hope he's careful enough to take that extra step. He'll lean over the wooden counter, match your name to your room number, and soon he'll be on the stairs, fixing a suppressor to a pistolbarrel, hiding the weapon with a glossy newsmagazine. The lock — quaint, old-fashioned — won't slow him down. The well-oiled door will swing open, and he'll see the neat berm your legs make on the bed.

By then, of course, you'll already be in the mirror.

It's not easy, but you've practiced. Quick trips at first: a few seconds, in and out. Then longer stretches, deep dives into un-space. Not unlike learning how to swim. What you recall from the other side is the *hugeness* of it. And the unity: coming back, the idea of separateness becomes laughable. If passing through is hard; returning is much harder. Because, why bother, frankly?

But you do come back. Surfacing in Curtis's suite, in Veronica's room, in the suite at Walter's joint. Letting people see you when you got confident enough. Their startled reactions proving that what you felt was true. Proving something, anyway.

This time will be different. More like learning to breathe water. You have been very patient. You have waited a long time.

Damon will stand over your body for a while. Sniffing the shitty air. He'll step to the bedside, sit lightly on the mattress. Watching you. Then he'll set his gun on the stacked blankets and flick a finger hard against the tip of your nose. He'll find a penlight in his coat, lift your eyelid with his thumb, and shine the beam into your slack clammy face. Then he'll sigh, and turn, and look out the window at the campo below.

Eventually he'll stand, pick up the pistol. He'll press the thick barrel against your head, resting it in the orbit of your left eye, and he'll hold the newsmagazine above it, opened to catch the spatter. *Der Spiegel:* you'll be able to read the cover over his shoulder. *In Göttlicher Mission,* it says.

He'll shoot your eyes out, one at a time. He'll drop the wet red magazine on your chest, wipe his hands on the blanket. On his way to the door he'll pick up the passport that he had his friends in D.C. make for you: it's on the chest of drawers, easy to find. On his way back to his own hotel he'll drop it in a canal, fastened with an elastic band to a palm-size chunk of stone.

You will not get the chance to make those two calls.

If Damon looks in the mirror on his way out of the room — is he the sort of person who would? — you won't let him see you. Not just yet.

Mirror. Three hundred twenty-nine: a sharp disciplinarian. Or: those exhausted by hunger. Or: in the land beyond the sea. In Hebrew, הארמ, which adds to fifty. Unwedded. Completeness. A citadel.

This is what you've wanted all along: freedom from what's trapped you in this world. Freedom from yourself. At the end, they say, your whole life's supposed to flash before your eyes. *Flash:* that's the word they always use. You hope like hell it isn't true. It's been a long time since looking last held any interest. Lately, what jazzes you is what you *can't* see: the way the spell of vision gets broken, the way your breath fogs the glass when you get too close. All these years, dragged around by your eyeballs: you've had about enough. A goddamn slideshow! What the hell kind of death is that for a person? You don't want it. You're ready for whatever's next.

Eye. Four hundred ten. A mounting-up of

smoke. To be hindered or restrained. To lay snares.

That was Crivano's escape: it says so in Welles's book. Took you long enough to figure it out. Part of you wishes you'd brought *The Mirror Thief* along — although that's silly, sentimental. Curtis will take care of it; here it'd just get thrown away. Besides, it's not like you don't remember every word. Over the years you have become the book: a lifetime of dreams and memories, braided through its lines.

In a way, it's not so bad that the trail in the Biblioteca ran cold. Isn't that exactly what you wanted to hear the night you stalked Welles on the beach? That he'd made Crivano up? That the world of his book overlapped with the real world hardly at all? Finding out otherwise became a problem for you, one you've been working for years to solve. But even if Welles *did* lie, even if Crivano never really existed, this trip hasn't been a waste of time. There's something here: you've felt it, even if you haven't seen it. Can't somebody still be a ghost, even if they were never born? Why not? Who made up that rule?

Yesterday, a final clue. You mentioned the name of the ship to a librarian — the ship Crivano escapes on — and she came back with something: a letter from a young merchant captain to his father, bringing news from the Dalmatian coast. *Very bad are the uskok pirates,* the librarian translated. *Last month they robbed two small ships en route to Spalato, and they burned a trabacolo — a trabacolo is a boat, yes? — that fought them with great valor.*

The *Lynceus.* You kept the girls busy till closing time, but they found nothing else: neither the date the ship was lost, nor where it had sailed from. It might have already stopped at Split, let Crivano off. Maybe, as its wreck lit up the ocean, he was already intriguing his way through the Croatian port, dodging the Council of Ten's assassins, seeking passage to Turkish lands. No doubt that city would have felt dreamlike to him: both strange and familiar. Diocletian's ancient palace was the model for this city's Piazza; the belltower in this city's Piazza is duplicated there. You would like to have seen that, too. But no matter. Cities appearing in other cities: a map of echoes, a pattern you know well.

You prefer to believe that Crivano burned. It's an end that fits him, a doom you can imagine. Trapped belowdecks, flames arcing overhead, his mind would have returned to Lepanto: what he did there, what he did not do. His lonely secret life would have seemed a peculiar circuit, beginning and ending in the hold of a burning ship.

With nothing to do but await the agonies — the blistering flesh, the smothering outrush of air — how would he have passed his final moments? Tincture of henbane, probably: to slow his pulse, to dull his senses, to free his mind to wander. And the magic mirror, of course: the trick he taught you. To meditate upon the talisman — to gaze upon the mirror's surface — is to arrange your mind to resemble the mind of God. You pass through the silvering, beyond all earthly torment, into the realm of pure idea. At last, all mysteries become clear.

By that point, you imagine, it'll be hard for you to care about any earthly thing: hard to convince yourself to come back, to finish your remaining task.

But when Damon returns to his own hotel, you'll be waiting. It might take him a moment to notice you, especially if he's avoiding his reflection; you'll bide your time until he does. With the benefit of perfect knowledge, you will not be unkind. If he shoots out the glass — as well he might — you will remain with him, even in the fallen shards. There was a time not long ago when you felt something for him akin to love.

Only one result is possible, so you hope it will come easily. Your ghost-hands will guide the pistol to his mouth, then steady it while his thumb locates the trigger.

Then it will be time for you to join Crivano: to stand with his shade on the blackened foredeck of the *Lynceus* while he signals to the full moon. The moon will answer through the smoke: *Imagine me not as a mirror, but as an opening, an aperture, a pupil admitting light. Imagine the earth curves around you, not under. Imagine this world to be the eye of God, and the ocean its retina. Know that you are always seen.*

But you are indeed a mirror, Crivano will say. And I, a stranger to myself, would be seen by no one. That is all I ask, and far more than I deserve.

The pillar of smoke will blot the moon; the flames will rise to erase him. The ship will burn to the waterline: hissing, then sunken, silent. Once the sky has cleared, the sea will betray nothing. *The Mirror Thief* will be gone.

So, in the end, only we two will remain: you and the ocean, you and the mirror, you and the story you've dreamed.

Listen, now: footfalls in the corridor. A cautious hand upon the knob.

No time remains to doubt. This, then, is the end of you — what you've feared, what you remember. All of it flashing. The faces and the colors. Watch closely: here they come.

ACKNOWLEDGMENTS

It took me five and a half years to write this book, and another seven and a half to find a publisher for it. During this time I benefited to a nearly immeasurable degree from the patience, guidance, and generosity of others, without whom this would not have been possible. I'd like to express my thanks to my spouse, Kathleen Rooney; my parents, David and Barbara Seay; my late grandfather Joe F. Boydstun; to Michael Seay, Jen Seay, Beth Rooney, Nick Super, Richard Rooney, Mary Ann Rooney, Megan Rooney, J. Mark Rooney, Karen Rooney, Cliff Turner, Kelly Seal, Richard Weil, Hester Arnold Farmer, Andrew Rash, Angela McClendon Ossar, Scott Blackwood, James Charlesworth, Carole Shepherd, David Spooner, Matthew MacGregor, Elisa Gabbert, John Cotter, Carrie Scanga, Jason Skipper, Warren Frazier, Mitchell Brown, Bob Drinan, Olivia Lilley, Shane Zimmer, Tovah Burstein, Timothy Moore, the faculty and my fellow students at Queens University of Charlotte's low-residency MFA program, and my colleagues at the Village of Wheeling, Illinois, especially Jon Sfondilis, Michael Crotty, and Lisa Leonteos.

As my collection of pages has grown closer to becoming a book, I have benefited from the hard work and good judgment of my agent Kent Wolf and my editor Mark Krotov, as well as his colleagues at Melville House, including, but not limited to, Dennis Loy Johnson, Valerie Merians, Julia Fleischaker, Liam O'Brien, Ena Brdjanovic, Chad Felix, and Eric Price.

A substantial portion of the manuscript was written at the Fine Arts Work Center in Provincetown, Massachusetts, where I had a 2005–2006 fiction fellowship. It's impossible to overstate the value of the support and encouragement that I received from this organization, its staff, and the other fellows.

Finally, I'm eternally indebted to Richard Peabody for starting me down the path that led here, and to Jane Alison for helping me map my route. If they're willing to claim it, this book is theirs as well as mine.

ABOUT THE AUTHOR

Martin Seay is the executive secretary for the village of Wheeling, Illinois. *The Mirror Thief* is his first novel.